MILES MORALES

SPIDER-MAN

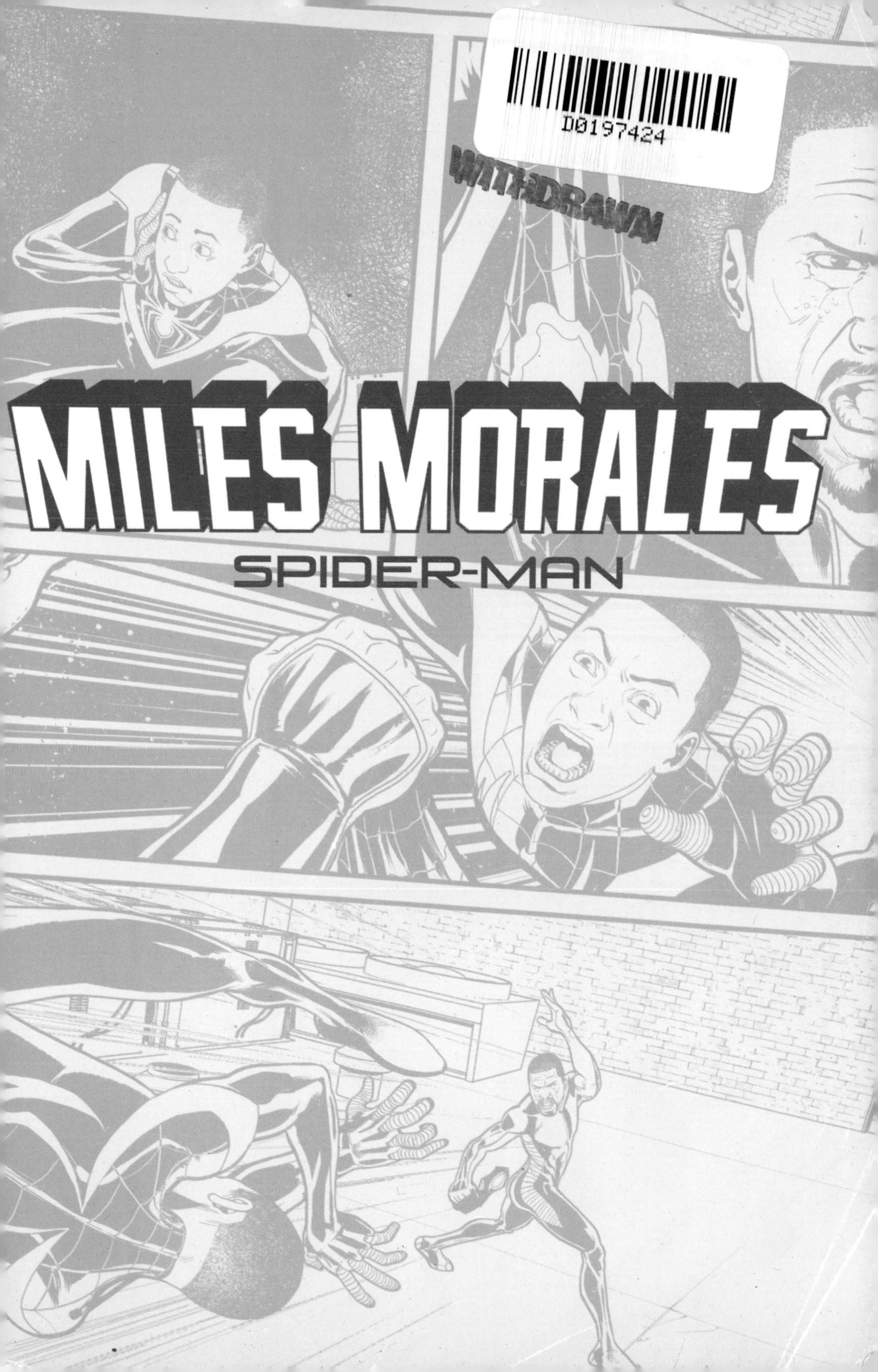

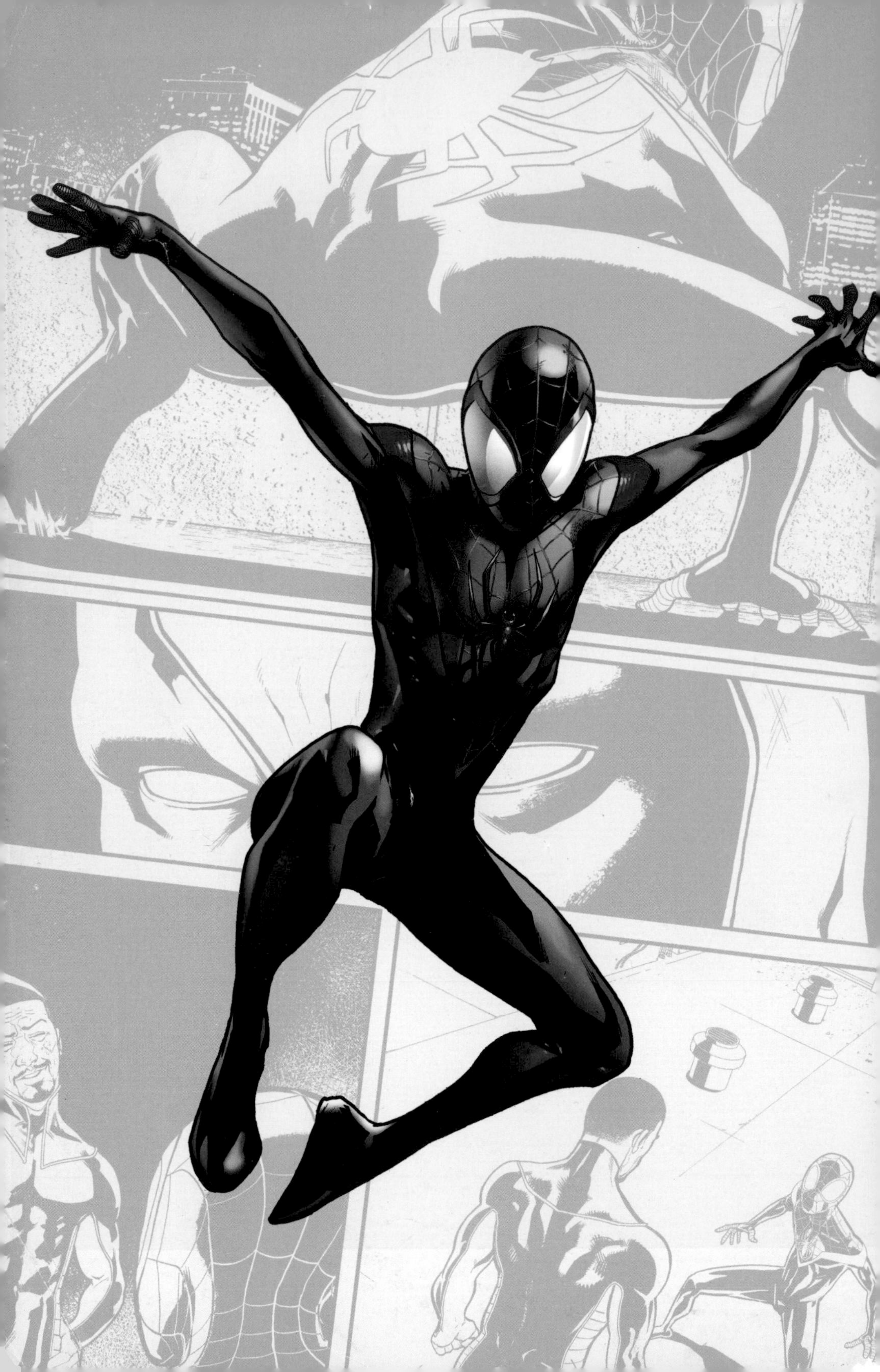

MILES MORALES

SPIDER-MAN

WRITER
BRIAN MICHAEL BENDIS

ARTISTS
SARA PICHELLI (#1-5, #8),
CHRIS SAMNEE (#6-7)
& DAVID MARQUEZ (#9-10)

FINISHES, #5
DAVID MESSINA

COLOR ARTIST
JUSTIN PONSOR

LETTERER
VC's CORY PETIT

COVER ART
KAARE ANDREWS

ASSISTANT EDITOR
JON MOISAN

ASSOCIATE EDITOR
SANA AMANAT

EXECUTIVE EDITOR
MARK PANICCIA

Spider-Man created by STAN LEE & STEVE DITKO

collection editor JENNIFER GRÜNWALD
assistant editor CAITLIN O'CONNELL • associate managing editor KATERI WOODY
editor, special projects MARK D. BEAZLEY • vp production & special projects JEFF YOUNGQUIST

director, licensed publishing SVEN LARSEN • svp print, sales & marketing DAVID GABRIEL
editor in chief C.B. CEBULSKI • chief creative officer JOE QUESADA
president DAN BUCKLEY • executive producer ALAN FINE

LES MORALES: SPIDER-MAN. Contains material originally published in magazine form as ULTIMATE COMICS SPIDER-MAN 1-10. First printing 2019. ISBN 978-1-302-91807-1. Published by
ARVEL WORLDWIDE, INC., a subsidiary of MARVEL ENTERTAINMENT, LLC. OFFICE OF PUBLICATION: 135 West 50th Street, New York, NY 10020. © 2019 MARVEL No similarity between any of the
mes, characters, persons, and/or institutions in this magazine with those of any living or dead person or institution is intended, and any such similarity which may exist is purely coincidental.
inted in Canada. DAN BUCKLEY, President, Marvel Entertainment; JOHN NEE, Publisher; JOE QUESADA, Chief Creative Officer; TOM BREVOORT, SVP of Publishing; DAVID BOGART, Associate
blisher & SVP of Talent Affairs; DAVID GABRIEL, SVP of Sales & Marketing, Publishing; JEFF YOUNGQUIST, VP of Production & Special Projects; DAN CARR, Executive Director of Pu
chnology; ALEX MORALES, Director of Publishing Operations; DAN EDINGTON, Managing Editor; SUSAN CRESPI, Production Manager; STAN LEE, Chairman Emeritus. For informatic
vertising in Marvel Comics or on Marvel.com, please contact Vit DeBellis, Custom Solutions & Integrated Advertising Manager, at vdebellis@marvel.com. For Marvel subscription
l 888-511-5480. Manufactured between 5/17/2019 and 6/18/2019 by SOLISCO PRINTERS, SCOTT, QC, CANADA.

9 8 7 6 5 4 3 2 1

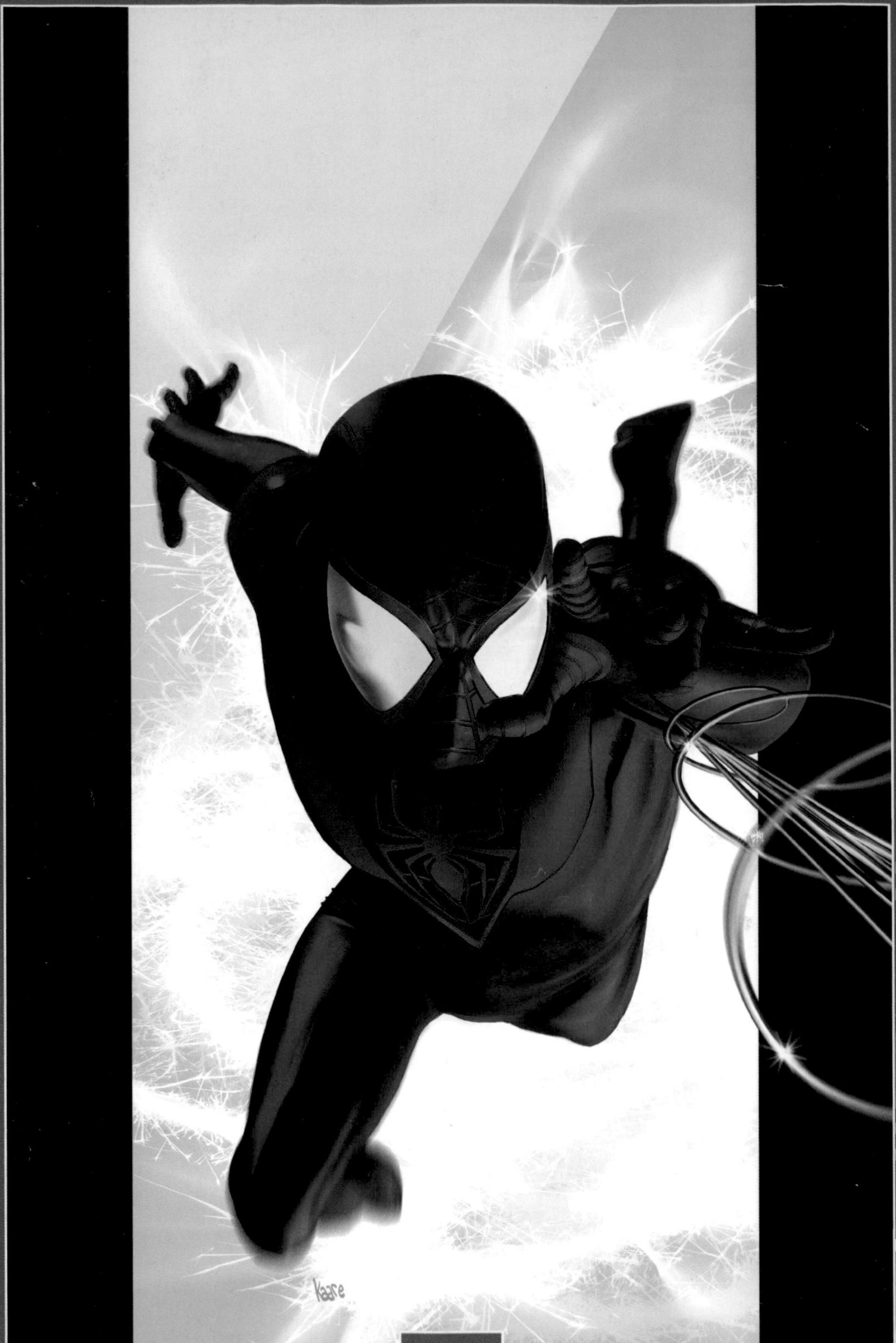
Kaare
1

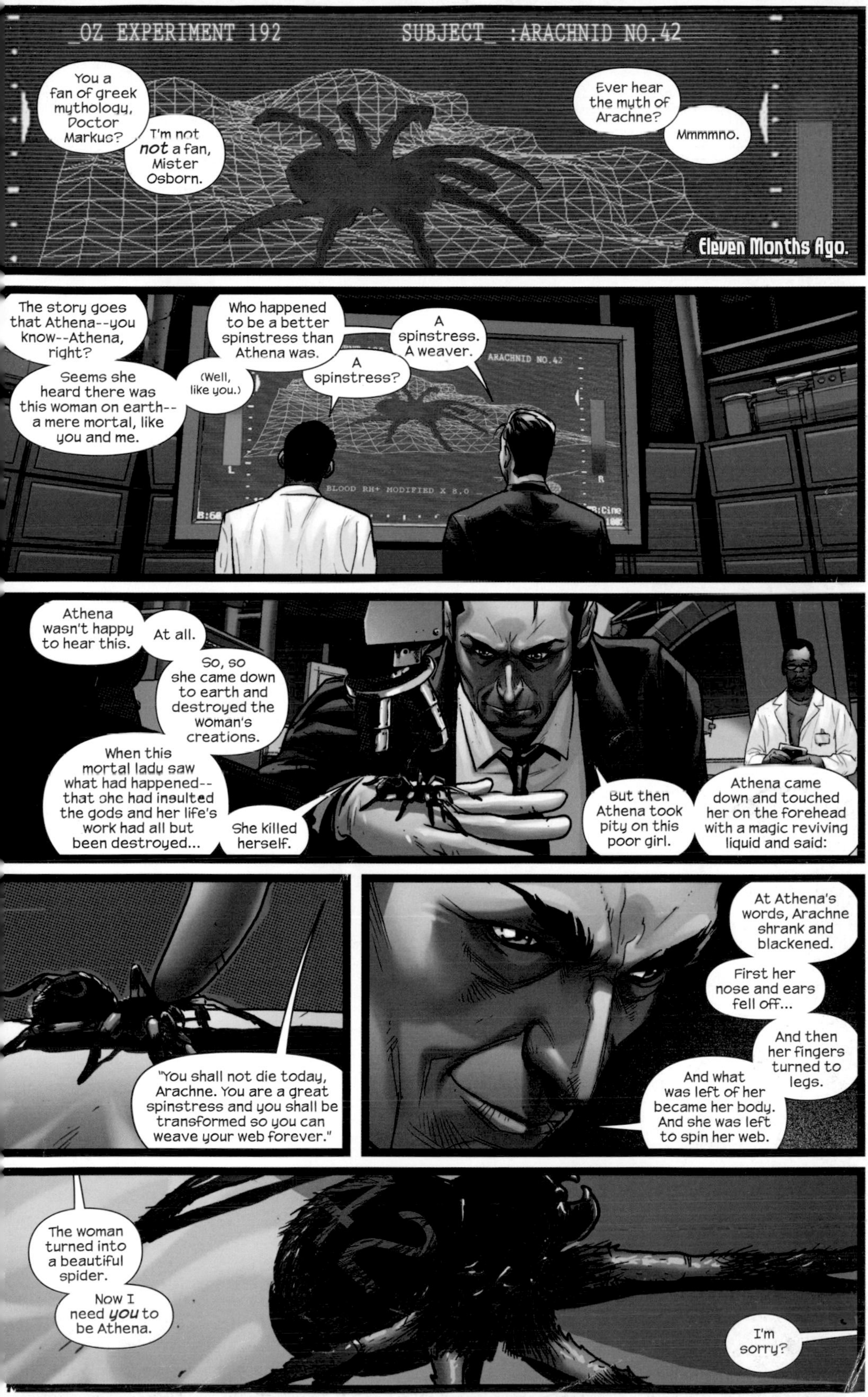
_OZ EXPERIMENT 192
SUBJECT_ :ARACHNID NO.42
You a fan of greek mythology, Doctor Markus?
I'm not not a fan, Mister Osborn.
Ever hear the myth of Arachne?
Mmmmno.
Eleven Months Ago.
The story goes that Athena--you know--Athena, right?
Seems she heard there was this woman on earth--a mere mortal, like you and me.
(Well, like you.)
Who happened to be a better spinstress than Athena was.
A spinstress?
A spinstress. A weaver.
ARACHNID NO.42
BLOOD RH+ MODIFIED X 8.0
Athena wasn't happy to hear this.
At all.
So, so she came down to earth and destroyed the woman's creations.
When this mortal lady saw what had happened--that she had insulted the gods and her life's work had all but been destroyed...
She killed herself.
But then Athena took pity on this poor girl.
Athena came down and touched her on the forehead with a magic reviving liquid and said:
"You shall not die today, Arachne. You are a great spinstress and you shall be transformed so you can weave your web forever."
At Athena's words, Arachne shrank and blackened.
First her nose and ears fell off...
And then her fingers turned to legs.
And what was left of her became her body. And she was left to spin her web.
The woman turned into a beautiful spider.
Now I need you to be Athena.
I'm sorry?

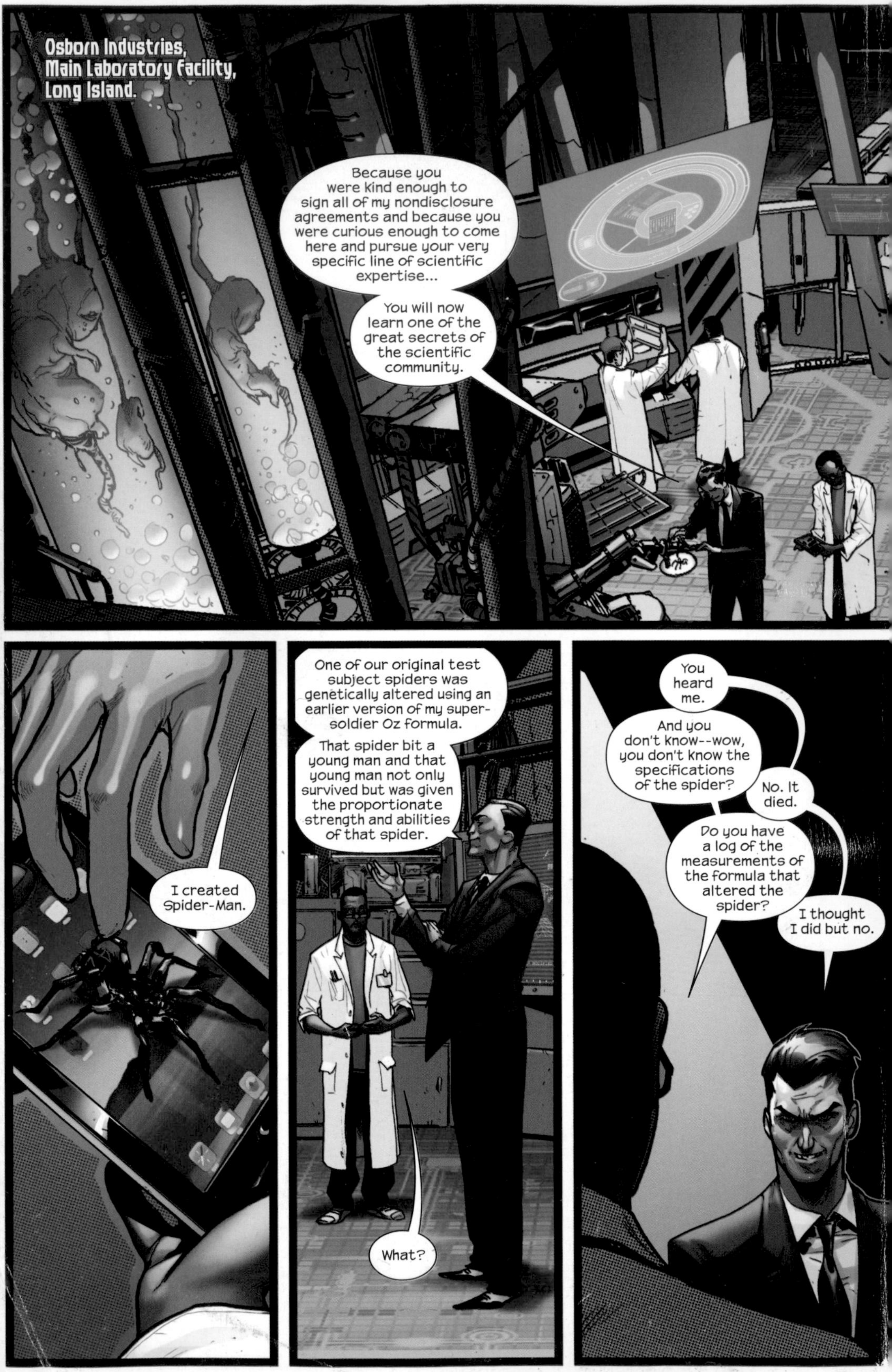
Osborn Industries, Main Laboratory Facility, Long Island.
Because you were kind enough to sign all of my nondisclosure agreements and because you were curious enough to come here and pursue your very specific line of scientific expertise...
You will now learn one of the great secrets of the scientific community.
I created Spider-Man.
One of our original test subject spiders was genetically altered using an earlier version of my super-soldier Oz formula.
That spider bit a young man and that young man not only survived but was given the proportionate strength and abilities of that spider.
What?
You heard me.
And you don't know--wow, you don't know the specifications of the spider?
No. It died.
Do you have a log of the measurements of the formula that altered the spider?
I thought I did but no.

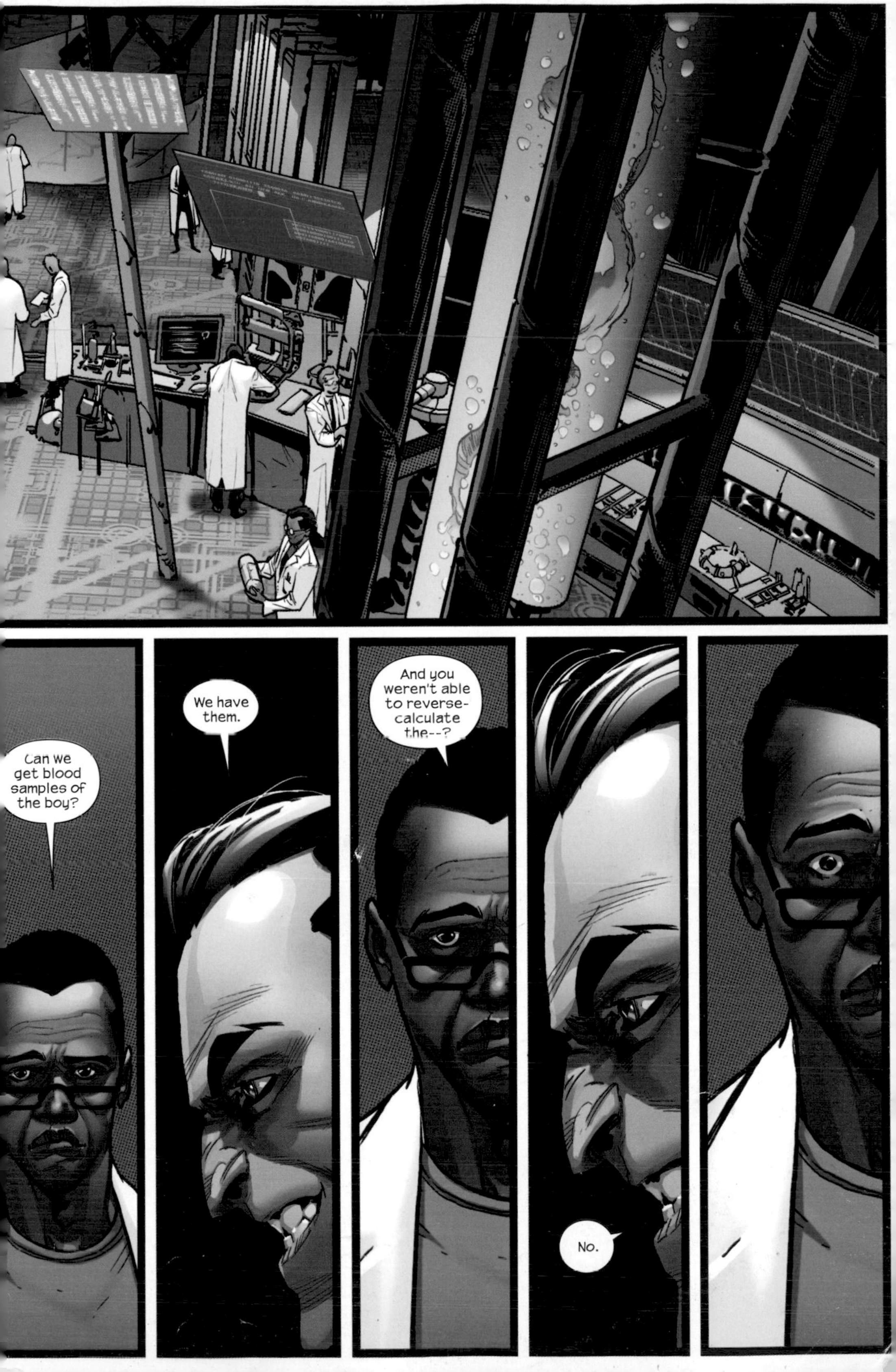
Can we get blood samples of the boy?
We have them.
And you weren't able to reverse-calculate the--?
No.

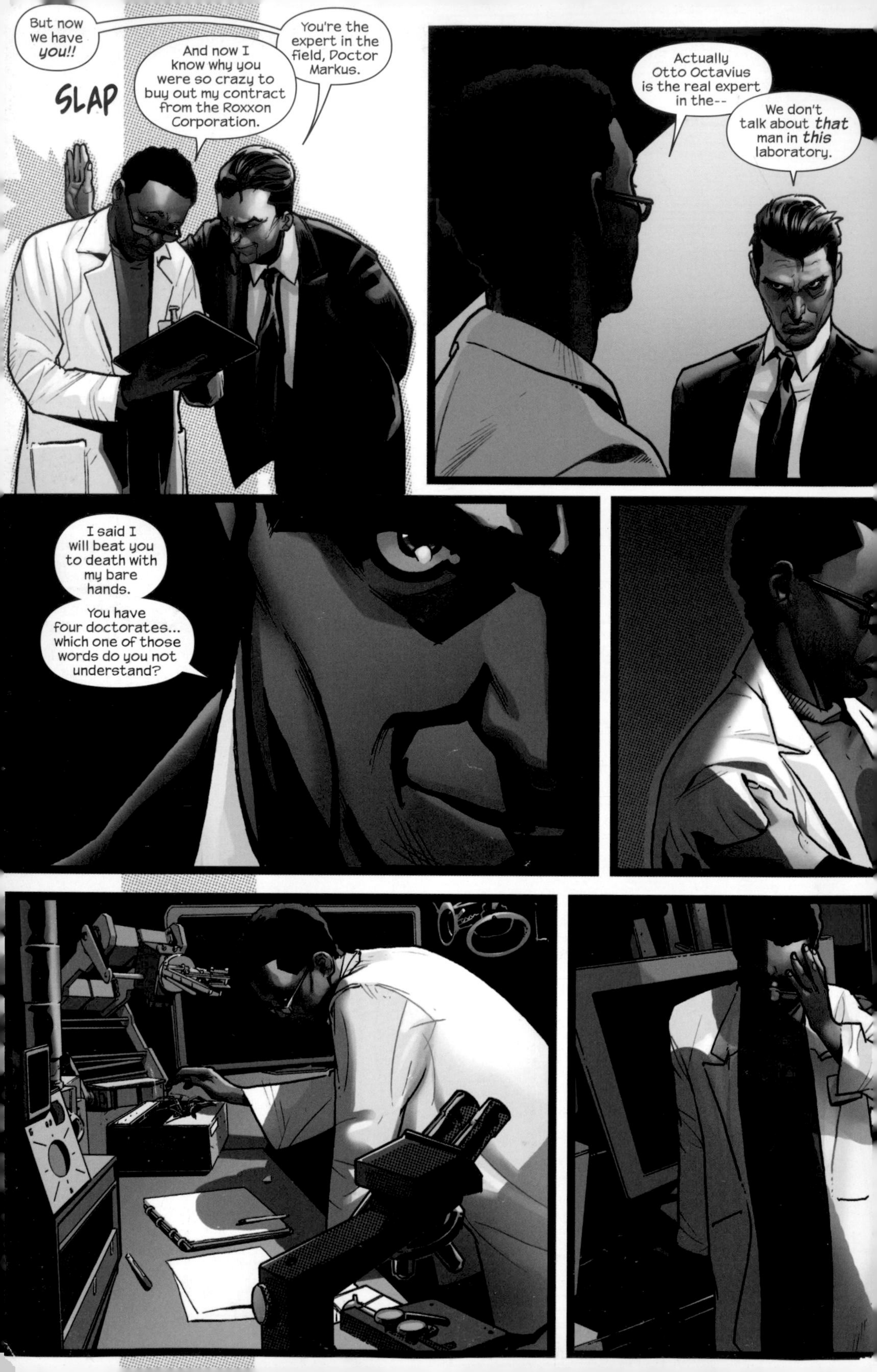
But now we have *you!!*
SLAP
You're the expert in the field, Doctor Markus.
And now I know why you were so crazy to buy out my contract from the Roxxon Corporation.
Actually Otto Octavius is the real expert in the--
We don't talk about *that* man in *this* laboratory.
I said I will beat you to death with my bare hands.
You have four doctorates... which one of those words do you not understand?

You created Spider-Man.
And I hope you understand that if this information leaves this building I will *kill* you.
Excuse me?
But if you solve this problem for me I will reward you to the point where I reinvent your life on every conceivable level.
n°43
n°44
n°42
n°42
n°42

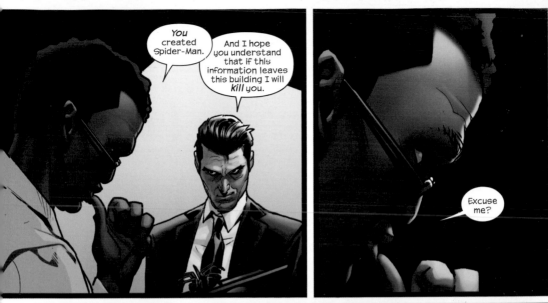

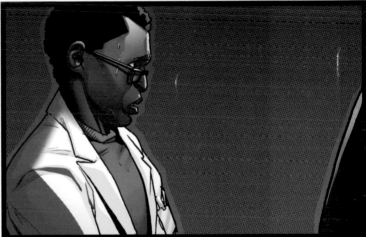

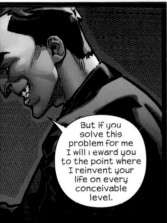

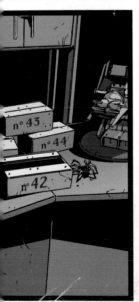

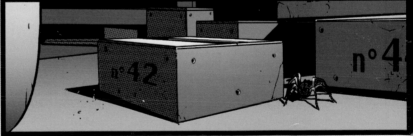

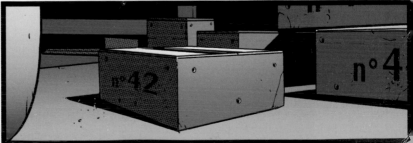

74º • LOG IN • REGISTER • ARCHIVES

DAILY BUGLE

LOCAL | INTERNATIONAL | ARTS & ENTERTAINMENT | OPINION | SPORTS

NORMAN OSBORN IS THE GREEN GOBLIN!

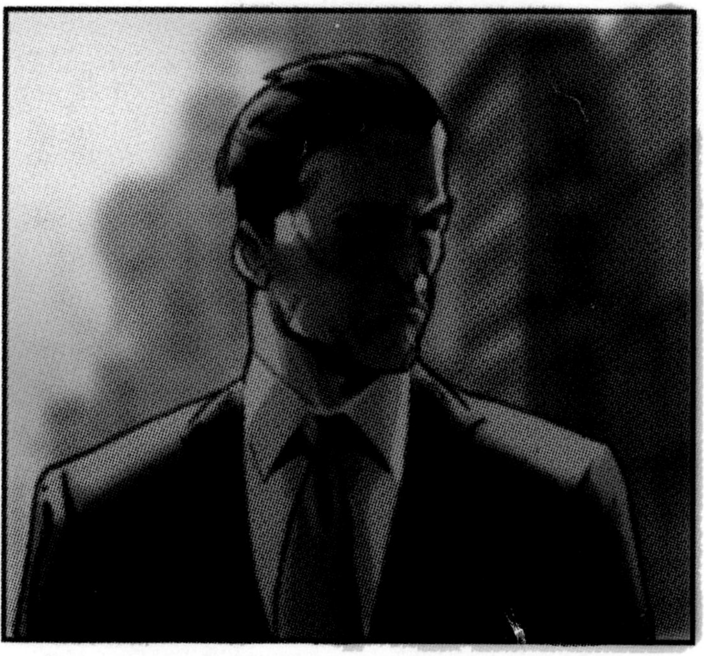

CONTROVERSIAL INDUSTRIALIST IS REVEALED TO BE GENETICALLY ALTERED MONSTER NOW IN THE CUSTODY OF S.H.I.E.L.D.

Reporting by Frederick Fosswell

Agents of the world peacekeeping task force S.H.I.E.L.D. have confirmed to the Daily Bugle that controversial industrialist Norman Osborn had infected his own body with one of his experiments altering himself into what one of our S.H.I.E.L.D. sources are referring to as the Green Goblin.

Sources also confirm that this Green Goblin is the same one that attacked Midtown High School a few months ago, shutting the school down for weeks. It is also referred to as the public debut of the mystery man called Spider-Man. Whether or not there is a connection between Spider-Man and Norman Osborn's double life has yet to be revealed.

Speculation continues as to why Norman Osborn would break one of the cardinal rules of science by experimenting on himself. Sources close to Norman say that certain pressures to create a workable version of his experimental "super-soldier" formula led him to use the formula on himself.

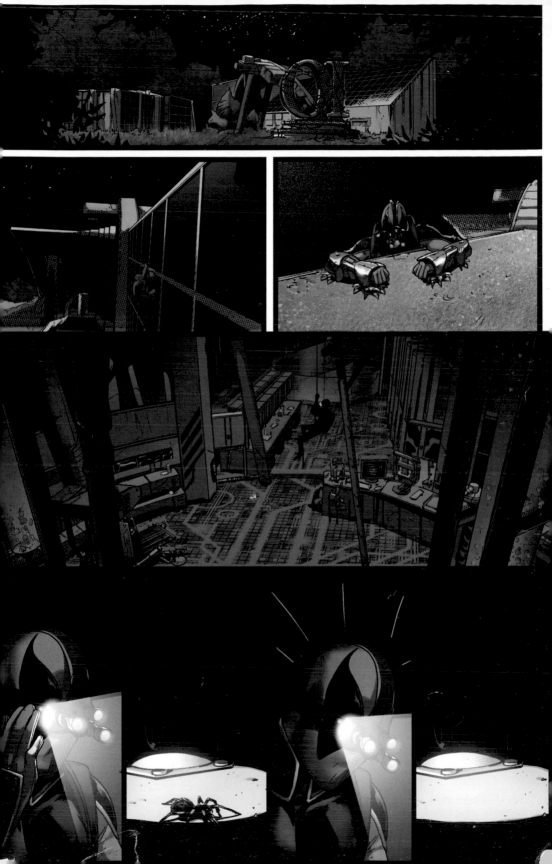

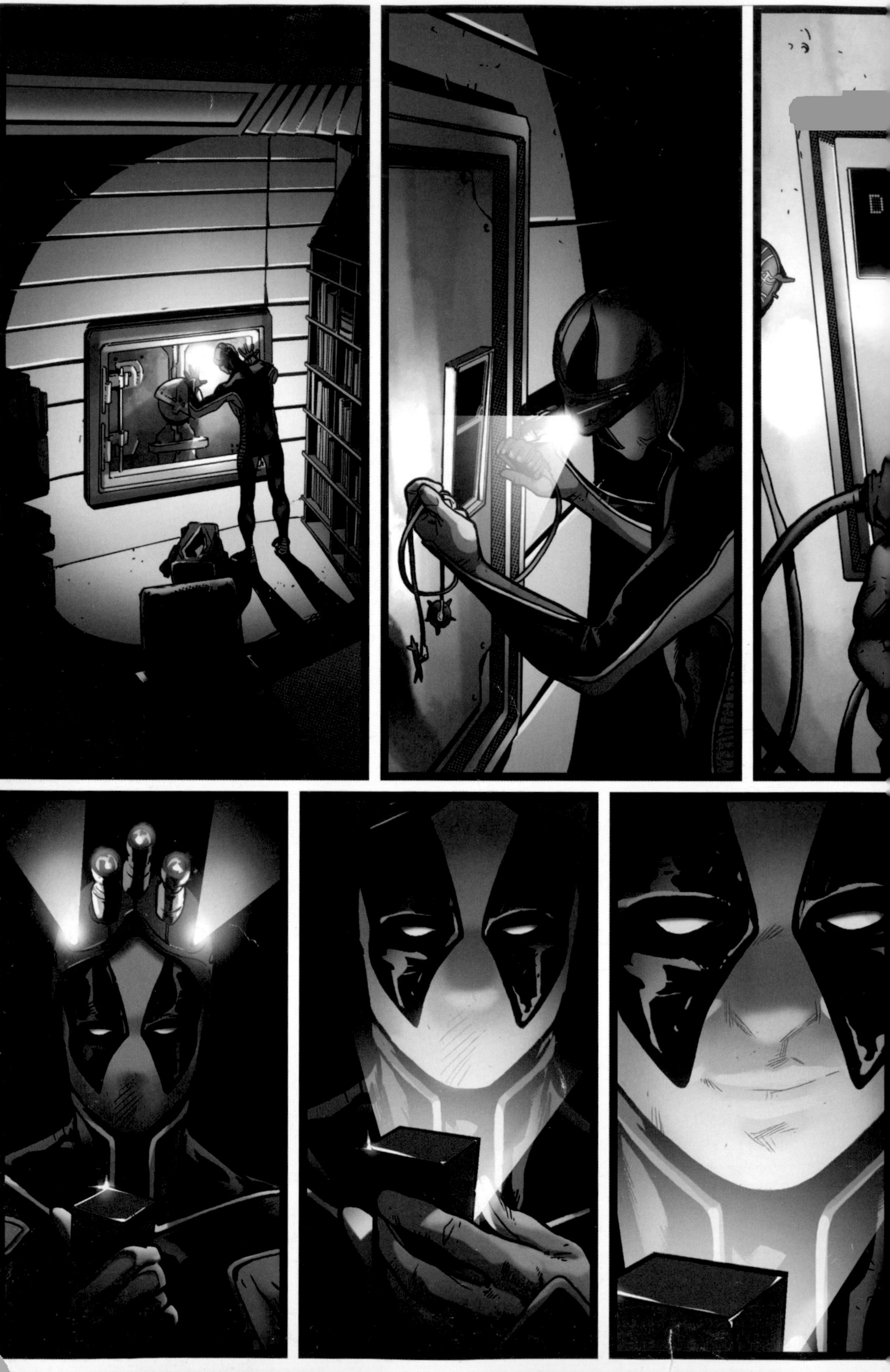

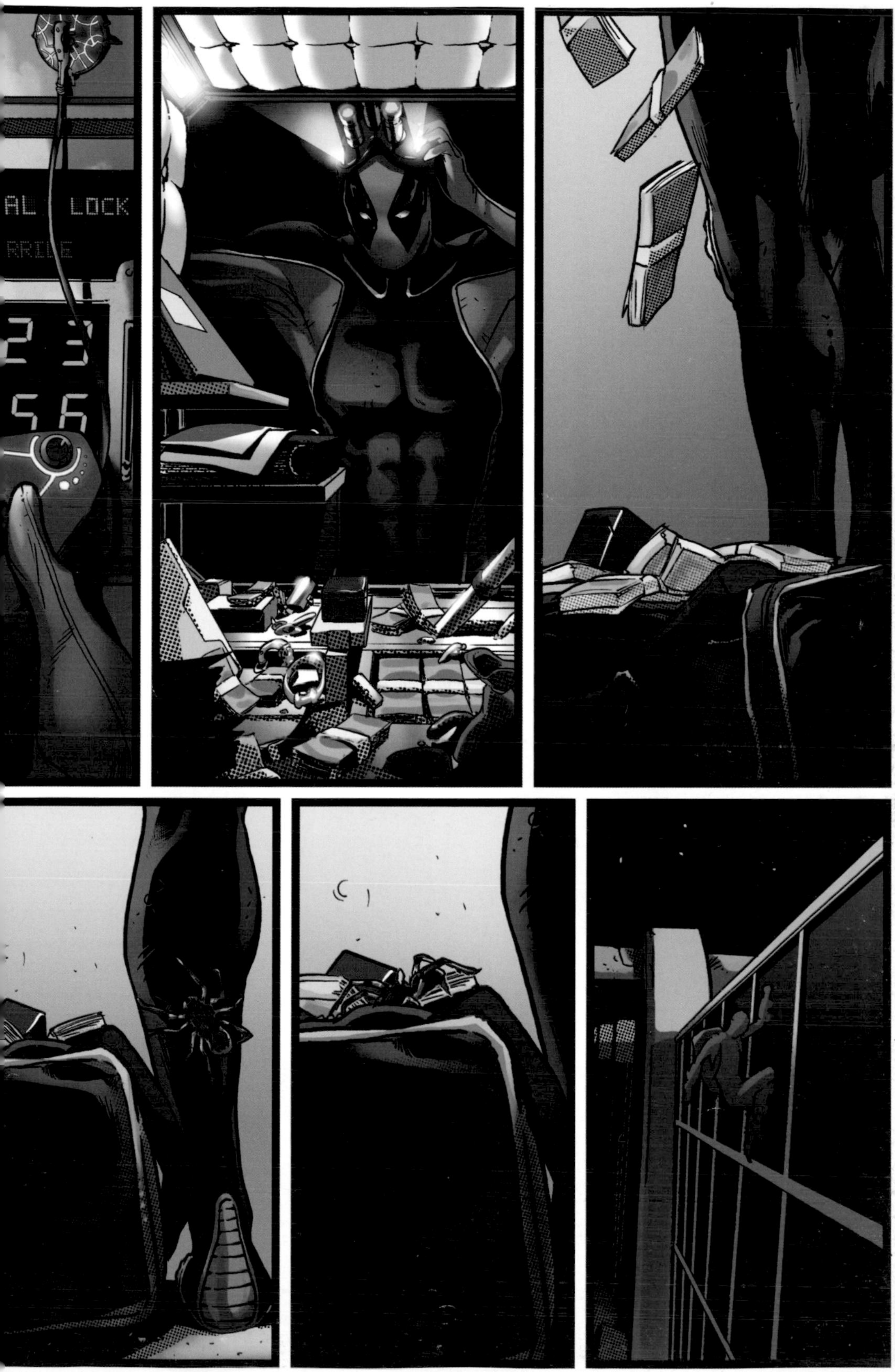
AL LOCK

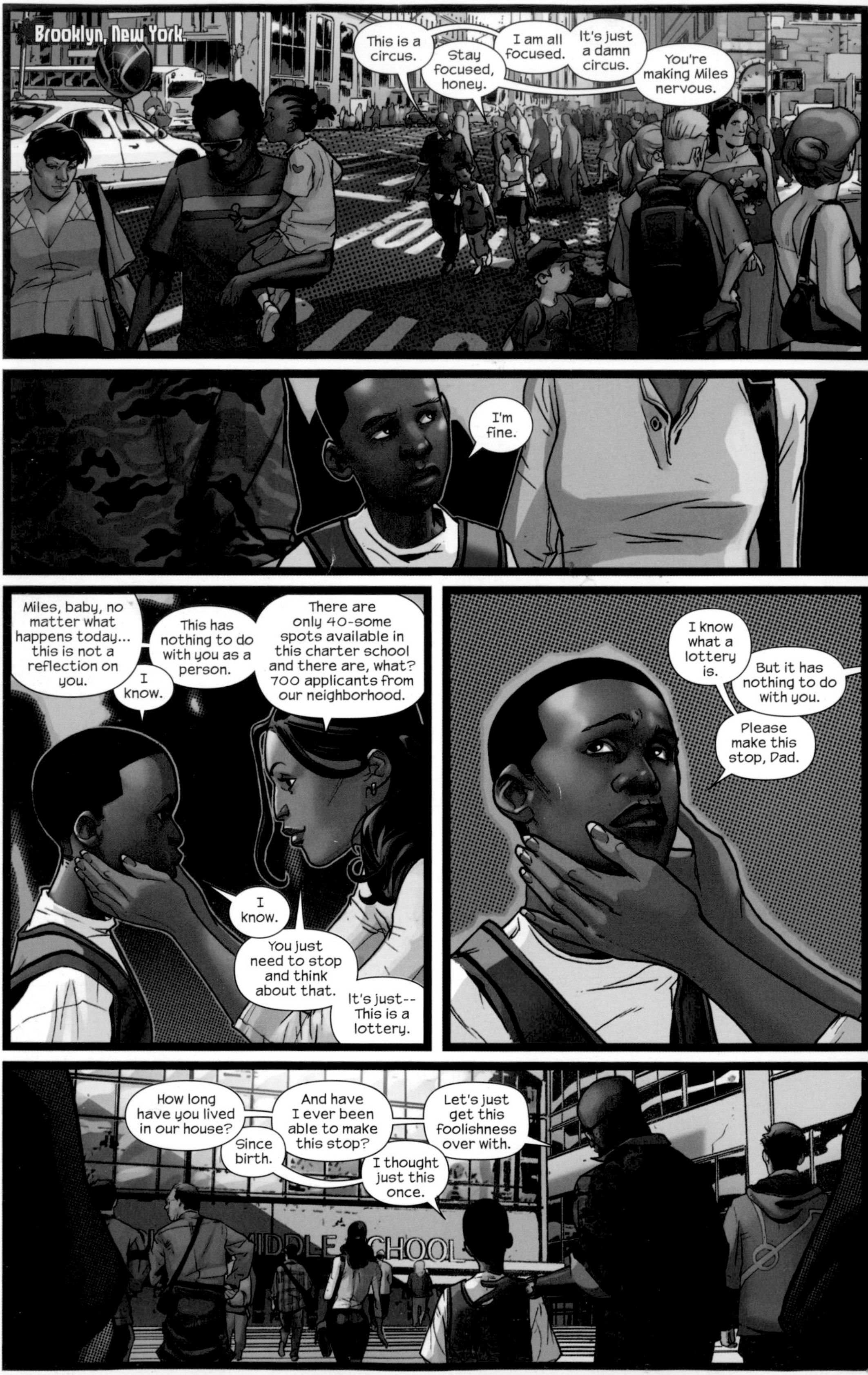
Brooklyn, New York.
This is a circus.
Stay focused, honey.
I am all focused.
It's just a damn circus.
You're making Miles nervous.
I'm fine.
Miles, baby, no matter what happens today... this is not a reflection on you.
I know.
This has nothing to do with you as a person.
There are only 40-some spots available in this charter school and there are, what? 700 applicants from our neighborhood.
I know.
You just need to stop and think about that.
It's just-- This is a lottery.
I know what a lottery is.
But it has nothing to do with you.
Please make this stop, Dad.
How long have you lived in our house?
Since birth.
And have I ever been able to make this stop?
I thought just this once.
Let's just get this foolishness over with.
MIDDLE SCHOOL

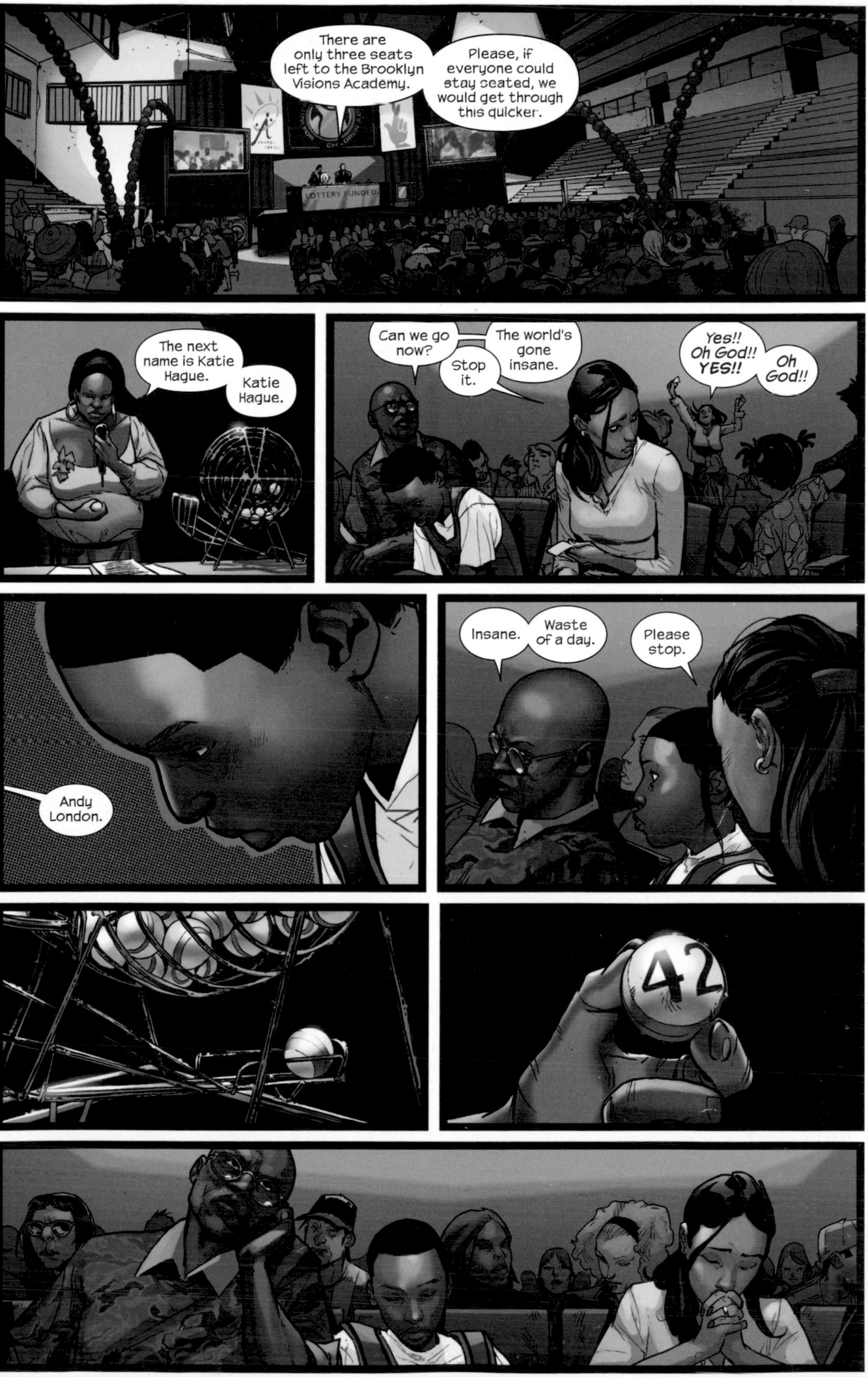
There are only three seats left to the Brooklyn Visions Academy.
Please, if everyone could stay seated, we would get through this quicker.
LOTTERY FUNDED
The next name is Katie Hague.
Katie Hague.
Can we go now?
The world's gone insane.
Stop it.
Yes!! Oh God!! YES!!
Oh God!!
Andy London.
Insane.
Waste of a day.
Please stop.
42

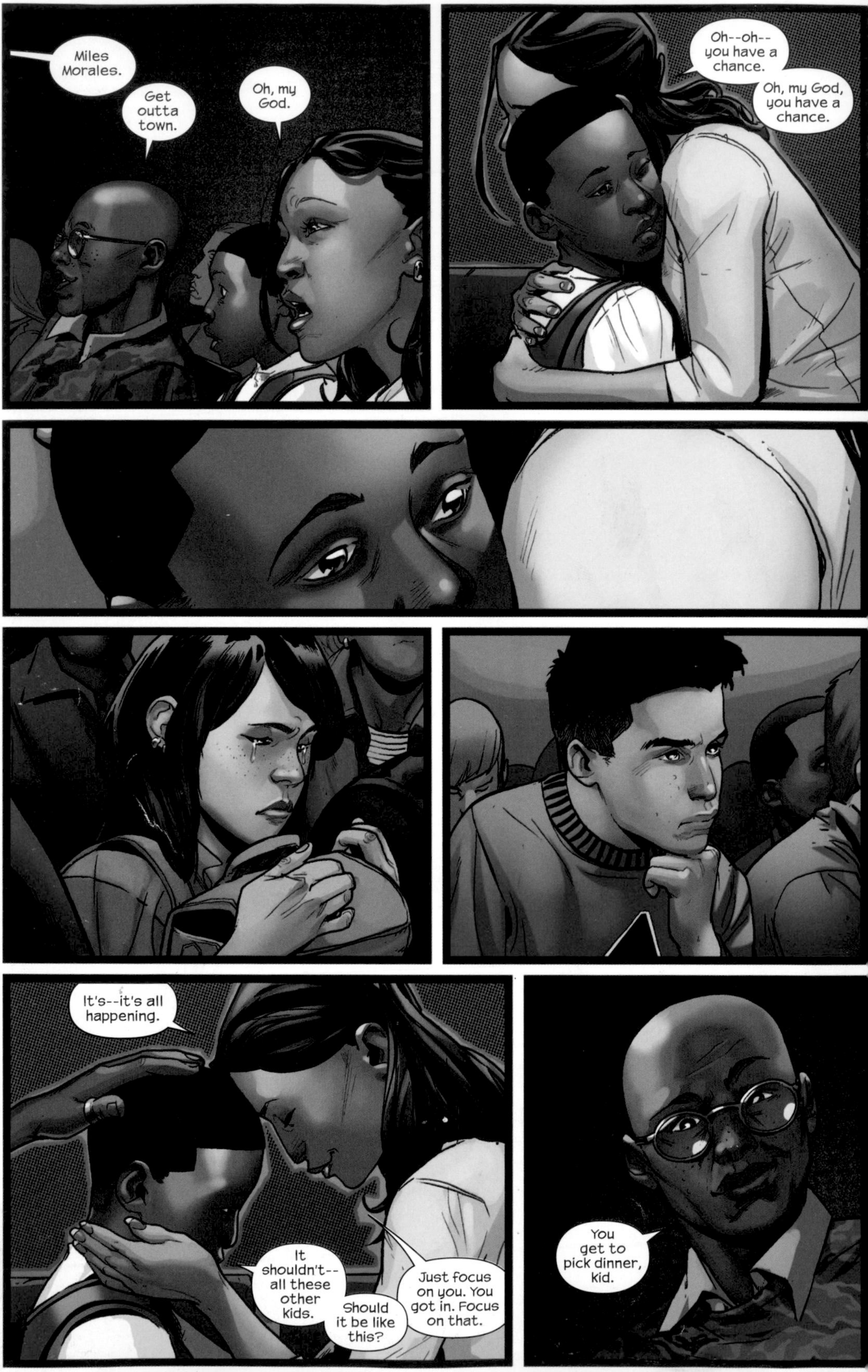
Miles Morales.
Get outta town.
Oh, my God.
Oh--oh-- you have a chance.
Oh, my God, you have a chance.
It's--it's all happening.
It shouldn't-- all these other kids.
Should it be like this?
Just focus on you. You got in. Focus on that.
You get to pick dinner, kid.

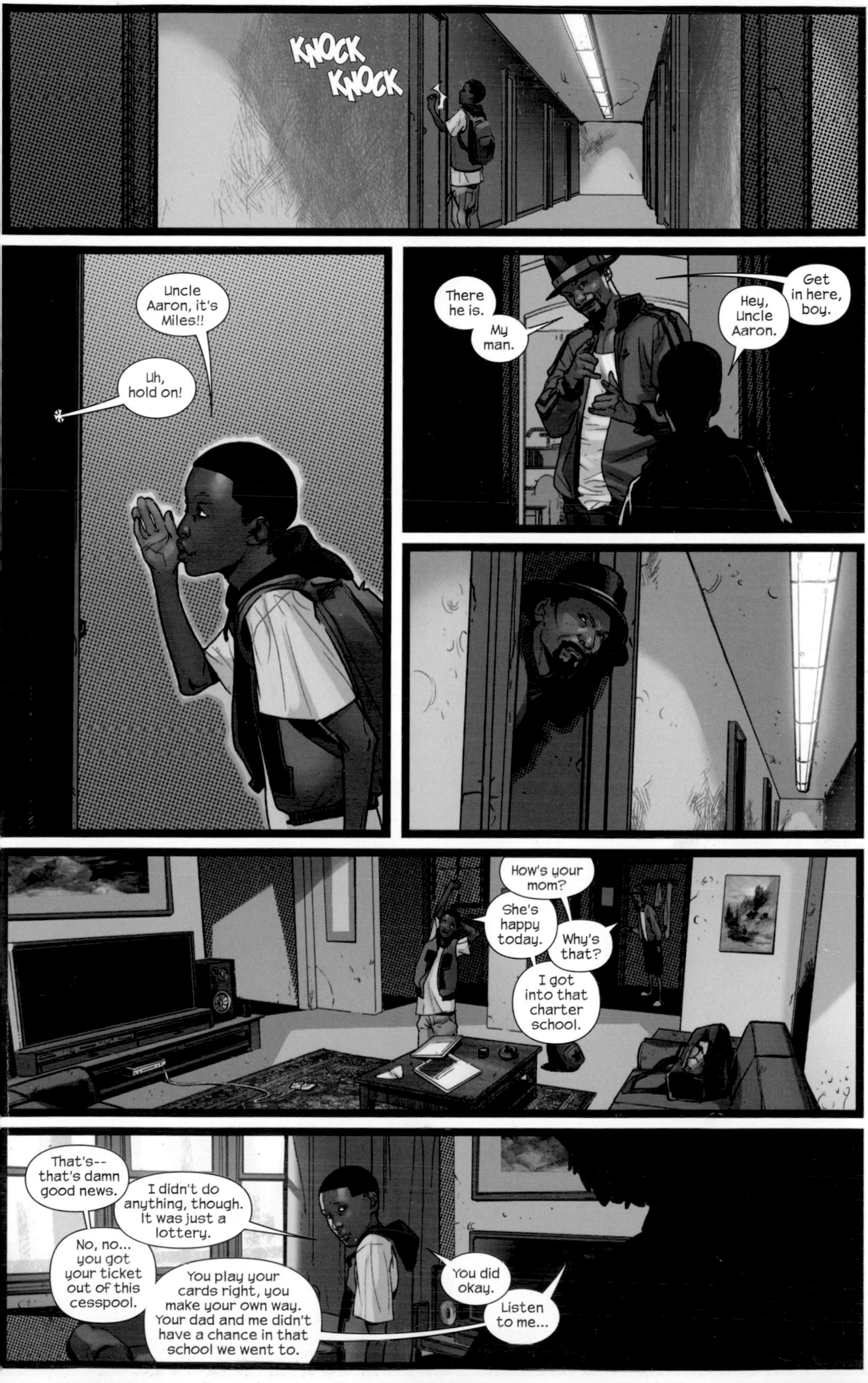
KNOCK KNOCK
Uncle Aaron, it's Miles!!
Uh, hold on!
There he is.
My man.
Hey, Uncle Aaron.
Get in here, boy.
How's your mom?
She's happy today.
Why's that?
I got into that charter school.
That's-- that's damn good news.
I didn't do anything, though. It was just a lottery.
No, no... you got your ticket out of this cesspool.
You did okay.
Listen to me...
You play your cards right, you make your own way. Your dad and me didn't have a chance in that school we went to.

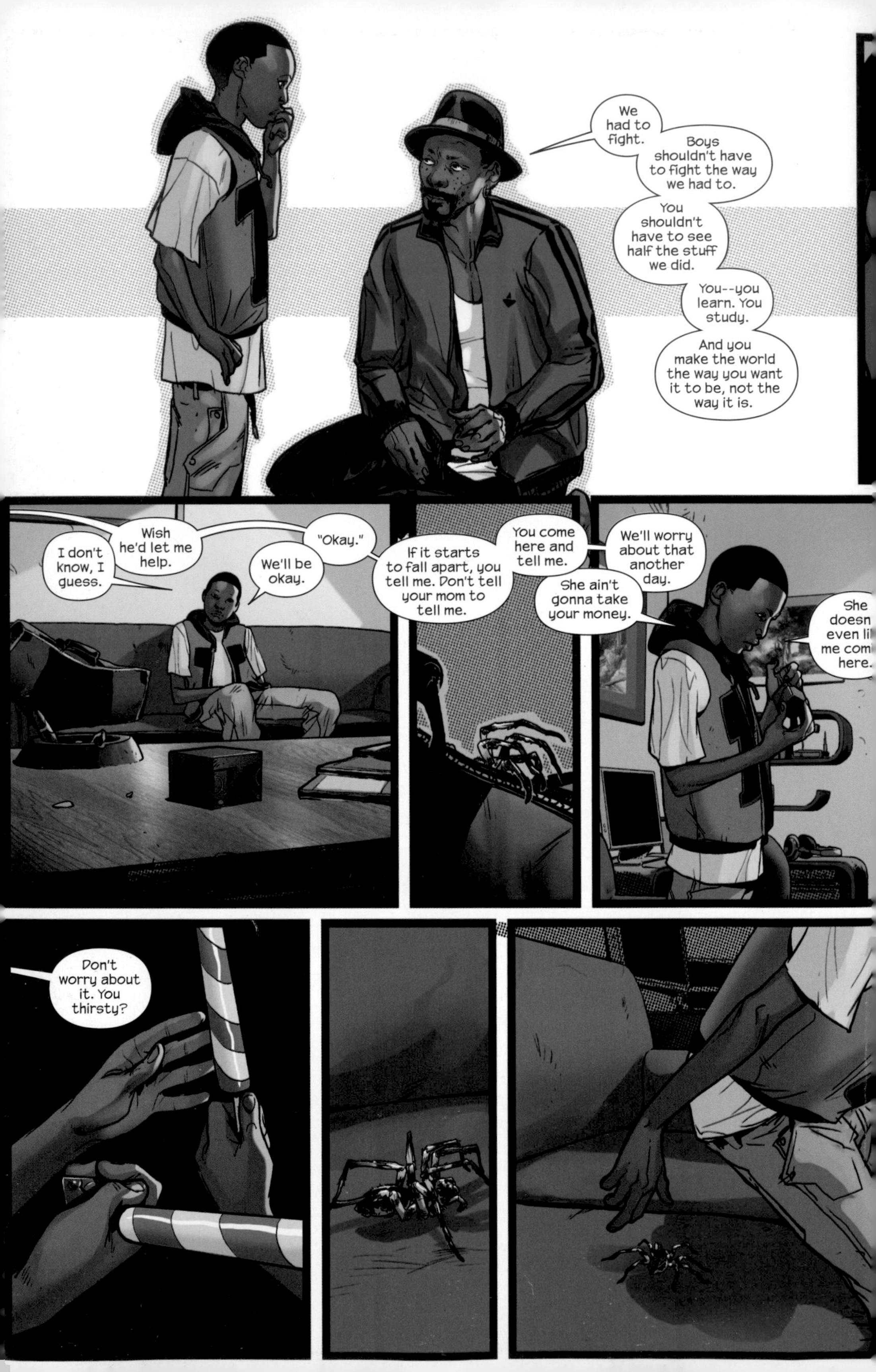
We had to fight.
Boys shouldn't have to fight the way we had to.
You shouldn't have to see half the stuff we did.
You--you learn. You study.
And you make the world the way you want it to be, not the way it is.
I don't know, I guess.
Wish he'd let me help.
We'll be okay.
"Okay."
If it starts to fall apart, you tell me. Don't tell your mom to tell me.
You come here and tell me.
We'll worry about that another day.
She ain't gonna take your money.
Don't worry about it. You thirsty?

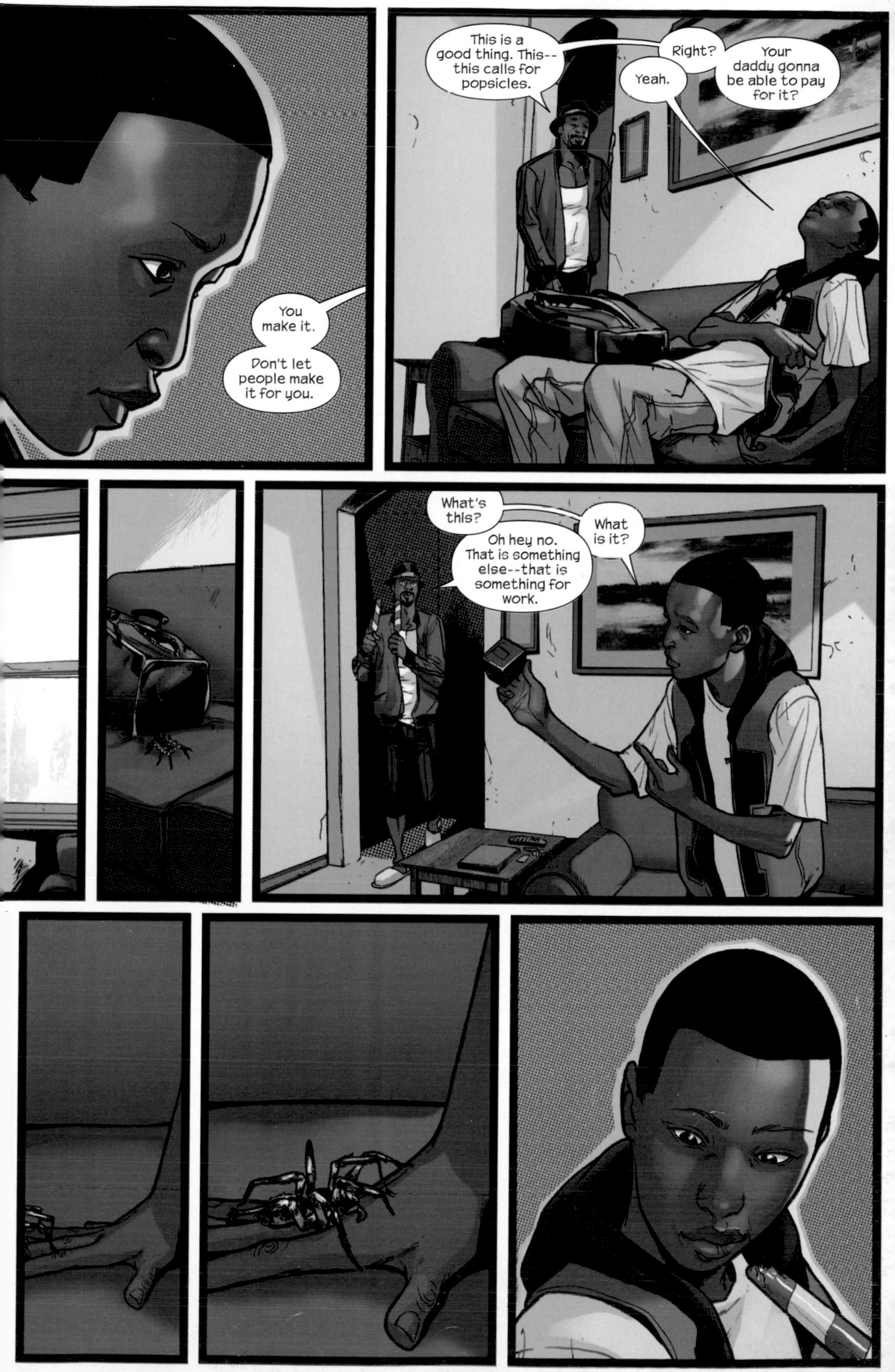
You make it.
Don't let people make it for you.
This is a good thing. This-- this calls for popsicles.
Right?
Yeah.
Your daddy gonna be able to pay for it?
What's this?
What is it?
Oh hey no. That is something else--that is something for work.

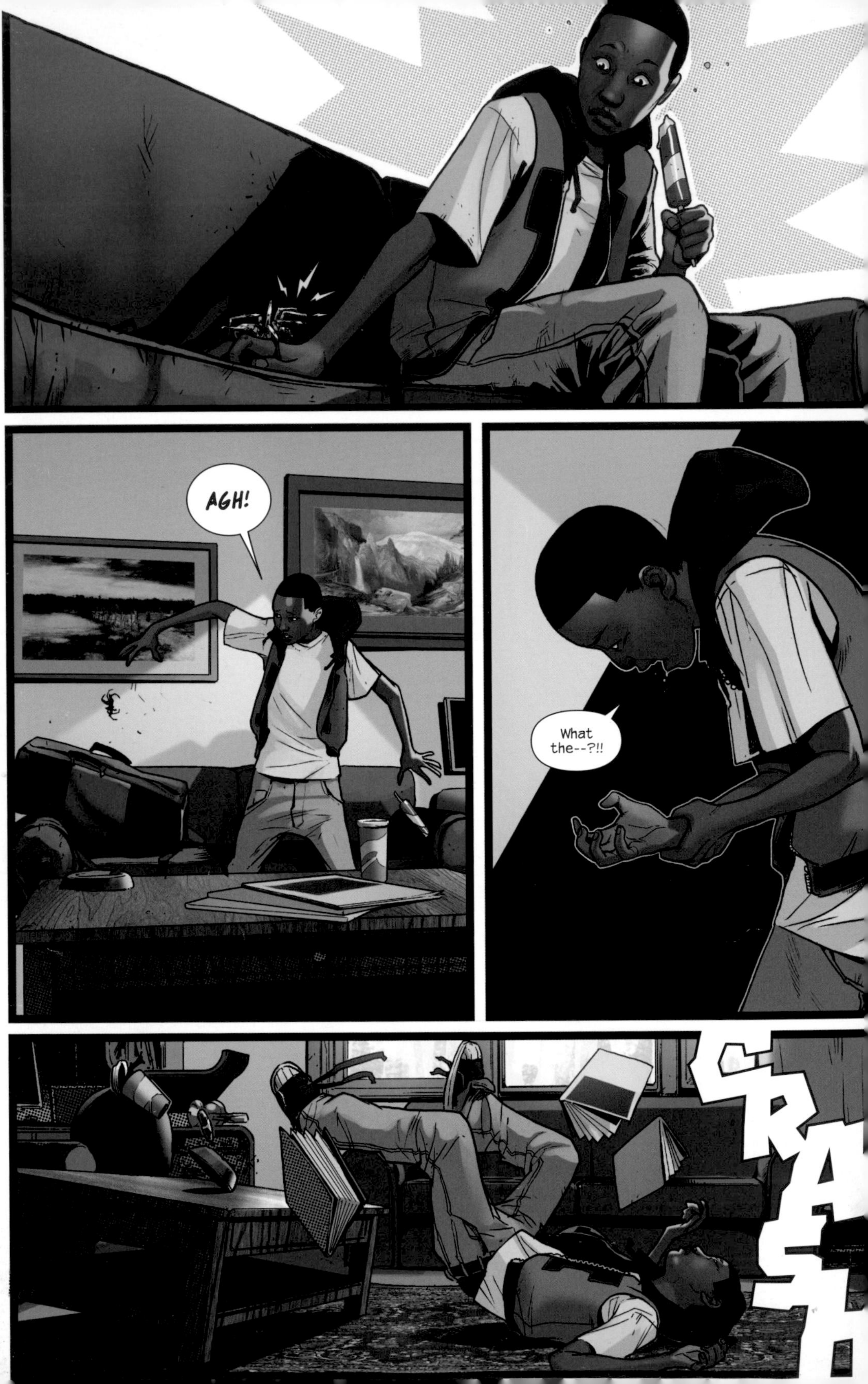

AGH!
What the--?!!
CRASH

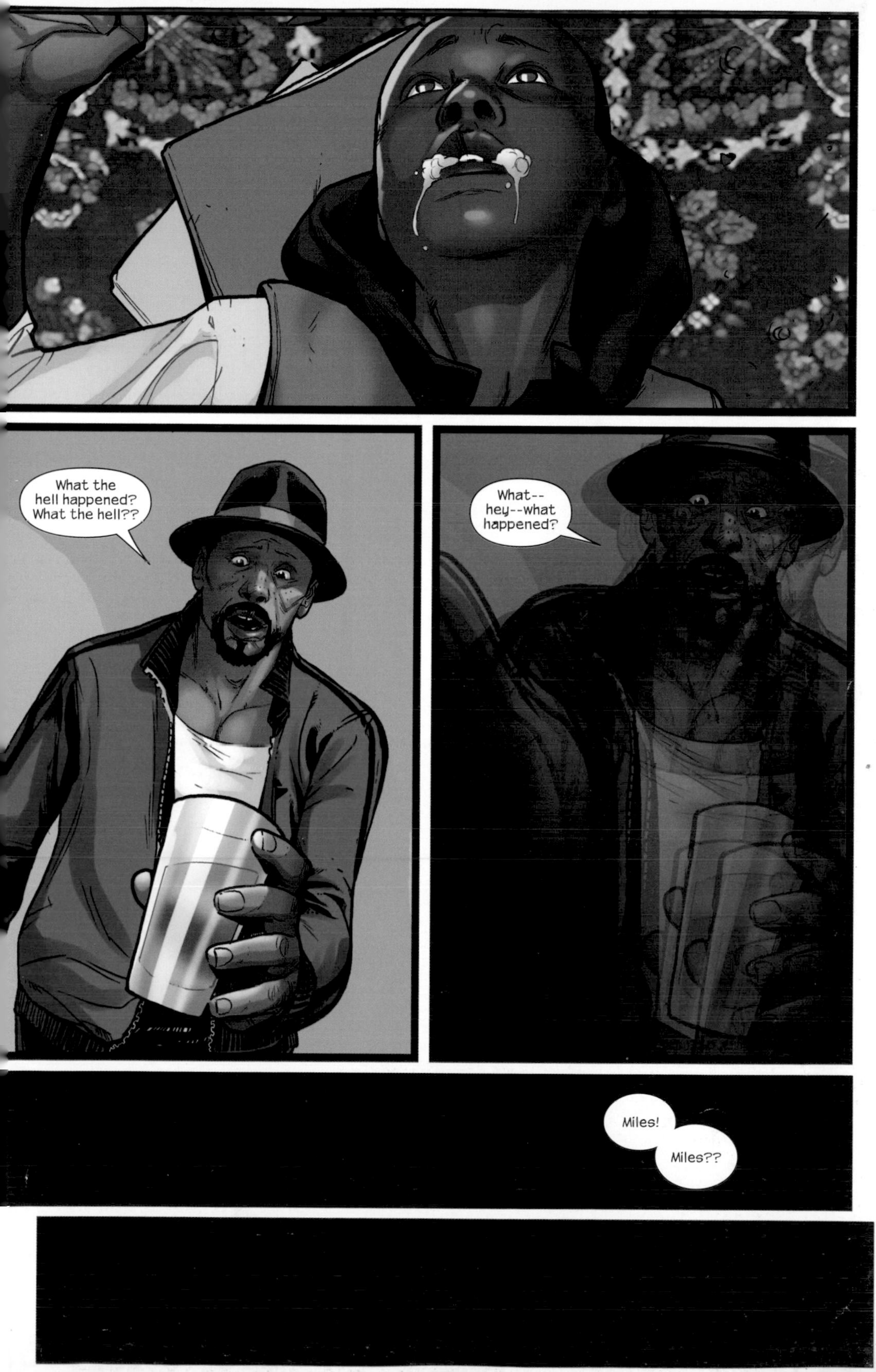
What the hell happened? What the hell??
What-- hey--what happened?
Miles!
Miles??

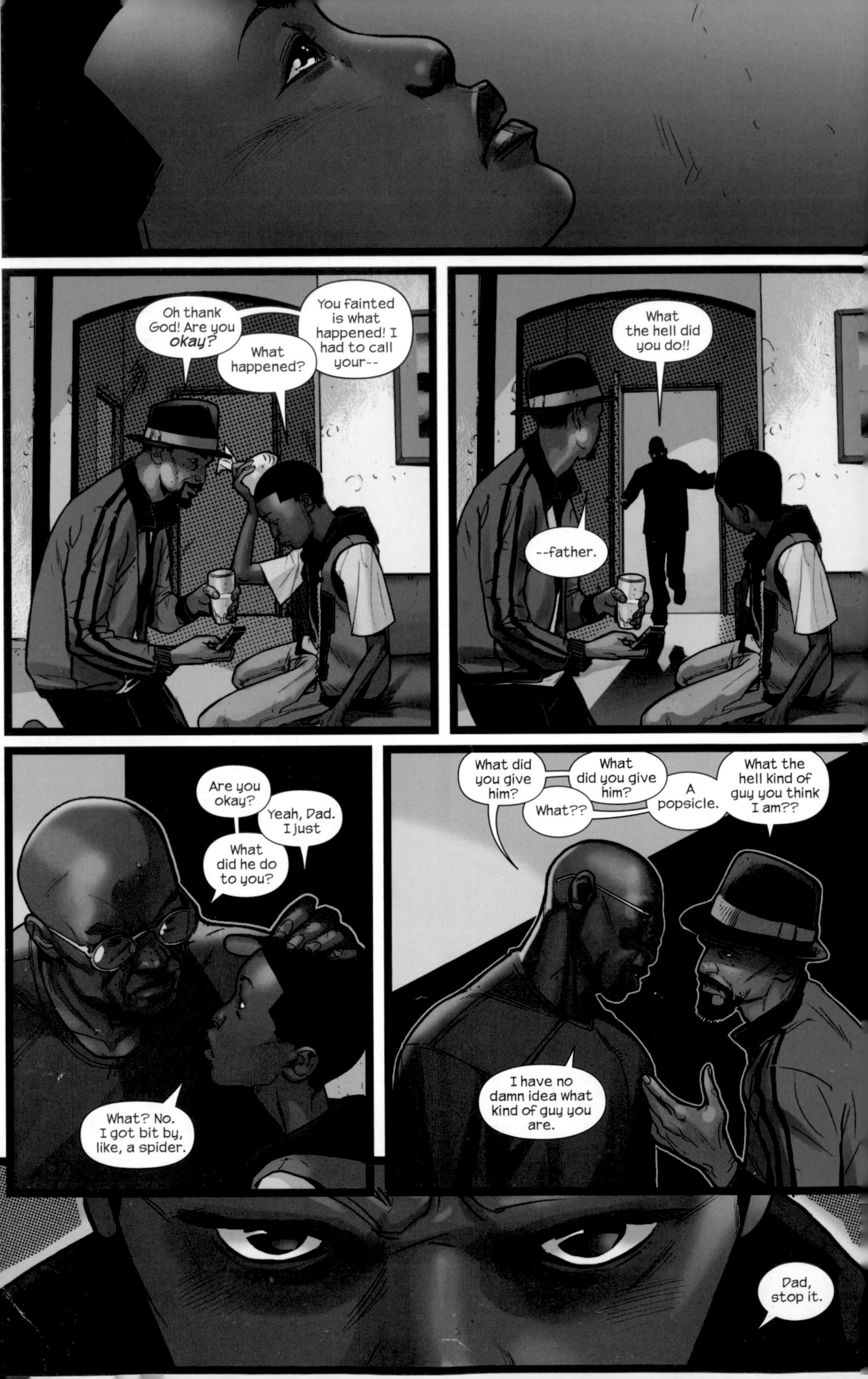
Oh thank God! Are you *okay?*
What happened?
You fainted is what happened! I had to call your--
What the hell did you do!!
--father.
Are you okay?
What did he do to you?
Yeah, Dad. I just
What? No. I got bit by, like, a spider.
What did you give him?
What did you give him?
What??
A popsicle.
What the hell kind of guy you think I am??
I have no damn idea what kind of guy you are.
Dad, stop it.

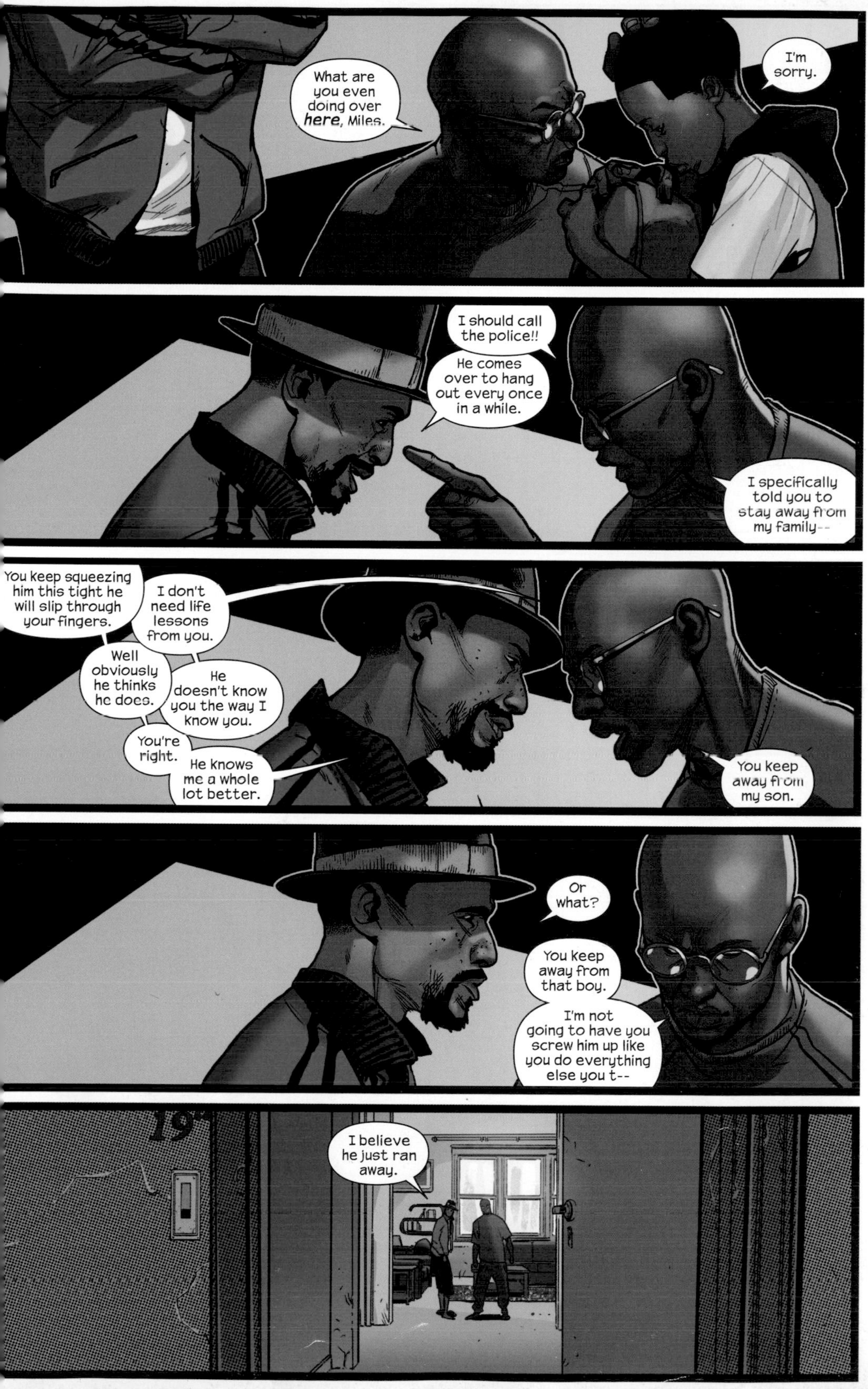

What are you even doing over *here*, Miles.
I'm sorry.
I should call the police!!
He comes over to hang out every once in a while.
I specifically told you to stay away from my family--
You keep squeezing him this tight he will slip through your fingers.
I don't need life lessons from you.
Well obviously he thinks he does.
He doesn't know you the way I know you.
You're right.
He knows me a whole lot better.
You keep away from my son.
Or what?
You keep away from that boy.
I'm not going to have you screw him up like you do everything else you t--
I believe he just ran away.

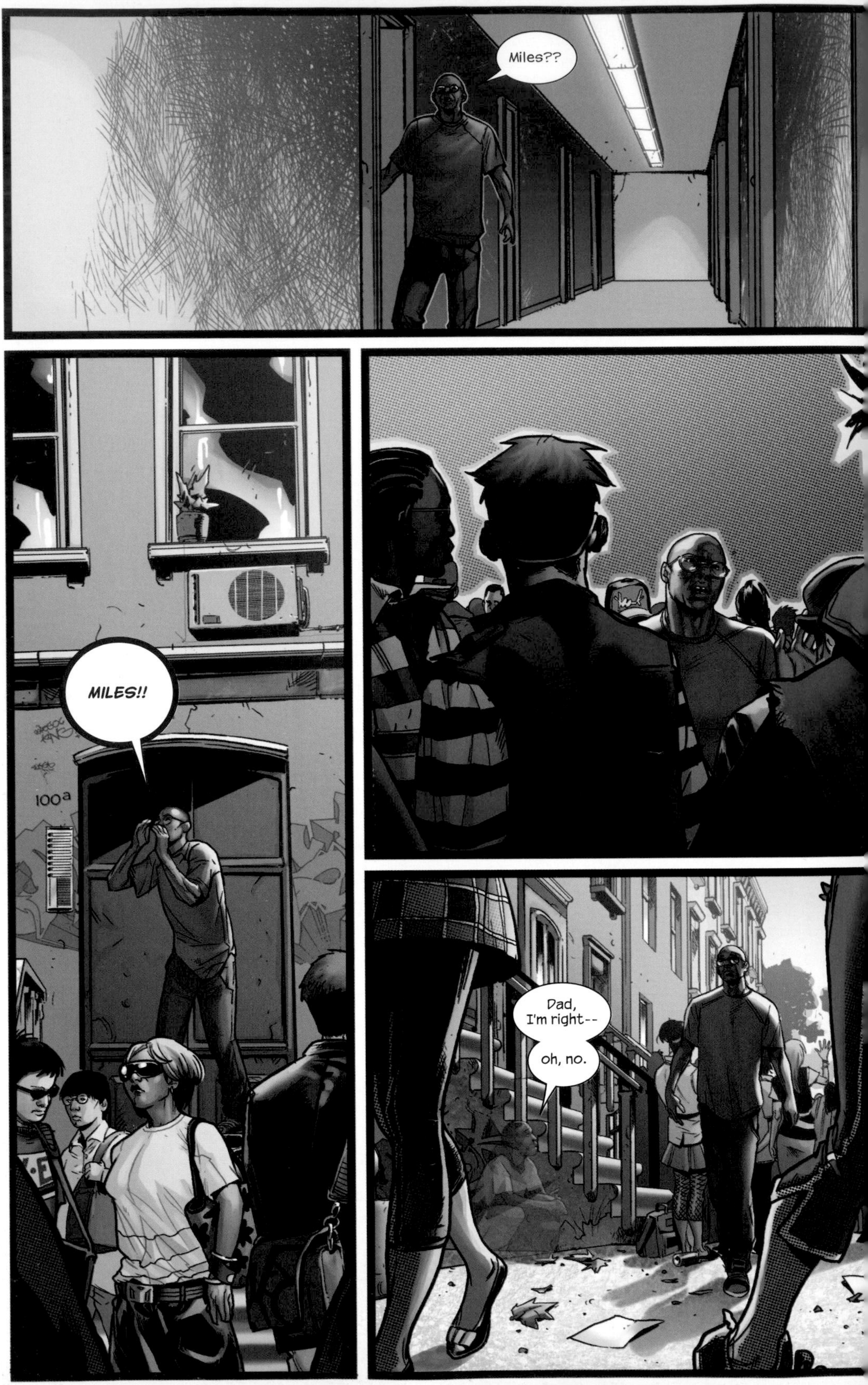
Miles??
100a
MILES!!
Dad,
I'm right--
oh, no.

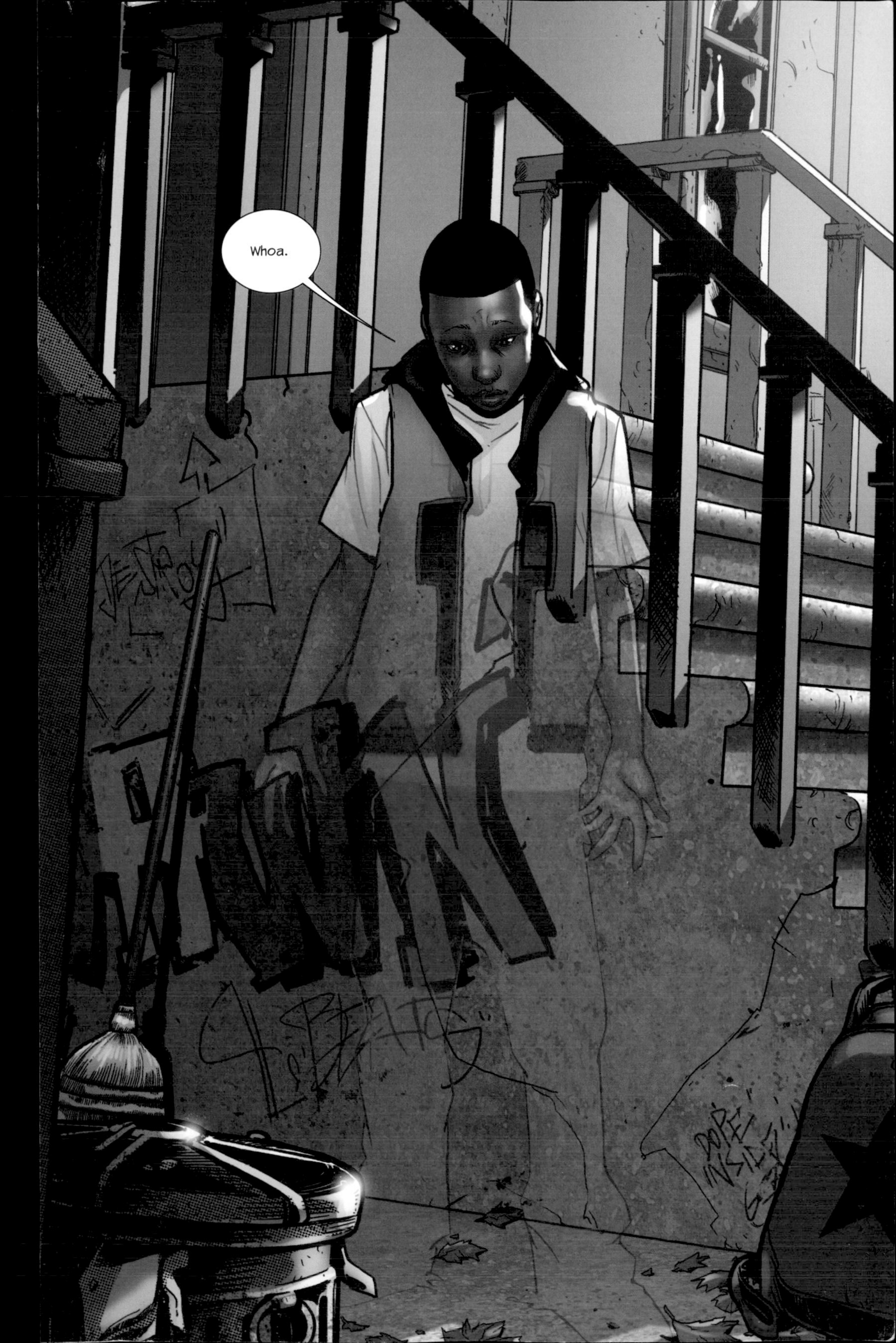
Whoa.

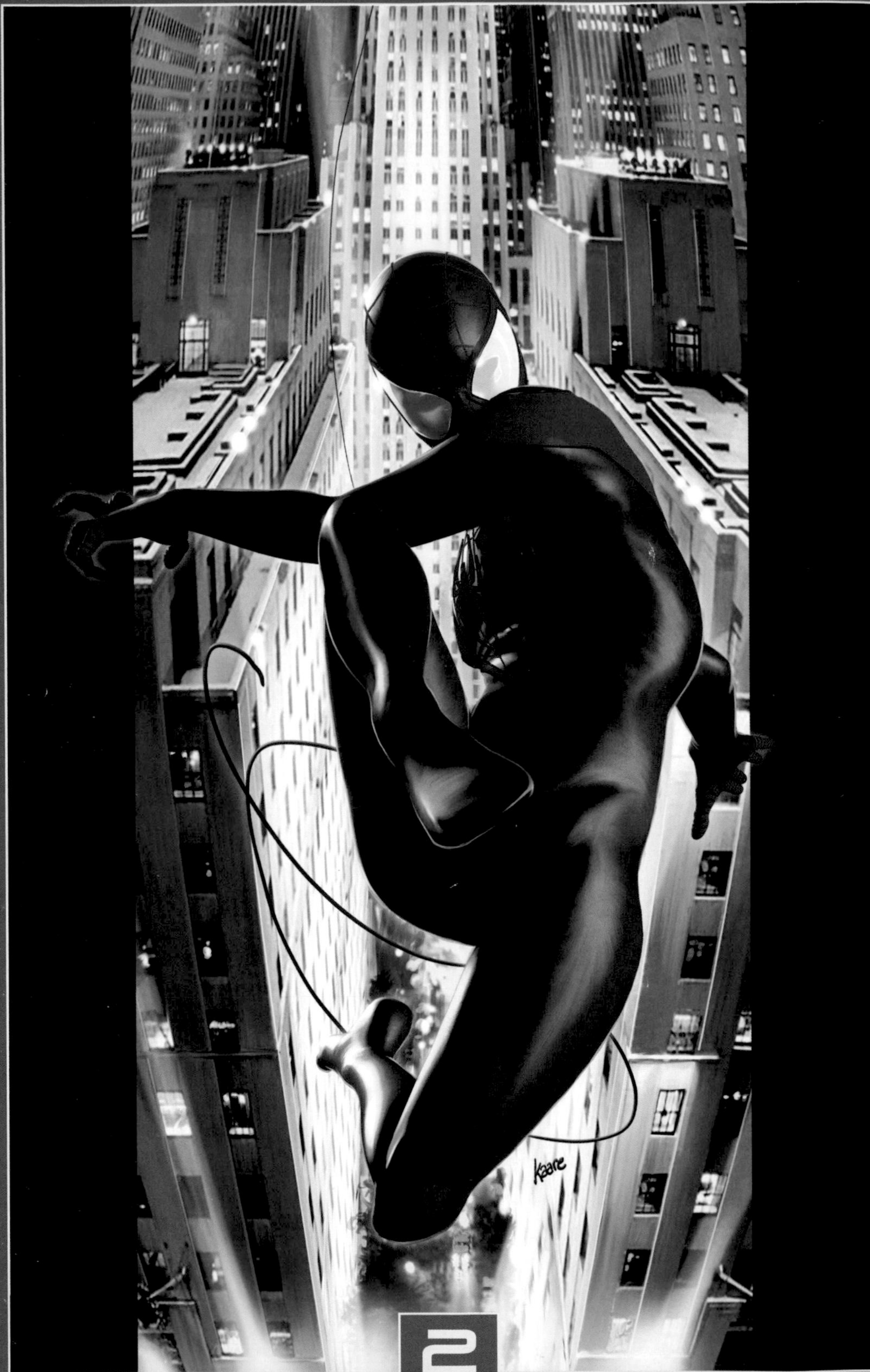
Kaare
2

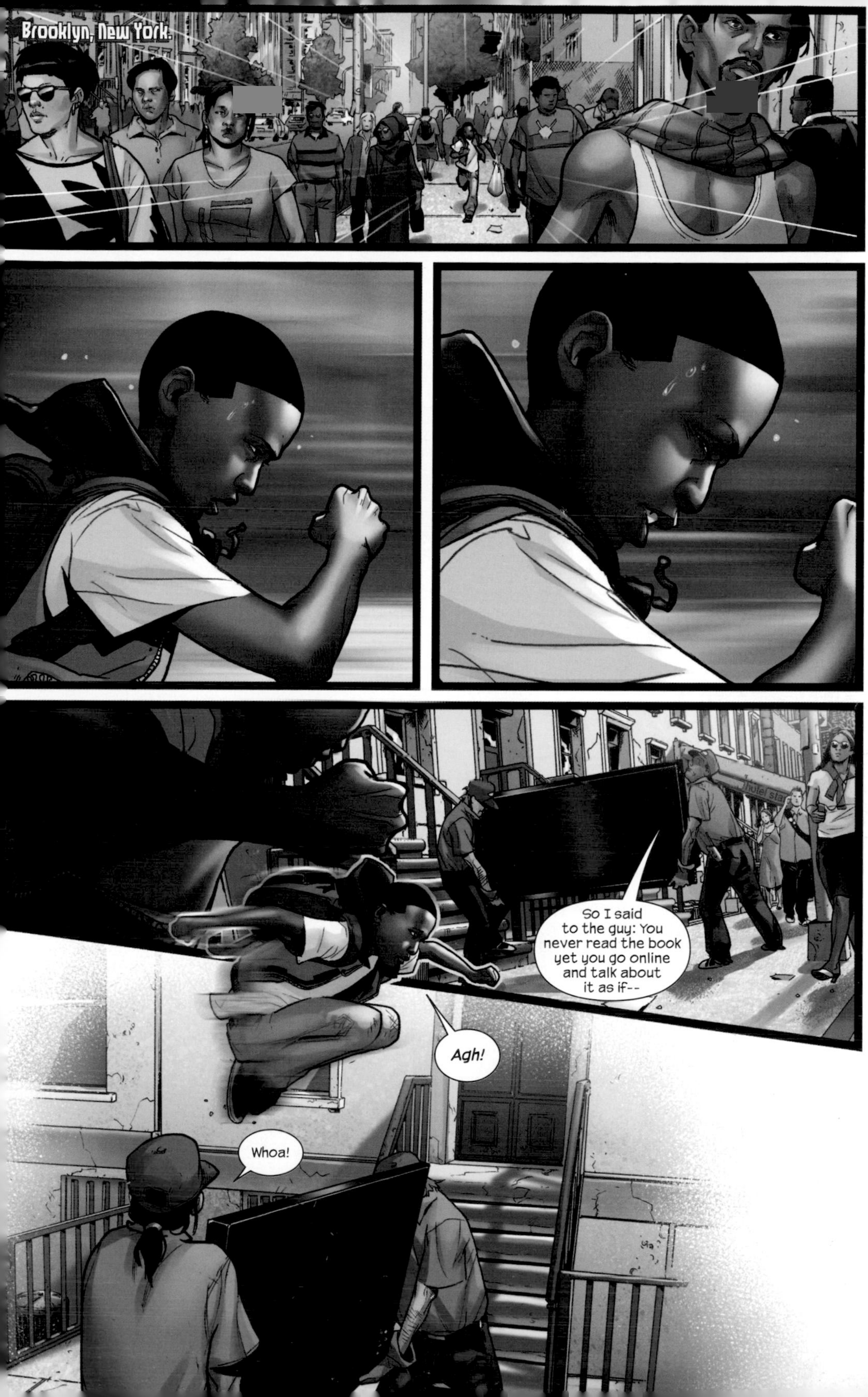
Brooklyn, New York.
So I said to the guy: You never read the book yet you go online and talk about it as if--
Agh!
Whoa!

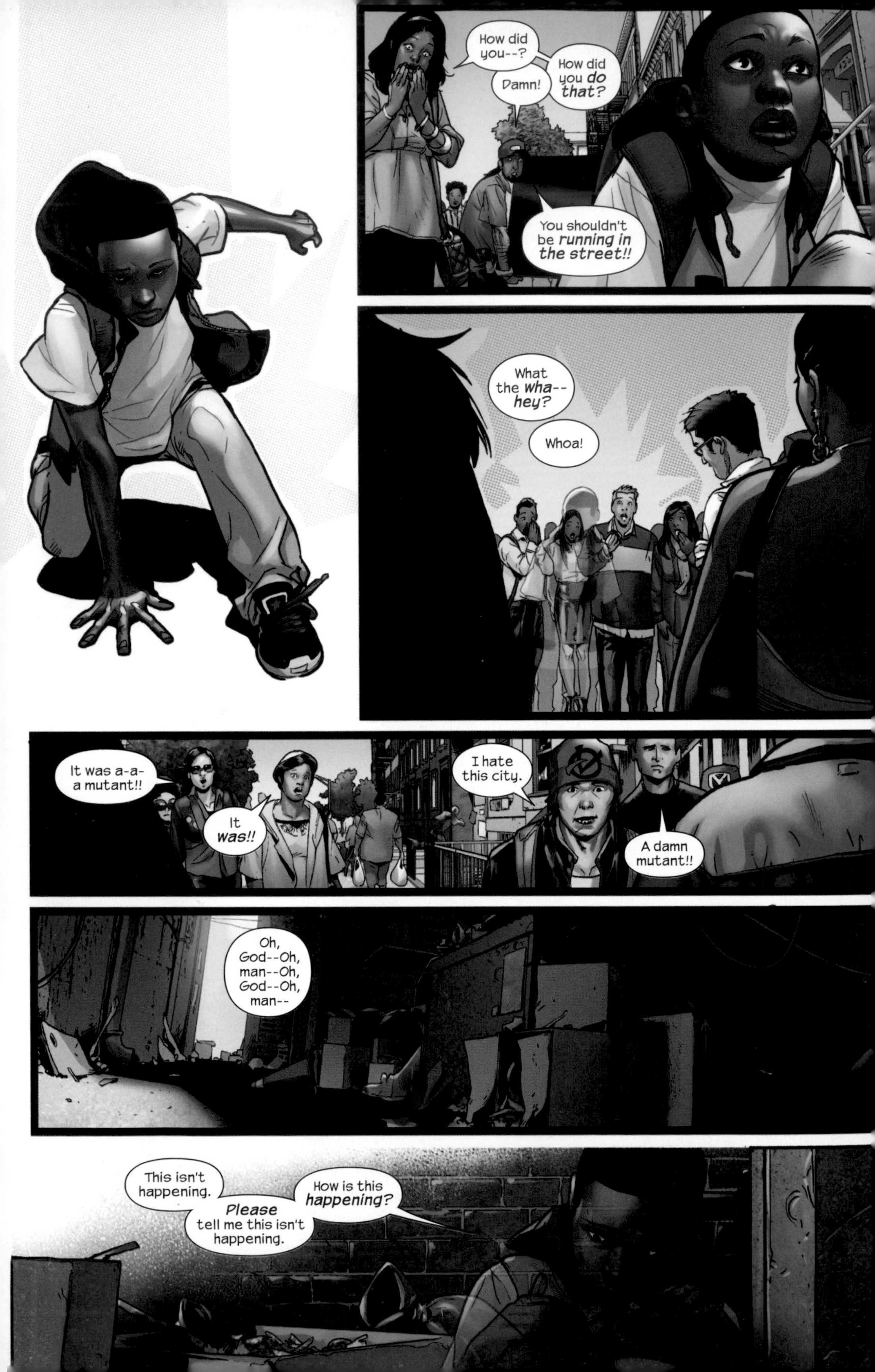
How did you--?
Damn!
How did you do that?
You shouldn't be running in the street!!
What the wha--hey?
Whoa!
It was a-a-a mutant!!
It was!!
I hate this city.
A damn mutant!!
Oh, God--Oh, man--Oh, God--Oh, man--
This isn't happening.
Please tell me this isn't happening.
How is this happening?

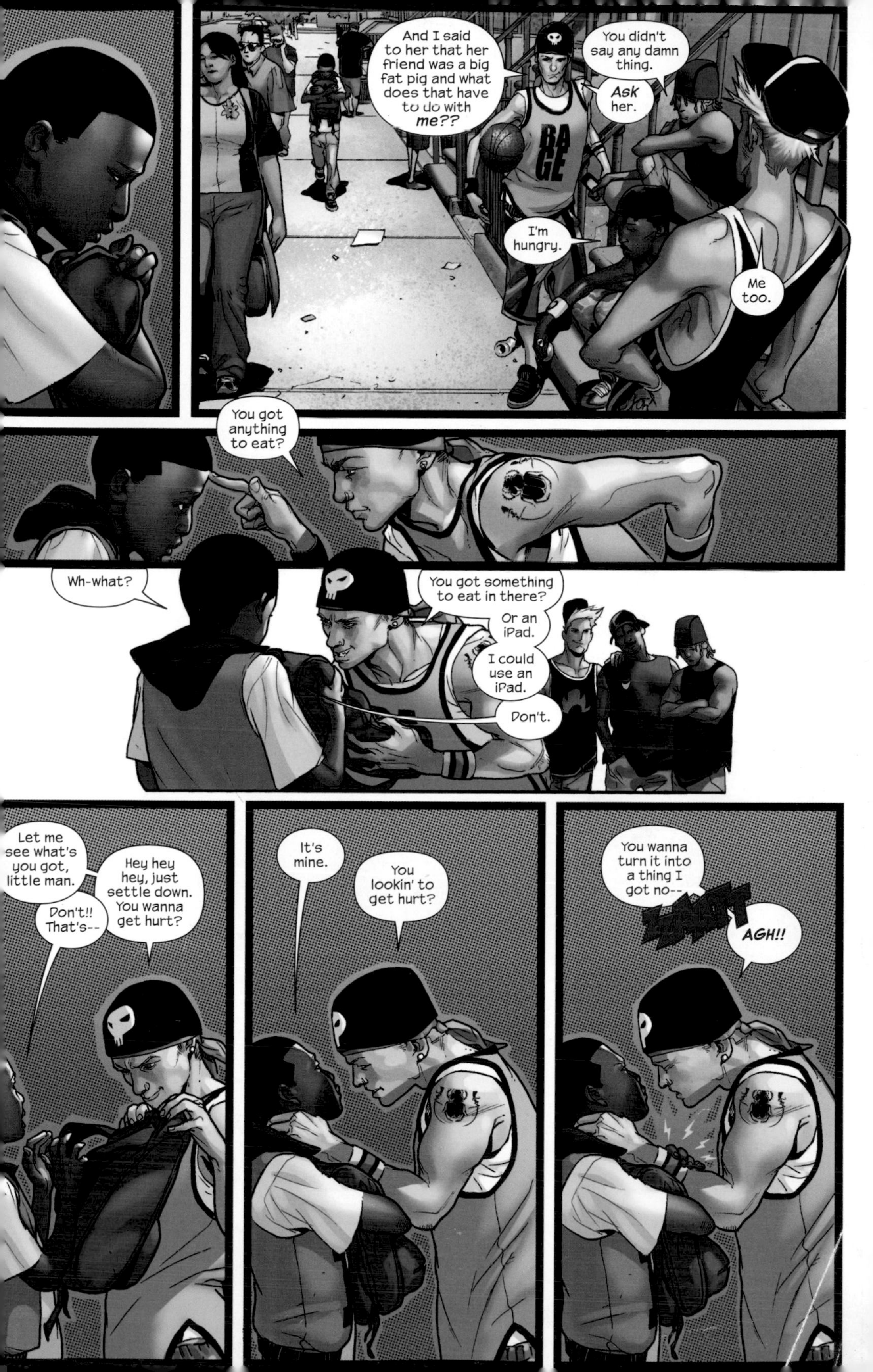
And I said to her that her friend was a big fat pig and what does that have to do with me??
You didn't say any damn thing.
Ask her.
RAGE
I'm hungry.
Me too.
You got anything to eat?
Wh-what?
You got something to eat in there?
Or an iPad.
I could use an iPad.
Don't.
Let me see what's you got, little man.
Hey hey hey, just settle down. You wanna get hurt?
Don't!! That's--
It's mine.
You lookin' to get hurt?
You wanna turn it into a thing I got no--
AGH!!

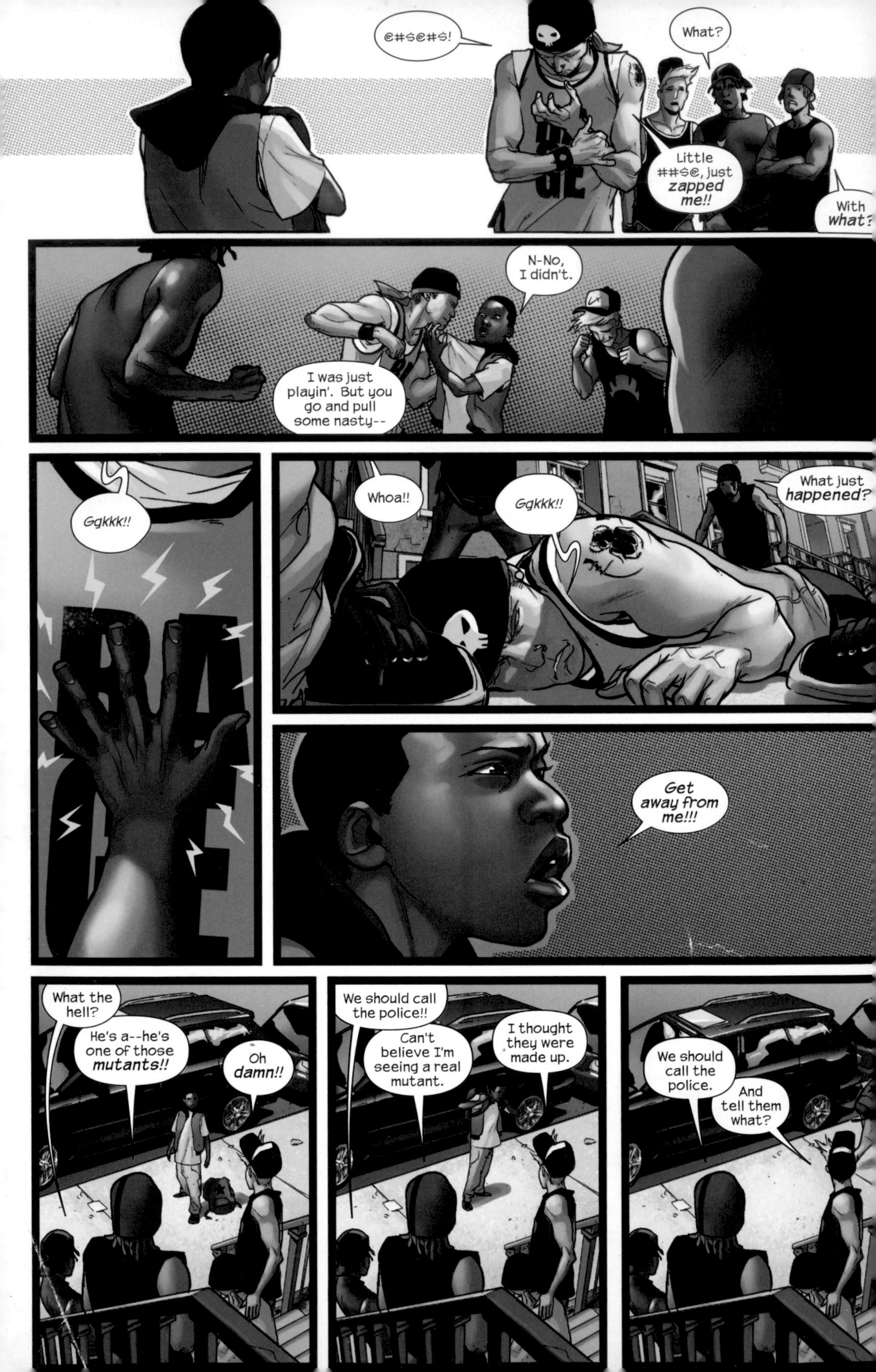

@#$@#$!
What?
Little ##$@, just zapped me!!
With what?
N-No, I didn't.
I was just playin'. But you go and pull some nasty--
Ggkkk!!
Whoa!!
Ggkkk!!
What just happened?
Get away from me!!!
What the hell?
He's a--he's one of those mutants!!
Oh damn!!
We should call the police!!
Can't believe I'm seeing a real mutant.
I thought they were made up.
We should call the police.
And tell them what?

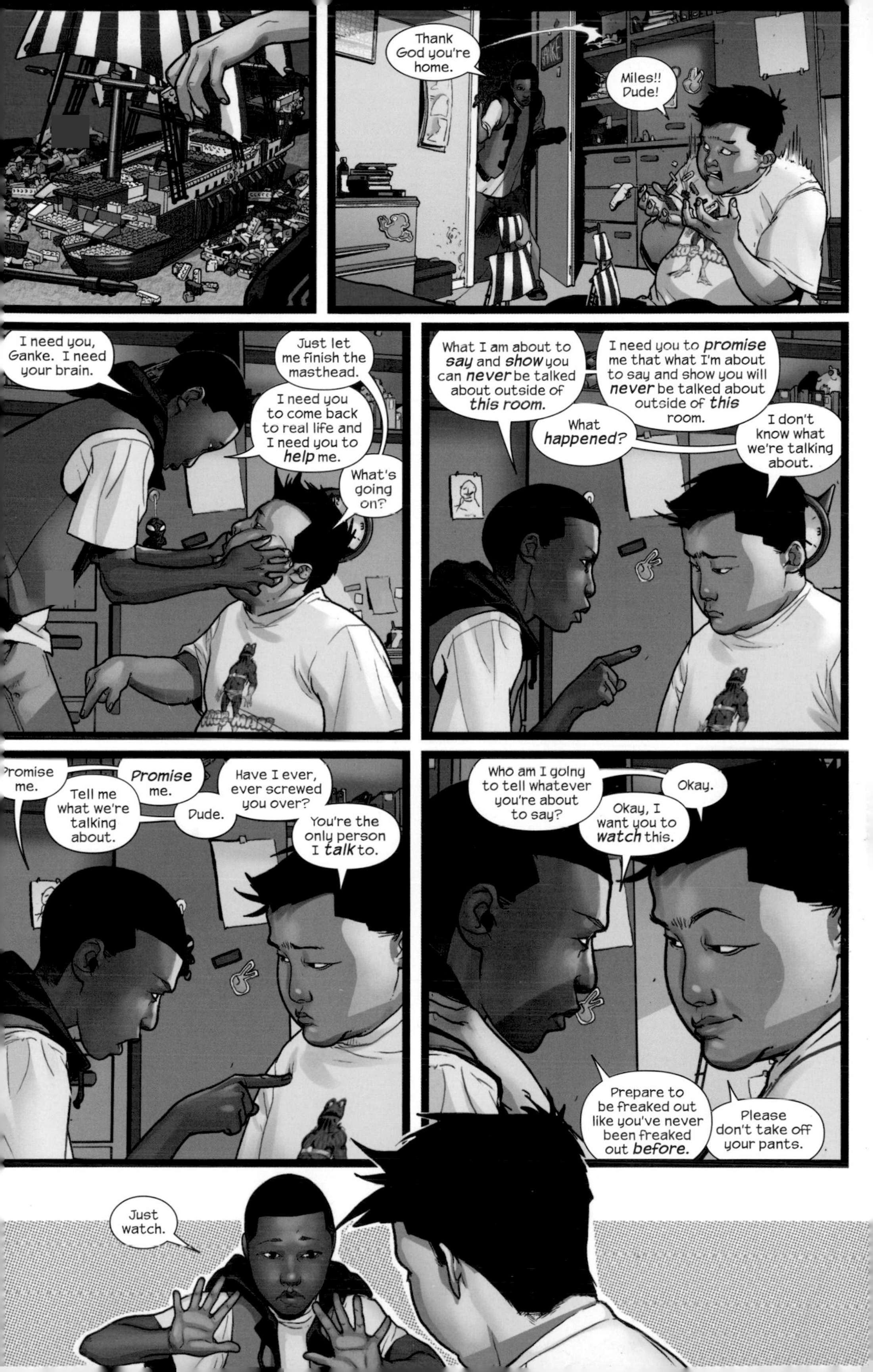
Thank God you're home.
Miles!! Dude!
I need you, Ganke. I need your brain.
Just let me finish the masthead.
I need you to come back to real life and I need you to *help* me.
What's going on?
What I am about to *say* and *show* you can *never* be talked about outside of *this room.*
I need you to *promise* me that what I'm about to say and show you will *never* be talked about outside of *this* room.
What *happened?*
I don't know what we're talking about.
romise me.
Promise me.
Tell me what we're talking about.
Dude.
Have I ever, ever screwed you over?
You're the only person I *talk* to.
Who am I going to tell whatever you're about to say?
Okay.
Okay, I want you to *watch* this.
Prepare to be freaked out like you've never been freaked out *before.*
Please don't take off your pants.
Just watch.

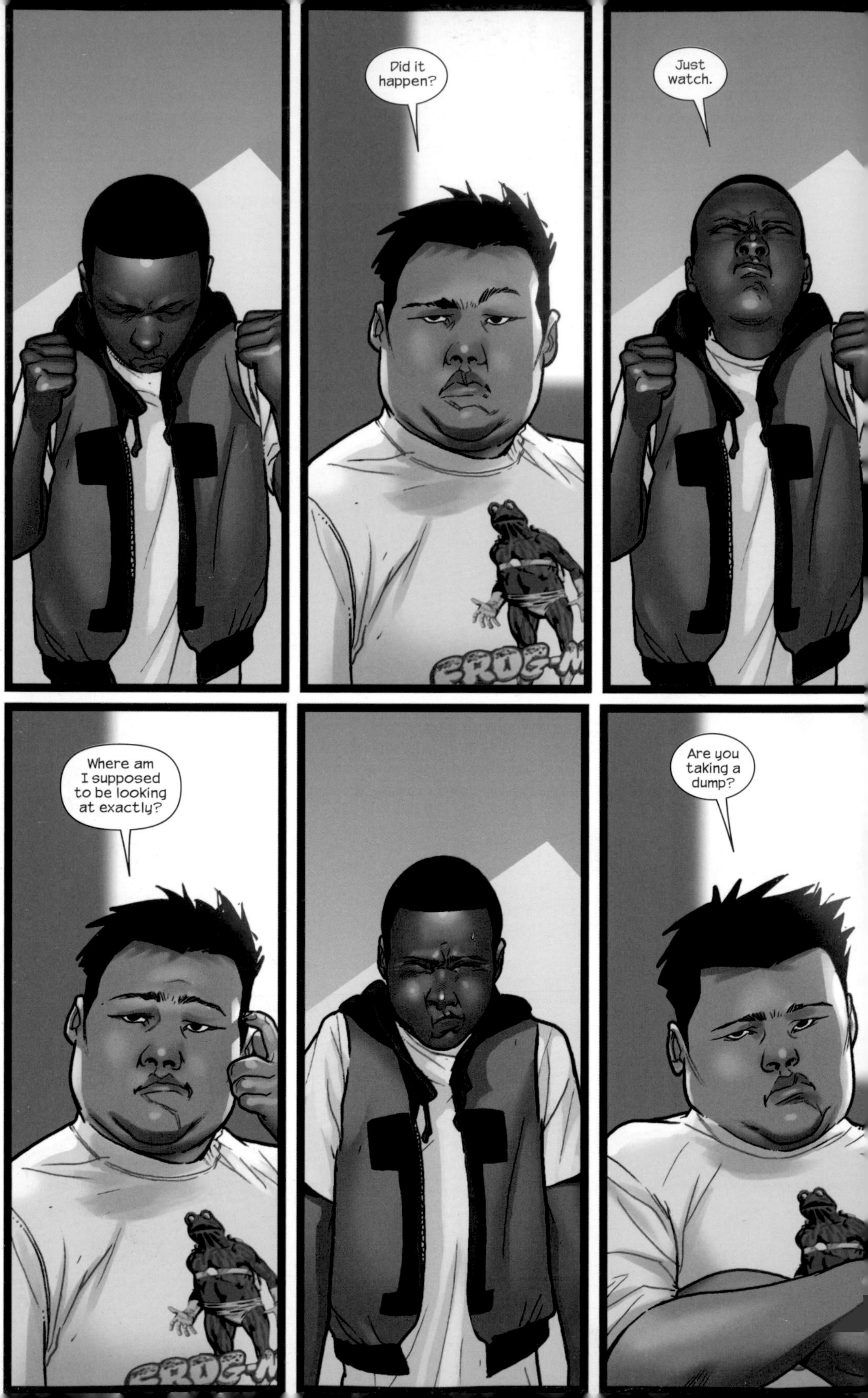
Did it happen?
Just watch.
Where am I supposed to be looking at exactly?
Are you taking a dump?

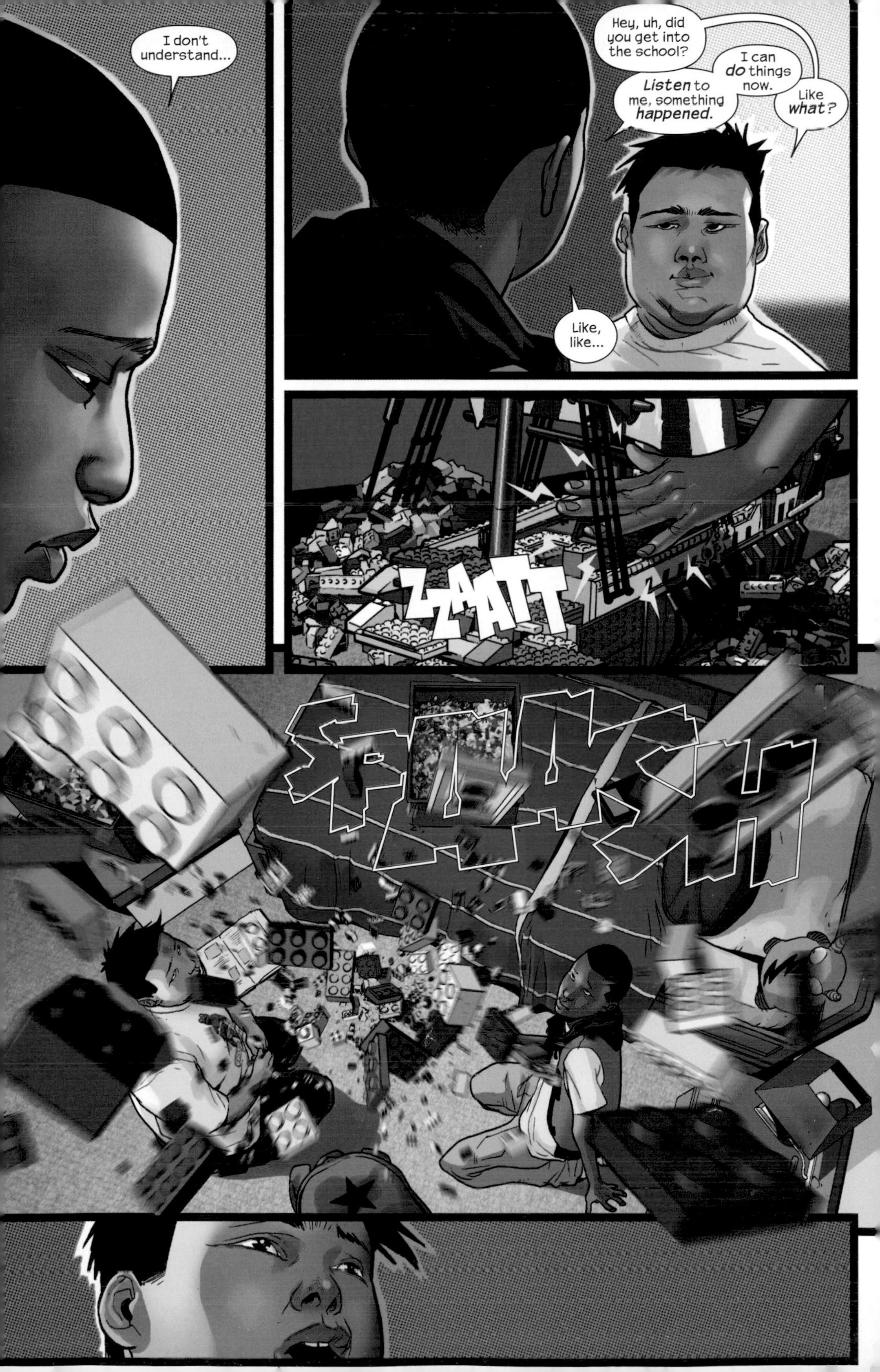

I don't understand...
Hey, uh, did you get into the school?
Listen to me, something happened.
I can do things now.
Like what?
Like, like...
ZZAATT

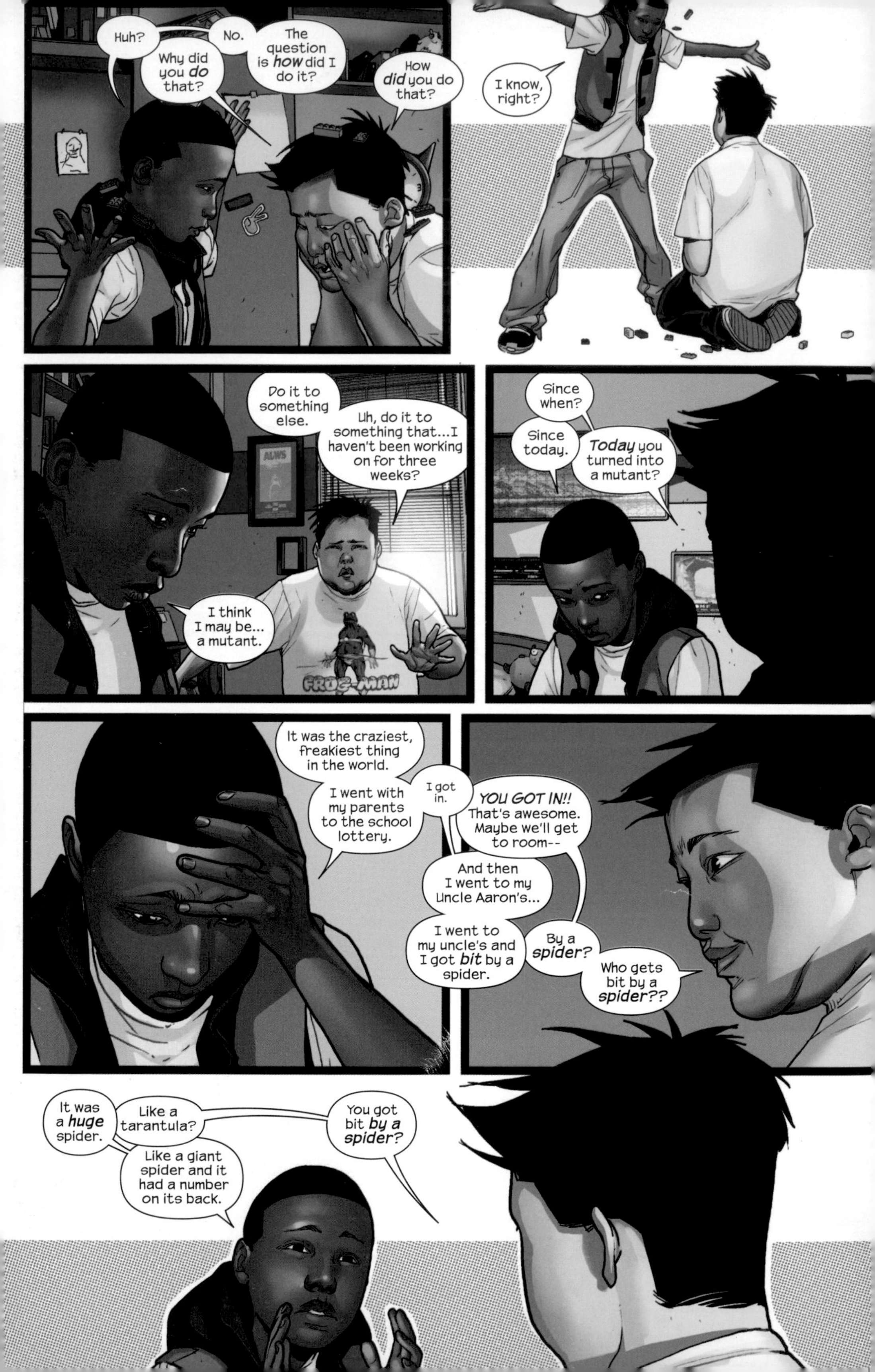

Huh?
Why did you do that?
No.
The question is how did I do it?
How did you do that?
I know, right?
Do it to something else.
Uh, do it to something that...I haven't been working on for three weeks?
I think I may be... a mutant.
ALWS
FROG-MAN
Since when?
Since today.
Today you turned into a mutant?
It was the craziest, freakiest thing in the world.
I went with my parents to the school lottery.
I got in.
YOU GOT IN!! That's awesome. Maybe we'll get to room--
And then I went to my Uncle Aaron's...
I went to my uncle's and I got bit by a spider.
By a spider?
Who gets bit by a spider??
It was a huge spider.
Like a tarantula?
Like a giant spider and it had a number on its back.
You got bit by a spider?

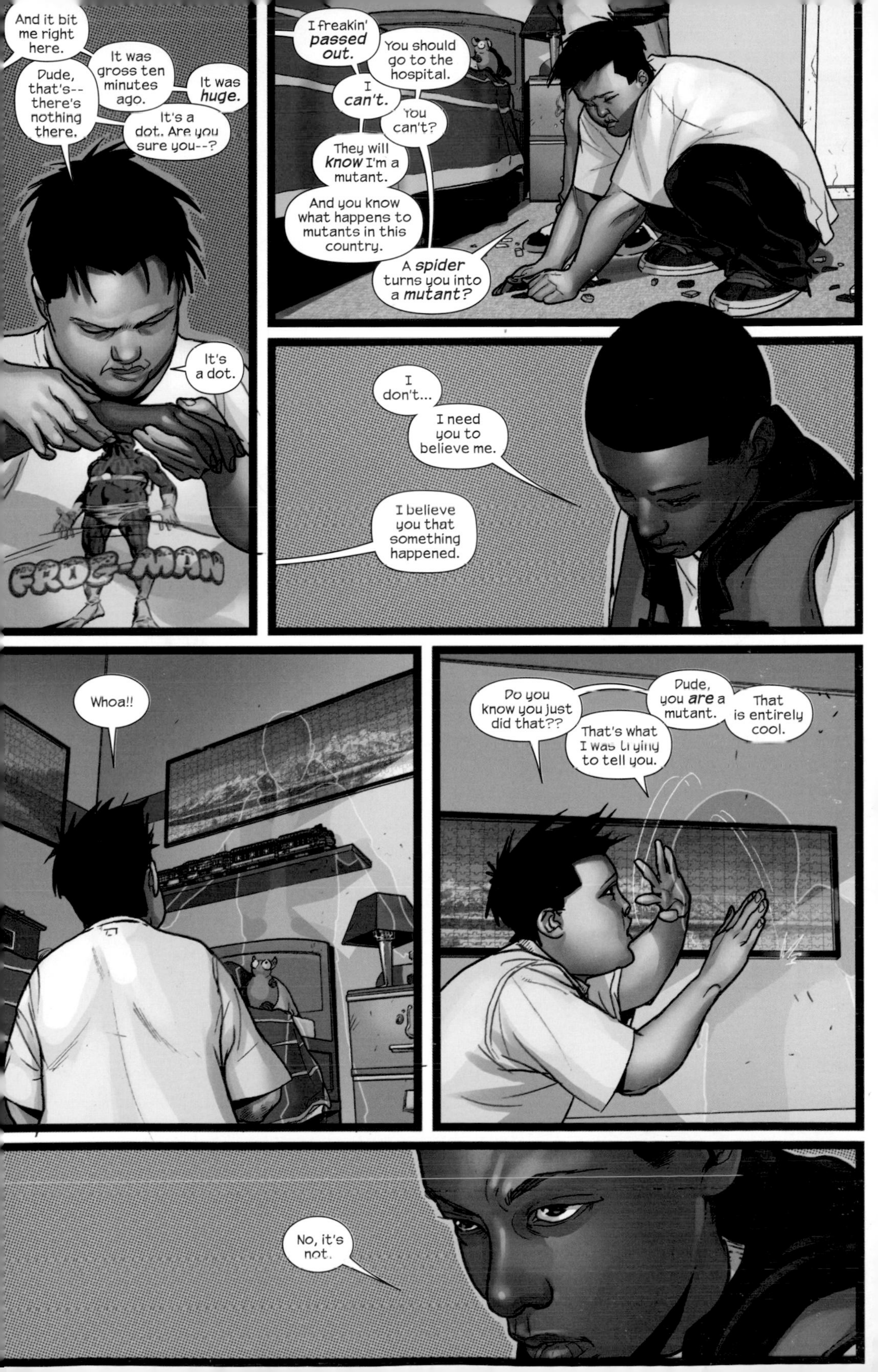
And it bit me right here.
It was gross ten minutes ago.
It was *huge.*
Dude, that's-- there's nothing there.
It's a dot. Are you sure you--?
It's a dot.
I freakin' *passed out.*
You should go to the hospital.
I *can't.*
You can't?
They will *know* I'm a mutant.
And you know what happens to mutants in this country.
A *spider* turns you into a *mutant?*
I don't...
I need you to believe me.
I believe you that something happened.
Whoa!!
Do you know you just did that??
Dude, you *are* a mutant.
That is entirely cool.
That's what I was trying to tell you.
No, it's not.

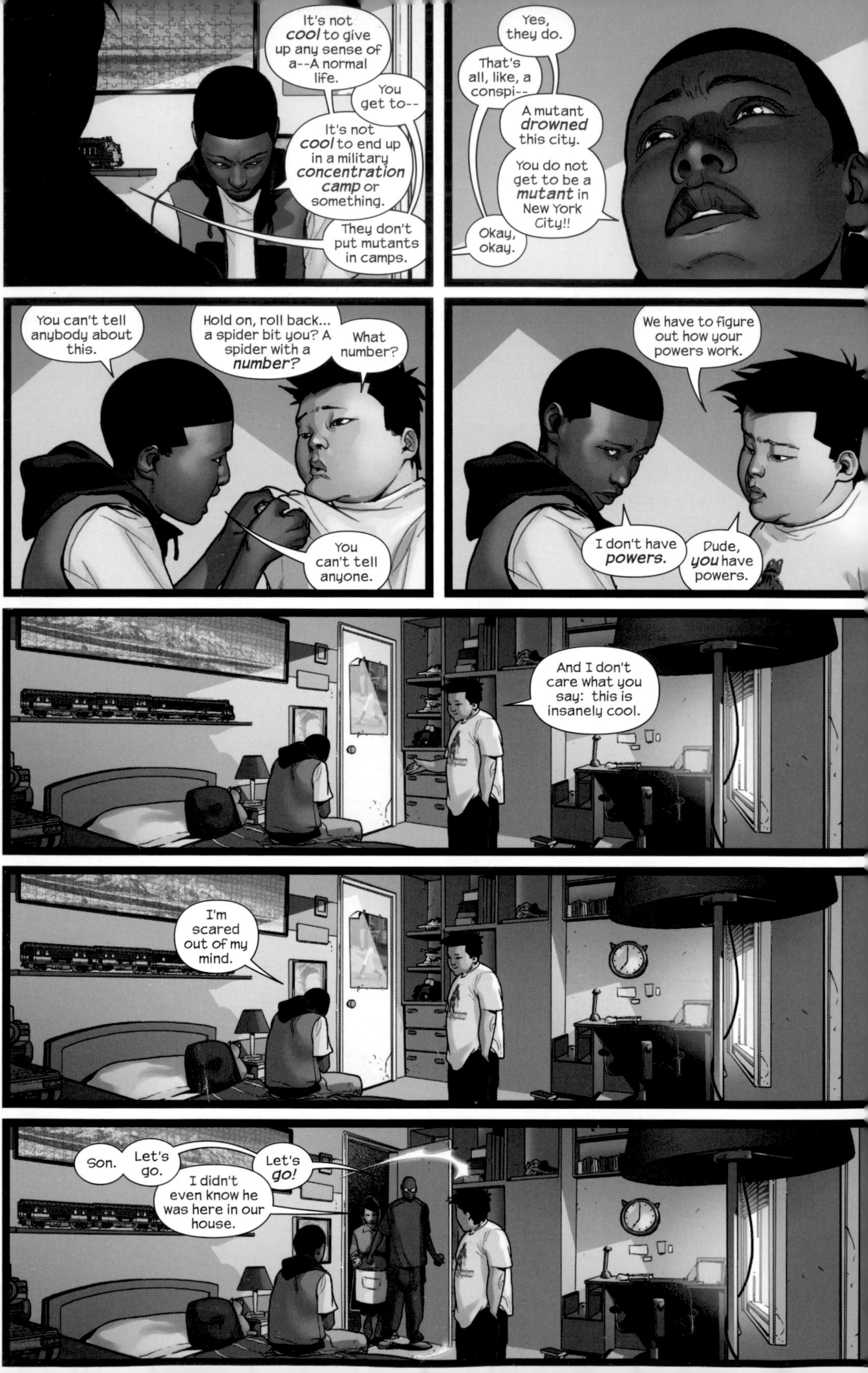
It's not *cool* to give up any sense of a--A normal life.
You get to--
It's not *cool* to end up in a military *concentration camp* or something.
They don't put mutants in camps.
Yes, they do.
That's all, like, a conspi--
A mutant *drowned* this city.
You do not get to be a *mutant* in New York City!!
Okay, okay.
You can't tell anybody about this.
Hold on, roll back... a spider bit you? A spider with a *number?*
What number?
You can't tell anyone.
We have to figure out how your powers work.
I don't have *powers.*
Dude, *you* have powers.
And I don't care what you say: this is insanely cool.
I'm scared out of my mind.
Son.
Let's go.
Let's *go!*
I didn't even know he was here in our house.

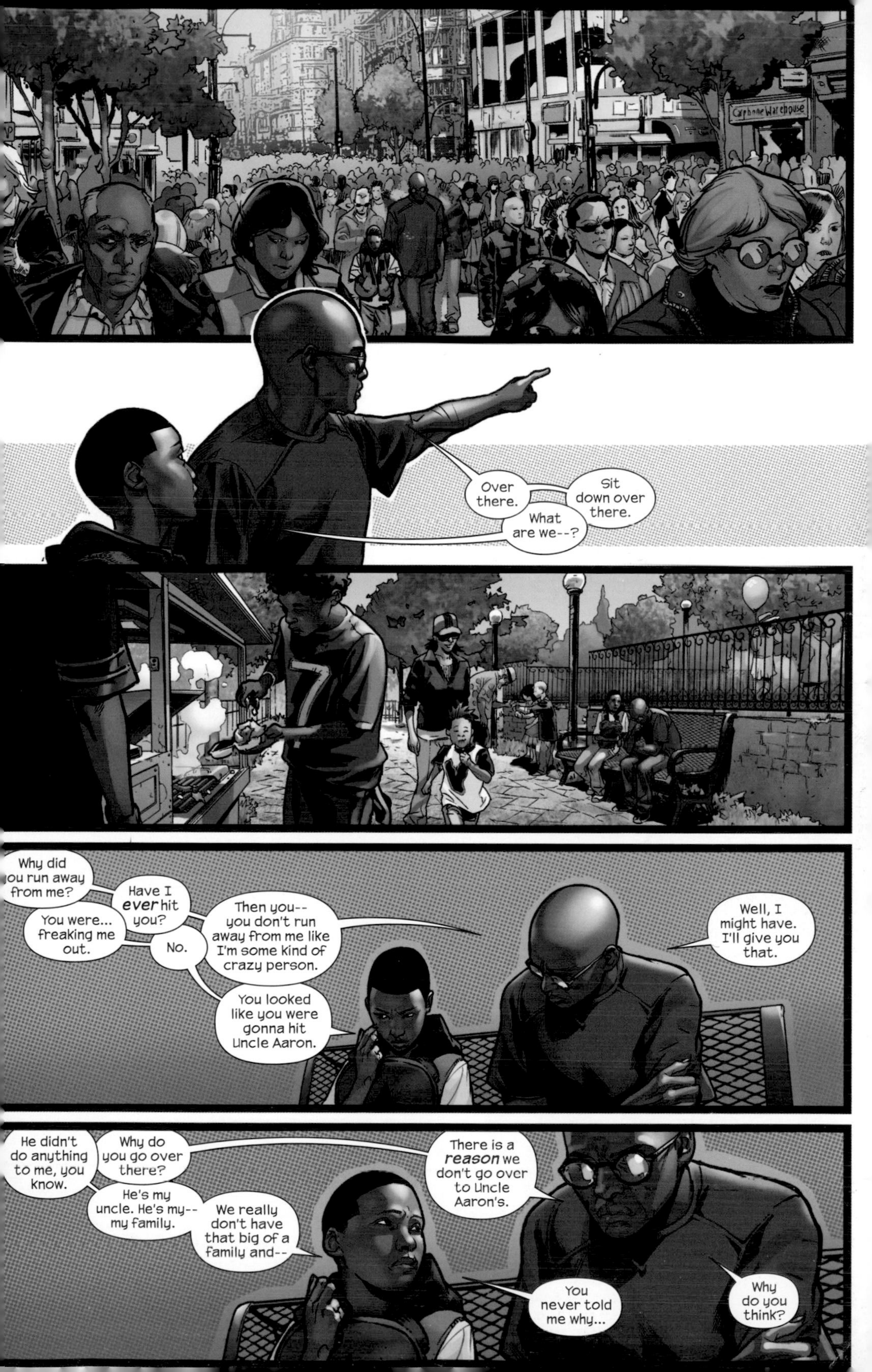
Carphone Warehouse
Over there.
Sit down over there.
What are we--?
Why did you run away from me?
You were... freaking me out.
Have I ever hit you?
No.
Then you-- you don't run away from me like I'm some kind of crazy person.
You looked like you were gonna hit Uncle Aaron.
Well, I might have. I'll give you that.
He didn't do anything to me, you know.
Why do you go over there?
He's my uncle. He's my-- my family.
We really don't have that big of a family and--
There is a reason we don't go over to Uncle Aaron's.
You never told me why...
Why do you think?

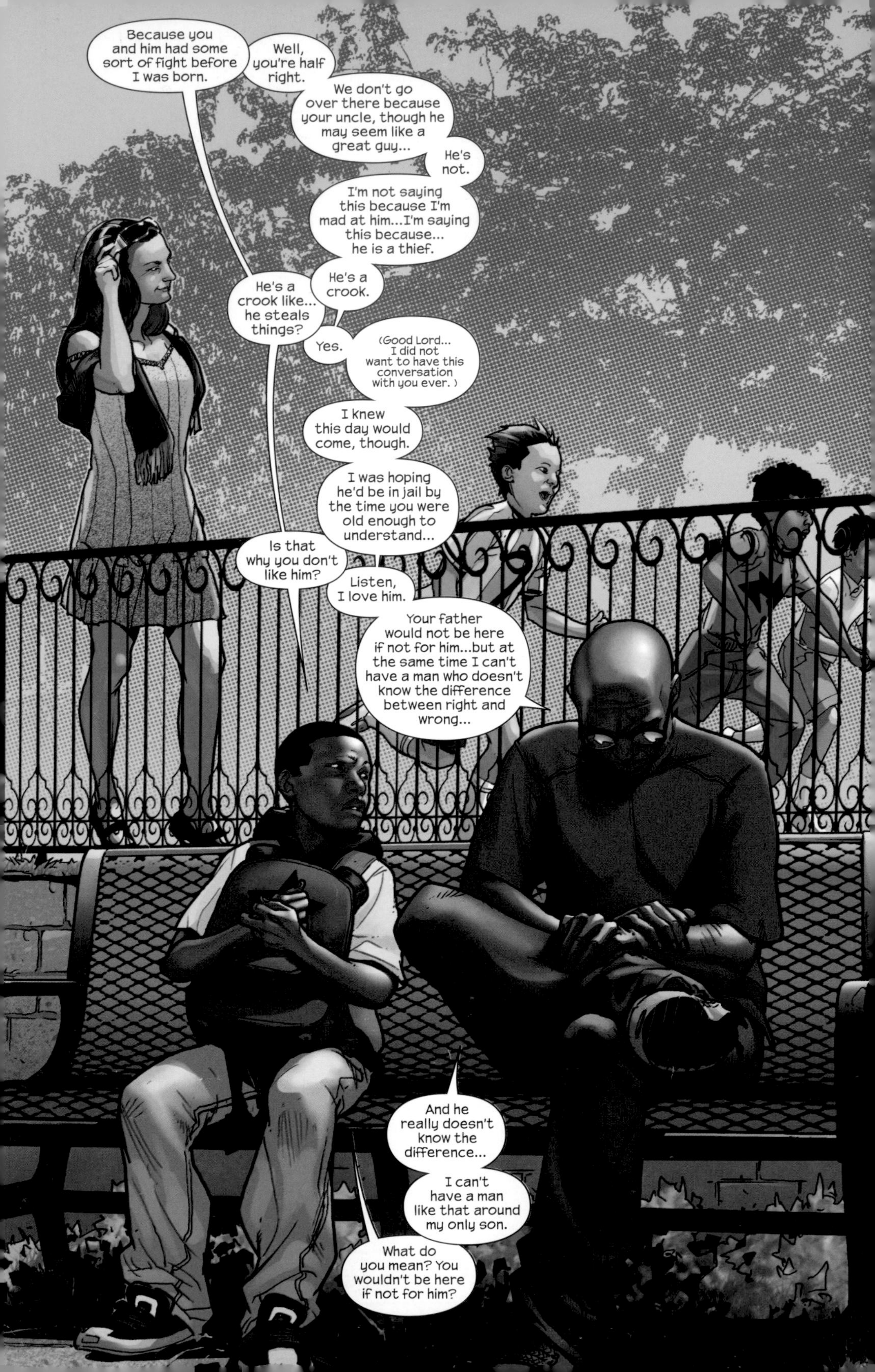
Because you and him had some sort of fight before I was born.
Well, you're half right.
We don't go over there because your uncle, though he may seem like a great guy...
He's not.
I'm not saying this because I'm mad at him...I'm saying this because... he is a thief.
He's a crook.
He's a crook like... he steals things?
Yes.
(Good Lord... I did not want to have this conversation with you ever.)
I knew this day would come, though.
I was hoping he'd be in jail by the time you were old enough to understand...
Is that why you don't like him?
Listen, I love him.
Your father would not be here if not for him...but at the same time I can't have a man who doesn't know the difference between right and wrong...
And he really doesn't know the difference...
I can't have a man like that around my only son.
What do you mean? You wouldn't be here if not for him?

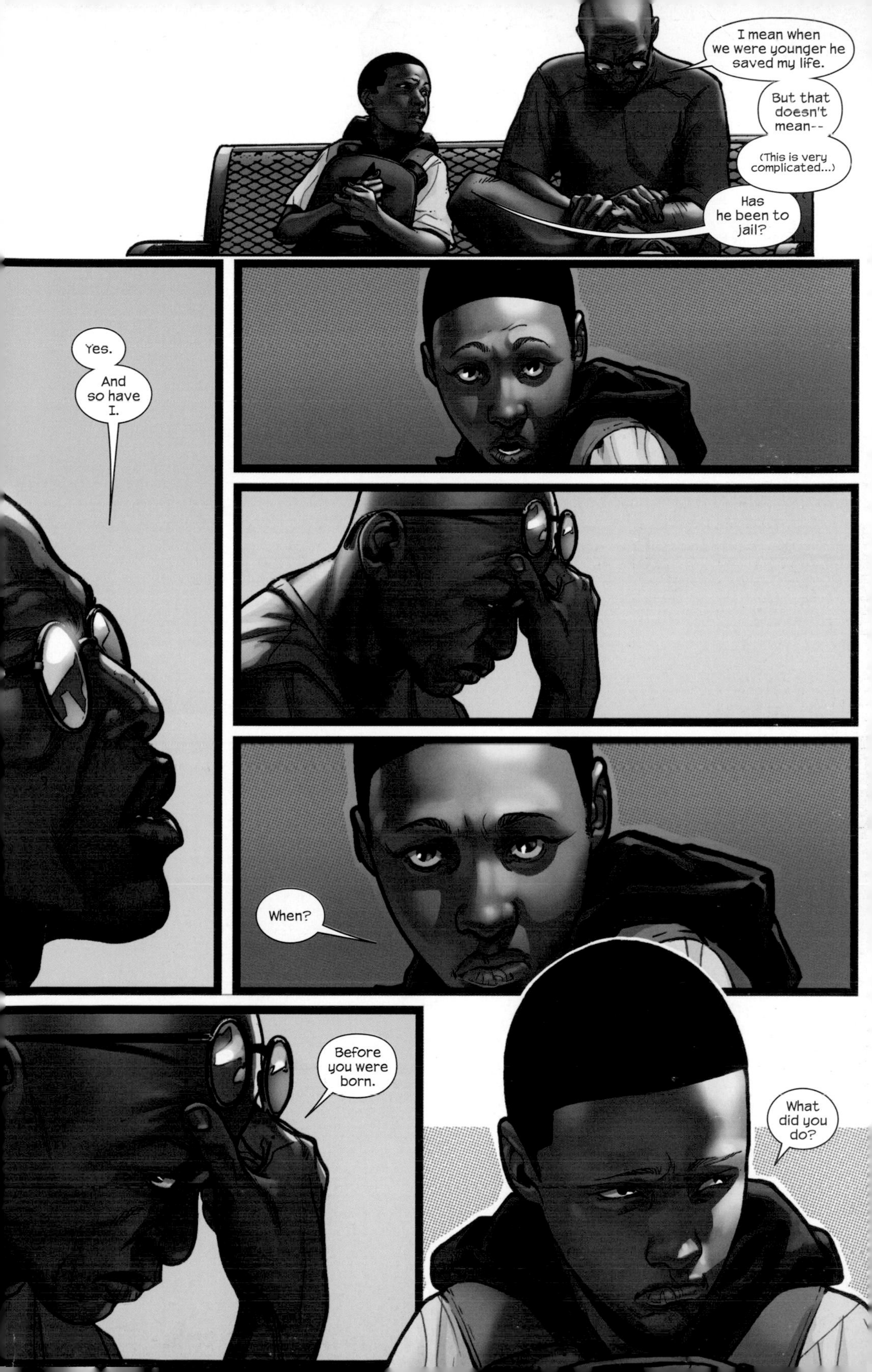

I mean when we were younger he saved my life.
But that doesn't mean--
(This is very complicated...)
Has he been to jail?
Yes.
And so have I.
When?
Before you were born.
What did you do?

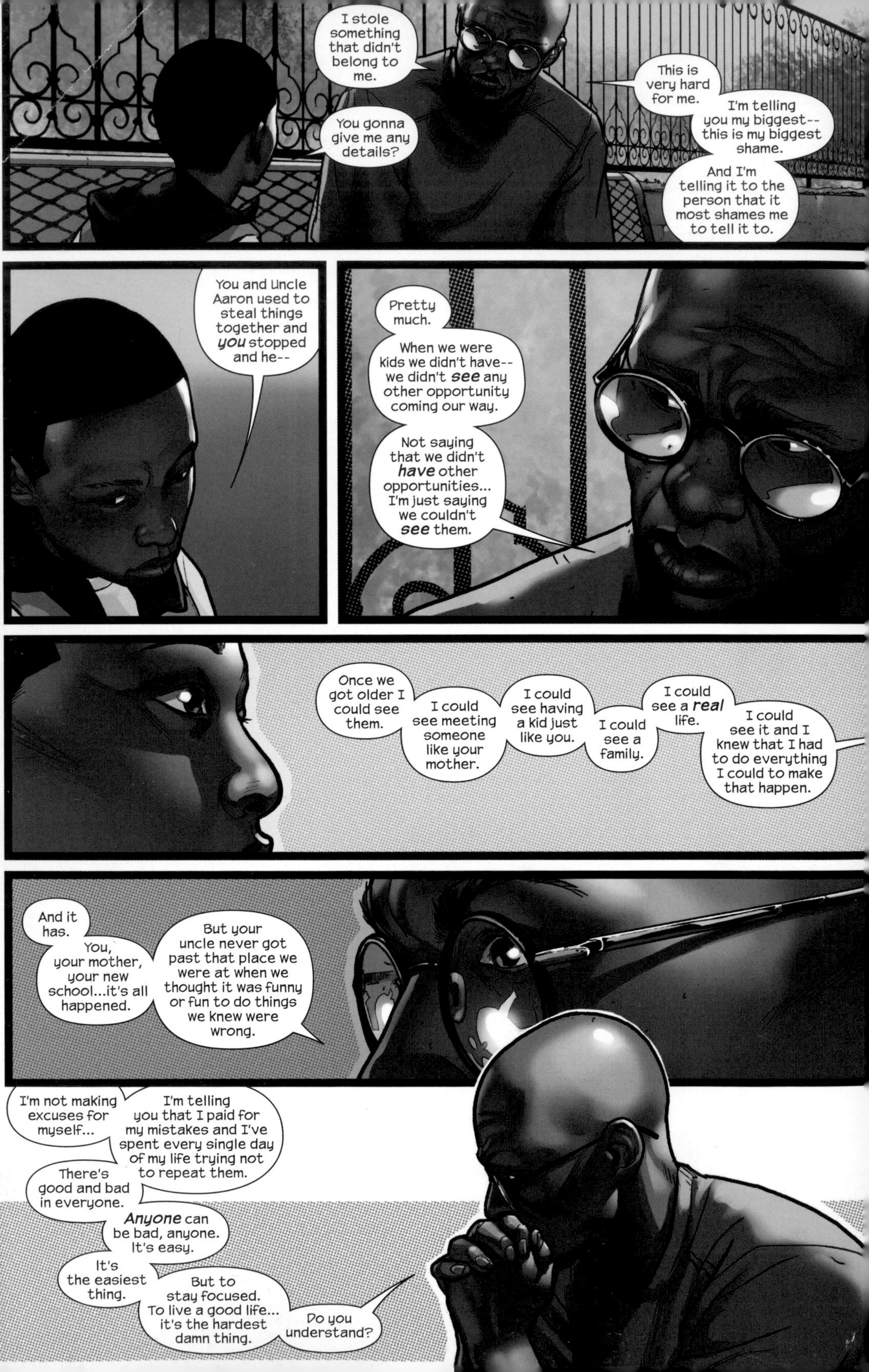

I stole something that didn't belong to me.
You gonna give me any details?
This is very hard for me.
I'm telling you my biggest-- this is my biggest shame.
And I'm telling it to the person that it most shames me to tell it to.
You and Uncle Aaron used to steal things together and *you* stopped and he--
Pretty much.
When we were kids we didn't have-- we didn't *see* any other opportunity coming our way.
Not saying that we didn't *have* other opportunities... I'm just saying we couldn't *see* them.
Once we got older I could see them.
I could see meeting someone like your mother.
I could see having a kid just like you.
I could see a family.
I could see a *real* life.
I could see it and I knew that I had to do everything I could to make that happen.
And it has.
You, your mother, your new school...it's all happened.
But your uncle never got past that place we were at when we thought it was funny or fun to do things we knew were wrong.
I'm not making excuses for myself...
I'm telling you that I paid for my mistakes and I've spent every single day of my life trying not to repeat them.
There's good and bad in everyone.
Anyone can be bad, anyone. It's easy.
It's the easiest thing.
But to stay focused. To live a good life... it's the hardest damn thing.
Do you understand?

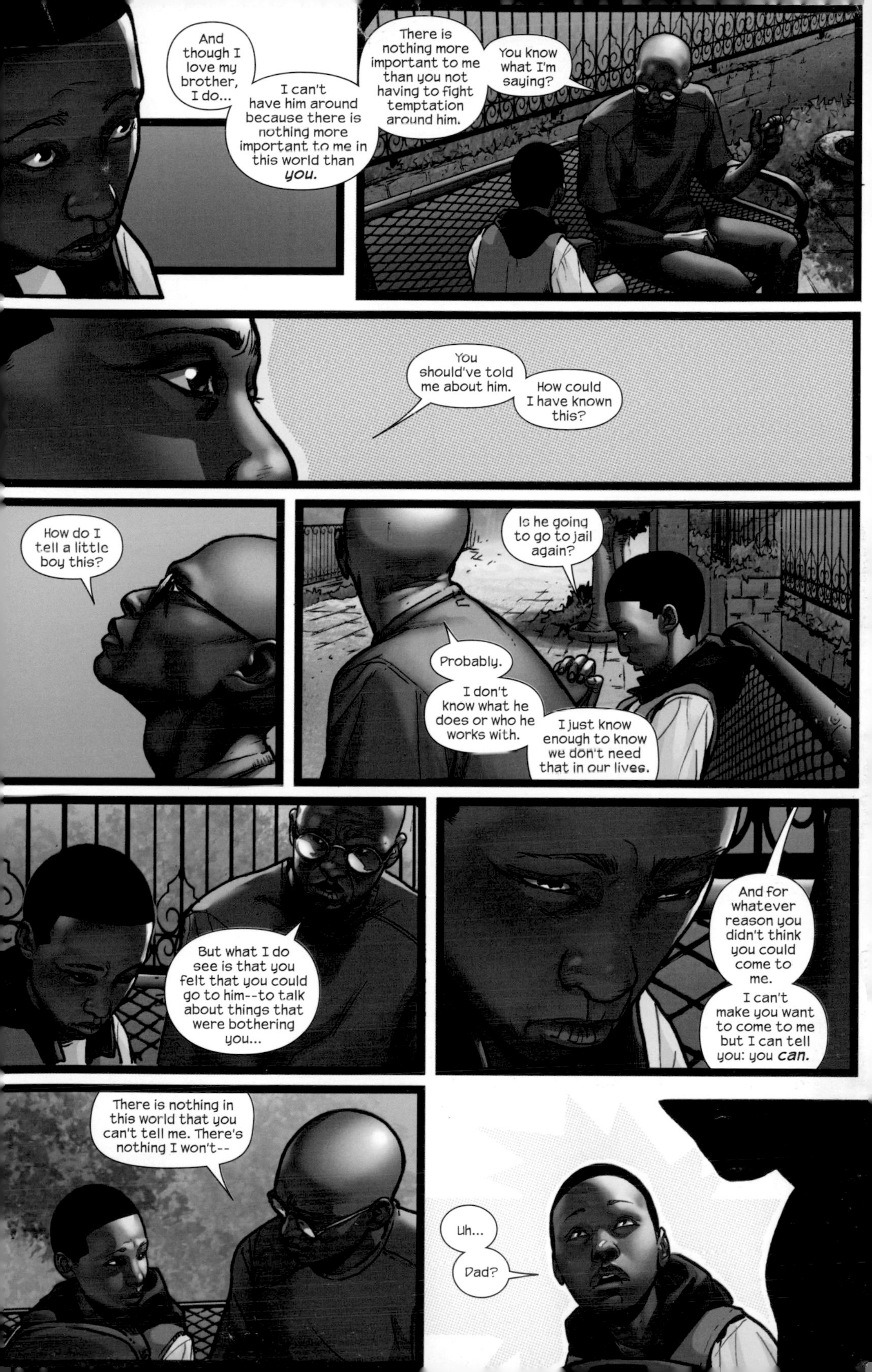
And though I love my brother, I do...
I can't have him around because there is nothing more important to me in this world than *you.*
There is nothing more important to me than you not having to fight temptation around him.
You know what I'm saying?
You should've told me about him.
How could I have known this?
How do I tell a little boy this?
Is he going to go to jail again?
Probably.
I don't know what he does or who he works with.
I just know enough to know we don't need that in our lives.
But what I do see is that you felt that you could go to him--to talk about things that were bothering you...
And for whatever reason you didn't think you could come to me.
I can't make you want to come to me but I can tell you: you *can.*
There is nothing in this world that you can't tell me. There's nothing I won't--
Uh...
Dad?

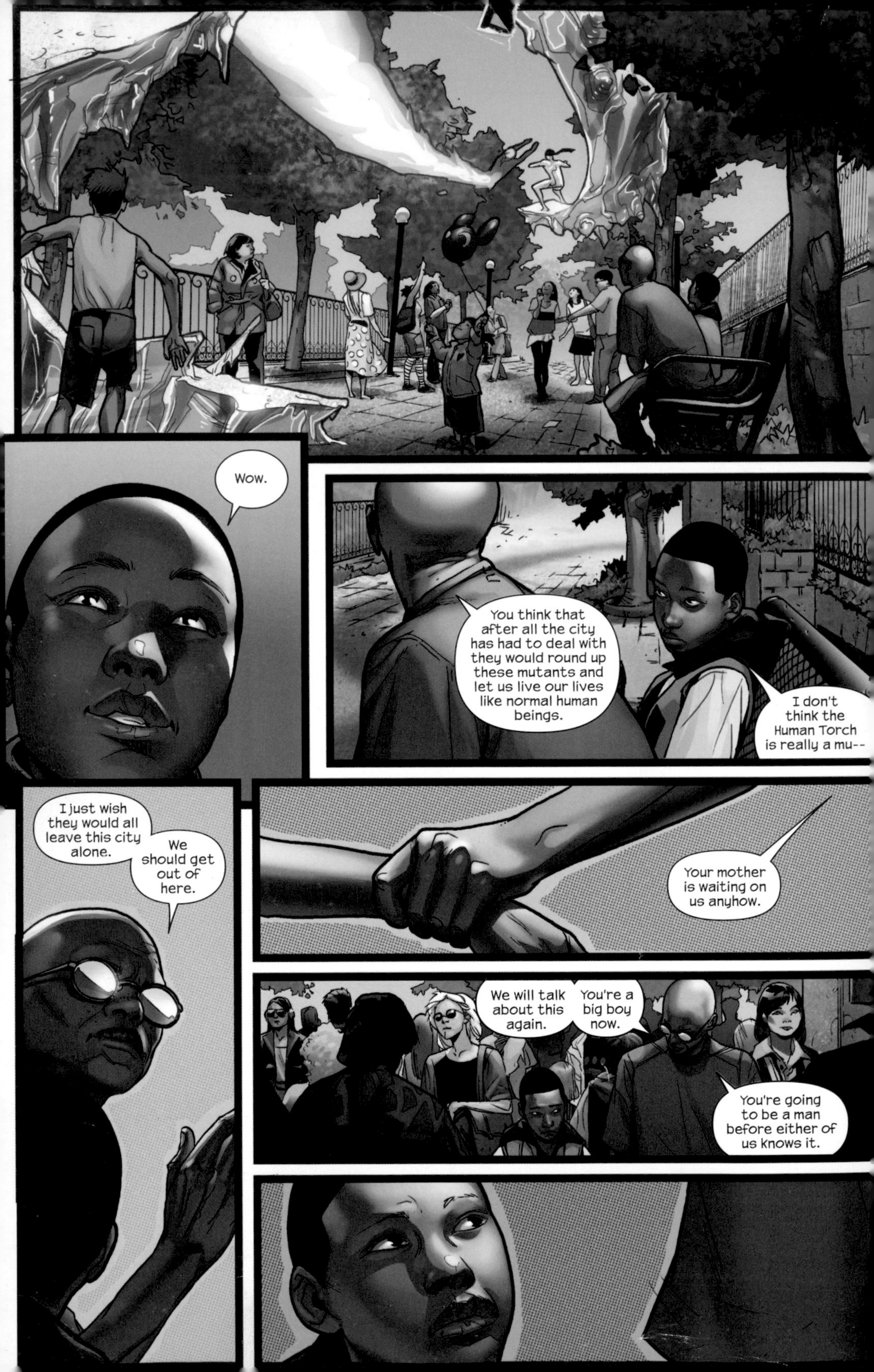
Wow.
You think that after all the city has had to deal with they would round up these mutants and let us live our lives like normal human beings.
I don't think the Human Torch is really a mu--
I just wish they would all leave this city alone.
We should get out of here.
Your mother is waiting on us anyhow.
We will talk about this again.
You're a big boy now.
You're going to be a man before either of us knows it.

Ganke THE AWESOME:
today,1:07 am

you're not a mutant.

Ganke THE AWESOME:
today,1:07 am

you're not a mutant.

Ganke THE AWESOME:
today,1:08 am

u have chameleon like powers like some spiders do- & u have a venom strike, like some spiders have.

u have chameleon like powers like some spiders do- & u have a venom strike, like some spiders have.

Sir MILES:
today,1:09 am

what r u talking about?

today,1:09 am

what r u talking about?

Ganke THE AWESOME:
today,1:10 am

Spider-Man was bit by a spider too.

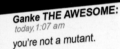

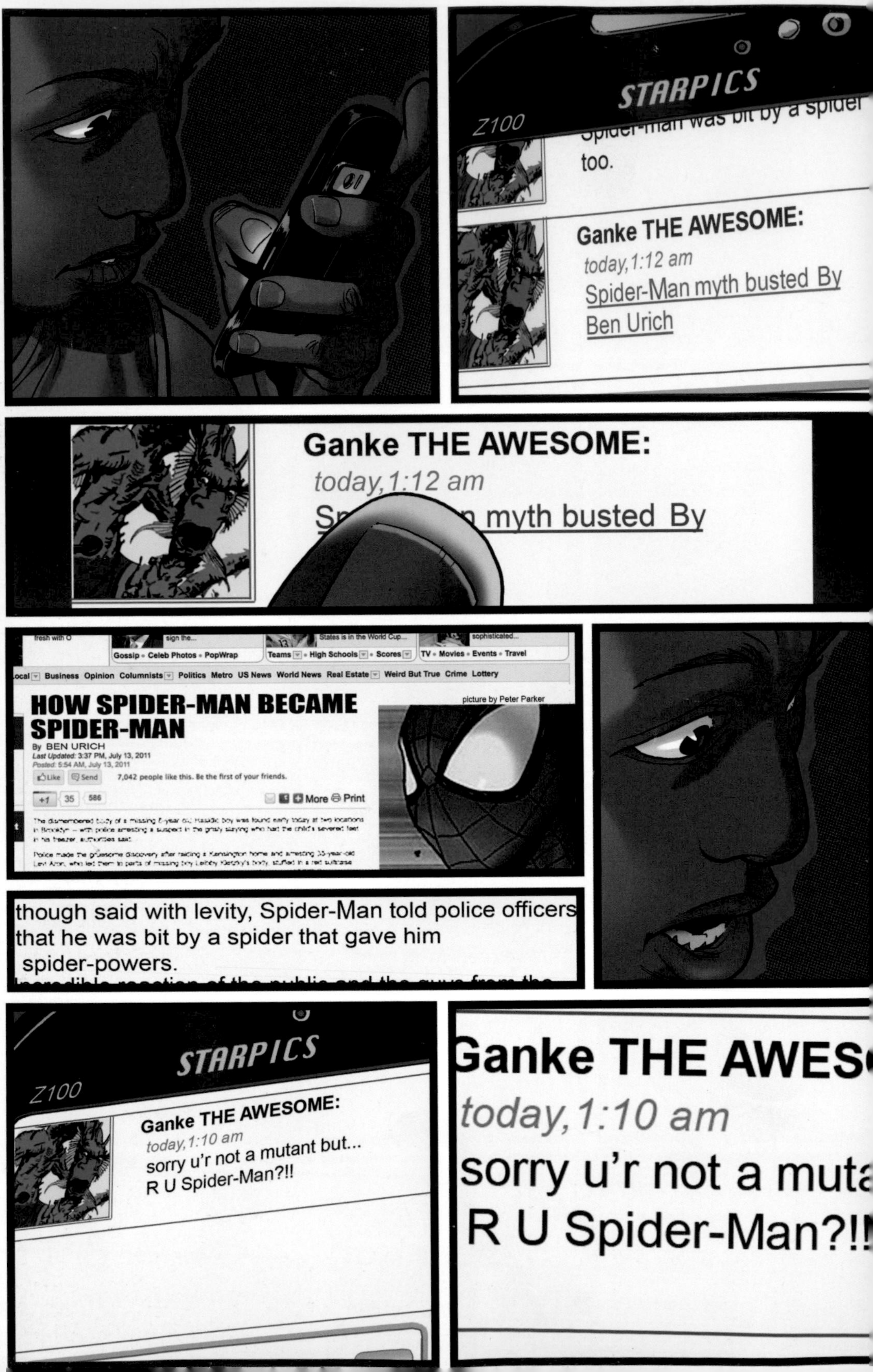
STARPICS
Z100
too.
Ganke THE AWESOME:
today,1:12 am
Spider-Man myth busted By
Ben Urich
Ganke THE AWESOME:
today,1:12 am
myth busted By
Gossip • Celeb Photos • PopWrap
Teams • High Schools • Scores
TV • Movies • Events • Travel
Business Opinion Columnists Politics Metro US News World News Real Estate Weird But True Crime Lottery
picture by Peter Parker
HOW SPIDER-MAN BECAME SPIDER-MAN
By BEN URICH
Last Updated: 3:37 PM, July 13, 2011
Posted: 5:54 AM, July 13, 2011
Like Send 7,042 people like this. Be the first of your friends.
+1 35 586
More Print
though said with levity, Spider-Man told police officers that he was bit by a spider that gave him spider-powers.
STARPICS
Z100
Ganke THE AWESOME:
today,1:10 am
sorry u'r not a mutant but...
R U Spider-Man?!!
today,1:10 am
R U Spider-Man?!!

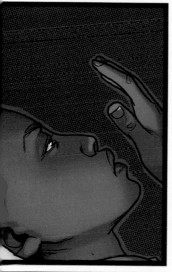

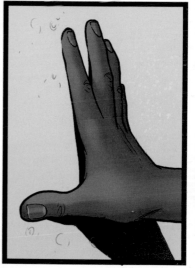

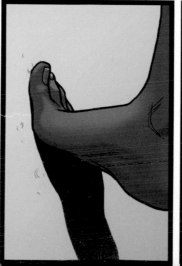
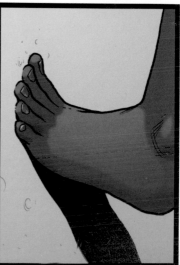
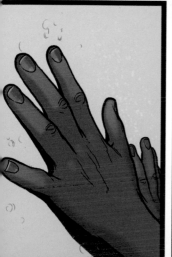

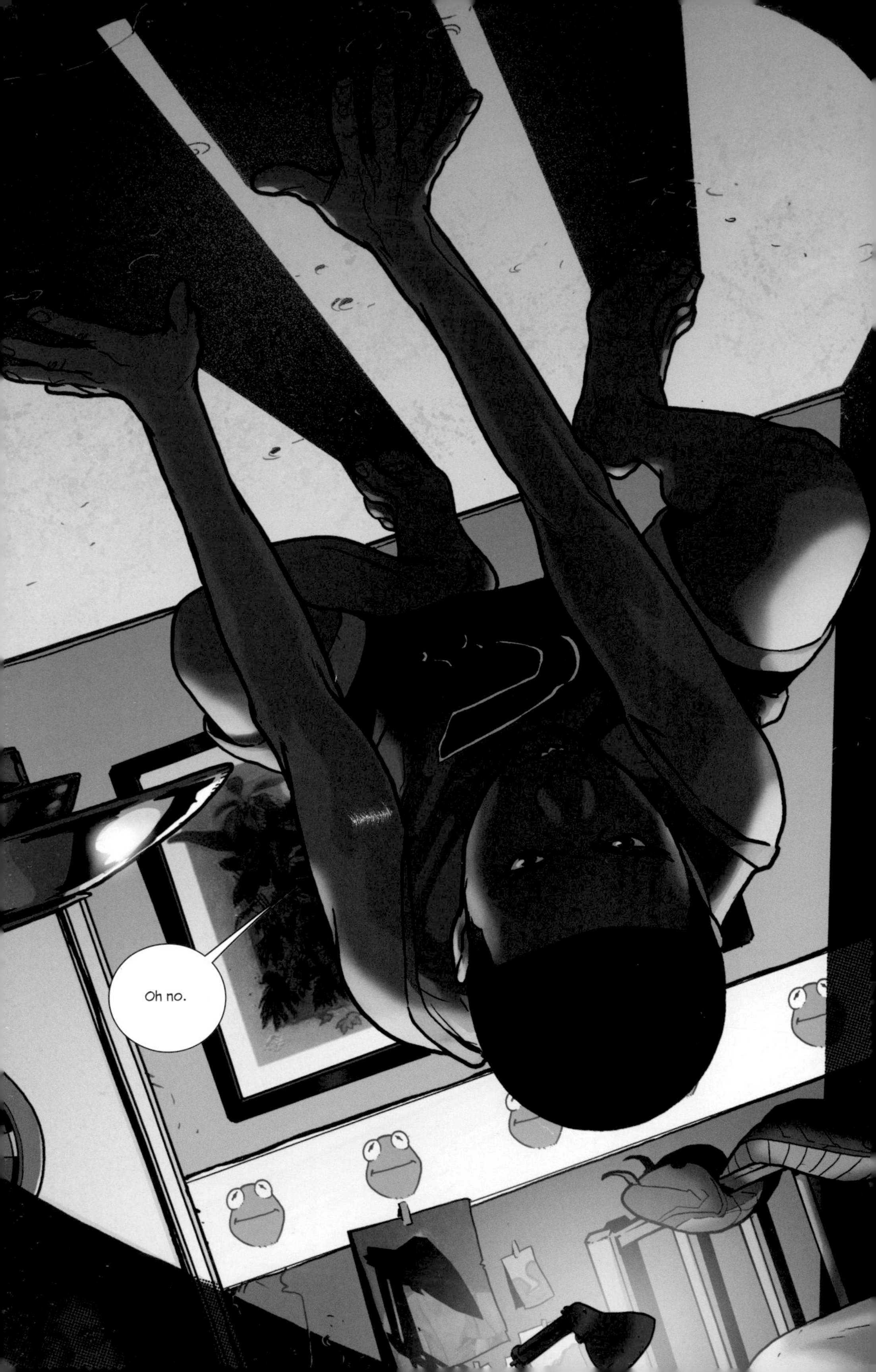
Oh no.

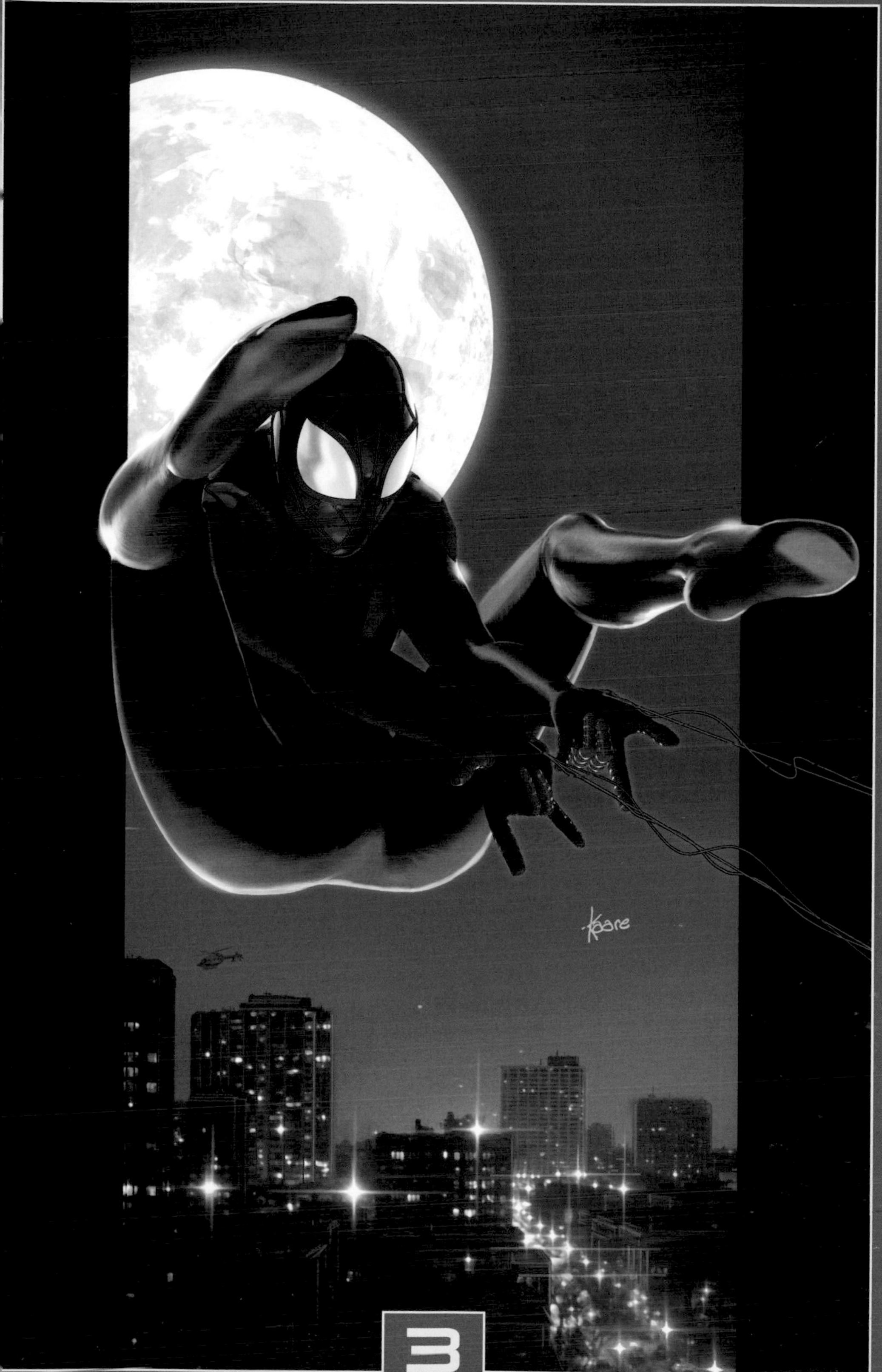
3

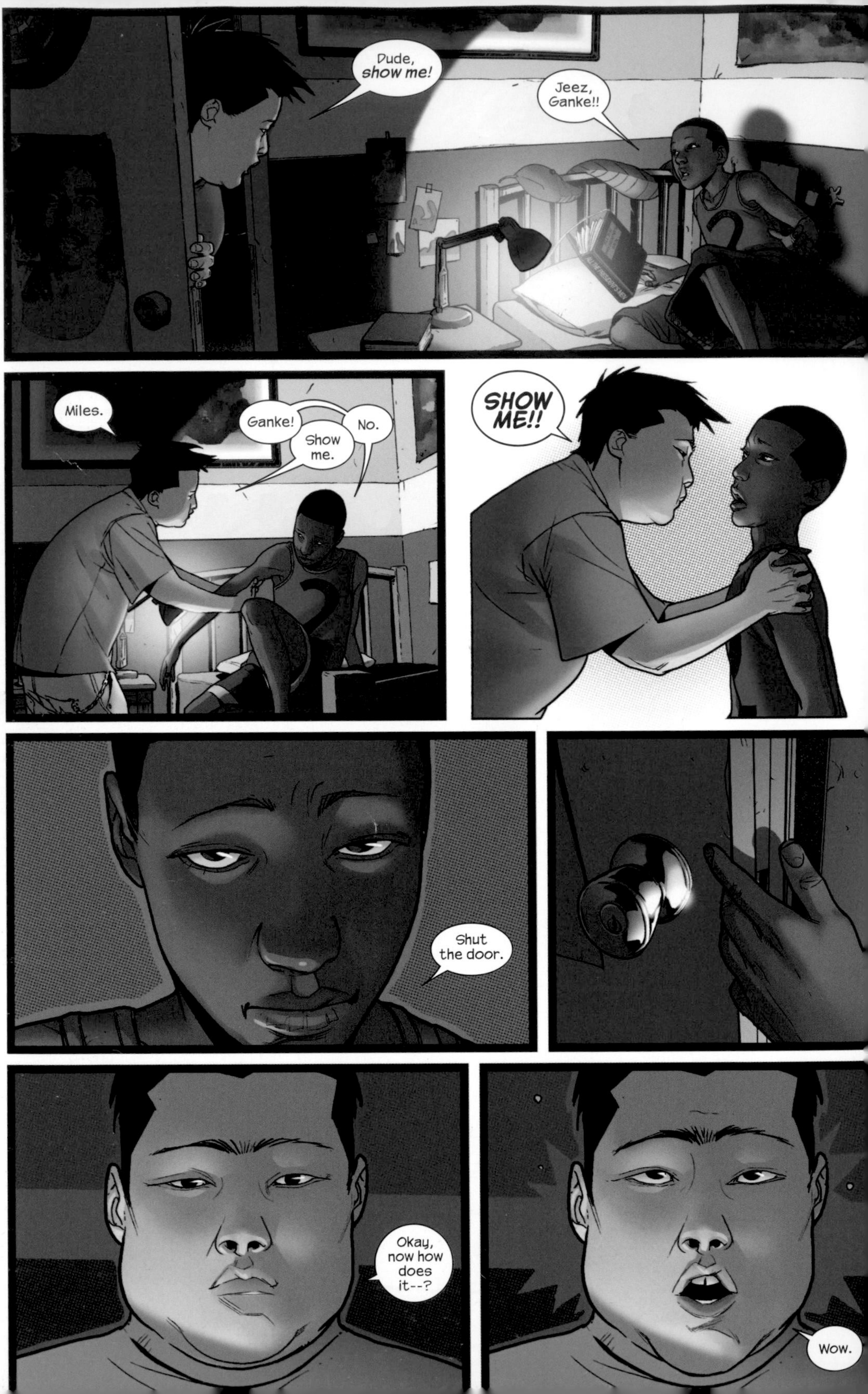
Dude, show me!
Jeez, Ganke!!
Miles.
Ganke!
No.
Show me.
SHOW ME!!
Shut the door.
Okay, now how does it--?
Wow.

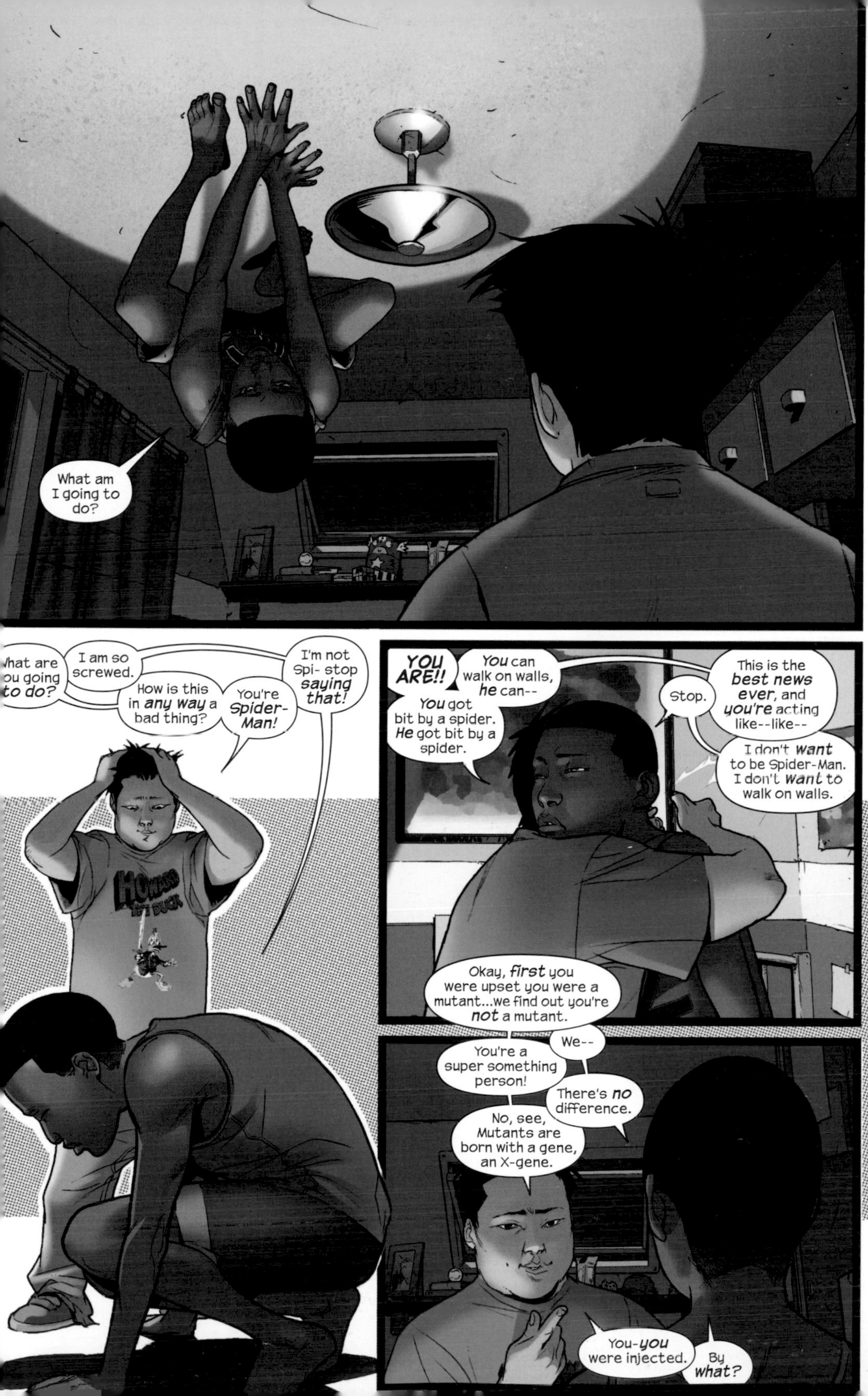
What am I going to do?
What are you going to do?
I am so screwed.
How is this in any way a bad thing?
You're Spider-Man!
I'm not Spi- stop saying that!
YOU ARE!!
You can walk on walls, he can--
You got bit by a spider. He got bit by a spider.
Stop.
This is the best news ever, and you're acting like--like--
I don't want to be Spider-Man. I don't want to walk on walls.
Okay, first you were upset you were a mutant...we find out you're not a mutant.
We--
You're a super something person!
There's no difference.
No, see, Mutants are born with a gene, an X-gene.
You-you were injected.
By what?

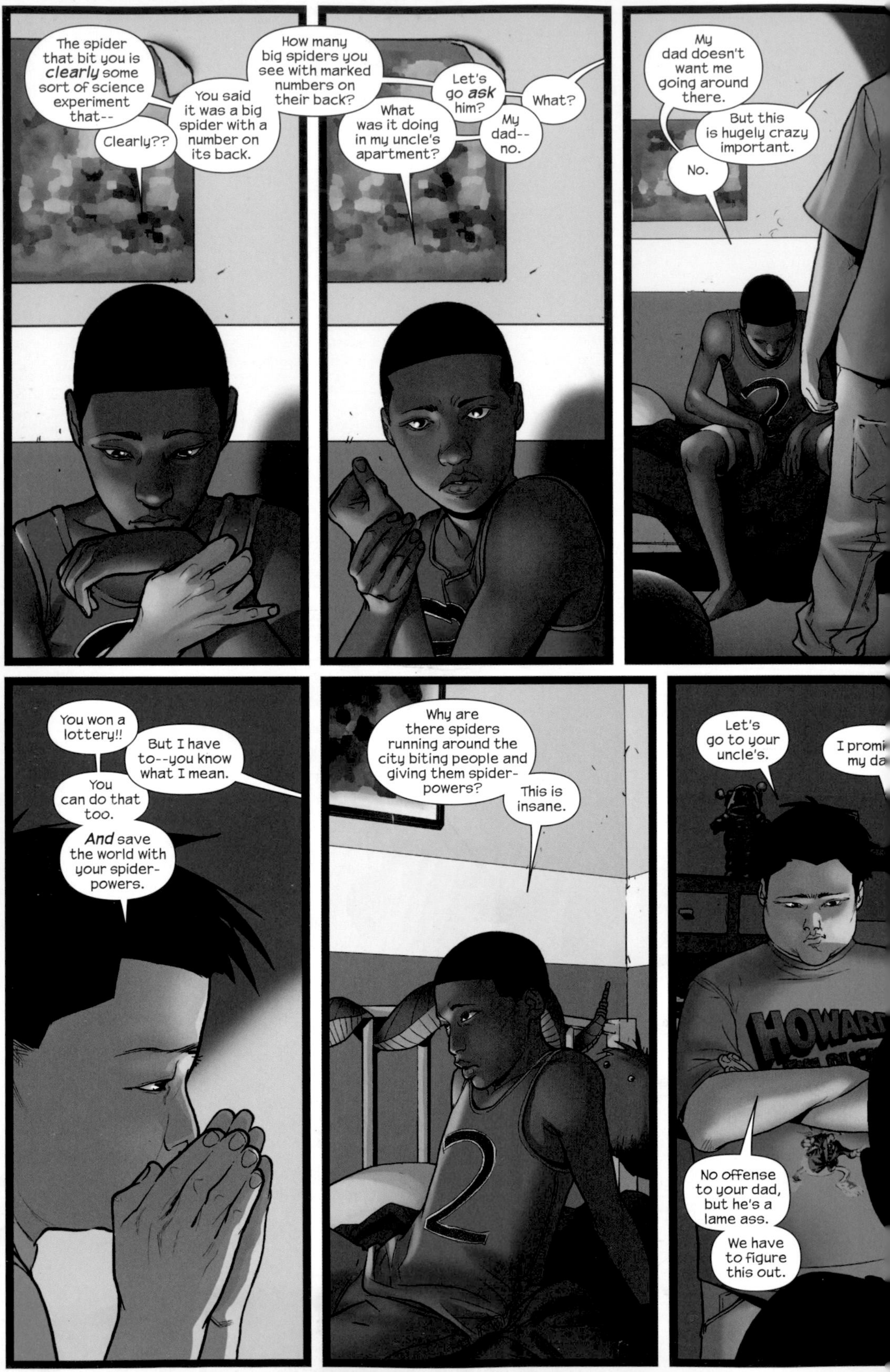

The spider that bit you is *clearly* some sort of science experiment that--
Clearly??
You said it was a big spider with a number on its back.
How many big spiders you see with marked numbers on their back?
What was it doing in my uncle's apartment?
Let's go *ask* him?
What?
My dad-- no.
My dad doesn't want me going around there.
But this is hugely crazy important.
No.
You won a lottery!!
But I have to--you know what I mean.
You can do that too.
And save the world with your spider-powers.
Why are there spiders running around the city biting people and giving them spider-powers?
This is insane.
Let's go to your uncle's.
No offense to your dad, but he's a lame ass.
We have to figure this out.
HOWARD

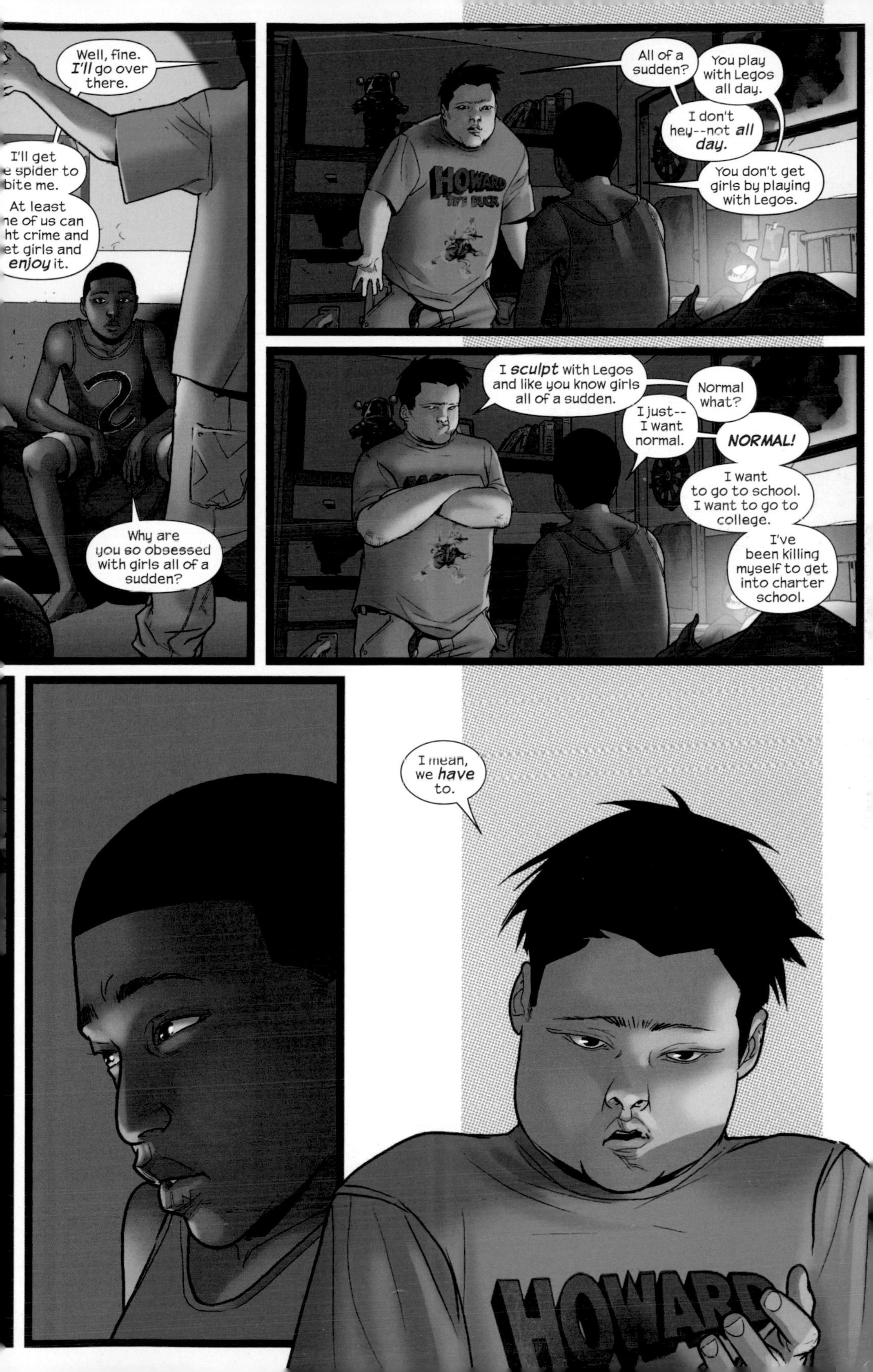
Well, fine. I'll go over there.
I'll get e spider to bite me.
At least ne of us can ht crime and et girls and enjoy it.
Why are you so obsessed with girls all of a sudden?
All of a sudden?
You play with Legos all day.
I don't hey--not all day.
You don't get girls by playing with Legos.
I sculpt with Legos and like you know girls all of a sudden.
Normal what?
I just-- I want normal.
NORMAL!
I want to go to school. I want to go to college.
I've been killing myself to get into charter school.
I mean, we have to.

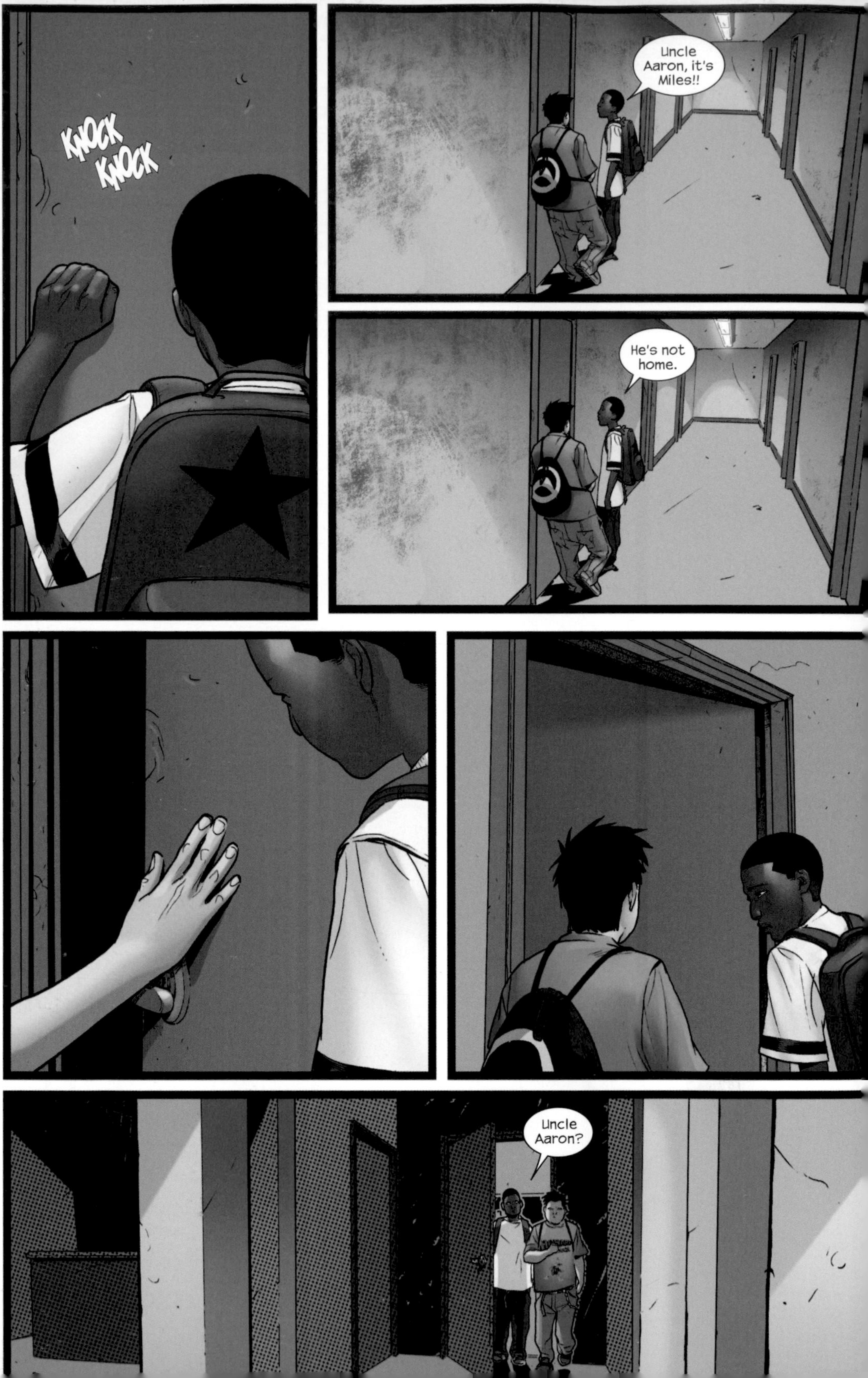
KNOCK
KNOCK
Uncle Aaron, it's Miles!!
He's not home.
Uncle Aaron?

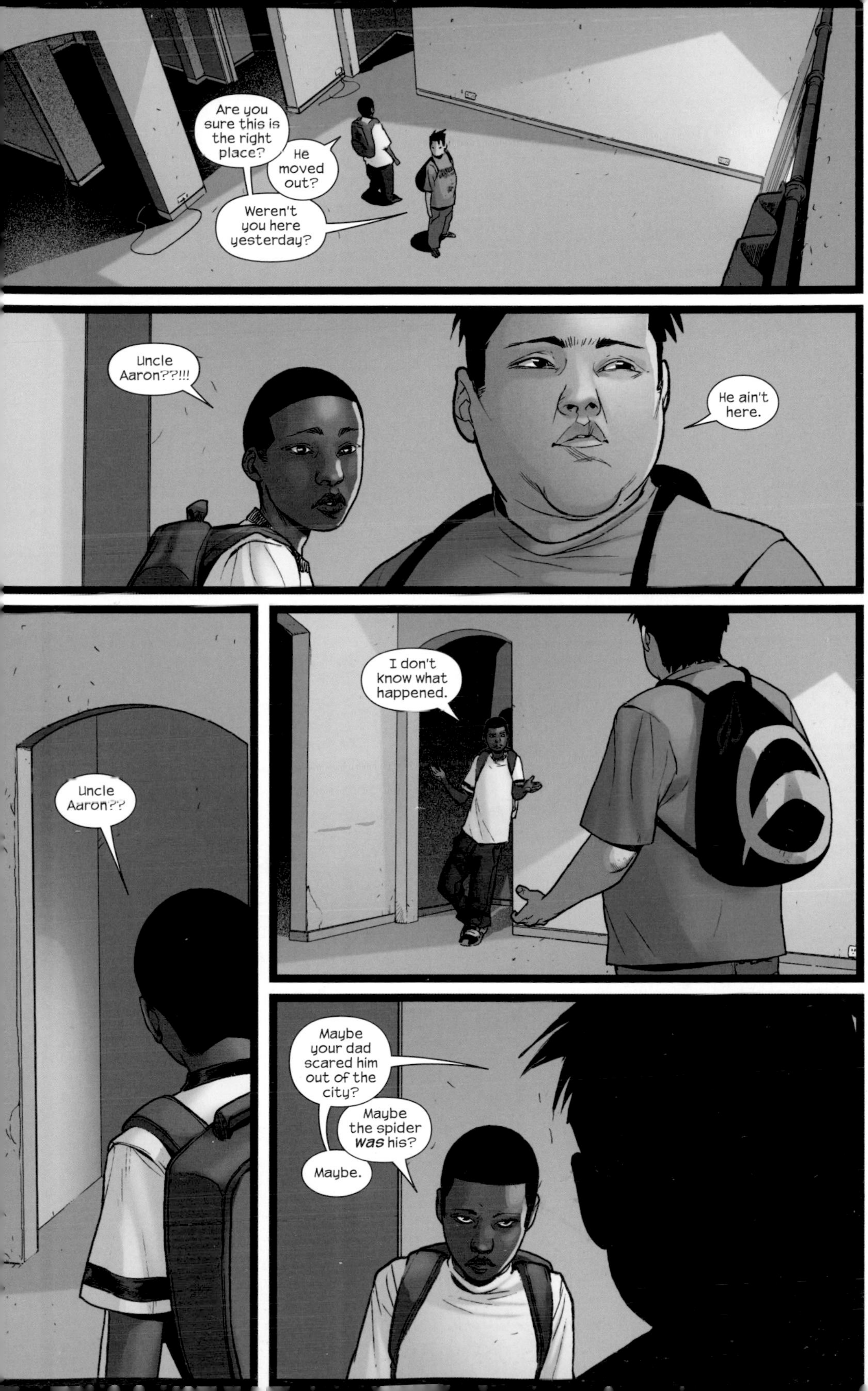
Are you sure this is the right place?
He moved out?
Weren't you here yesterday?
Uncle Aaron??!!!
He ain't here.
Uncle Aaron??
I don't know what happened.
Maybe your dad scared him out of the city?
Maybe the spider *was* his?
Maybe.

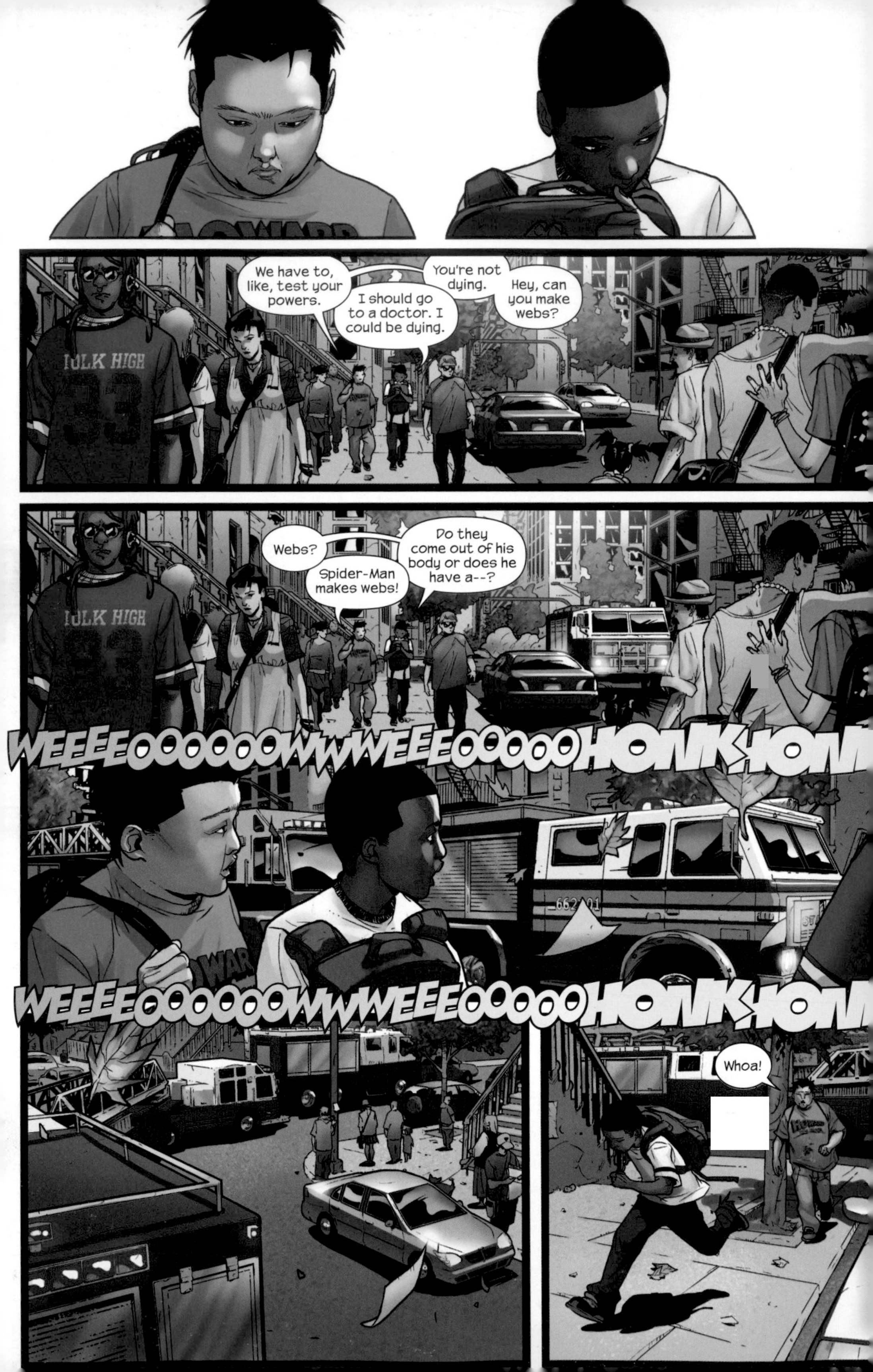
We have to, like, test your powers.
I should go to a doctor. I could be dying.
You're not dying.
Hey, can you make webs?
Webs?
Spider-Man makes webs!
Do they come out of his body or does he have a--?
WEEEEOOOOOOWWWEEEOOOOOHONKHON
WEEEEOOOOOOWWWEEEOOOOOHONKHON
Whoa!

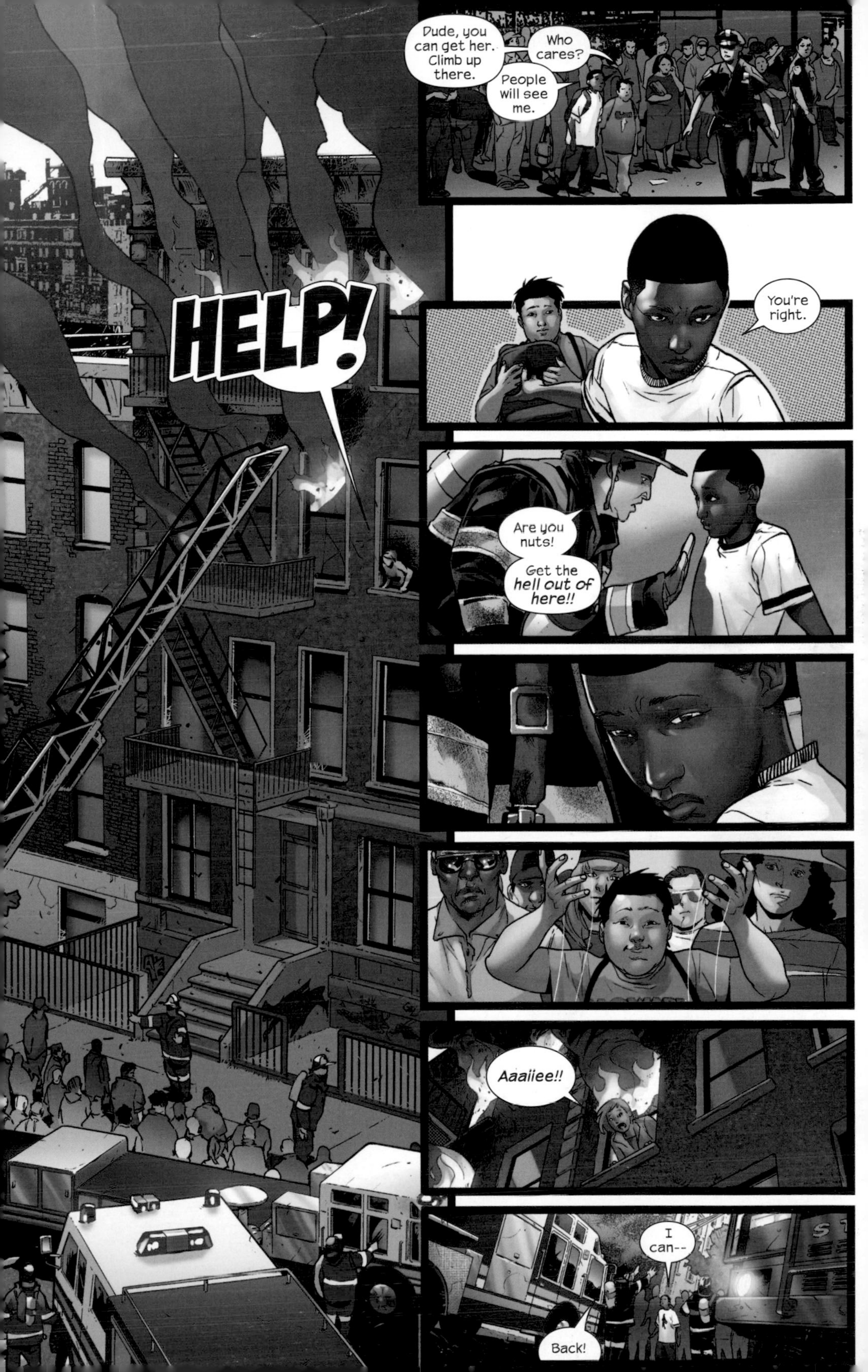
HELP!
Dude, you can get her. Climb up there.
Who cares?
People will see me.
You're right.
Are you nuts!
Get the *hell out of here!!*
Aaaiiee!!
I can--
Back!

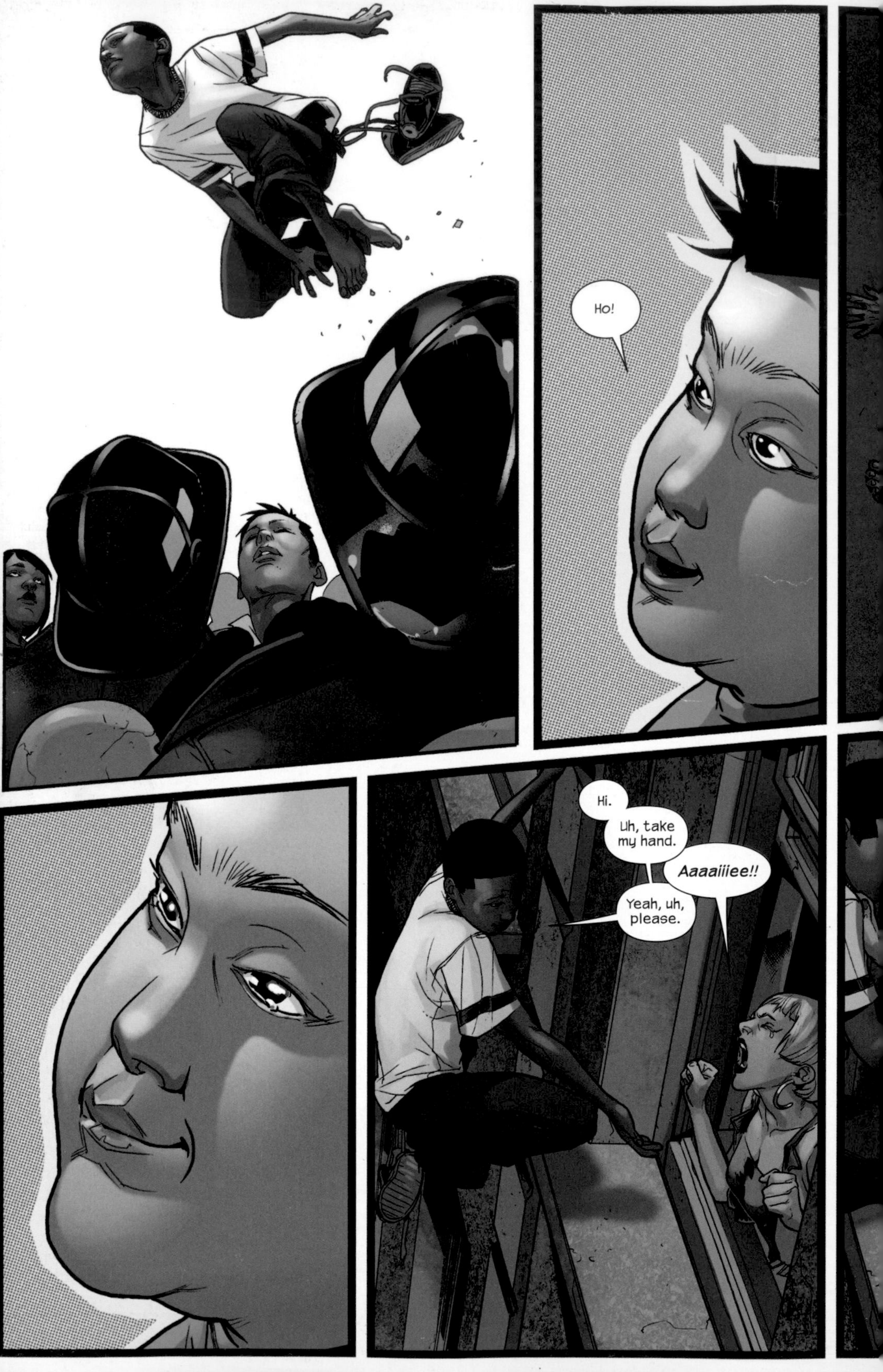
Ho!
Hi.
Uh, take my hand.
Aaaaiiiee!!
Yeah, uh, please.

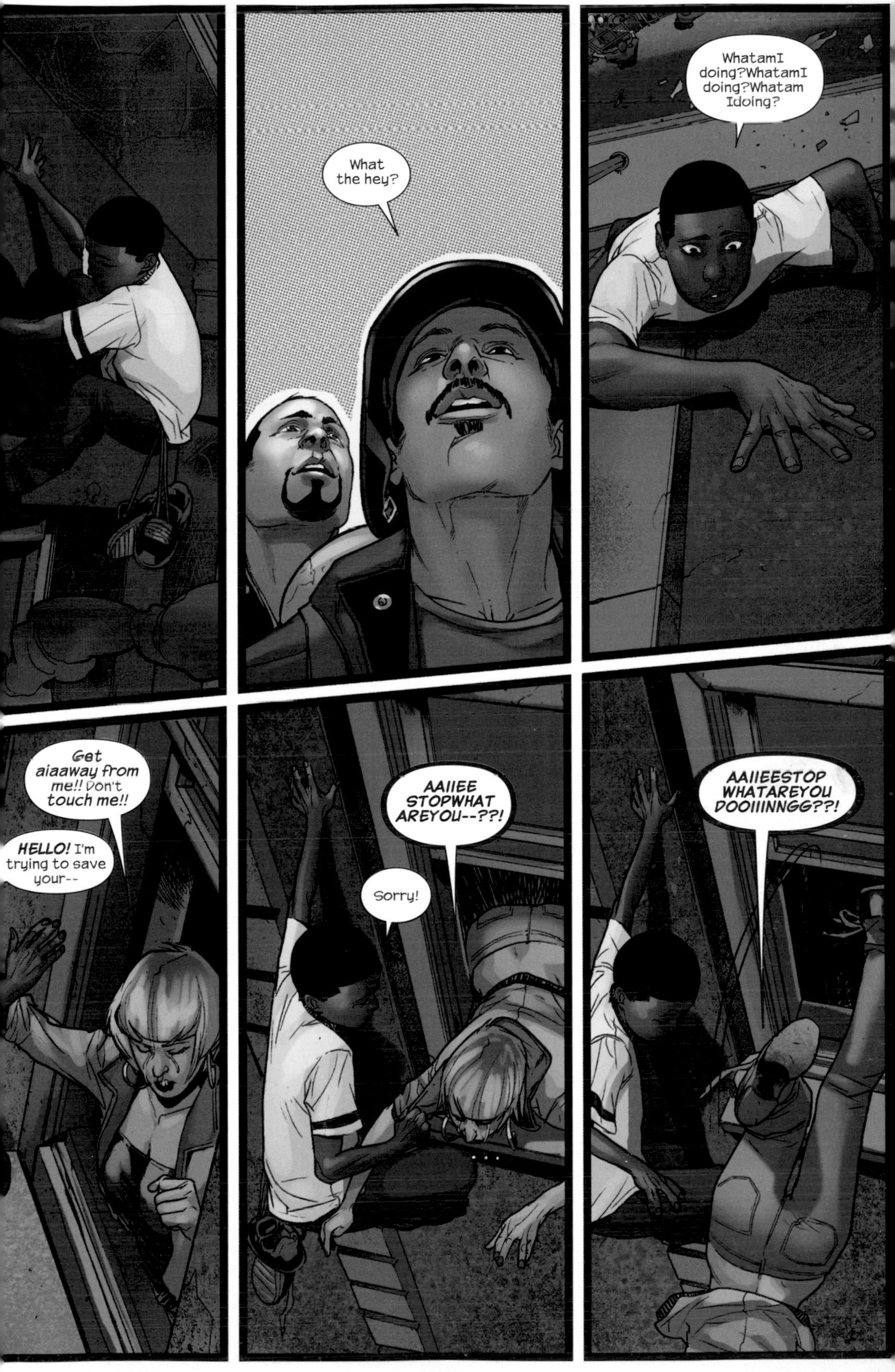
What the hey?
WhatamI doing?WhatamI doing?Whatam Idoing?
Get aiaaway from me!! Don't touch me!!
HELLO! I'm trying to save your--
AAIIEE STOPWHAT AREYOU--??!
Sorry!
AAIIEESTOP WHATAREYOU DOOIIINNGG??!

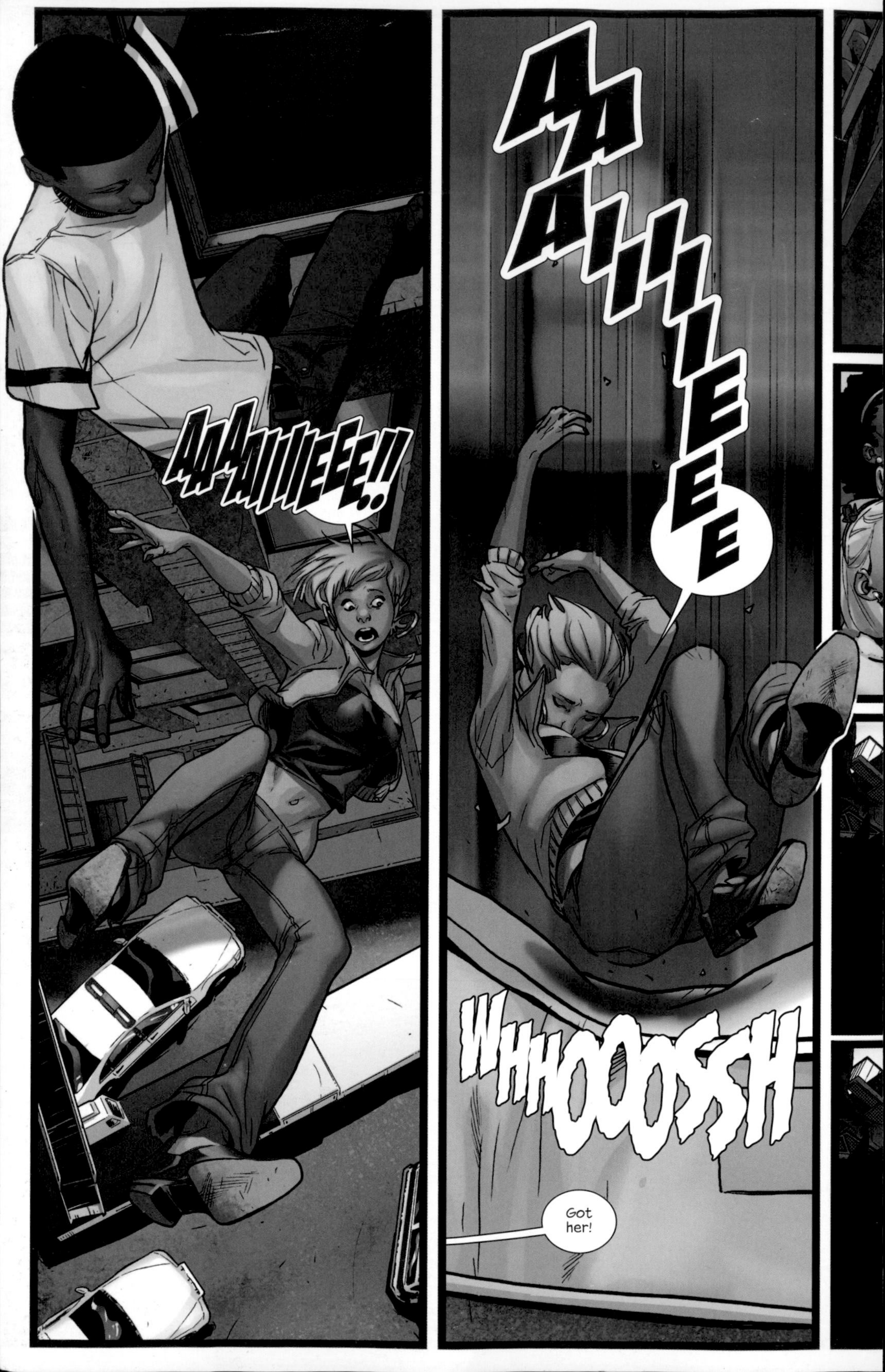
AAAAIIIIEEE!!
AAAIIIIIEEEE
WHHOOOSSH
Got her!

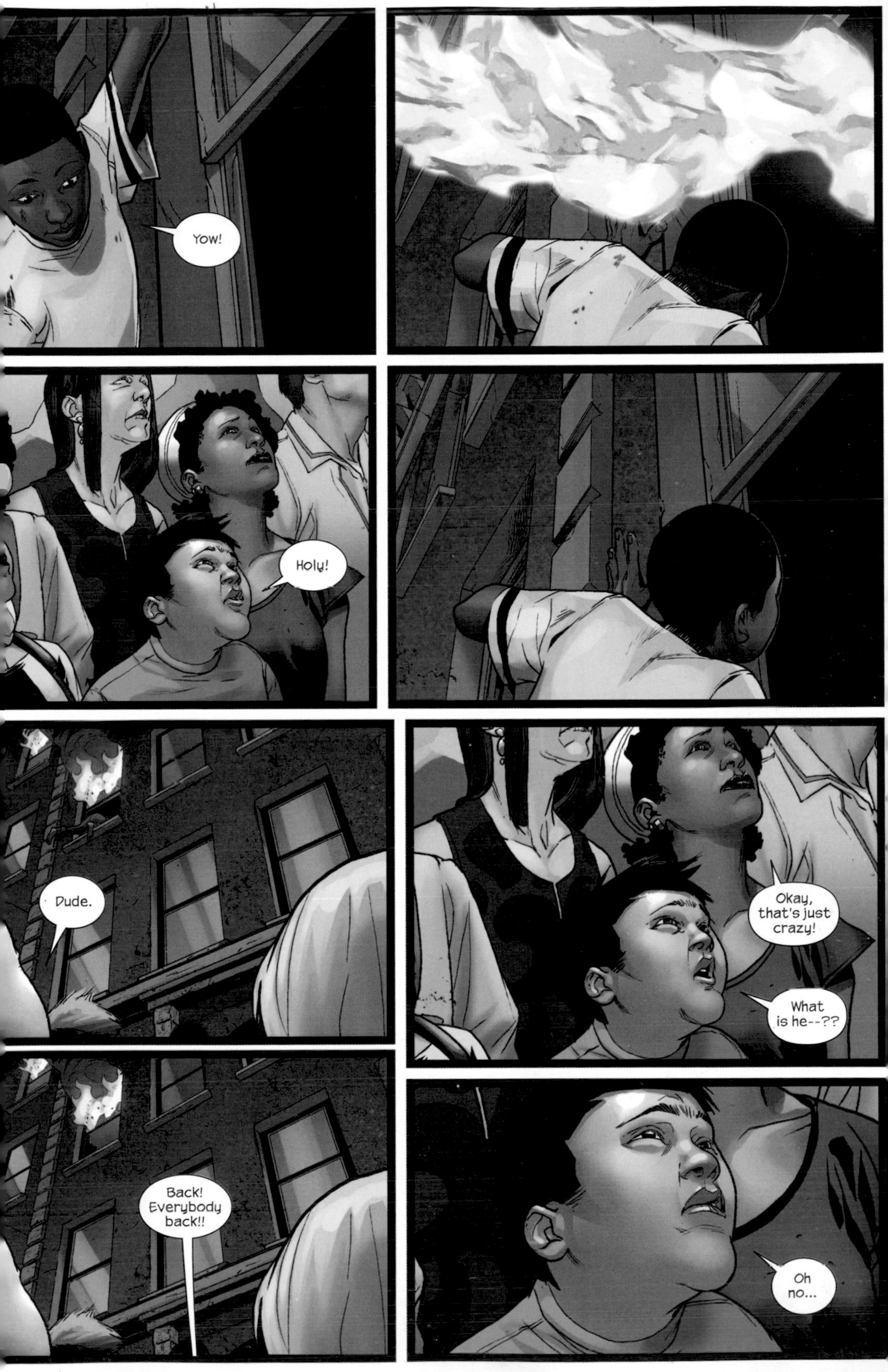
Yow!
Holy!
Dude.
Okay, that's just crazy!
What is he--??
Back! Everybody back!!
Oh no...

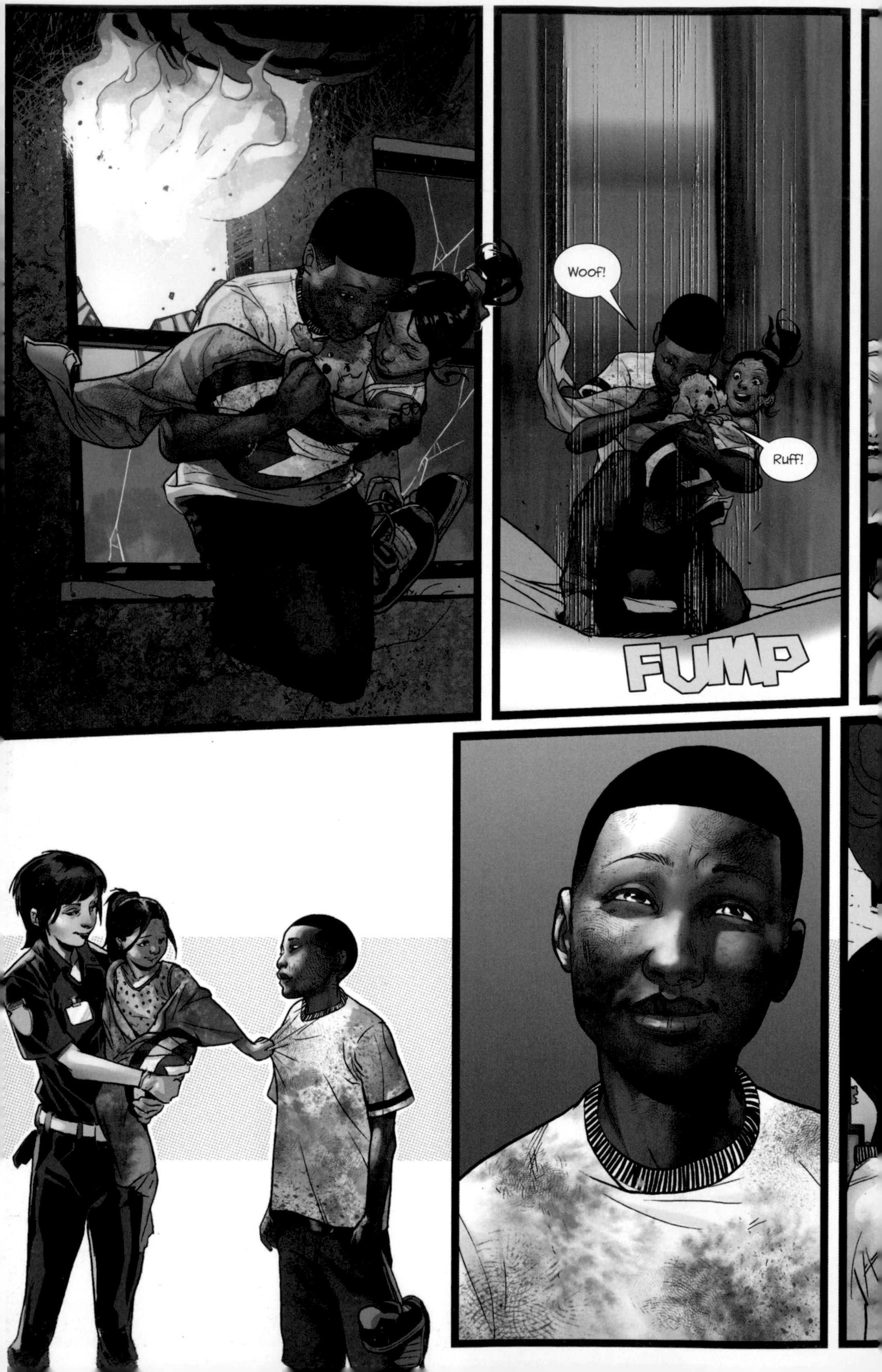
Woof!
Ruff!
FUMP

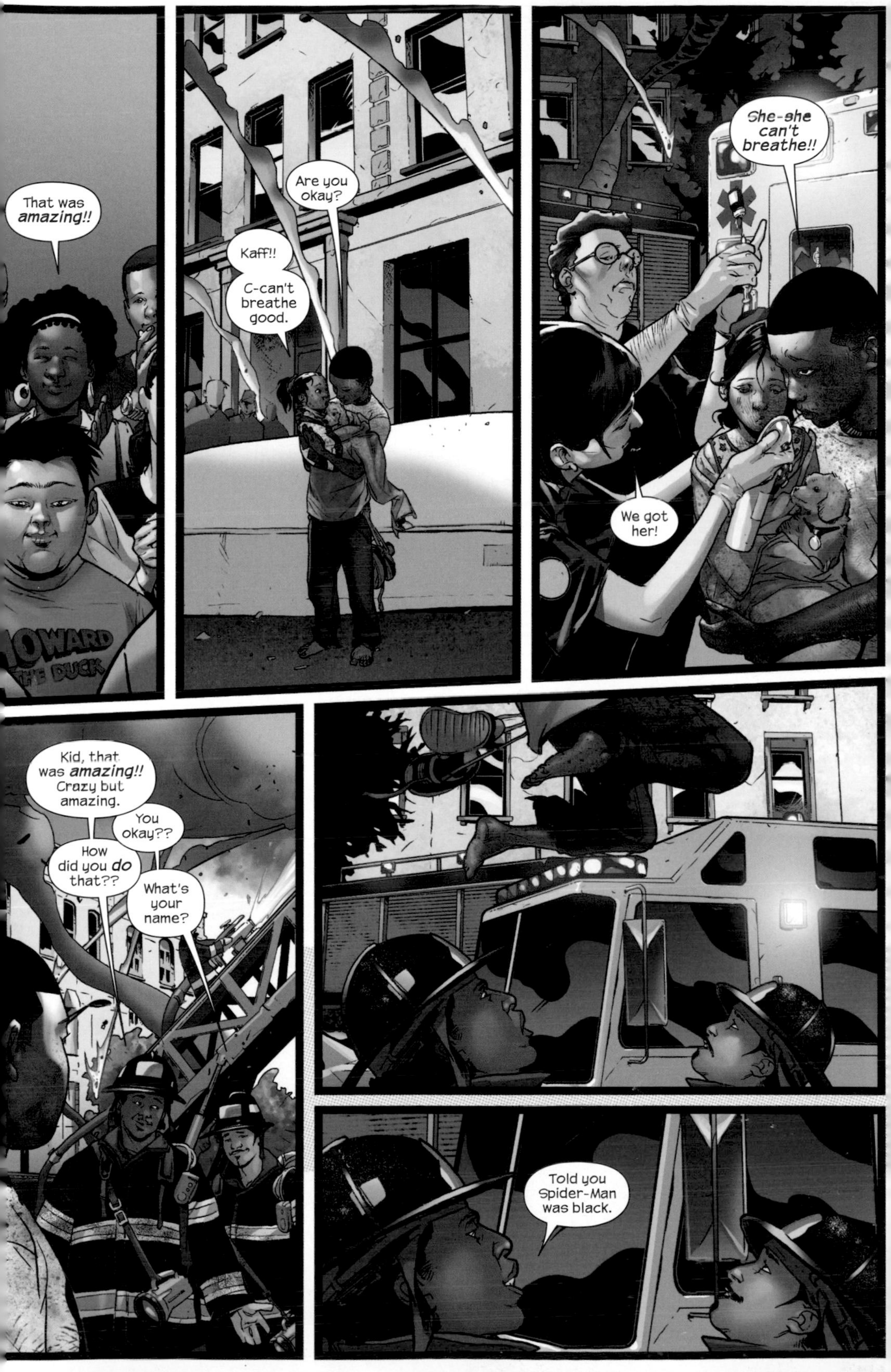
That was amazing!!
Are you okay?
Kaff!!
C-can't breathe good.
She-she can't breathe!!
We got her!
Kid, that was amazing!! Crazy but amazing.
You okay??
How did you do that??
What's your name?
HOWARD THE DUCK
Told you Spider-Man was black.

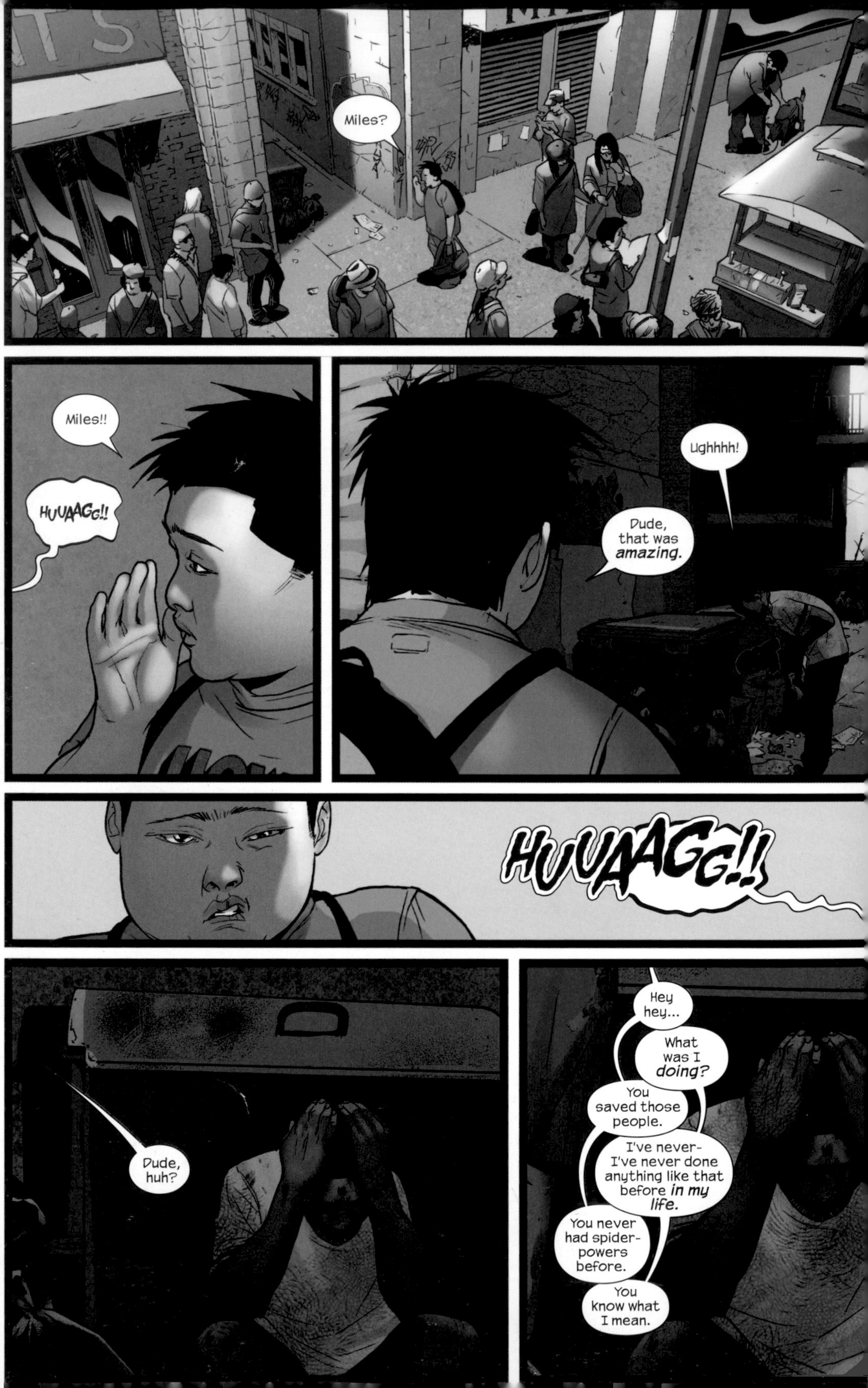
Miles?
Miles!!
HUUAAGG!!
Ughhhh!
Dude, that was amazing.
HUUAAGG!!
Dude, huh?
Hey hey...
What was I doing?
You saved those people.
I've never- I've never done anything like that before in my life.
You never had spider-powers before.
You know what I mean.

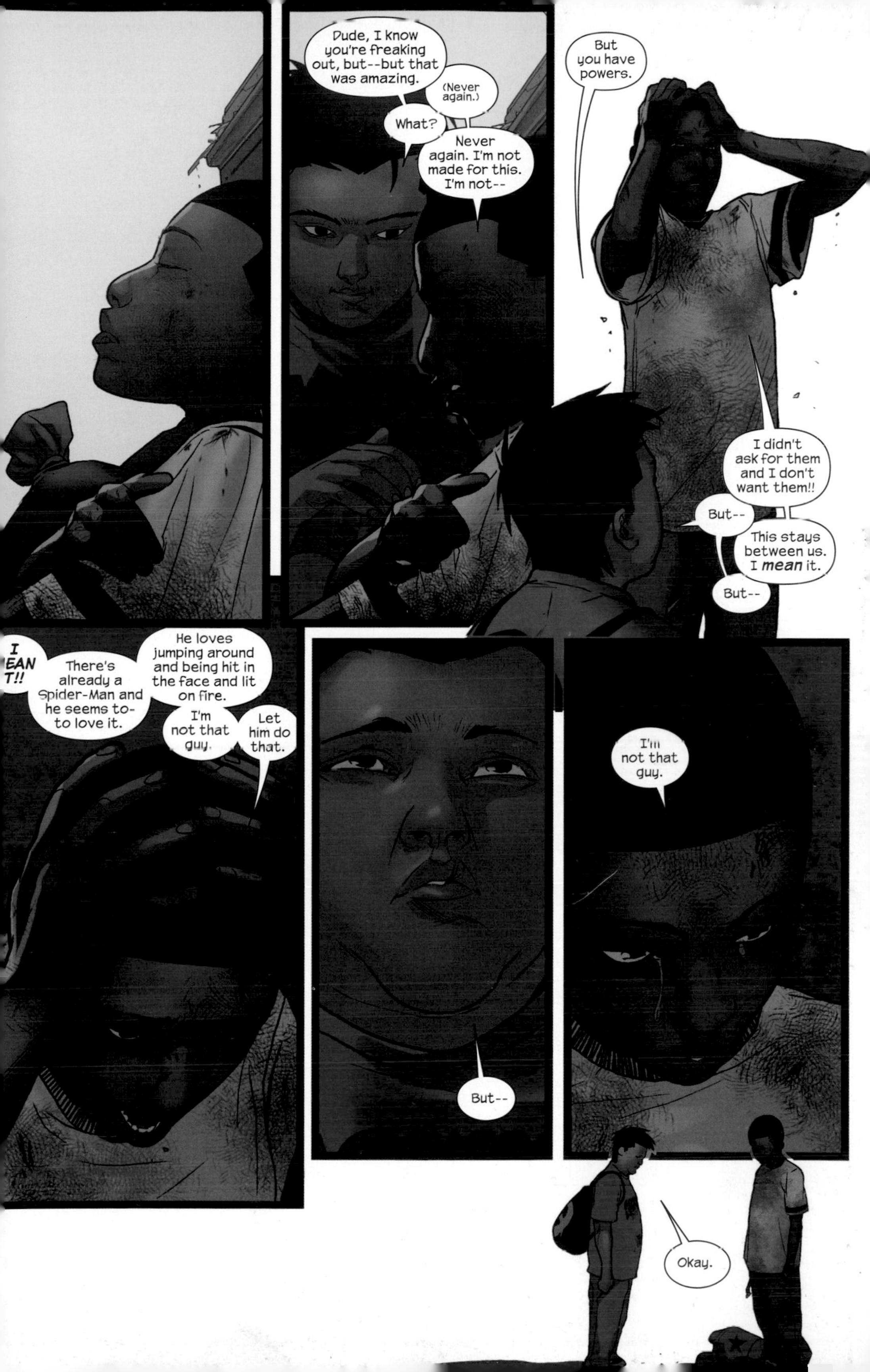
Dude, I know you're freaking out, but--but that was amazing.
(Never again.)
What?
Never again. I'm not made for this. I'm not--
But you have powers.
I didn't ask for them and I don't want them!!
But--
This stays between us. I *mean* it.
But--
I MEAN IT!!
There's already a Spider-Man and he seems to-to love it.
He loves jumping around and being hit in the face and lit on fire.
I'm not that guy.
Let him do that.
But--
I'm not that guy.
Okay.

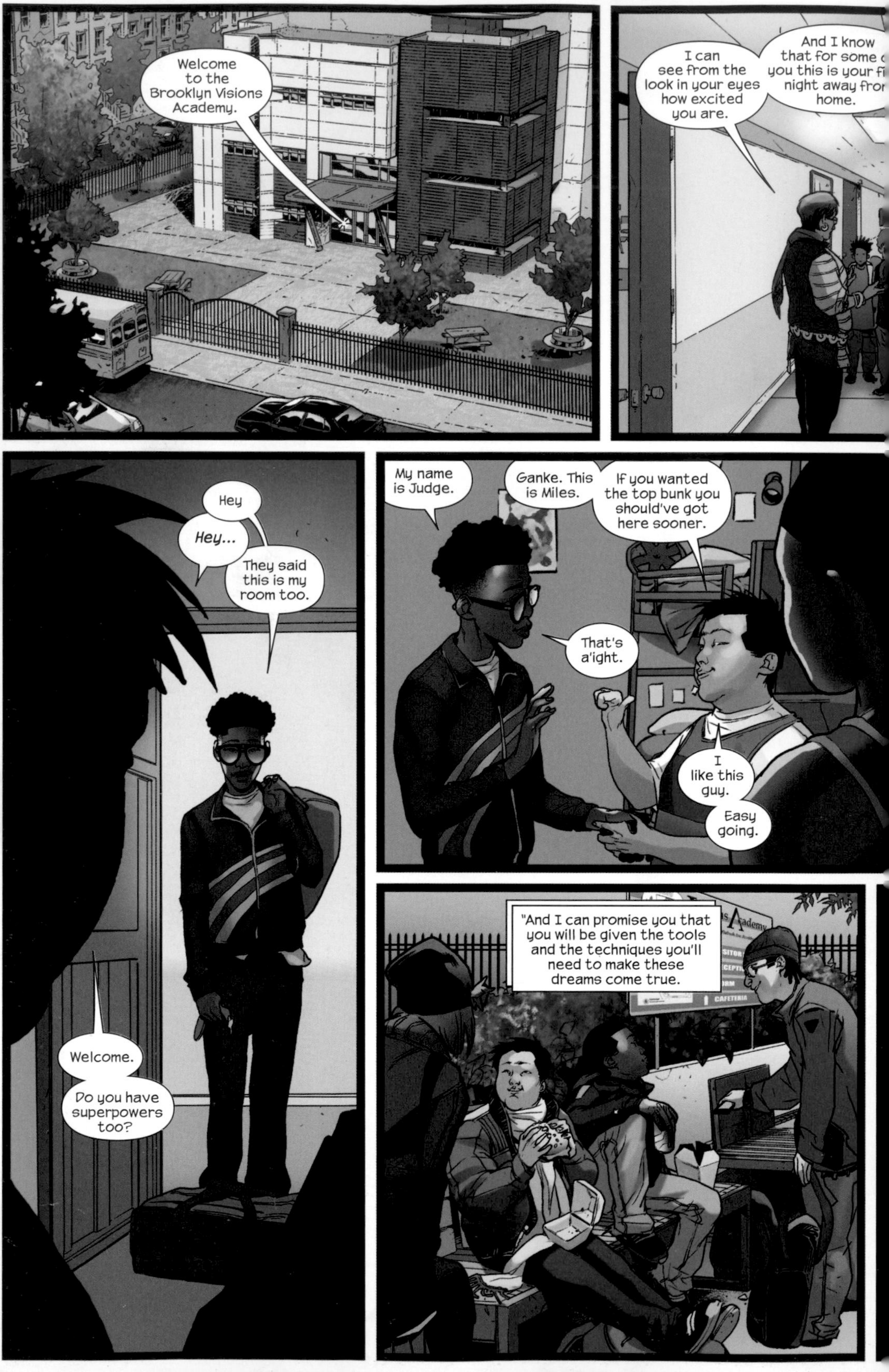

Welcome to the Brooklyn Visions Academy.
I can see from the look in your eyes how excited you are.
And I know that for some o you this is your fi night away fror home.
Hey
Hey...
They said this is my room too.
Welcome.
Do you have superpowers too?
My name is Judge.
Ganke. This is Miles.
If you wanted the top bunk you should've got here sooner.
That's a'ight.
I like this guy.
Easy going.
"And I can promise you that you will be given the tools and the techniques you'll need to make these dreams come true.
CAFETERIA

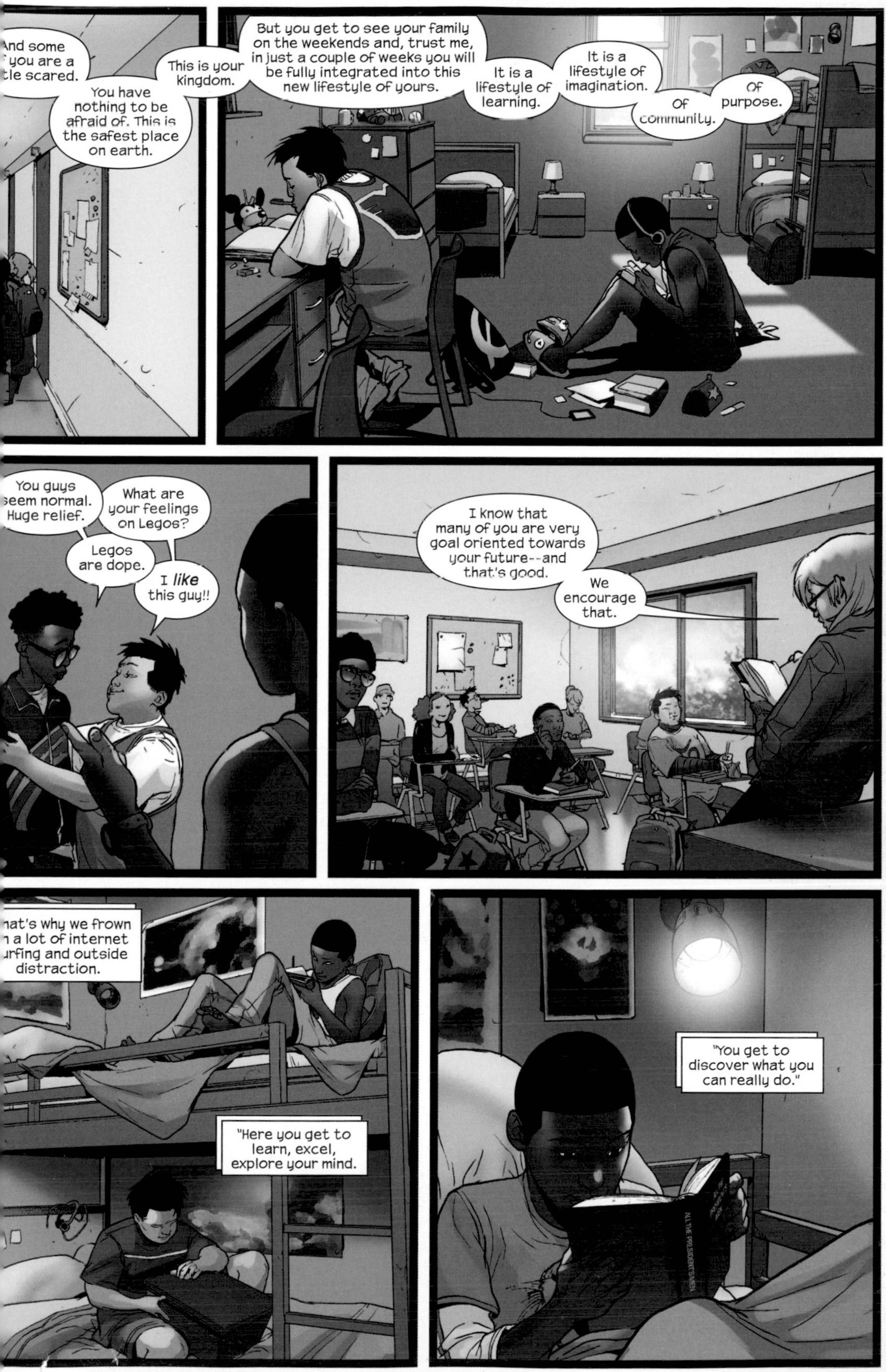

And some
you are a
tle scared.
You have nothing to be afraid of. This is the safest place on earth.
This is your kingdom.
But you get to see your family on the weekends and, trust me, in just a couple of weeks you will be fully integrated into this new lifestyle of yours.
It is a lifestyle of learning.
It is a lifestyle of imagination.
Of community.
Of purpose.
You guys seem normal. Huge relief.
What are your feelings on Legos?
Legos are dope.
I *like* this guy!!
I know that many of you are very goal oriented towards your future--and that's good.
We encourage that.
hat's why we frown
n a lot of internet
urfing and outside
distraction.
"Here you get to learn, excel, explore your mind.
"You get to discover what you can really do."
ALL THE PRESIDENT'S MEN

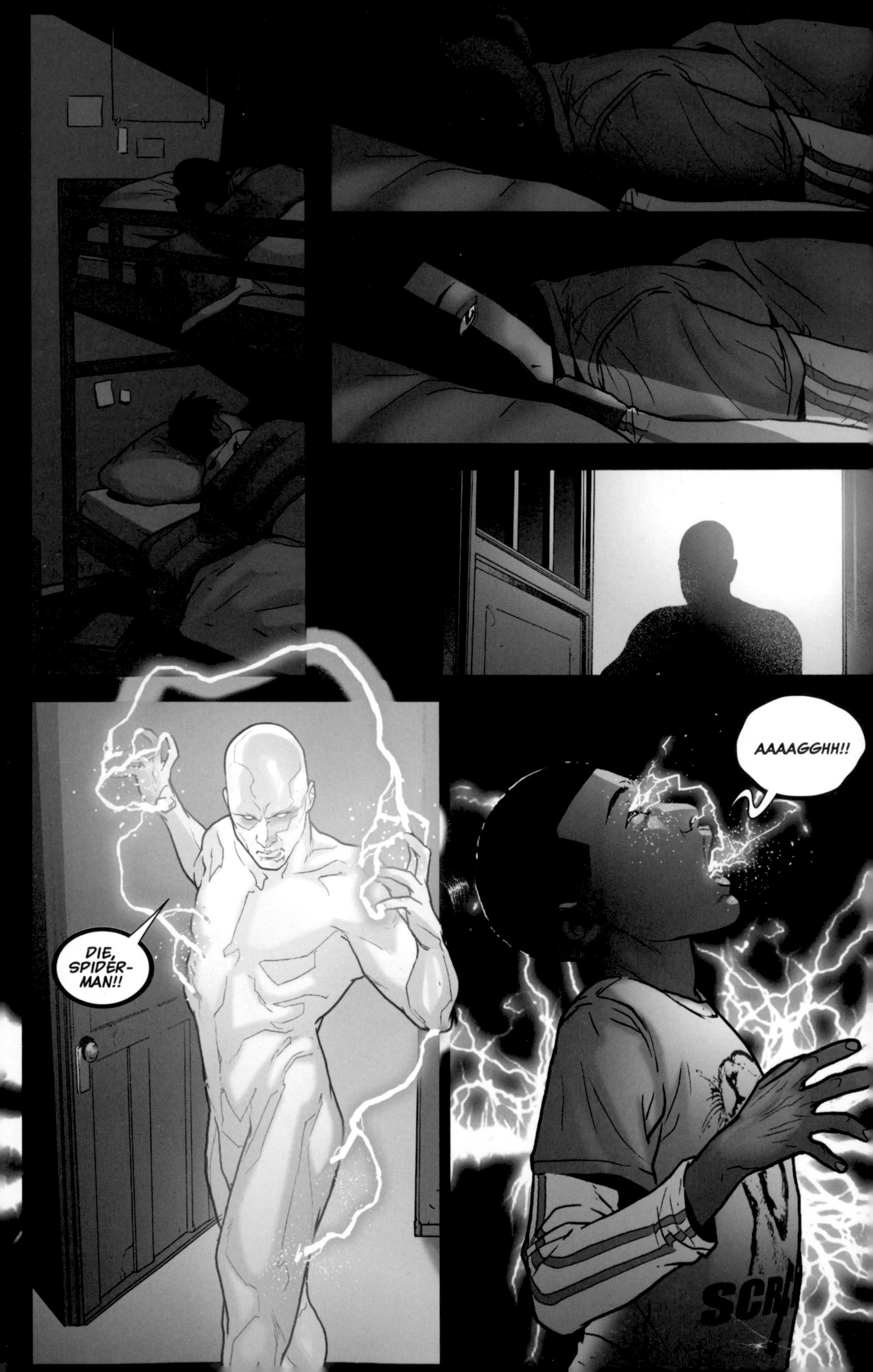
DIE, SPIDER-MAN!!
AAAAGGHH!!
SCR

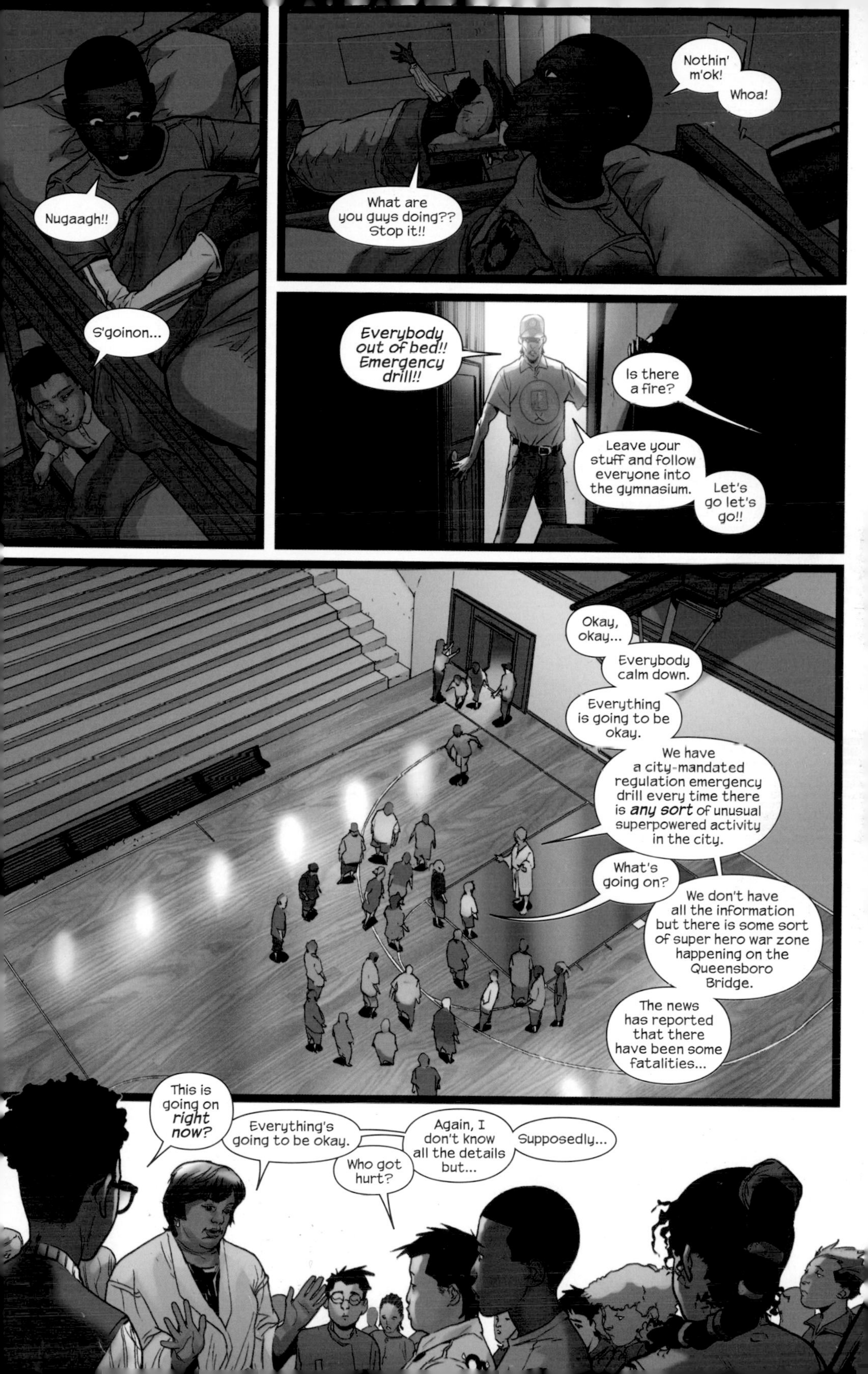

Nugaagh!!
S'goinon...
What are you guys doing?? Stop it!!
Nothin' m'ok!
Whoa!
Everybody out of bed!! Emergency drill!!
Is there a fire?
Leave your stuff and follow everyone into the gymnasium.
Let's go let's go!!
Okay, okay...
Everybody calm down.
Everything is going to be okay.
We have a city-mandated regulation emergency drill every time there is any sort of unusual superpowered activity in the city.
What's going on?
We don't have all the information but there is some sort of super hero war zone happening on the Queensboro Bridge.
The news has reported that there have been some fatalities...
This is going on right now?
Everything's going to be okay.
Who got hurt?
Again, I don't know all the details but...
Supposedly...

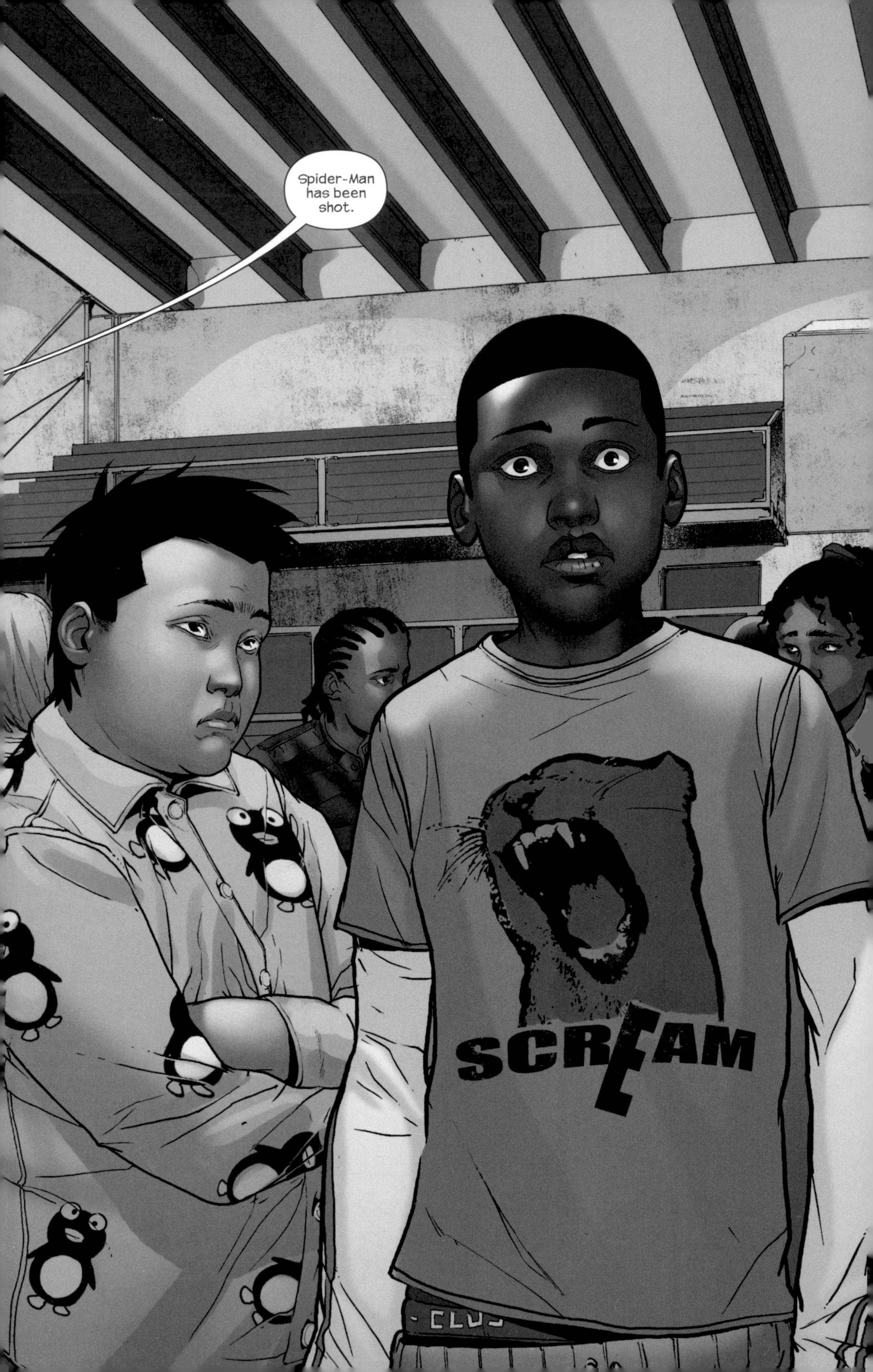
Spider-Man has been shot.
SCREAM

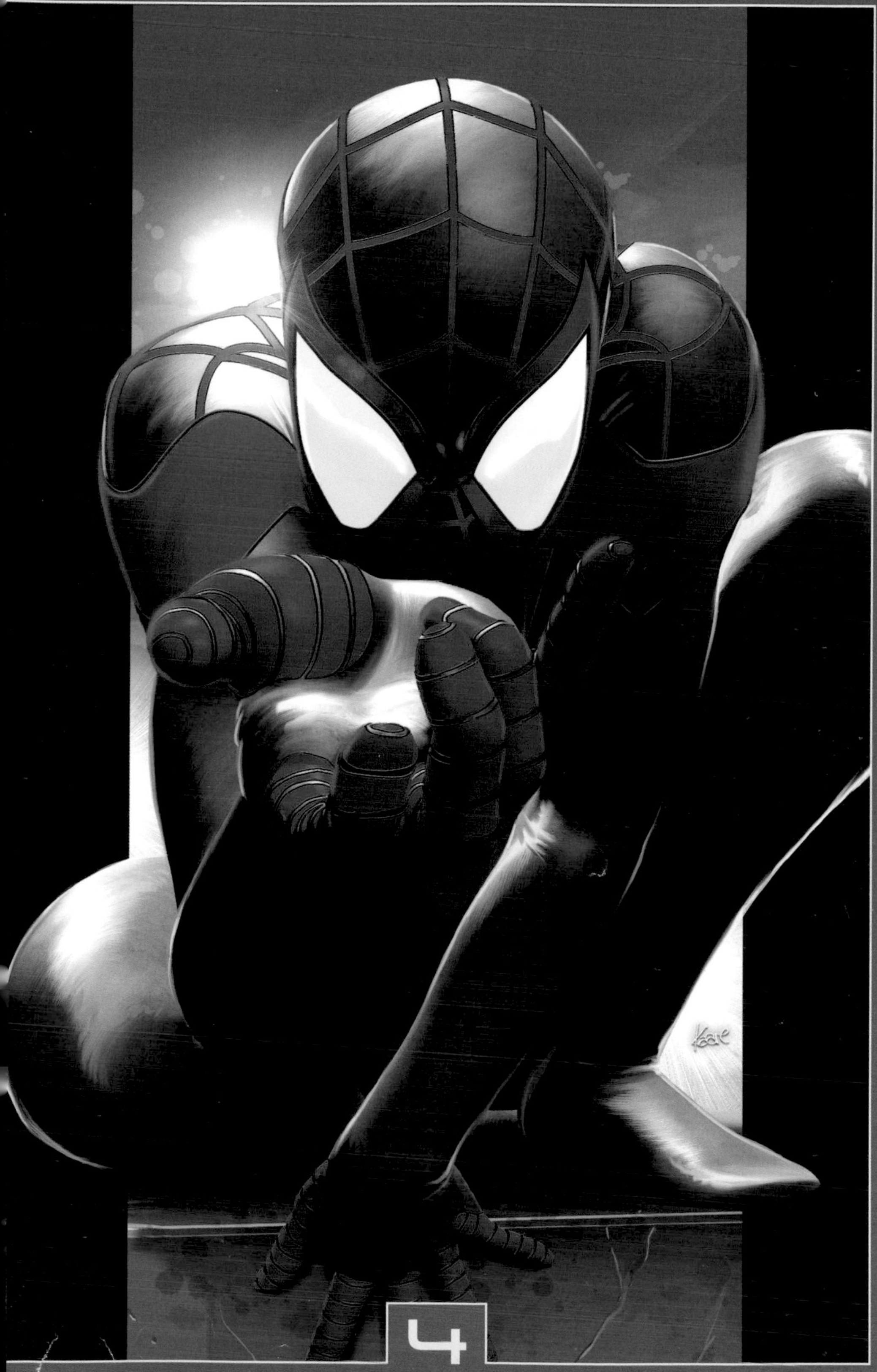

4

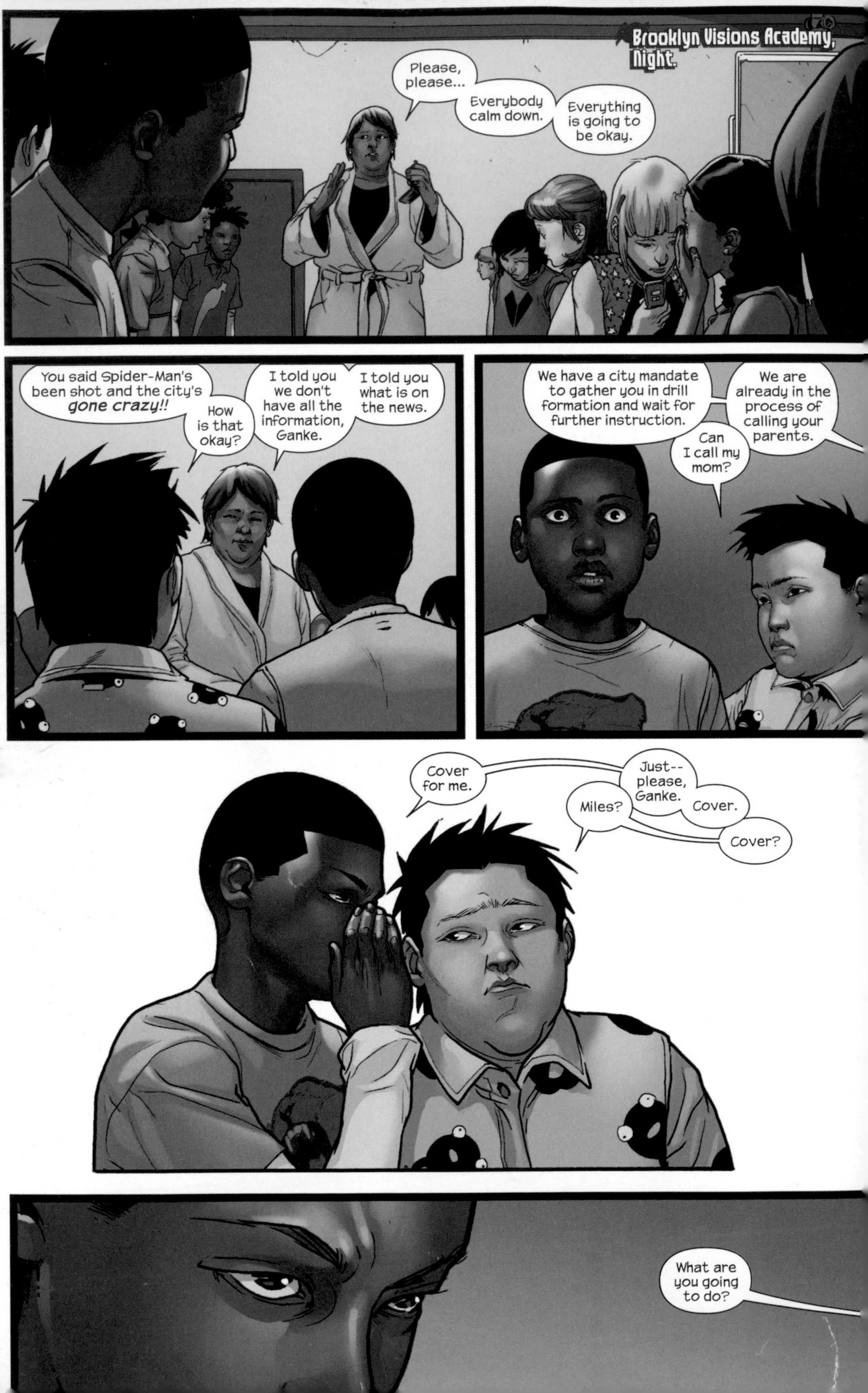

Brooklyn Visions Academy, Night.
Please, please...
Everybody calm down.
Everything is going to be okay.
You said Spider-Man's been shot and the city's *gone crazy!!*
How is that okay?
I told you we don't have all the information, Ganke.
I told you what is on the news.
We have a city mandate to gather you in drill formation and wait for further instruction.
We are already in the process of calling your parents.
Can I call my mom?
Cover for me.
Just-- please, Ganke.
Cover.
Miles?
Cover?
What are you going to do?

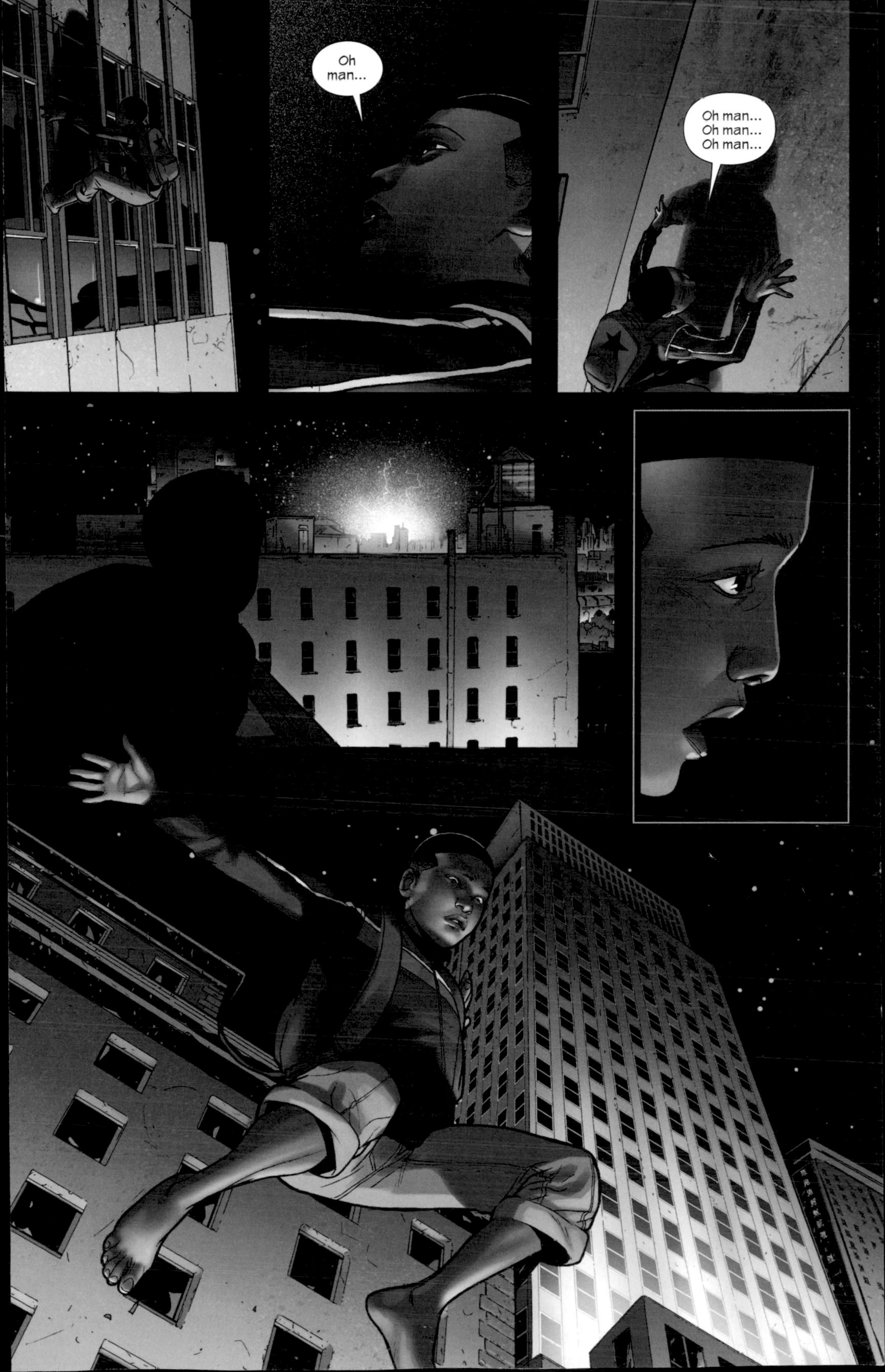
Oh man...
Oh man...
Oh man...
Oh man...

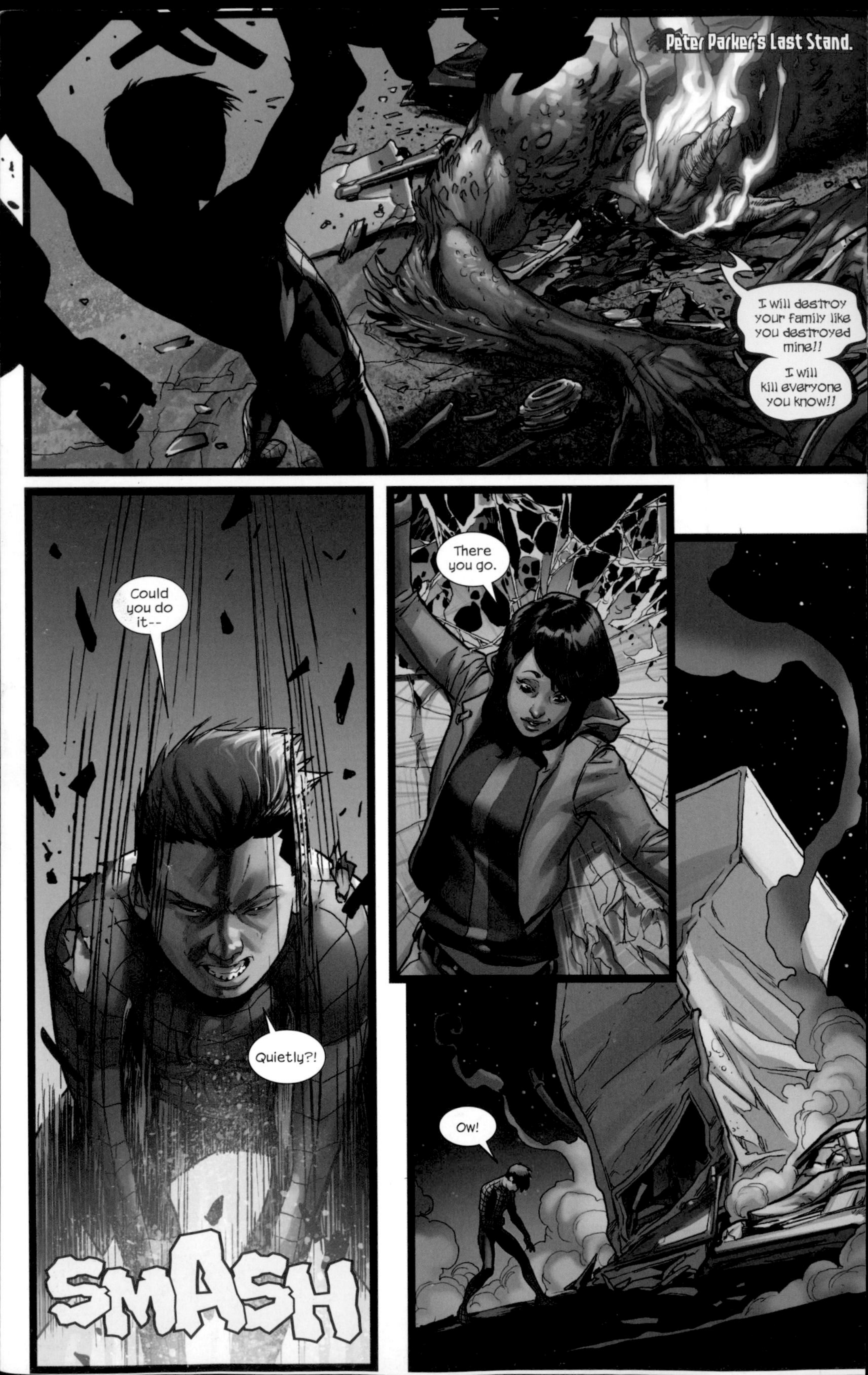
Peter Parker's Last Stand.
I will destroy your family like you destroyed mine!!
I will kill everyone you know!!
Could you do it--
Quietly?!
SMASH
There you go.
Ow!

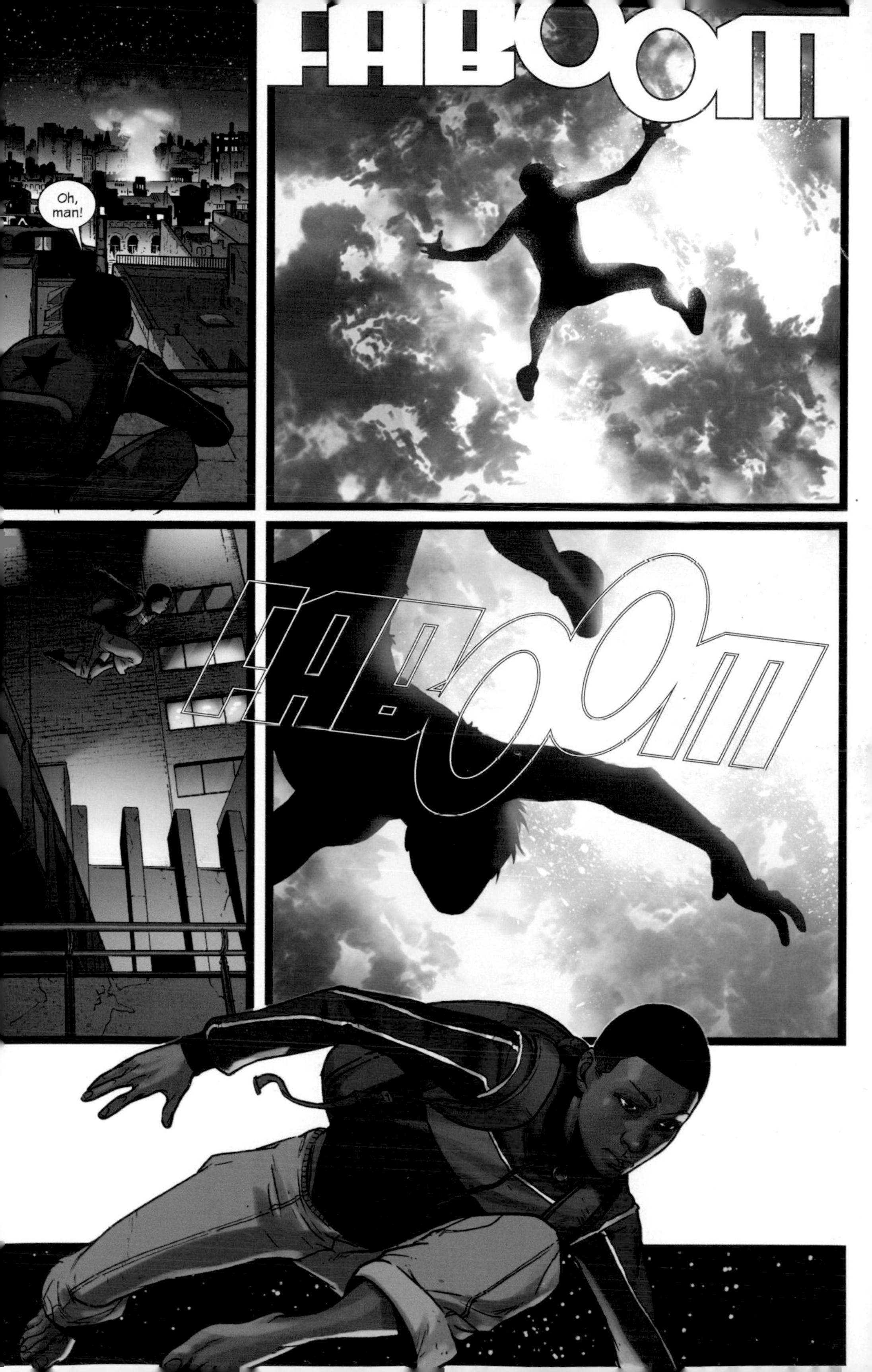

Oh, man!
KABOOM
KABOOM

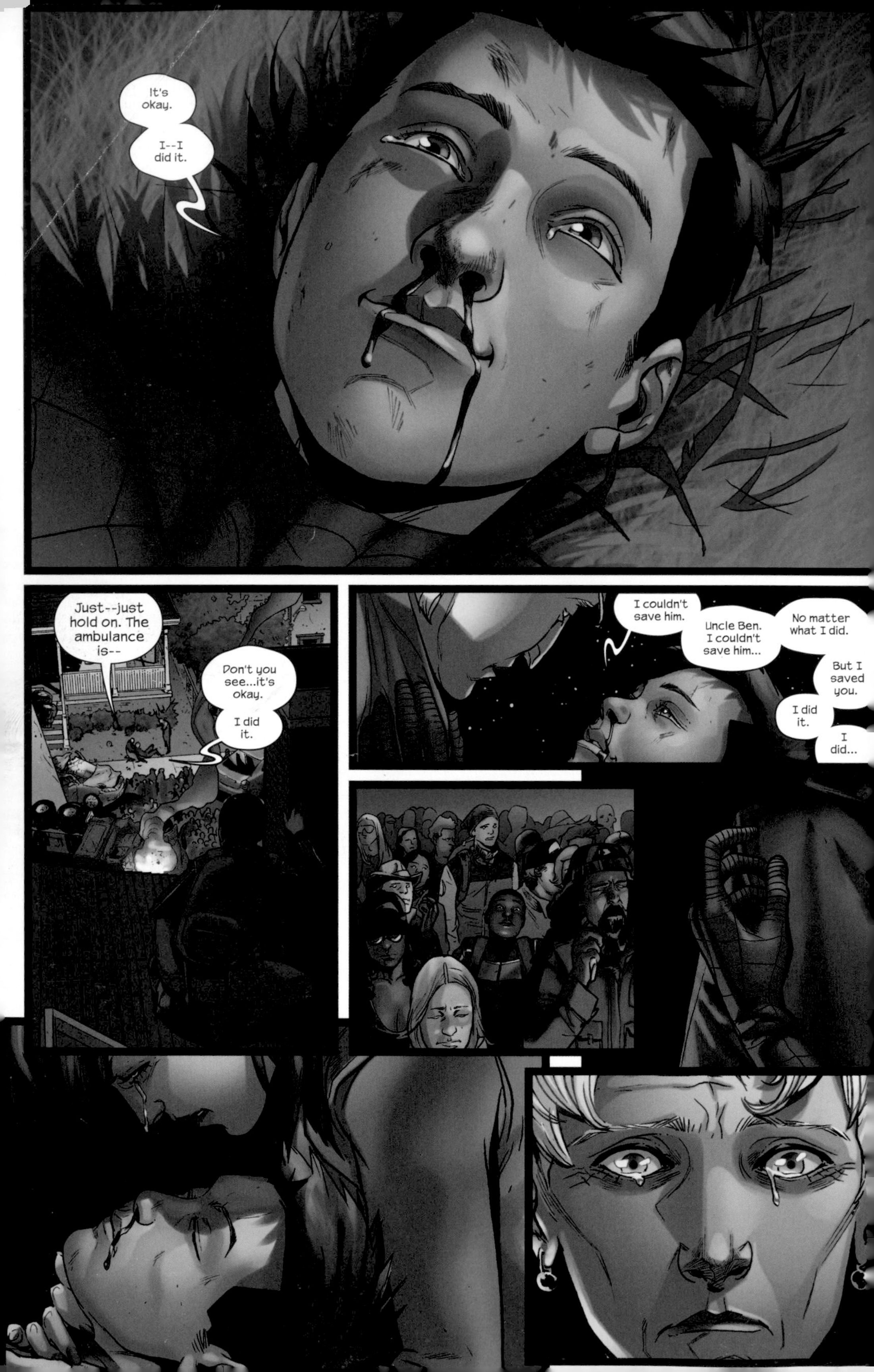
It's okay.
I--I did it.
Just--just hold on. The ambulance is--
Don't you see...it's okay.
I did it.
I couldn't save him.
Uncle Ben. I couldn't save him...
No matter what I did.
But I saved you.
I did it.
I did...

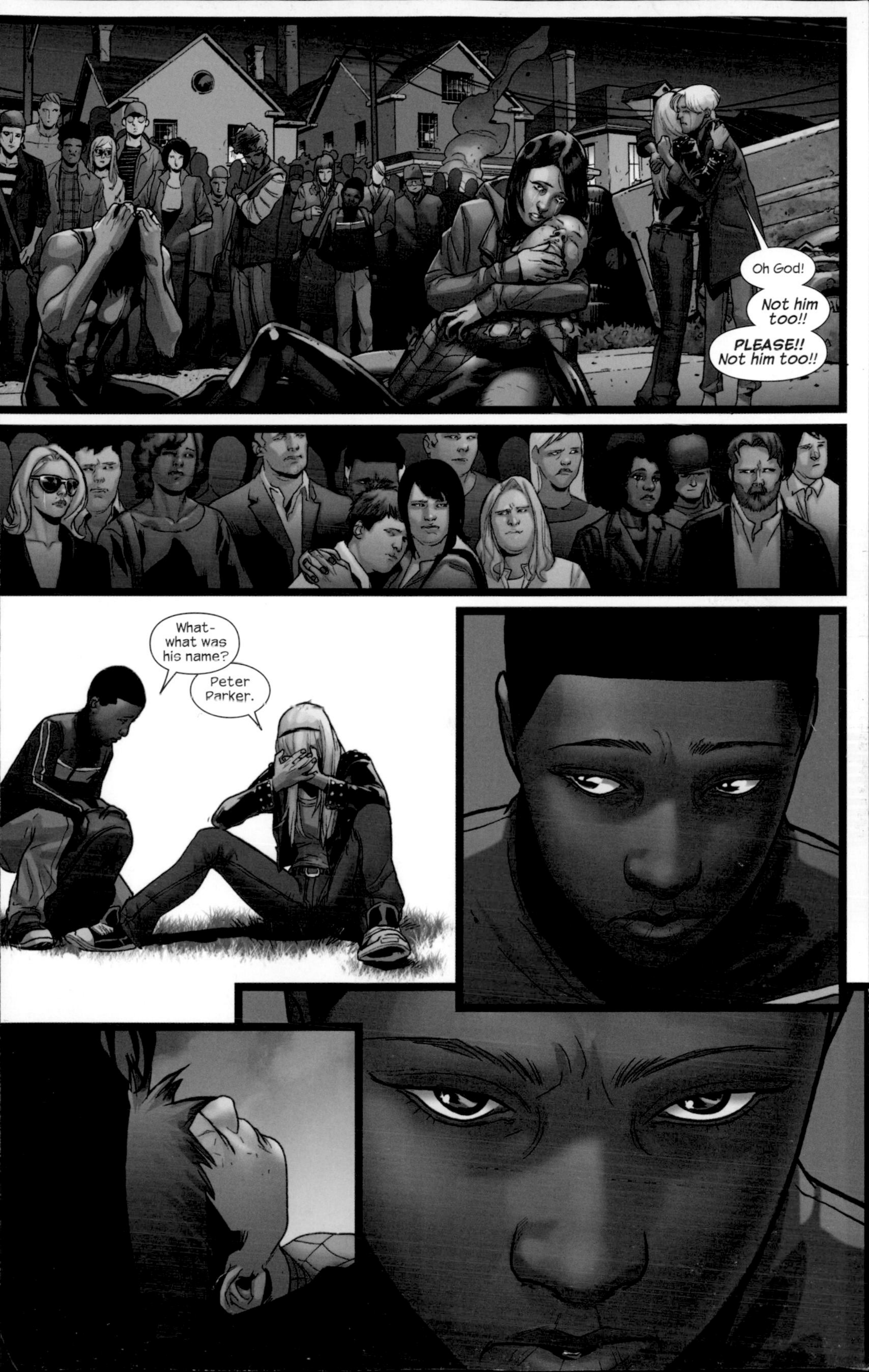
Oh God!
Not him too!!
PLEASE!! Not him too!!
What- what was his name?
Peter Parker.

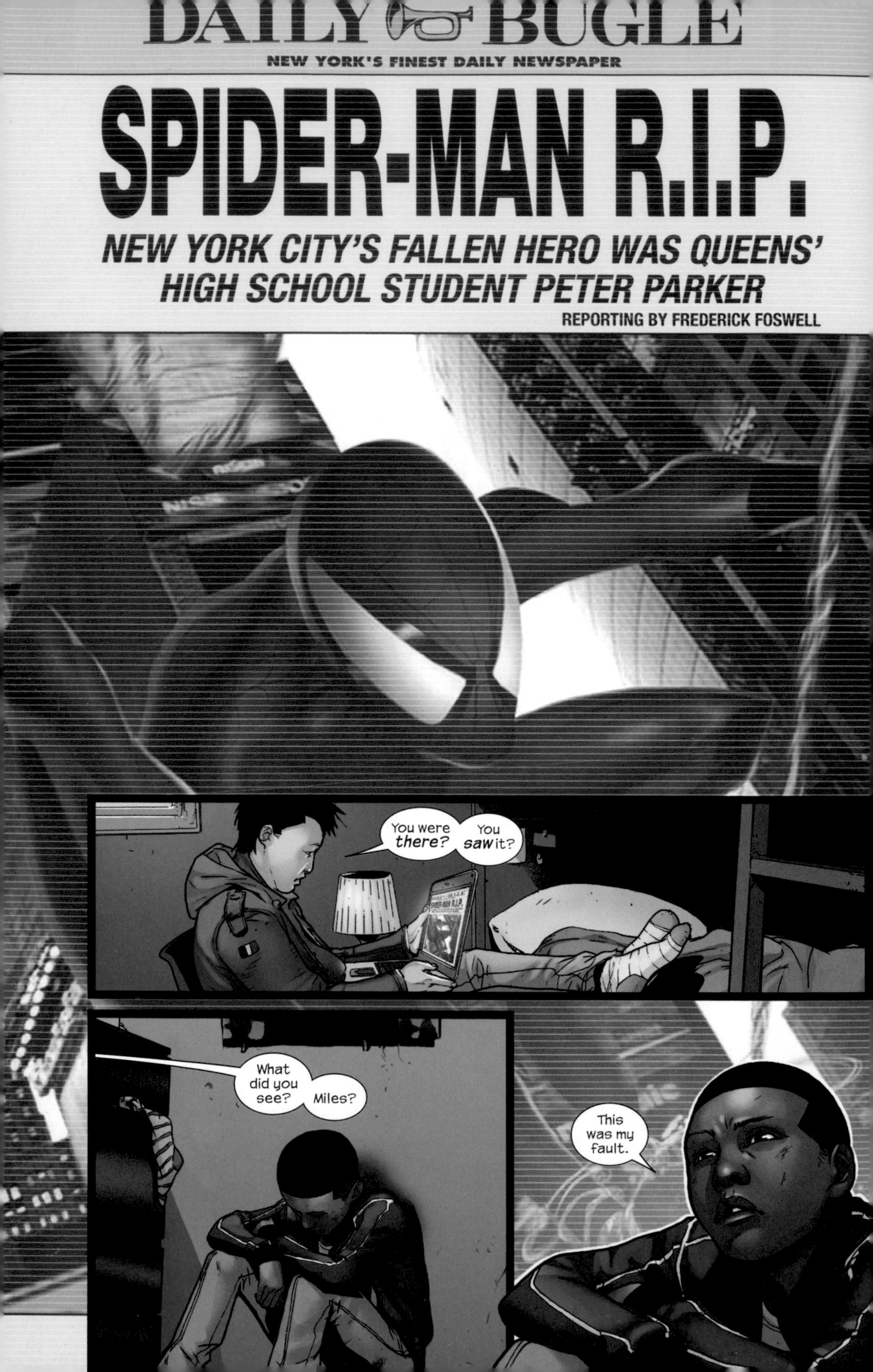
DAILY BUGLE
NEW YORK'S FINEST DAILY NEWSPAPER
SPIDER-MAN R.I.P.
NEW YORK CITY'S FALLEN HERO WAS QUEENS' HIGH SCHOOL STUDENT PETER PARKER
REPORTING BY FREDERICK FOSWELL
You were *there?*
You *saw* it?
What did you see?
Miles?
This was my fault.

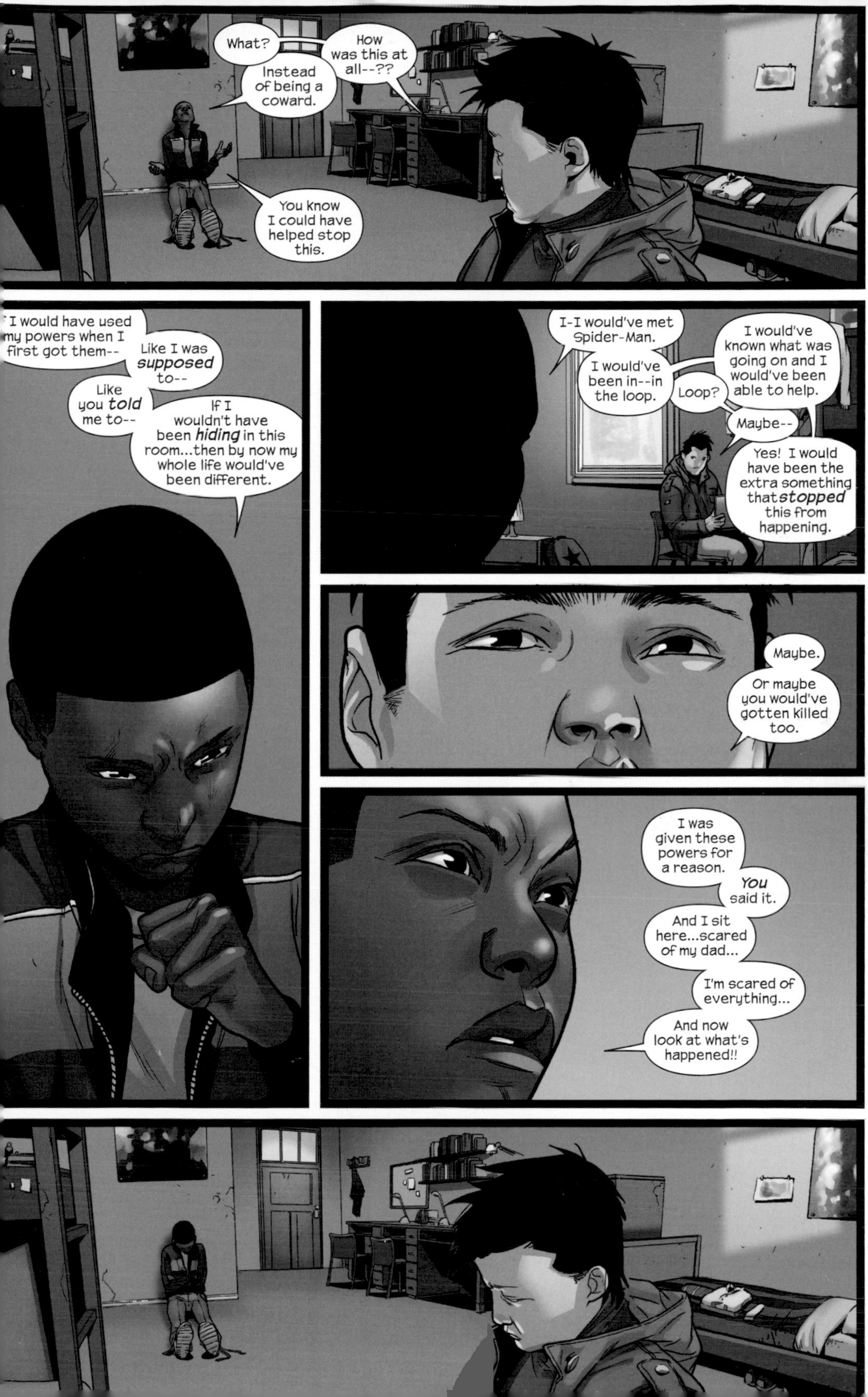
What?
How was this at all--??
Instead of being a coward.
You know I could have helped stop this.
I would have used my powers when I first got them--
Like I was *supposed* to--
Like you *told* me to--
If I wouldn't have been *hiding* in this room...then by now my whole life would've been different.
I-I would've met Spider-Man.
I would've been in--in the loop.
I would've known what was going on and I would've been able to help.
Loop?
Maybe--
Yes! I would have been the extra something that *stopped* this from happening.
Maybe.
Or maybe you would've gotten killed too.
I was given these powers for a reason.
You said it.
And I sit here...scared of my dad...
I'm scared of everything...
And now look at what's happened!!

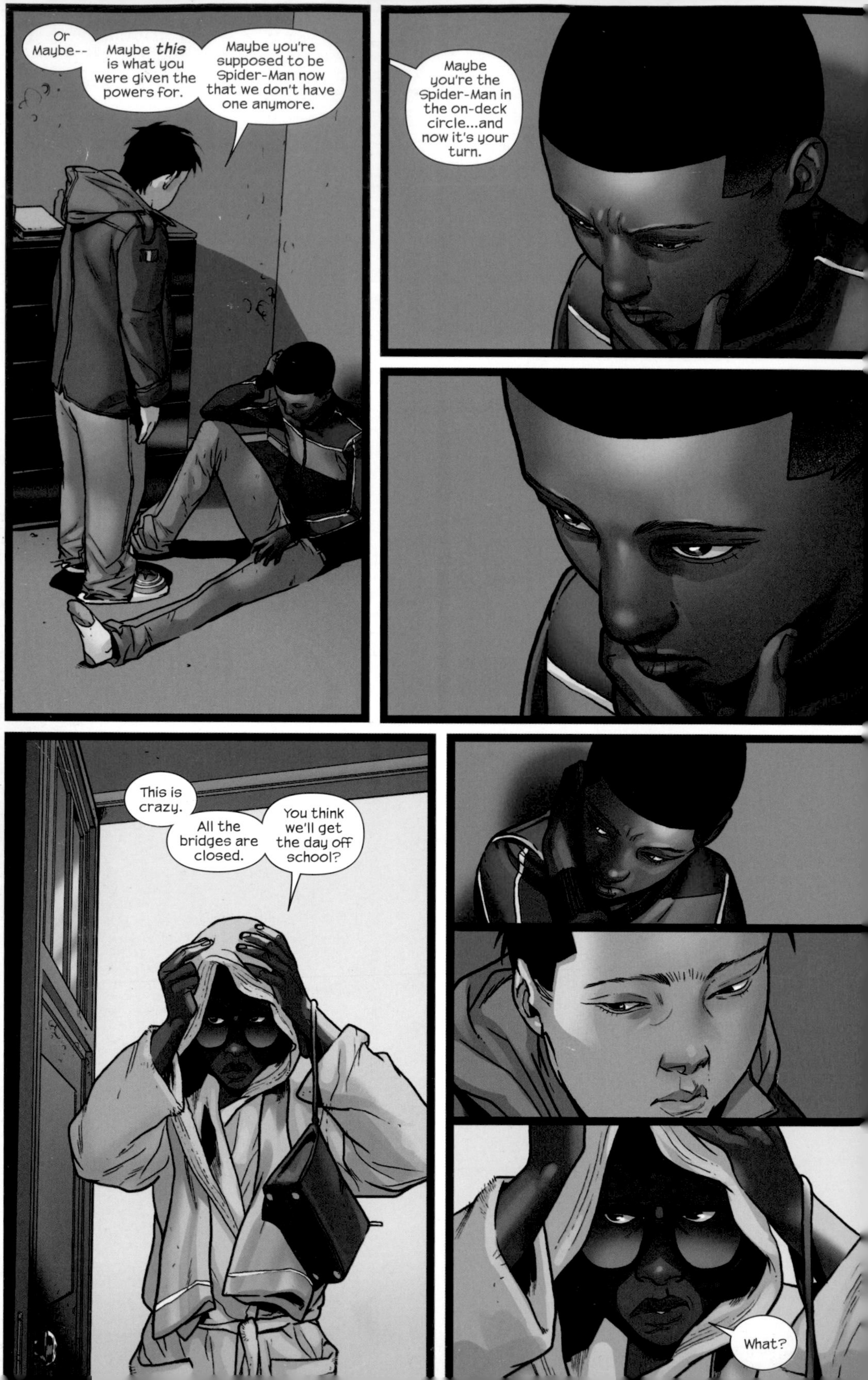
Or Maybe--
Maybe *this* is what you were given the powers for.
Maybe you're supposed to be Spider-Man now that we don't have one anymore.
Maybe you're the Spider-Man in the on-deck circle...and now it's your turn.
This is crazy.
All the bridges are closed.
You think we'll get the day off school?
What?

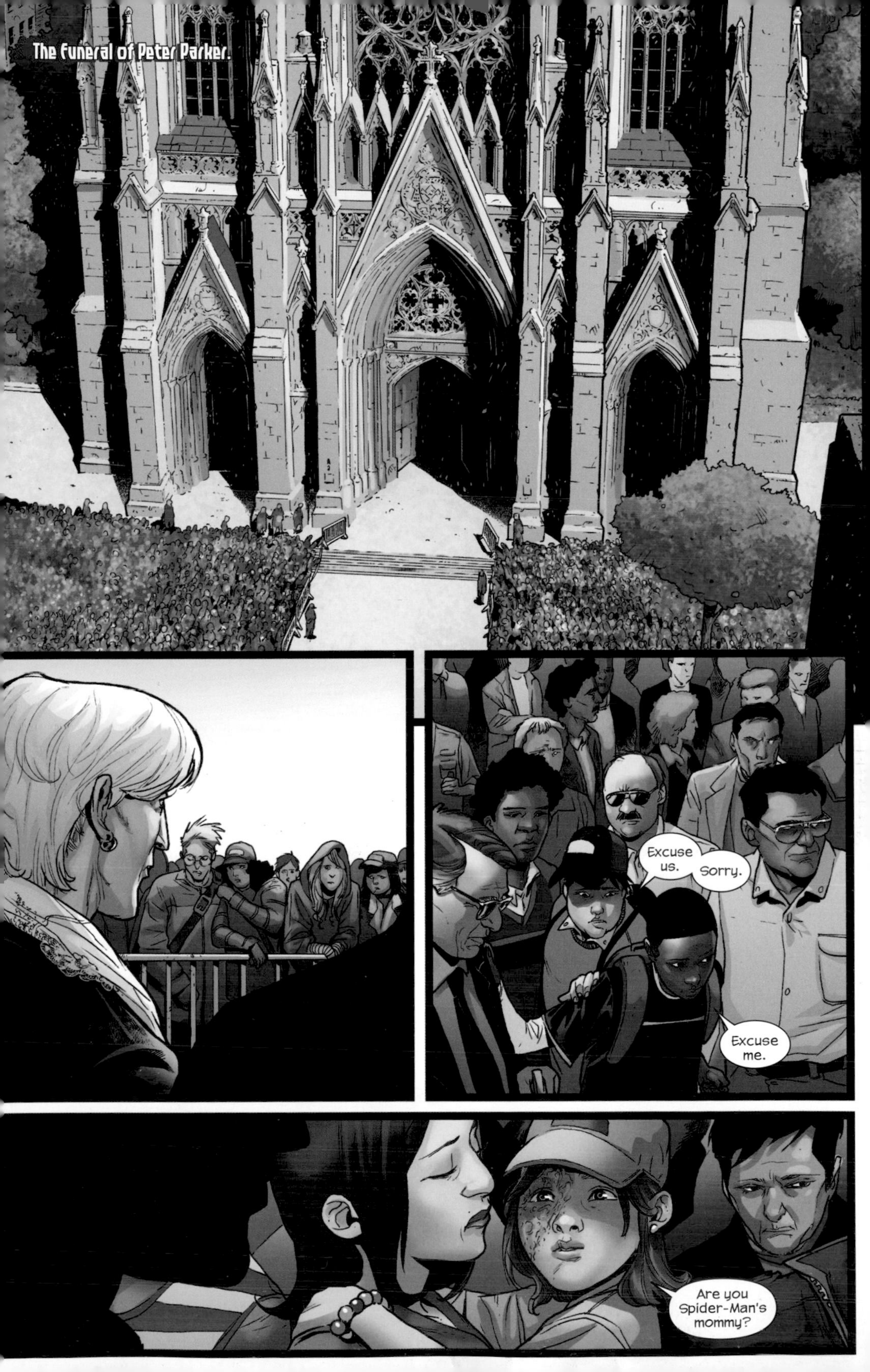
The Funeral of Peter Parker.
Excuse us.
Sorry.
Excuse me.
Are you Spider-Man's mommy?

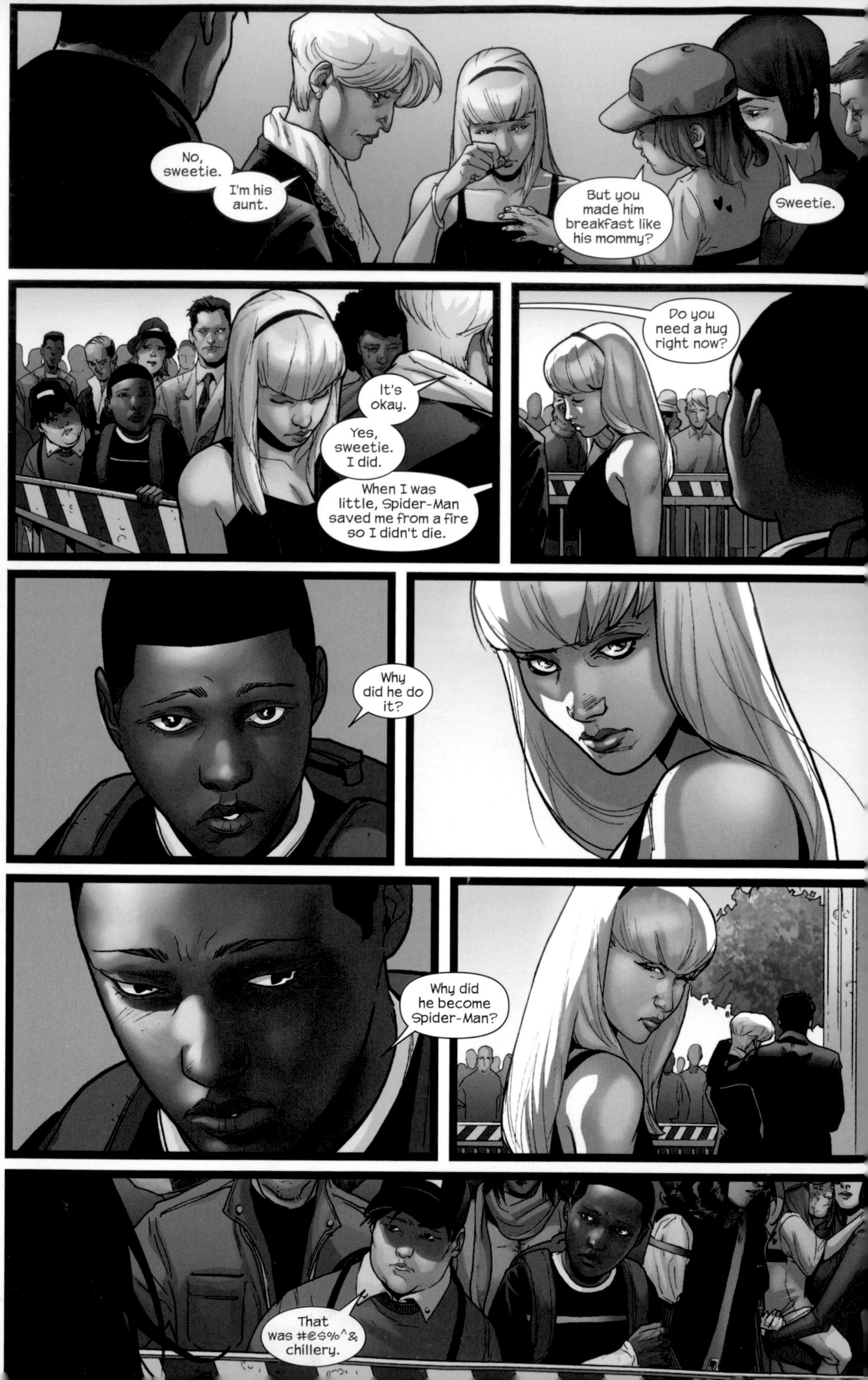
No, sweetie.
I'm his aunt.
But you made him breakfast like his mommy?
Sweetie.
It's okay.
Yes, sweetie. I did.
When I was little, Spider-Man saved me from a fire so I didn't die.
Do you need a hug right now?
Why did he do it?
Why did he become Spider-Man?
That was #@$%^& chillery.

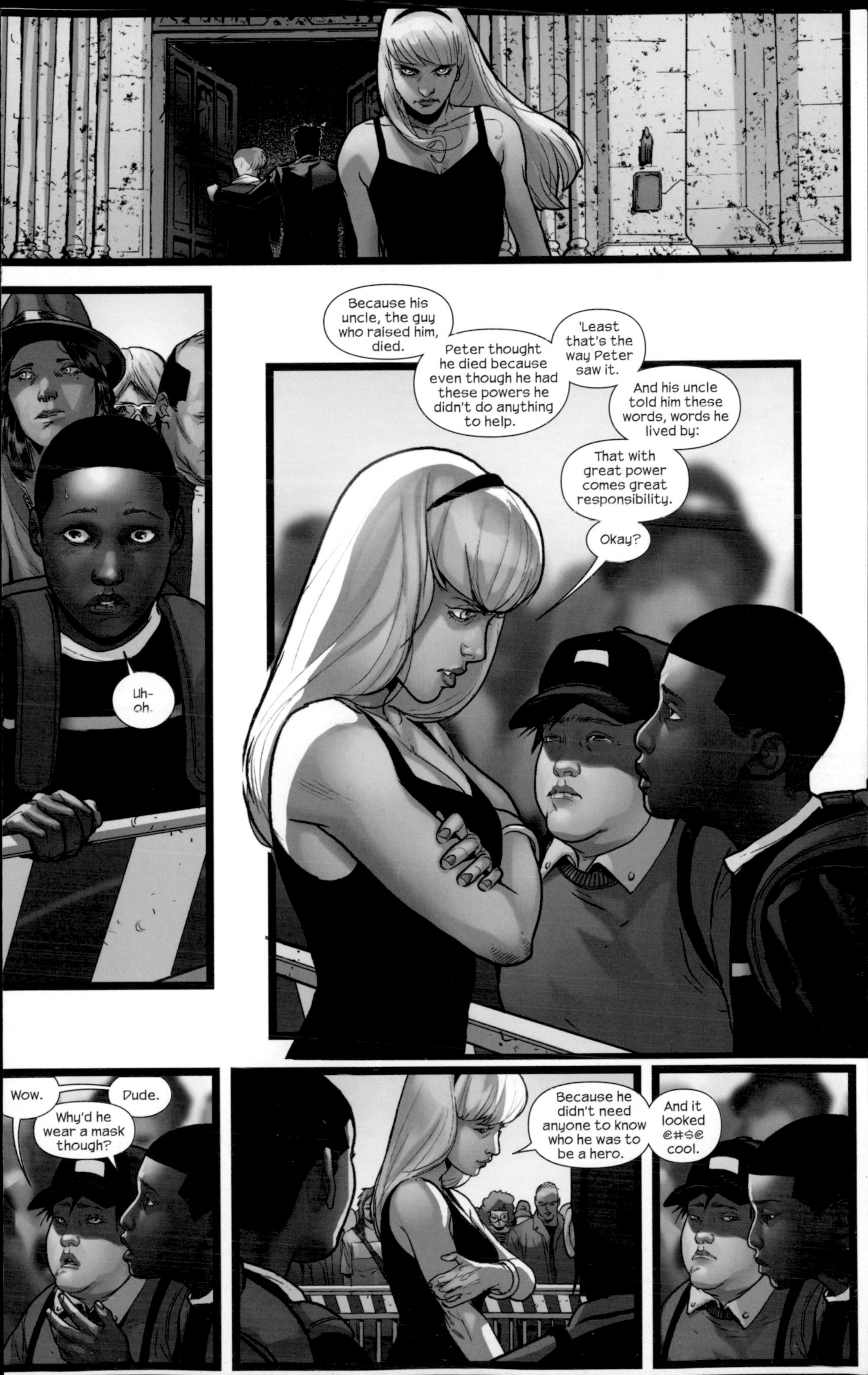
Because his uncle, the guy who raised him, died.
Peter thought he died because even though he had these powers he didn't do anything to help.
'Least that's the way Peter saw it.
And his uncle told him these words, words he lived by:
That with great power comes great responsibility.
Okay?
Uh-oh.
Wow.
Dude.
Why'd he wear a mask though?
Because he didn't need anyone to know who he was to be a hero.
And it looked @#$@ cool.

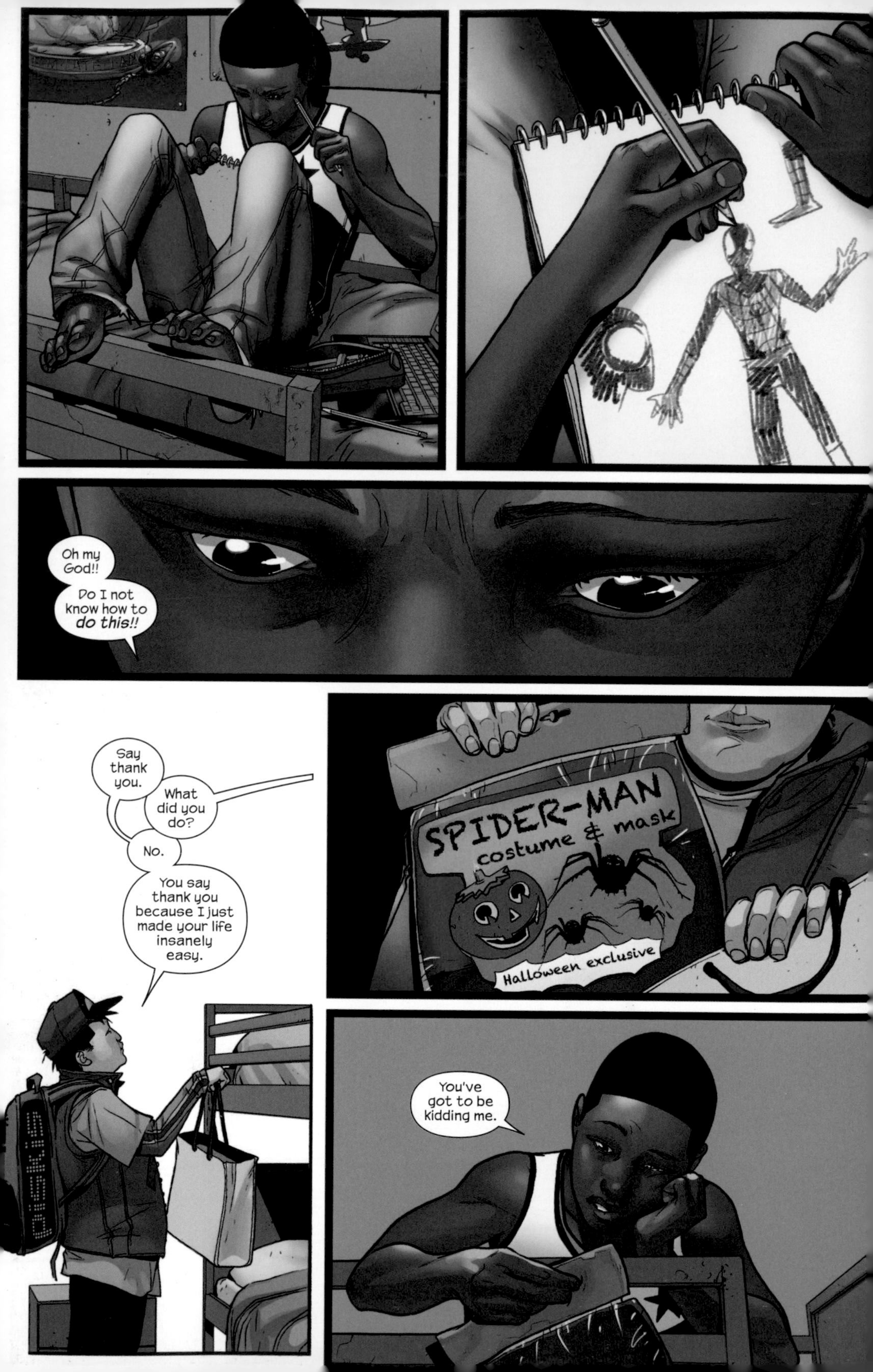
Oh my God!!
Do I not know how to do this!!
Say thank you.
What did you do?
No.
You say thank you because I just made your life insanely easy.
SPIDER-MAN costume & mask
Halloween exclusive
You've got to be kidding me.

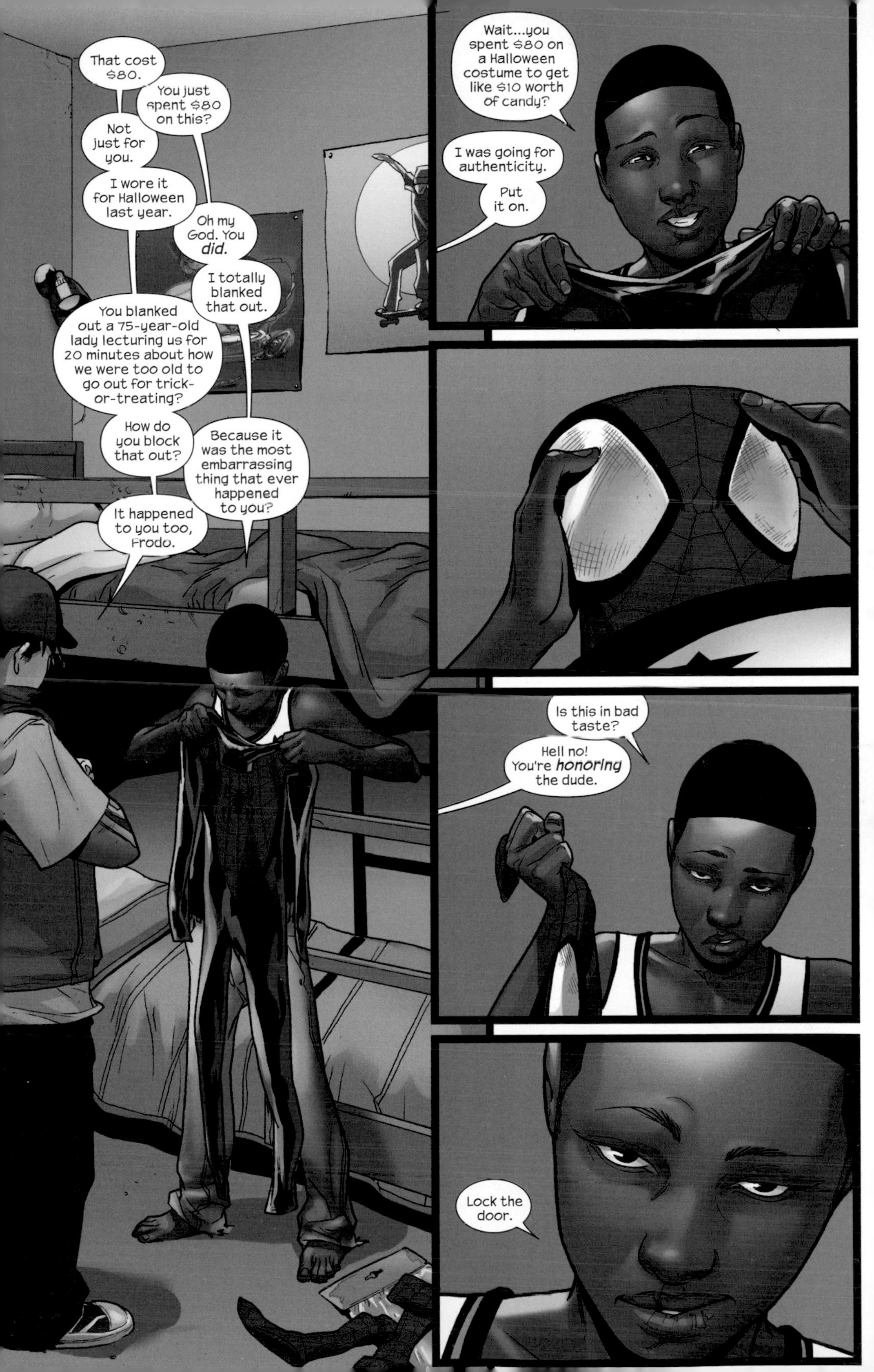
That cost $80.
You just spent $80 on this?
Not just for you.
I wore it for Halloween last year.
Oh my God. You *did.*
I totally blanked that out.
You blanked out a 75-year-old lady lecturing us for 20 minutes about how we were too old to go out for trick-or-treating?
How do you block that out?
Because it was the most embarrassing thing that ever happened to you?
It happened to you too, Frodo.
Wait...you spent $80 on a Halloween costume to get like $10 worth of candy?
I was going for authenticity.
Put it on.
Is this in bad taste?
Hell no! You're ***honoring*** the dude.
Lock the door.

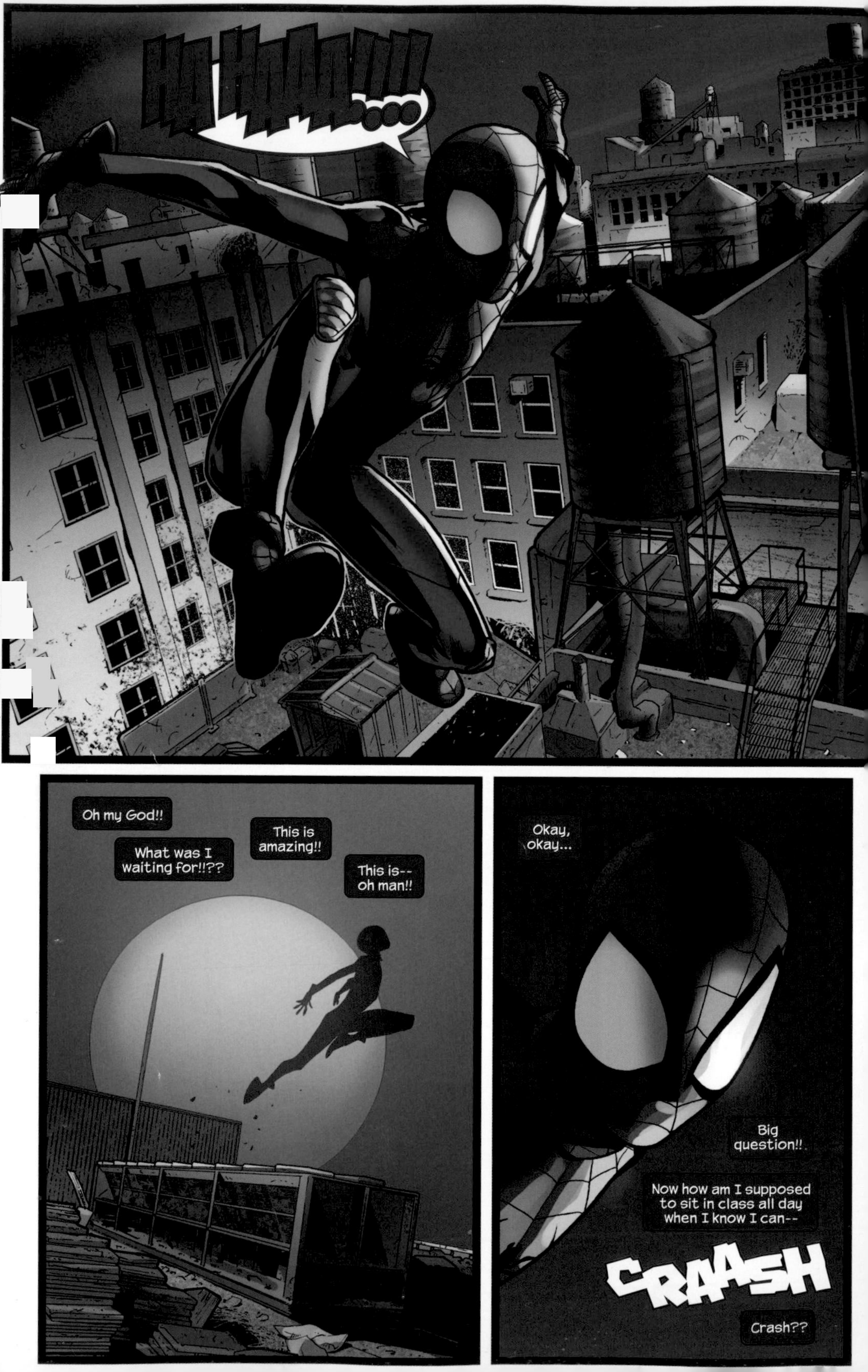
HA HAAA!!!....
Oh my God!!
What was I waiting for!!??
This is amazing!!
This is-- oh man!!
Okay, okay...
Big question!!
Now how am I supposed to sit in class all day when I know I can--
CRAASH
Crash??

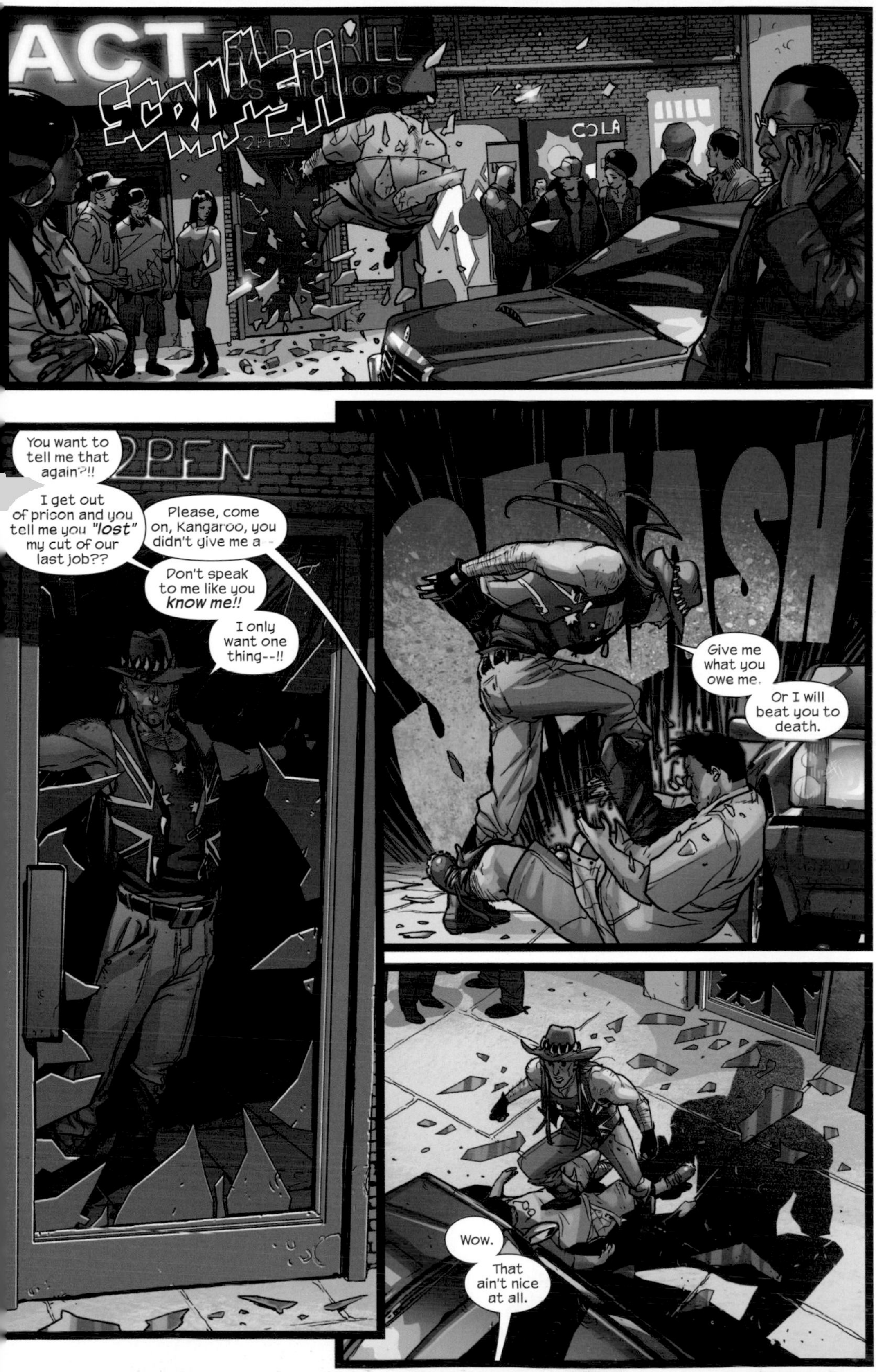

ACT
BAR & GRILL
wines & liquors
SCRAAASH
OPEN
COLA
You want to tell me that again?!!
I get out of prison and you tell me you "lost" my cut of our last job??
Please, come on, Kangaroo, you didn't give me a--
Don't speak to me like you know me!!
I only want one thing--!!
SMASH
Give me what you owe me.
Or I will beat you to death.
Wow.
That ain't nice at all.

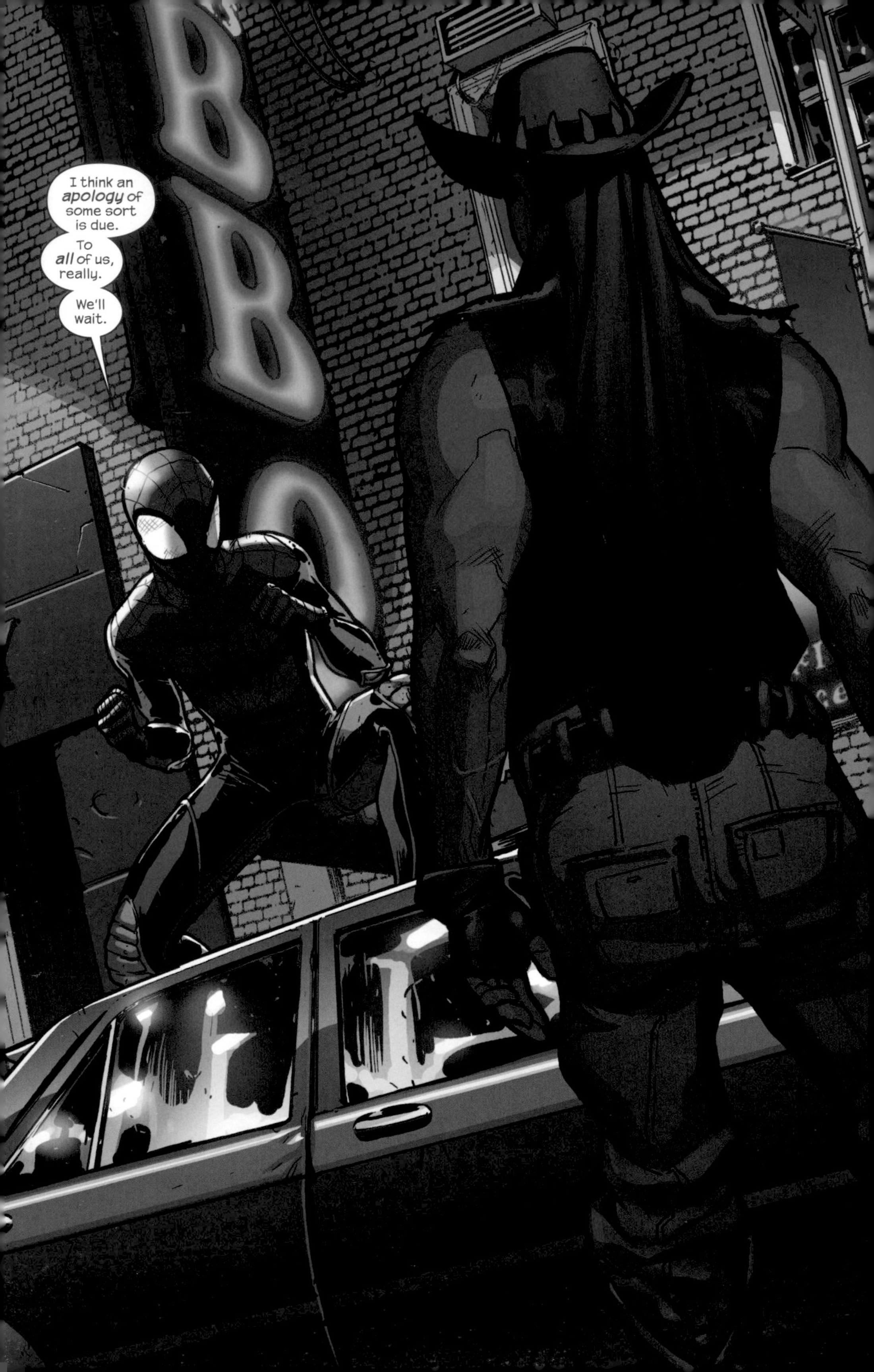
I think an *apology* of some sort is due.
To *all* of us, really.
We'll wait.

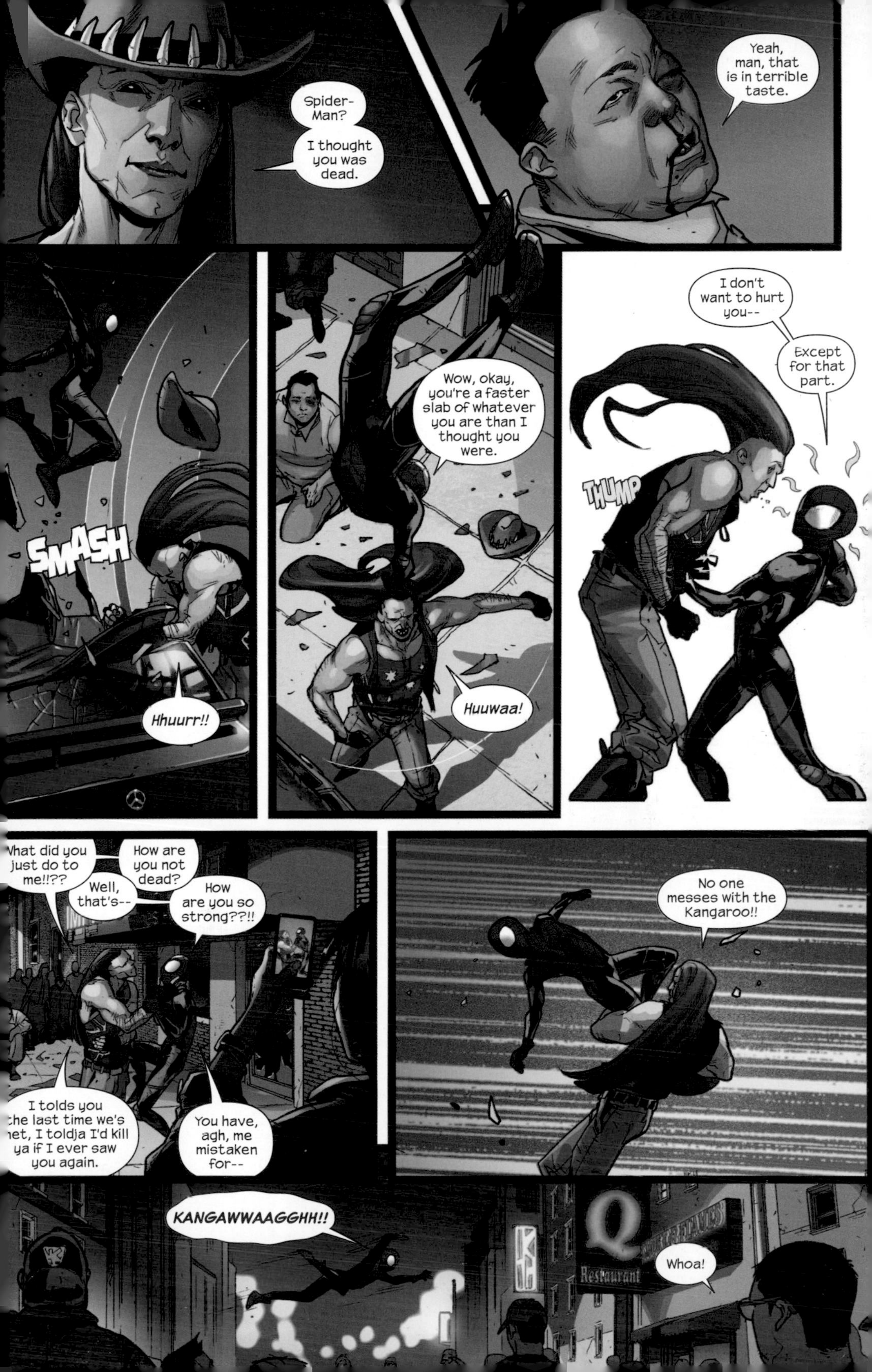

Spider-Man?
I thought you was dead.
Yeah, man, that is in terrible taste.
SMASH
Hhuurr!!
Wow, okay, you're a faster slab of whatever you are than I thought you were.
Huuwaa!
I don't want to hurt you--
Except for that part.
THUMP
What did you just do to me!!??
How are you not dead?
Well, that's--
How are you so strong??!!
I tolds you the last time we's met, I toldja I'd kill ya if I ever saw you again.
You have, agh, me mistaken for--
No one messes with the Kangaroo!!
KANGAWWAAGGHH!!
Restaurant
Whoa!

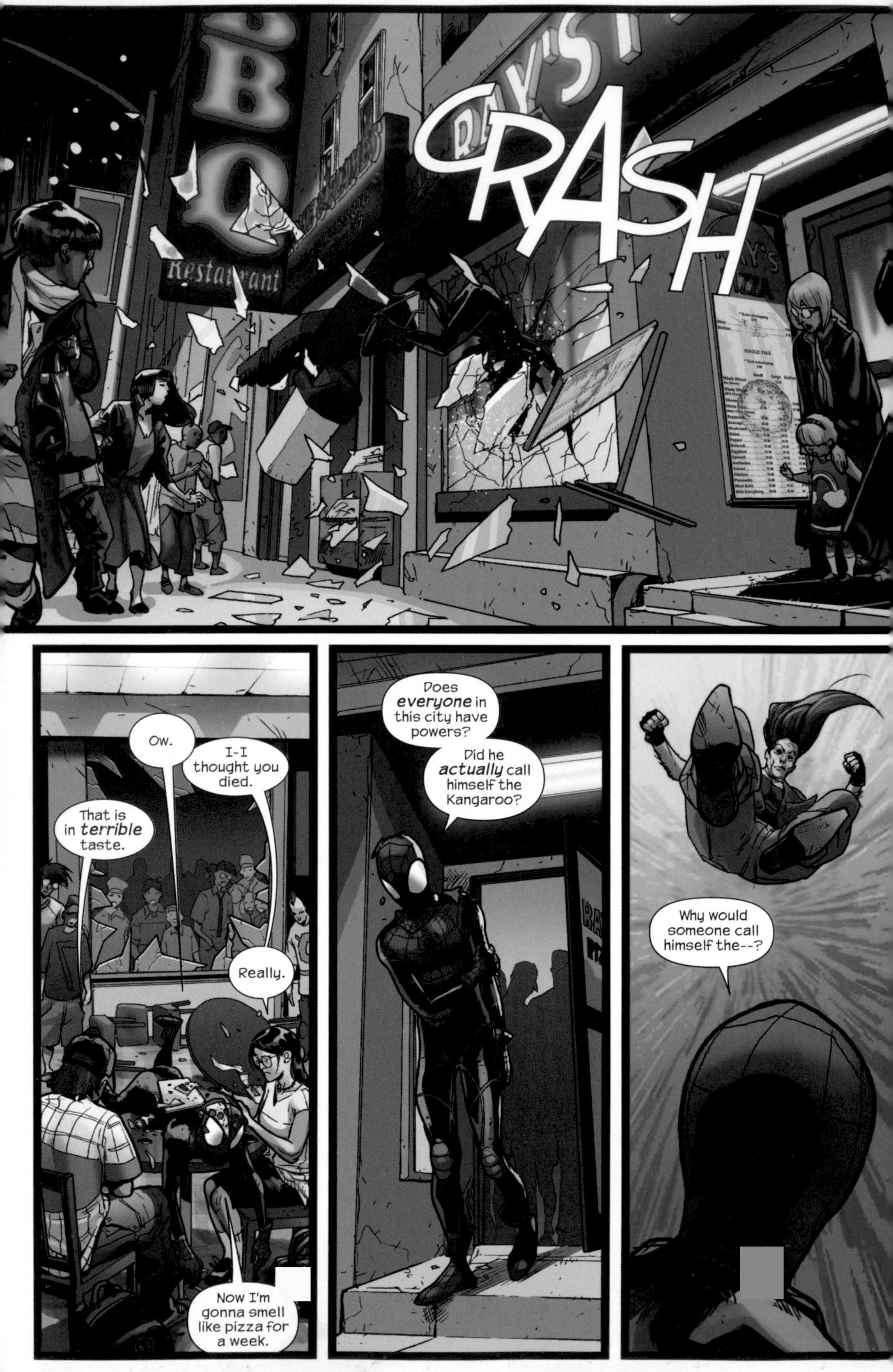

CRASH
Ow.
I-I thought you died.
That is in *terrible* taste.
Really.
Now I'm gonna smell like pizza for a week.
Does *everyone* in this city have powers?
Did he *actually* call himself the Kangaroo?
Why would someone call himself the--?

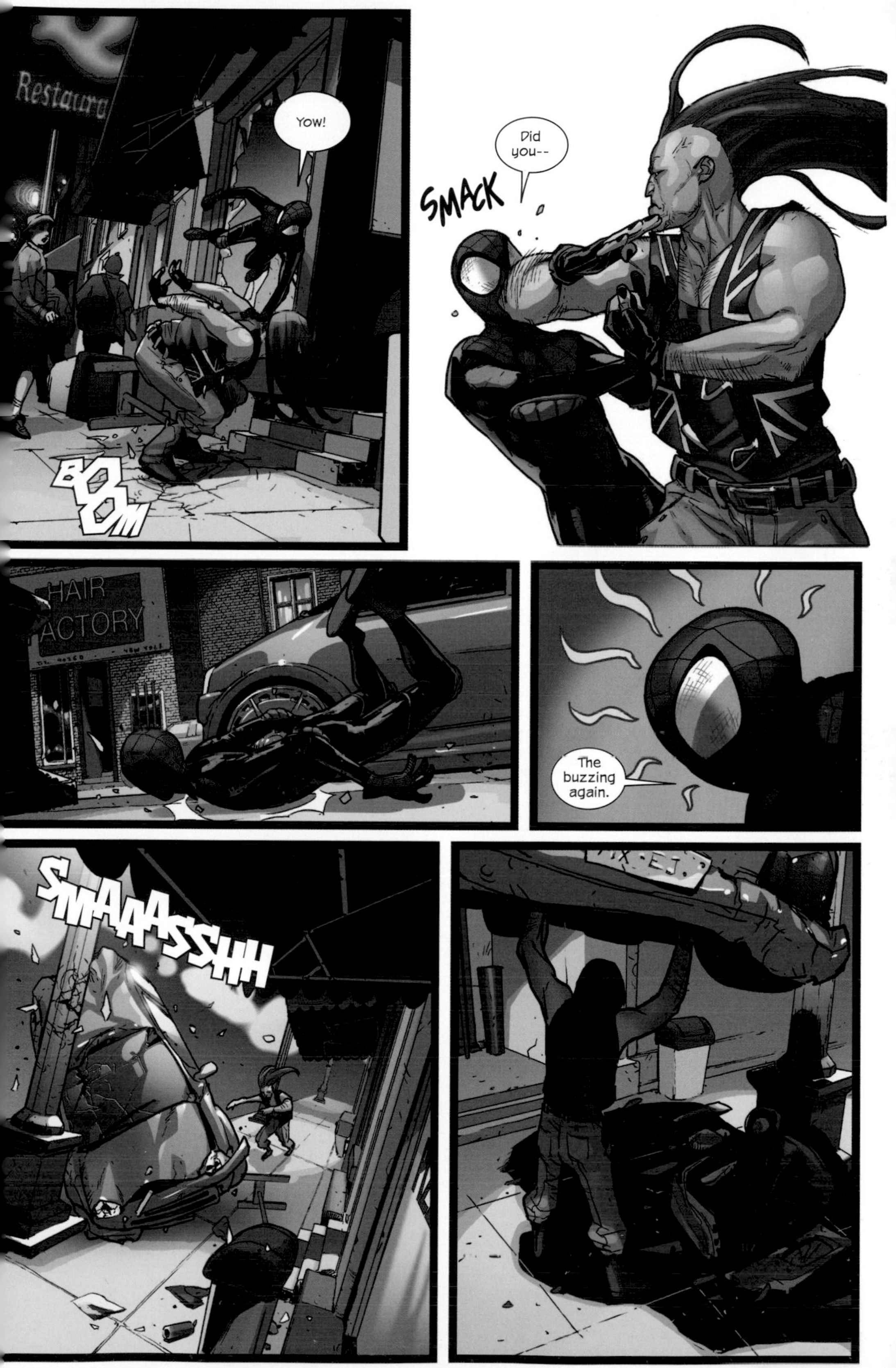
Restaura
Yow!
BOOM
SMACK
Did you--
HAIR FACTORY
The buzzing again.
SMAAASSHH

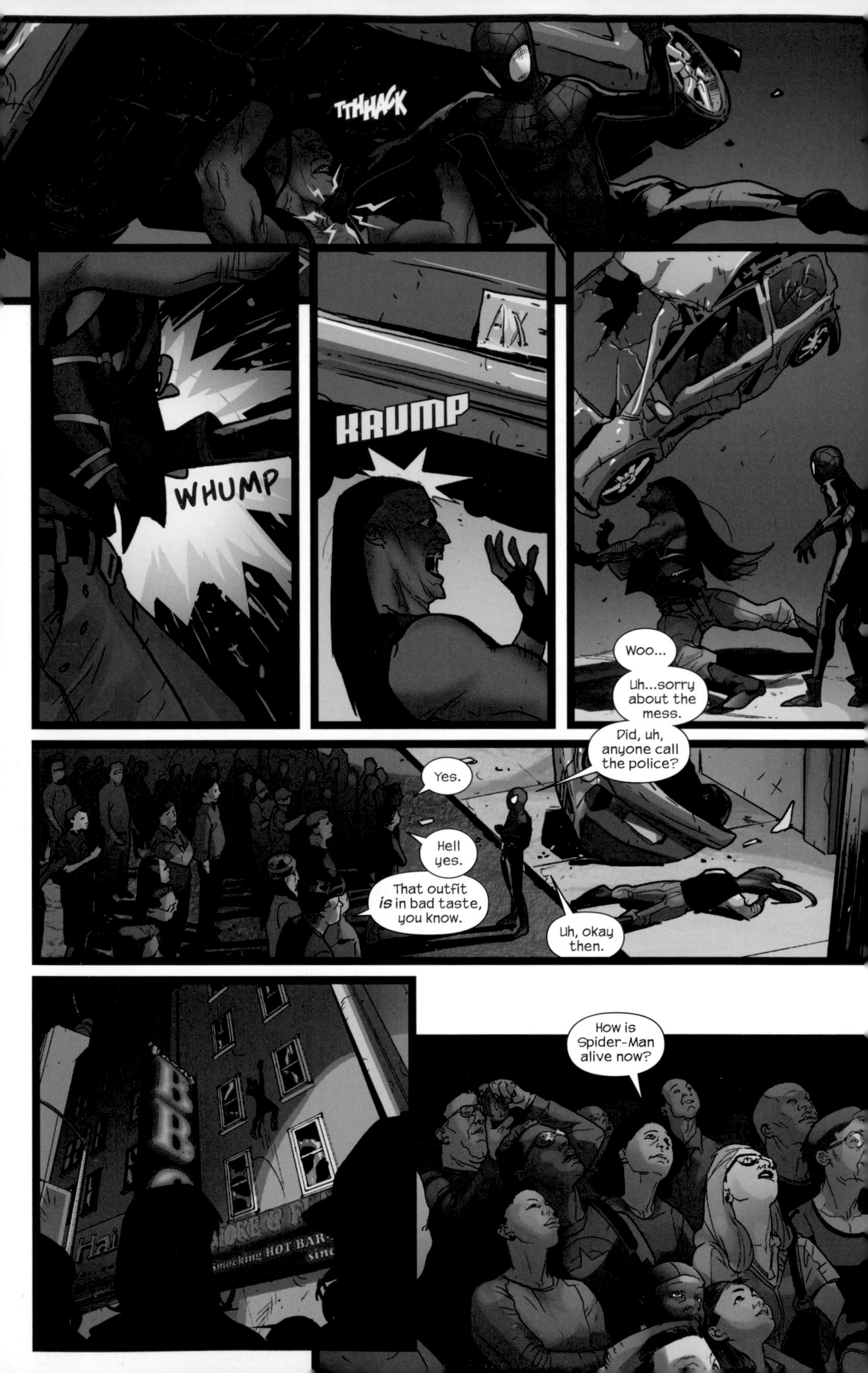
TTHHACK
WHUMP
KRUMP
Woo...
Uh...sorry about the mess.
Did, uh, anyone call the police?
Yes.
Hell yes.
That outfit *is* in bad taste, you know.
Uh, okay then.
How is Spider-Man alive now?

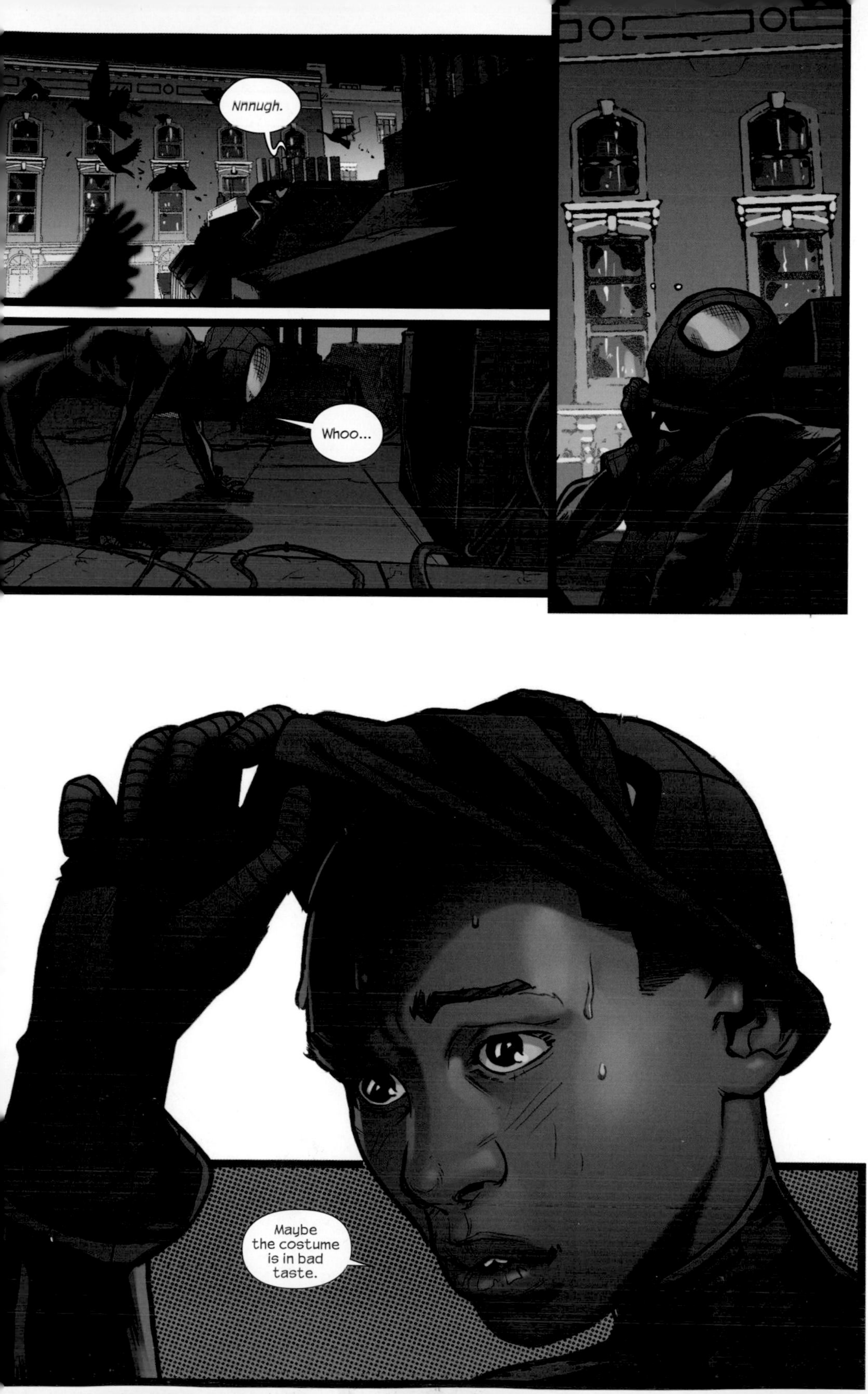
Nnnugh.
Whoo...
Maybe the costume is in bad taste.

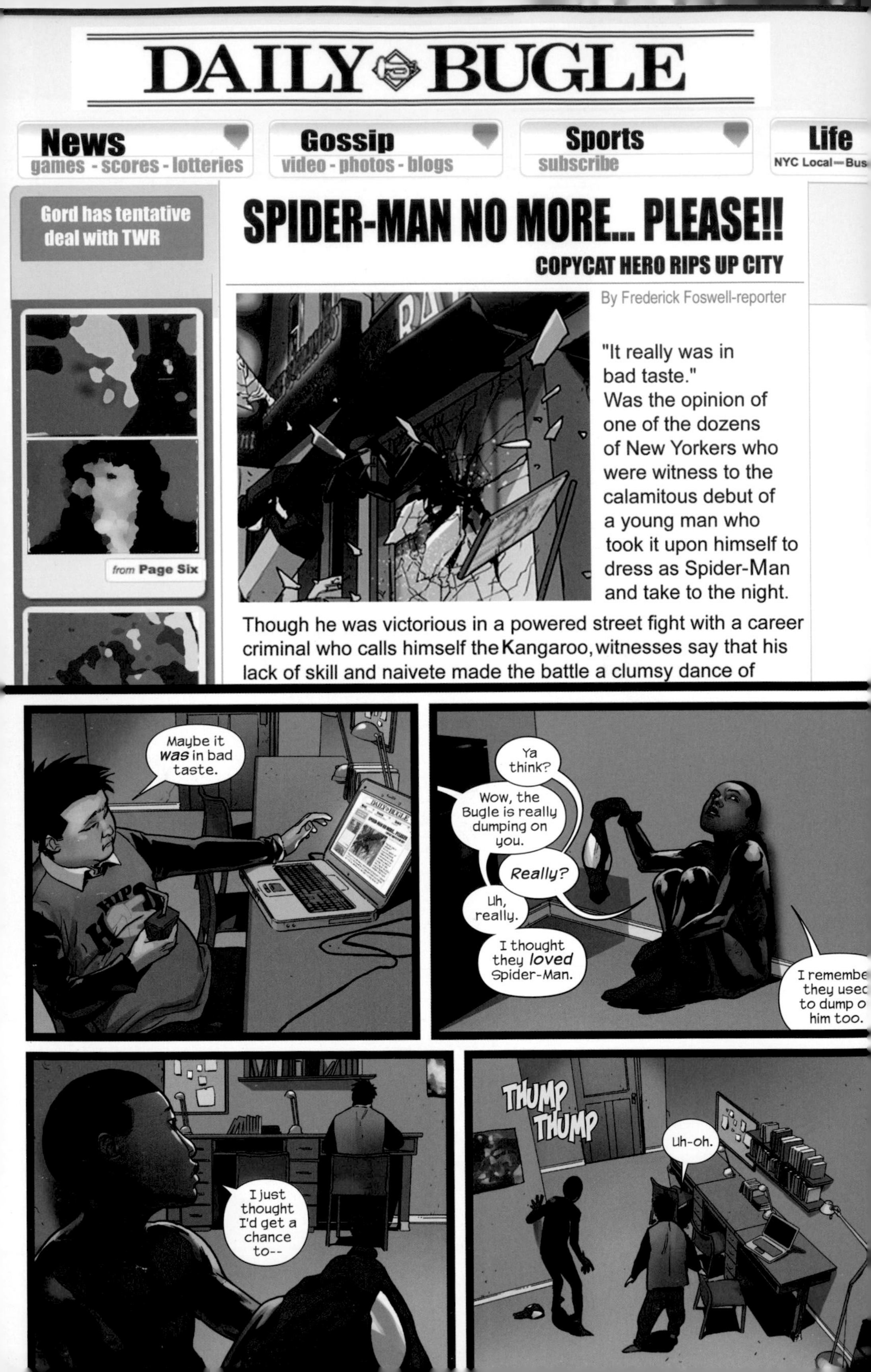
DAILY BUGLE
News
games - scores - lotteries
Gossip
video - photos - blogs
Sports
subscribe
Life
NYC Local—Bus
Gord has tentative deal with TWR
from Page Six
SPIDER-MAN NO MORE... PLEASE!!
COPYCAT HERO RIPS UP CITY
By Frederick Foswell-reporter
"It really was in bad taste."
Was the opinion of one of the dozens of New Yorkers who were witness to the calamitous debut of a young man who took it upon himself to dress as Spider-Man and take to the night.
Though he was victorious in a powered street fight with a career criminal who calls himself the Kangaroo, witnesses say that his lack of skill and naivete made the battle a clumsy dance of
Maybe it *was* in bad taste.
Ya think?
Wow, the Bugle is really dumping on you.
Really?
Uh, really.
I thought they *loved* Spider-Man.
I remembe
they usec
to dump o
him too.
I just thought I'd get a chance to--
THUMP THUMP
Uh-oh.

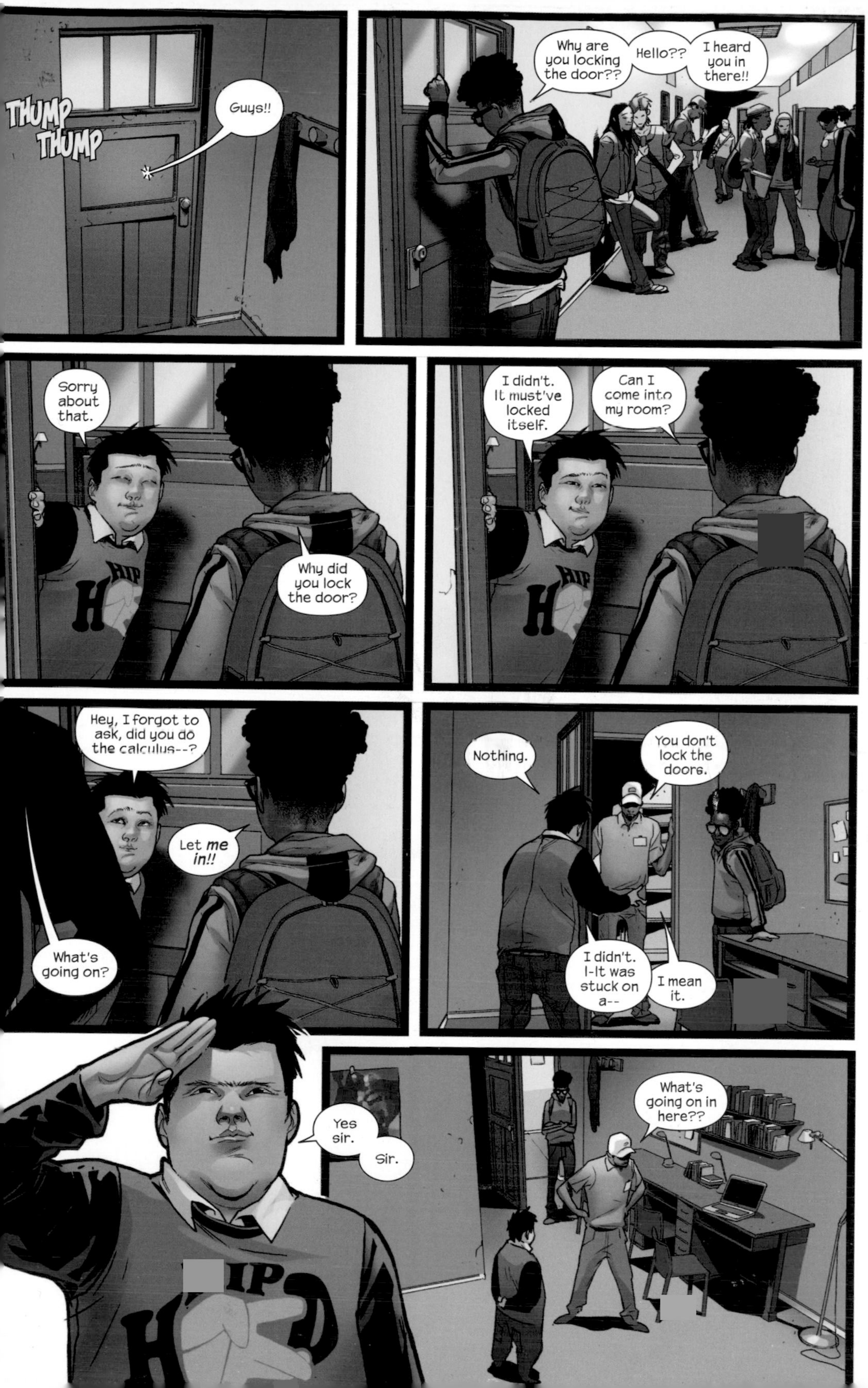
THUMP
THUMP
Guys!!
Why are you locking the door??
Hello??
I heard you in there!!
Sorry about that.
Why did you lock the door?
I didn't. It must've locked itself.
Can I come into my room?
Hey, I forgot to ask, did you do the calculus--?
Let *me in!!*
What's going on?
Nothing.
You don't lock the doors.
I didn't. I-It was stuck on a--
I mean it.
Yes sir.
Sir.
What's going on in here??

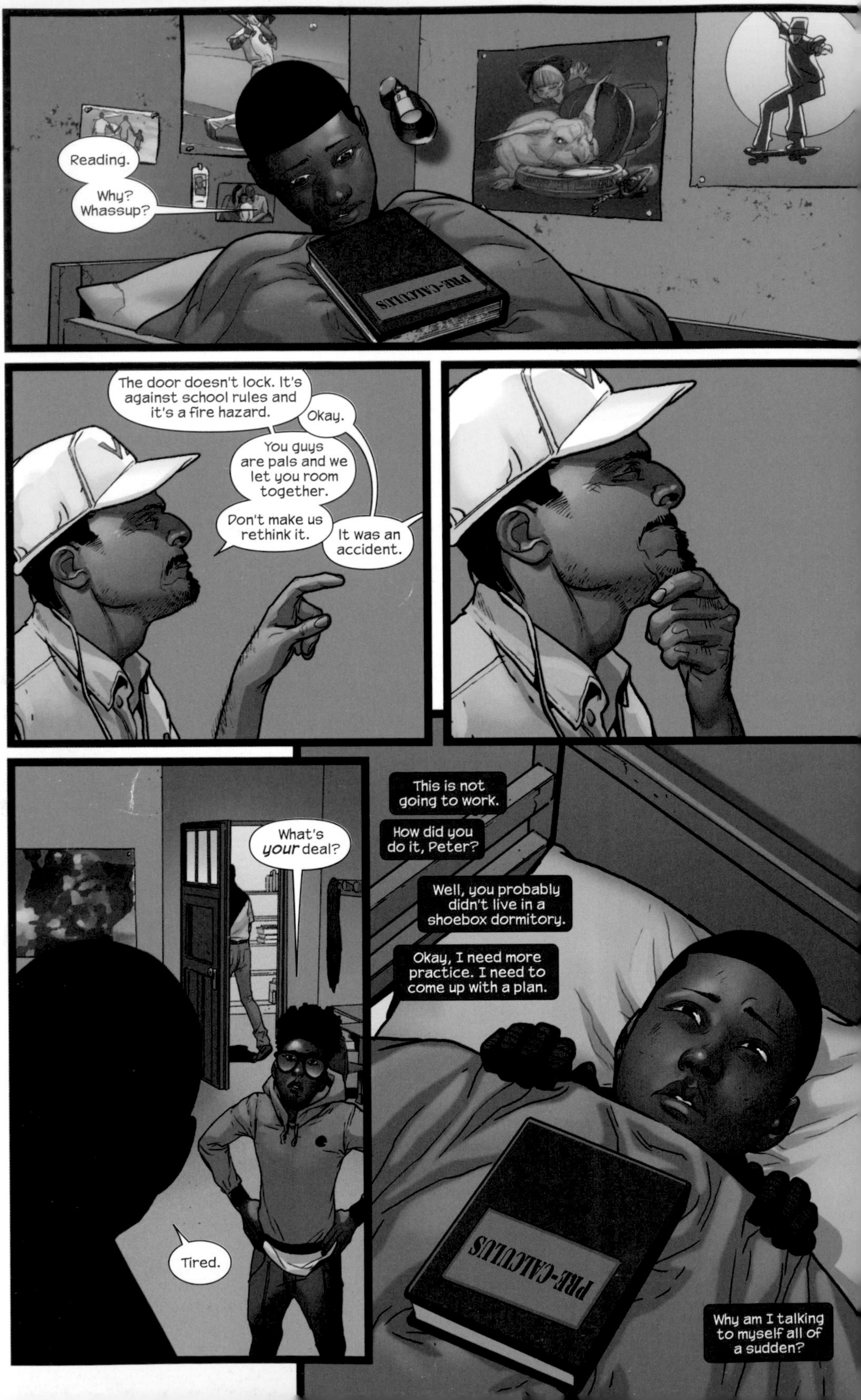

Reading.
Why? Whassup?
The door doesn't lock. It's against school rules and it's a fire hazard.
Okay.
You guys are pals and we let you room together.
Don't make us rethink it.
It was an accident.
PRE-CALCULUS
What's *your* deal?
Tired.
This is not going to work.
How did you do it, Peter?
Well, you probably didn't live in a shoebox dormitory.
Okay, I need more practice. I need to come up with a plan.
PRE-CALCULUS
Why am I talking to myself all of a sudden?

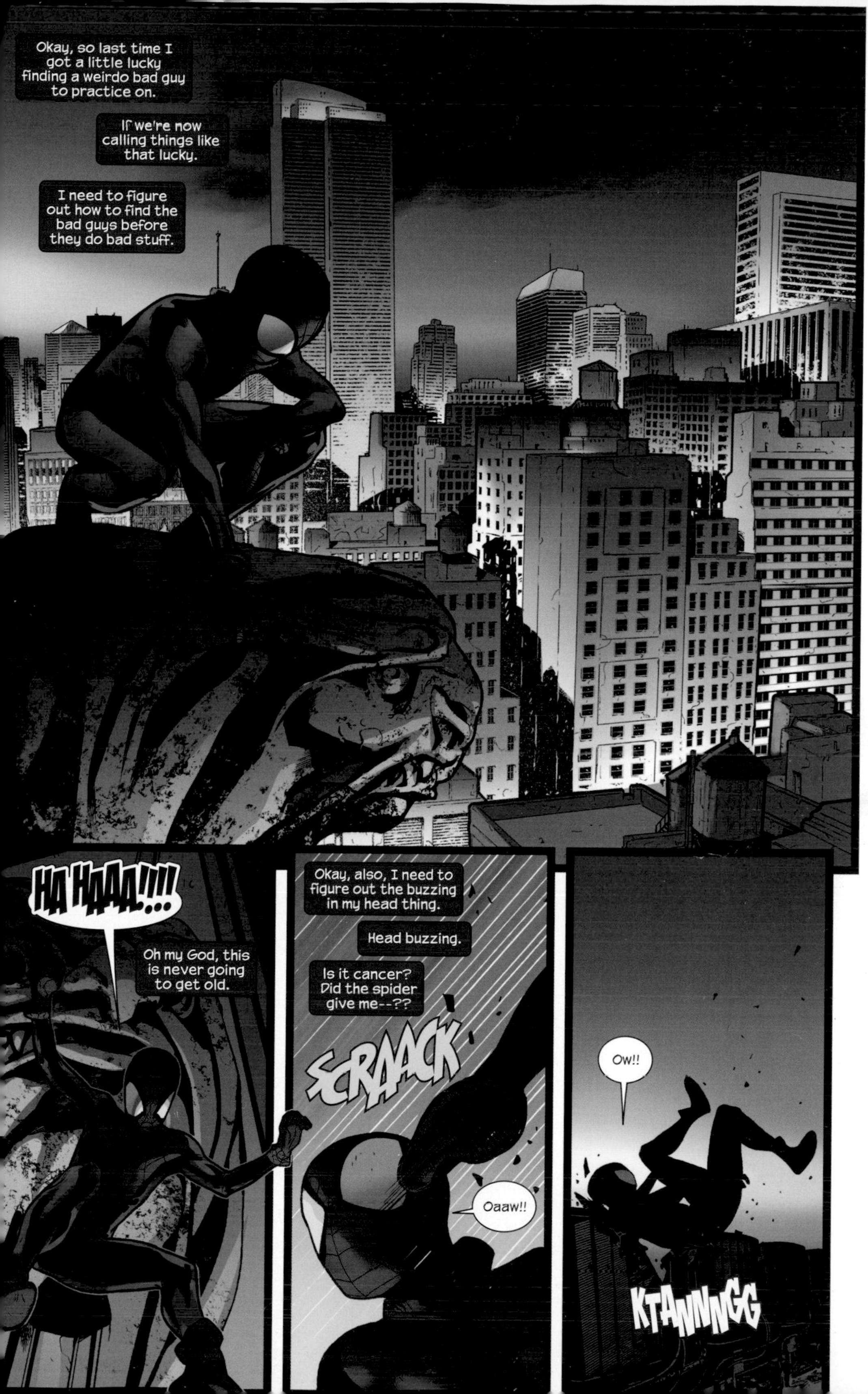
Okay, so last time I got a little lucky finding a weirdo bad guy to practice on.
If we're now calling things like that lucky.
I need to figure out how to find the bad guys before they do bad stuff.
HA HAAA!!!!...
Oh my God, this is never going to get old.
Okay, also, I need to figure out the buzzing in my head thing.
Head buzzing.
Is it cancer? Did the spider give me--??
SCRAACK
Oaaw!!
Ow!!
KTANNNGG

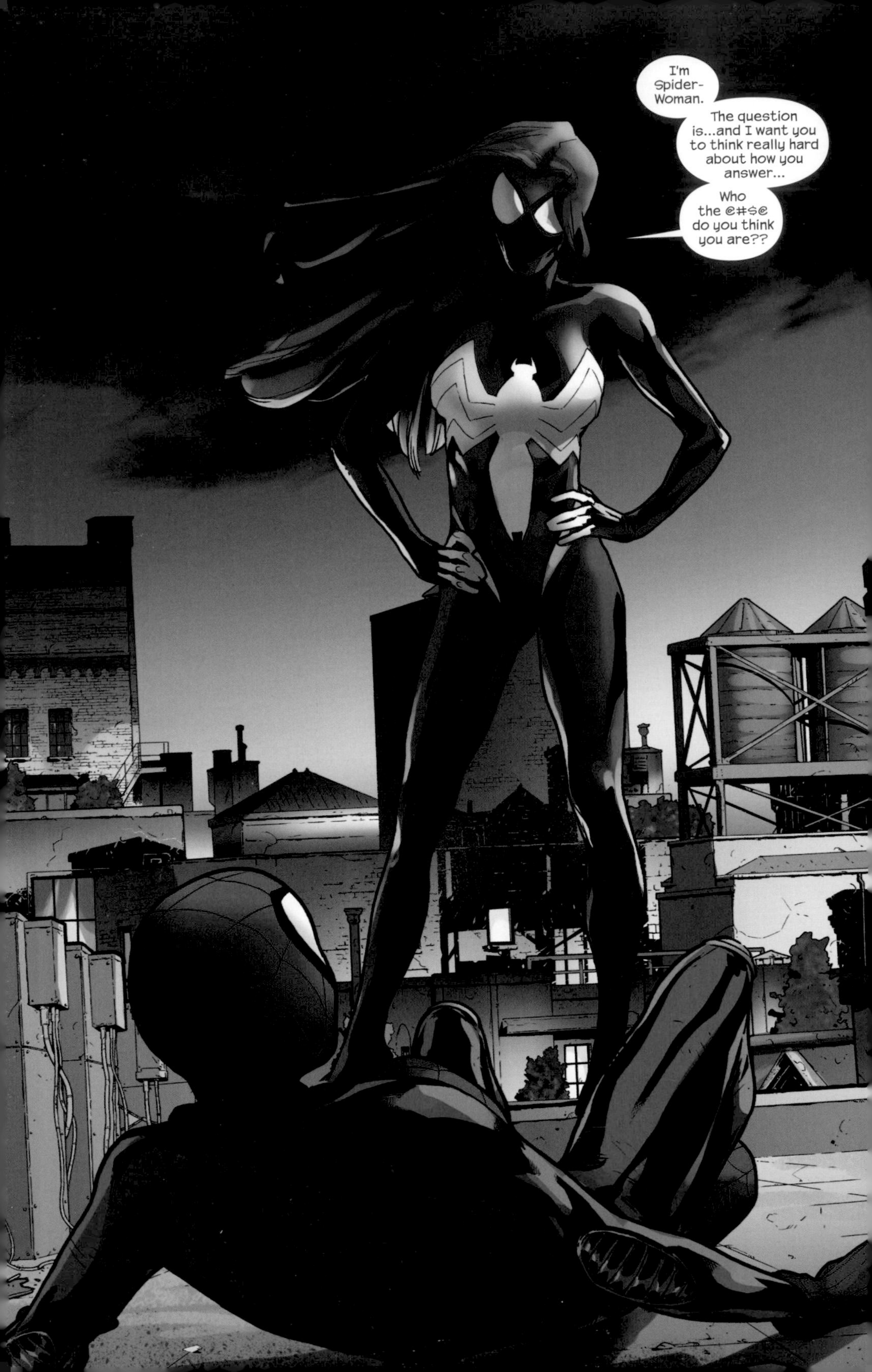
I'm Spider-Woman.
The question is...and I want you to think really hard about how you answer...
Who the @#$@ do you think you are??

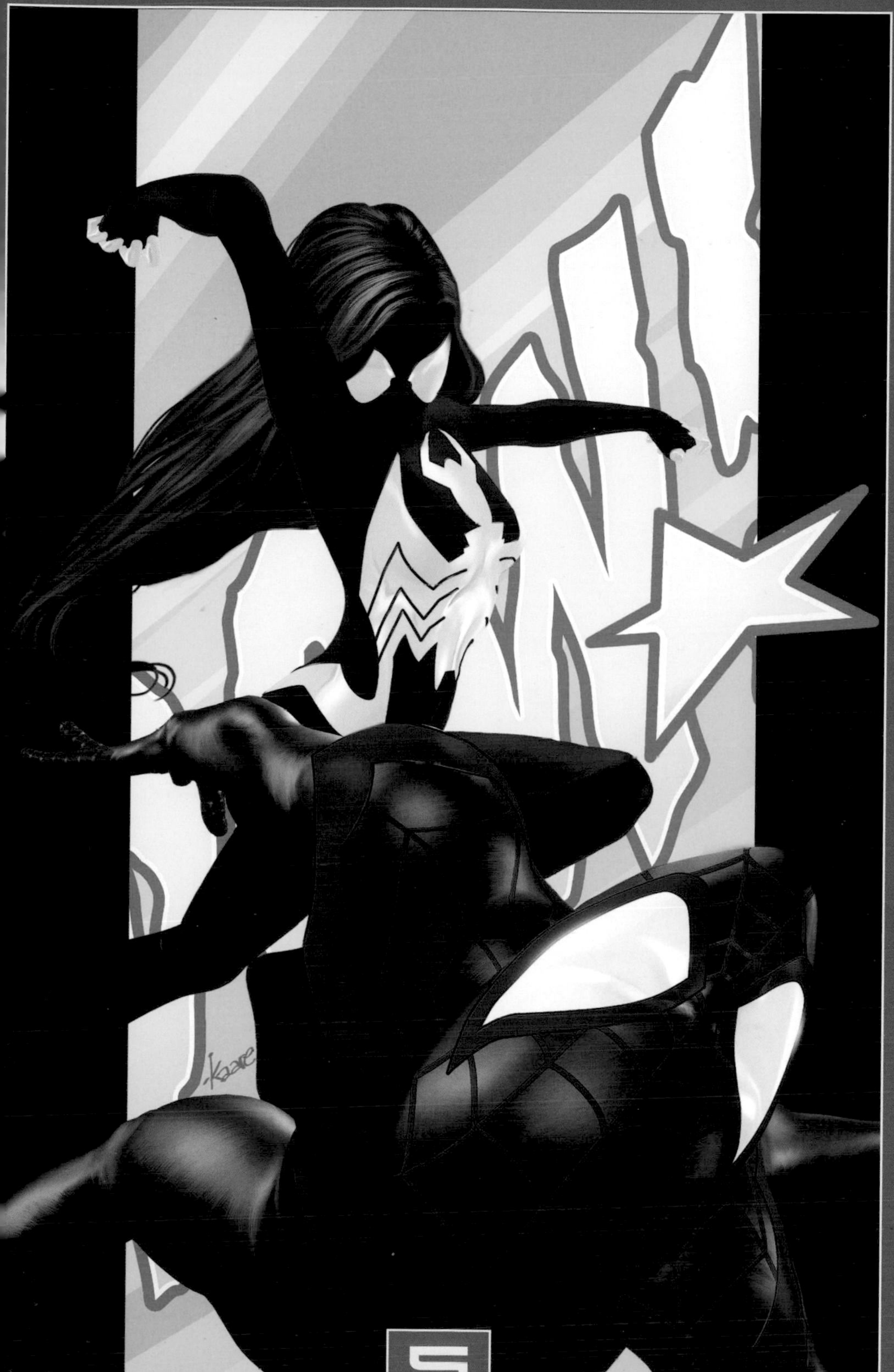
Kaare
5

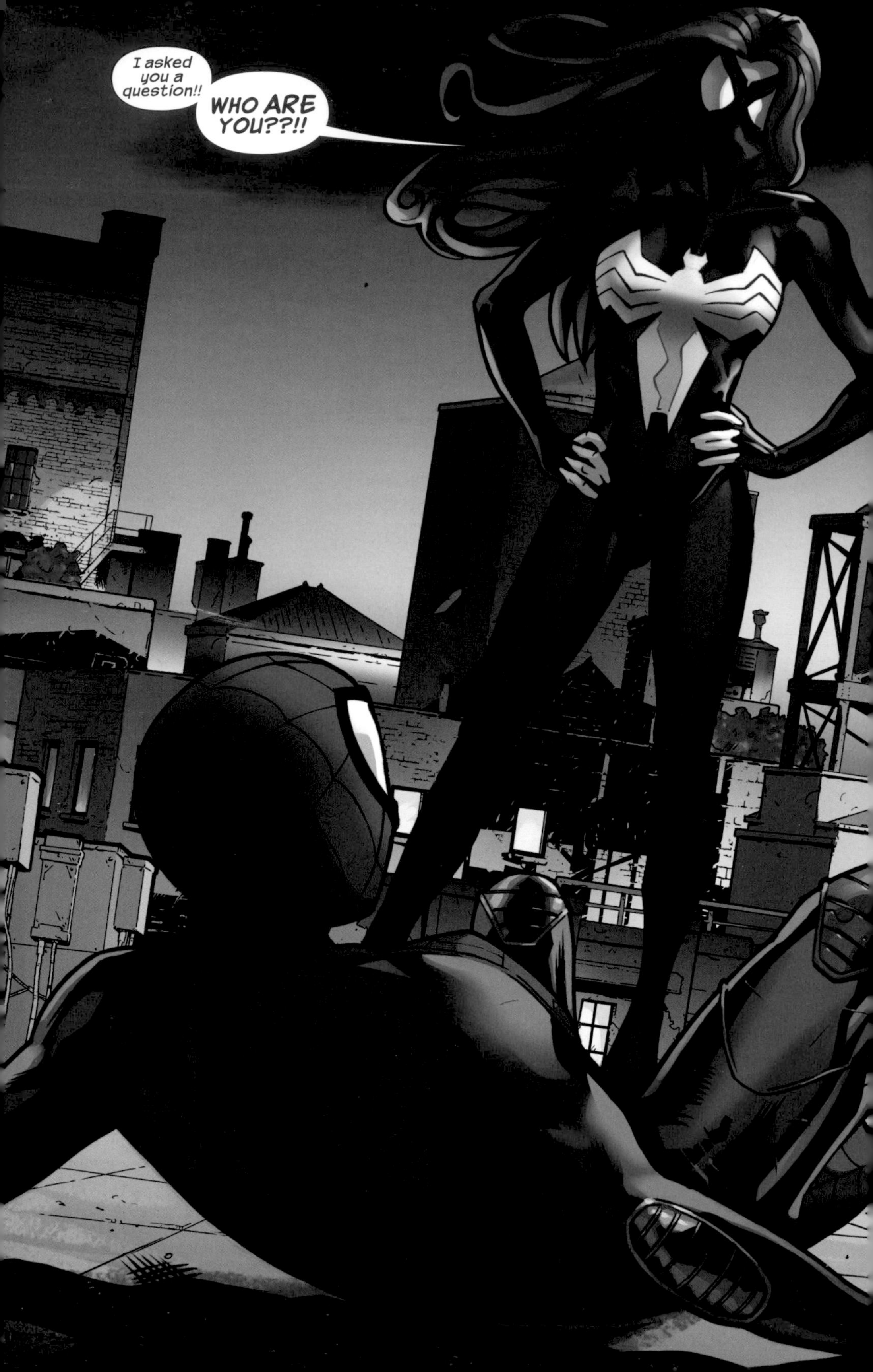
I asked you a question!!
WHO ARE YOU??!!

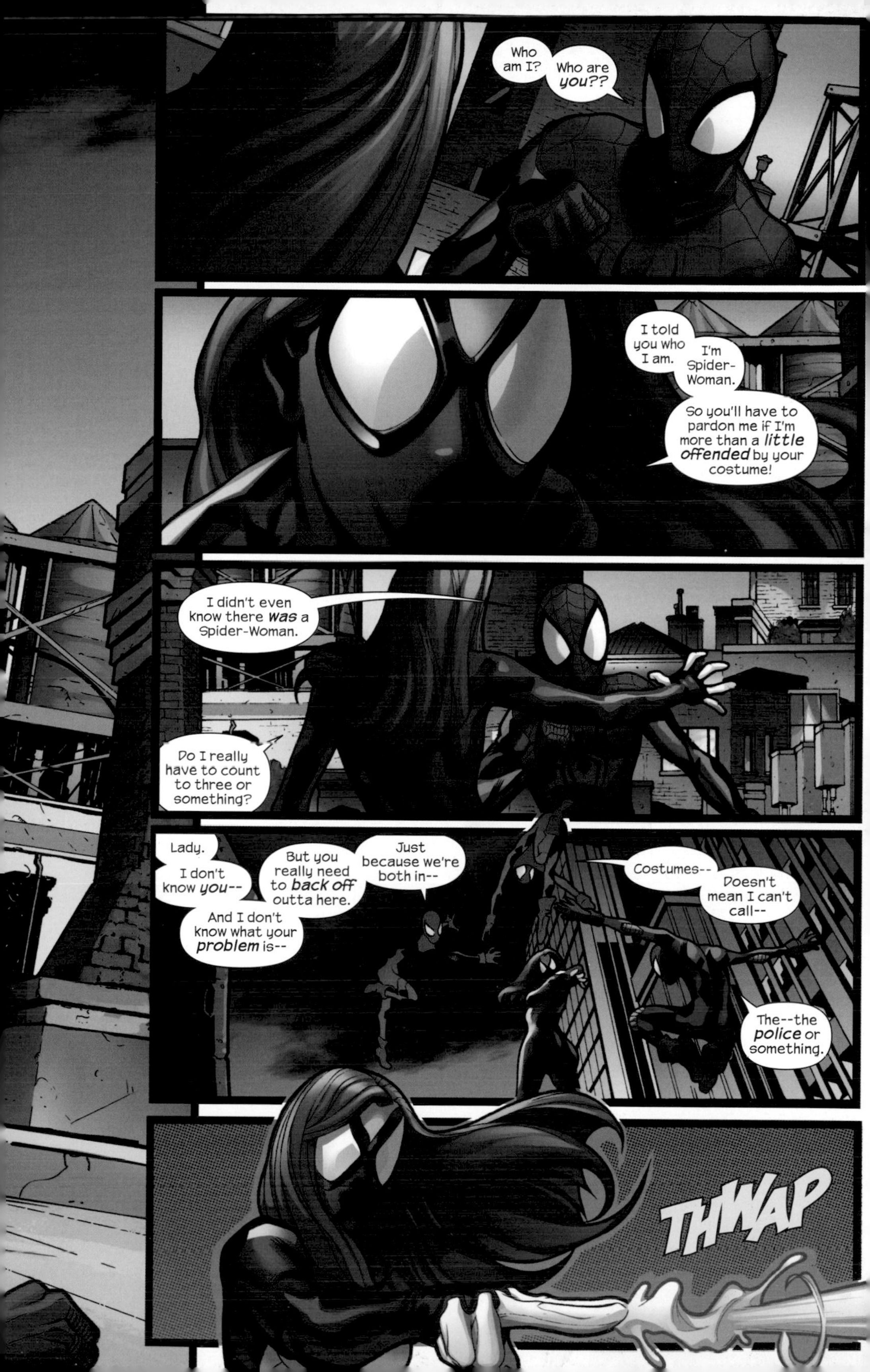

Who am I?
Who are *you??*
I told you who I am.
I'm Spider-Woman.
So you'll have to pardon me if I'm more than a *little offended* by your costume!
I didn't even know there *was* a Spider-Woman.
Do I really have to count to three or something?
Lady.
I don't know *you--*
And I don't know what your *problem* is--
But you really need to *back off* outta here.
Just because we're both in--
Costumes--
Doesn't mean I can't call--
The--the *police* or something.
THWAP

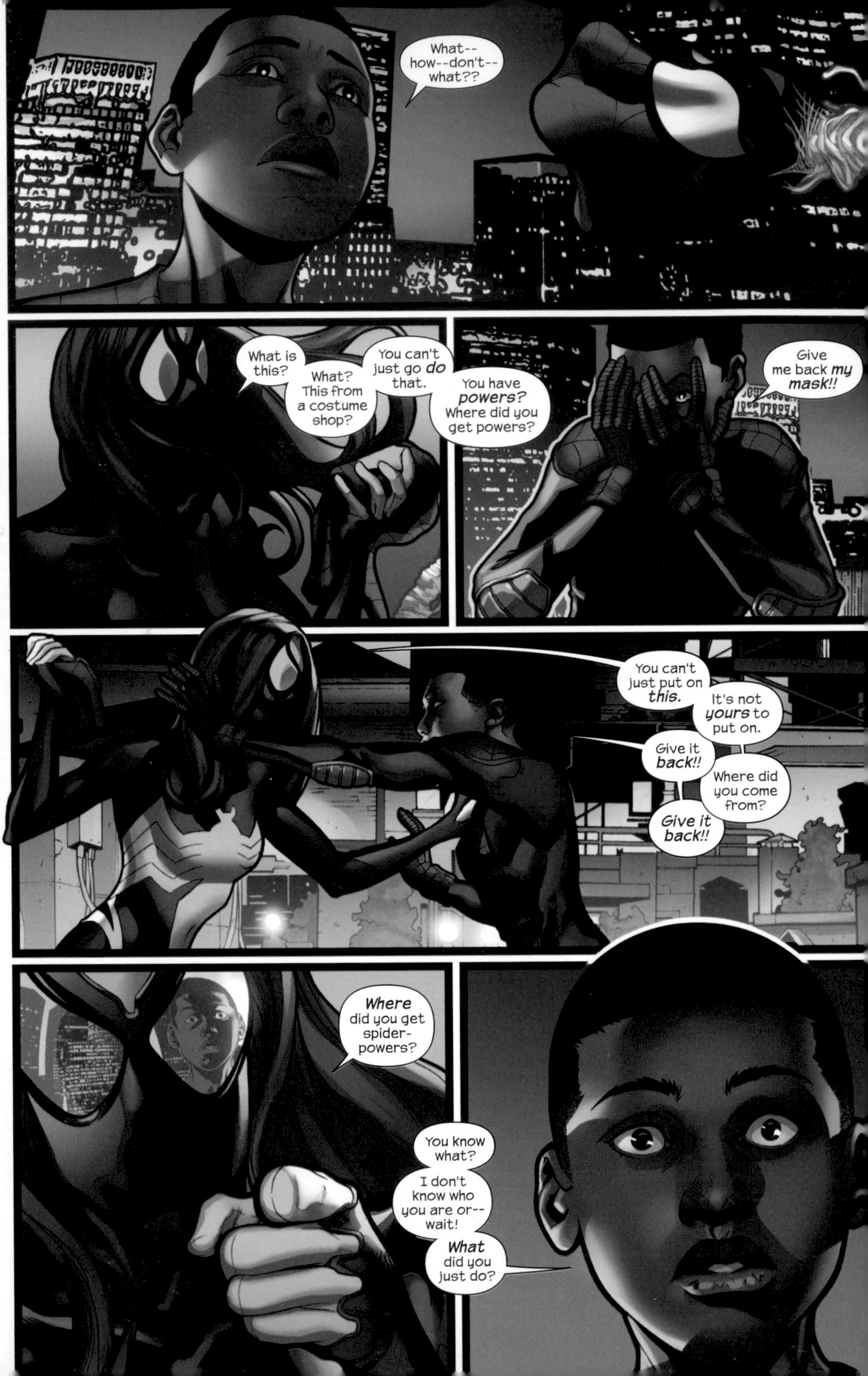
What--
how--don't--
what??
What is this?
What? This from a costume shop?
You can't just go *do* that.
You have *powers?* Where did you get powers?
Give me back *my mask!!*
You can't just put on *this.*
It's not *yours* to put on.
Give it *back!!*
Where did you come from?
Give it back!!
Where did you get spider-powers?
You know what?
I don't know who you are or--
wait!
What did you just do?

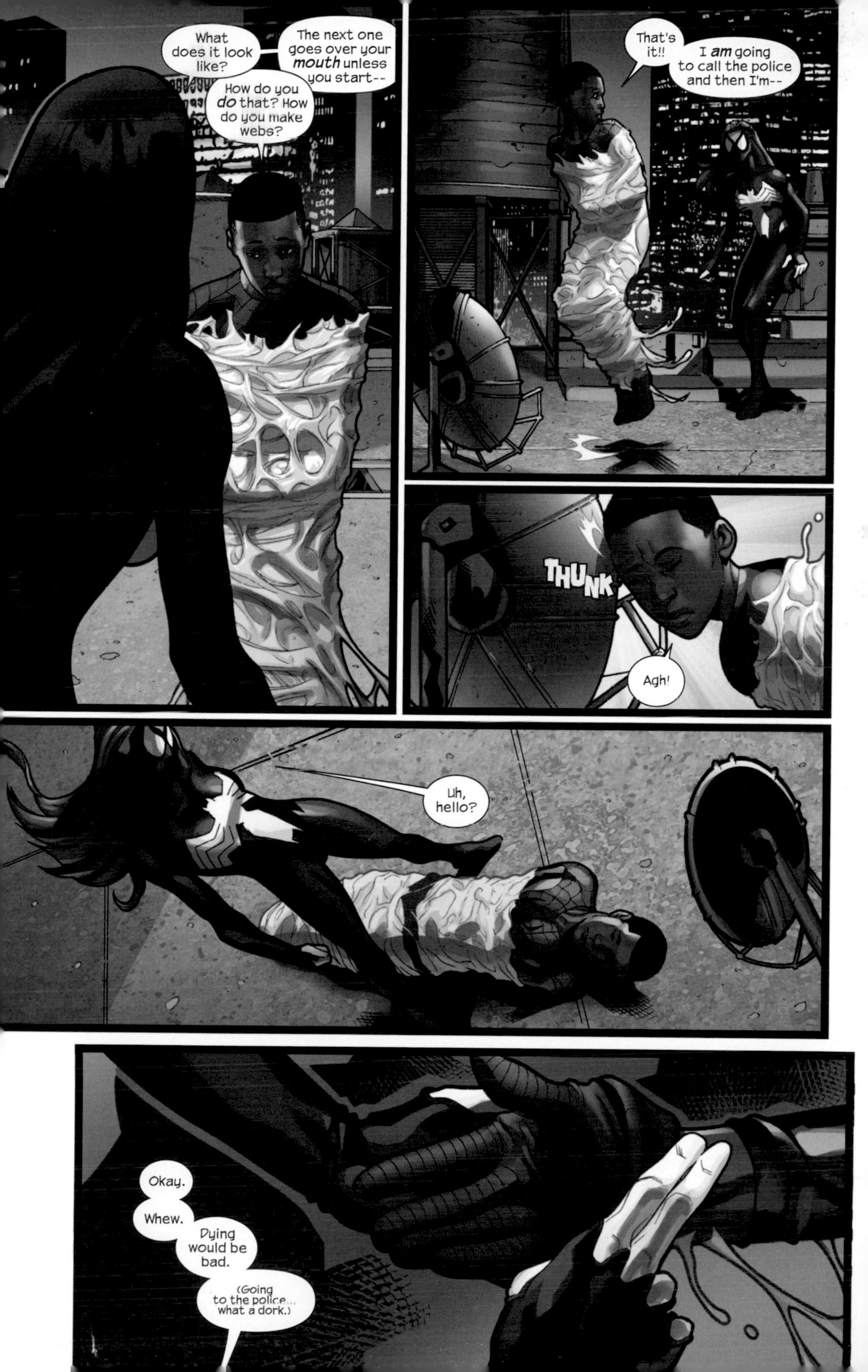

What does it look like?
The next one goes over your *mouth* unless you start--
How do you *do* that? How do you make webs?
That's it!!
I *am* going to call the police and then I'm--
THUNK
Agh!
Uh, hello?
Okay.
Whew.
Dying would be bad.
(Going to the police... what a dork.)

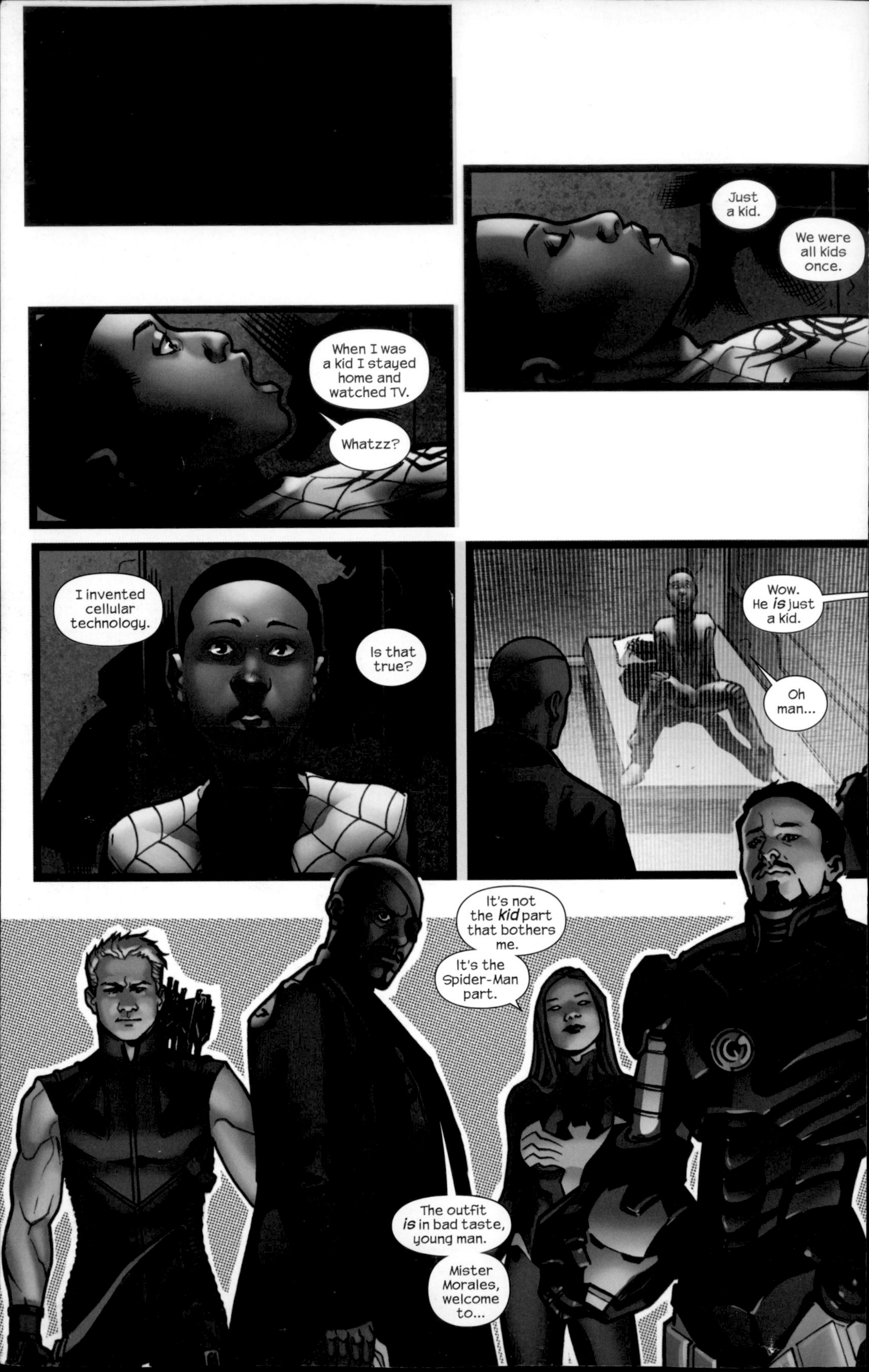
Just
a kid.
We were
all kids
once.
When I was
a kid I stayed
home and
watched TV.
Whatzz?
I invented
cellular
technology.
Is that
true?
Wow.
He *is* just
a kid.
Oh
man...
It's not
the *kid* part
that bothers
me.
It's the
Spider-Man
part.
The outfit
is in bad taste,
young man.
Mister
Morales,
welcome
to...

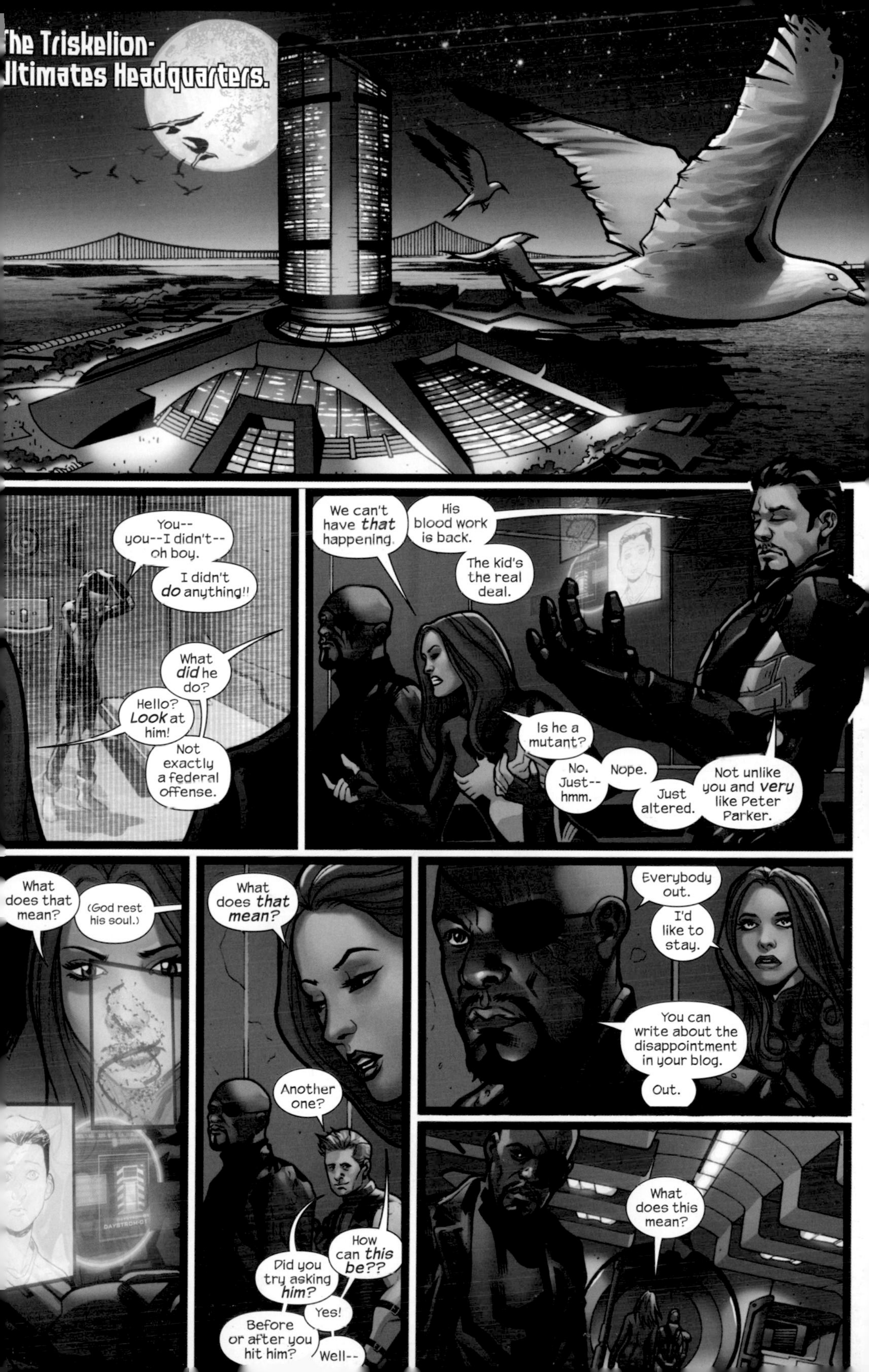

The Triskelion-
Ultimates Headquarters.
You--
you--I didn't--
oh boy.
I didn't do anything!!
What did he do?
Hello? Look at him!
Not exactly a federal offense.
We can't have that happening.
His blood work is back.
The kid's the real deal.
Is he a mutant?
No. Just--hmm.
Nope.
Just altered.
Not unlike you and very like Peter Parker.
What does that mean?
(God rest his soul.)
What does that mean?
Another one?
How can this be??
Did you try asking him?
Yes!
Before or after you hit him?
Well--
Everybody out.
I'd like to stay.
You can write about the disappointment in your blog.
Out.
What does this mean?

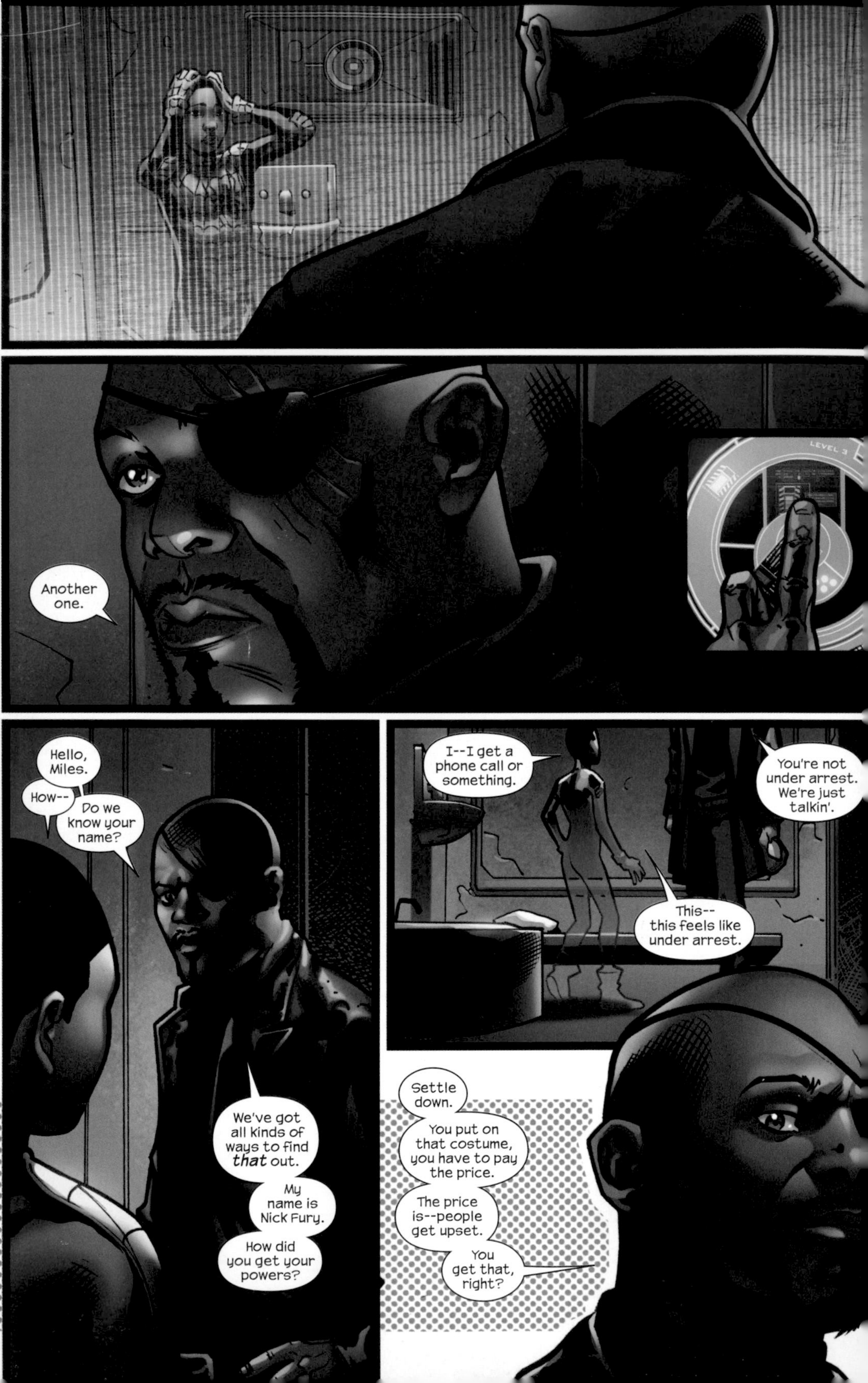
LEVEL 3
Another one.
Hello, Miles.
How--
Do we know your name?
We've got all kinds of ways to find *that* out.
My name is Nick Fury.
How did you get your powers?
I--I get a phone call or something.
You're not under arrest. We're just talkin'.
This-- this feels like under arrest.
Settle down.
You put on that costume, you have to pay the price.
The price is--people get upset.
You get that, right?

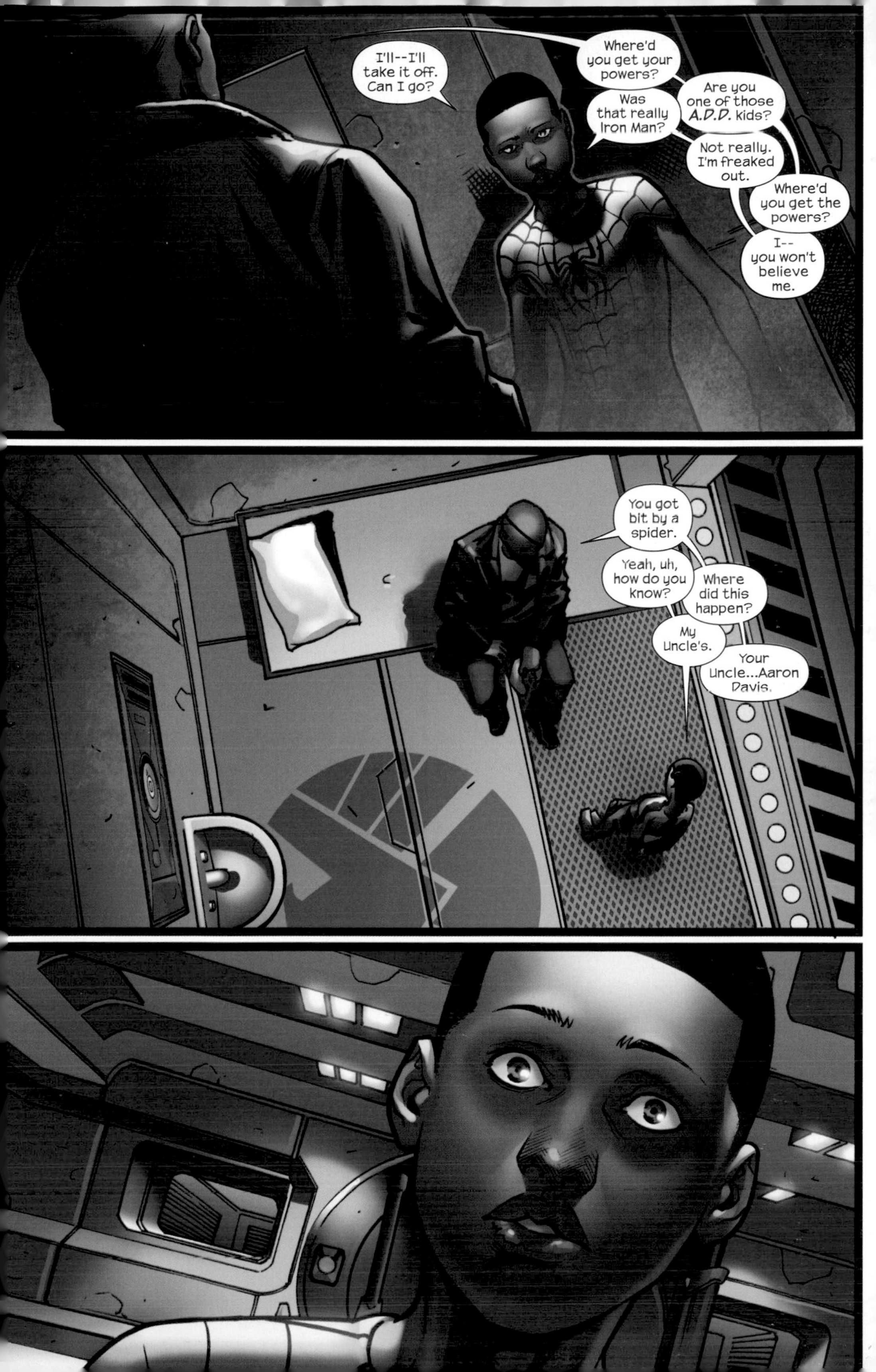
Where'd you get your powers?
I'll--I'll take it off. Can I go?
Are you one of those A.D.D. kids?
Was that really Iron Man?
Not really. I'm freaked out.
Where'd you get the powers?
I-- you won't believe me.
You got bit by a spider.
Yeah, uh, how do you know?
Where did this happen?
My Uncle's.
Your Uncle...Aaron Davis.

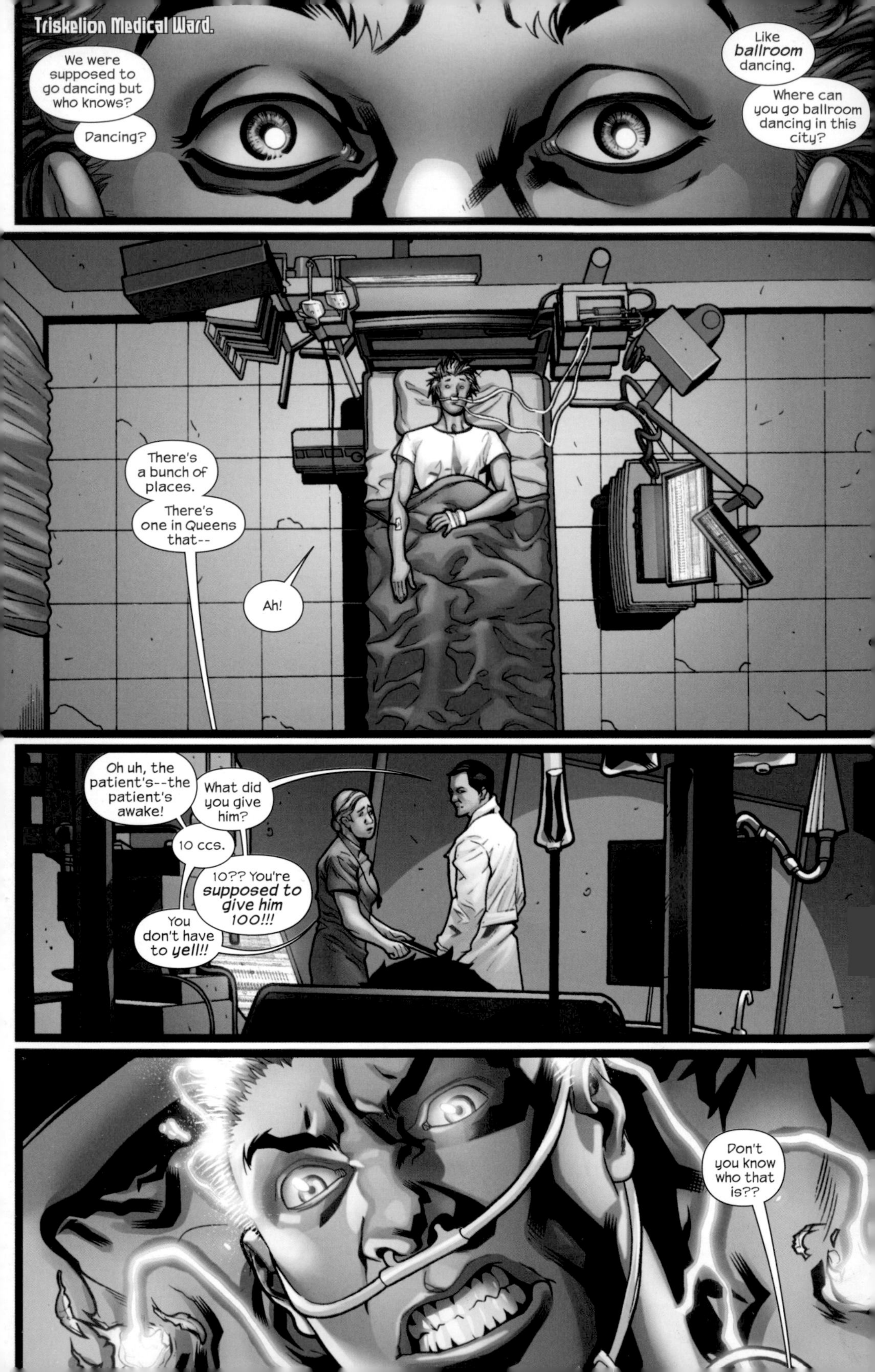
Triskelion Medical Ward.
We were supposed to go dancing but who knows?
Dancing?
Like ballroom dancing.
Where can you go ballroom dancing in this city?
There's a bunch of places.
There's one in Queens that--
Ah!
Oh uh, the patient's--the patient's awake!
What did you give him?
10 ccs.
10?? You're supposed to give him 100!!!
You don't have to yell!!
Don't you know who that is??

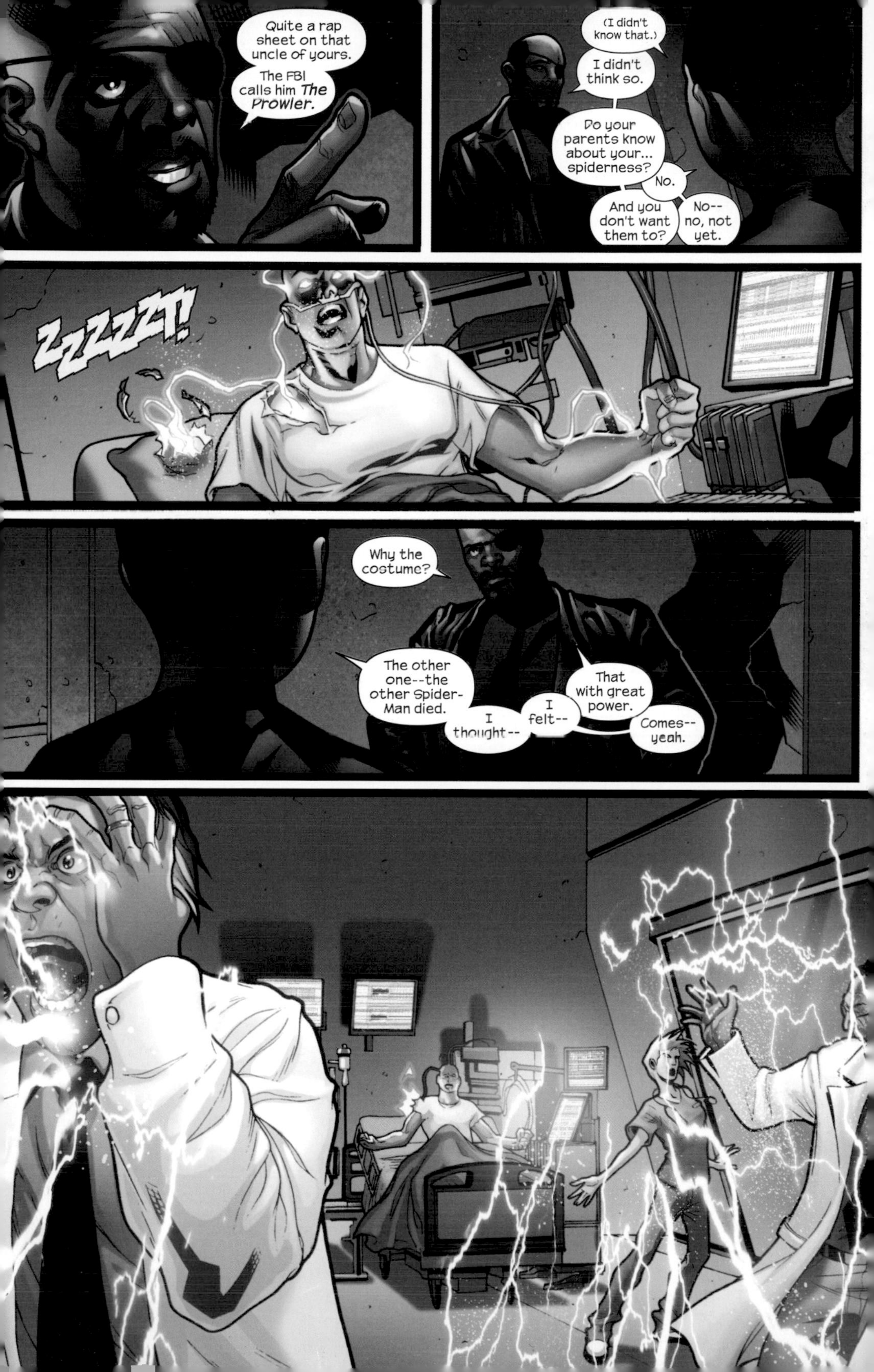
Quite a rap sheet on that uncle of yours.
The FBI calls him The Prowler.
(I didn't know that.)
I didn't think so.
Do your parents know about your... spiderness?
No.
And you don't want them to?
No-- no, not yet.
ZZZZZT!
Why the costume?
The other one--the other Spider-Man died.
I thought--
I felt--
That with great power.
Comes-- yeah.

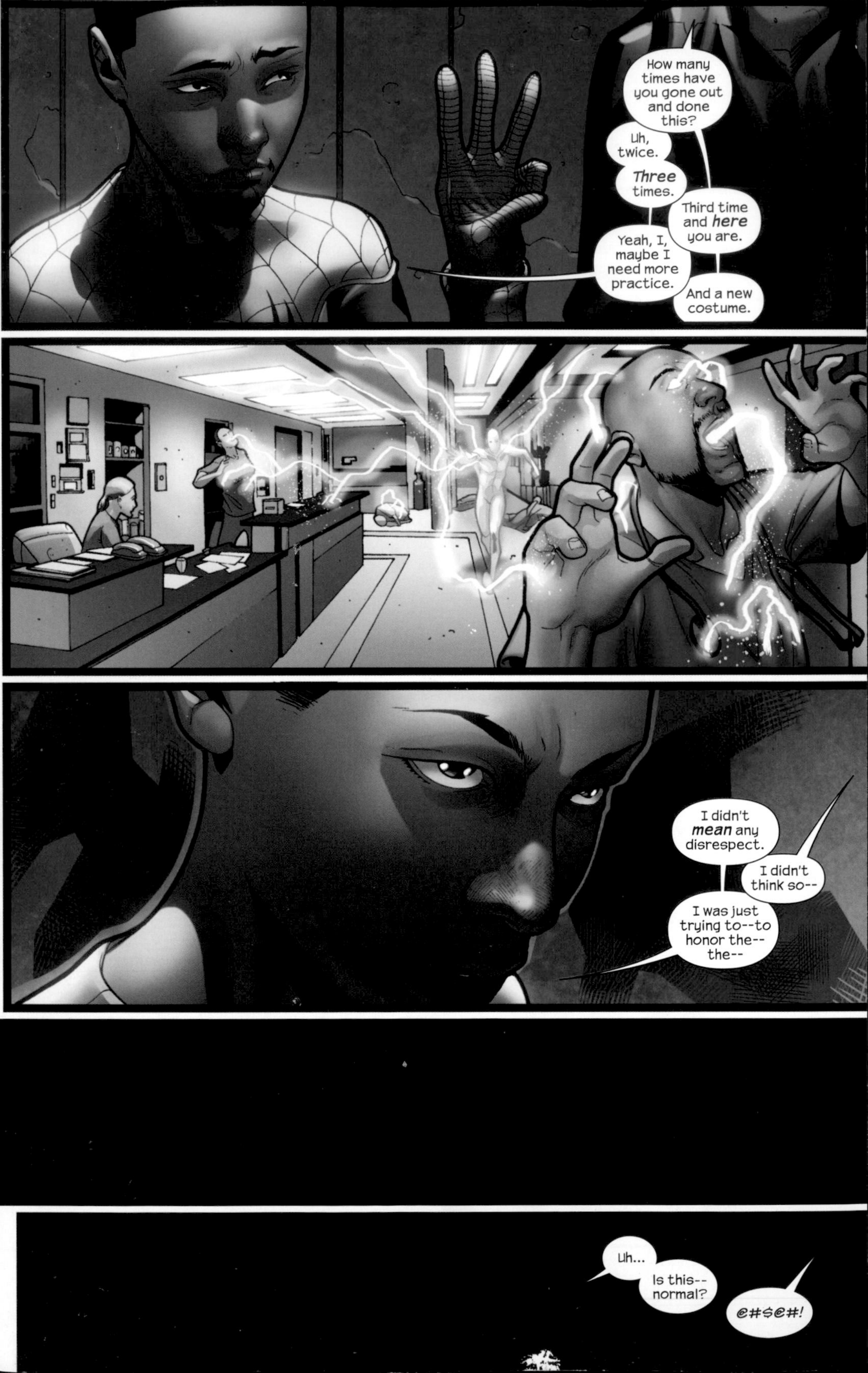
How many times have you gone out and done this?
Uh, twice.
Three times.
Third time and here you are.
Yeah, I, maybe I need more practice.
And a new costume.
I didn't mean any disrespect.
I didn't think so--
I was just trying to--to honor the-- the--
Uh...
Is this-- normal?
@#$@#!

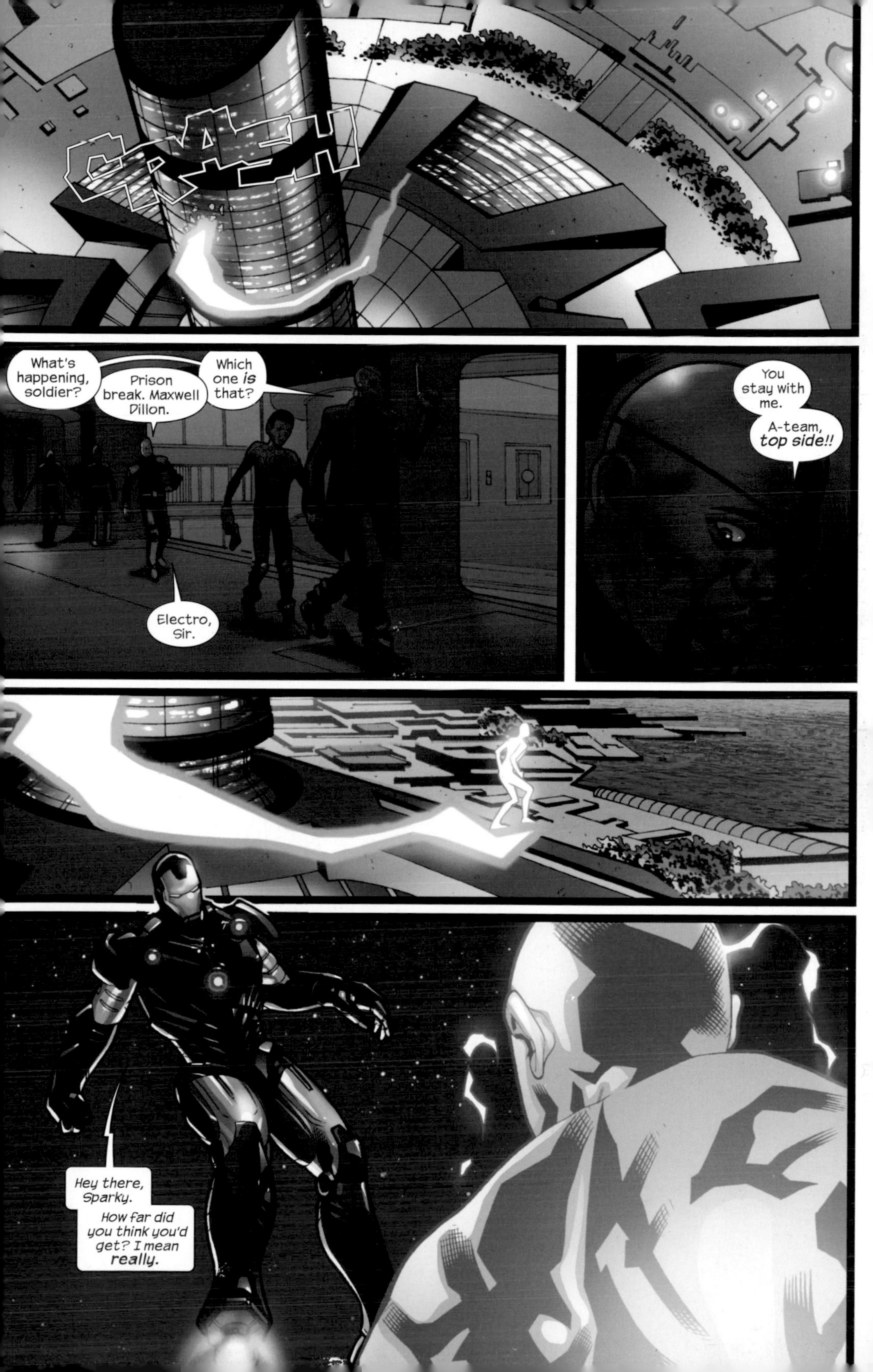
CRASH
What's happening, soldier?
Prison break. Maxwell Dillon.
Which one *is* that?
Electro, Sir.
You stay with me.
A-team, ***top side!!***
Hey there, Sparky.
How far did you think you'd get? I mean **really.**

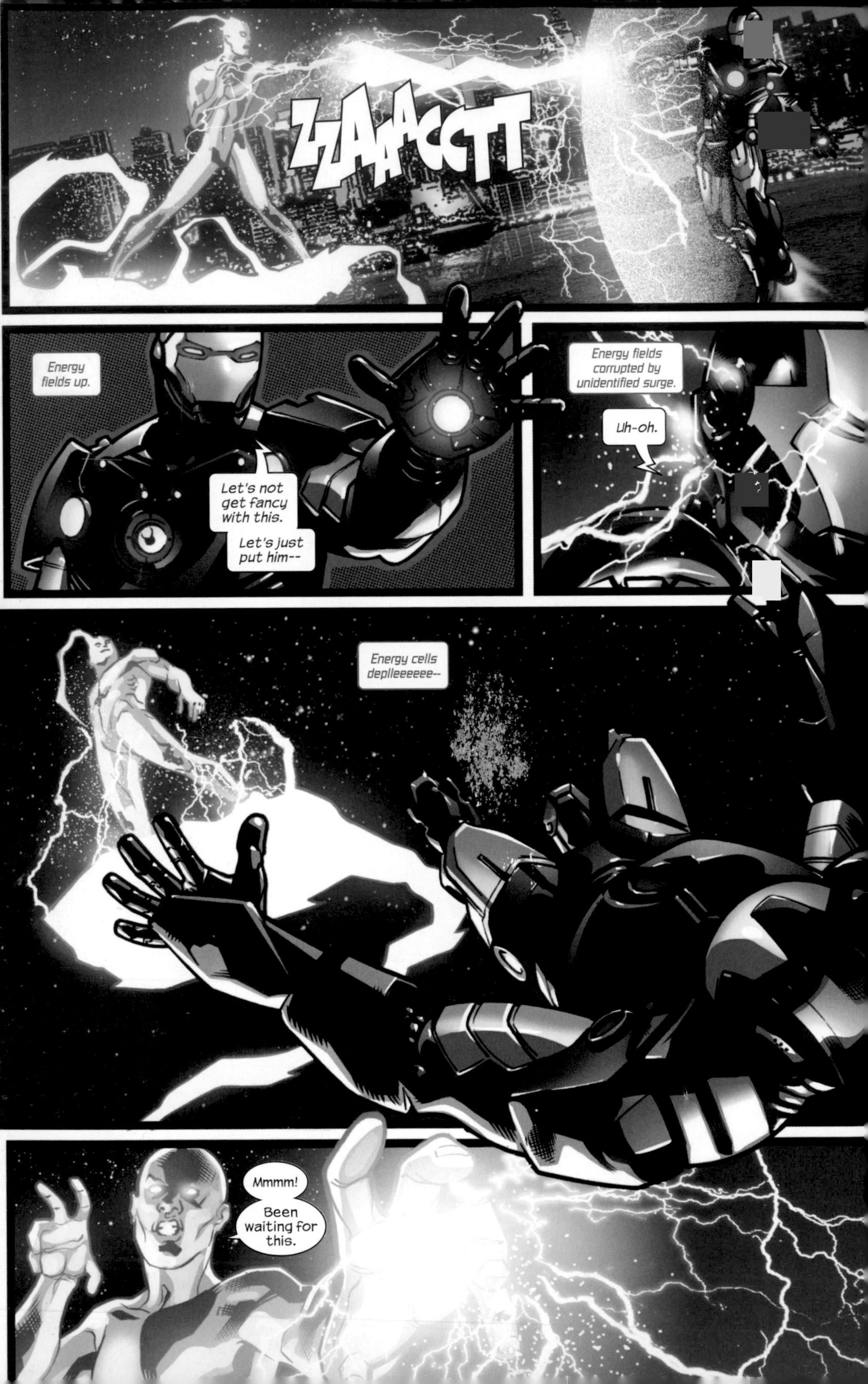
ZZAAACCTT
Energy fields up.
Let's not get fancy with this.
Let's just put him--
Energy fields corrupted by unidentified surge.
Uh-oh.
Energy cells deplleeeeee--
Mmmm!
Been waiting for this.

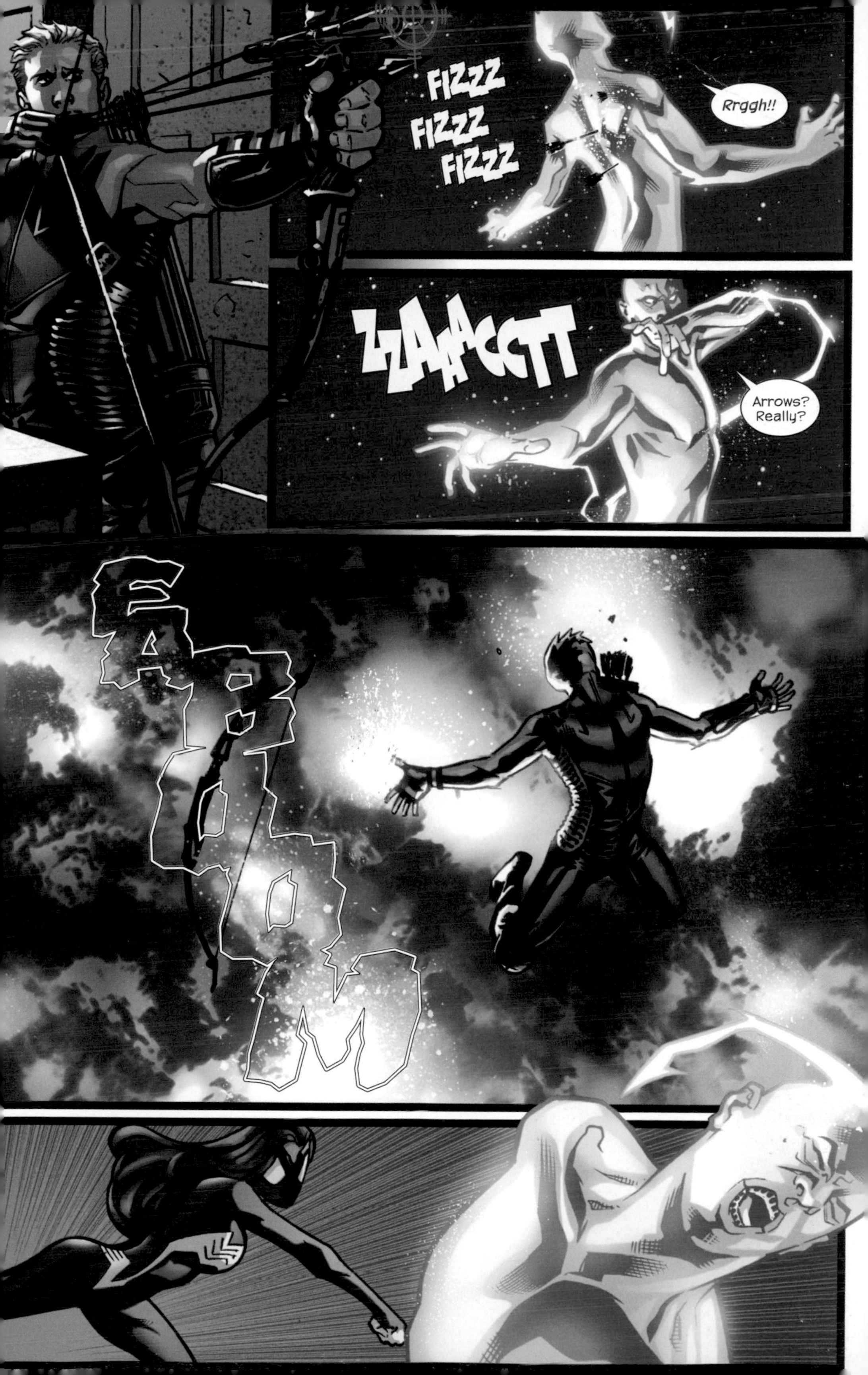
FIZZZ
FIZZZ
FIZZZ
Rrggh!!
ZZAAACCTT
Arrows? Really?
FABOOM

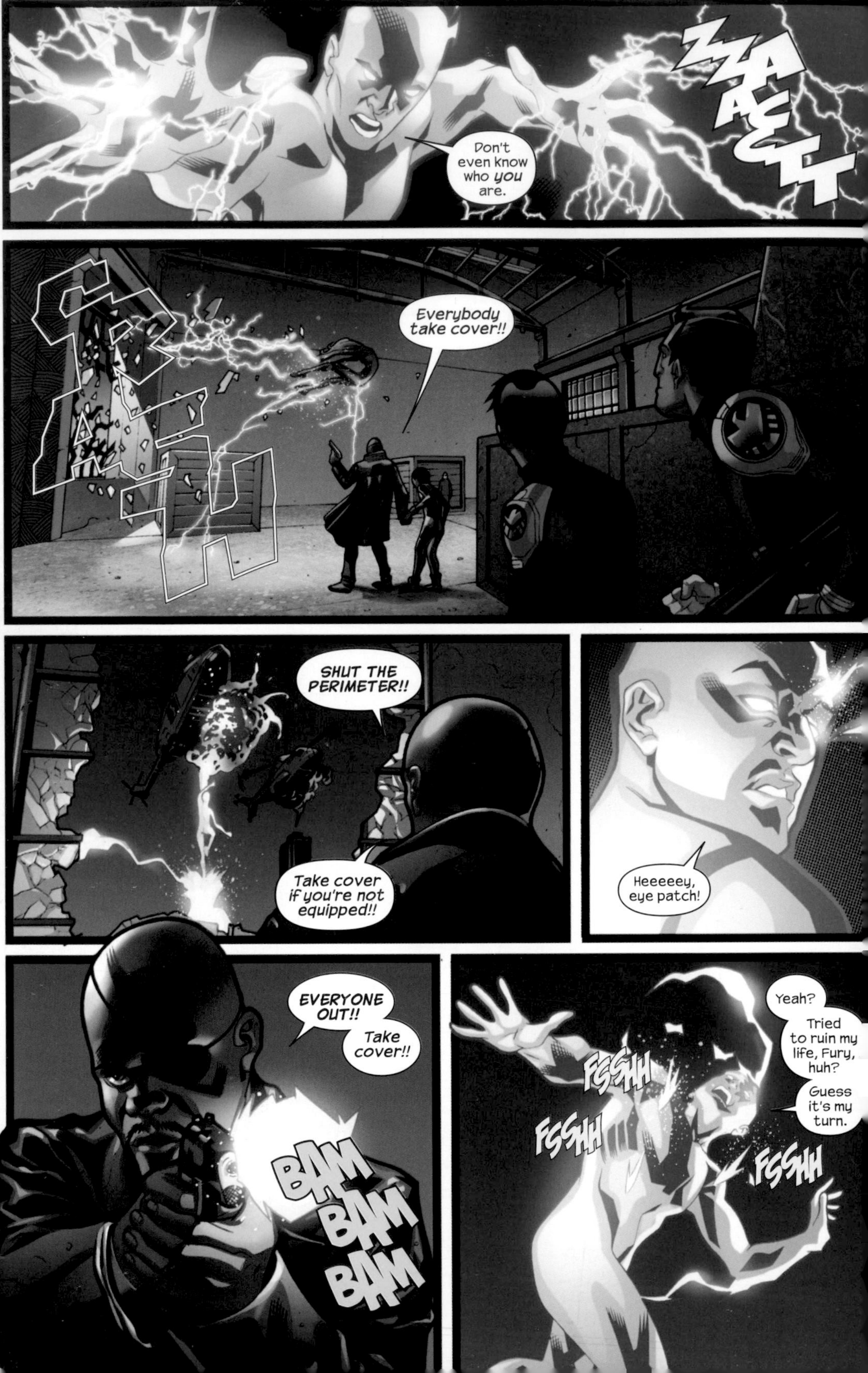
Don't even know who *you* are.
ZZAACCTT
CRAKKH
Everybody take cover!!
SHUT THE PERIMETER!!
Take cover if you're not equipped!!
Heeeeey, eye patch!
EVERYONE OUT!!
Take cover!!
BAM BAM BAM
Yeah?
Tried to ruin my life, Fury, huh?
Guess it's my turn.
FSSHH
FSSHH
FSSHH

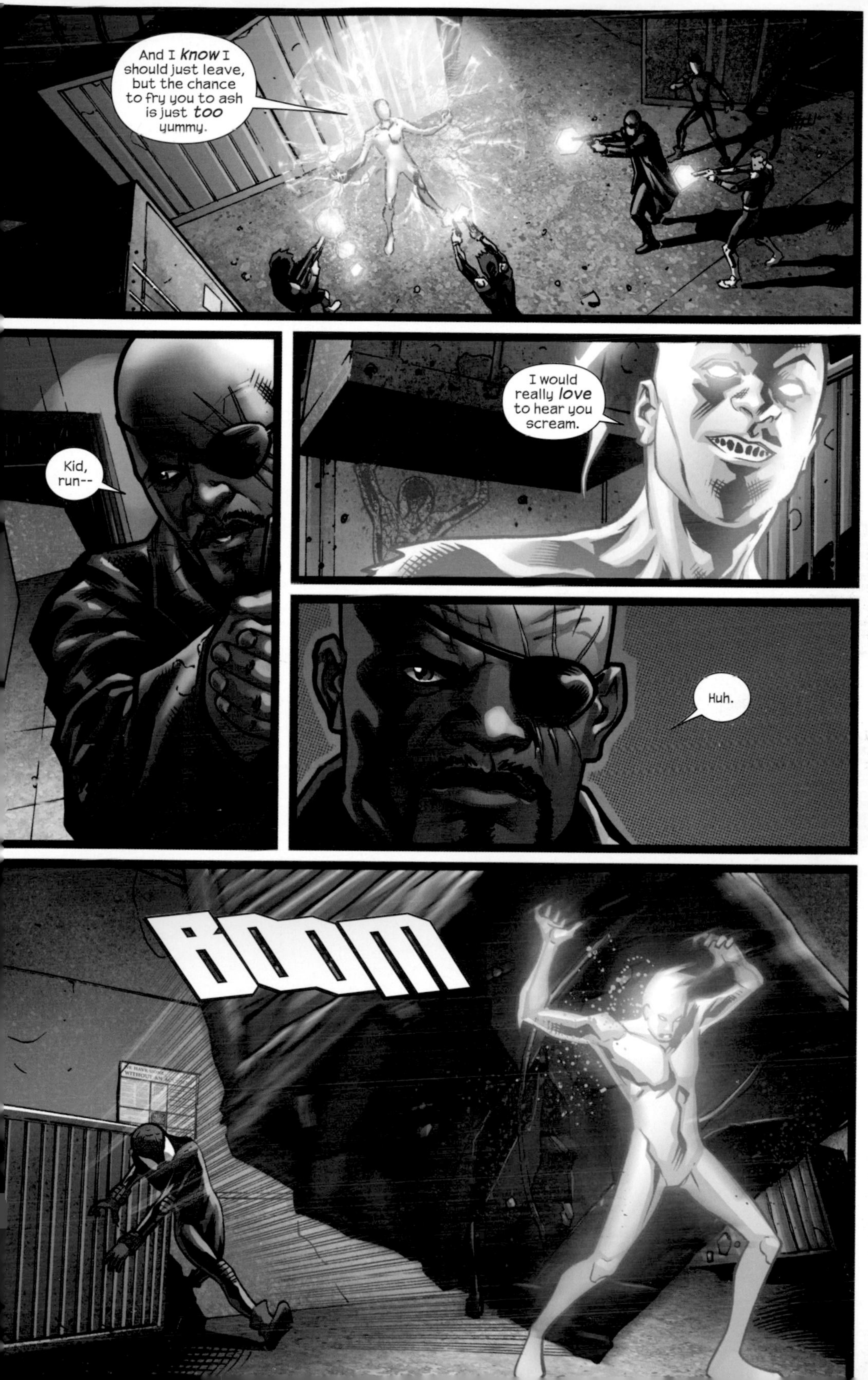
And I know I should just leave, but the chance to fry you to ash is just too yummy.
Kid, run--
I would really love to hear you scream.
Huh.
BOOM

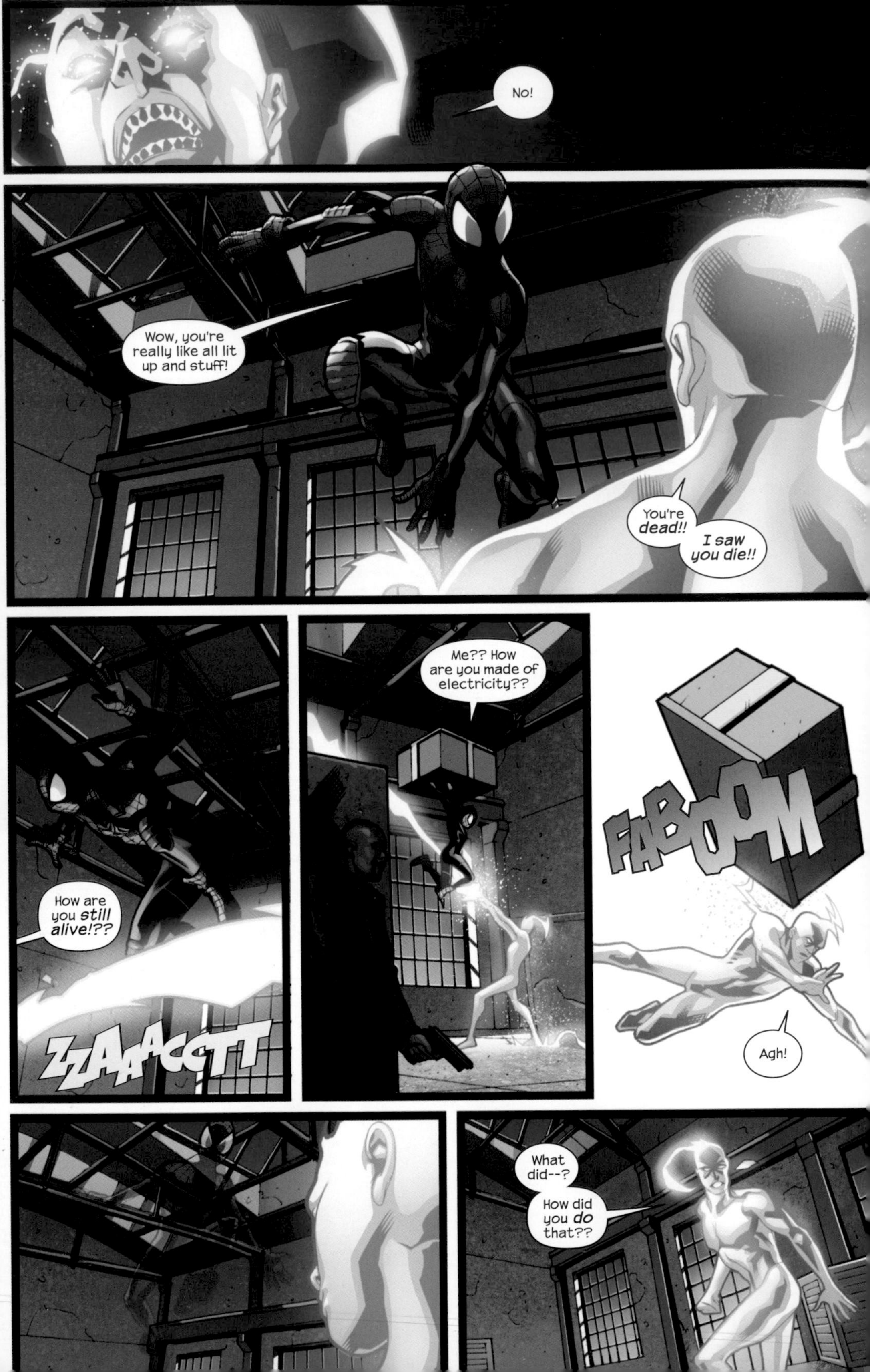
No!
Wow, you're really like all lit up and stuff!
You're dead!!
I saw you die!!
How are you still alive!??
ZZAAACCTT
Me?? How are you made of electricity??
FABOOM
Agh!
What did--?
How did you do that??

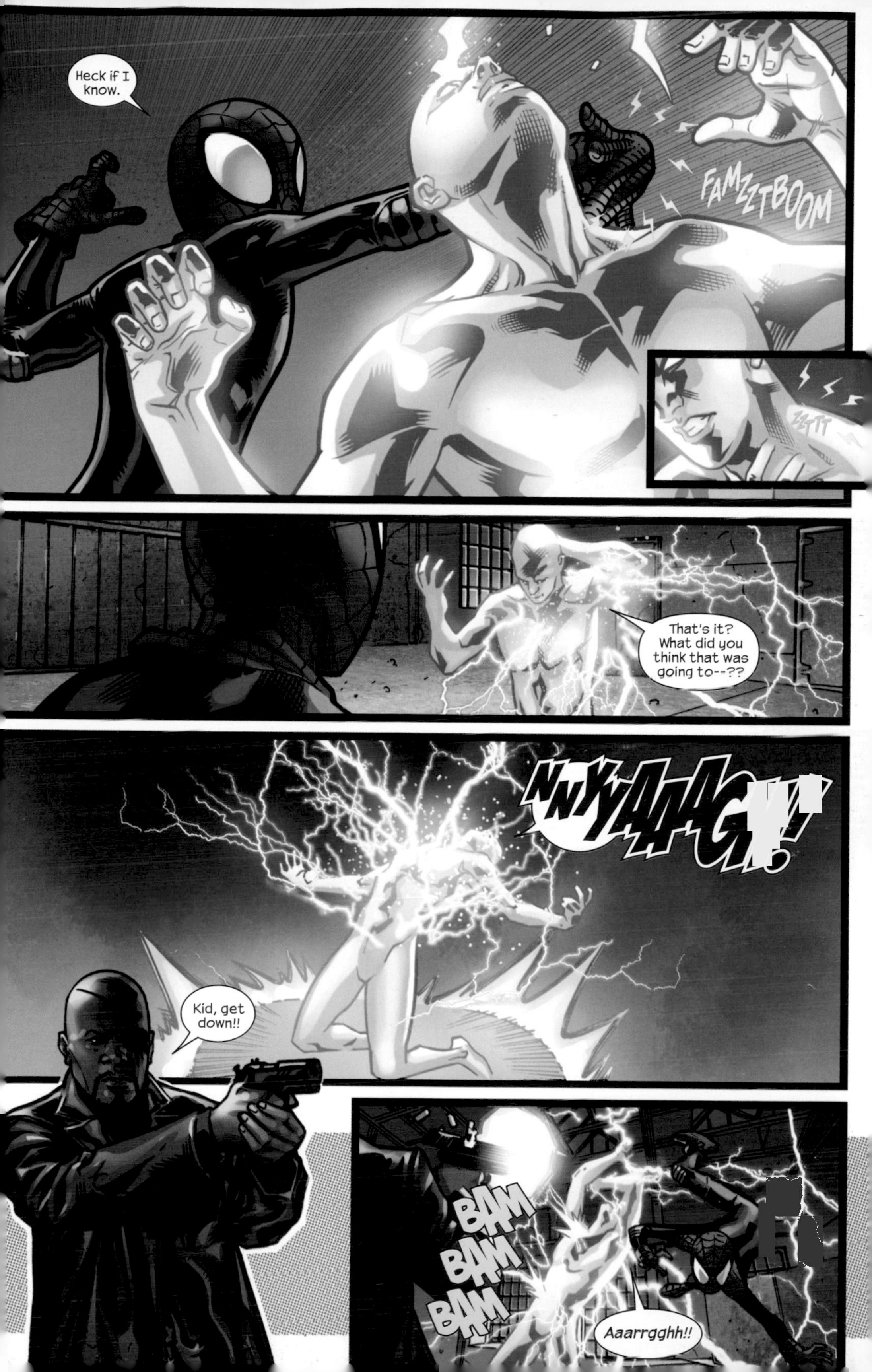
Heck if I know.
FAMZZTBOOM
ZZZTTT
That's it? What did you think that was going to--??
NNYYAAAGH!
Kid, get down!!
BAM
BAM
BAM
Aaarrgghh!!

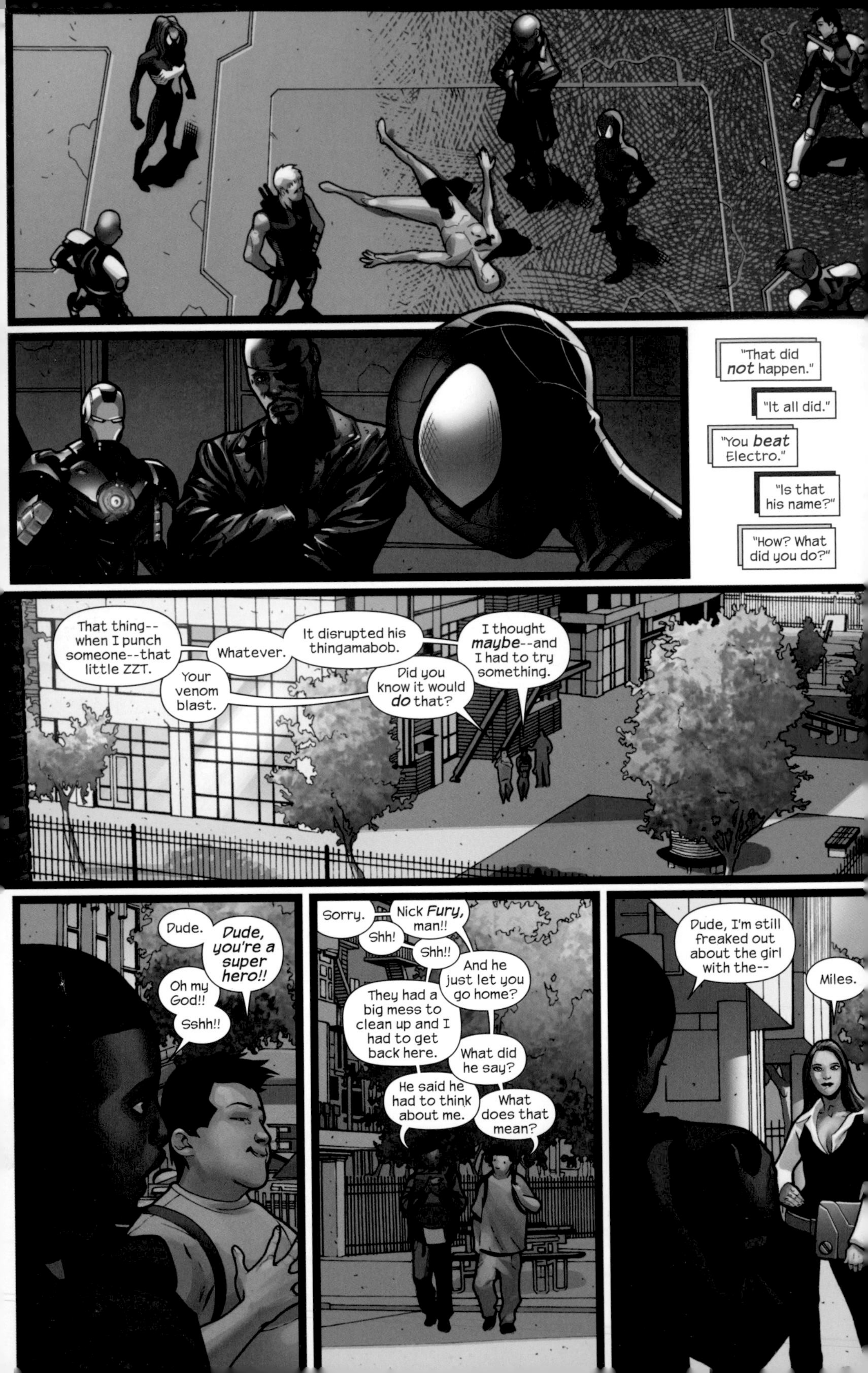
"That did not happen."
"It all did."
"You beat Electro."
"Is that his name?"
"How? What did you do?"
That thing--when I punch someone--that little ZZT.
Whatever.
Your venom blast.
It disrupted his thingamabob.
Did you know it would do that?
I thought maybe--and I had to try something.
Dude.
Dude, you're a super hero!!
Oh my God!!
Sshh!!
Sorry.
Nick Fury, man!!
Shh!
Shh!!
And he just let you go home?
They had a big mess to clean up and I had to get back here.
What did he say?
He said he had to think about me.
What does that mean?
Dude, I'm still freaked out about the girl with the--
Miles.

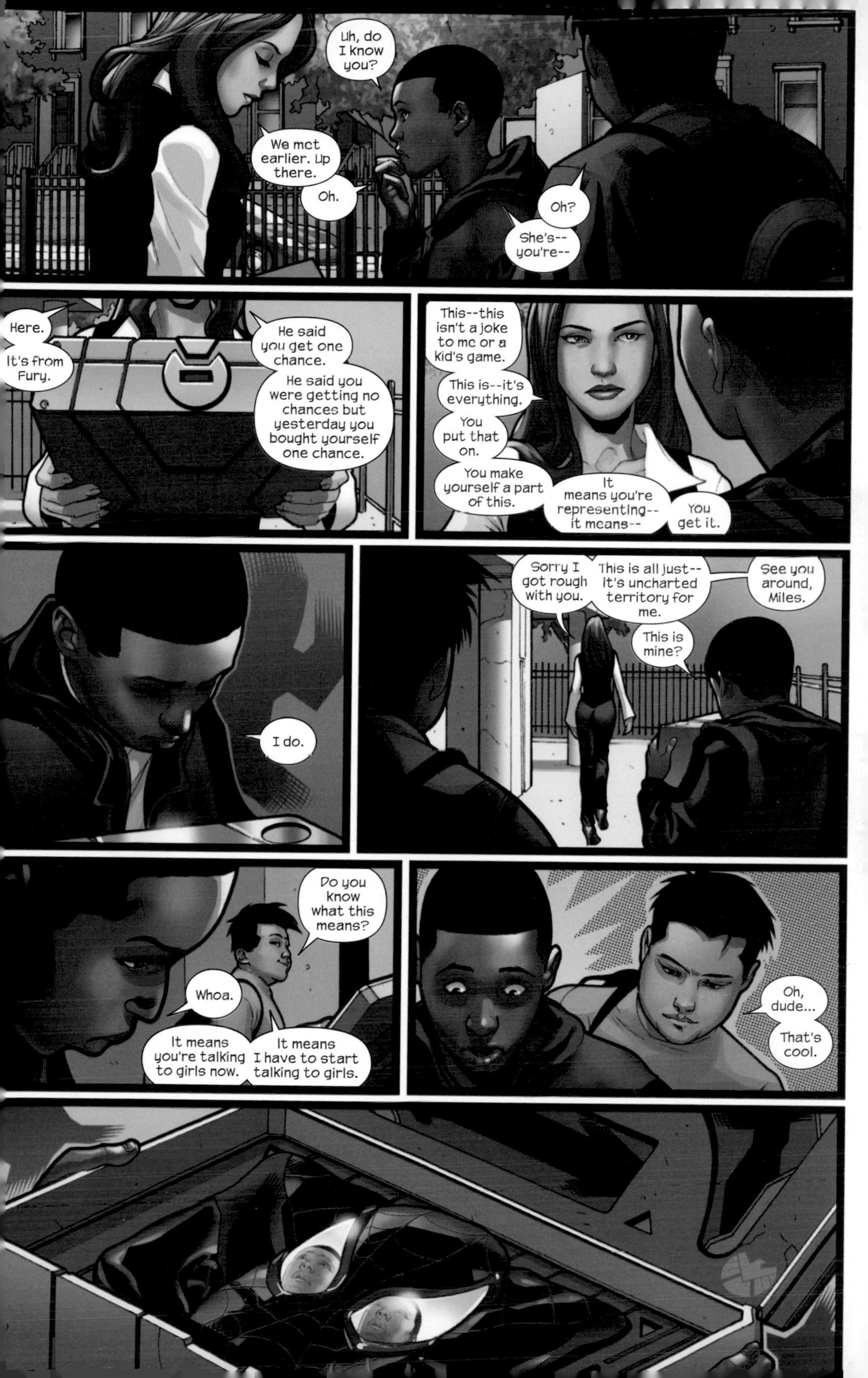
Uh, do I know you?
We met earlier. Up there.
Oh.
Oh?
She's-- you're--
Here.
It's from Fury.
He said you get one chance.
He said you were getting no chances but yesterday you bought yourself one chance.
This--this isn't a joke to me or a kid's game.
This is--it's everything.
You put that on.
You make yourself a part of this.
It means you're representing-- it means--
You get it.
I do.
Sorry I got rough with you.
This is all just-- It's uncharted territory for me.
See you around, Miles.
This is mine?
Do you know what this means?
Whoa.
It means you're talking to girls now.
It means I have to start talking to girls.
Oh, dude...
That's cool.

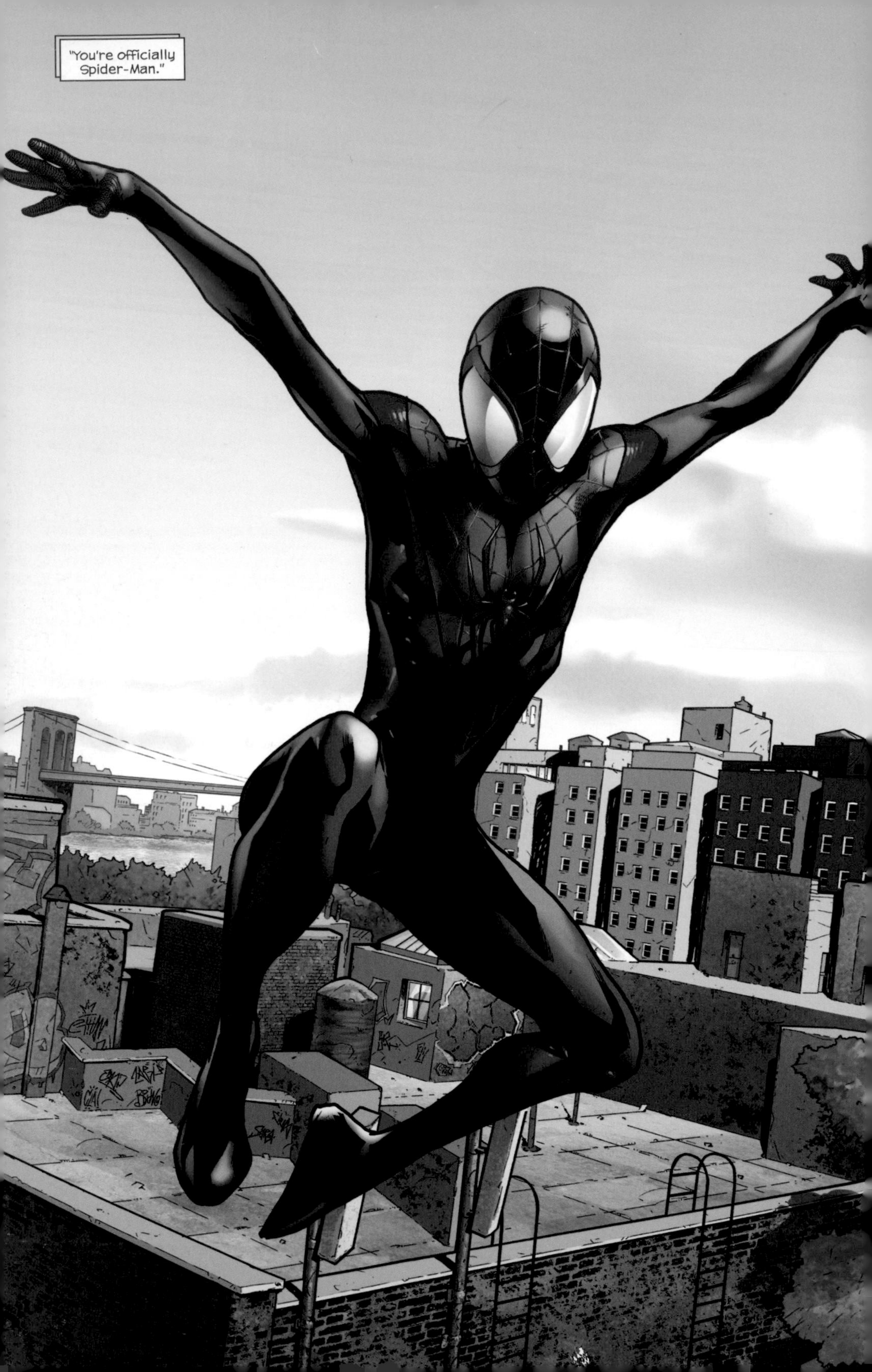
"You're officially Spider-Man."

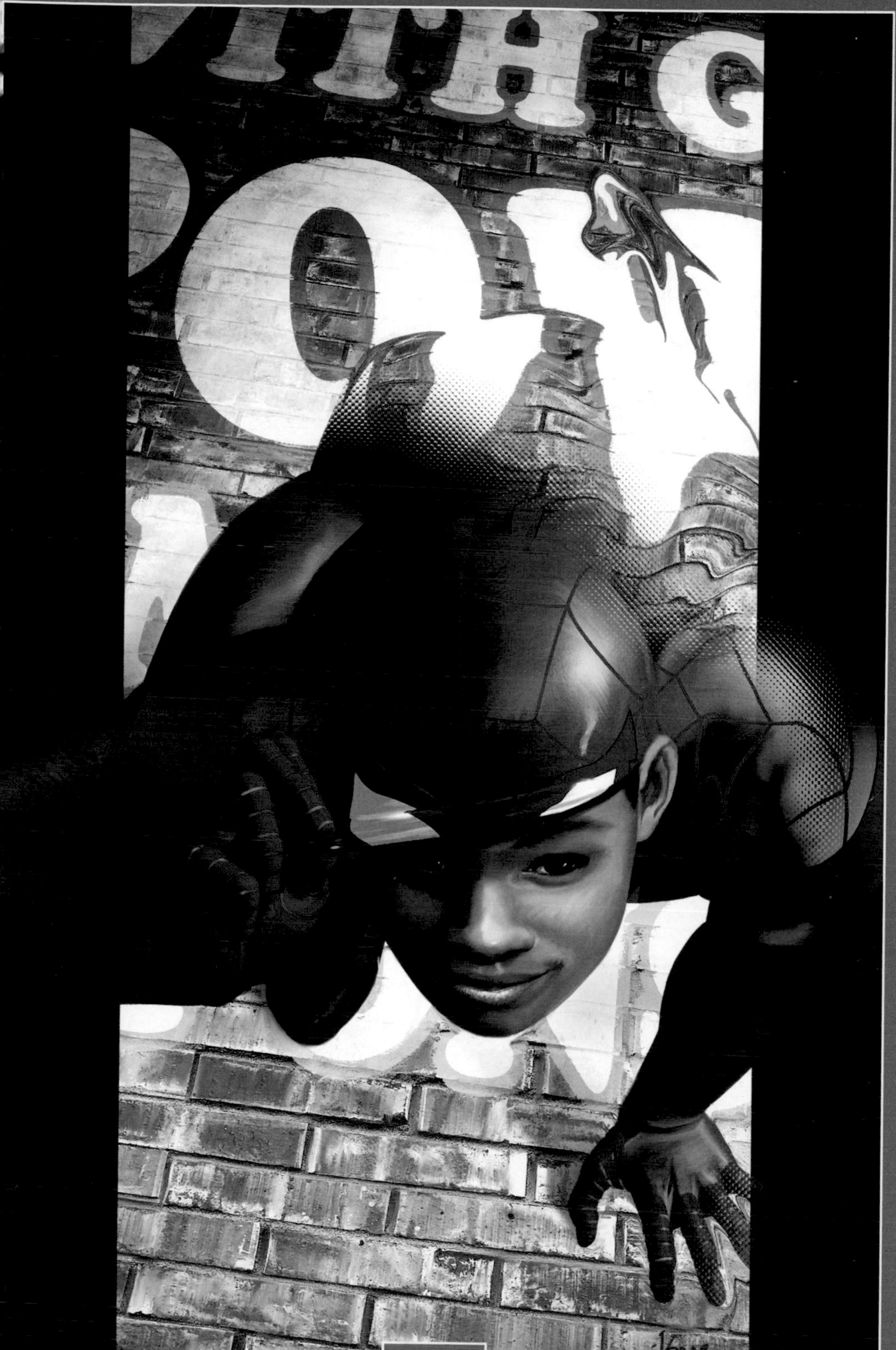
6

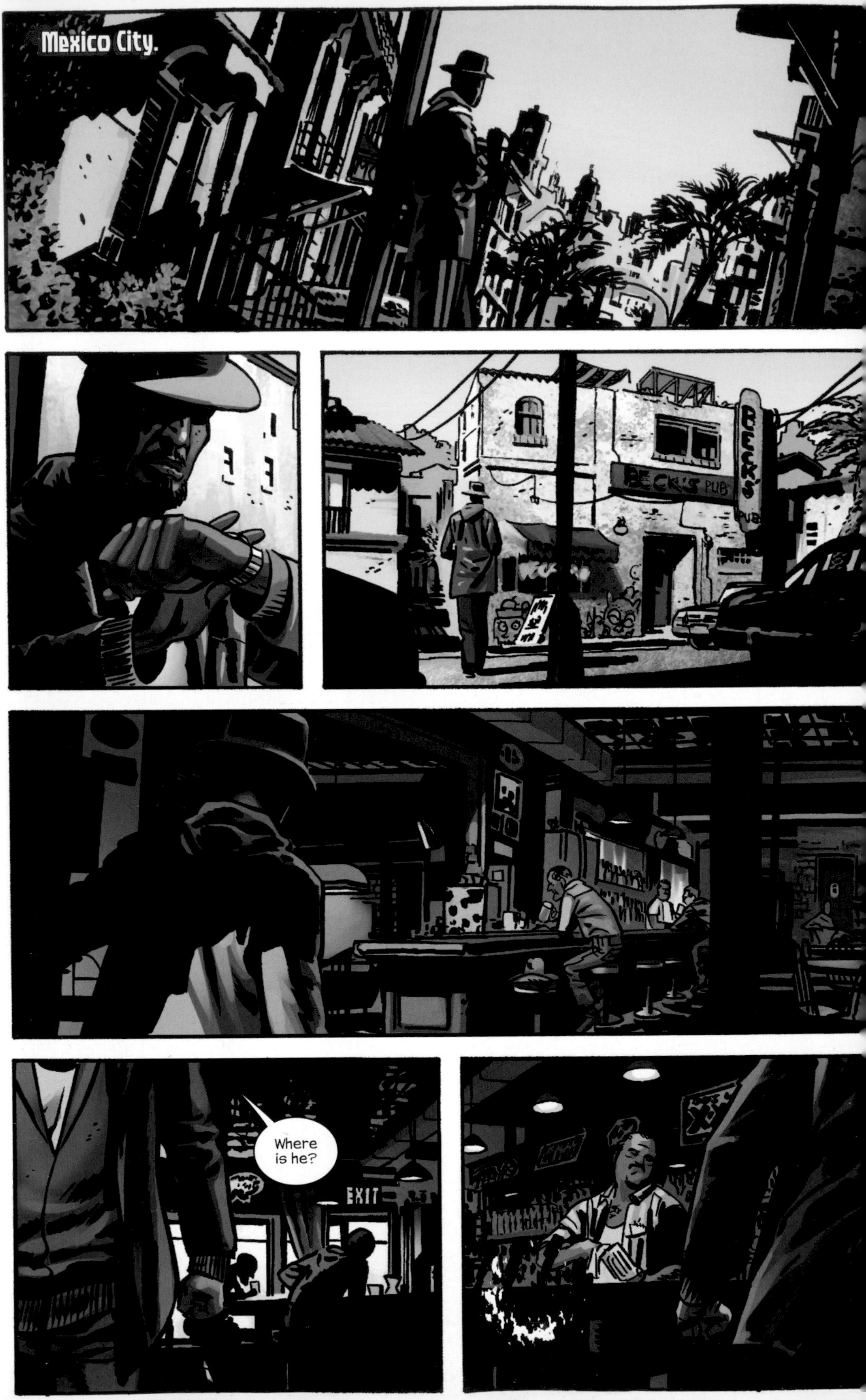
Mexico City.
BECK'S PUB
BECK'S PUB
Where is he?
EXIT

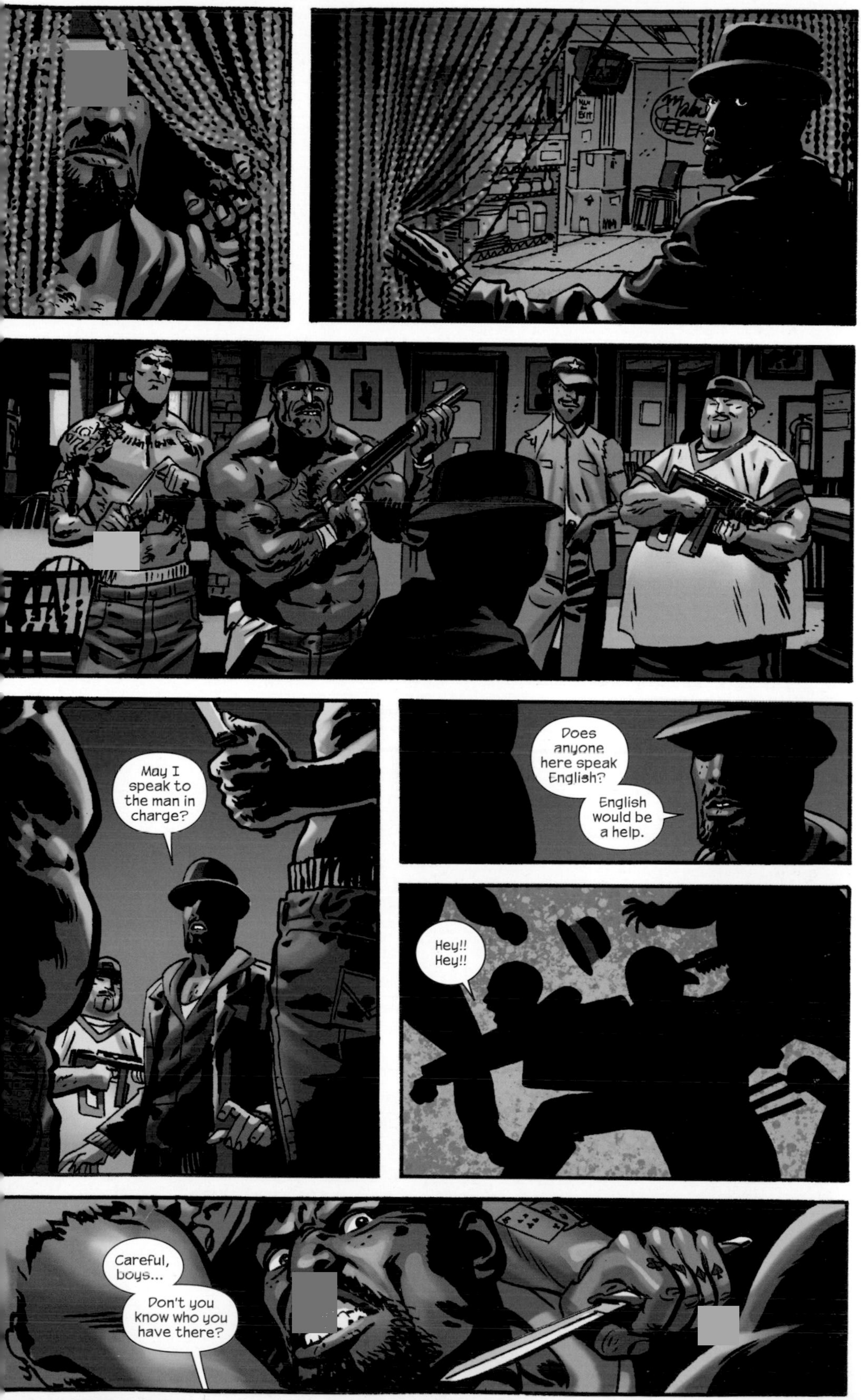
May I speak to the man in charge?
Does anyone here speak English?
English would be a help.
Hey!! Hey!!
Careful, boys...
Don't you know who you have there?

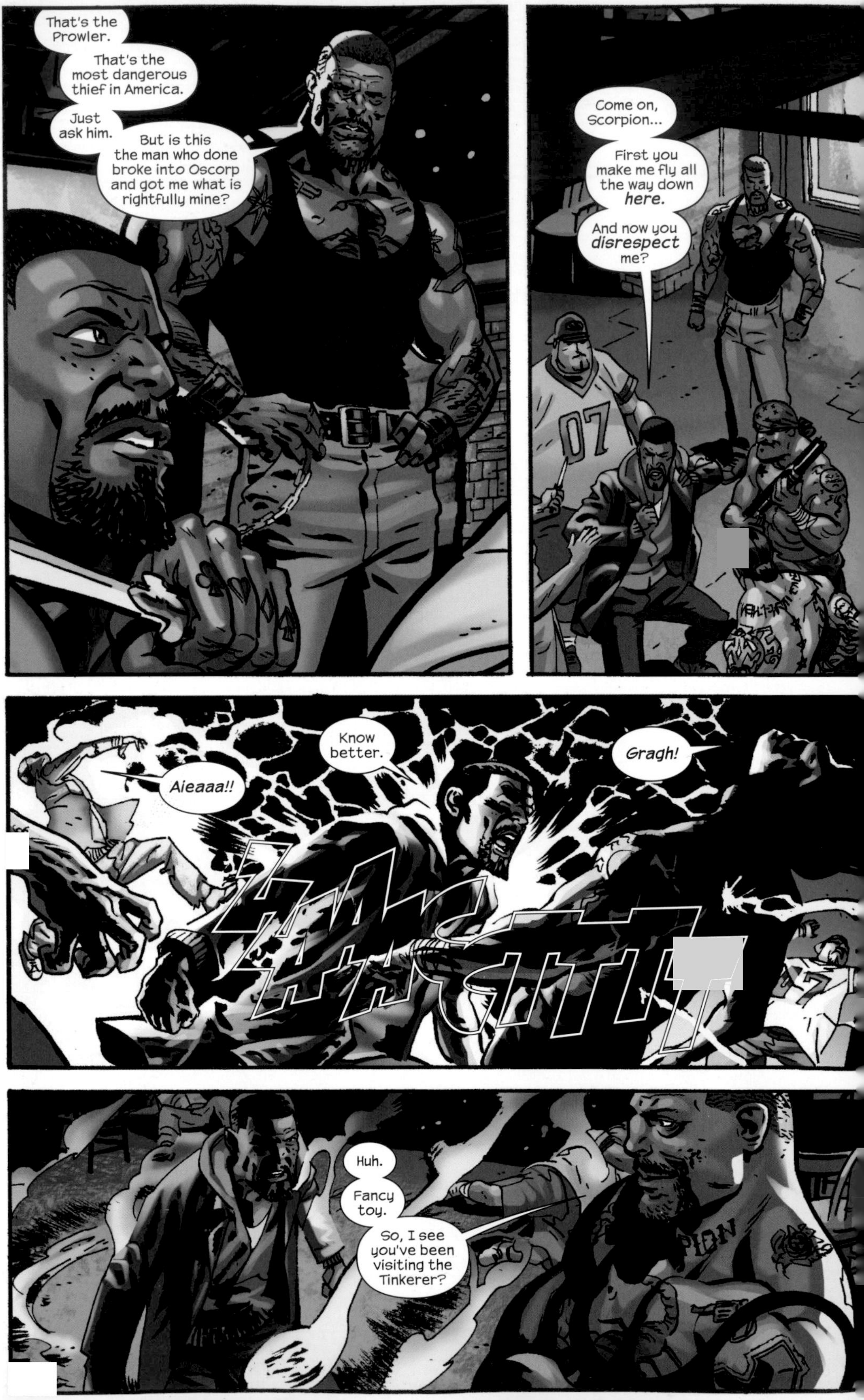
That's the Prowler.
That's the most dangerous thief in America.
Just ask him.
But is this the man who done broke into Oscorp and got me what is rightfully mine?
Come on, Scorpion...
First you make me fly all the way down *here.*
And now you *disrespect* me?
Aieaaa!!
Know better.
Gragh!
Huh.
Fancy toy.
So, I see you've been visiting the Tinkerer?

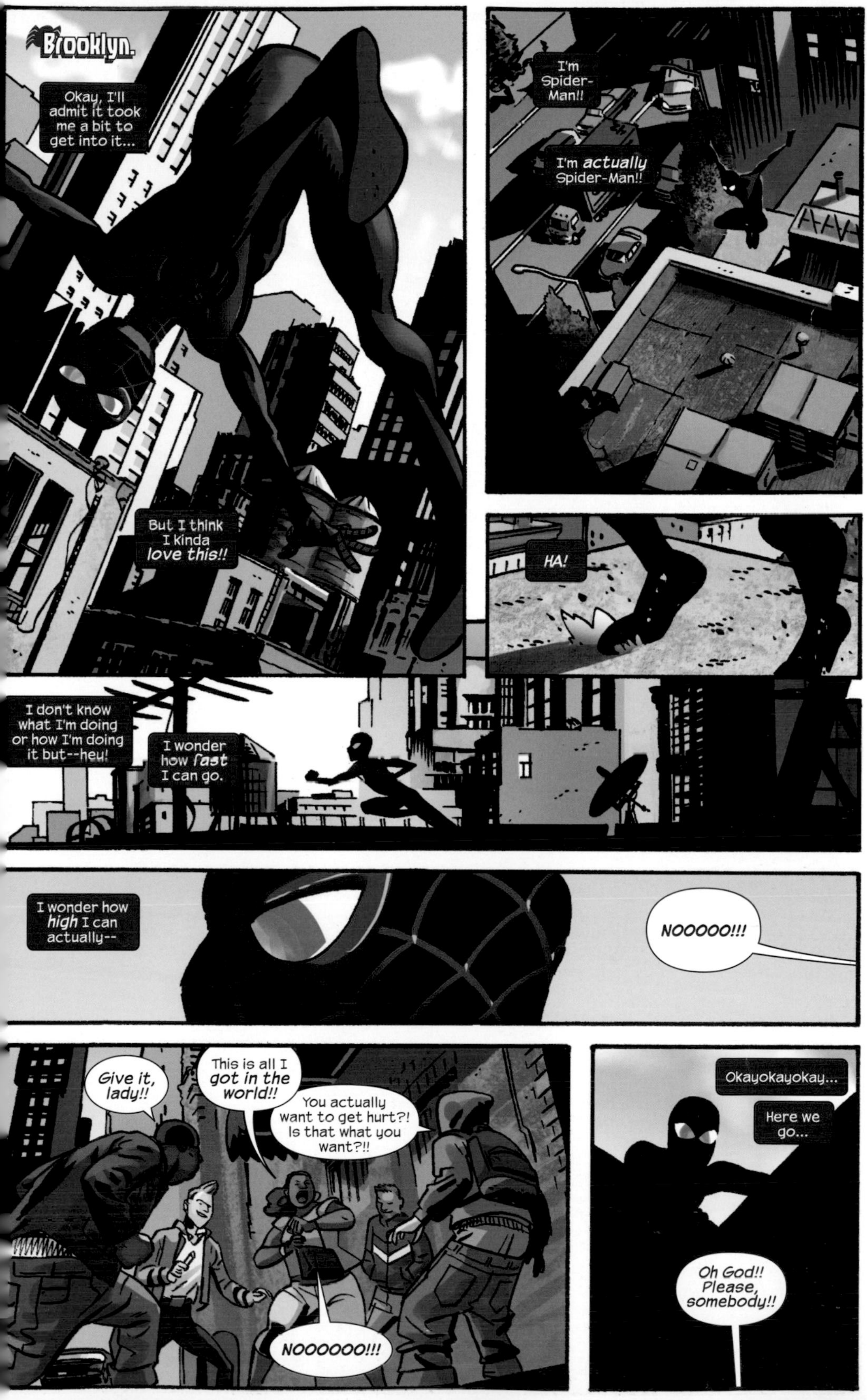
Brooklyn.
Okay, I'll admit it took me a bit to get into it...
But I think I kinda love this!!
I'm Spider-Man!!
I'm actually Spider-Man!!
HA!
I don't know what I'm doing or how I'm doing it but--hey!
I wonder how fast I can go.
I wonder how high I can actually--
NOOOOO!!!
Give it, lady!!
This is all I got in the world!!
You actually want to get hurt?! Is that what you want?!!
NOOOOOO!!!
Okayokayokay...
Here we go...
Oh God!! Please, somebody!!

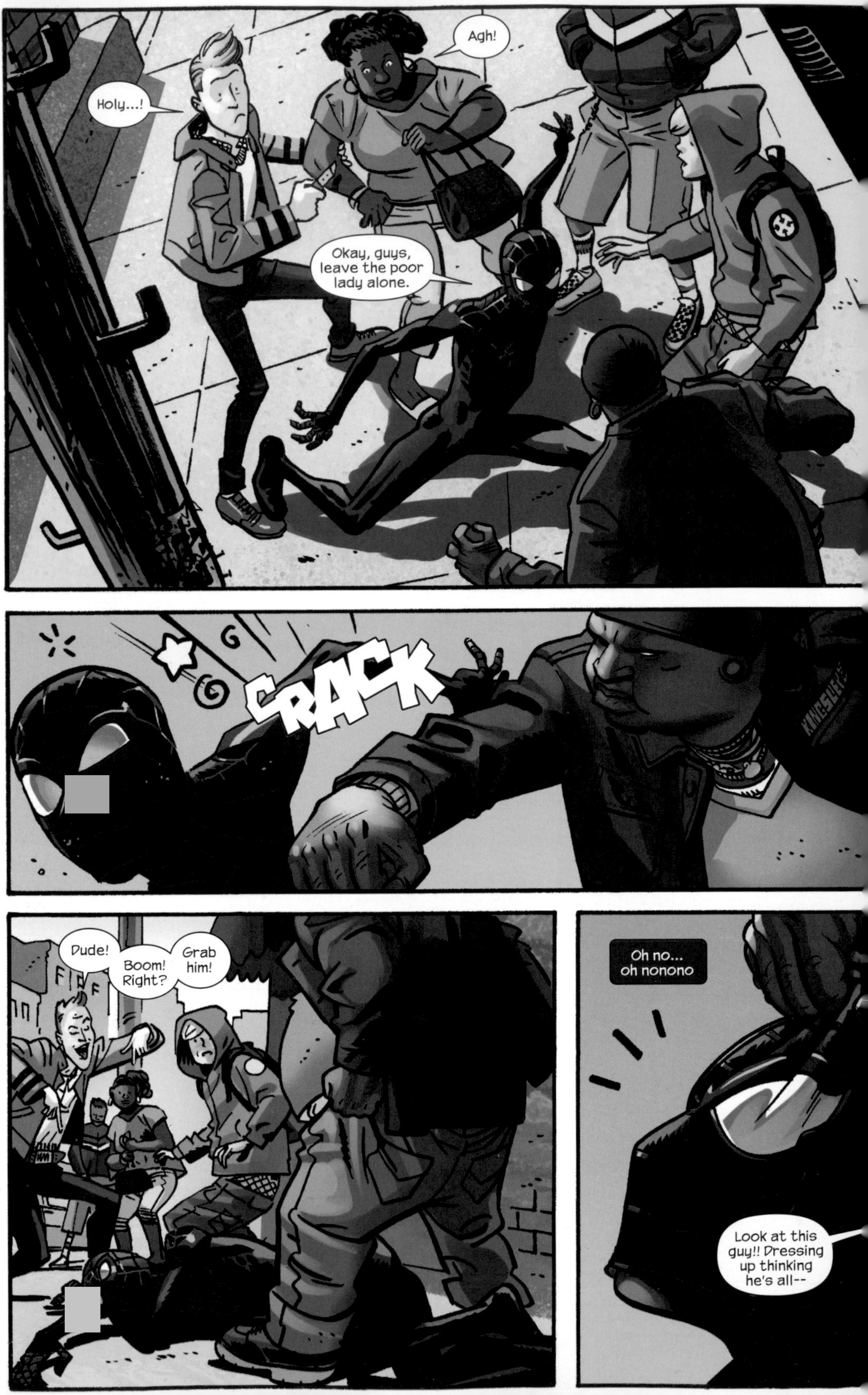
Agh!
Holy...!
Okay, guys, leave the poor lady alone.
CRACK
Dude!
Boom! Right?
Grab him!
Oh no... oh nonono
Look at this guy!! Dressing up thinking he's all--

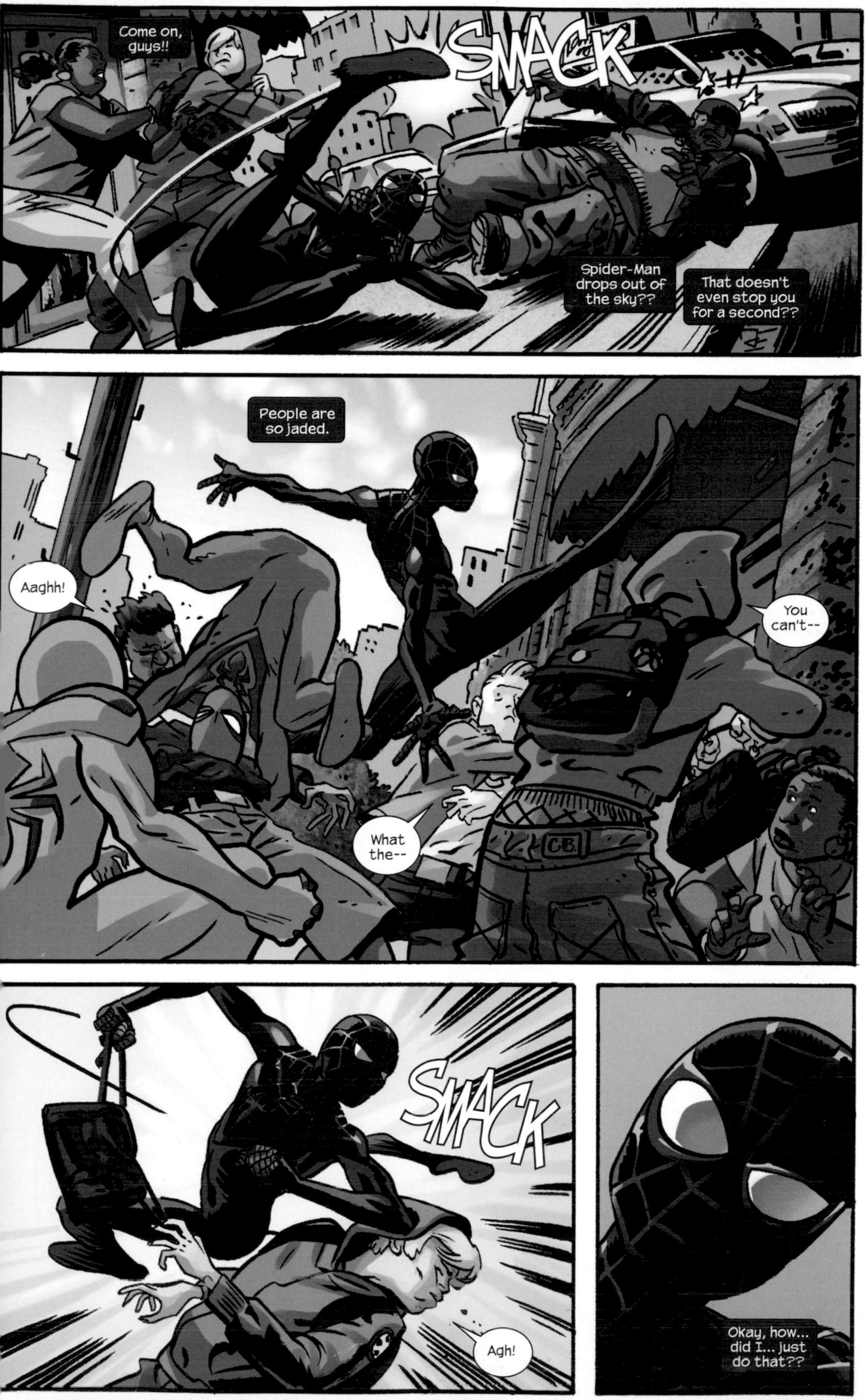

Come on, guys!!
SMACK
Spider-Man drops out of the sky??
That doesn't even stop you for a second??
People are so jaded.
Aaghh!
You can't--
What the--
SMACK
Agh!
Okay, how... did I... just do that??

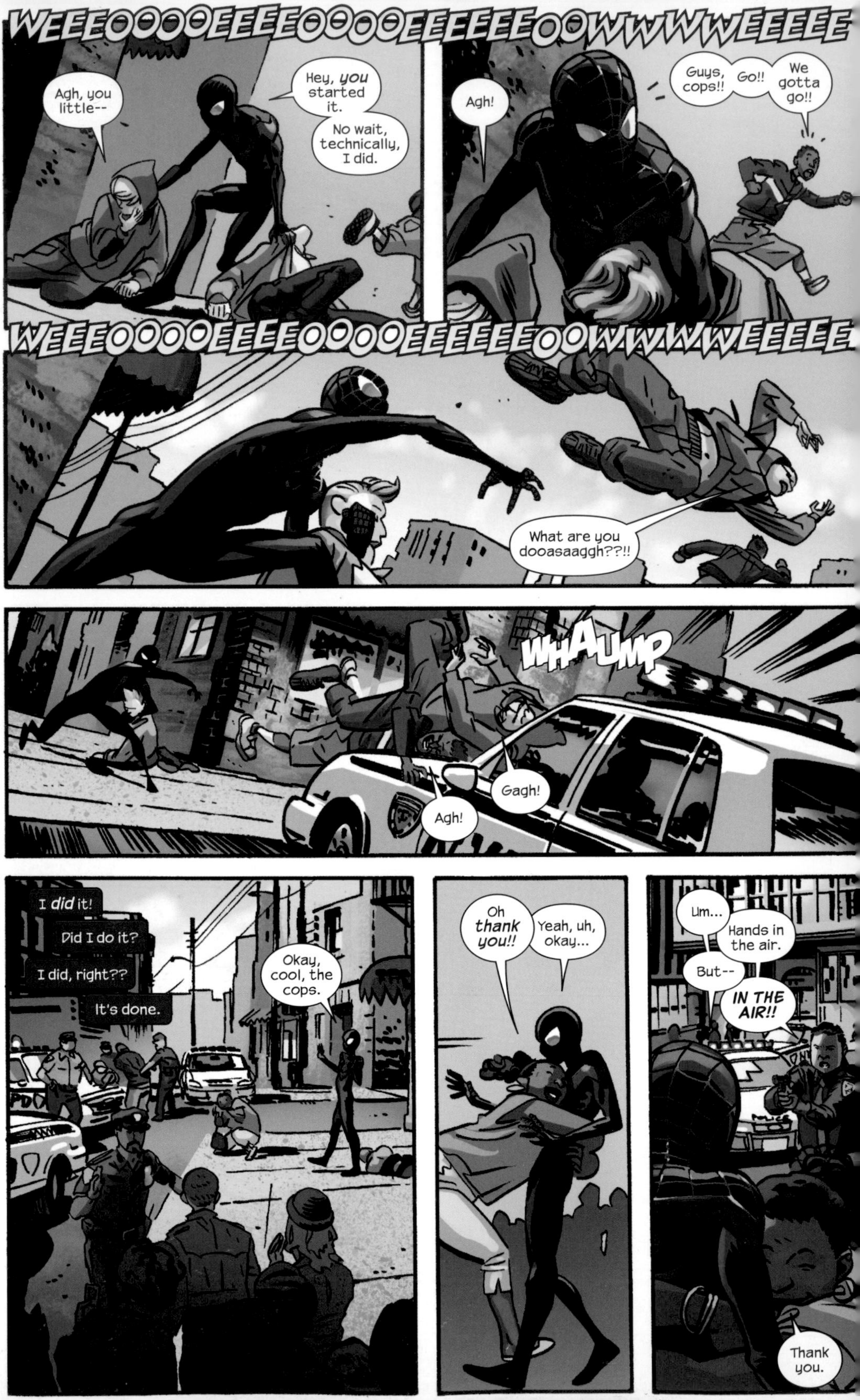
WEEEOOOOEEEEOOOOEEEEEEOOWWWWWEEEEE
Agh, you little--
Hey, you started it.
No wait, technically, I did.
Agh!
Guys, cops!!
Go!!
We gotta go!!
WEEEOOOOEEEEOOOOEEEEEEOOWWWWWEEEEE
What are you dooasaaggh??!!
WHAUMP
Gagh!
Agh!
I did it!
Did I do it?
I did, right??
It's done.
Okay, cool, the cops.
Oh thank you!!
Yeah, uh, okay...
Um...
Hands in the air.
But--
IN THE AIR!!
Thank you.

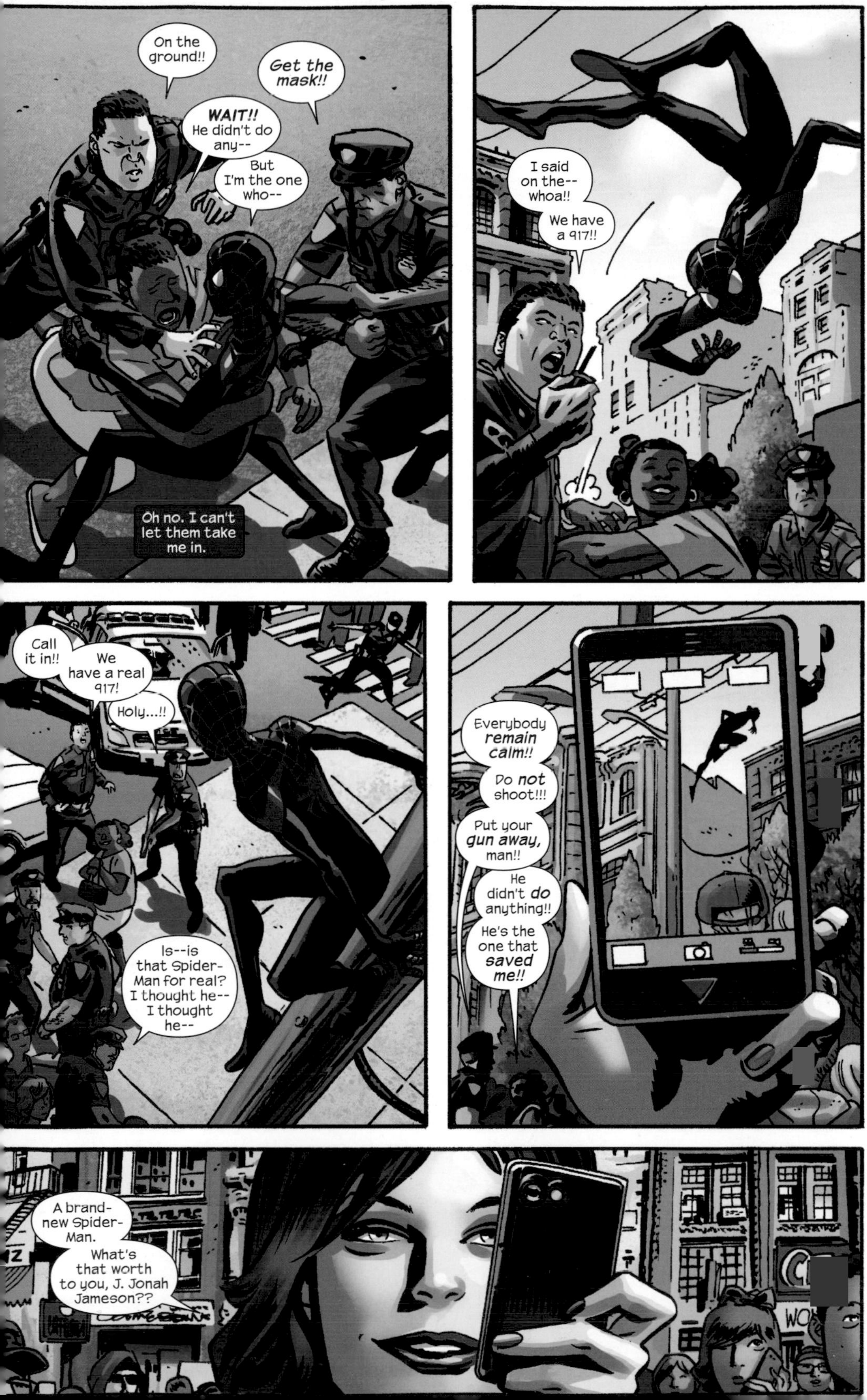
On the ground!!
Get the mask!!
WAIT!! He didn't do any--
But I'm the one who--
Oh no. I can't let them take me in.
I said on the-- whoa!!
We have a 917!!
Call it in!!
We have a real 917!
Holy...!!
Is--is that Spider-Man for real? I thought he-- I thought he--
Everybody remain calm!!
Do not shoot!!!
Put your gun away, man!!
He didn't do anything!!
He's the one that saved me!!
A brand-new Spider-Man.
What's that worth to you, J. Jonah Jameson??

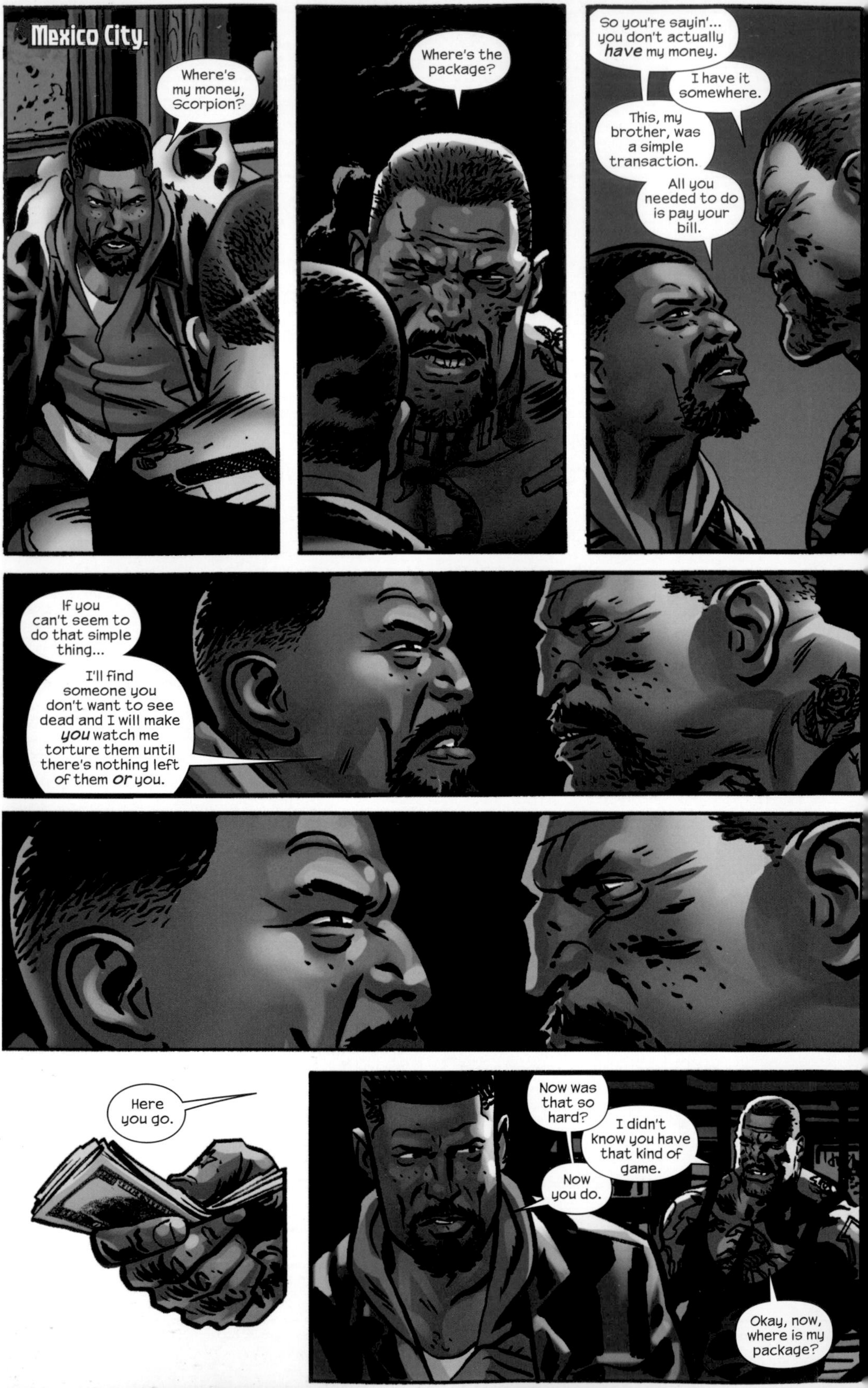
Mexico City.
Where's my money, Scorpion?
Where's the package?
So you're sayin'... you don't actually have my money.
I have it somewhere.
This, my brother, was a simple transaction.
All you needed to do is pay your bill.
If you can't seem to do that simple thing...
I'll find someone you don't want to see dead and I will make you watch me torture them until there's nothing left of them or you.
Here you go.
Now was that so hard?
I didn't know you have that kind of game.
Now you do.
Okay, now, where is my package?

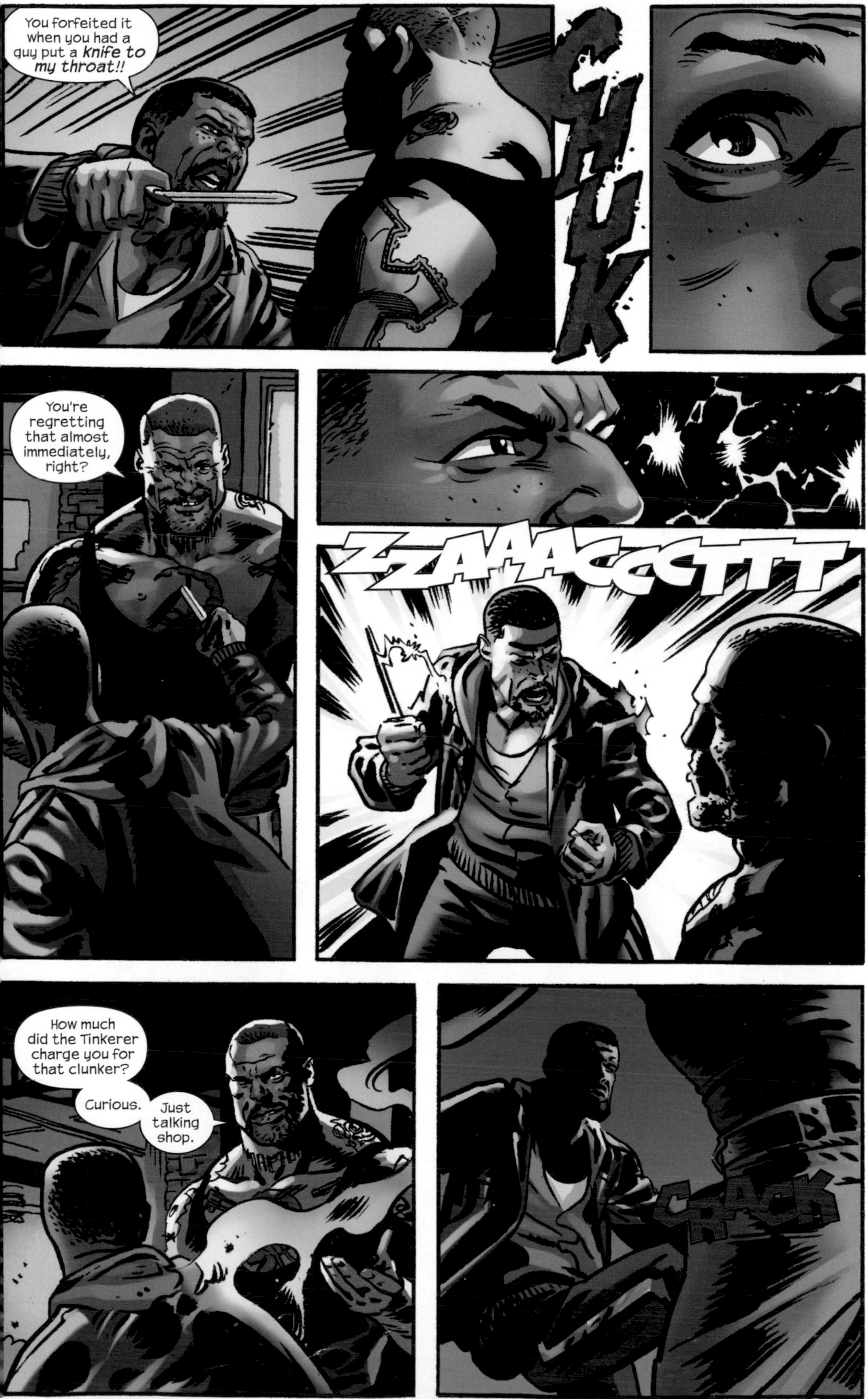
You forfeited it when you had a guy put a *knife to my throat!!*
CHUK
You're regretting that almost immediately, right?
ZZAAACCCTTT
How much did the Tinkerer charge you for that clunker?
Curious.
Just talking shop.
CRACK

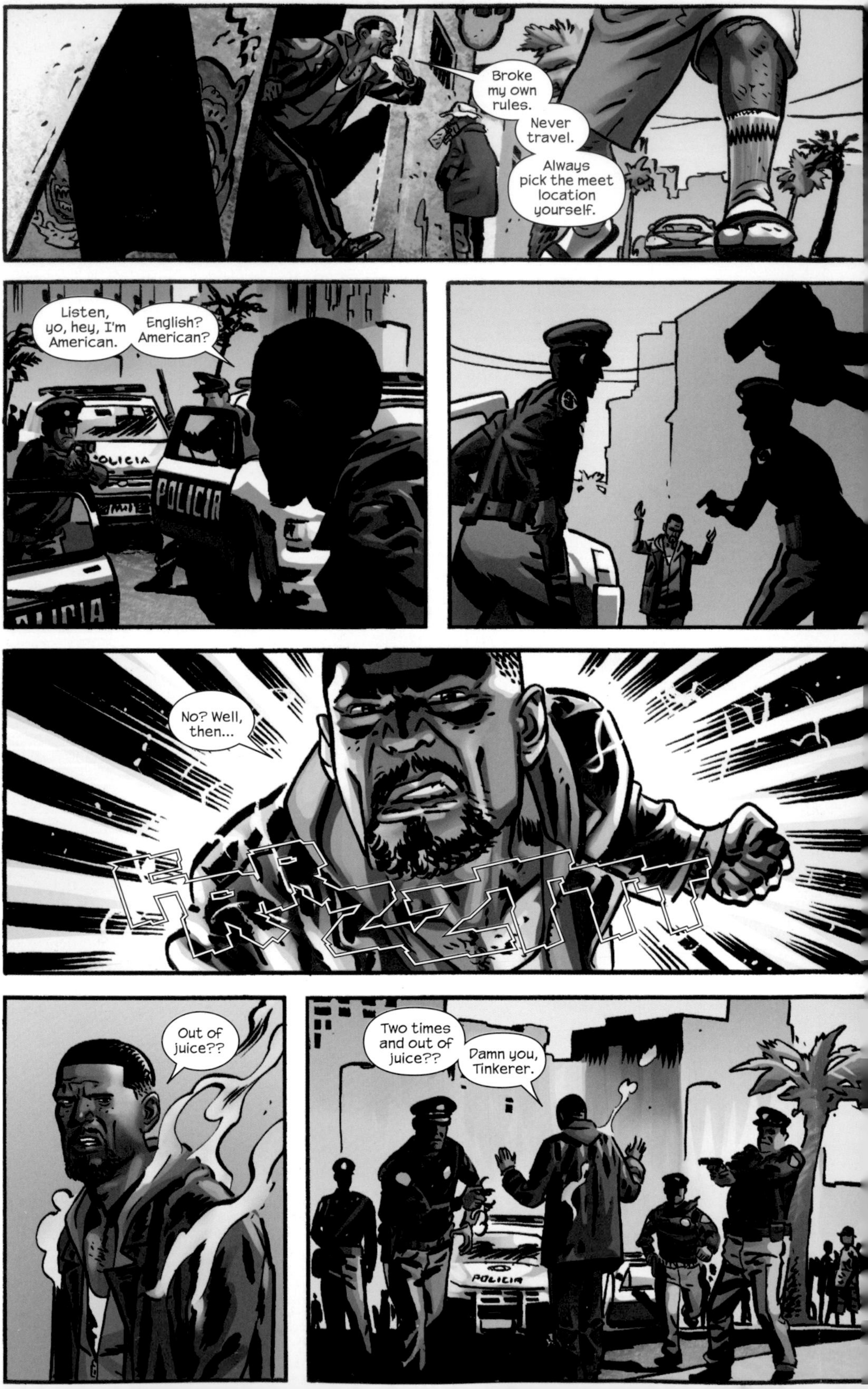

Broke my own rules.
Never travel.
Always pick the meet location yourself.
Listen, yo, hey, I'm American.
English? American?
POLICIA
POLICIA
No? Well, then...
Out of juice??
Two times and out of juice??
Damn you, Tinkerer.
POLICIA

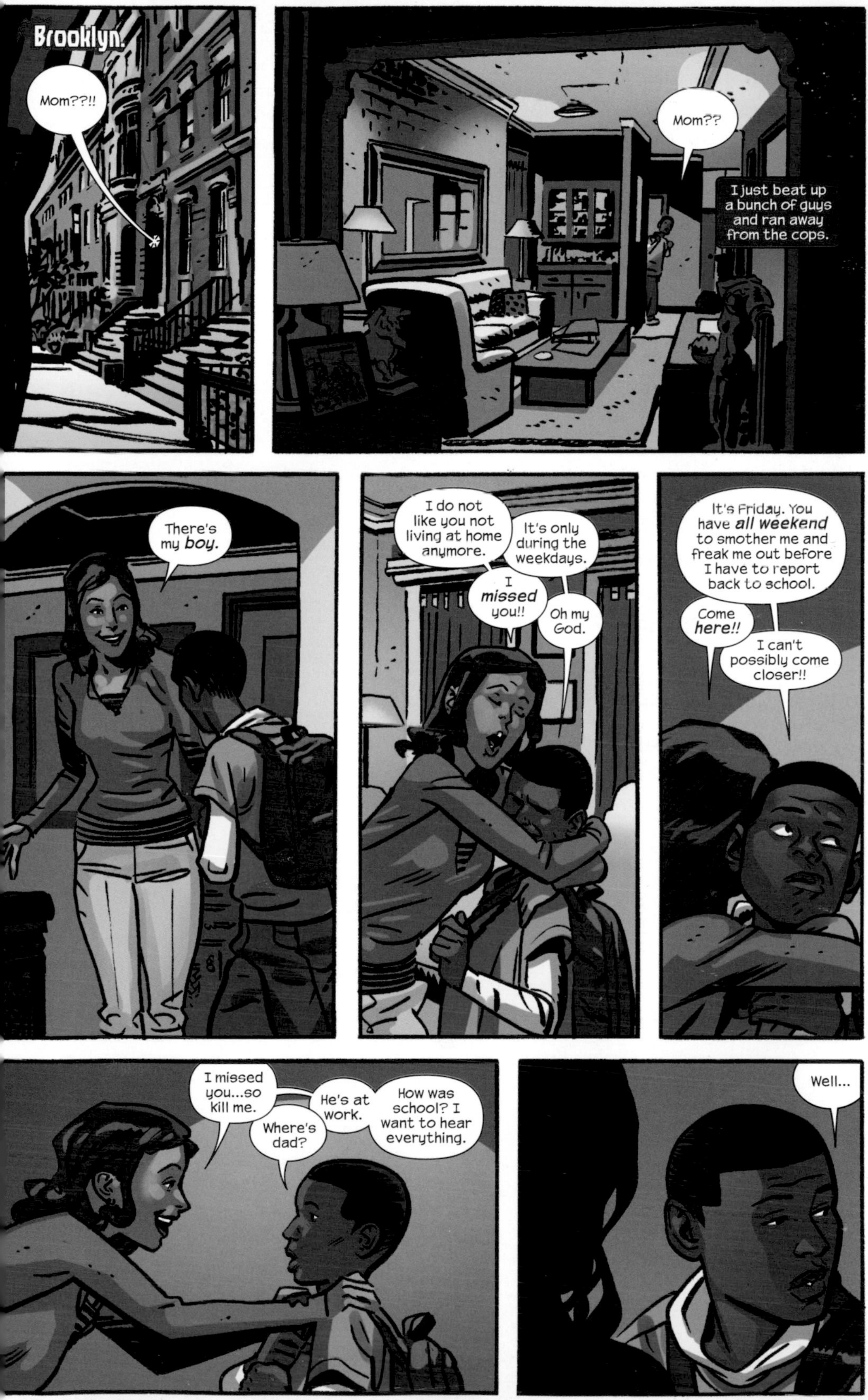
Brooklyn.
Mom??!!
Mom??
I just beat up a bunch of guys and ran away from the cops.
There's my *boy.*
I do not like you not living at home anymore.
It's only during the weekdays.
I *missed* you!!
Oh my God.
It's Friday. You have *all weekend* to smother me and freak me out before I have to report back to school.
Come *here!!*
I can't possibly come closer!!
I missed you...so kill me.
Where's dad?
He's at work.
How was school? I want to hear everything.
Well...

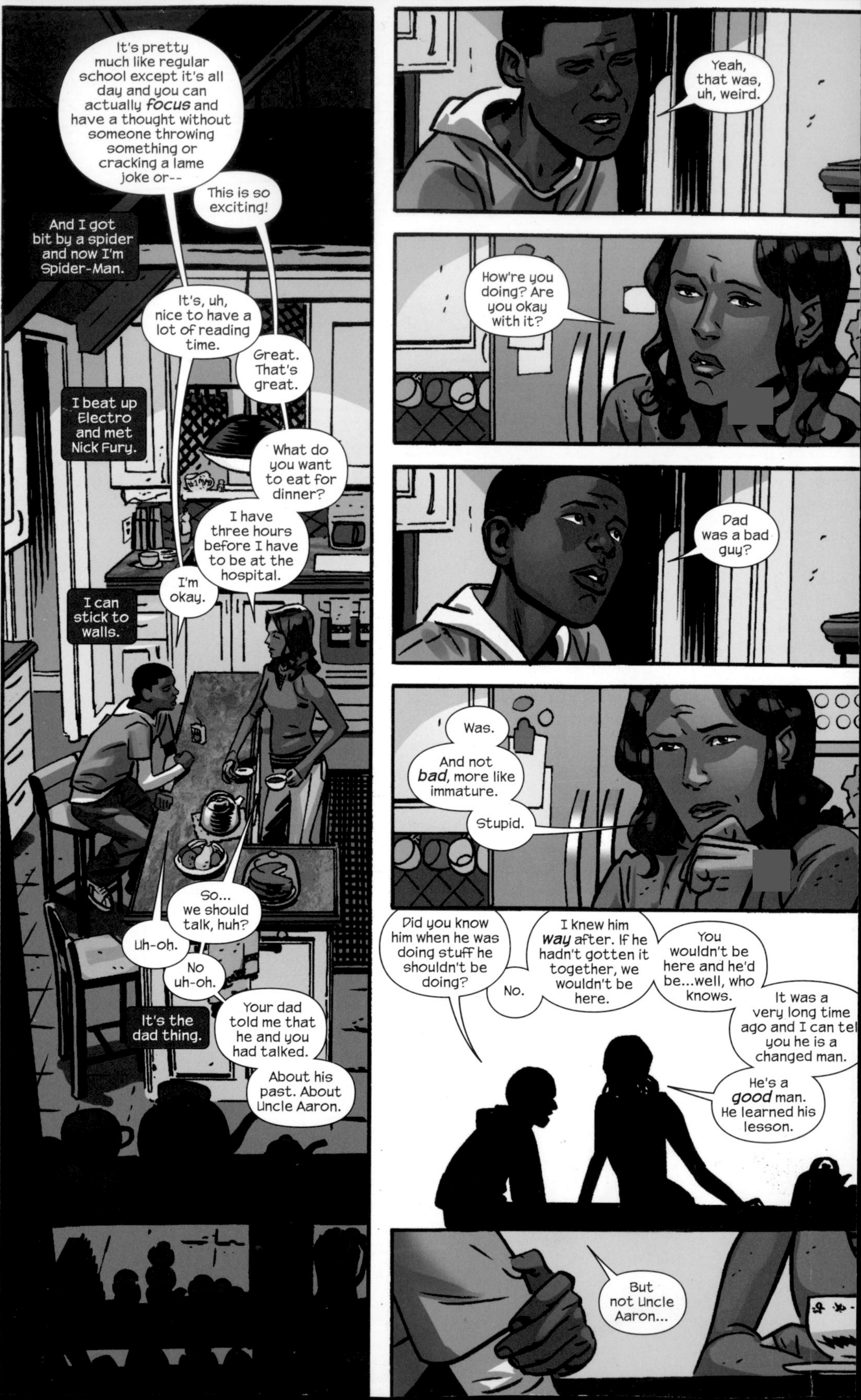

It's pretty much like regular school except it's all day and you can actually *focus* and have a thought without someone throwing something or cracking a lame joke or--
This is so exciting!
And I got bit by a spider and now I'm Spider-Man.
It's, uh, nice to have a lot of reading time.
Great. That's great.
I beat up Electro and met Nick Fury.
What do you want to eat for dinner?
I have three hours before I have to be at the hospital.
I'm okay.
I can stick to walls.
So... we should talk, huh?
Uh-oh.
No uh-oh.
It's the dad thing.
Your dad told me that he and you had talked.
About his past. About Uncle Aaron.
Yeah, that was, uh, weird.
How're you doing? Are you okay with it?
Dad was a bad guy?
Was.
And not **bad**, more like immature.
Stupid.
Did you know him when he was doing stuff he shouldn't be doing?
No.
I knew him **way** after. If he hadn't gotten it together, we wouldn't be here.
You wouldn't be here and he'd be...well, who knows.
It was a very long time ago and I can tell you he is a changed man.
He's a **good** man. He learned his lesson.
But not Uncle Aaron...

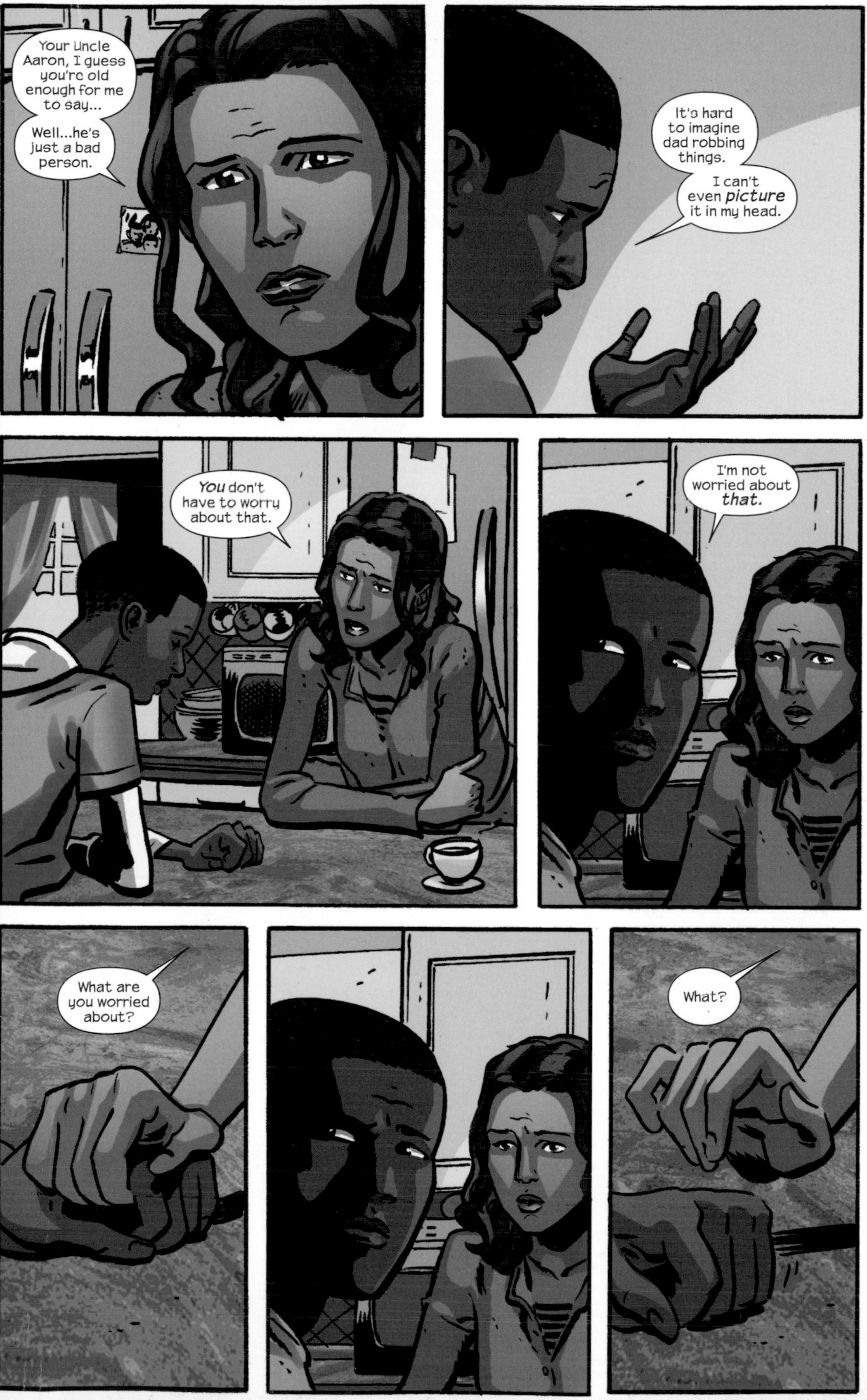
Your Uncle Aaron, I guess you're old enough for me to say...
Well...he's just a bad person.
It's hard to imagine dad robbing things.
I can't even *picture* it in my head.
You don't have to worry about that.
I'm not worried about ***that.***
What are you worried about?
What?

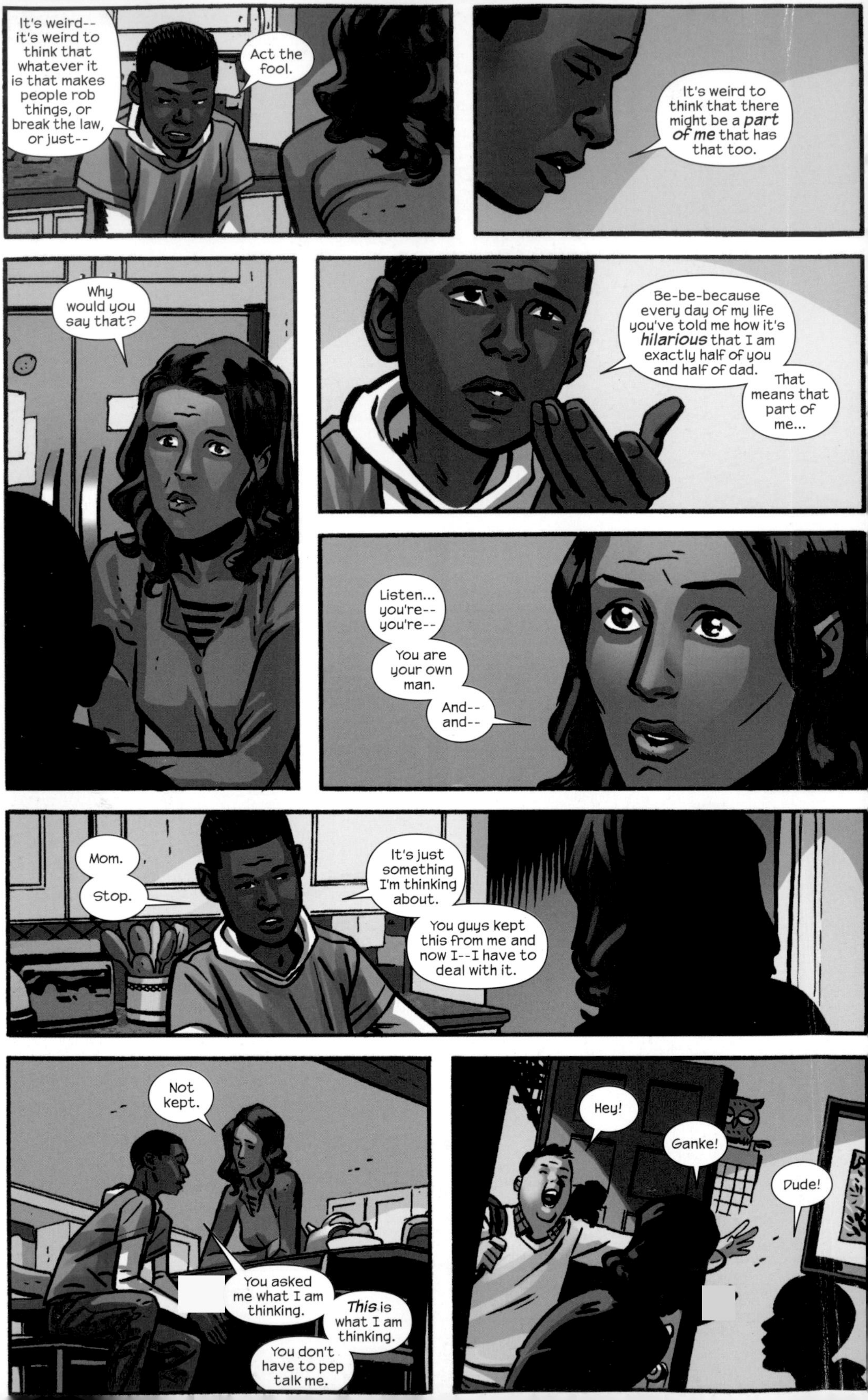
It's weird-- it's weird to think that whatever it is that makes people rob things, or break the law, or just--
Act the fool.
It's weird to think that there might be a *part of me* that has that too.
Why would you say that?
Be-be-because every day of my life you've told me how it's *hilarious* that I am exactly half of you and half of dad.
That means that part of me...
Listen... you're-- you're--
You are your own man.
And-- and--
Mom.
Stop.
It's just something I'm thinking about.
You guys kept this from me and now I--I have to deal with it.
Not kept.
You asked me what I am thinking.
This is what I am thinking.
You don't have to pep talk me.
Hey!
Ganke!
Dude!

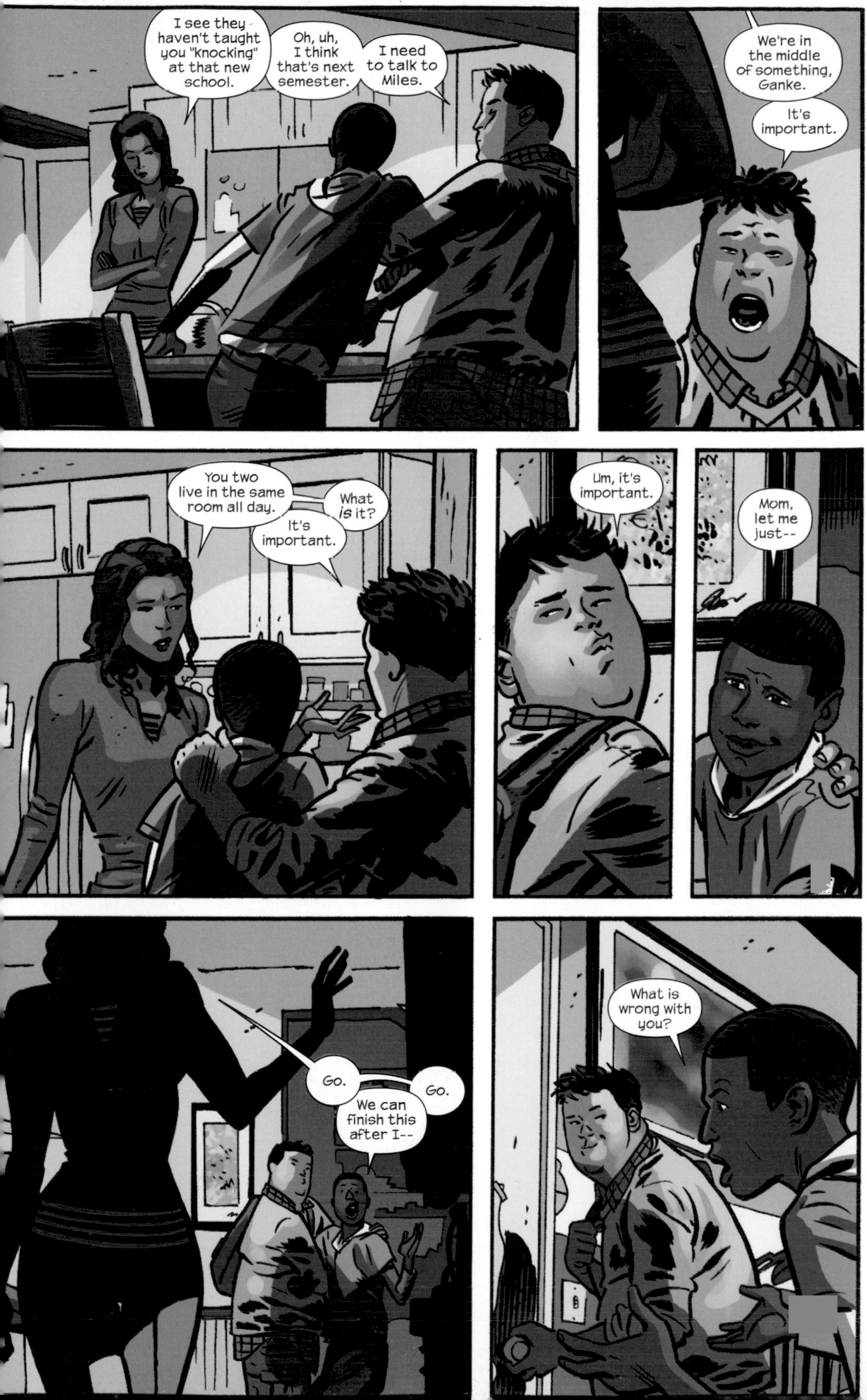
I see they haven't taught you "knocking" at that new school.
Oh, uh, I think that's next semester.
I need to talk to Miles.
We're in the middle of something, Ganke.
It's important.
You two live in the same room all day.
What *is* it?
It's important.
Um, it's important.
Mom, let me just--
Go.
Go.
We can finish this after I--
What is wrong with you?

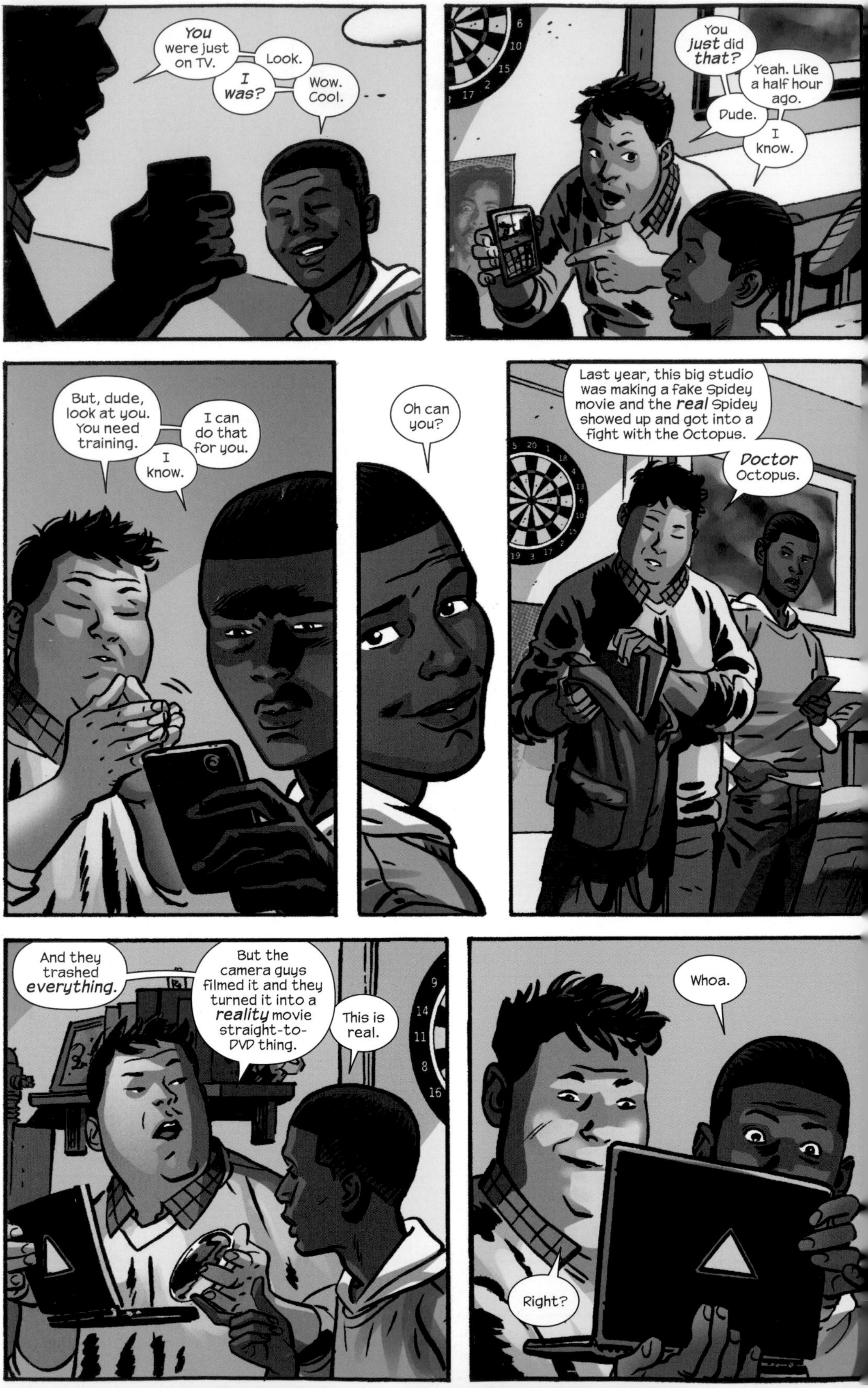
You were just on TV.
Look.
I was?
Wow. Cool.
You just did that?
Yeah. Like a half hour ago.
Dude.
I know.
But, dude, look at you. You need training.
I can do that for you.
I know.
Oh can you?
Last year, this big studio was making a fake Spidey movie and the real Spidey showed up and got into a fight with the Octopus.
Doctor Octopus.
And they trashed everything.
But the camera guys filmed it and they turned it into a reality movie straight-to-DVD thing.
This is real.
Whoa.
Right?

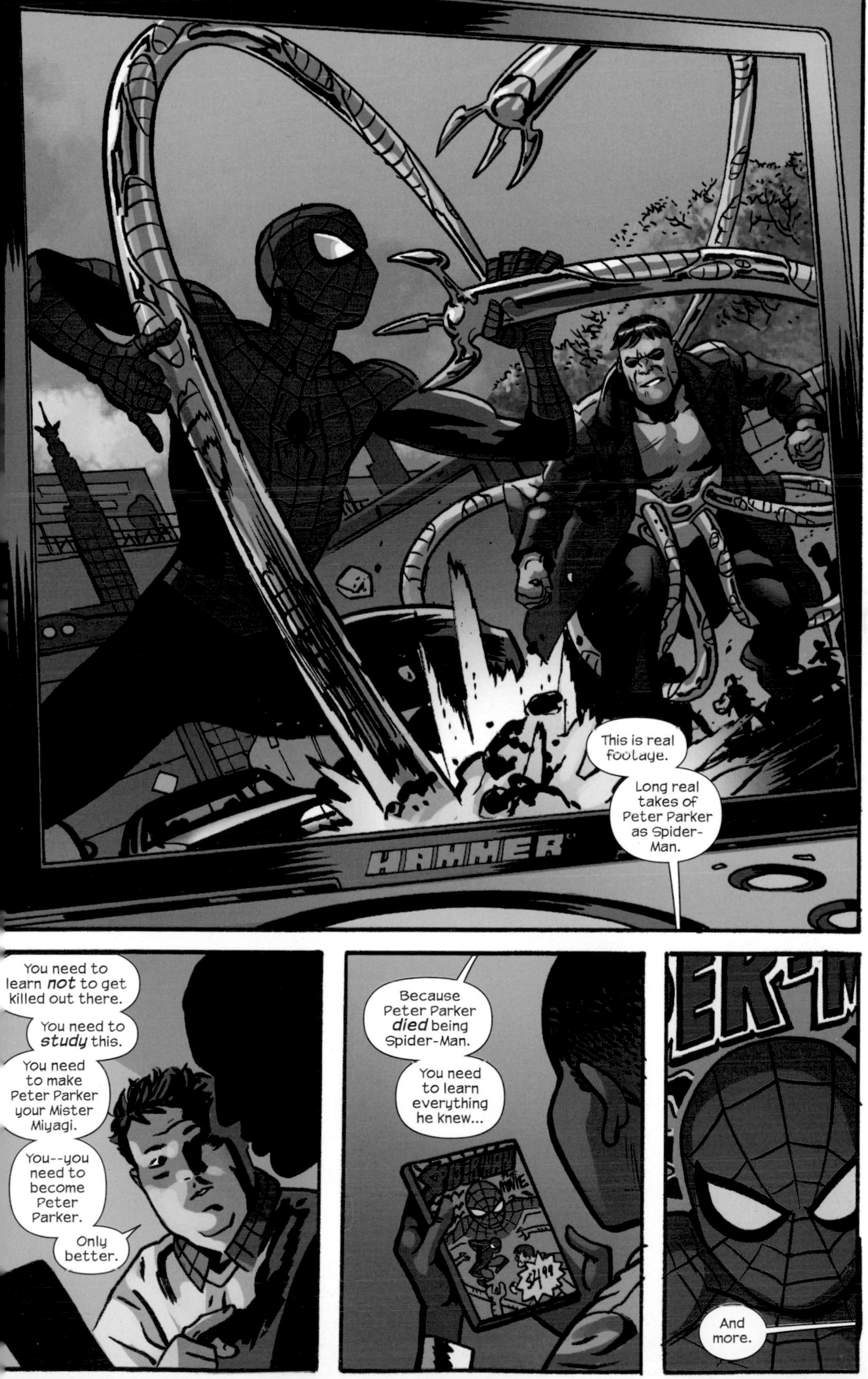
HAMMER
This is real footage.
Long real takes of Peter Parker as Spider-Man.
You need to learn *not* to get killed out there.
You need to *study* this.
You need to make Peter Parker your Mister Miyagi.
You--you need to become Peter Parker.
Only better.
Because Peter Parker *died* being Spider-Man.
You need to learn everything he knew...
And more.

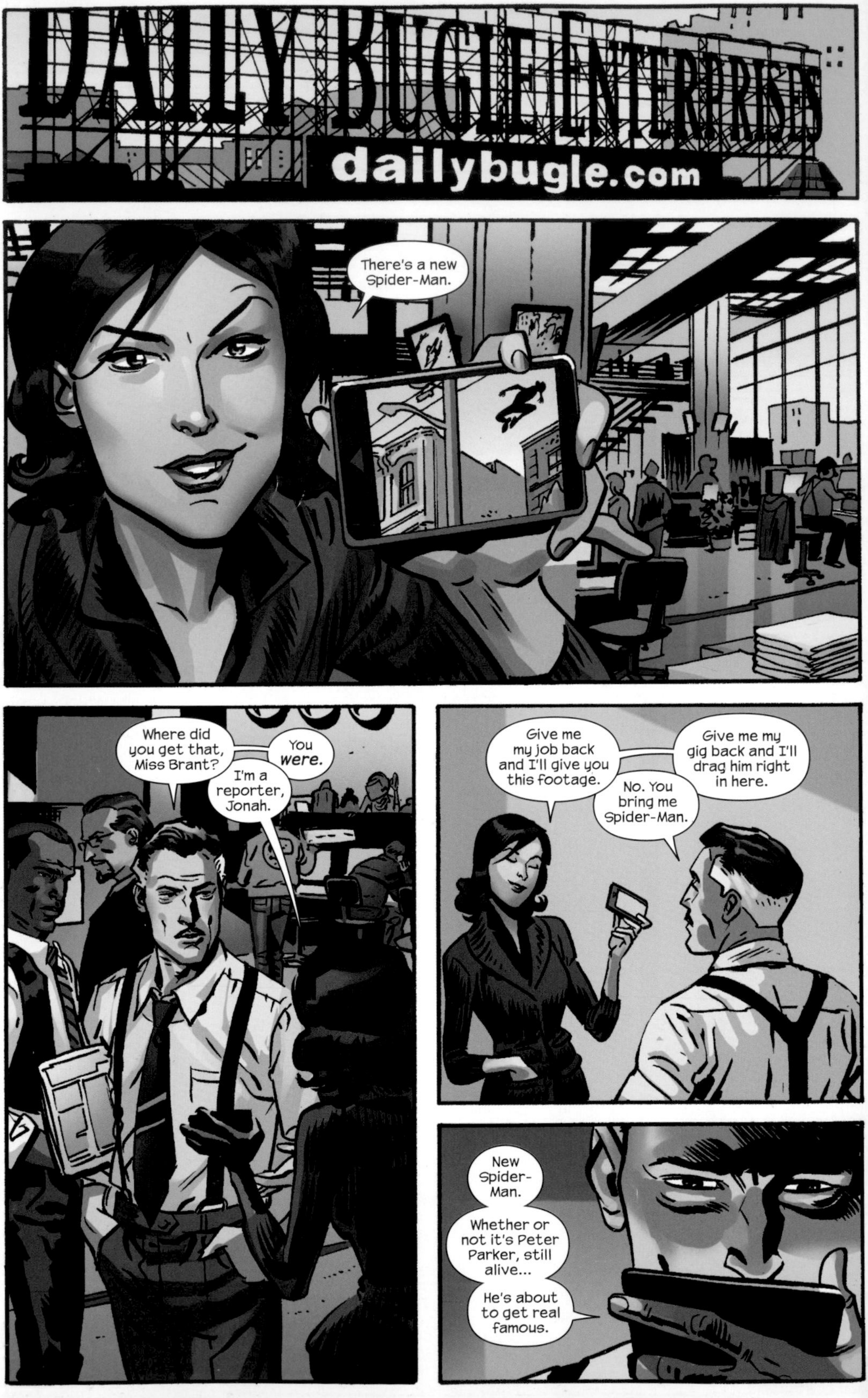

DAILY BUGLE ENTERPRISES
dailybugle.com
There's a new Spider-Man.
Where did you get that, Miss Brant?
You were.
I'm a reporter, Jonah.
Give me my job back and I'll give you this footage.
Give me my gig back and I'll drag him right in here.
No. You bring me Spider-Man.
New Spider-Man.
Whether or not it's Peter Parker, still alive...
He's about to get real famous.

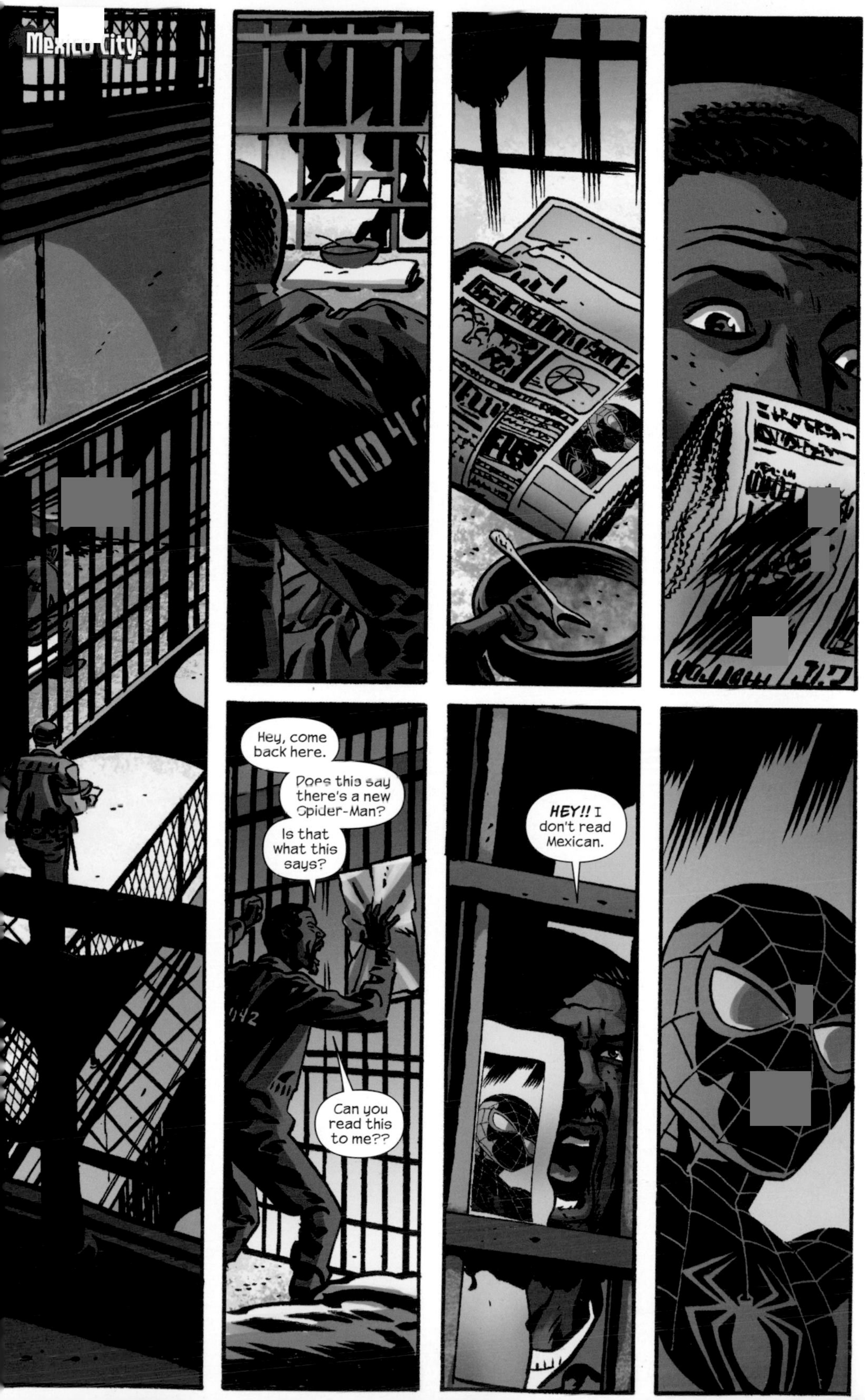
Mexico City.
Hey, come back here.
Does this say there's a new Spider-Man?
Is that what this says?
Can you read this to me??
HEY!! I don't read Mexican.

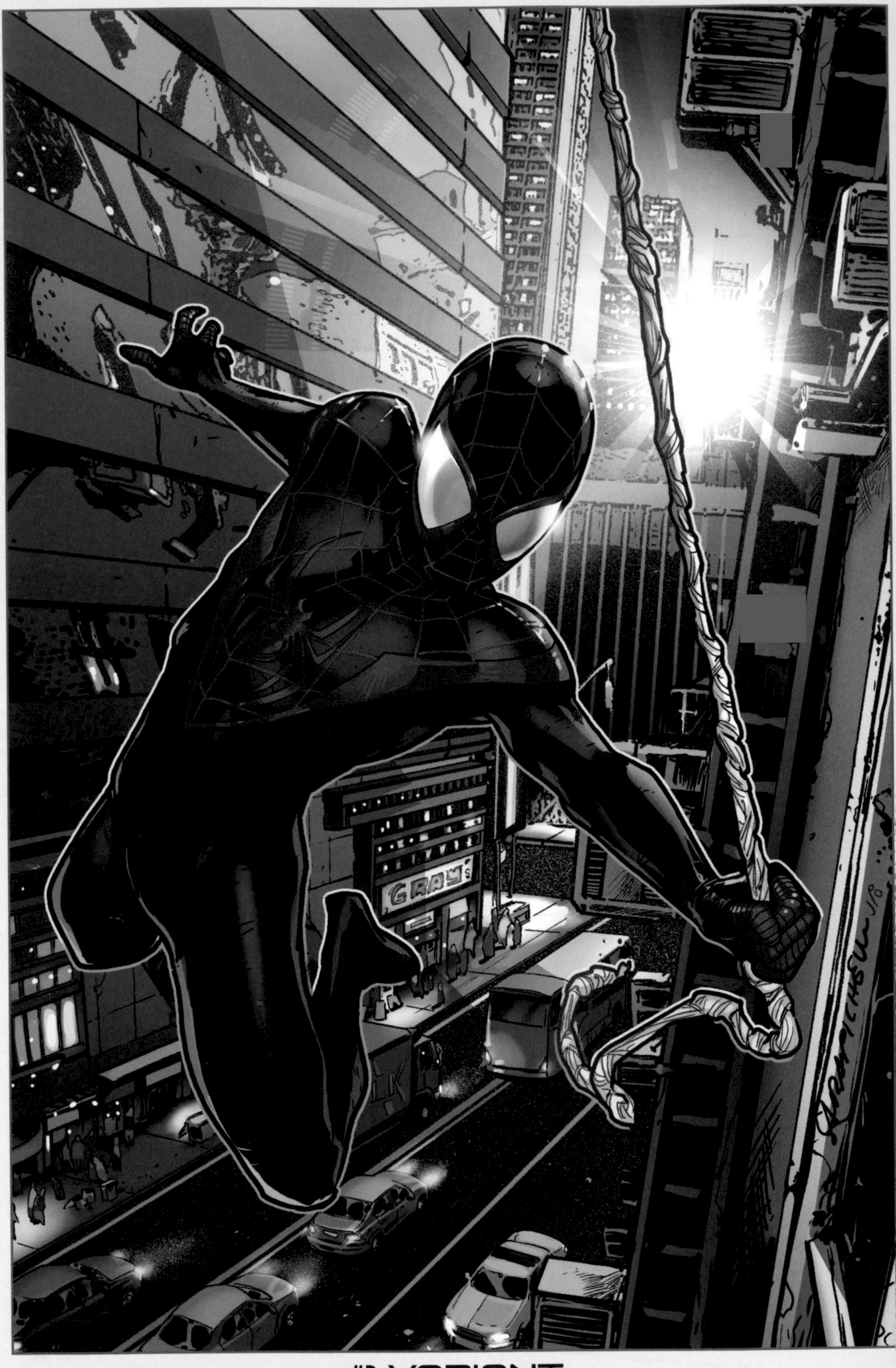
GRAY'S

#1 VARIANT
BY SARA PICHELLI & JUSTIN PONSOR

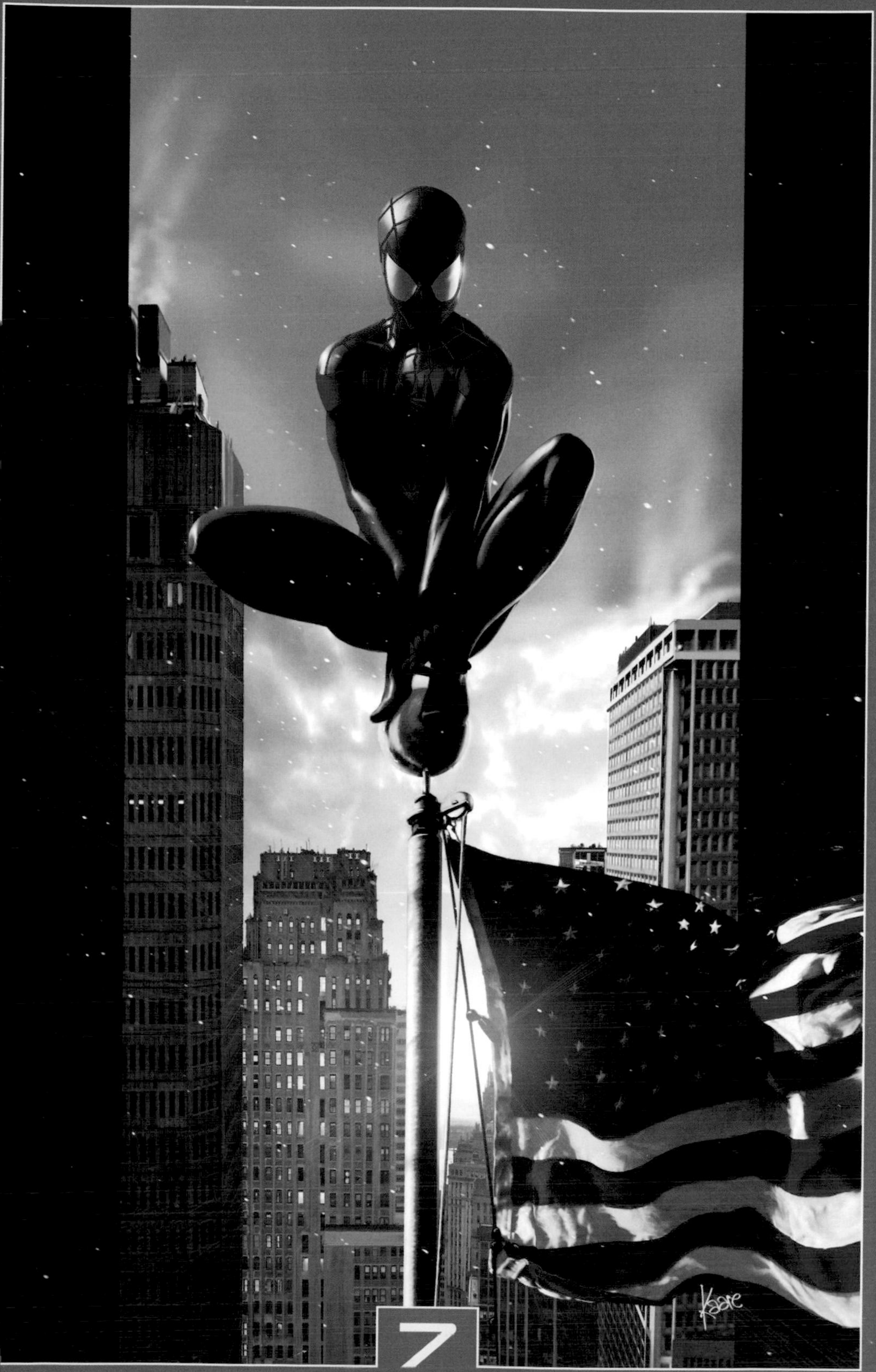
7

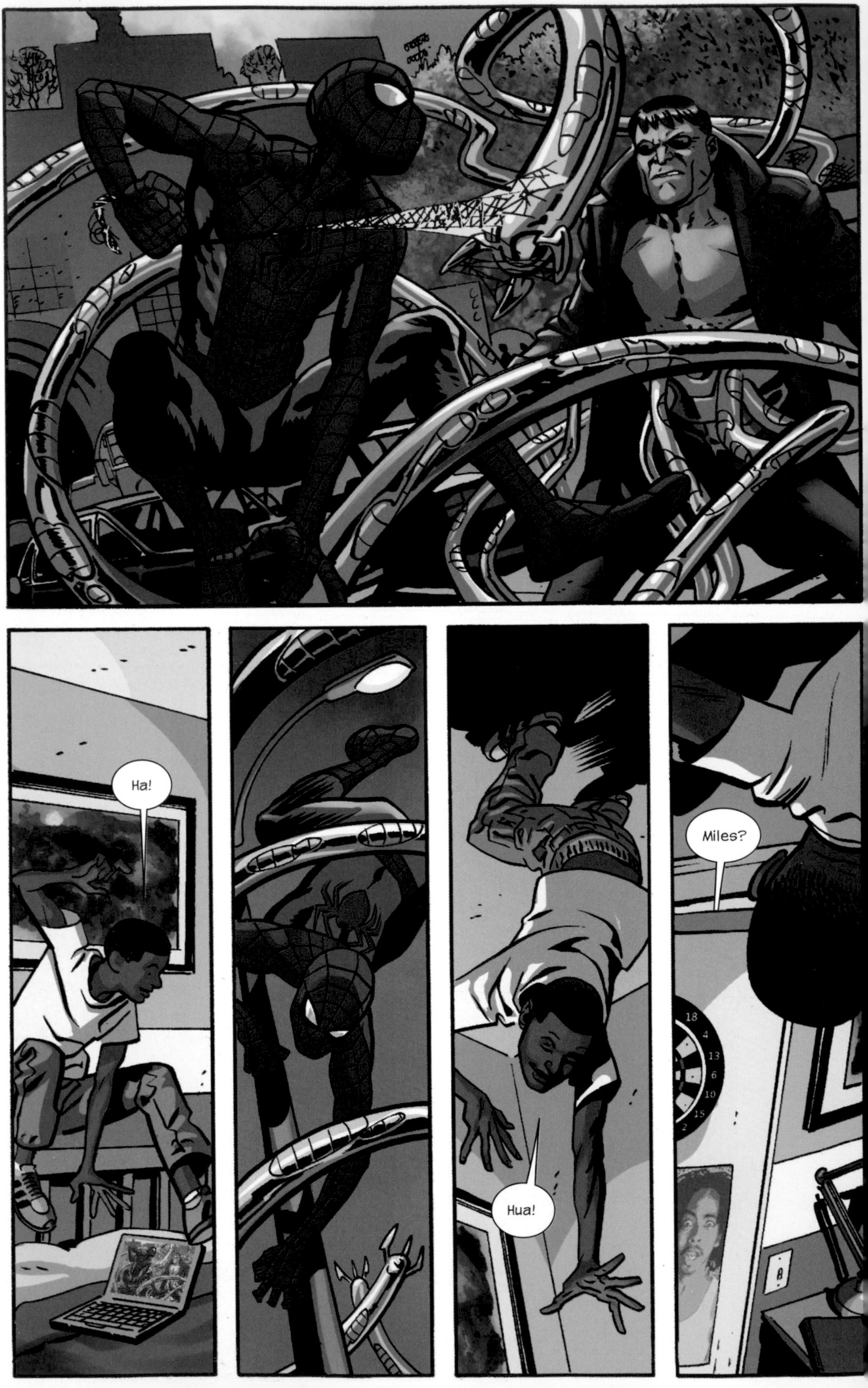
Ha!
Hua!
Miles?

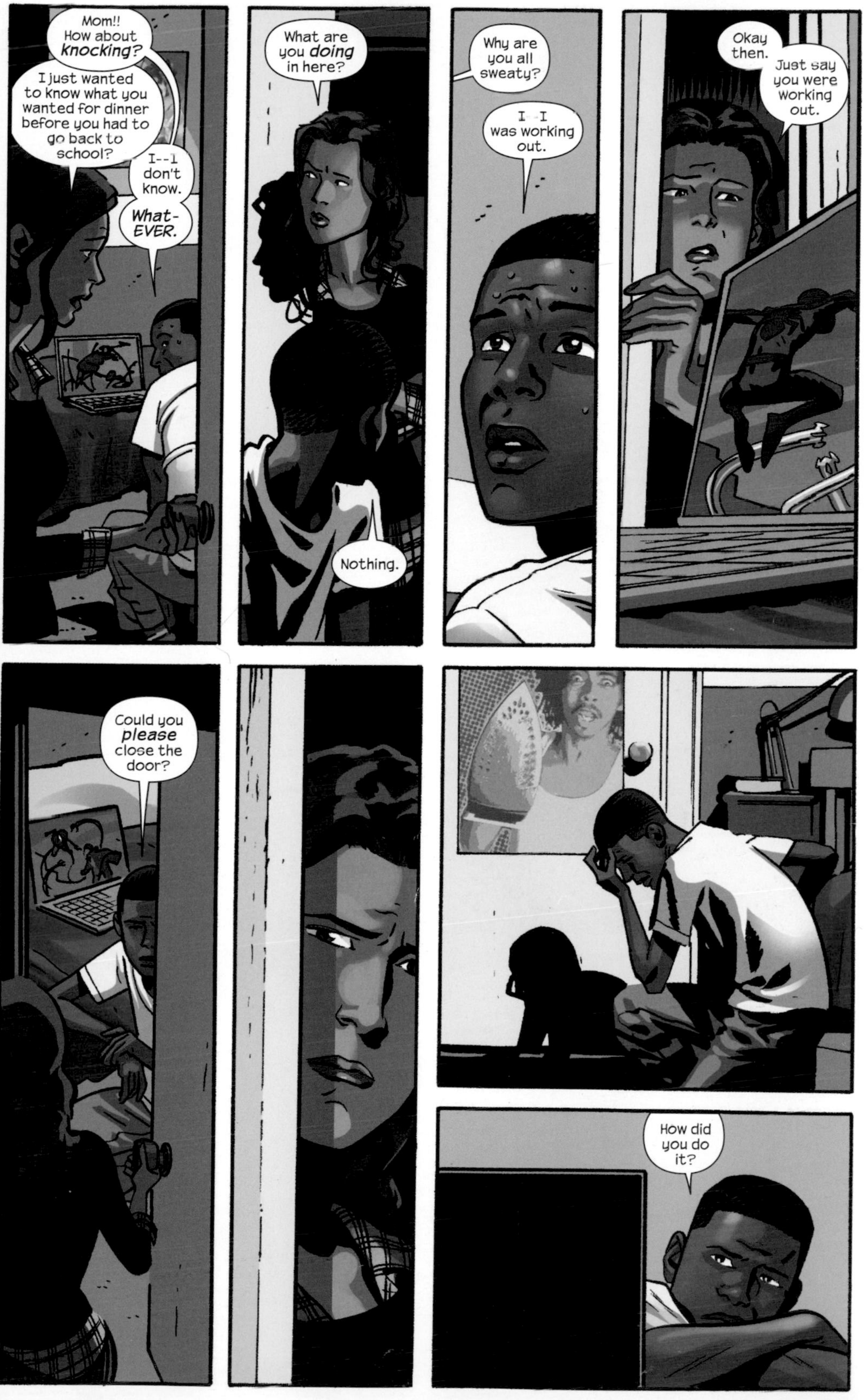
Mom!! How about *knocking*?
I just wanted to know what you wanted for dinner before you had to go back to school?
I--I don't know.
What-EVER.
What are you *doing* in here?
Nothing.
Why are you all sweaty?
I--I was working out.
Okay then.
Just say you were working out.
Could you *please* close the door?
How did you do it?

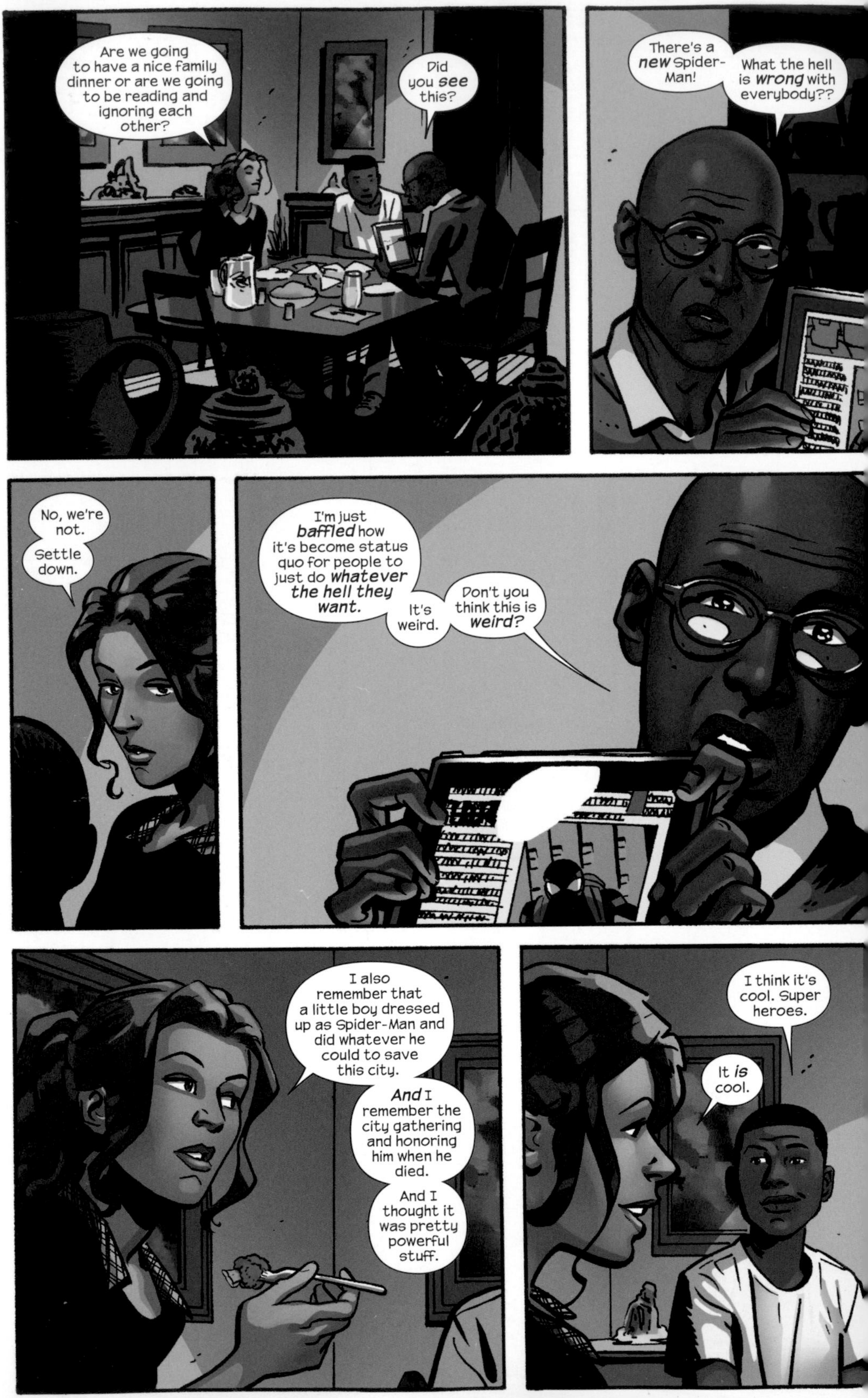

Are we going to have a nice family dinner or are we going to be reading and ignoring each other?
Did you see this?
There's a new Spider-Man!
What the hell is wrong with everybody??
No, we're not.
Settle down.
I'm just baffled how it's become status quo for people to just do whatever the hell they want.
It's weird.
Don't you think this is weird?
I also remember that a little boy dressed up as Spider-Man and did whatever he could to save this city.
And I remember the city gathering and honoring him when he died.
And I thought it was pretty powerful stuff.
I think it's cool. Super heroes.
It is cool.

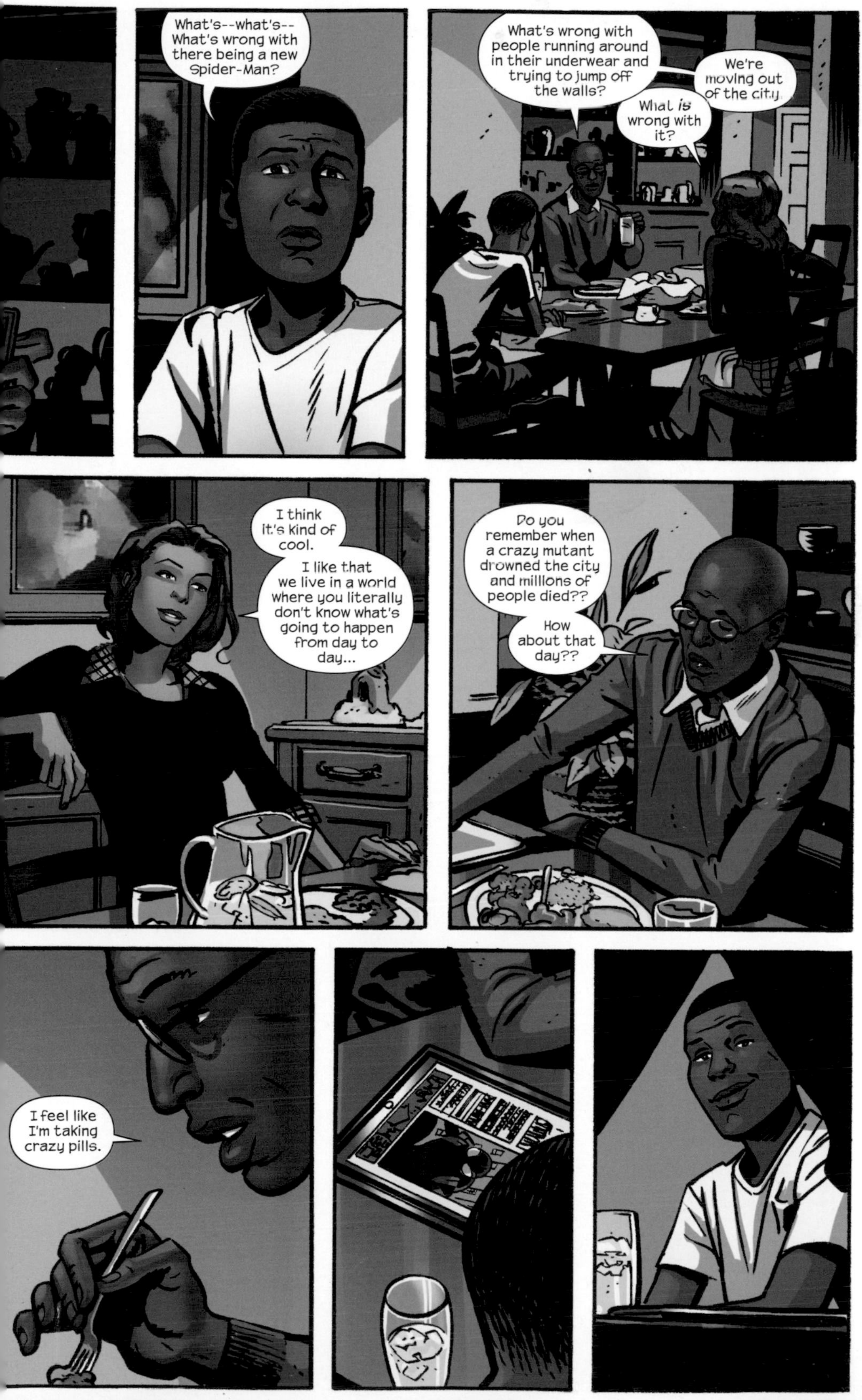

What's--what's--What's wrong with there being a new Spider-Man?
What's wrong with people running around in their underwear and trying to jump off the walls?
What *is* wrong with it?
We're moving out of the city.
I think it's kind of cool.
I like that we live in a world where you literally don't know what's going to happen from day to day...
Do you remember when a crazy mutant drowned the city and millions of people died??
How about that day??
I feel like I'm taking crazy pills.

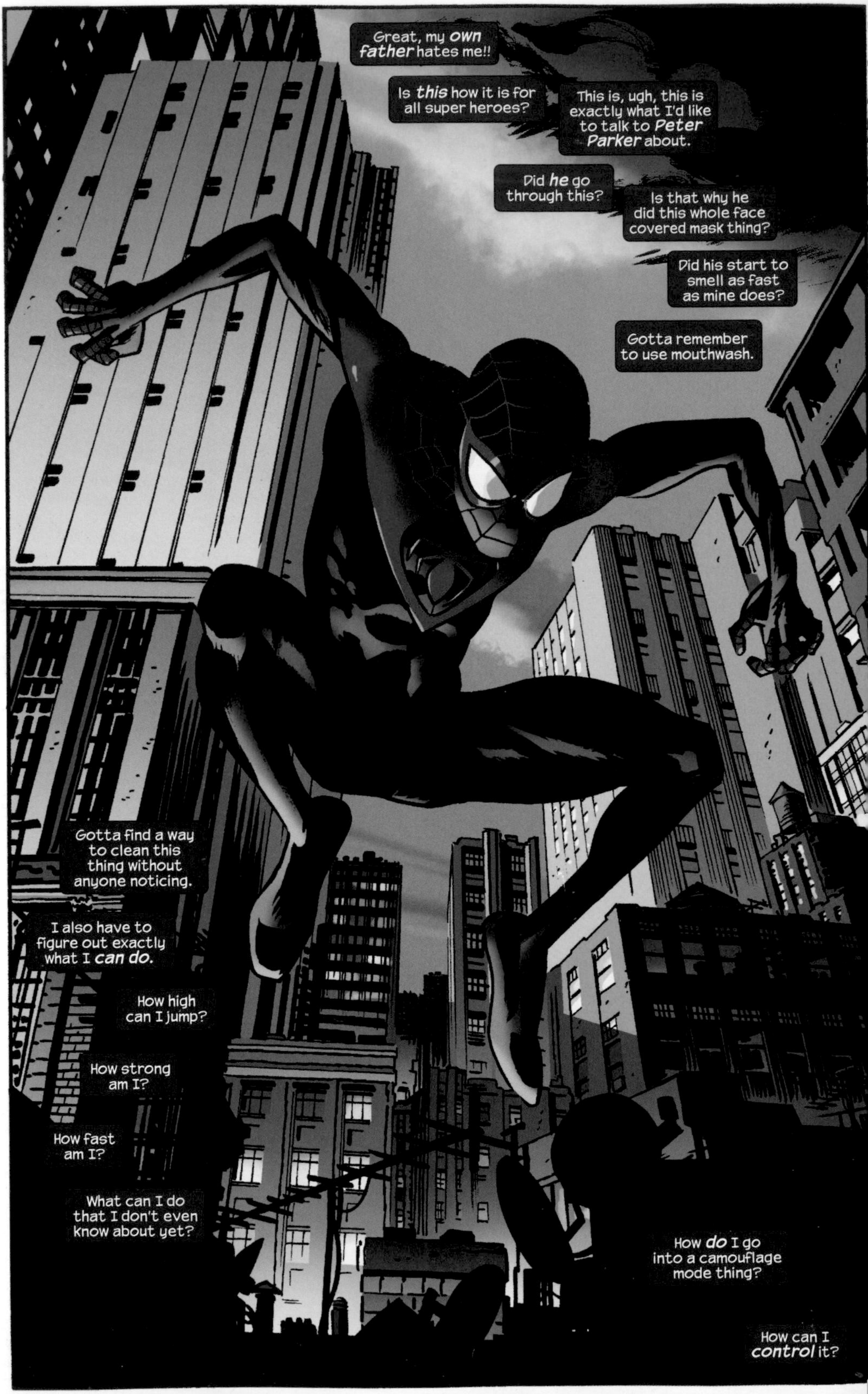
Great, my own father hates me!!
Is this how it is for all super heroes?
This is, ugh, this is exactly what I'd like to talk to Peter Parker about.
Did he go through this?
Is that why he did this whole face covered mask thing?
Did his start to smell as fast as mine does?
Gotta remember to use mouthwash.
Gotta find a way to clean this thing without anyone noticing.
I also have to figure out exactly what I can do.
How high can I jump?
How strong am I?
How fast am I?
What can I do that I don't even know about yet?
How do I go into a camouflage mode thing?
How can I control it?

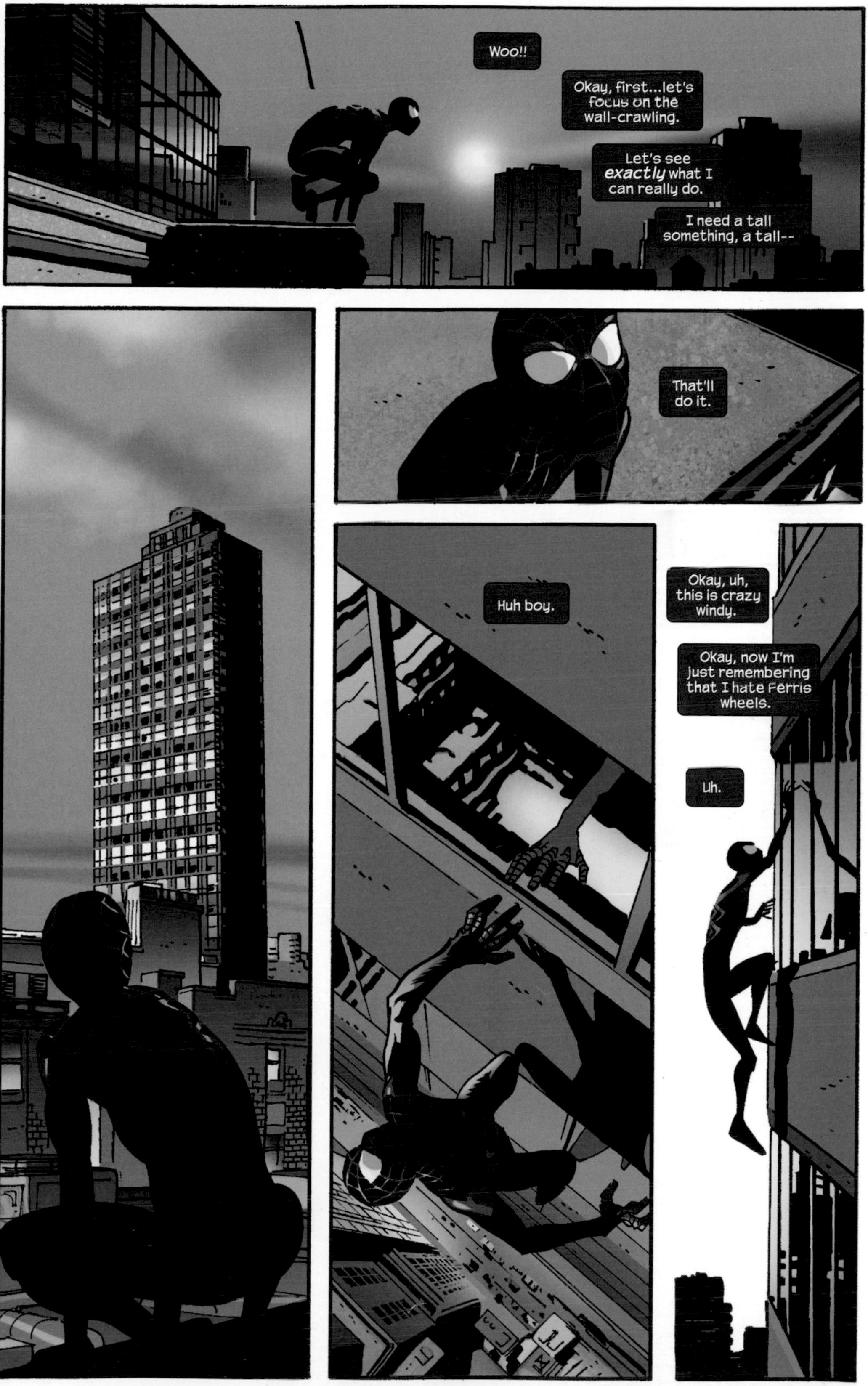
Woo!!
Okay, first...let's focus on the wall-crawling.
Let's see exactly what I can really do.
I need a tall something, a tall--
That'll do it.
Huh boy.
Okay, uh, this is crazy windy.
Okay, now I'm just remembering that I hate Ferris wheels.
Uh.

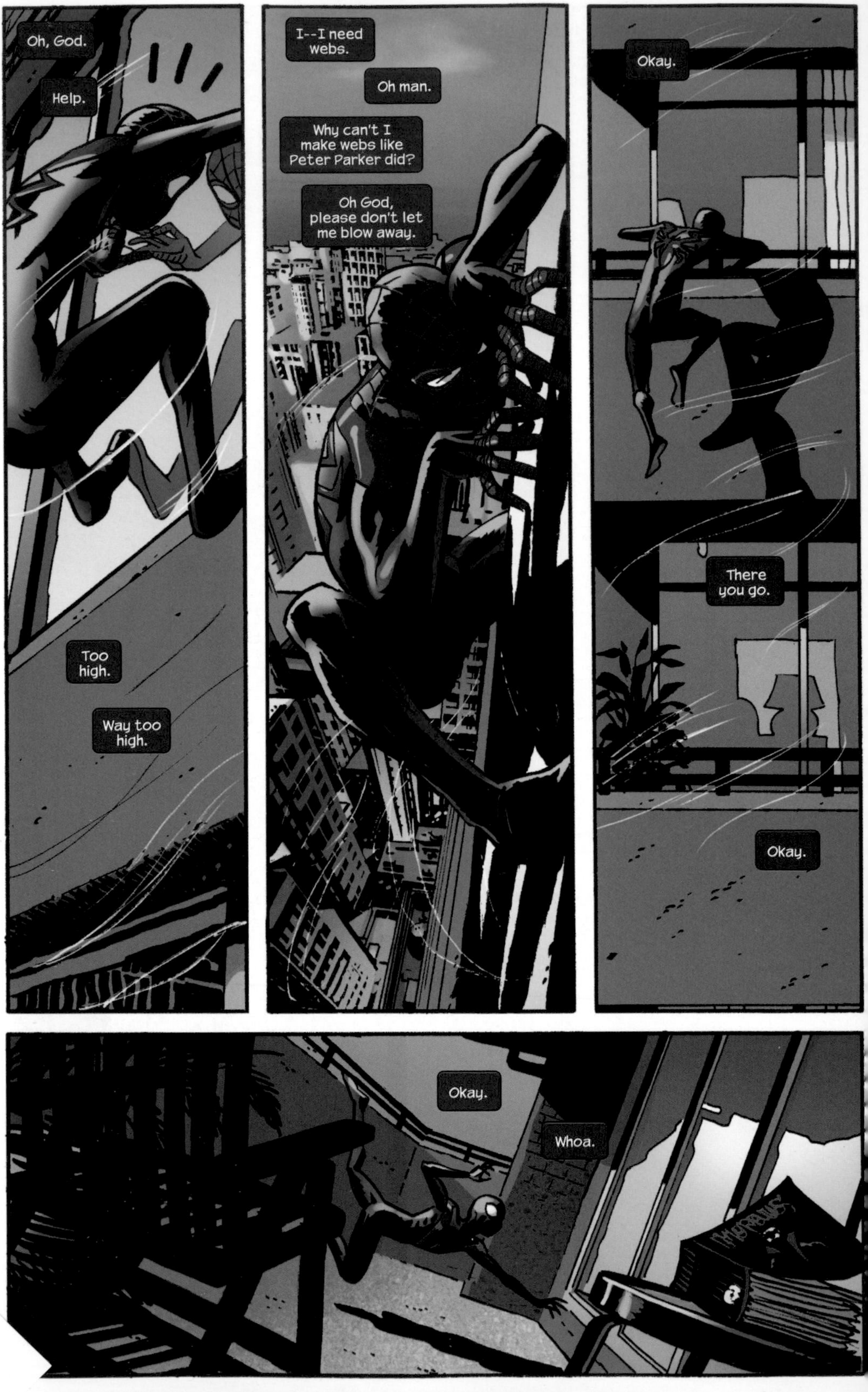
Oh, God.
Help.
Too high.
Way too high.
I--I need webs.
Oh man.
Why can't I make webs like Peter Parker did?
Oh God, please don't let me blow away.
Okay.
There you go.
Okay.
Okay.
Whoa.

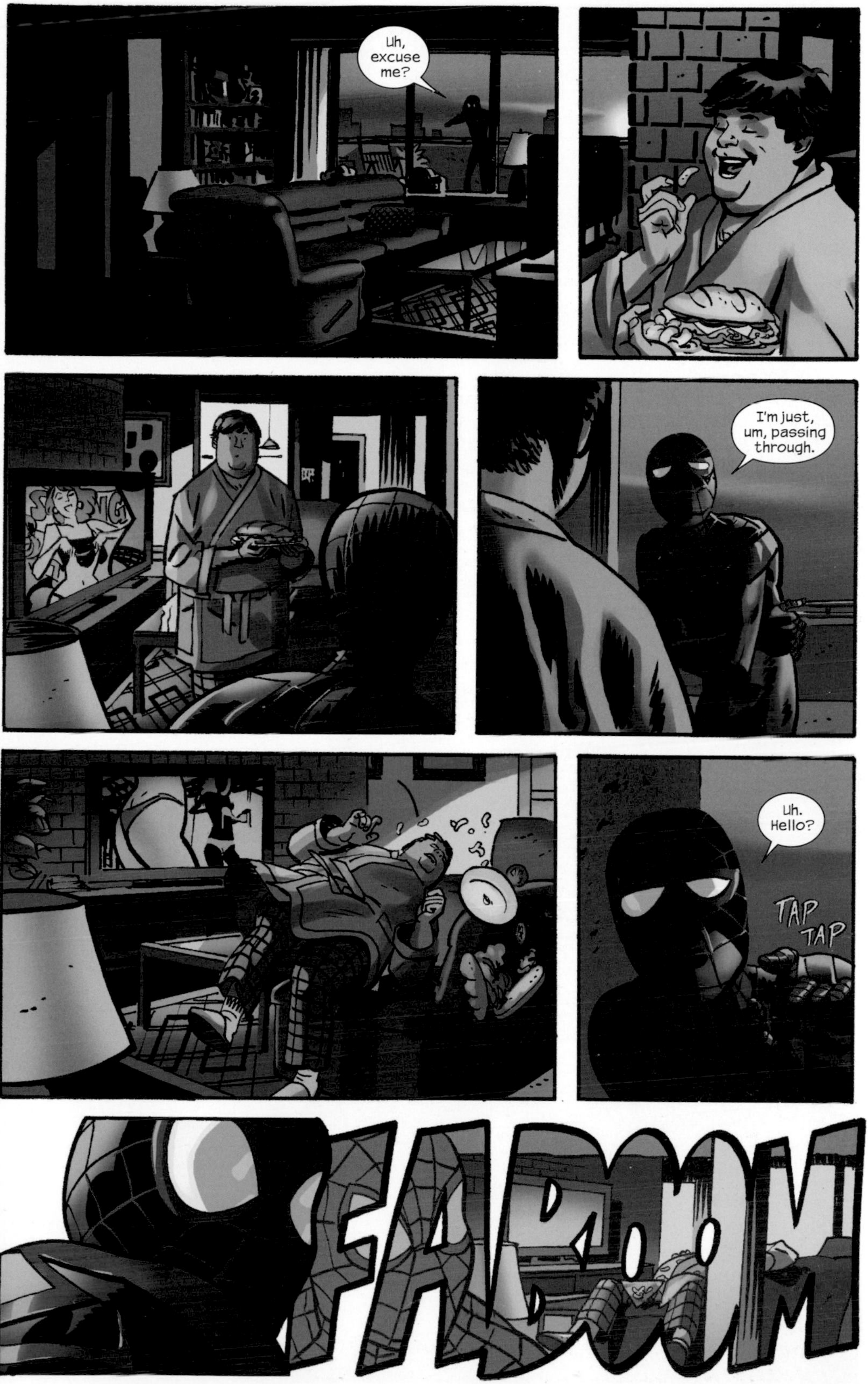
Uh, excuse me?
I'm just, um, passing through.
Uh. Hello?
TAP TAP
FADOOM

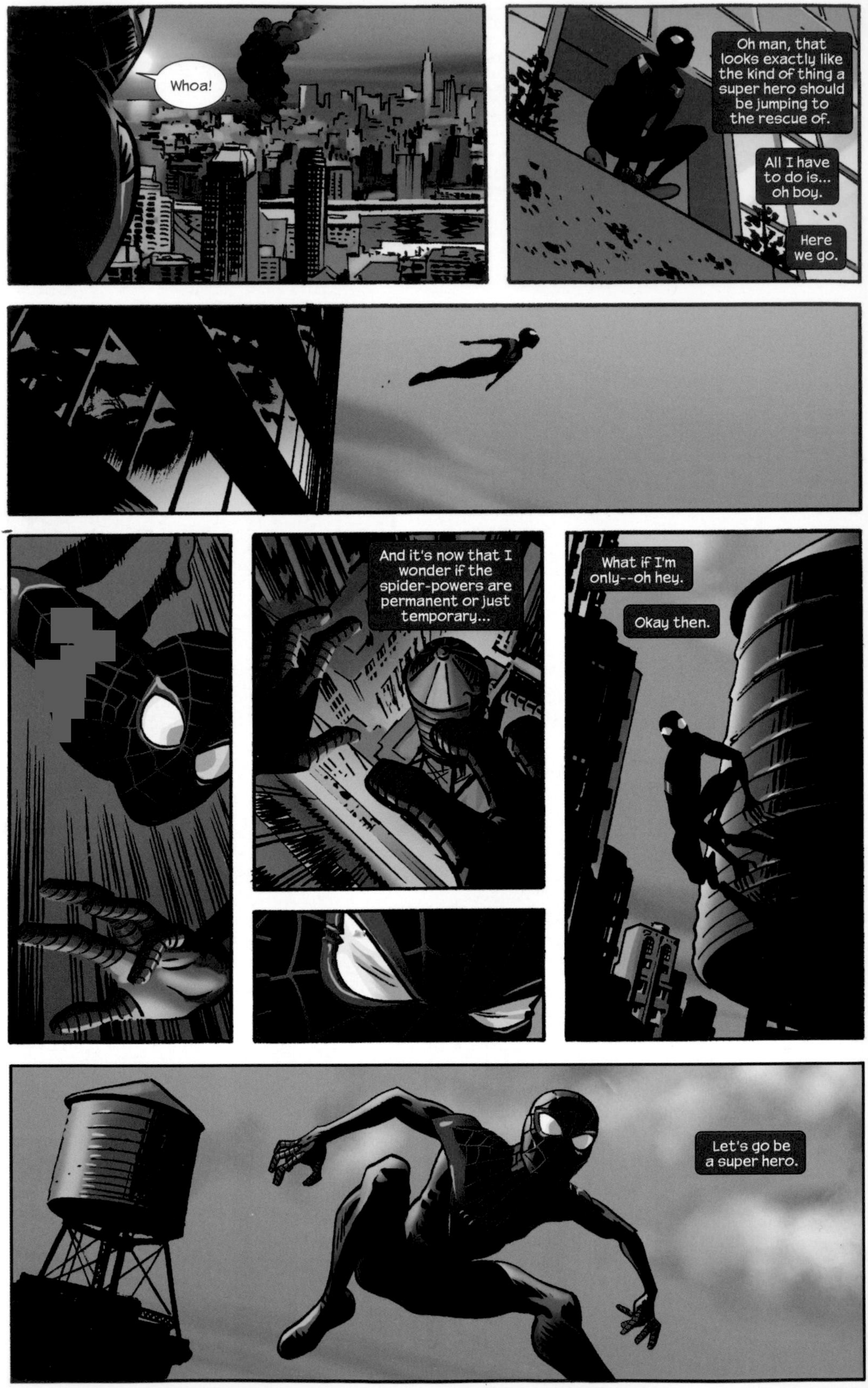
Whoa!
Oh man, that looks exactly like the kind of thing a super hero should be jumping to the rescue of.
All I have to do is... oh boy.
Here we go.
And it's now that I wonder if the spider-powers are permanent or just temporary...
What if I'm only--oh hey.
Okay then.
Let's go be a super hero.

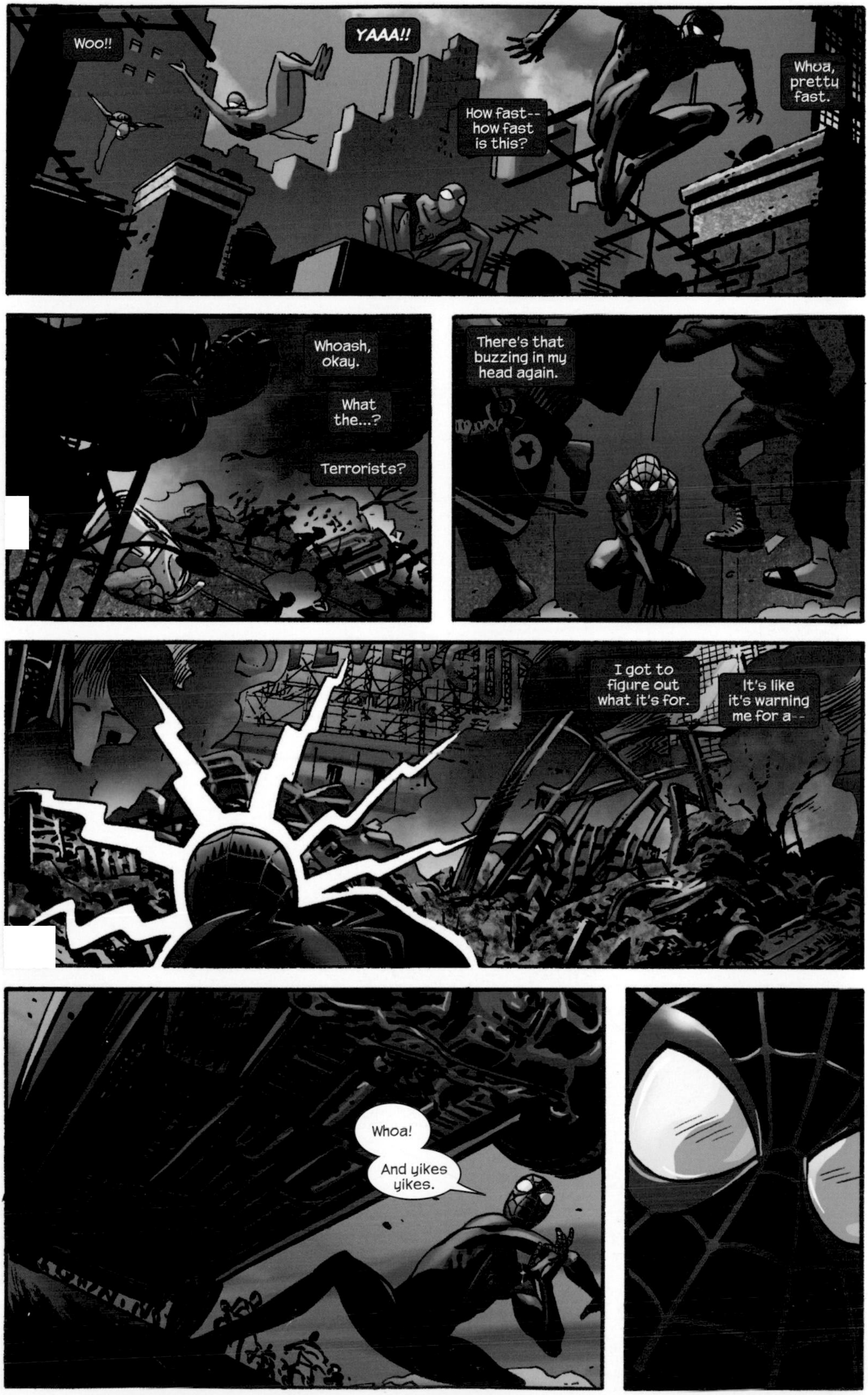
Woo!!
YAAA!!
How fast--how fast is this?
Whoa, pretty fast.
Whoash, okay.
What the...?
Terrorists?
There's that buzzing in my head again.
I got to figure out what it's for.
It's like it's warning me for a--
Whoa!
And yikes yikes.

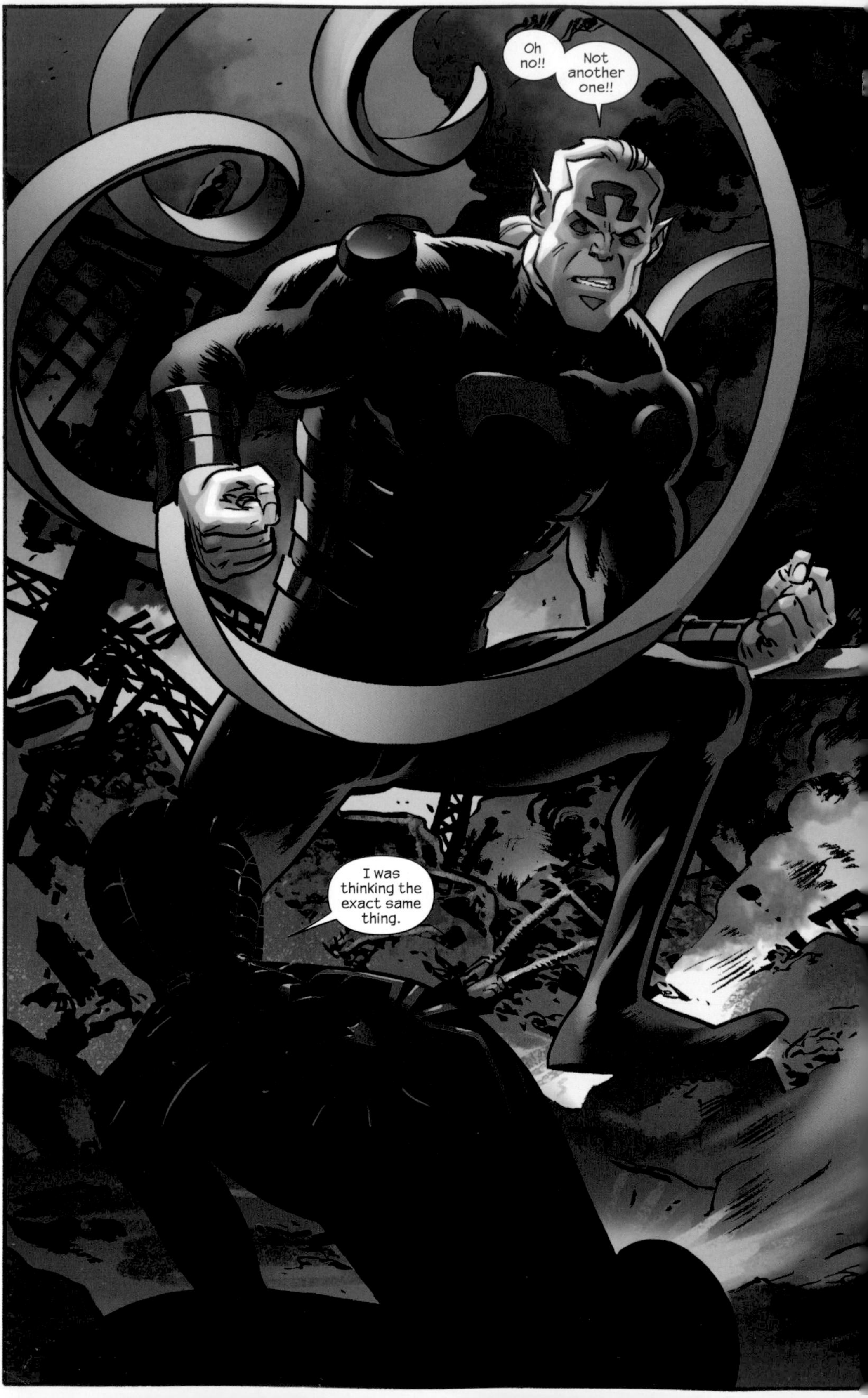

Oh no!!
Not another one!!
I was thinking the exact same thing.

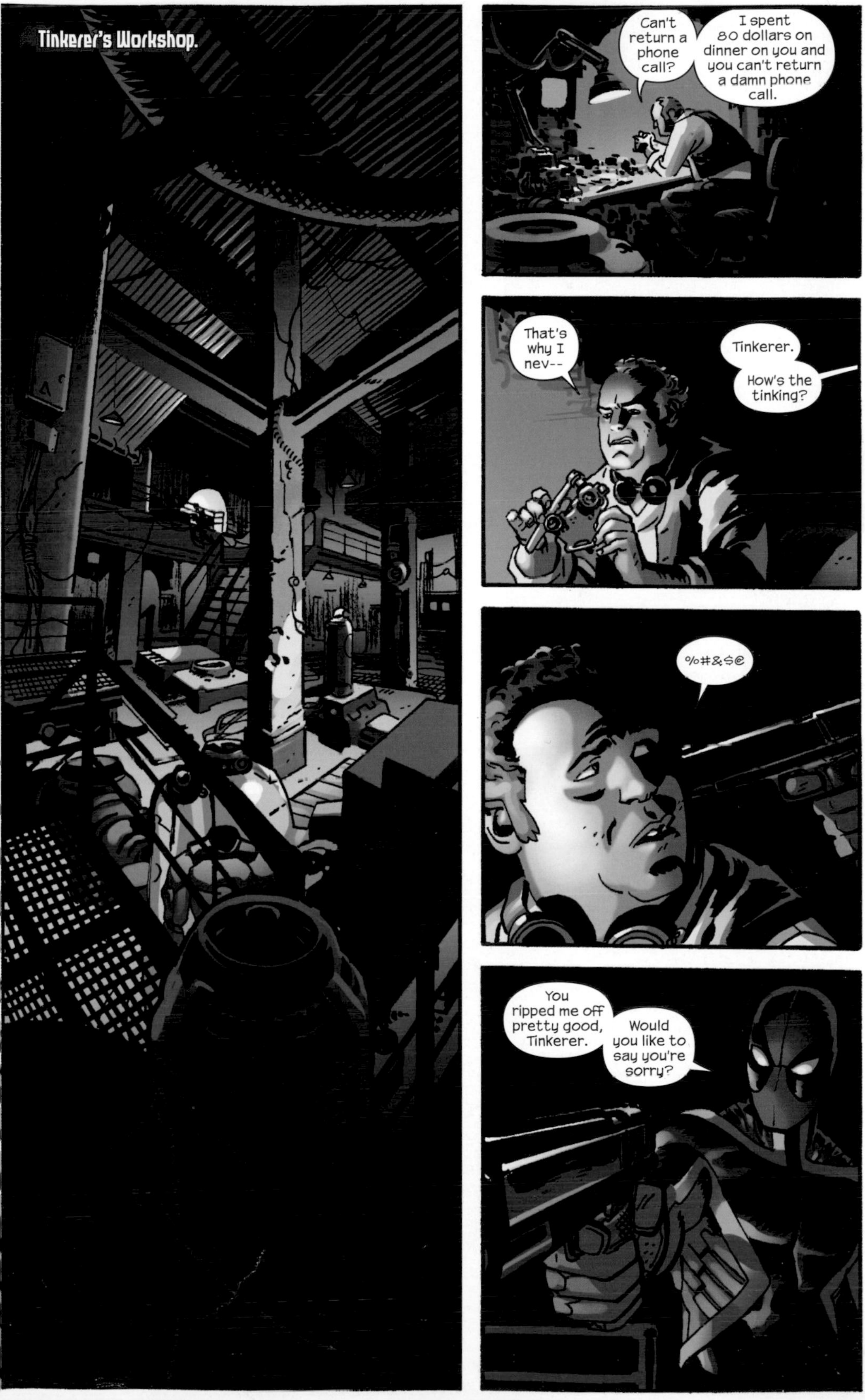
Tinkerer's Workshop.
Can't return a phone call?
I spent 80 dollars on dinner on you and you can't return a damn phone call.
That's why I nev--
Tinkerer.
How's the tinking?
%#&$@
You ripped me off pretty good, Tinkerer.
Would you like to say you're sorry?

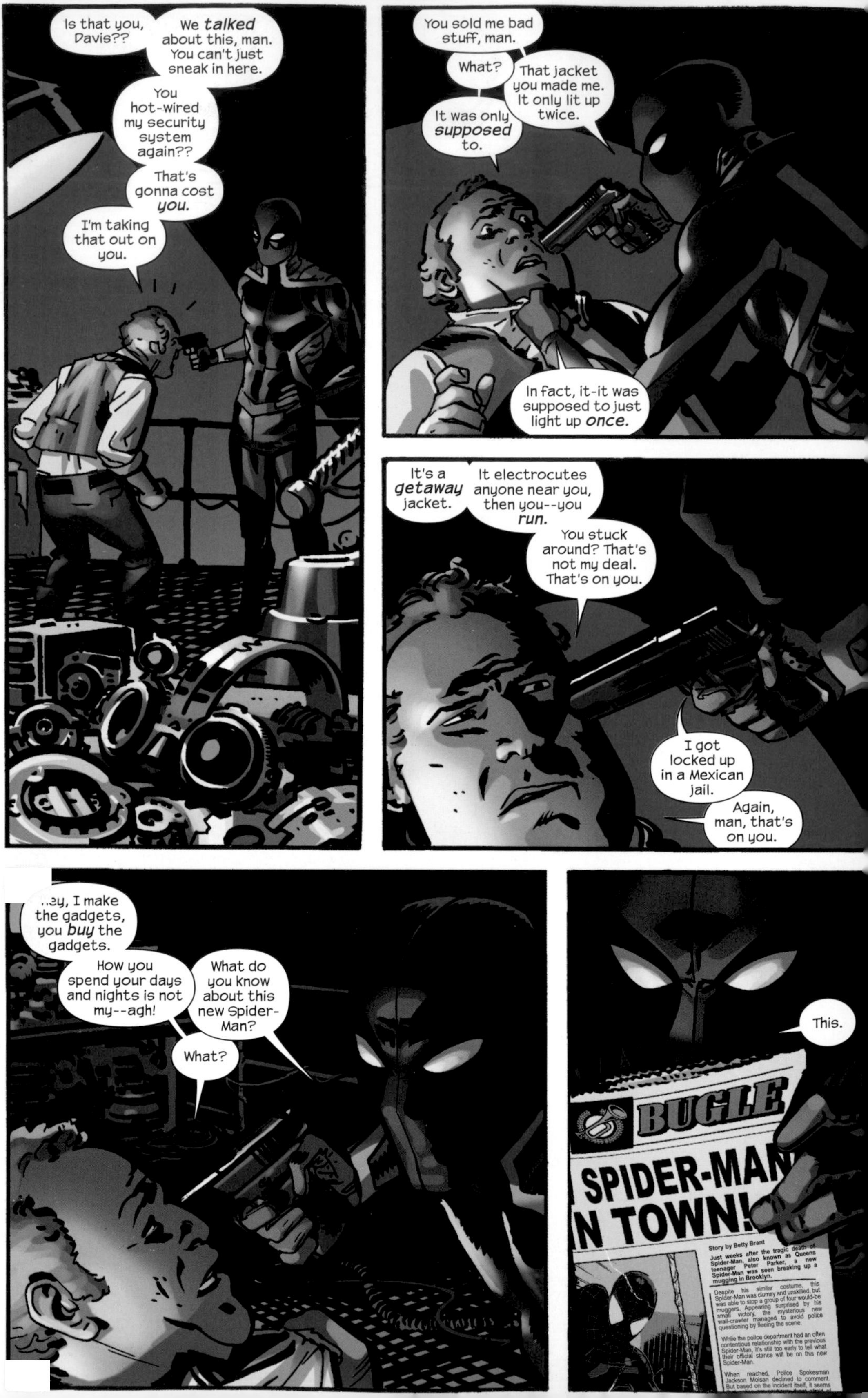

Is that you, Davis??
We talked about this, man. You can't just sneak in here.
You hot-wired my security system again??
That's gonna cost you.
I'm taking that out on you.
You sold me bad stuff, man.
What?
That jacket you made me. It only lit up twice.
It was only supposed to.
In fact, it-it was supposed to just light up once.
It's a getaway jacket.
It electrocutes anyone near you, then you--you run.
You stuck around? That's not my deal. That's on you.
I got locked up in a Mexican jail.
Again, man, that's on you.
ey, I make the gadgets, you buy the gadgets.
How you spend your days and nights is not my--agh!
What do you know about this new Spider-Man?
What?
This.
BUGLE
SPIDER-MAN
N TOWN!
Story by Betty Brant
Just weeks after the tragic death of Spider-Man, also known as Queens teenager Peter Parker, a new Spider-Man was seen breaking up a mugging in Brooklyn.
Despite his similar costume, this Spider-Man was clumsy and unskilled, but was able to stop a group of four would-be muggers. Appearing surprised by his small victory, the mysterious new wall-crawler managed to avoid police questioning by fleeing the scene.
While the police department had an often contentious relationship with the previous Spider-Man, it's still too early to tell what their official stance will be on this new Spider-Man.
When reached, Police Spokesman Jackson Moisan declined to comment. But based on the incident itself, it seems

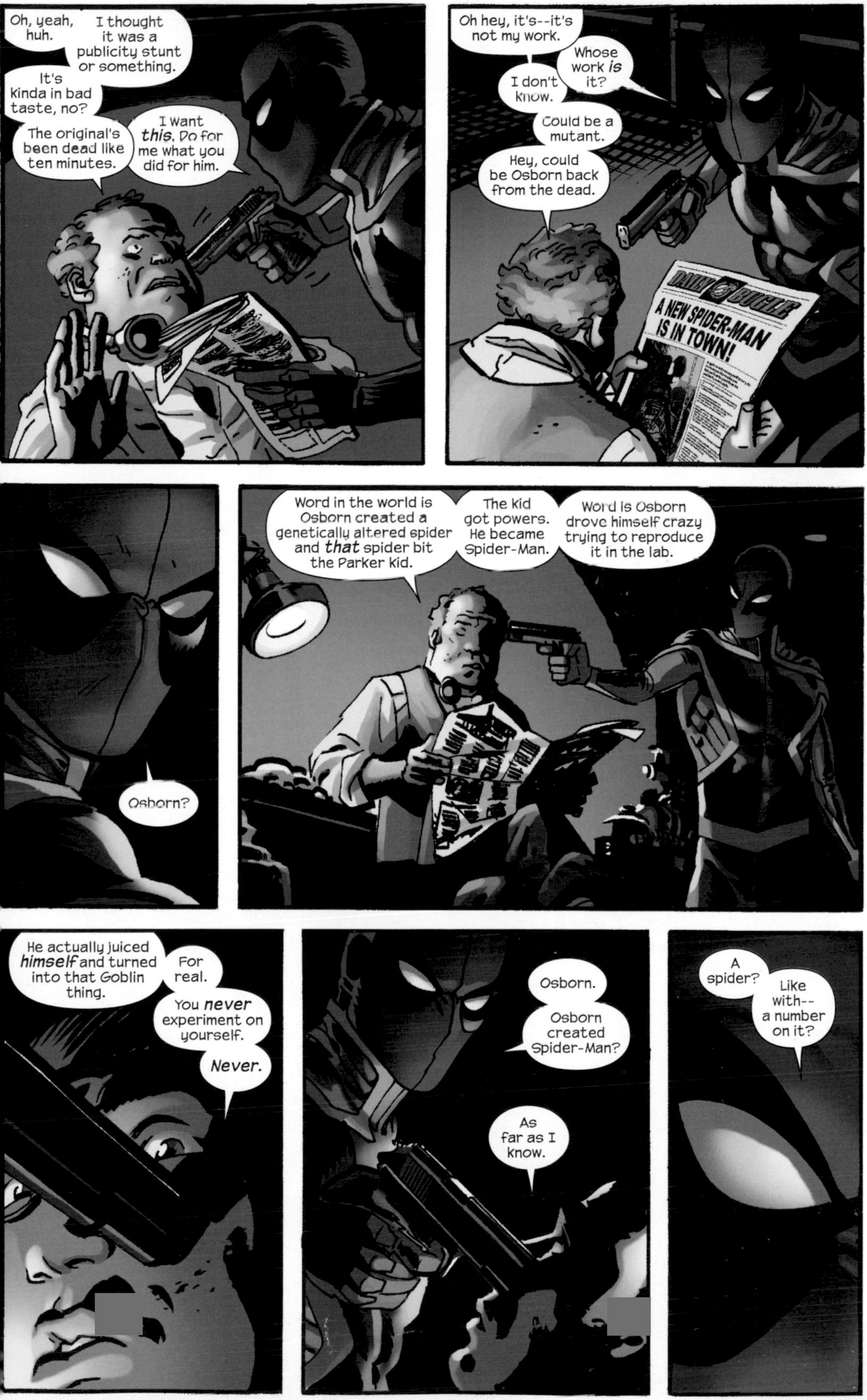
Oh, yeah, huh.
I thought it was a publicity stunt or something.
It's kinda in bad taste, no?
The original's been dead like ten minutes.
I want *this*. Do for me what you did for him.
Oh hey, it's--it's not my work.
Whose work *is* it?
I don't know.
Could be a mutant.
Hey, could be Osborn back from the dead.
DAILY BUGLE
A NEW SPIDER-MAN IS IN TOWN!
Osborn?
Word in the world is Osborn created a genetically altered spider and *that* spider bit the Parker kid.
The kid got powers. He became Spider-Man.
Word is Osborn drove himself crazy trying to reproduce it in the lab.
He actually juiced *himself* and turned into that Goblin thing.
For real.
You *never* experiment on yourself.
Never.
Osborn.
Osborn created Spider-Man?
As far as I know.
A spider?
Like with--a number on it?

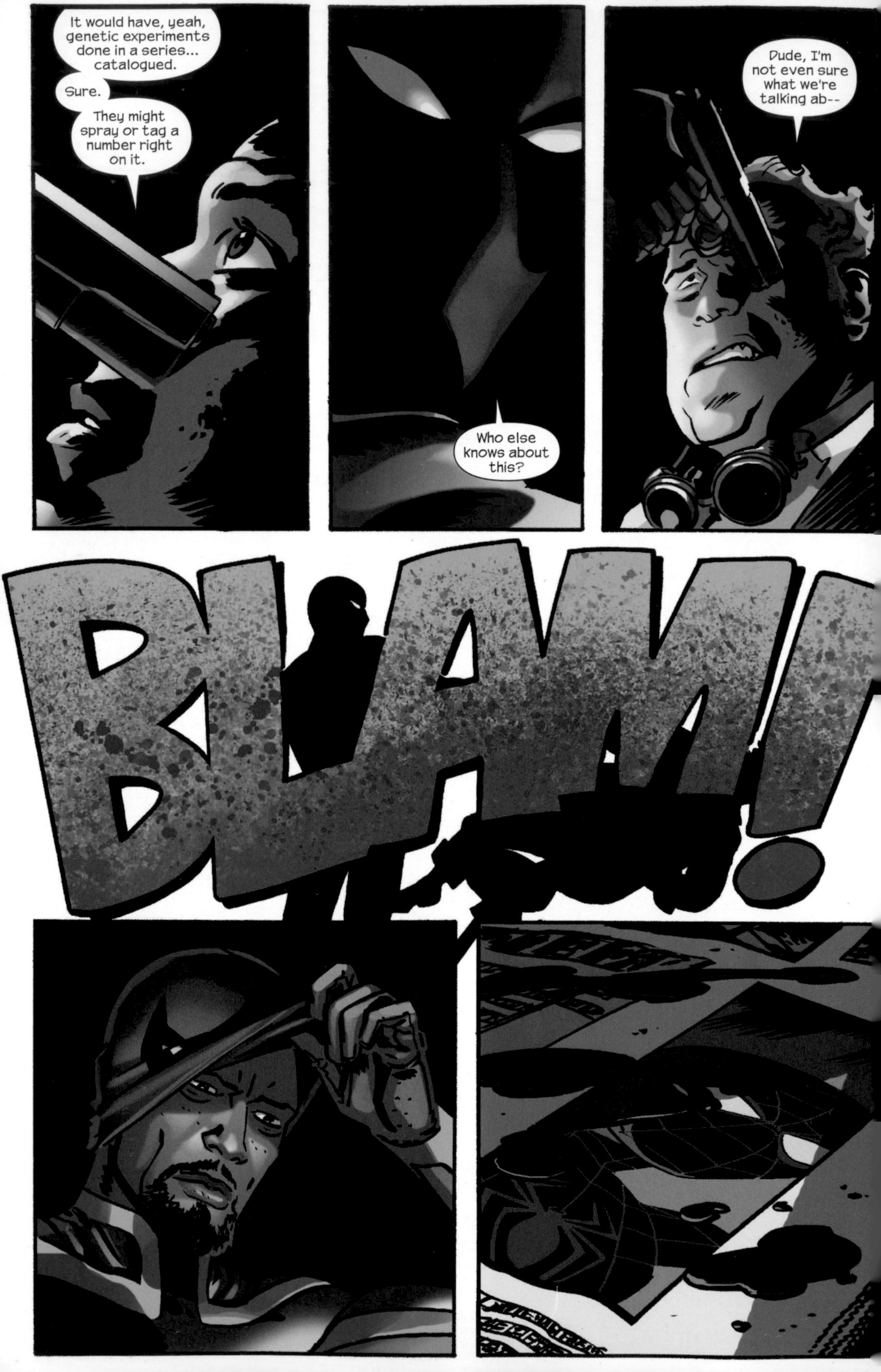
It would have, yeah, genetic experiments done in a series... catalogued.
Sure.
They might spray or tag a number right on it.
Who else knows about this?
Dude, I'm not even sure what we're talking ab--
BLAM!

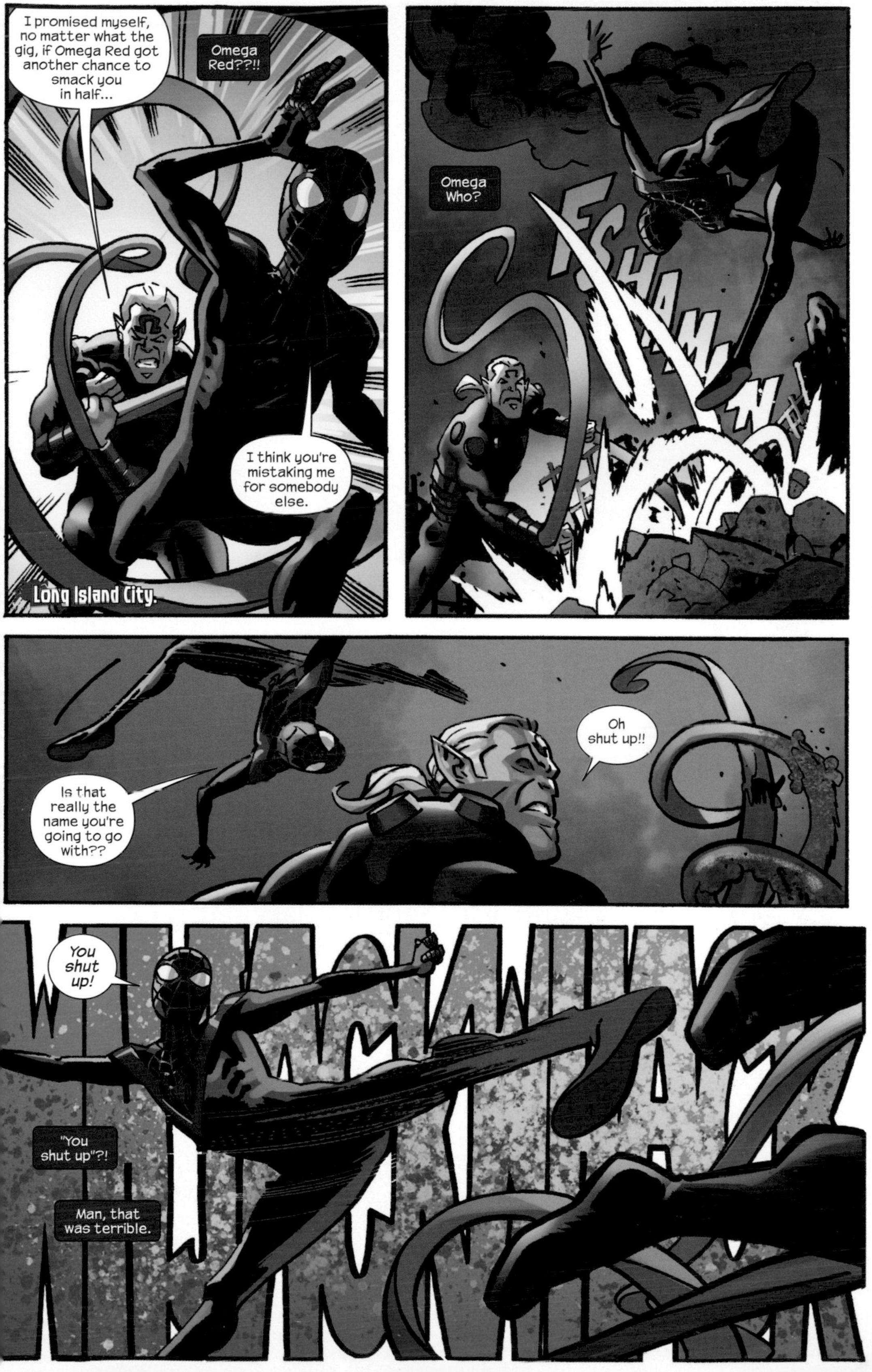
I promised myself, no matter what the gig, if Omega Red got another chance to smack you in half...
Omega Red??!!
I think you're mistaking me for somebody else.
Long Island City.
Omega Who?
FSHAMM!
Is that really the name you're going to go with??
Oh shut up!!
You shut up!
"You shut up"?!
Man, that was terrible.

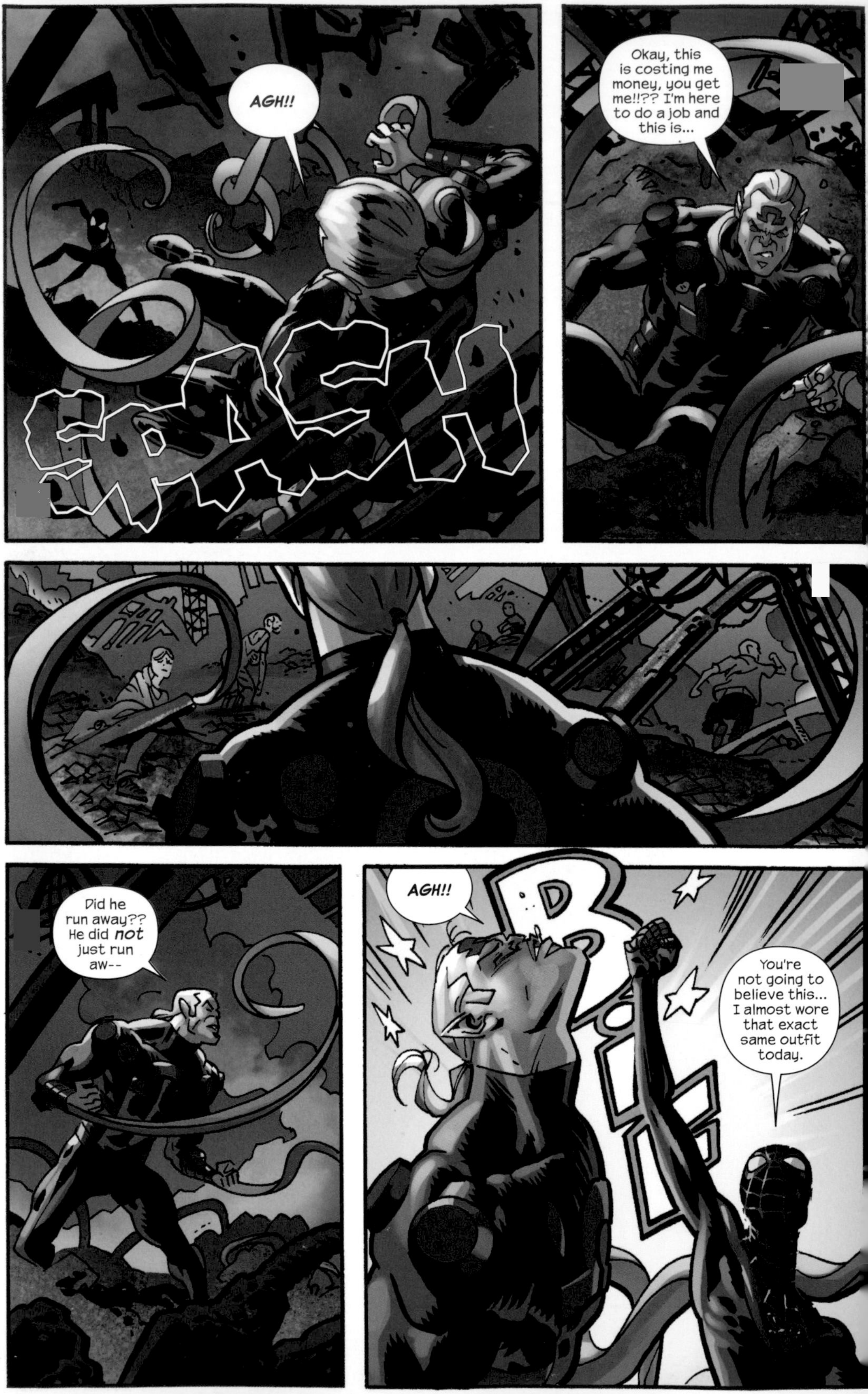
AGH!!
SPASH
Okay, this is costing me money, you get me!!?? I'm here to do a job and this is...
Did he run away?? He did *not* just run aw--
AGH!!
You're not going to believe this... I almost wore that exact same outfit today.

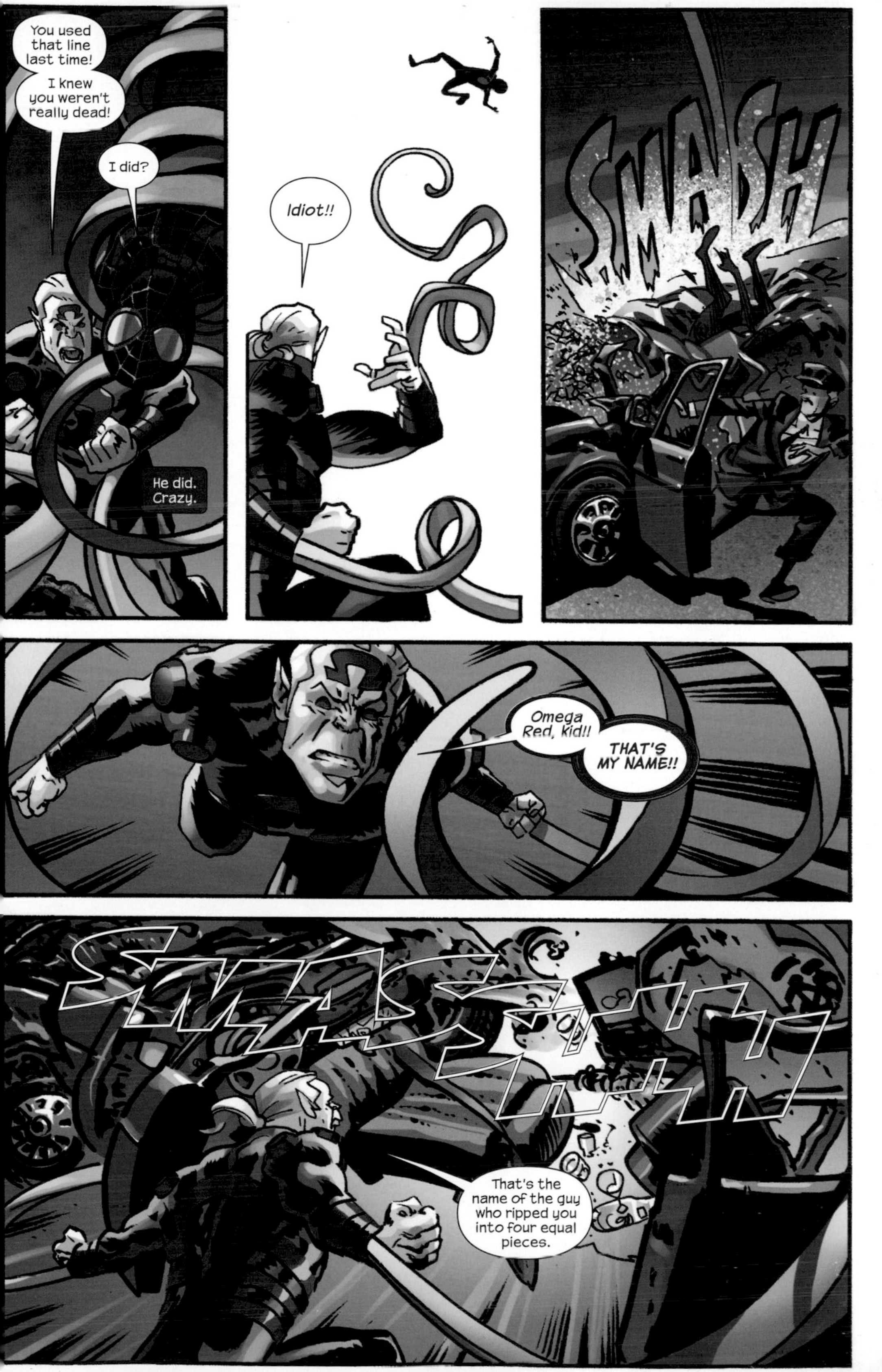

You used that line last time!
I knew you weren't really dead!
I did?
He did. Crazy.
Idiot!!
SMASH
Omega Red, kid!!
THAT'S MY NAME!!
SMASSHH
That's the name of the guy who ripped you into four equal pieces.

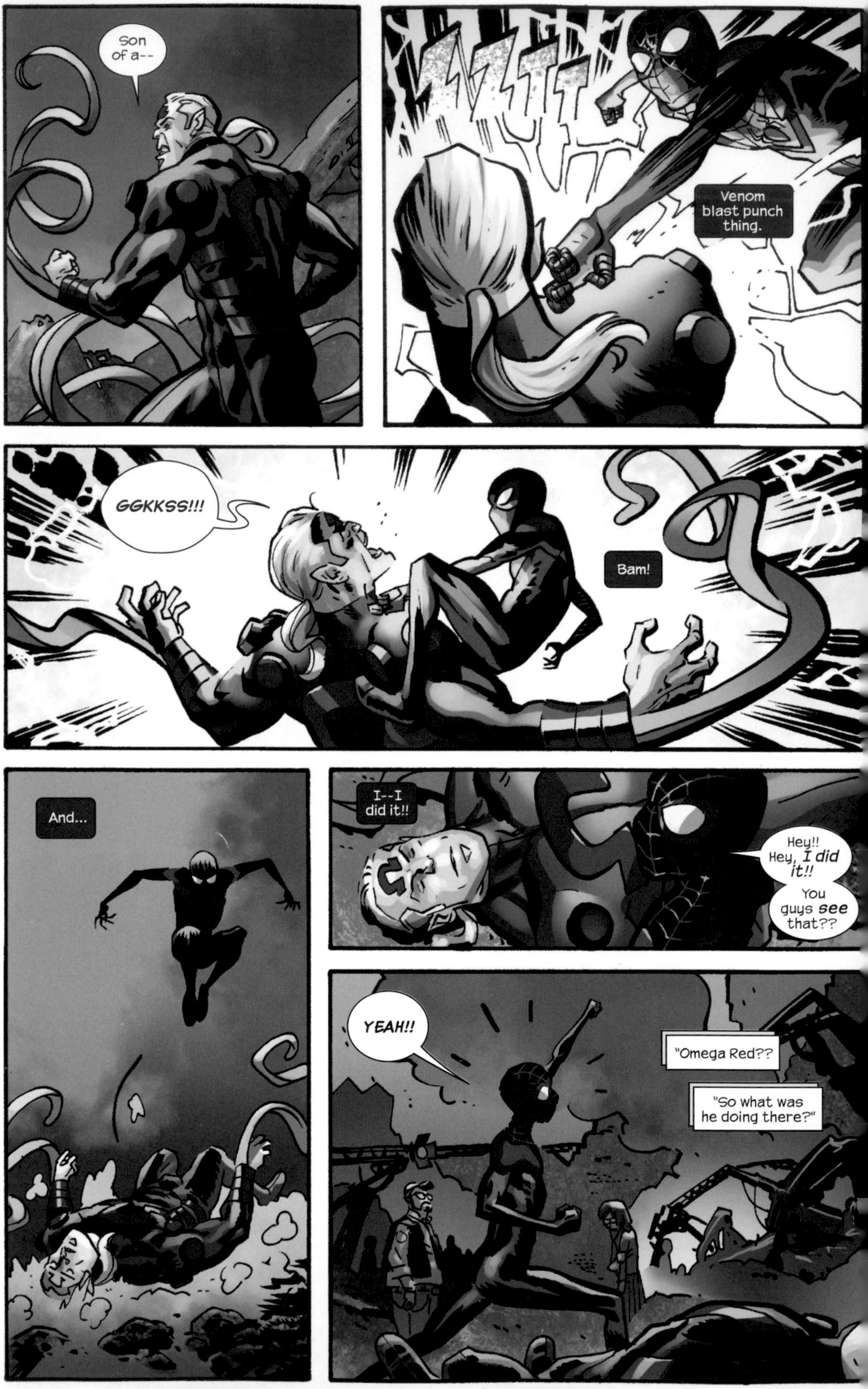
Son of a--
Venom blast punch thing.
GGKKSS!!!
Bam!
And...
I--I did it!!
Hey!! Hey, *I did it!!*
You guys *see* that??
YEAH!!
"Omega Red??
"So what was he doing there?"

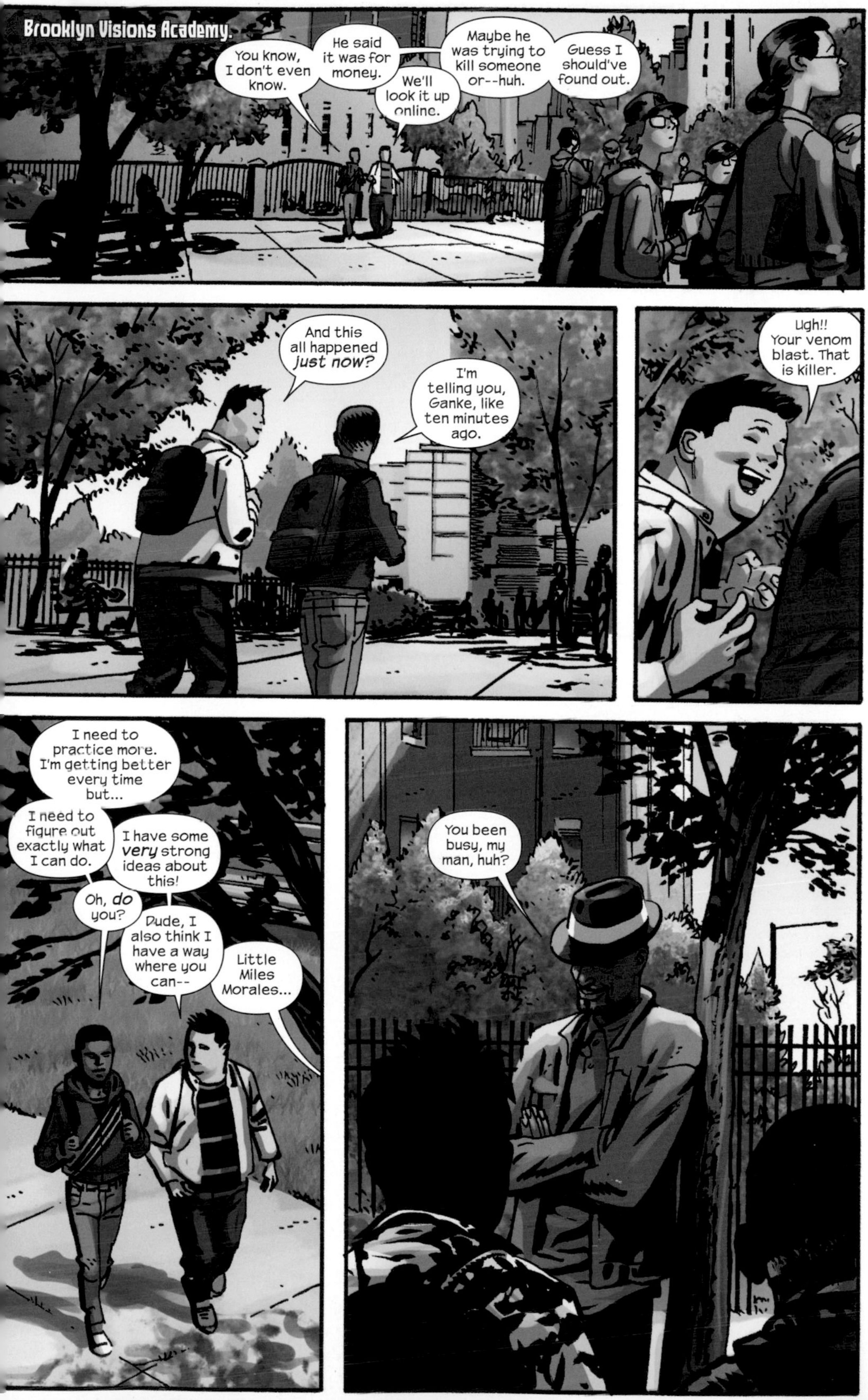
Brooklyn Visions Academy.
You know, I don't even know.
He said it was for money.
We'll look it up online.
Maybe he was trying to kill someone or--huh.
Guess I should've found out.
And this all happened just now?
I'm telling you, Ganke, like ten minutes ago.
Ugh!! Your venom blast. That is killer.
I need to practice more. I'm getting better every time but...
I need to figure out exactly what I can do.
I have some very strong ideas about this!
Oh, do you?
Dude, I also think I have a way where you can--
Little Miles Morales...
You been busy, my man, huh?

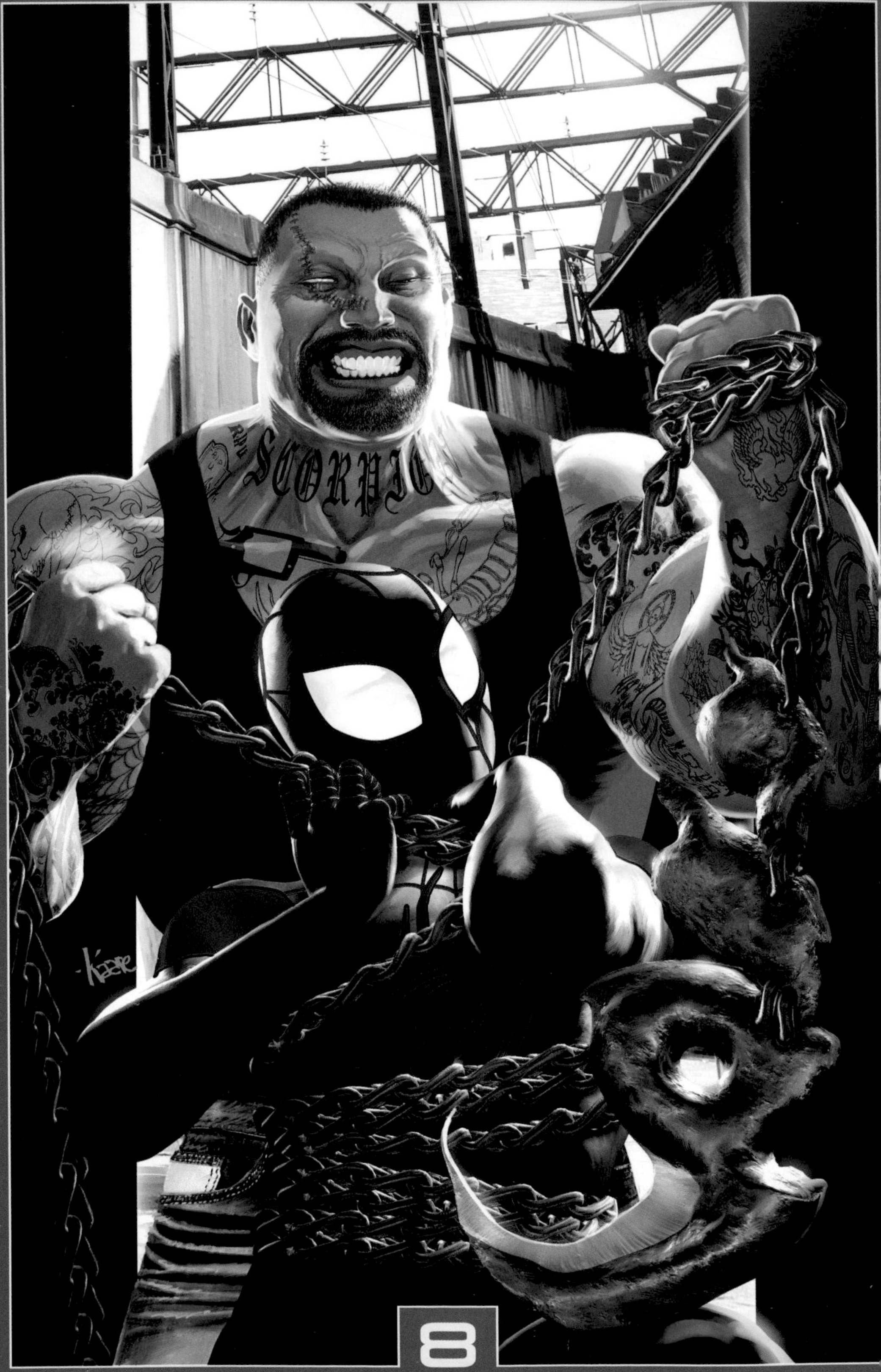

8

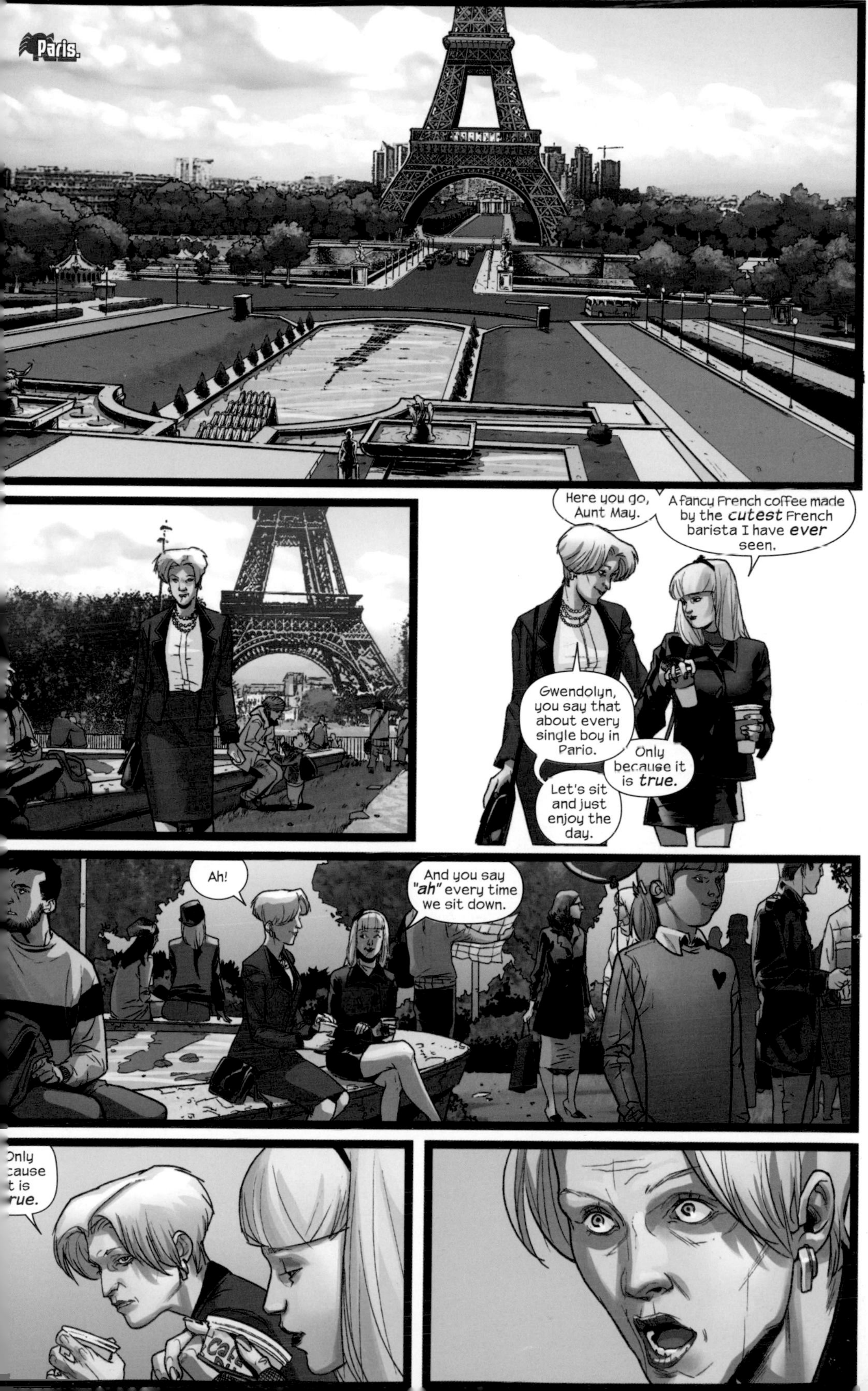
Paris.
Here you go, Aunt May.
A fancy French coffee made by the cutest French barista I have ever seen.
Gwendolyn, you say that about every single boy in Paris.
Only because it is true.
Let's sit and just enjoy the day.
Ah!
And you say "ah" every time we sit down.
Only cause t is rue.

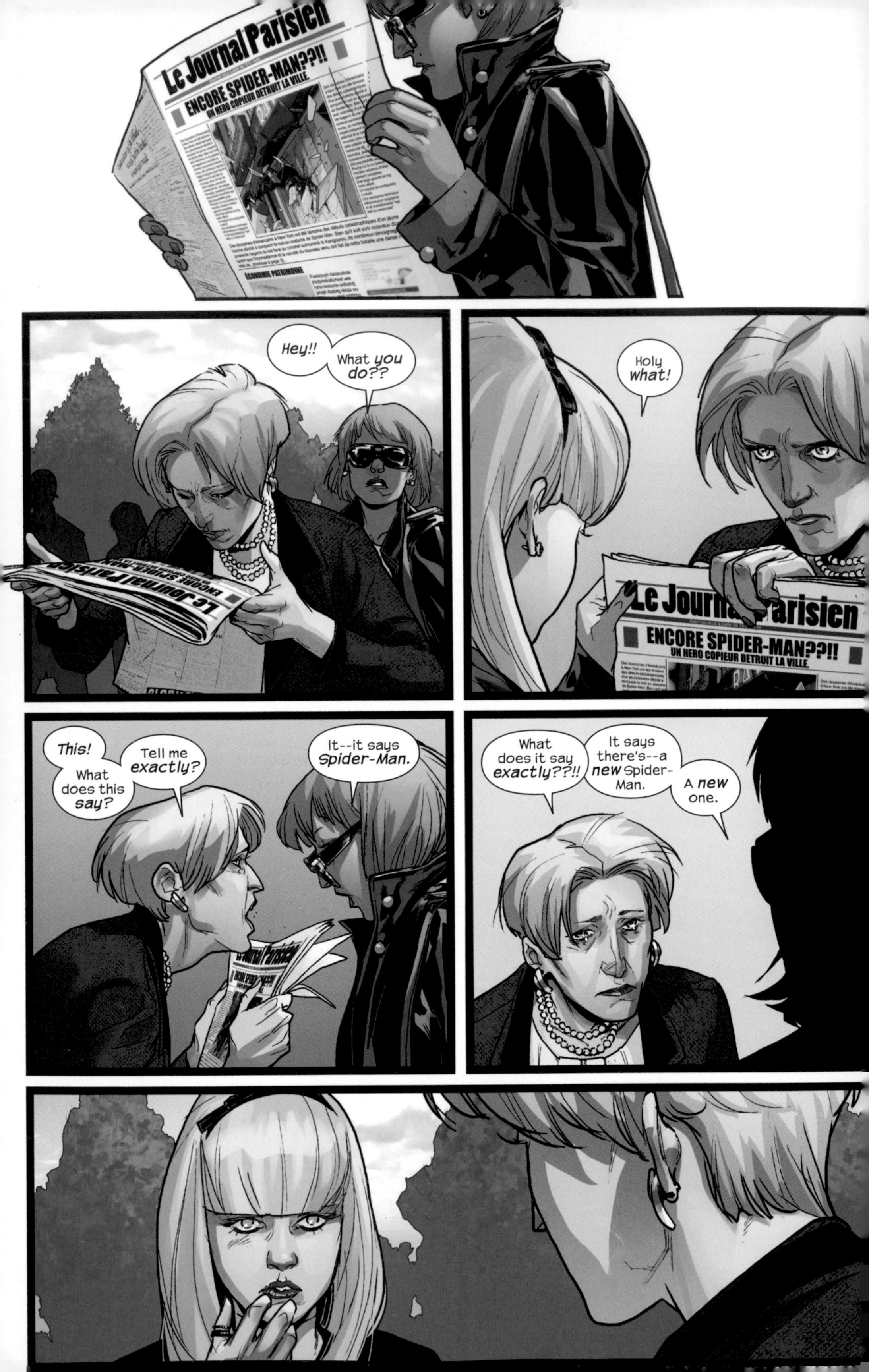

Le Journal Parisien
ENCORE SPIDER-MAN??!!
UN HERO COPIEUR DETRUIT LA VILLE.
ÉCONOMIE PATRIMOINE
Hey!!
What you do??
Holy what!
Le Journal Parisien
ENCORE SPIDER-MAN??!!
UN HERO COPIEUR DETRUIT LA VILLE.
This!
What does this say?
Tell me exactly?
It--it says Spider-Man.
What does it say exactly??!!
It says there's--a new Spider-Man.
A new one.

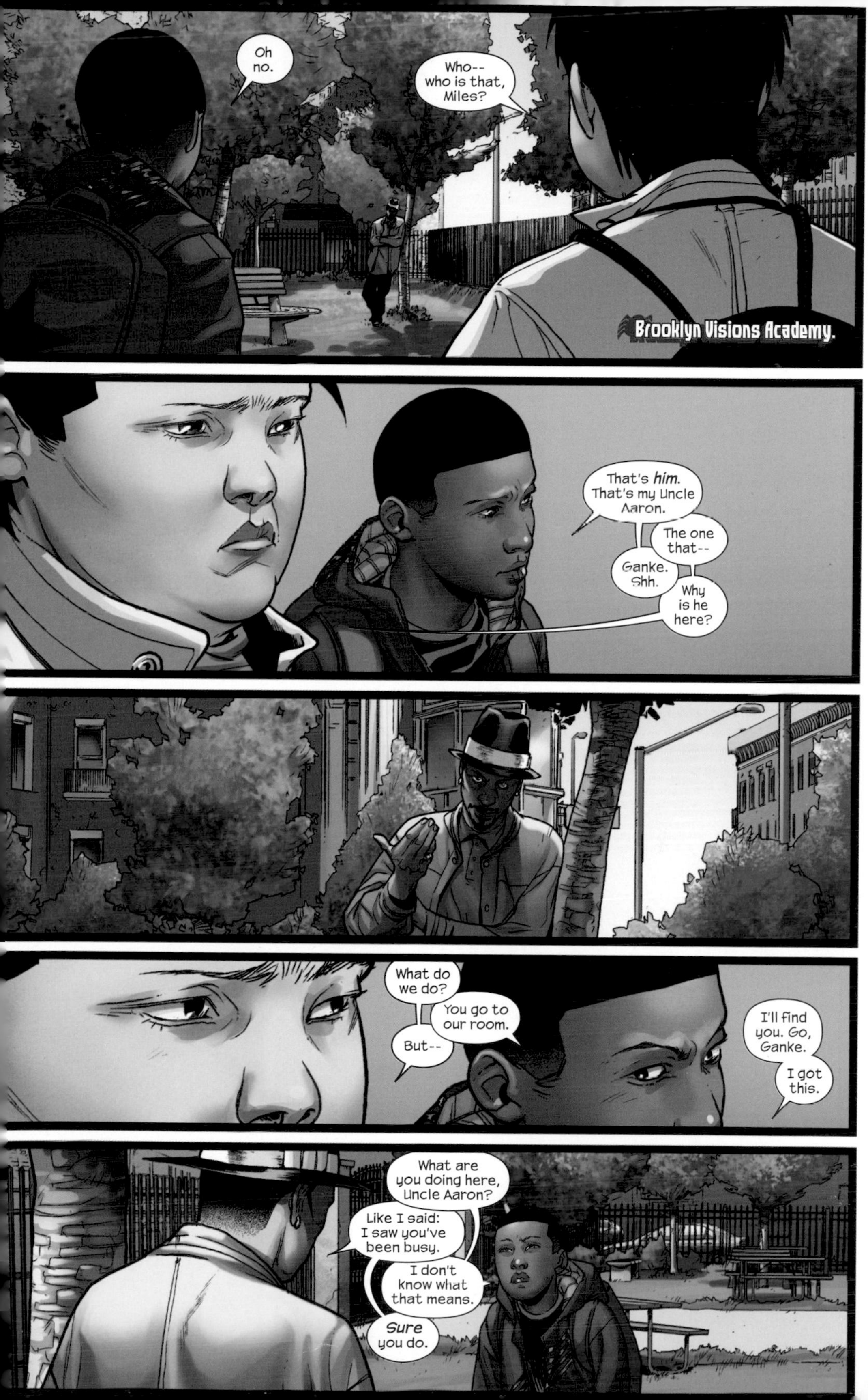
Oh no.
Who-- who is that, Miles?
Brooklyn Visions Academy.
That's *him.* That's my Uncle Aaron.
The one that--
Ganke. Shh.
Why is he here?
What do we do?
You go to our room.
But--
I'll find you. Go, Ganke.
I got this.
What are you doing here, Uncle Aaron?
Like I said: I saw you've been busy.
I don't know what that means.
Sure you do.

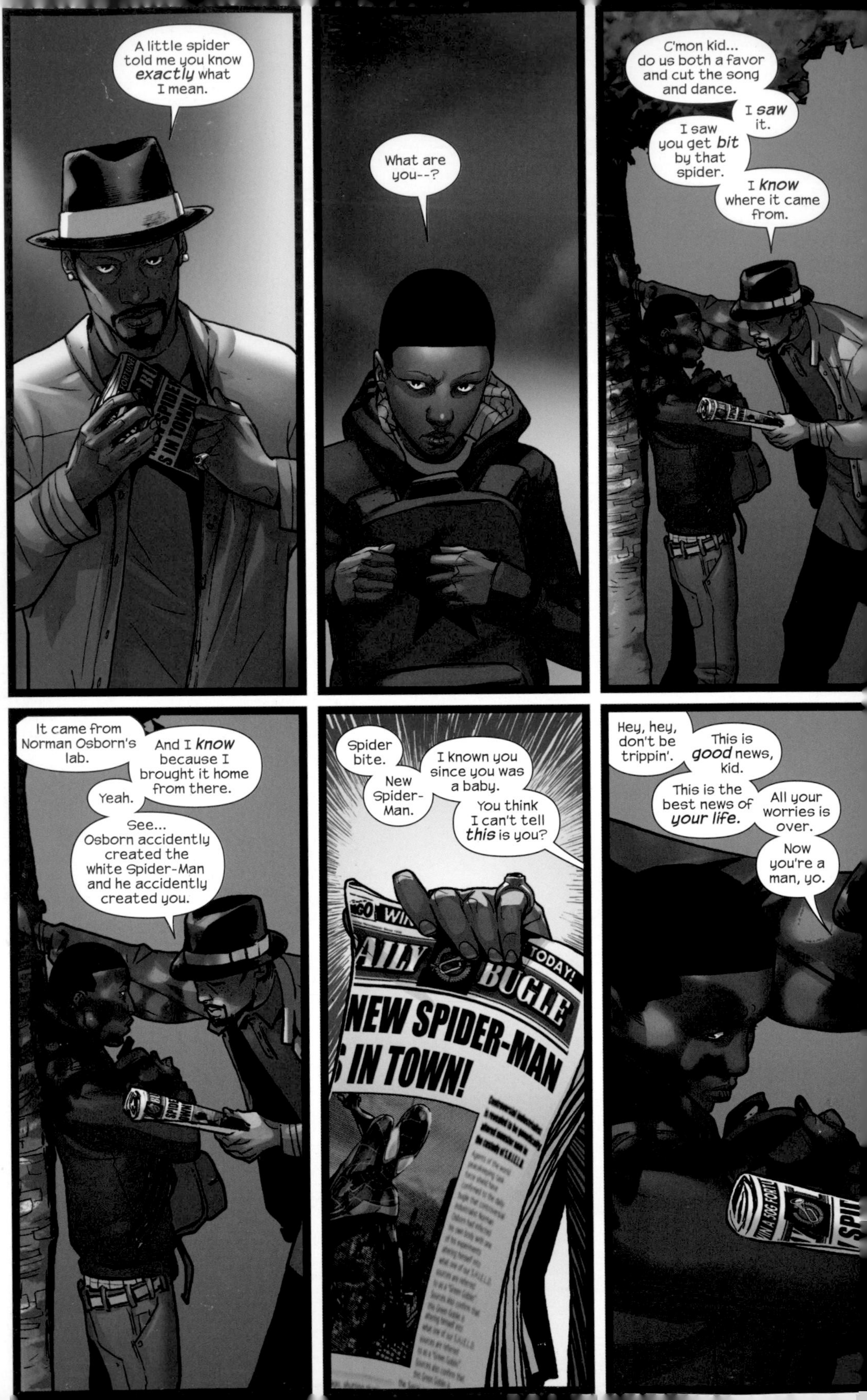
A little spider told me you know *exactly* what I mean.
What are you--?
C'mon kid... do us both a favor and cut the song and dance.
I *saw* it.
I saw you get *bit* by that spider.
I *know* where it came from.
It came from Norman Osborn's lab.
And I *know* because I brought it home from there.
Yeah.
See... Osborn accidently created the white Spider-Man and he accidently created you.
Spider bite.
New Spider-Man.
I known you since you was a baby.
You think I can't tell *this* is you?
DAILY BUGLE
TODAY!
NEW SPIDER-MAN IS IN TOWN!
Hey, hey, don't be trippin'.
This is *good* news, kid.
This is the best news of *your life.*
All your worries is over.
Now you're a man, yo.

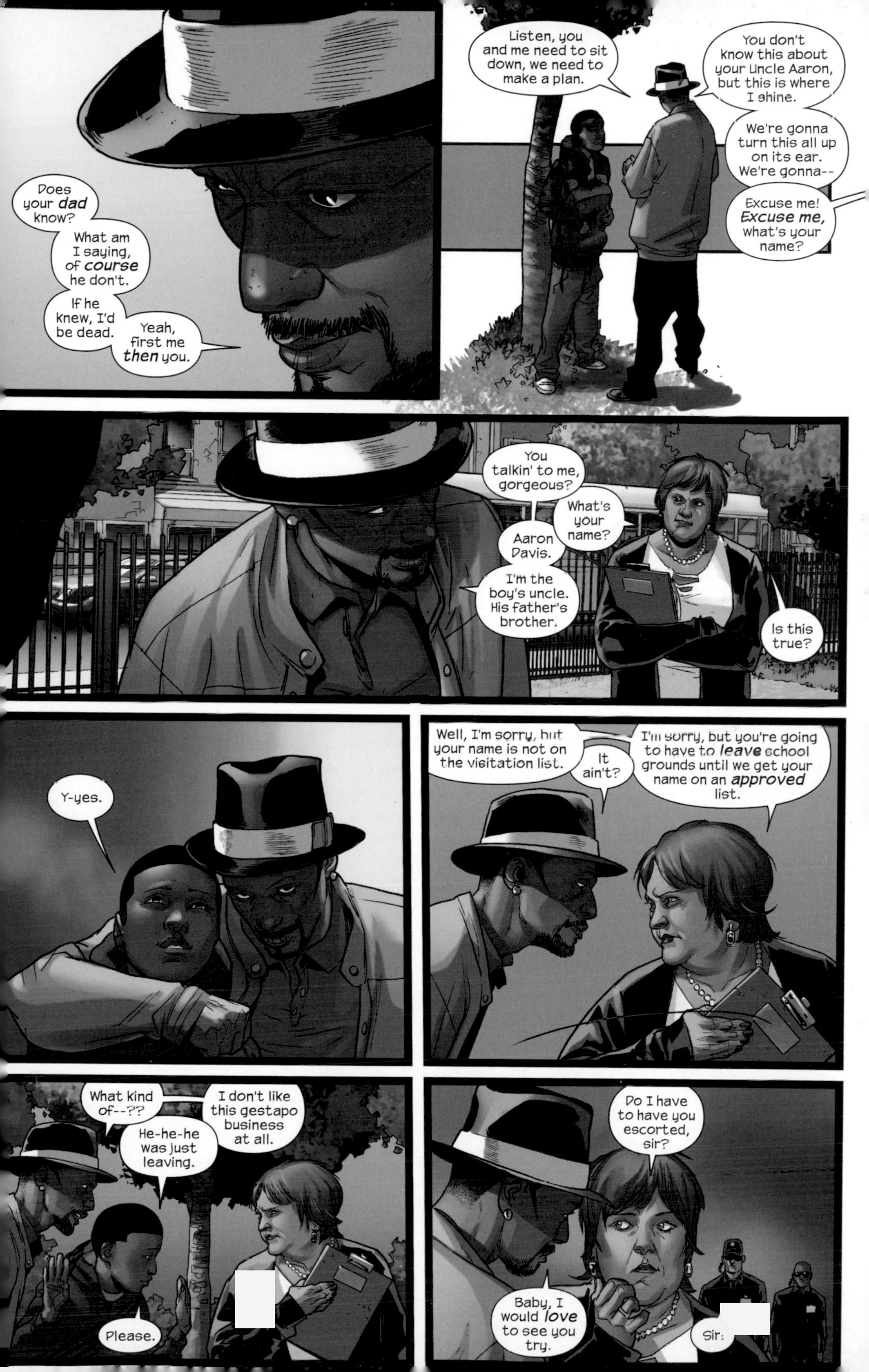
Does your dad know?
What am I saying, of course he don't.
If he knew, I'd be dead.
Yeah, first me then you.
Listen, you and me need to sit down, we need to make a plan.
You don't know this about your Uncle Aaron, but this is where I shine.
We're gonna turn this all up on its ear. We're gonna--
Excuse me! Excuse me, what's your name?
You talkin' to me, gorgeous?
What's your name?
Aaron Davis.
I'm the boy's uncle. His father's brother.
Is this true?
Y-yes.
Well, I'm sorry, but your name is not on the visitation list.
It ain't?
I'm sorry, but you're going to have to leave school grounds until we get your name on an approved list.
What kind of--??
I don't like this gestapo business at all.
He-he-he was just leaving.
Please.
Do I have to have you escorted, sir?
Baby, I would love to see you try.
Sir:

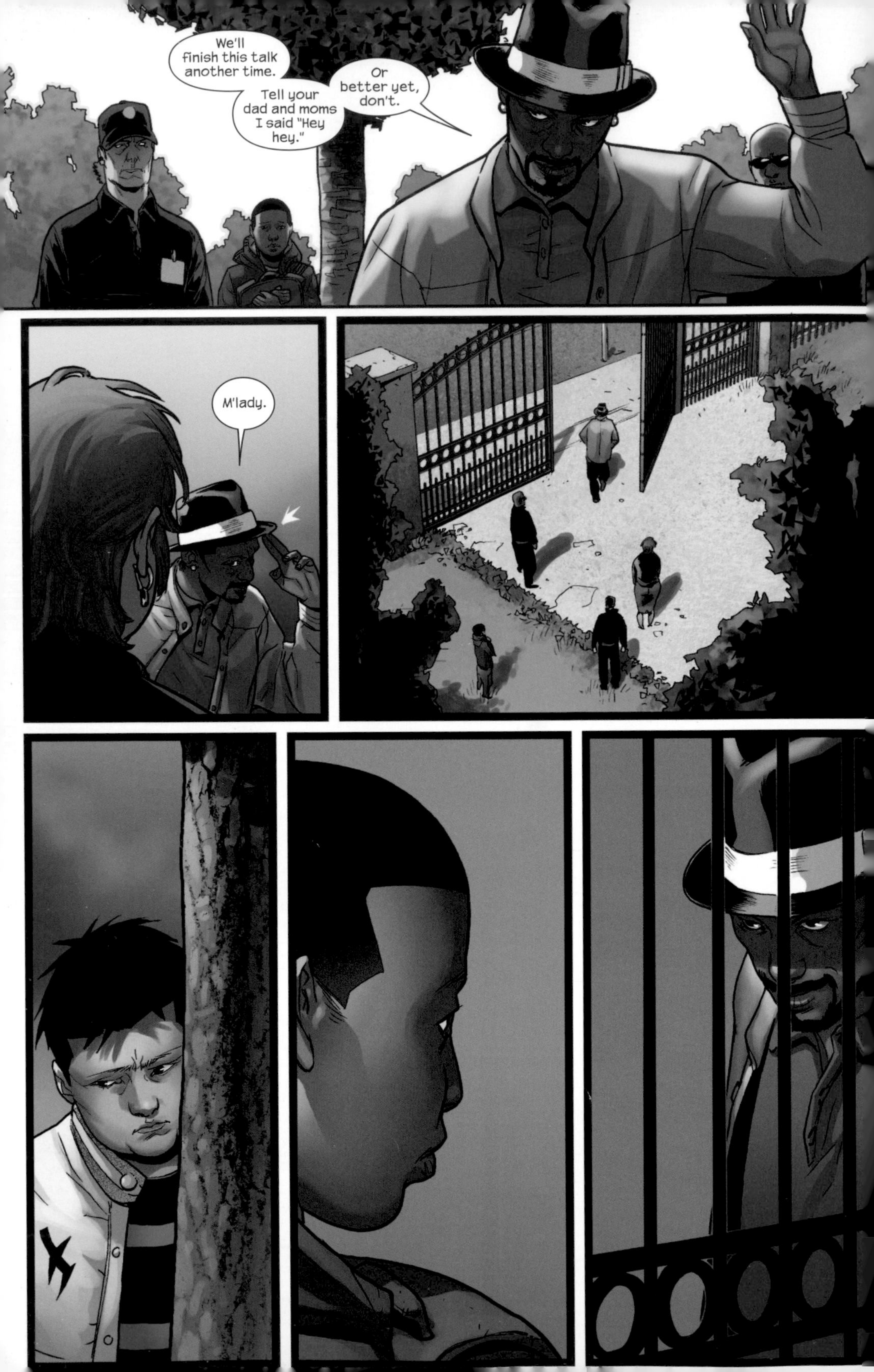
We'll finish this talk another time.
Tell your dad and moms I said "Hey hey."
Or better yet, don't.
M'lady.

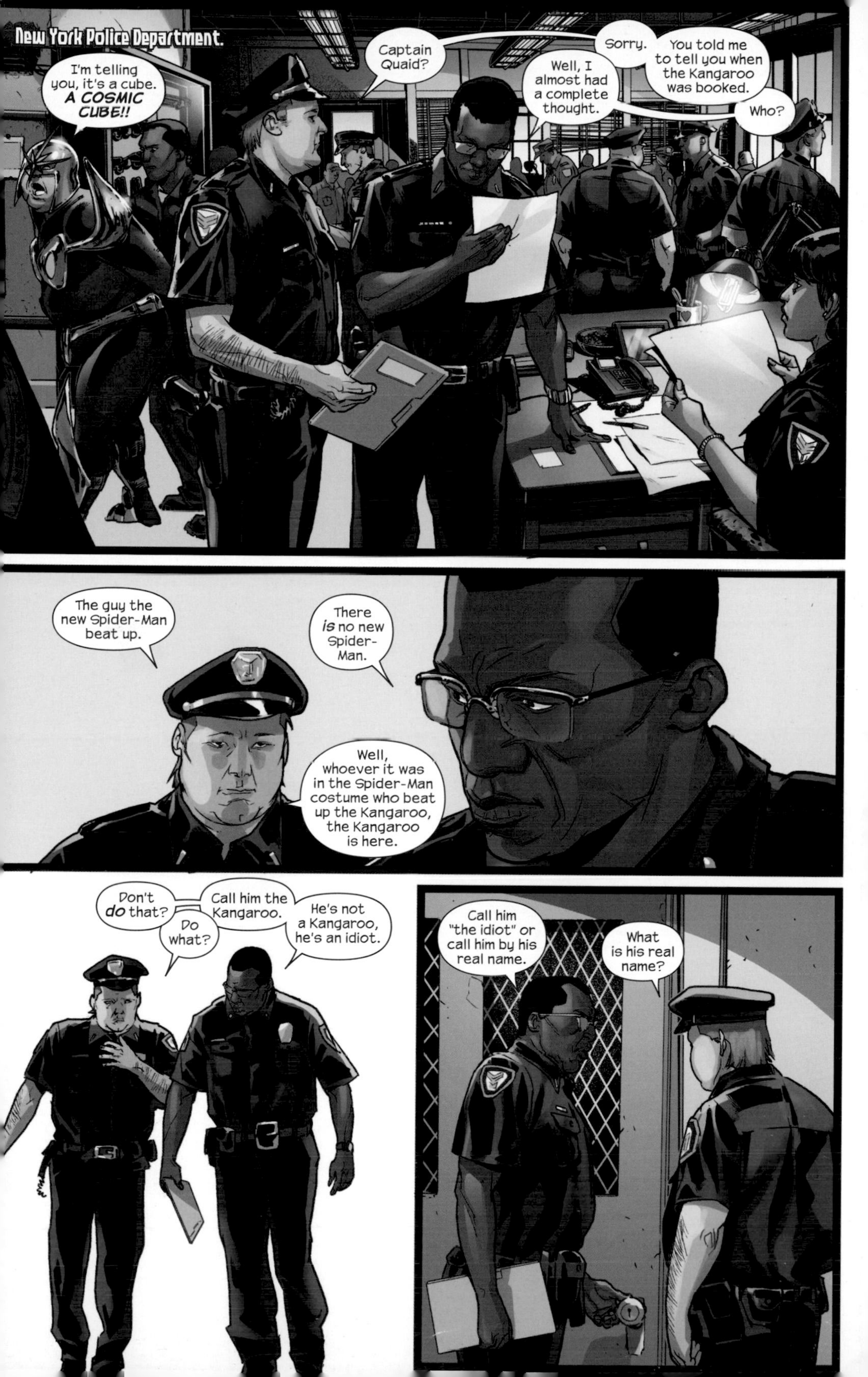
New York Police Department.
I'm telling you, it's a cube. A COSMIC CUBE!!
Captain Quaid?
Sorry.
Well, I almost had a complete thought.
You told me to tell you when the Kangaroo was booked.
Who?
The guy the new Spider-Man beat up.
There *is* no new Spider-Man.
Well, whoever it was in the Spider-Man costume who beat up the Kangaroo, the Kangaroo is here.
Call him the Kangaroo.
Don't *do* that?
Do what?
He's not a Kangaroo, he's an idiot.
Call him "the idiot" or call him by his real name.
What is his real name?

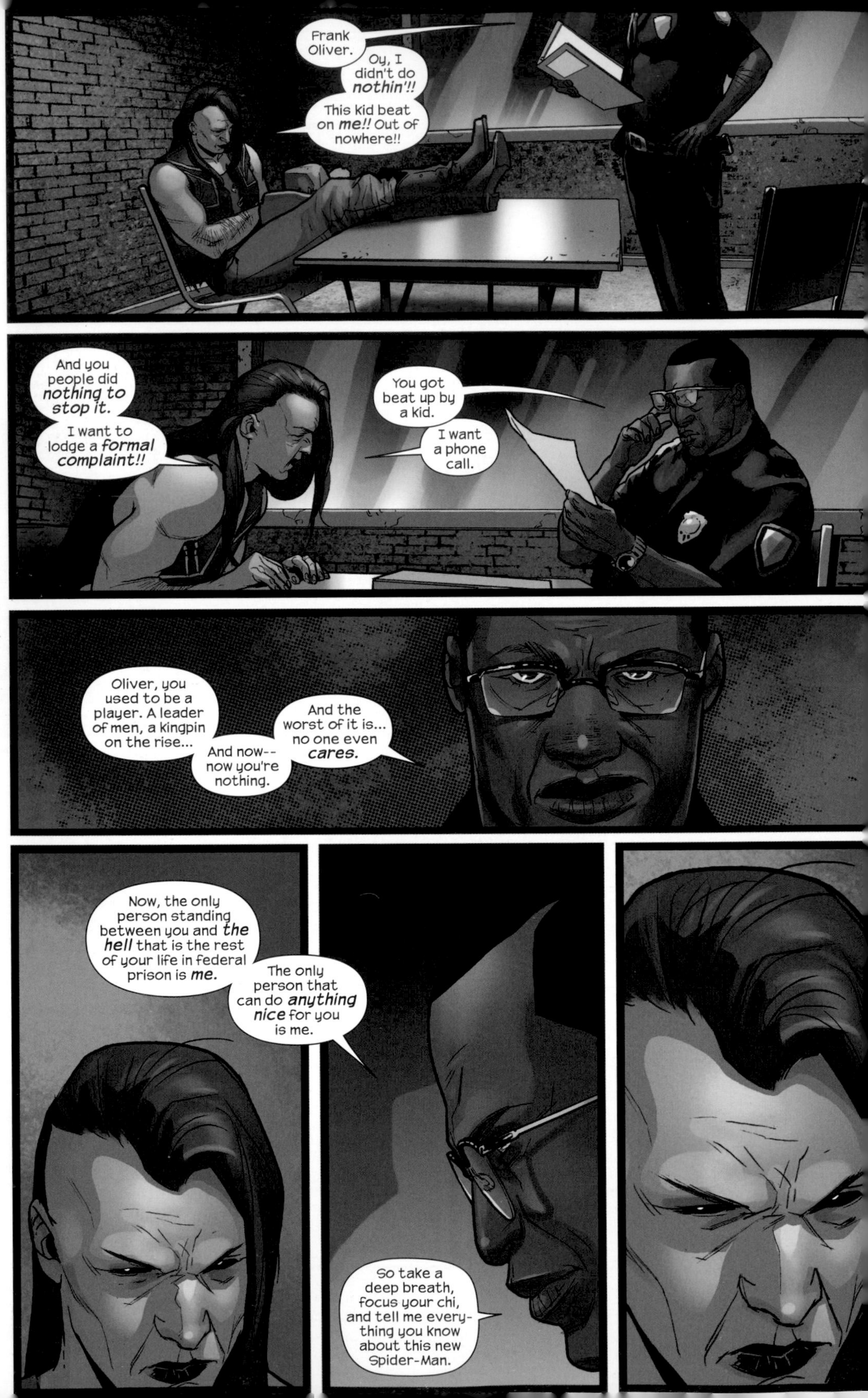
Frank Oliver.
Oy, I didn't do nothin'!!
This kid beat on me!! Out of nowhere!!
And you people did nothing to stop it.
I want to lodge a formal complaint!!
You got beat up by a kid.
I want a phone call.
Oliver, you used to be a player. A leader of men, a kingpin on the rise...
And now-- now you're nothing.
And the worst of it is... no one even cares.
Now, the only person standing between you and the hell that is the rest of your life in federal prison is me.
The only person that can do anything nice for you is me.
So take a deep breath, focus your chi, and tell me every-thing you know about this new Spider-Man.

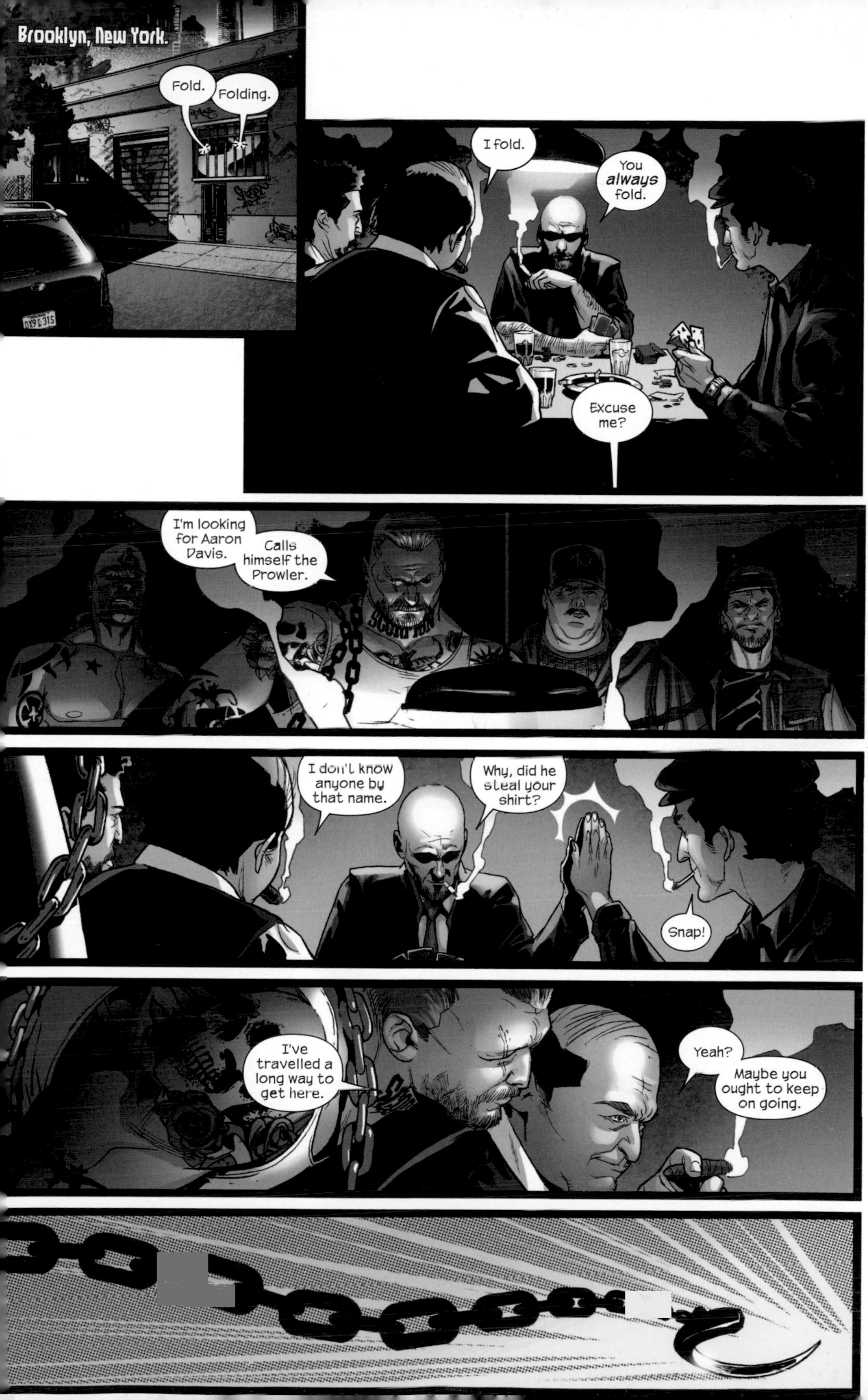
Brooklyn, New York.
Fold.
Folding.
I fold.
You always fold.
Excuse me?
I'm looking for Aaron Davis.
Calls himself the Prowler.
I don't know anyone by that name.
Why, did he steal your shirt?
Snap!
I've travelled a long way to get here.
Yeah?
Maybe you ought to keep on going.

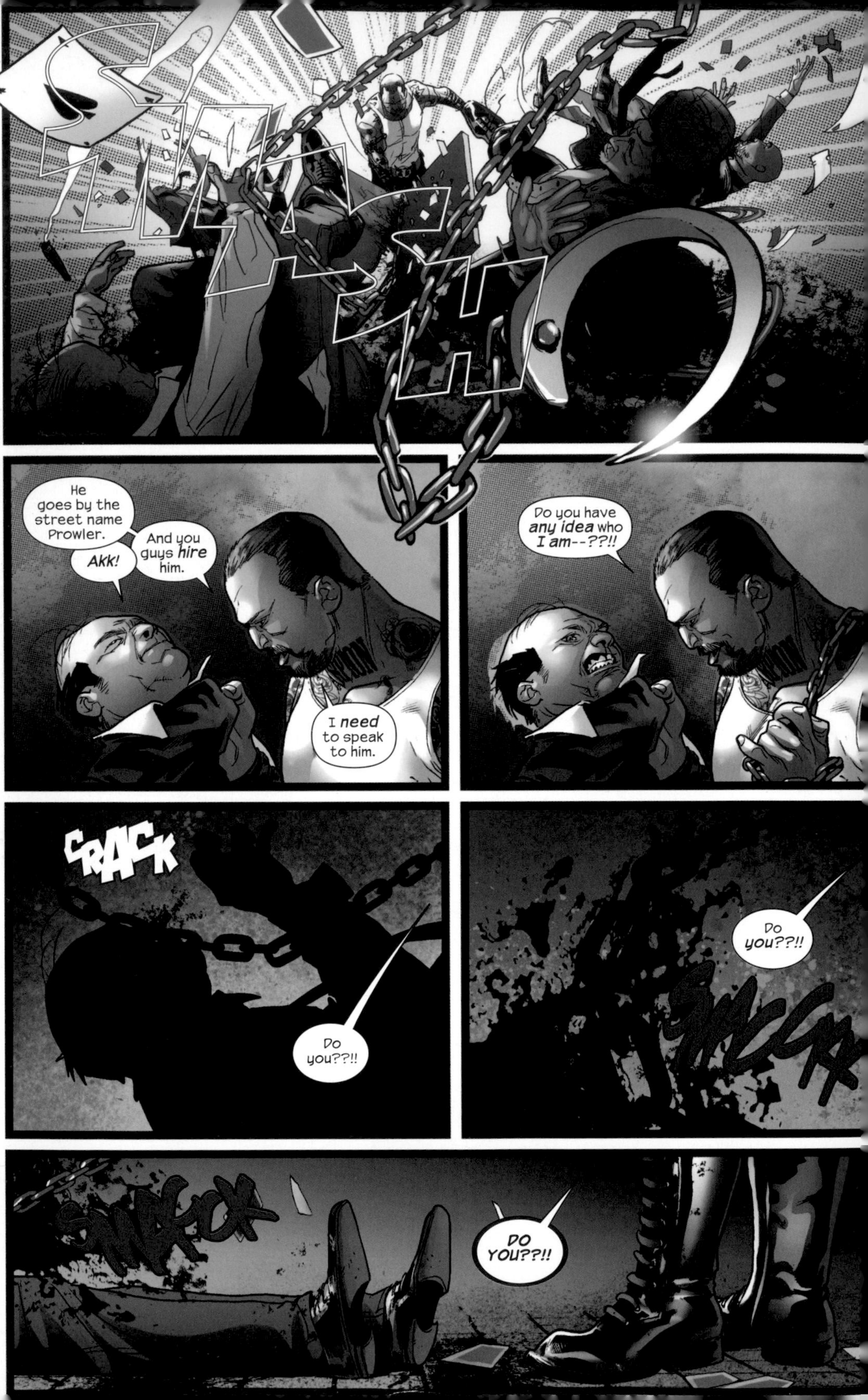
SHASH
He goes by the street name Prowler.
Akk!
And you guys hire him.
I need to speak to him.
Do you have any idea who I am--??!!
CRACK
Do you??!!
Do you??!!
DO YOU??!!

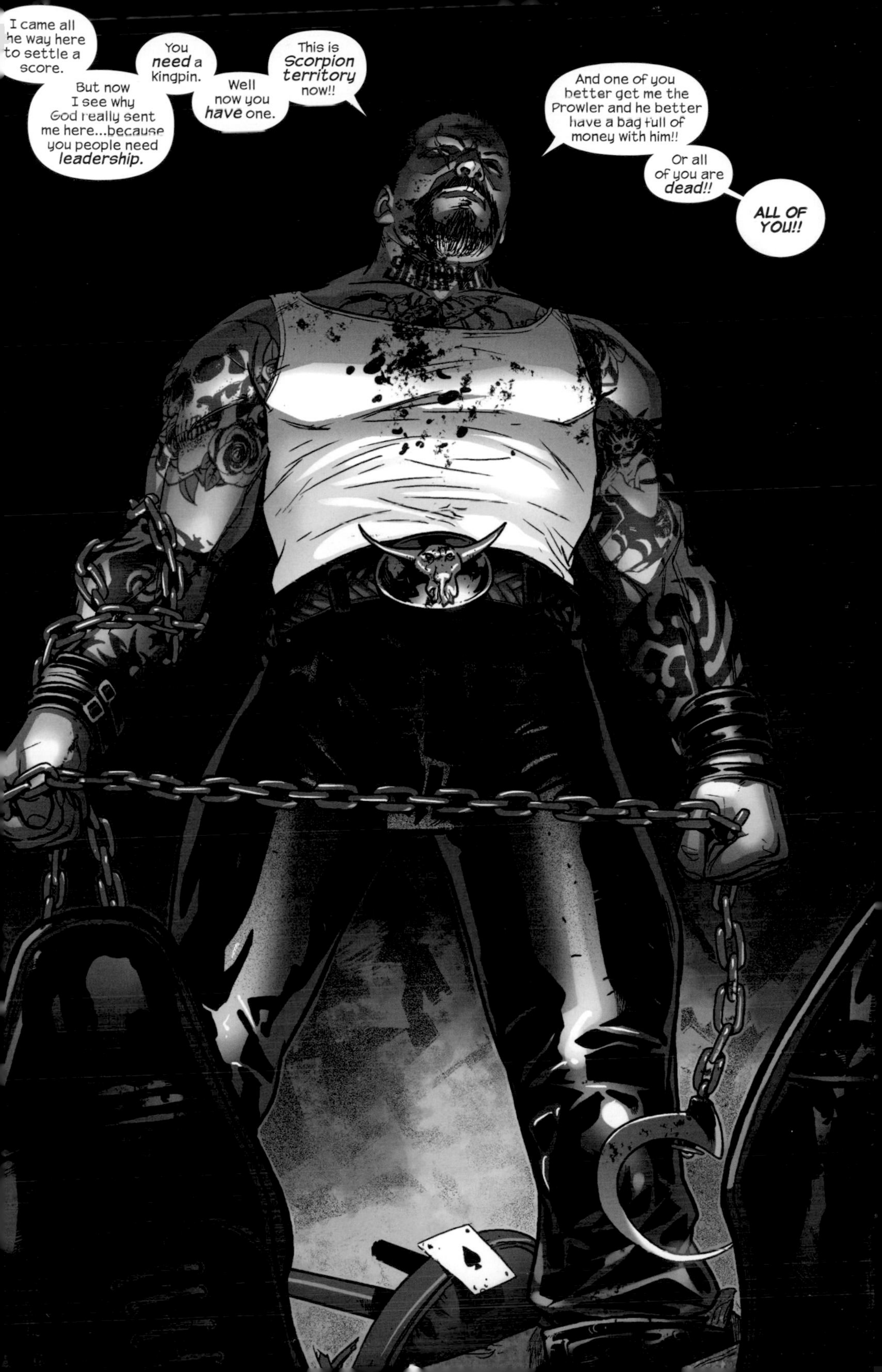
I came all the way here to settle a score.
But now I see why God really sent me here...because you people need leadership.
You need a kingpin.
Well now you have one.
This is Scorpion territory now!!
And one of you better get me the Prowler and he better have a bag full of money with him!!
Or all of you are dead!!
ALL OF YOU!!

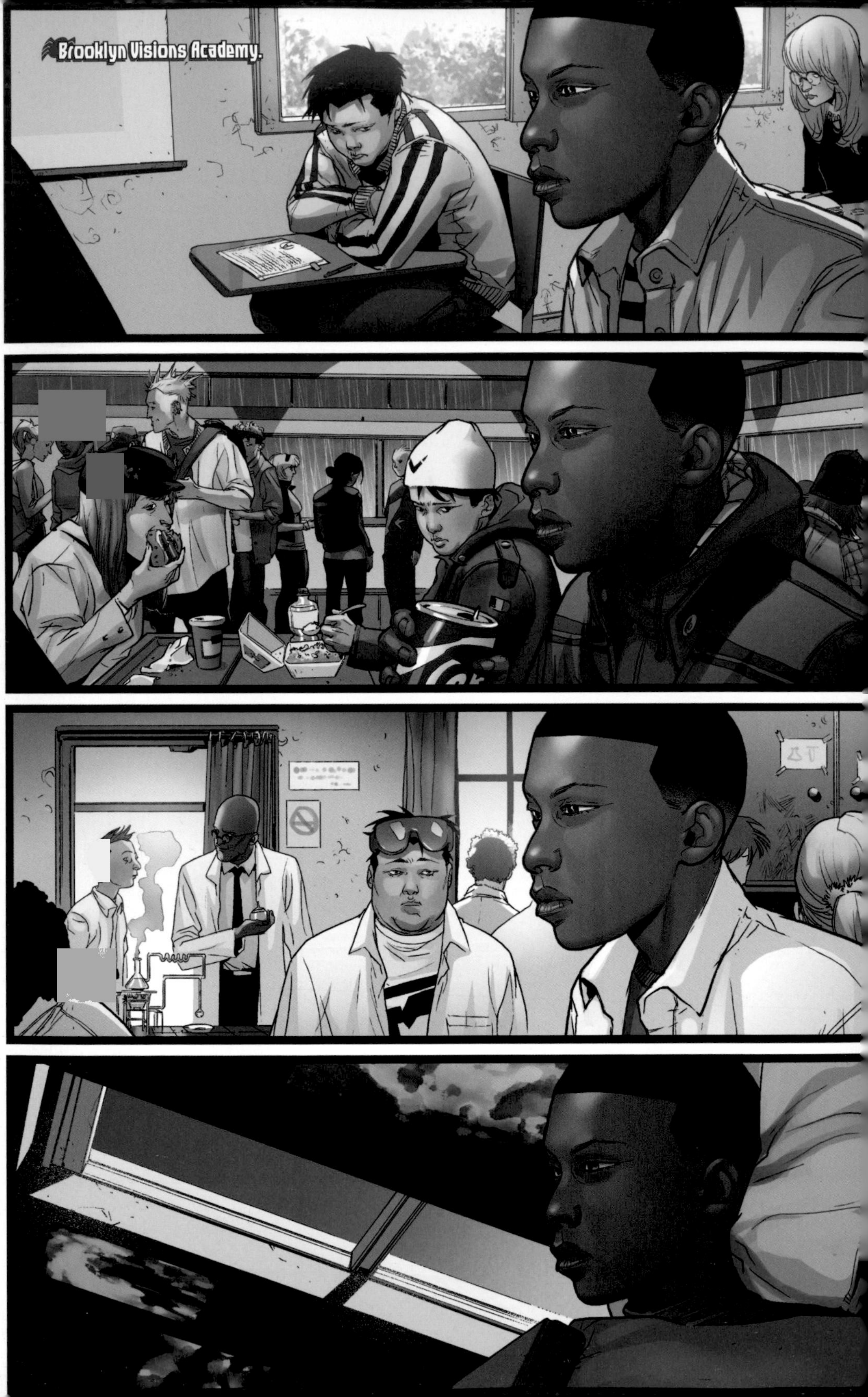
Brooklyn Visions Academy.

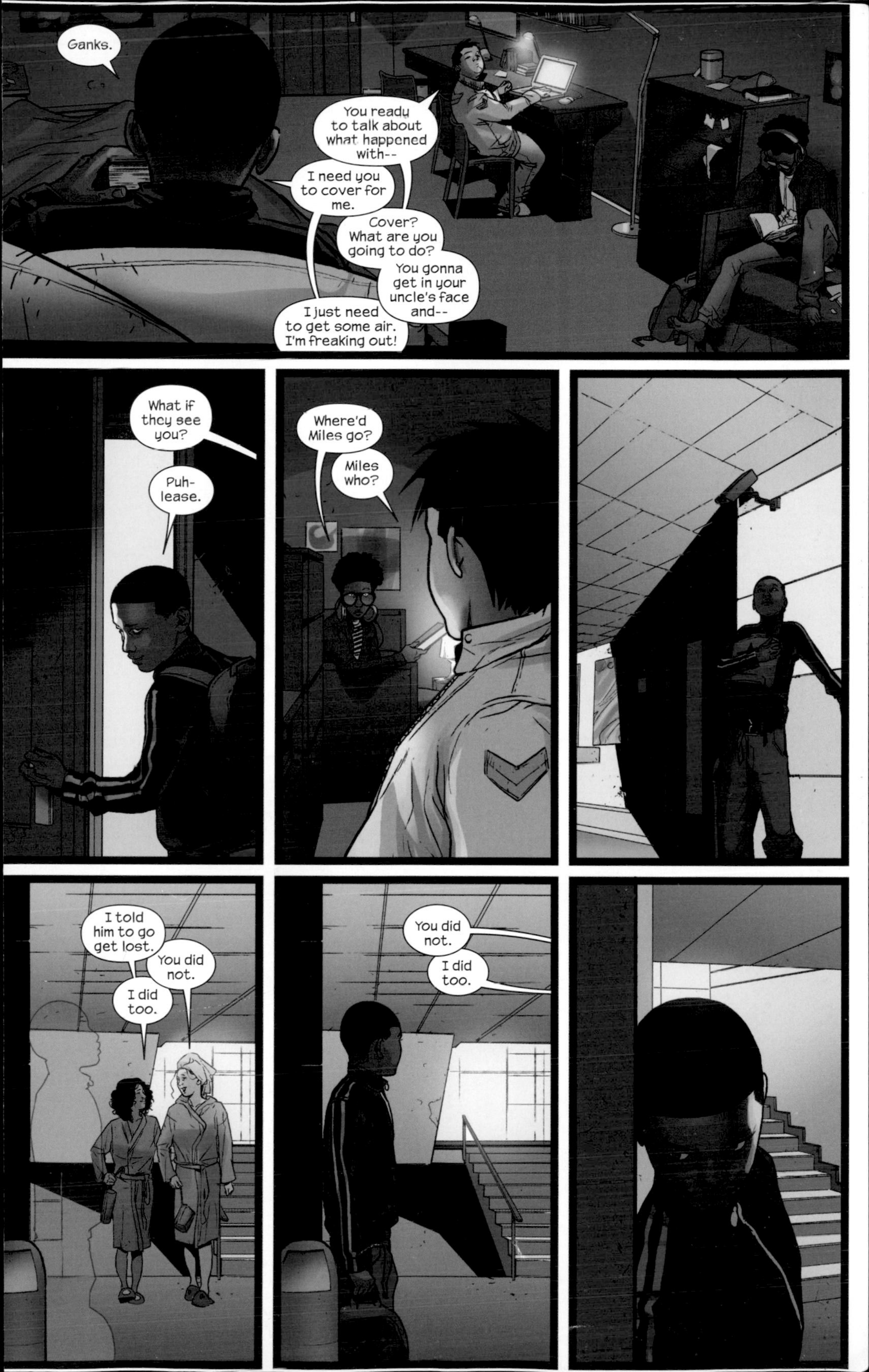
Ganks.
You ready to talk about what happened with--
I need you to cover for me.
Cover? What are you going to do?
You gonna get in your uncle's face and--
I just need to get some air. I'm freaking out!
What if they see you?
Puh-lease.
Where'd Miles go?
Miles who?
I told him to go get lost.
You did not.
I did too.
You did not.
I did too.

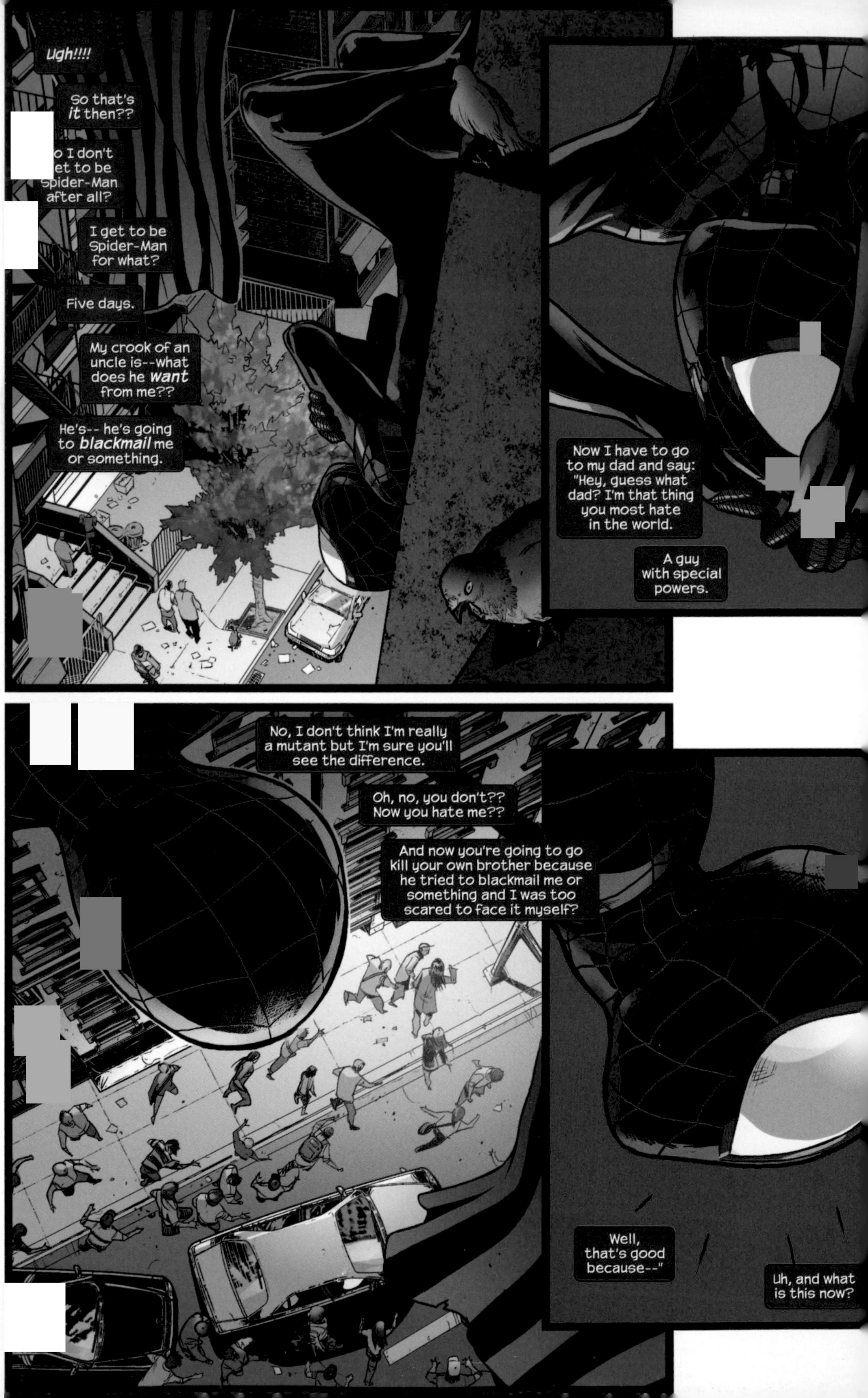

Ugh!!!!
So that's *it* then??
o I don't et to be Spider-Man after all?
I get to be Spider-Man for what?
Five days.
My crook of an uncle is--what does he *want* from me??
He's-- he's going to **blackmail** me or something.
Now I have to go to my dad and say: "Hey, guess what dad? I'm that thing you most hate in the world.
A guy with special powers.
No, I don't think I'm really a mutant but I'm sure you'll see the difference.
Oh, no, you don't?? Now you hate me??
And now you're going to go kill your own brother because he tried to blackmail me or something and I was too scared to face it myself?
Well, that's good because--"
Uh, and what is this now?

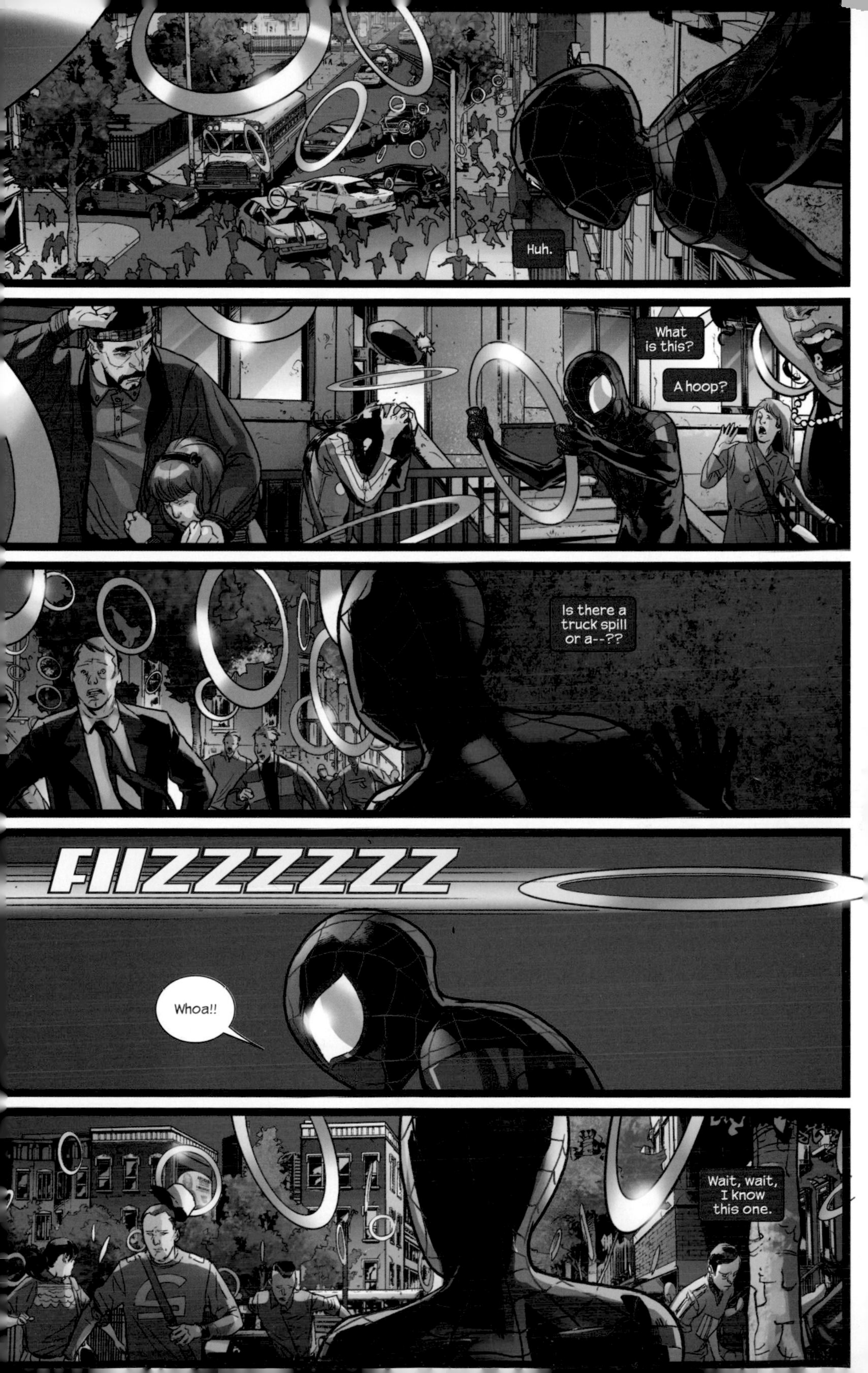
Huh.
What is this?
A hoop?
Is there a truck spill or a--??
FIIZZZZZZ
Whoa!!
Wait, wait, I know this one.

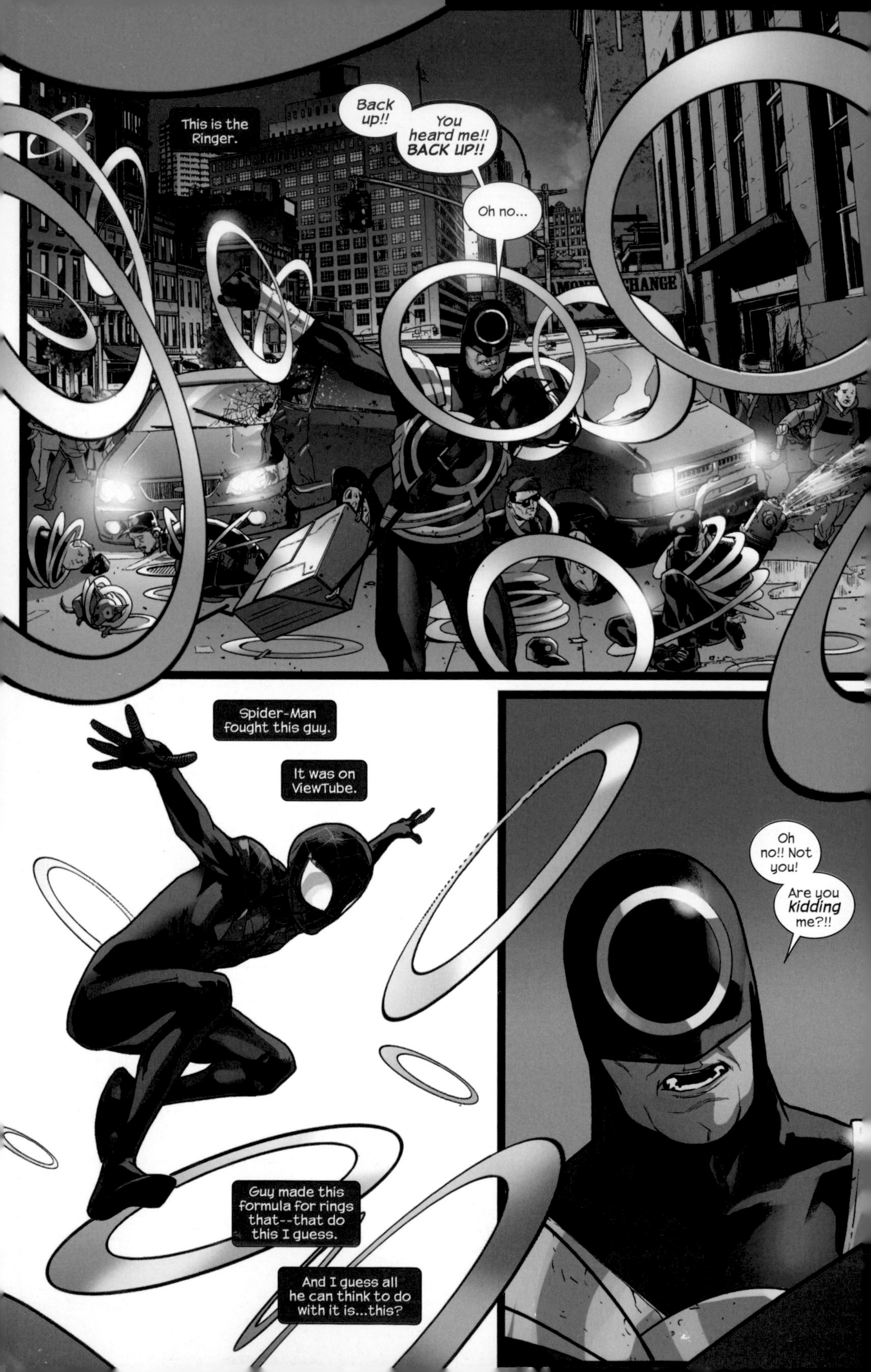
This is the Ringer.
Back up!!
You heard me!! BACK UP!!
Oh no...
Spider-Man fought this guy.
It was on ViewTube.
Guy made this formula for rings that--that do this I guess.
And I guess all he can think to do with it is...this?
Oh no!! Not you!
Are you *kidding* me?!!

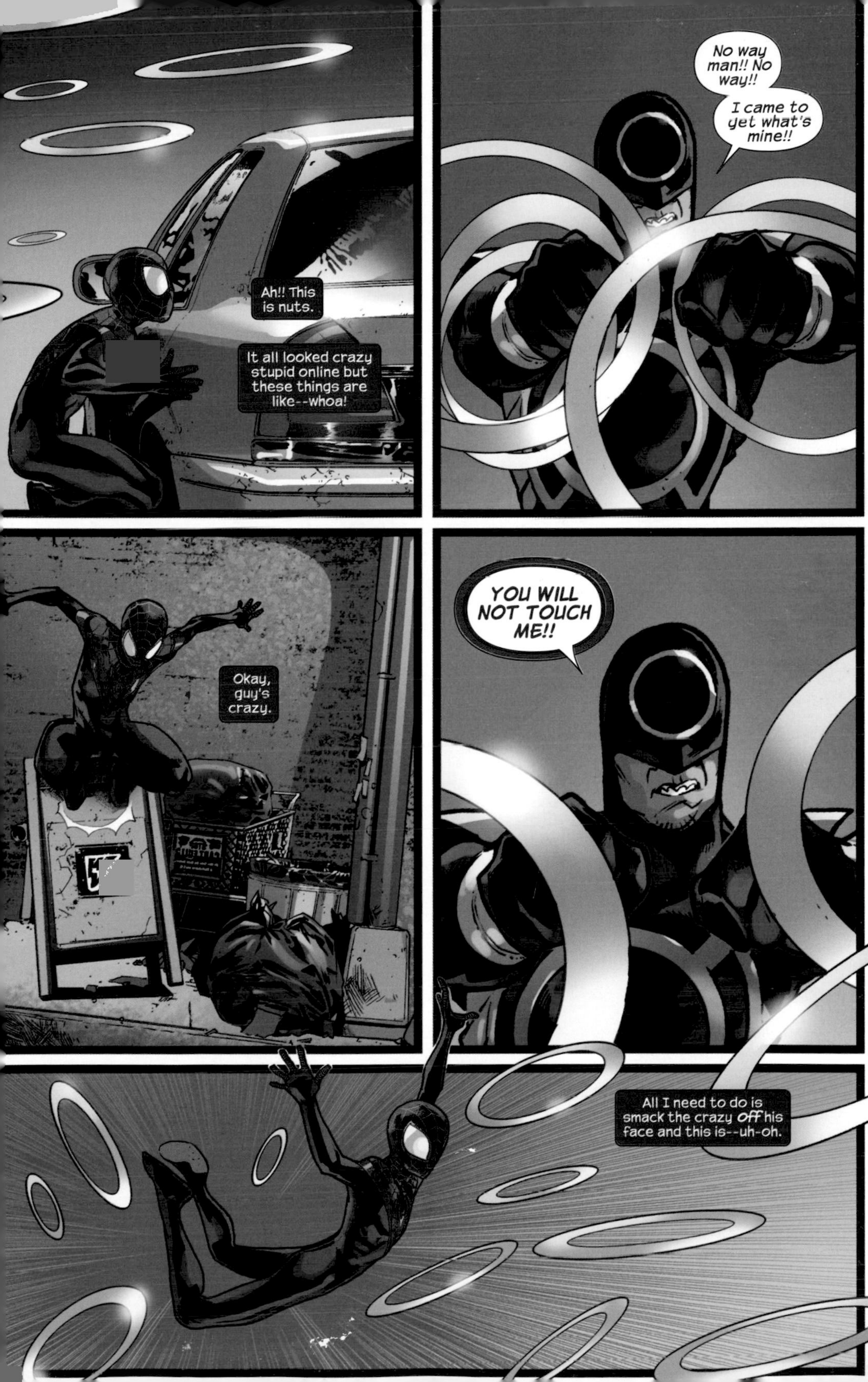
Ah!! This is nuts.
It all looked crazy stupid online but these things are like--whoa!
No way man!! No way!!
I came to get what's mine!!
Okay, guy's crazy.
YOU WILL NOT TOUCH ME!!
All I need to do is smack the crazy *off* his face and this is--uh-oh.

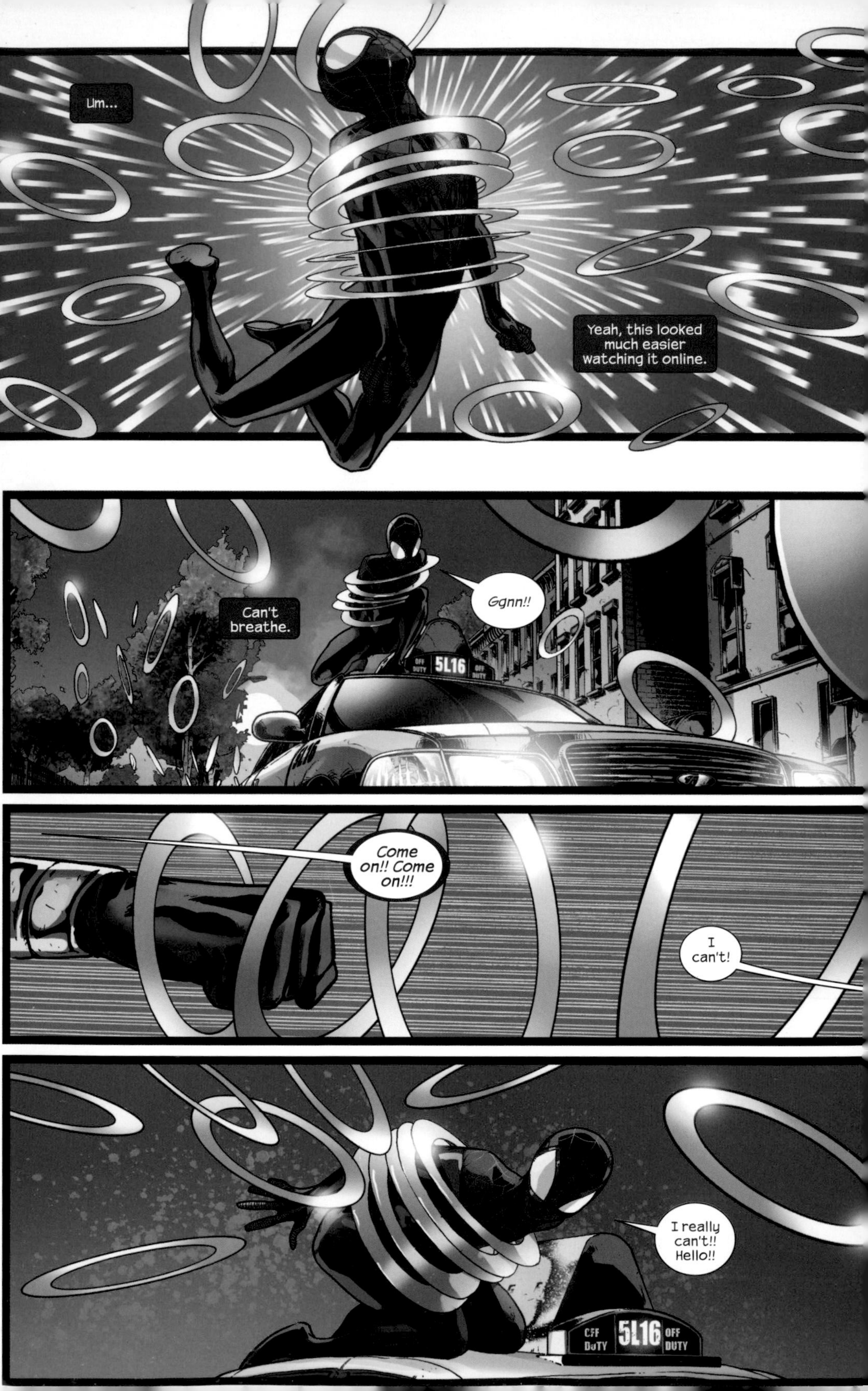
Um...
Yeah, this looked much easier watching it online.
Can't breathe.
Ggnn!!
OFF DUTY 5L16 OFF DUTY
Come on!! Come on!!!
I can't!
I really can't!! Hello!!
OFF DUTY 5L16 OFF DUTY

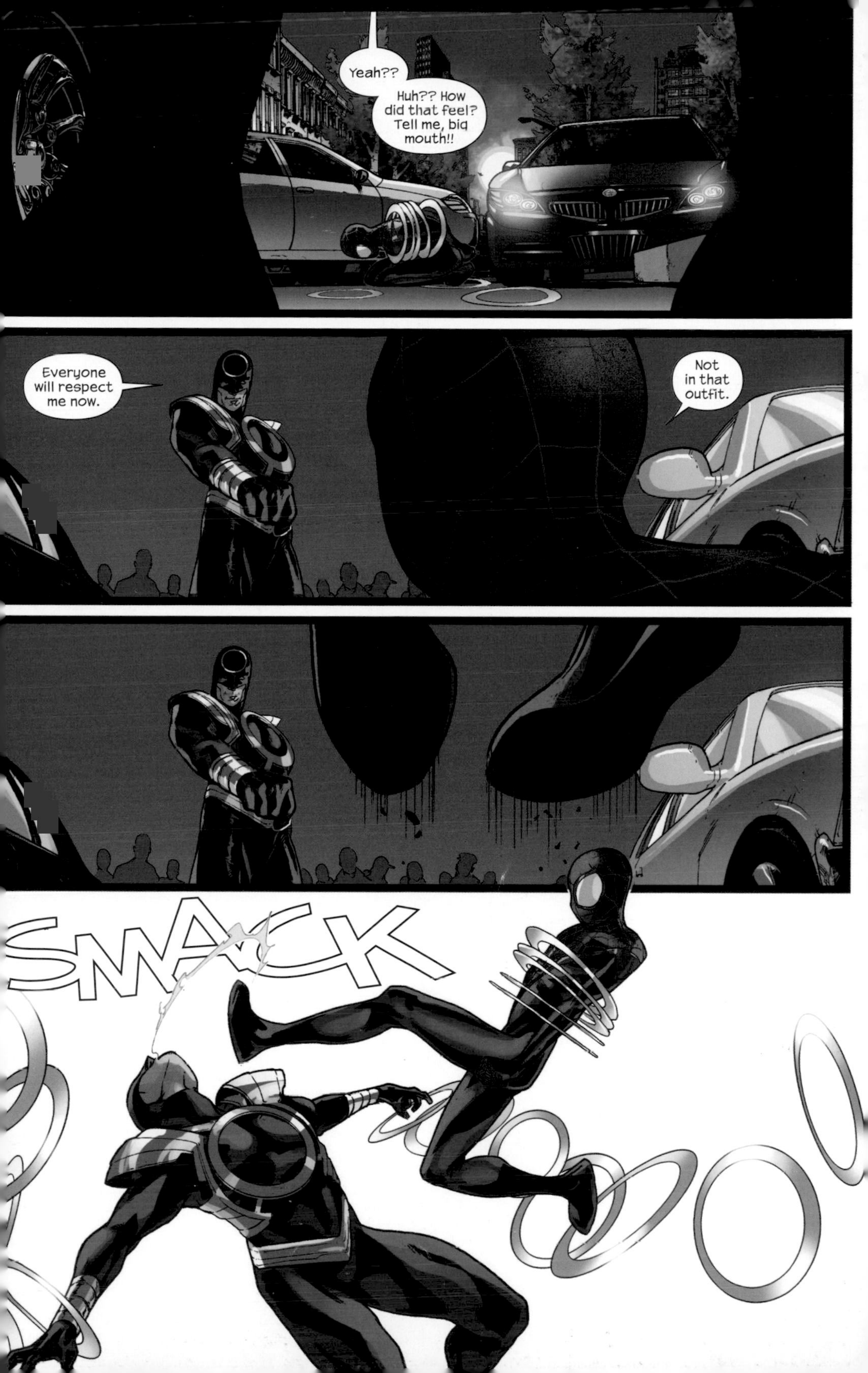
Yeah??
Huh?? How did that feel? Tell me, big mouth!!
Everyone will respect me now.
Not in that outfit.
SMACK

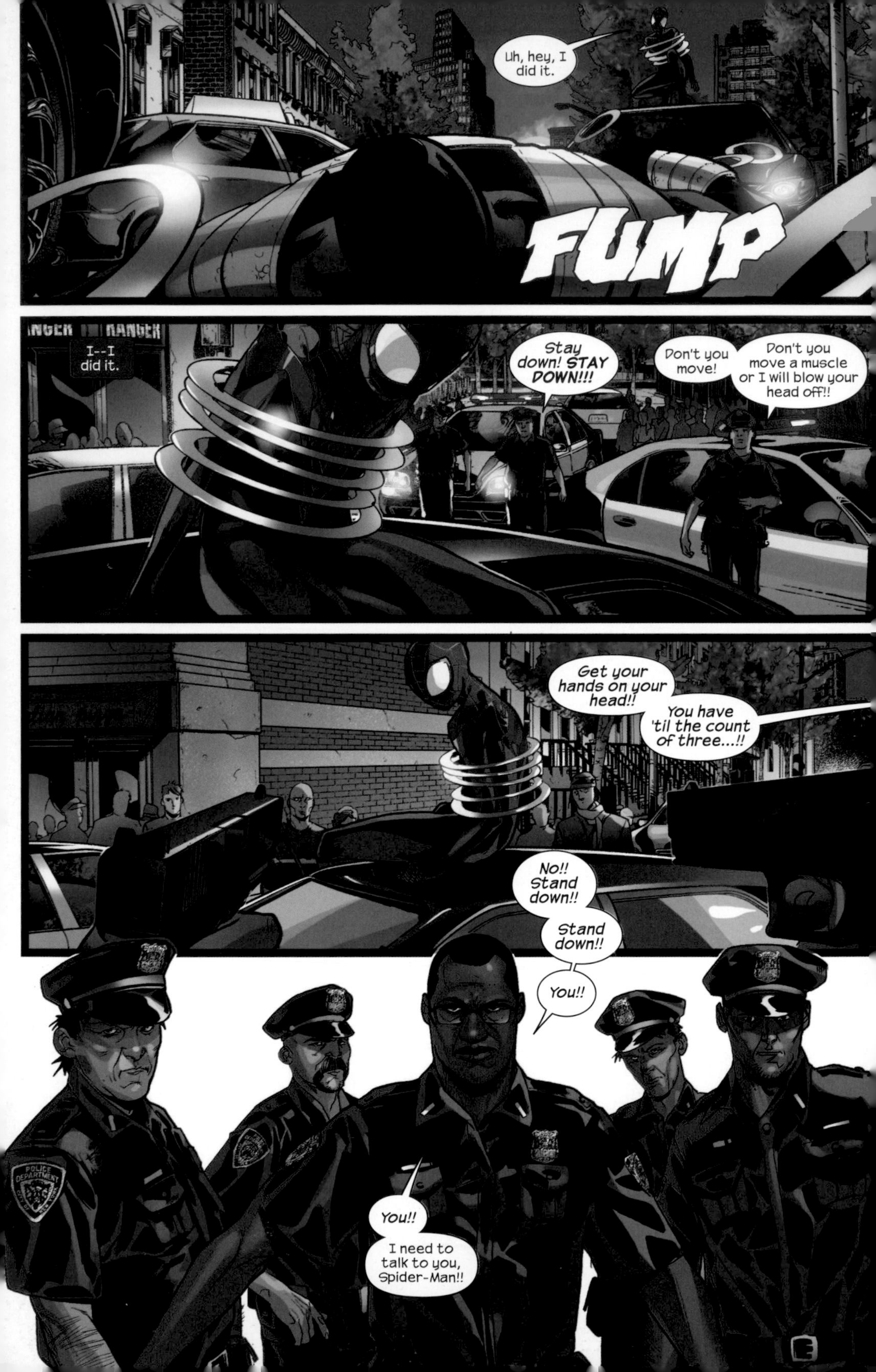
Uh, hey, I did it.
FUMP
I--I did it.
Stay down! STAY DOWN!!!
Don't you move!
Don't you move a muscle or I will blow your head off!!
Get your hands on your head!!
You have 'til the count of three...!!
No!! Stand down!!
Stand down!!
You!!
You!!
I need to talk to you, Spider-Man!!

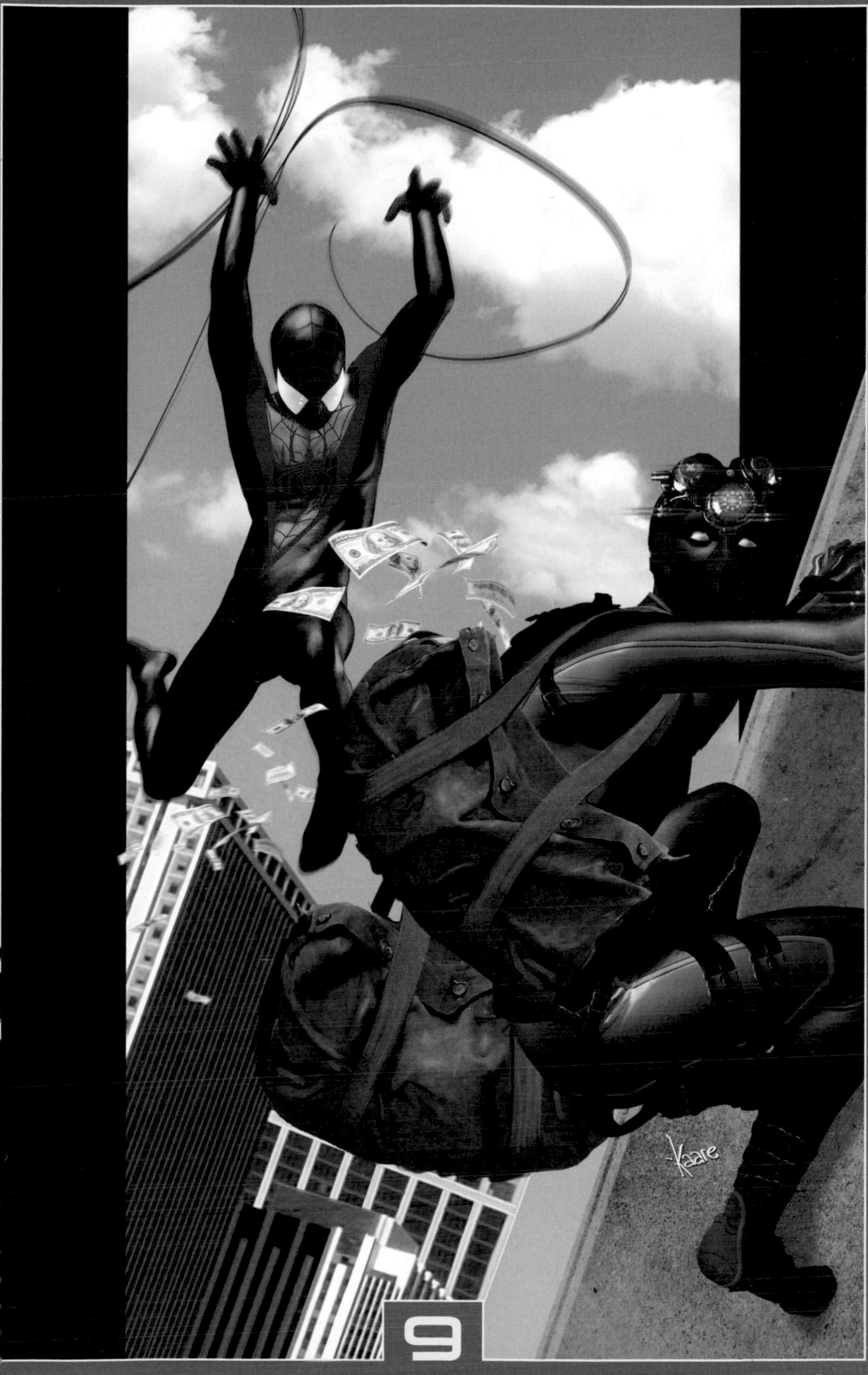
9
Kaare

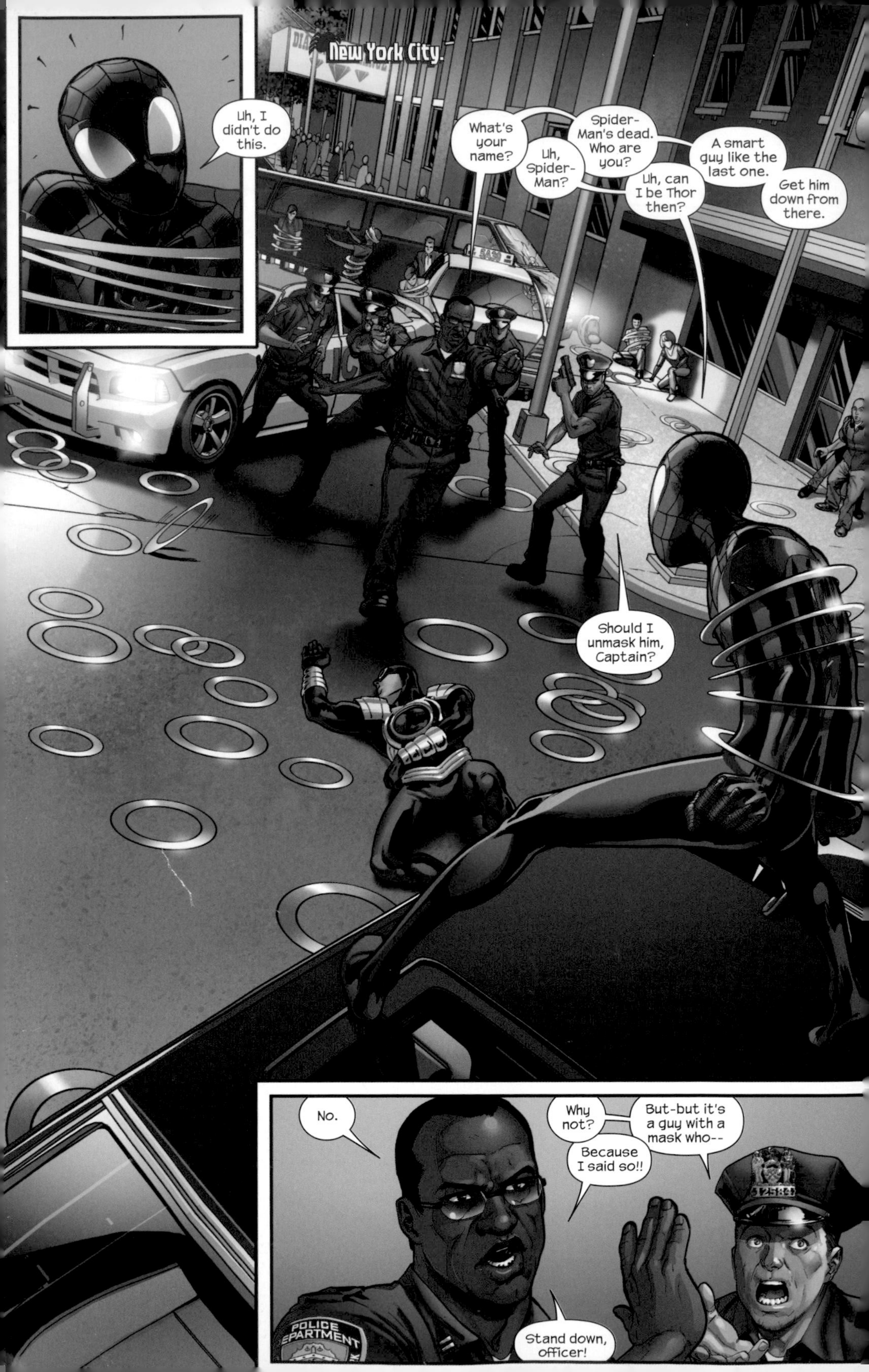
Uh, I didn't do this.
New York City.
What's your name?
Uh, Spider-Man?
Spider-Man's dead. Who are you?
Uh, can I be Thor then?
A smart guy like the last one.
Get him down from there.
Should I unmask him, Captain?
No.
Why not?
But-but it's a guy with a mask who--
Because I said so!!
Stand down, officer!
POLICE DEPARTMENT

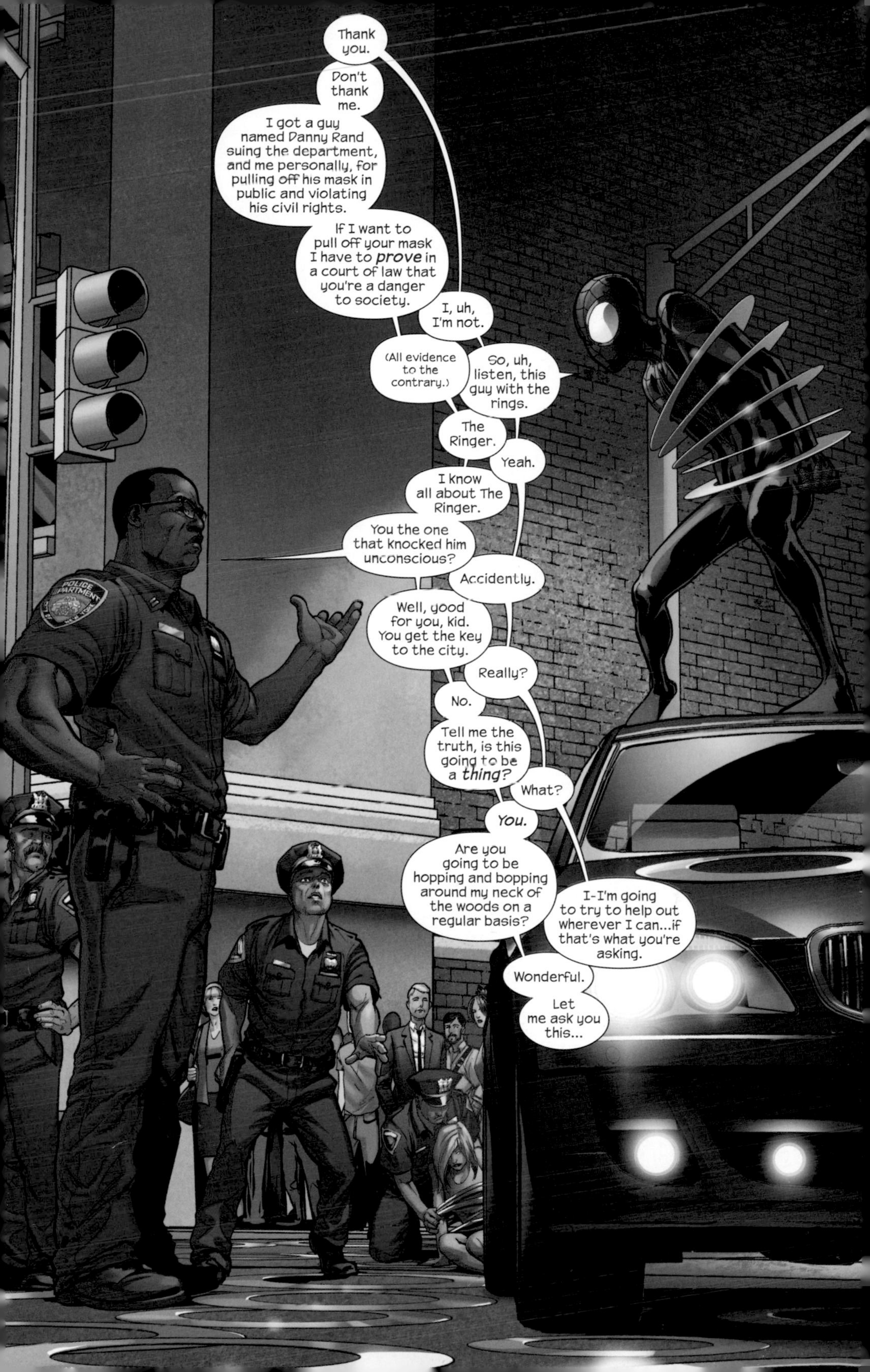
Thank you.
Don't thank me.
I got a guy named Danny Rand suing the department, and me personally, for pulling off his mask in public and violating his civil rights.
If I want to pull off your mask I have to *prove* in a court of law that you're a danger to society.
I, uh, I'm not.
(All evidence to the contrary.)
So, uh, listen, this guy with the rings.
The Ringer.
Yeah.
I know all about The Ringer.
You the one that knocked him unconscious?
Accidently.
Well, good for you, kid. You get the key to the city.
Really?
No.
Tell me the truth, is this going to be a *thing?*
What?
You.
Are you going to be hopping and bopping around my neck of the woods on a regular basis?
I-I'm going to try to help out wherever I can...if that's what you're asking.
Wonderful.
Let me ask you this...

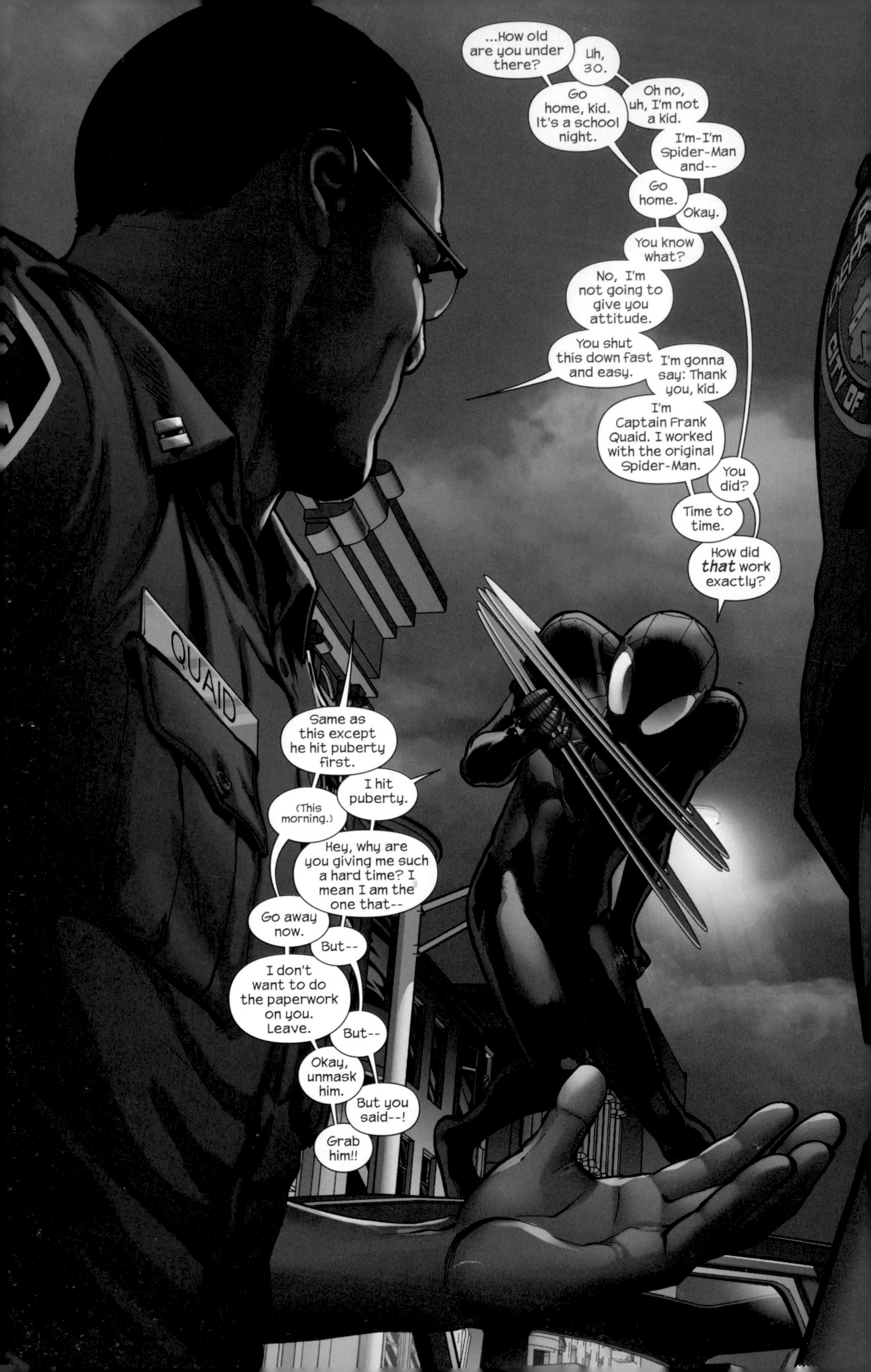
...How old are you under there?
Uh, 30.
Go home, kid. It's a school night.
Oh no, uh, I'm not a kid.
I'm-I'm Spider-Man and--
Go home.
Okay.
You know what?
No, I'm not going to give you attitude.
You shut this down fast and easy.
I'm gonna say: Thank you, kid.
I'm Captain Frank Quaid. I worked with the original Spider-Man.
You did?
Time to time.
How did *that* work exactly?
QUAID
Same as this except he hit puberty first.
I hit puberty.
(This morning.)
Hey, why are you giving me such a hard time? I mean I am the one that--
Go away now.
But--
I don't want to do the paperwork on you. Leave.
But--
Okay, unmask him.
But you said--!
Grab him!!

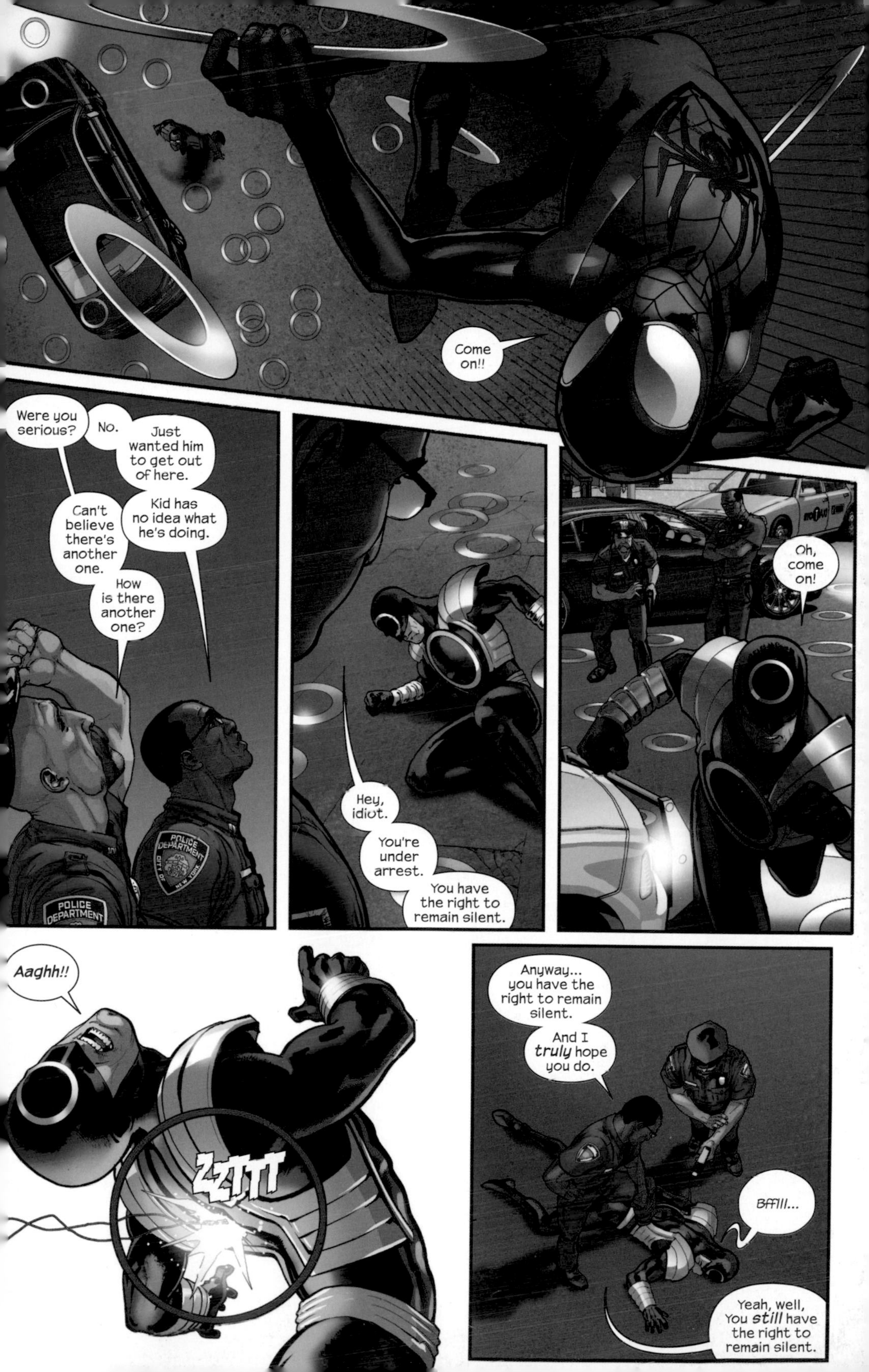
Come on!!
Were you serious?
No.
Just wanted him to get out of here.
Can't believe there's another one.
Kid has no idea what he's doing.
How is there another one?
Hey, idiot.
You're under arrest.
You have the right to remain silent.
Oh, come on!
Aaghh!!
ZZTTT
Anyway... you have the right to remain silent.
And I *truly* hope you do.
Bffill...
Yeah, well, You *still* have the right to remain silent.

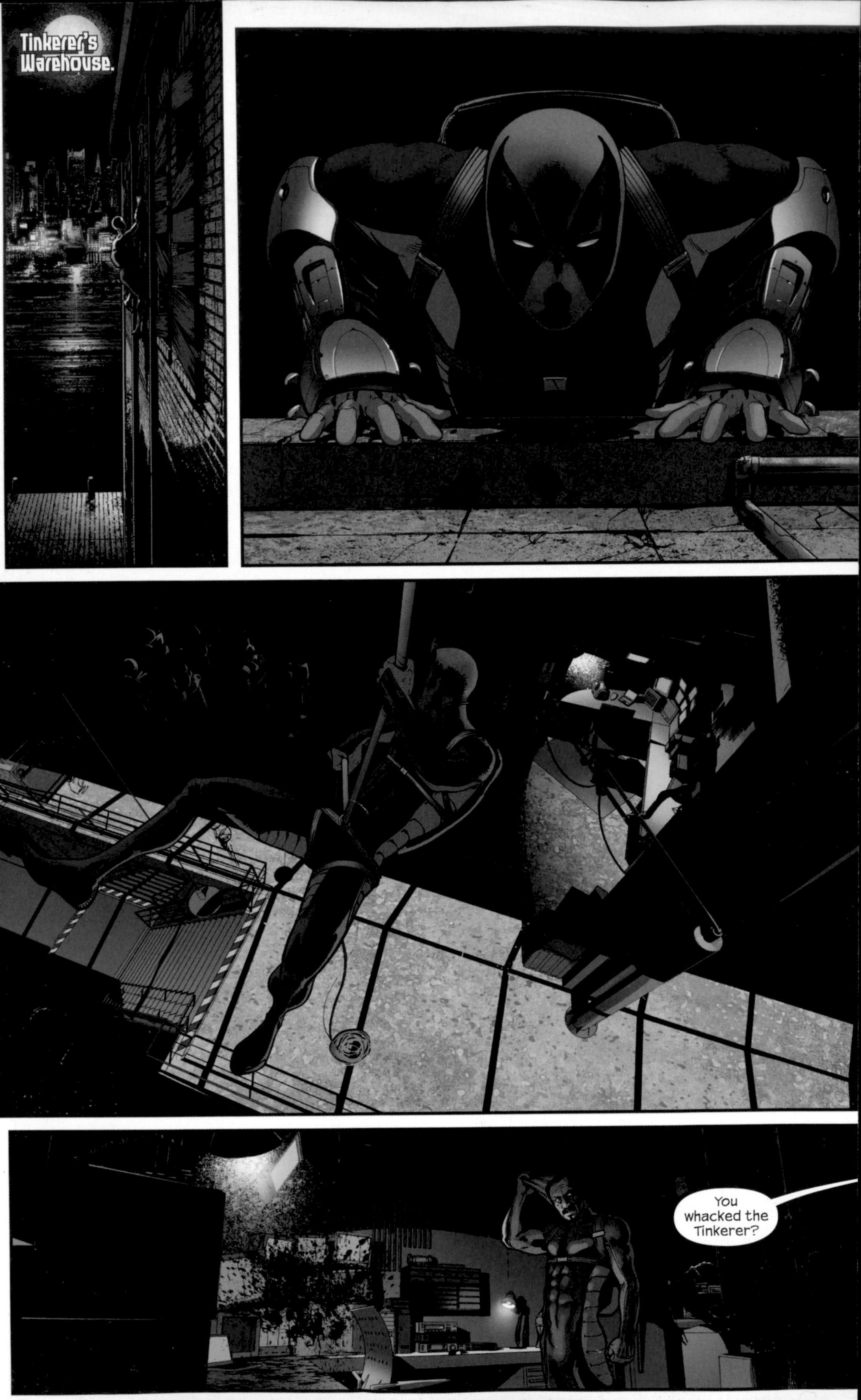

Tinkerer's Warehouse.
You whacked the Tinkerer?

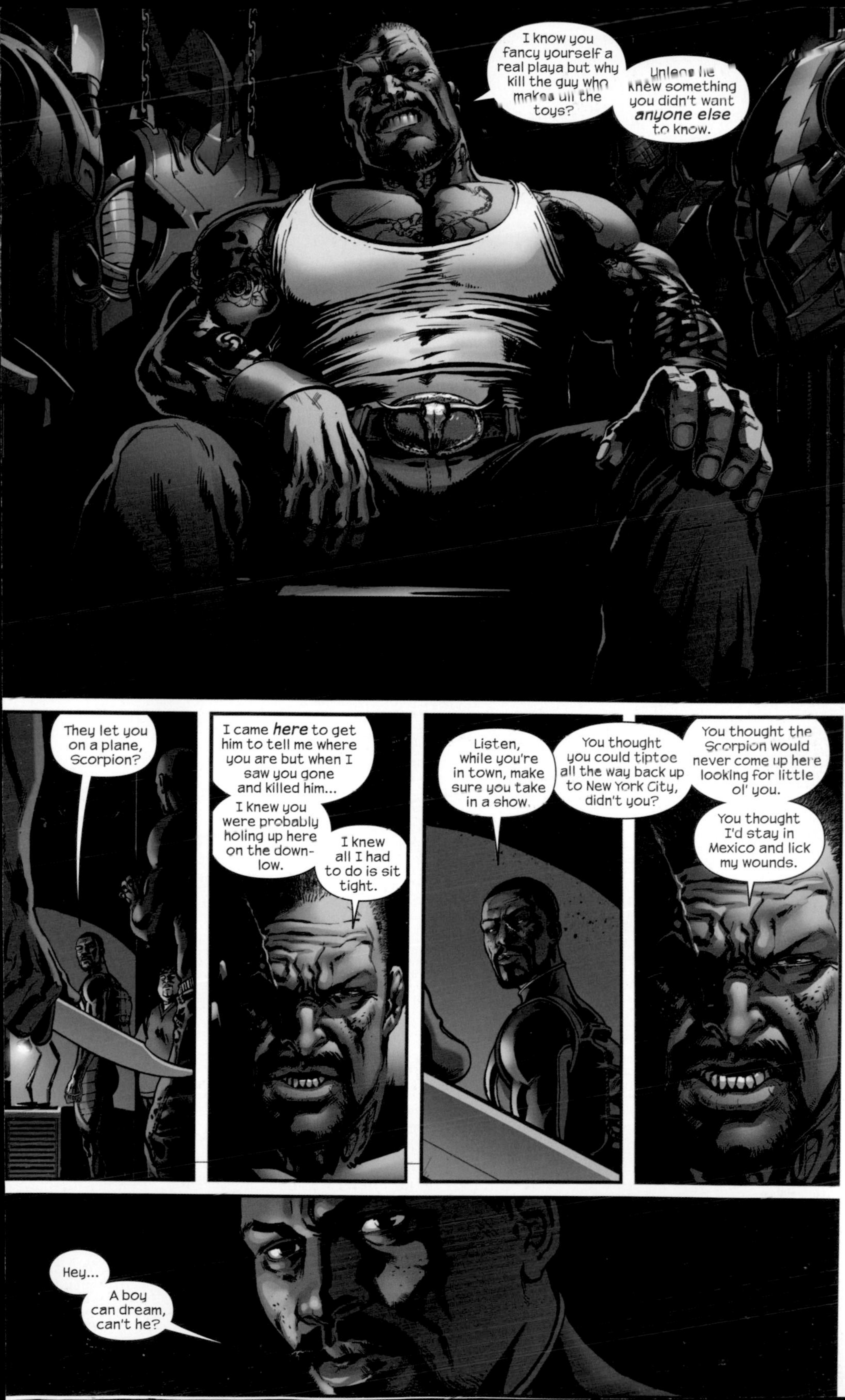
I know you fancy yourself a real playa but why kill the guy who makes all the toys?
Unless he knew something you didn't want *anyone else* to know.
They let you on a plane, Scorpion?
I came *here* to get him to tell me where you are but when I saw you gone and killed him...
I knew you were probably holing up here on the down-low.
I knew all I had to do is sit tight.
Listen, while you're in town, make sure you take in a show.
You thought you could tiptoe all the way back up to New York City, didn't you?
You thought the Scorpion would never come up here looking for little ol' you.
You thought I'd stay in Mexico and lick my wounds.
Hey...
A boy can dream, can't he?

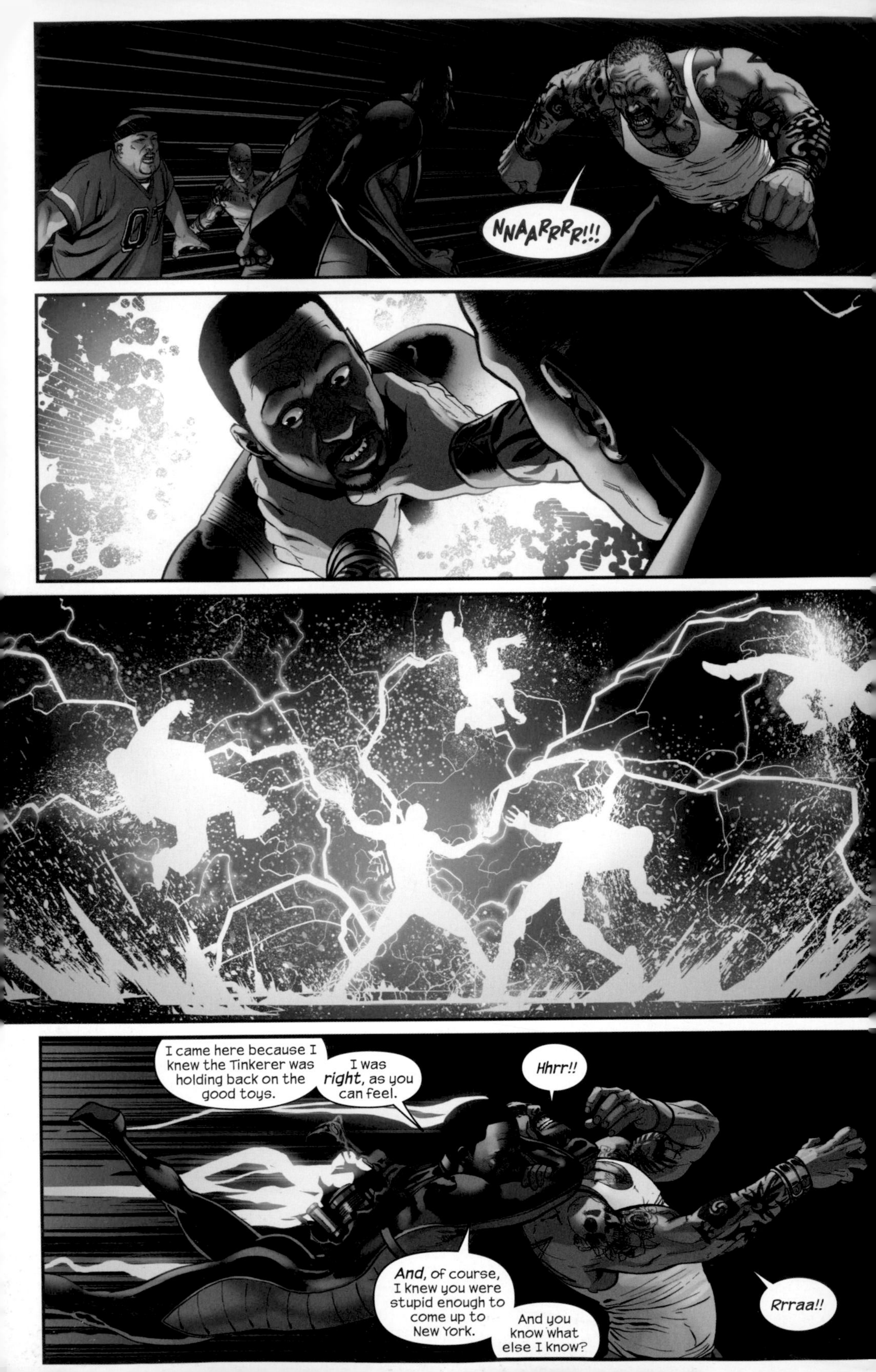
NNAARRRR!!!
I came here because I knew the Tinkerer was holding back on the good toys.
I was right, as you can feel.
Hhrr!!
And, of course, I knew you were stupid enough to come up to New York.
And you know what else I know?
Rrraa!!

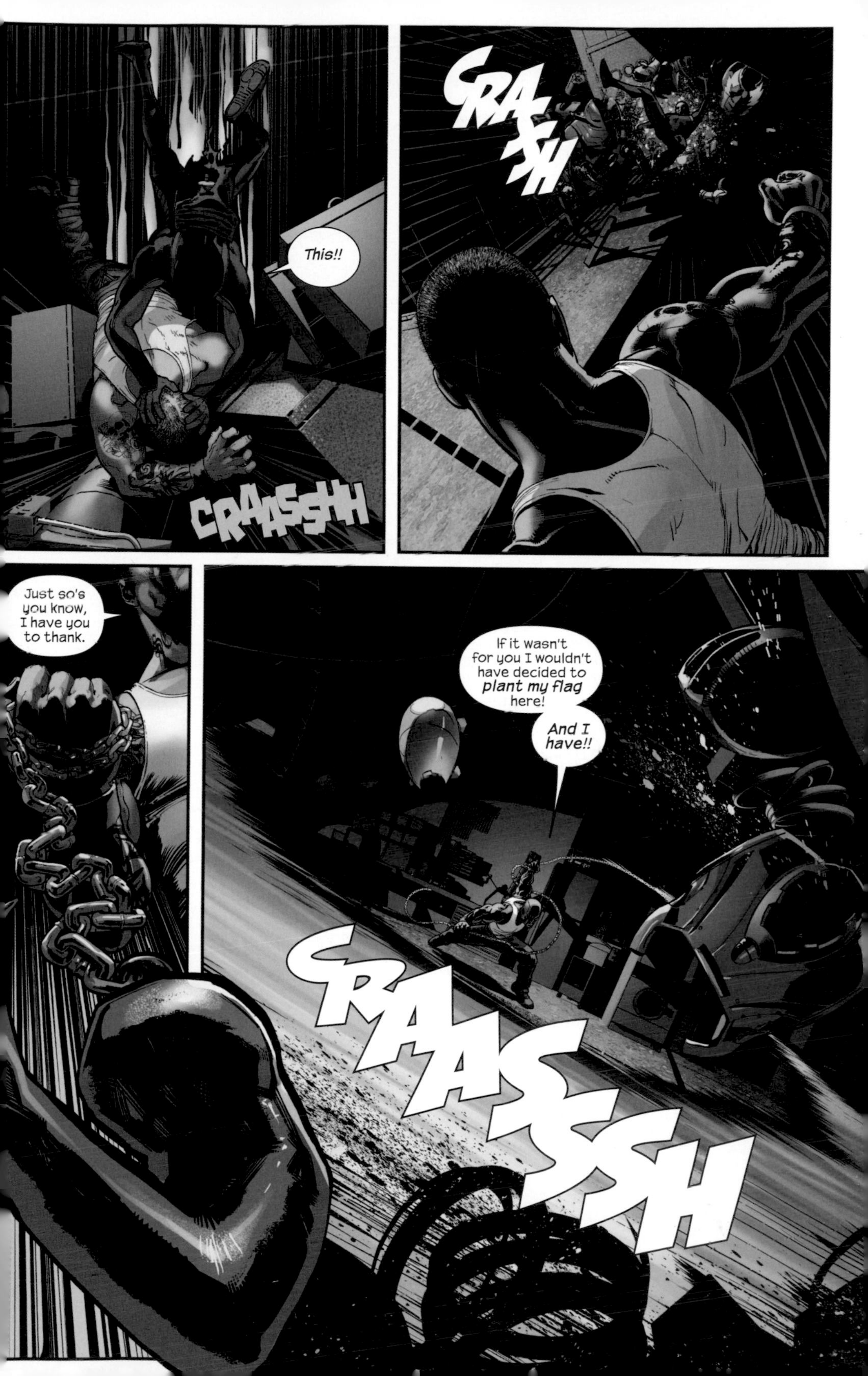
This!!
CRAASSHH
CRASH
Just so's you know, I have you to thank.
If it wasn't for you I wouldn't have decided to plant my flag here!
And I have!!
CRAASSSH

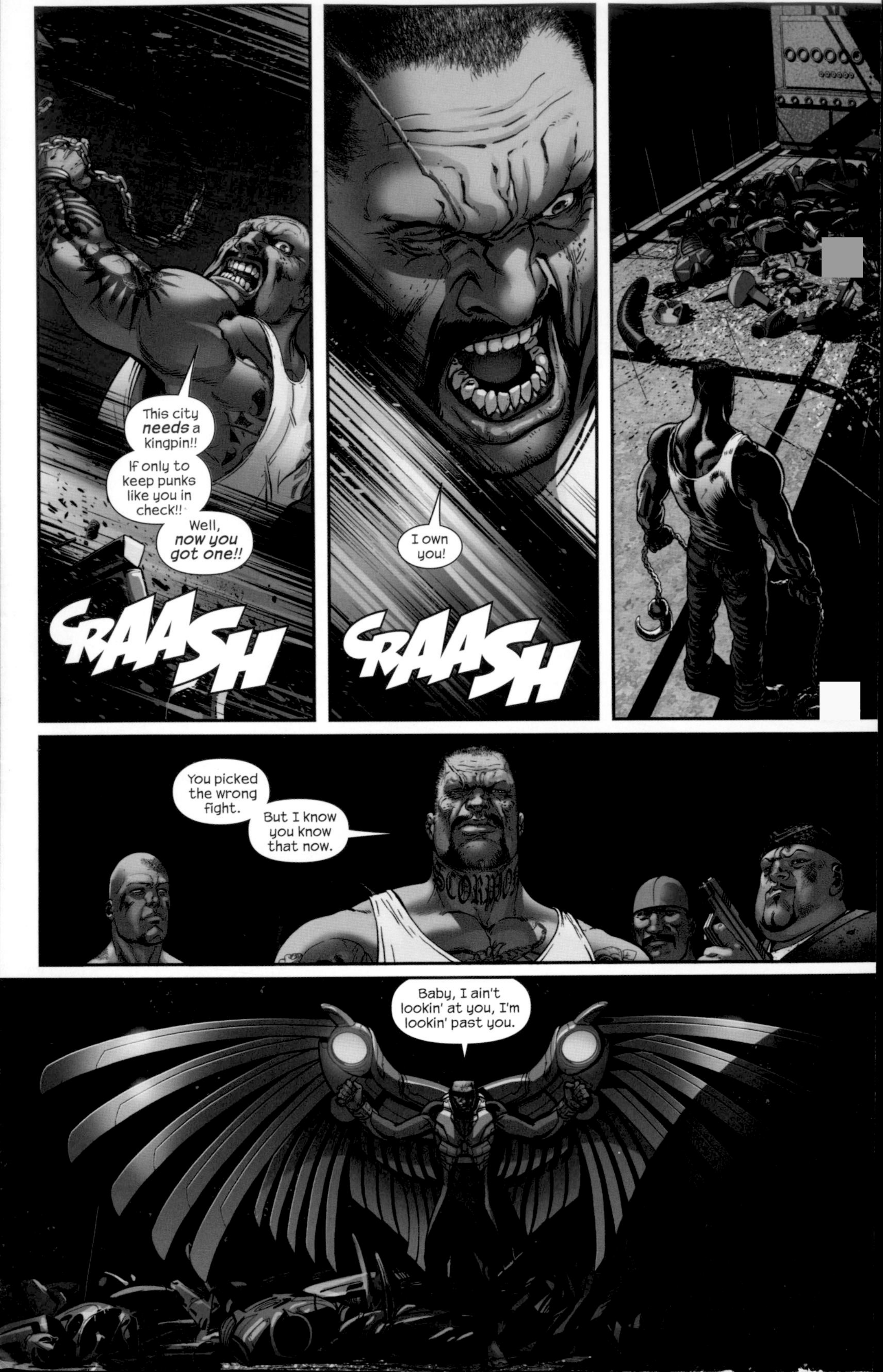
This city *needs* a kingpin!!
If only to keep punks like you in check!!
Well, *now you got one!!*
CRAASH
I own you!
CRAASH
You picked the wrong fight.
But I know you know that now.
SCORPION
Baby, I ain't lookin' at you, I'm lookin' past you.

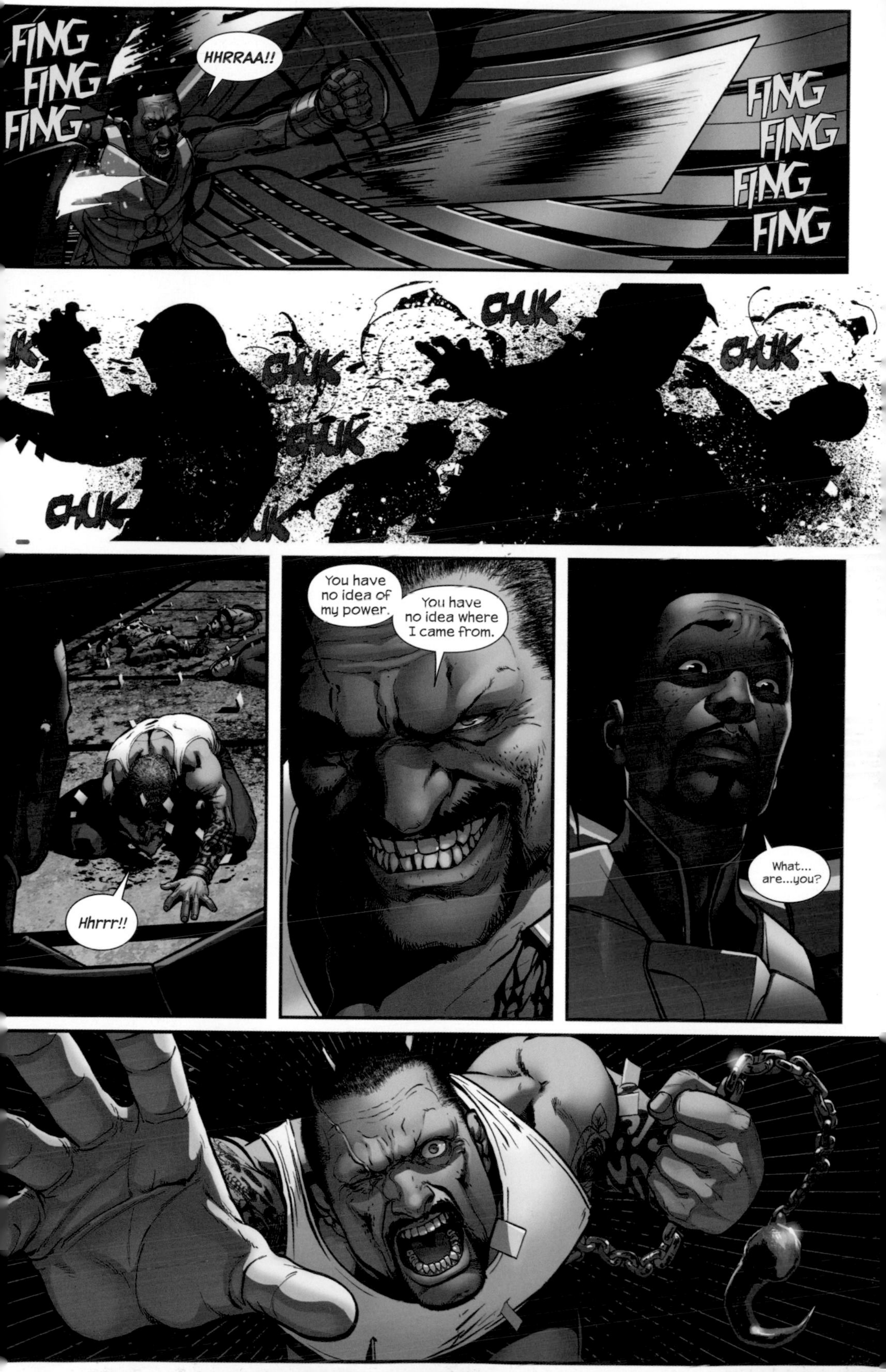
FING
FING
FING
HHRRAA!!
FING
FING
FING
FING
CHUK
CHUK
CHUK
CHUK
CHUK
Hhrrr!!
You have no idea of my power.
You have no idea where I came from.
What... are...you?

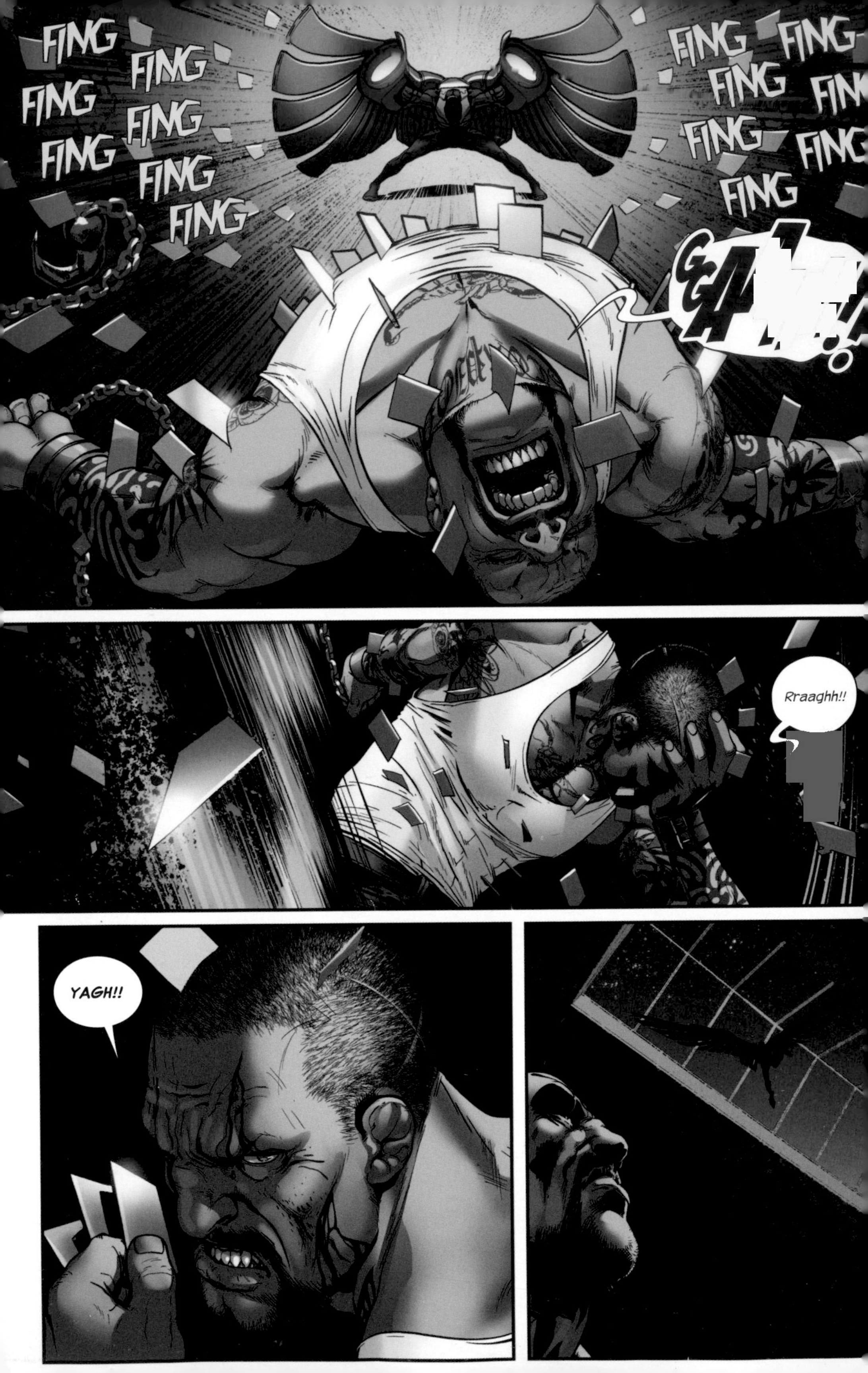
FING FING FING FING FING FING FING
FING FING FING FING FING FING FING
Rraaghh!!
YAGH!!

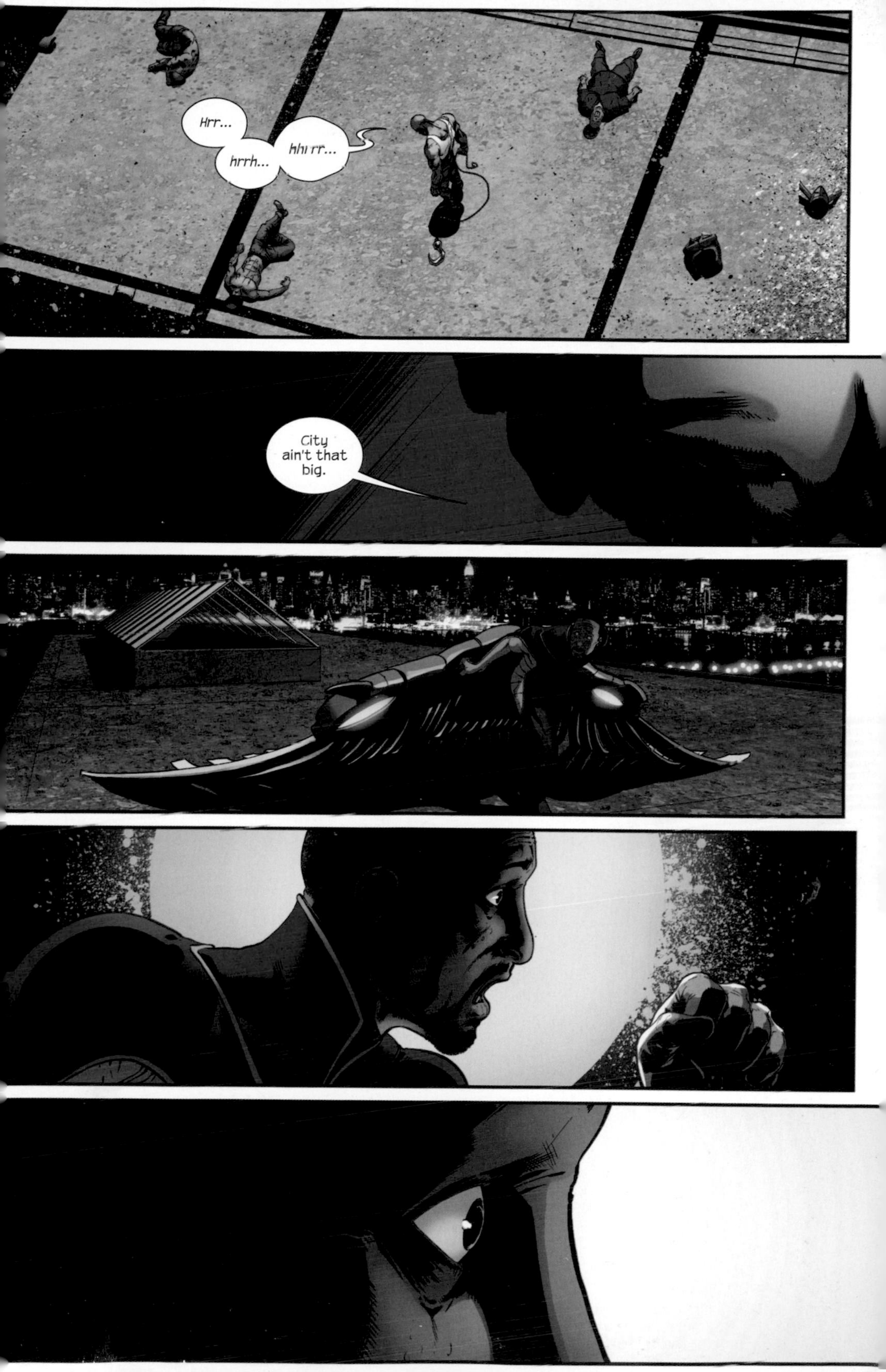
Hrr...
hrrh...
hhrrr...
City ain't that big.

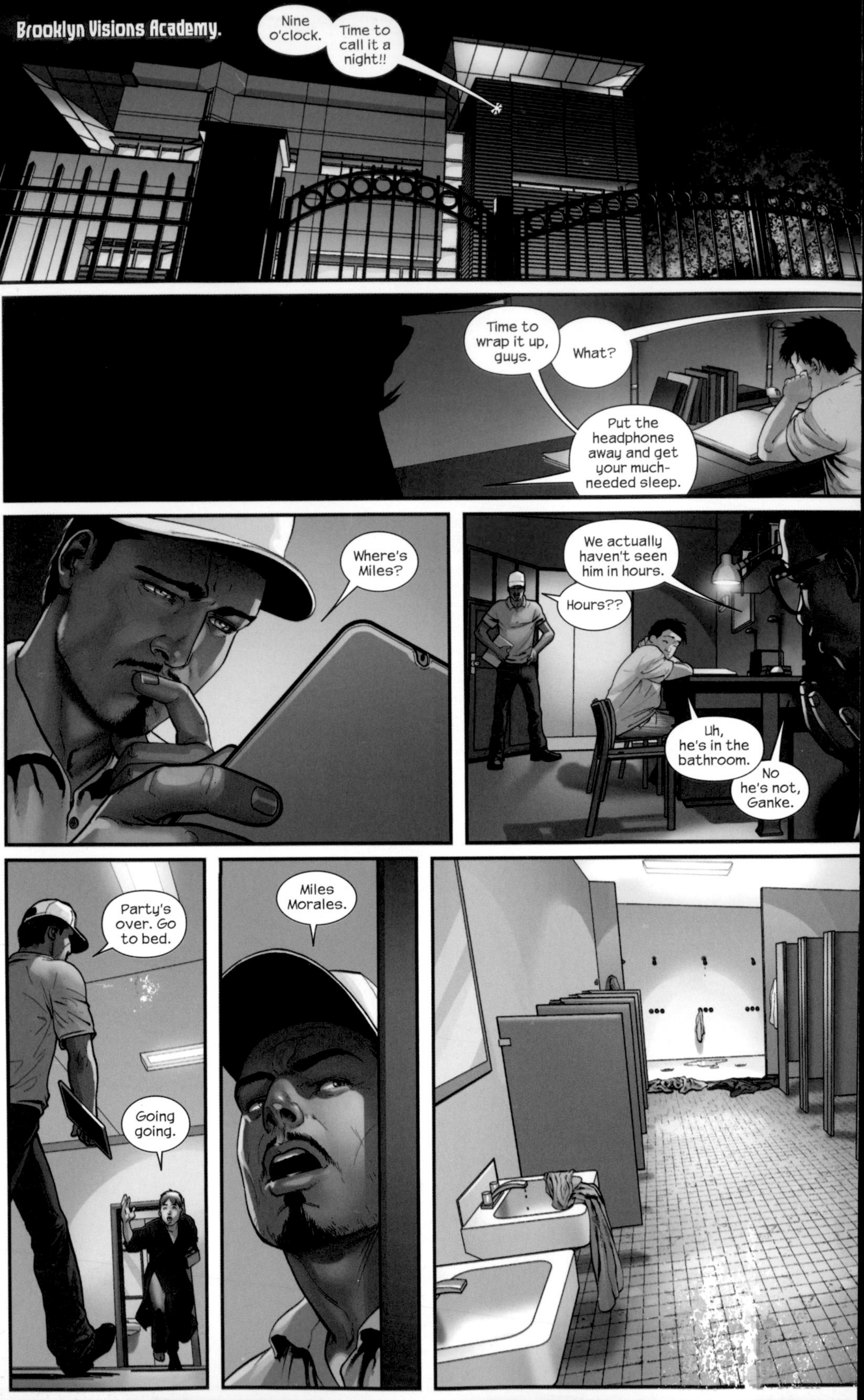
Brooklyn Visions Academy.
Nine o'clock.
Time to call it a night!!
Time to wrap it up, guys.
What?
Put the headphones away and get your much-needed sleep.
Where's Miles?
We actually haven't seen him in hours.
Hours??
Uh, he's in the bathroom.
No he's not, Ganke.
Party's over. Go to bed.
Going going.
Miles Morales.

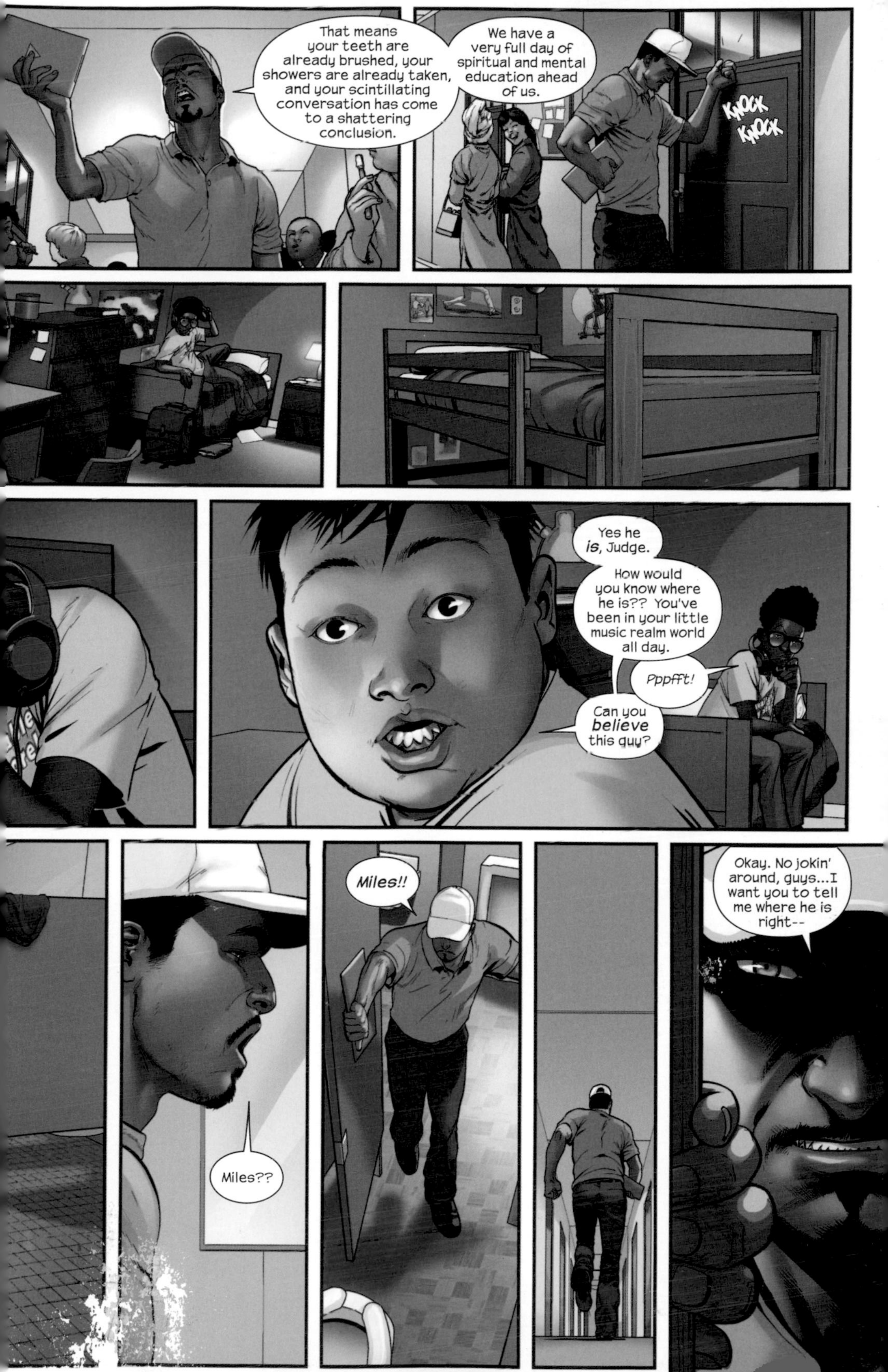
That means your teeth are already brushed, your showers are already taken, and your scintillating conversation has come to a shattering conclusion.
We have a very full day of spiritual and mental education ahead of us.
KNOCK KNOCK
Yes he is, Judge.
How would you know where he is?? You've been in your little music realm world all day.
Pppfft!
Can you believe this guy?
Miles??
Miles!!
Okay. No jokin' around, guys...I want you to tell me where he is right--

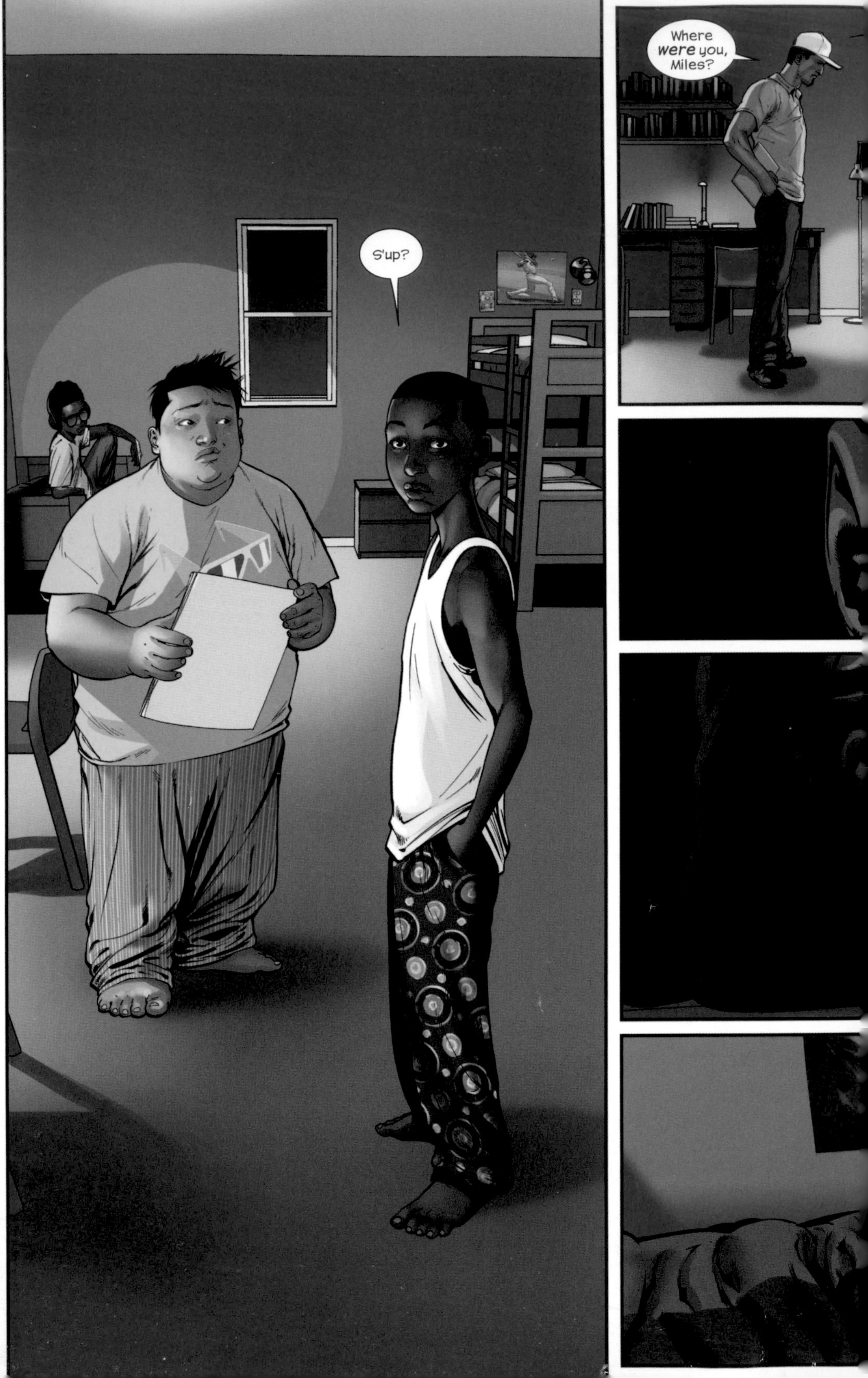
S'up?
Where *were* you, Miles?

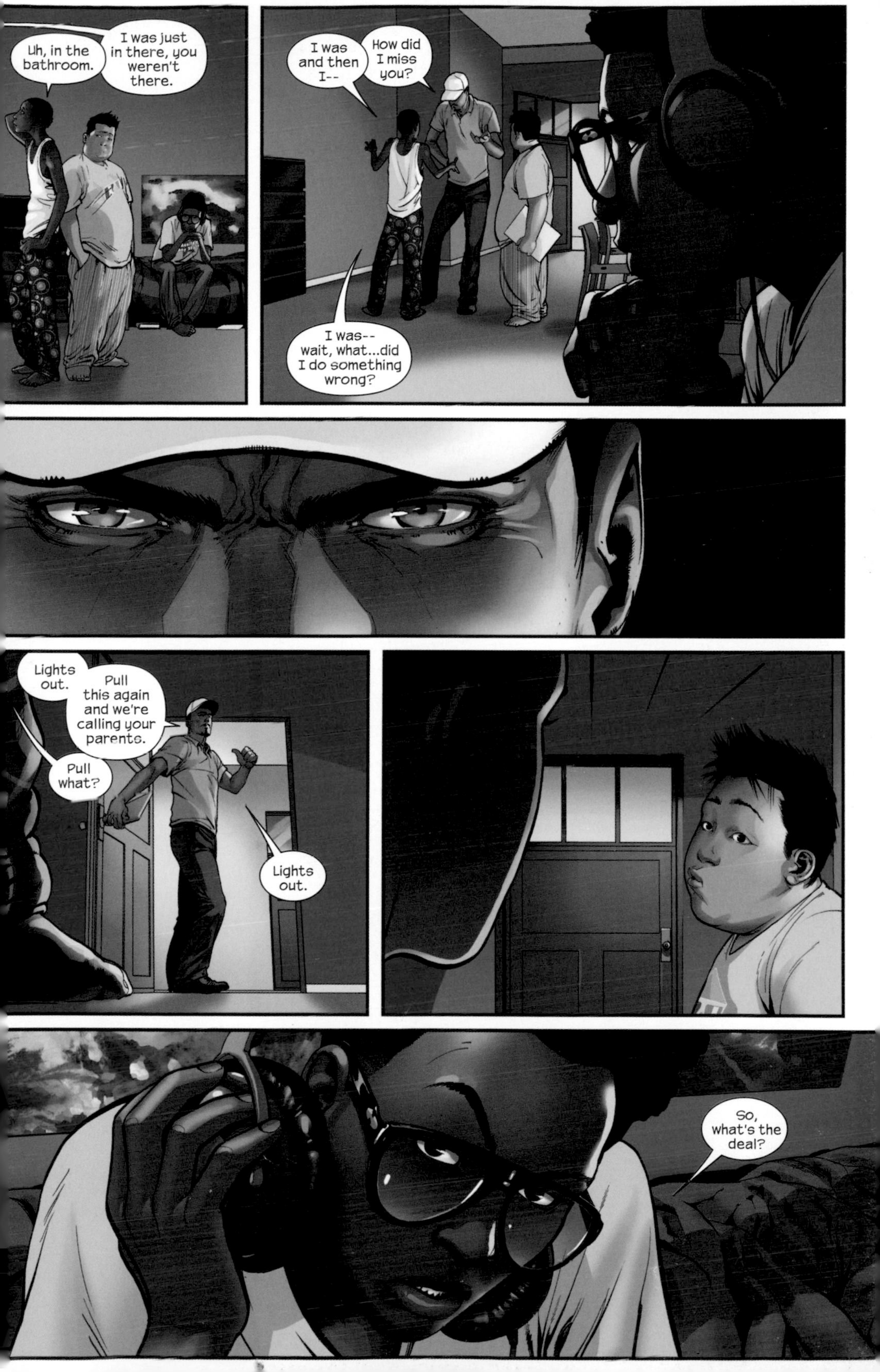
Uh, in the bathroom.
I was just in there, you weren't there.
I was and then I--
How did I miss you?
I was-- wait, what...did I do something wrong?
Lights out.
Pull this again and we're calling your parents.
Pull what?
Lights out.
So, what's the deal?

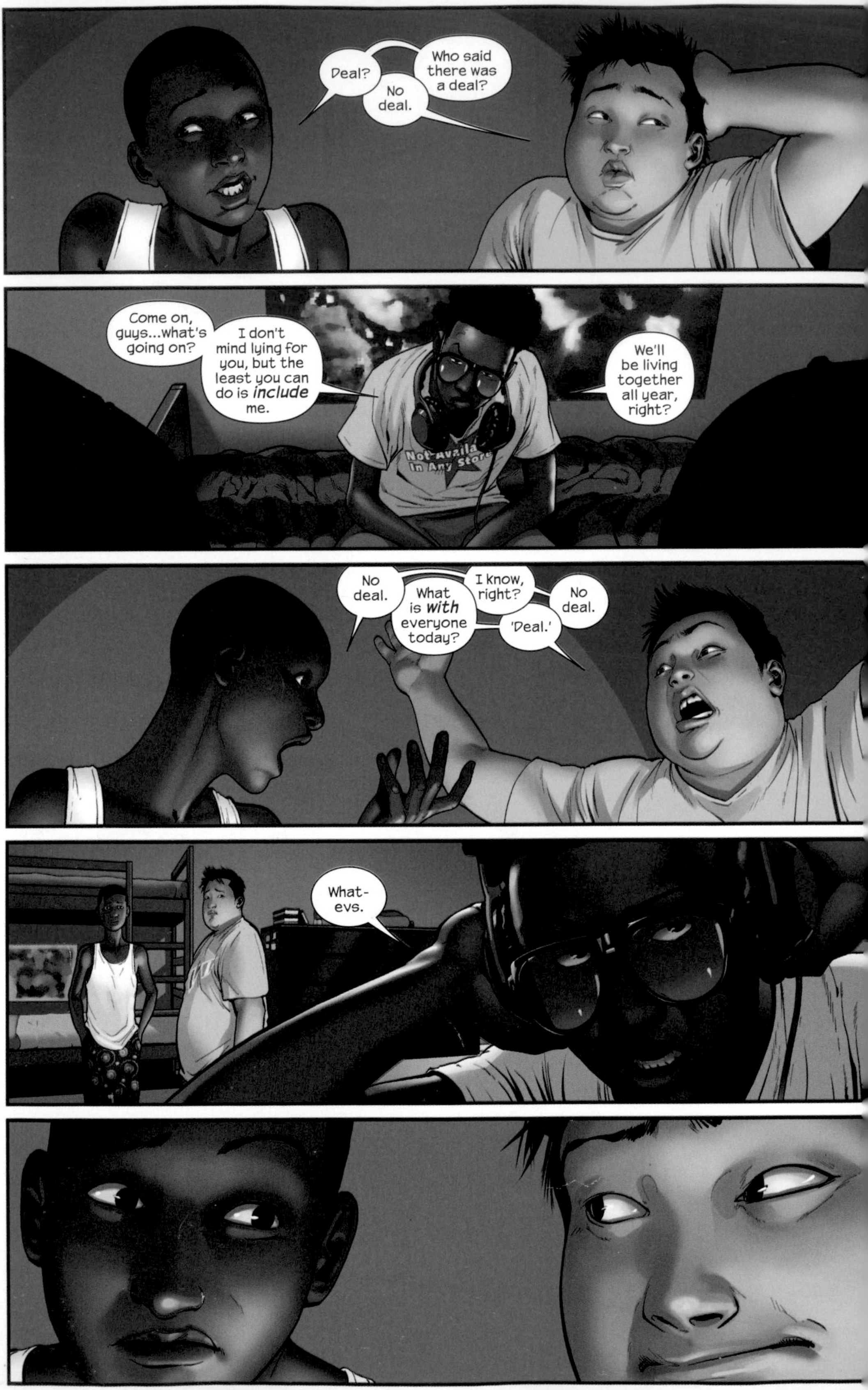
Deal?
No deal.
Who said there was a deal?
Come on, guys...what's going on?
I don't mind lying for you, but the least you can do is *include* me.
We'll be living together all year, right?
No deal.
What is *with* everyone today?
I know, right?
'Deal.'
No deal.
What-evs.

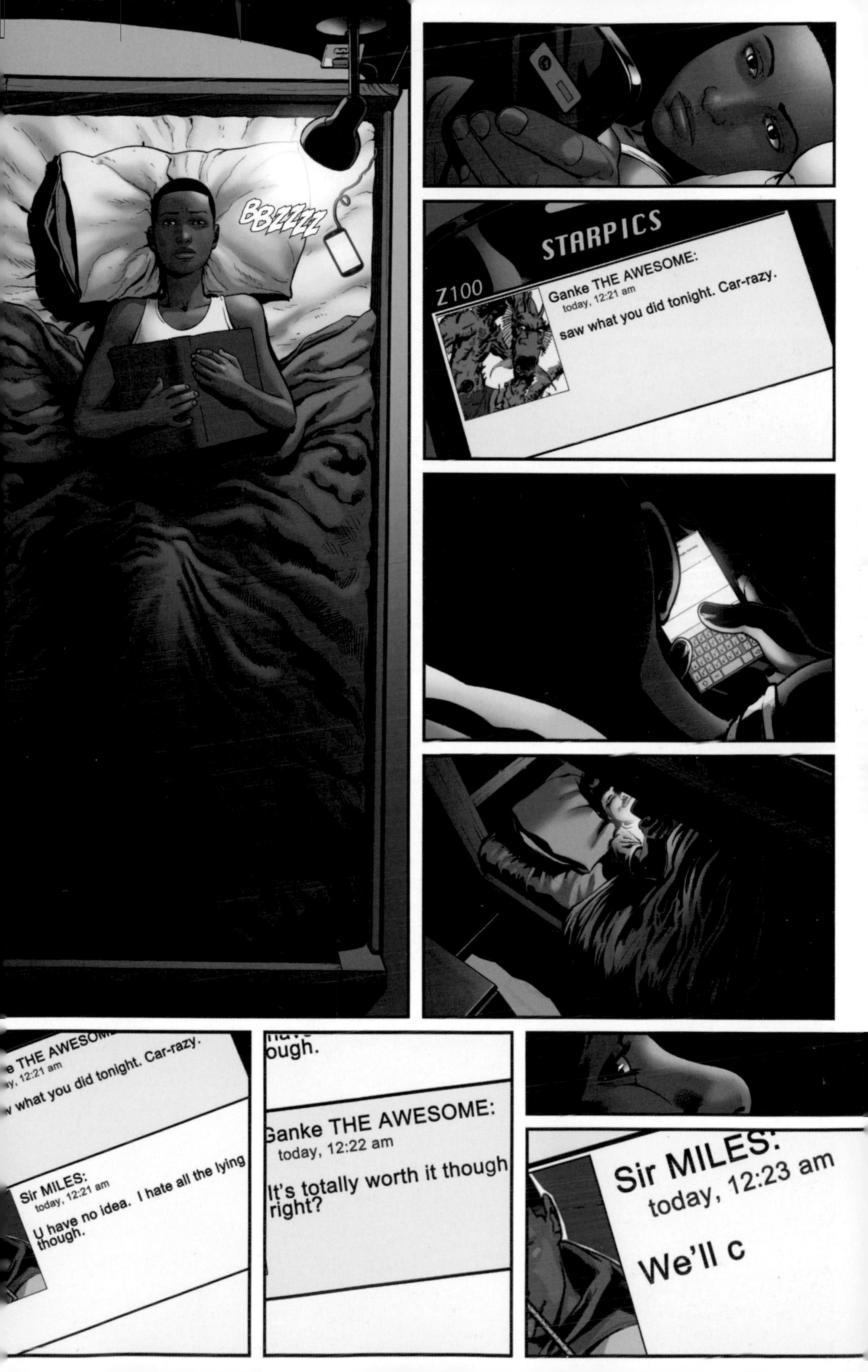
BBZZZZZ
STARPICS
Z100
Ganke THE AWESOME:
today, 12:21 am
saw what you did tonight. Car-razy.
Sir MILES:
today, 12:21 am
U have no idea. I hate all the lying though.
Ganke THE AWESOME:
today, 12:22 am
It's totally worth it though right?
Sir MILES:
today, 12:23 am
We'll c

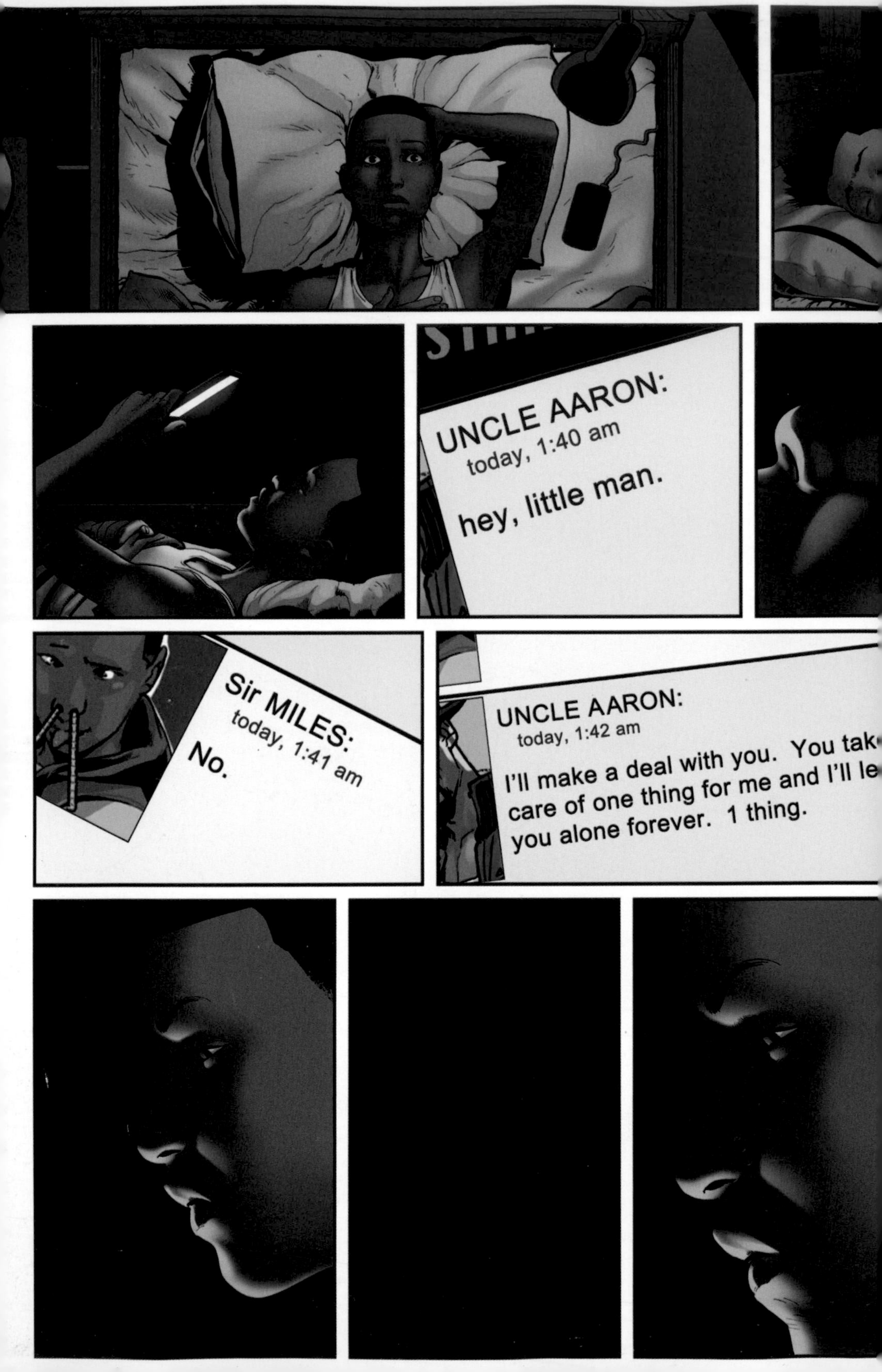
UNCLE AARON:
today, 1:40 am
hey, little man.
Sir MILES:
today, 1:41 am
No.
UNCLE AARON:
today, 1:42 am
I'll make a deal with you. You tak
care of one thing for me and I'll le
you alone forever. 1 thing.

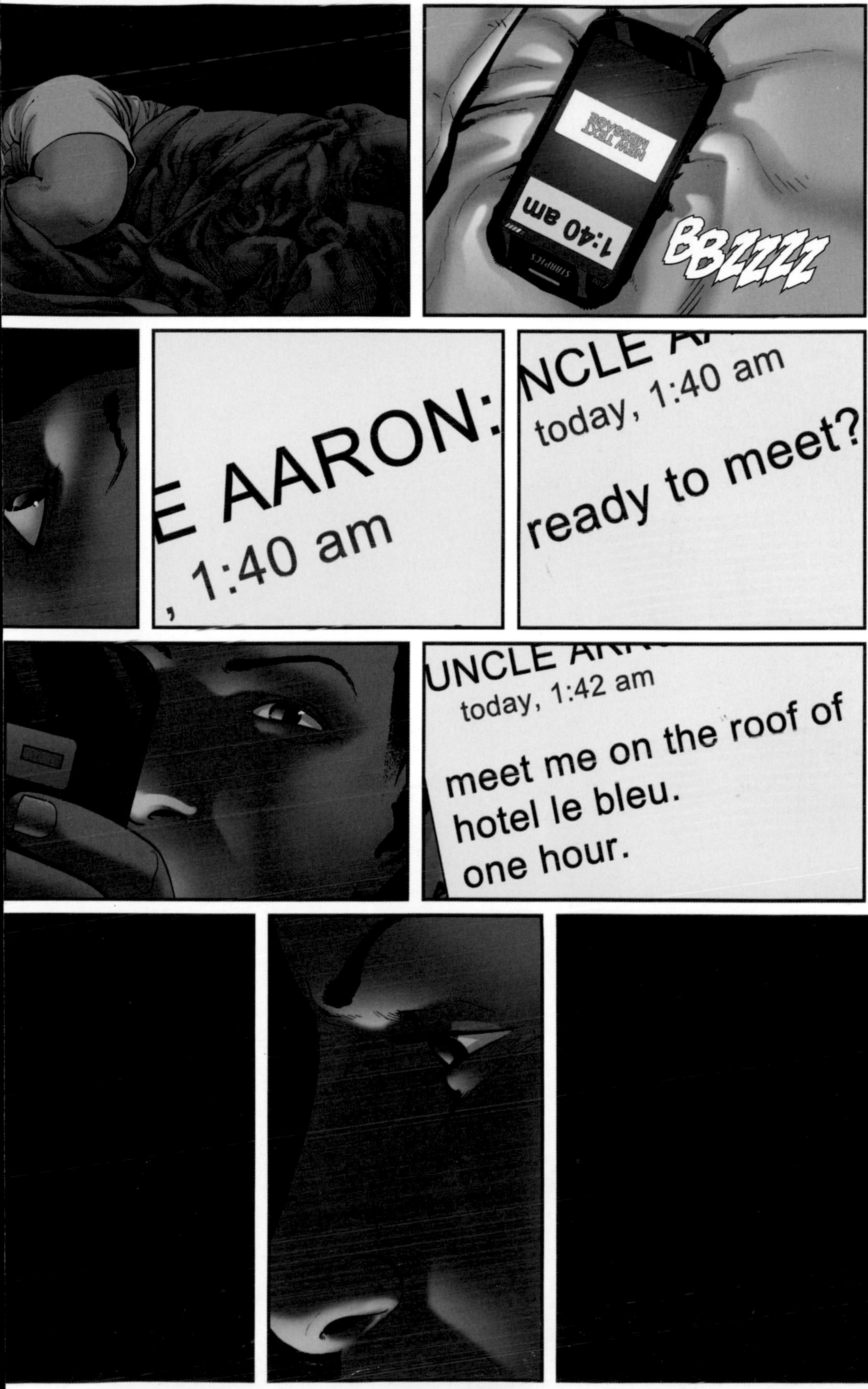
NEW TEXT MESSAGE
1:40 am
BBZZZZZ
E AARON:
, 1:40 am
NCLE A
today, 1:40 am
ready to meet?
UNCLE AAR
today, 1:42 am
meet me on the roof of
hotel le bleu.
one hour.

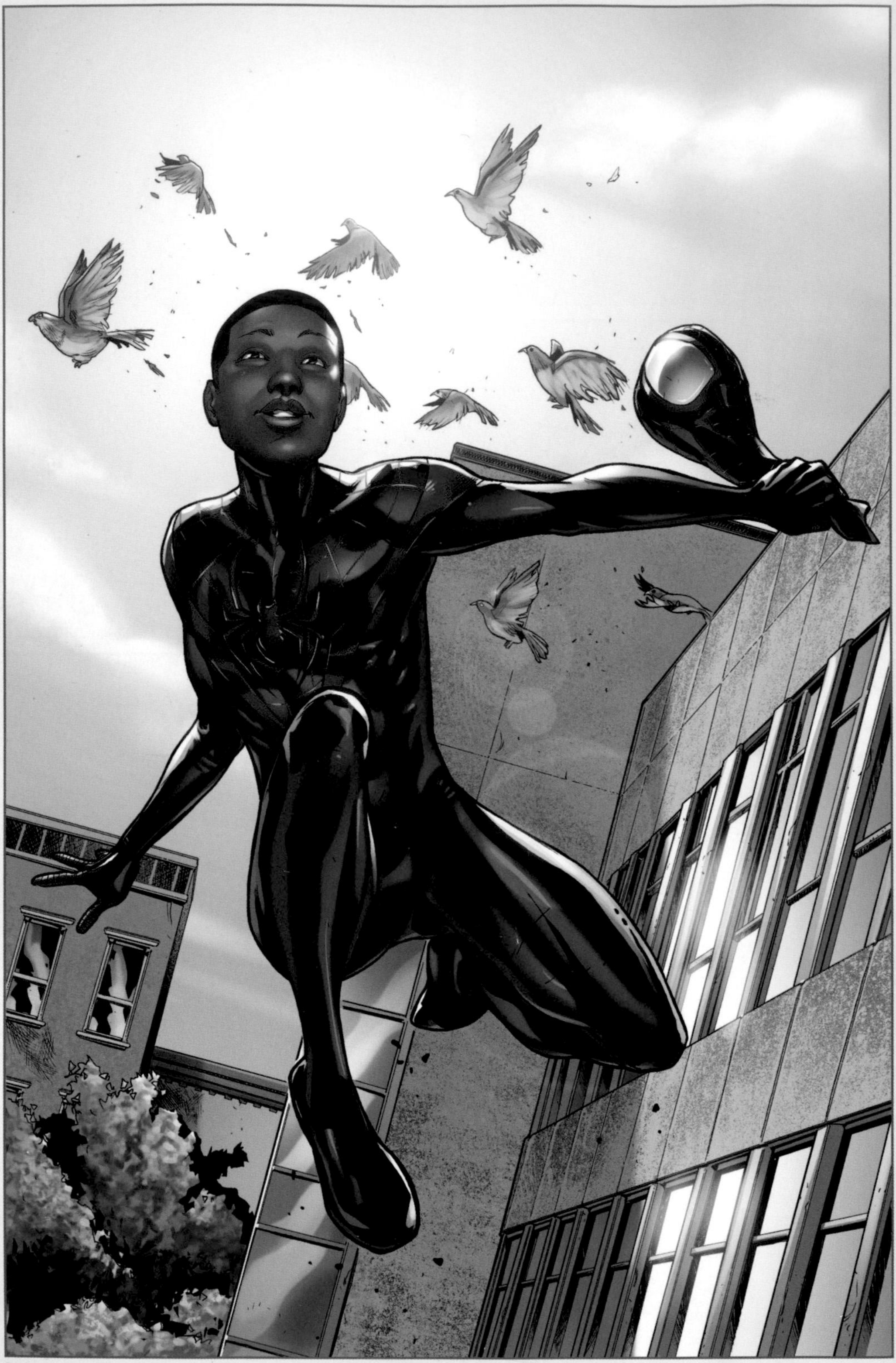

#1 VARIANT
BY SARA PICHELLI & JUSTIN PONSOR

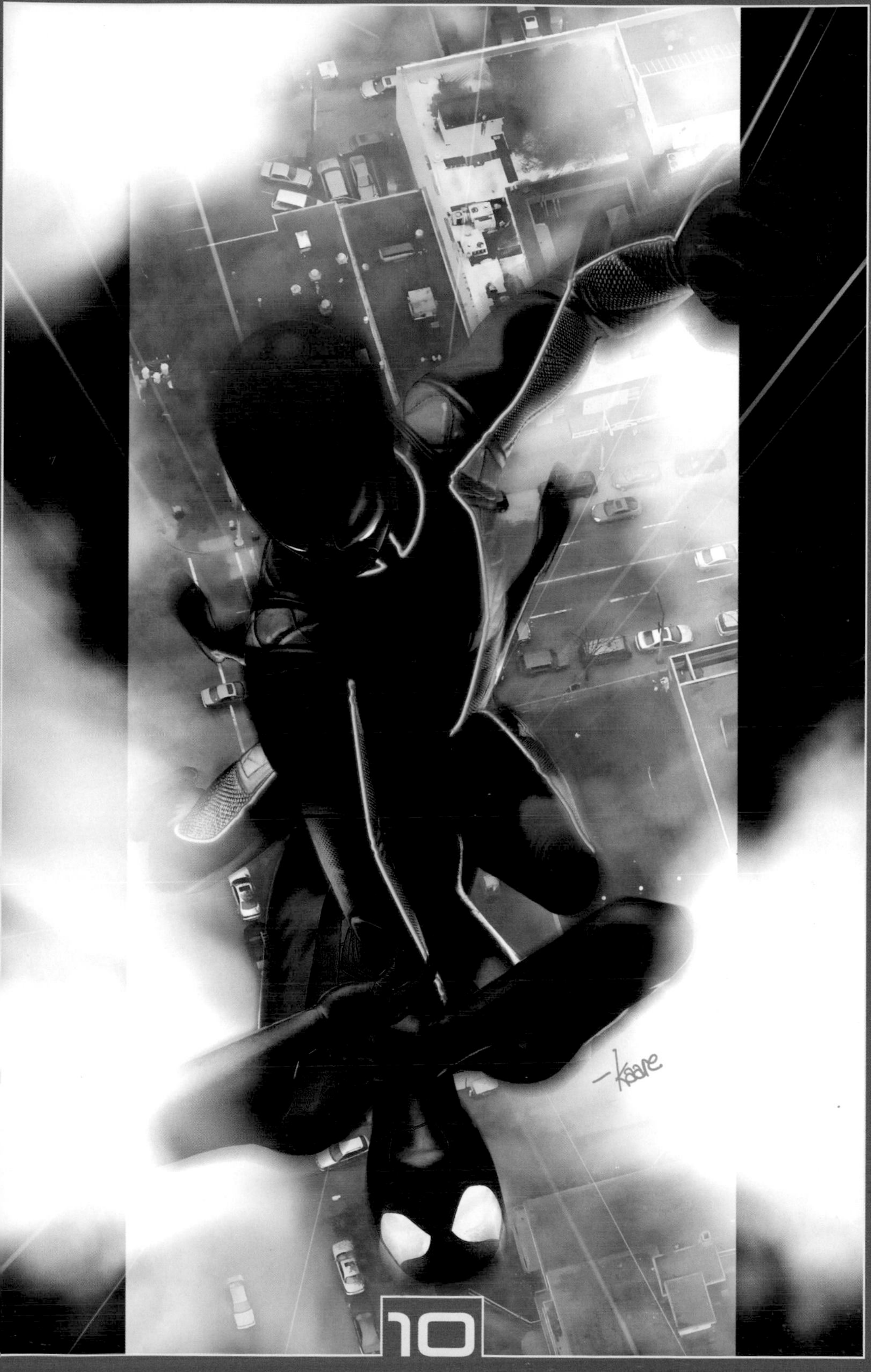
— Kaare
10

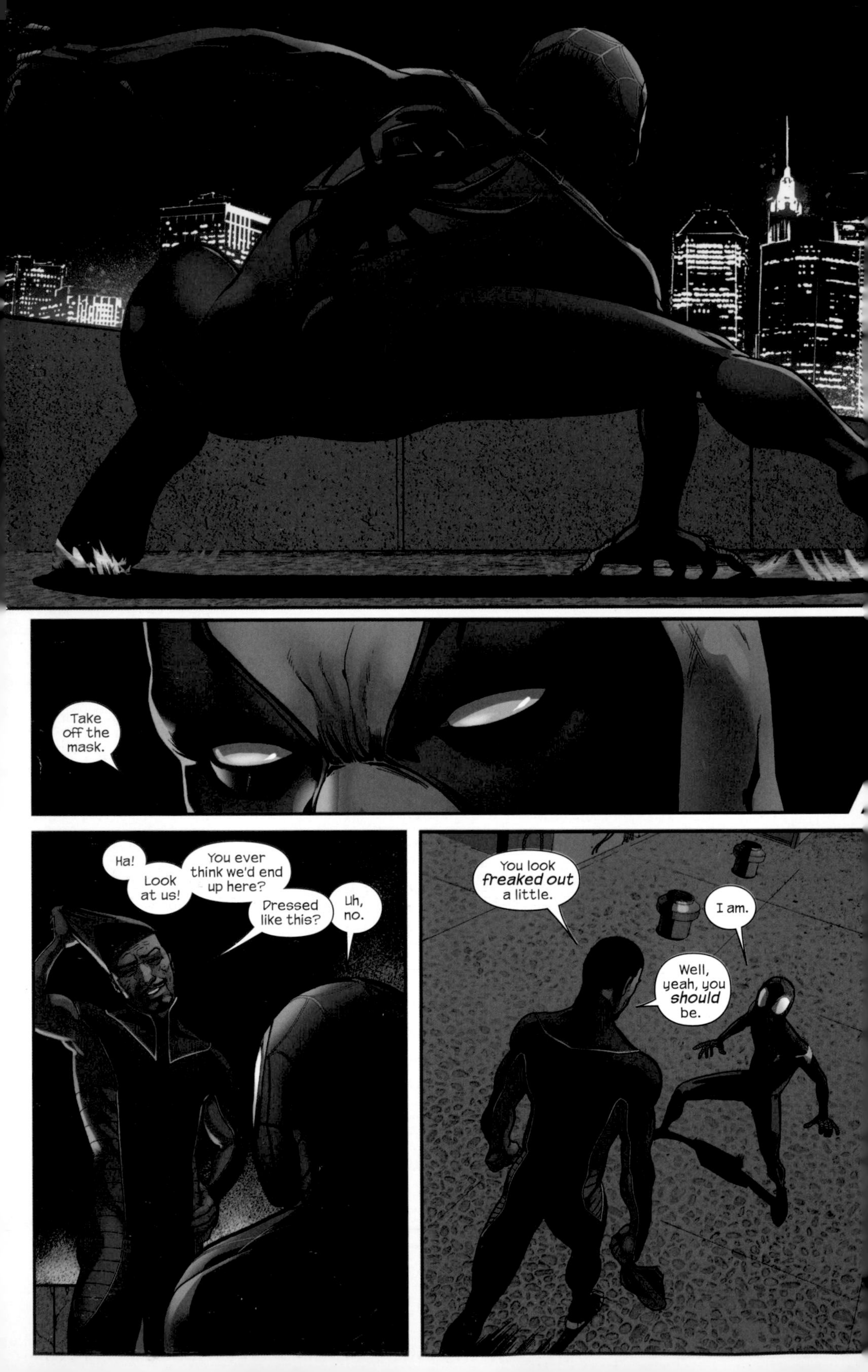
Take off the mask.
Ha!
Look at us!
You ever think we'd end up here?
Dressed like this?
Uh, no.
You look *freaked out* a little.
I am.
Well, yeah, you *should* be.

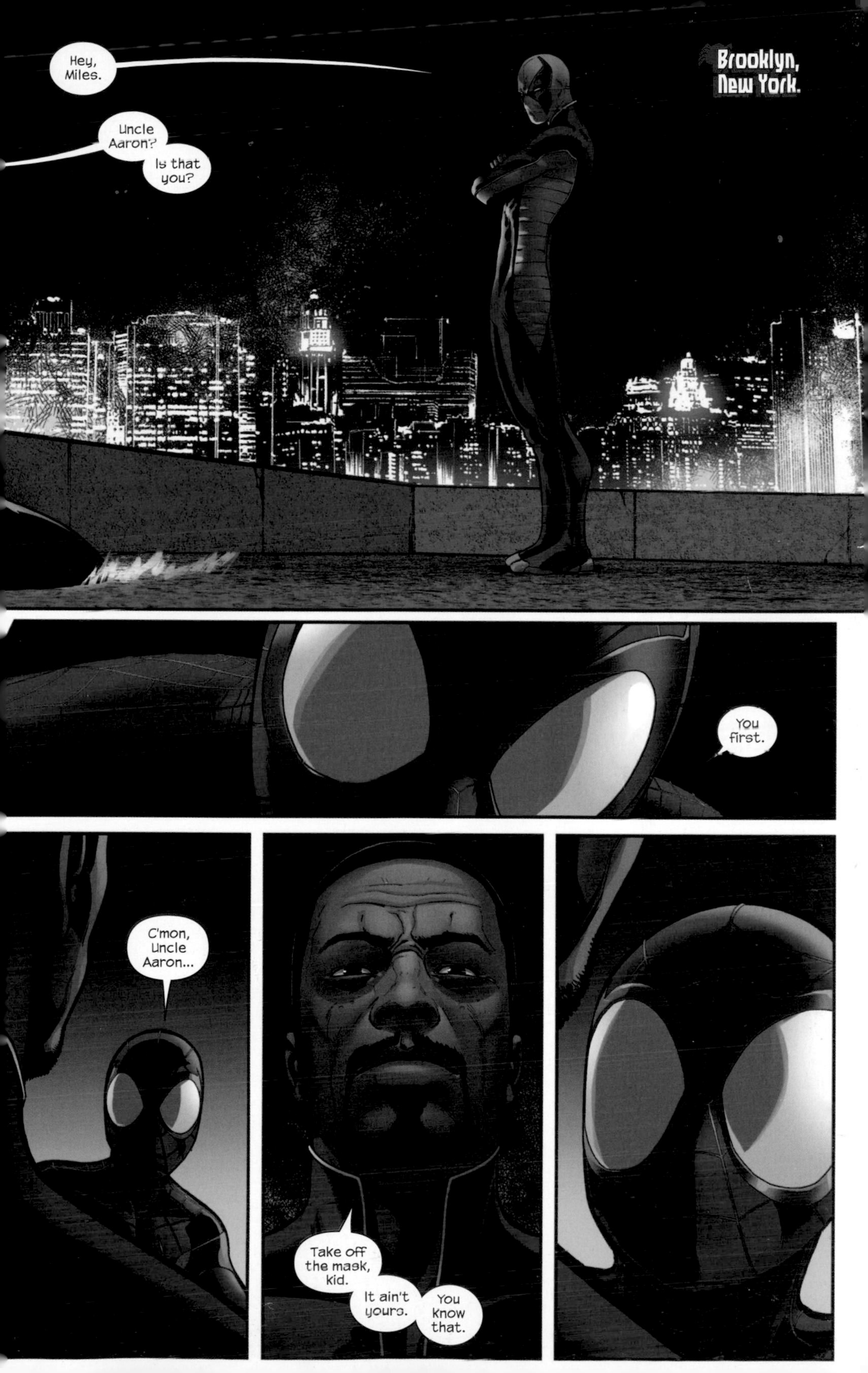

Brooklyn, New York.
Hey, Miles.
Uncle Aaron?
Is that you?
You first.
C'mon, Uncle Aaron...
Take off the mask, kid.
It ain't yours.
You know that.

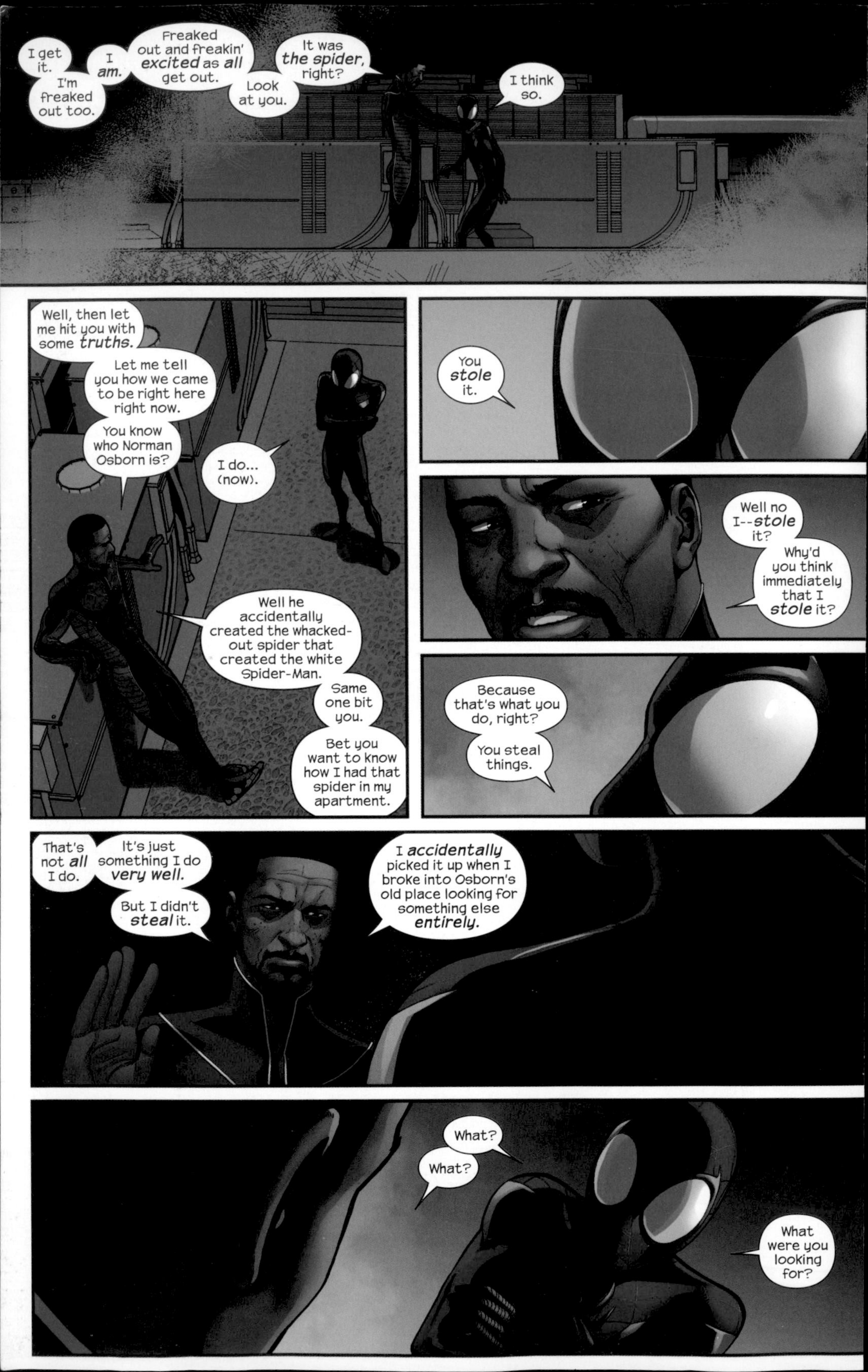
I get it.
I'm freaked out too.
I am.
Freaked out and freakin' excited as all get out.
Look at you.
It was the spider, right?
I think so.
Well, then let me hit you with some truths.
Let me tell you how we came to be right here right now.
You know who Norman Osborn is?
I do... (now).
Well he accidentally created the whacked-out spider that created the white Spider-Man.
Same one bit you.
Bet you want to know how I had that spider in my apartment.
You stole it.
Well no I--stole it?
Why'd you think immediately that I stole it?
Because that's what you do, right?
You steal things.
That's not all I do.
It's just something I do very well.
But I didn't steal it.
I accidentally picked it up when I broke into Osborn's old place looking for something else entirely.
What?
What?
What were you looking for?

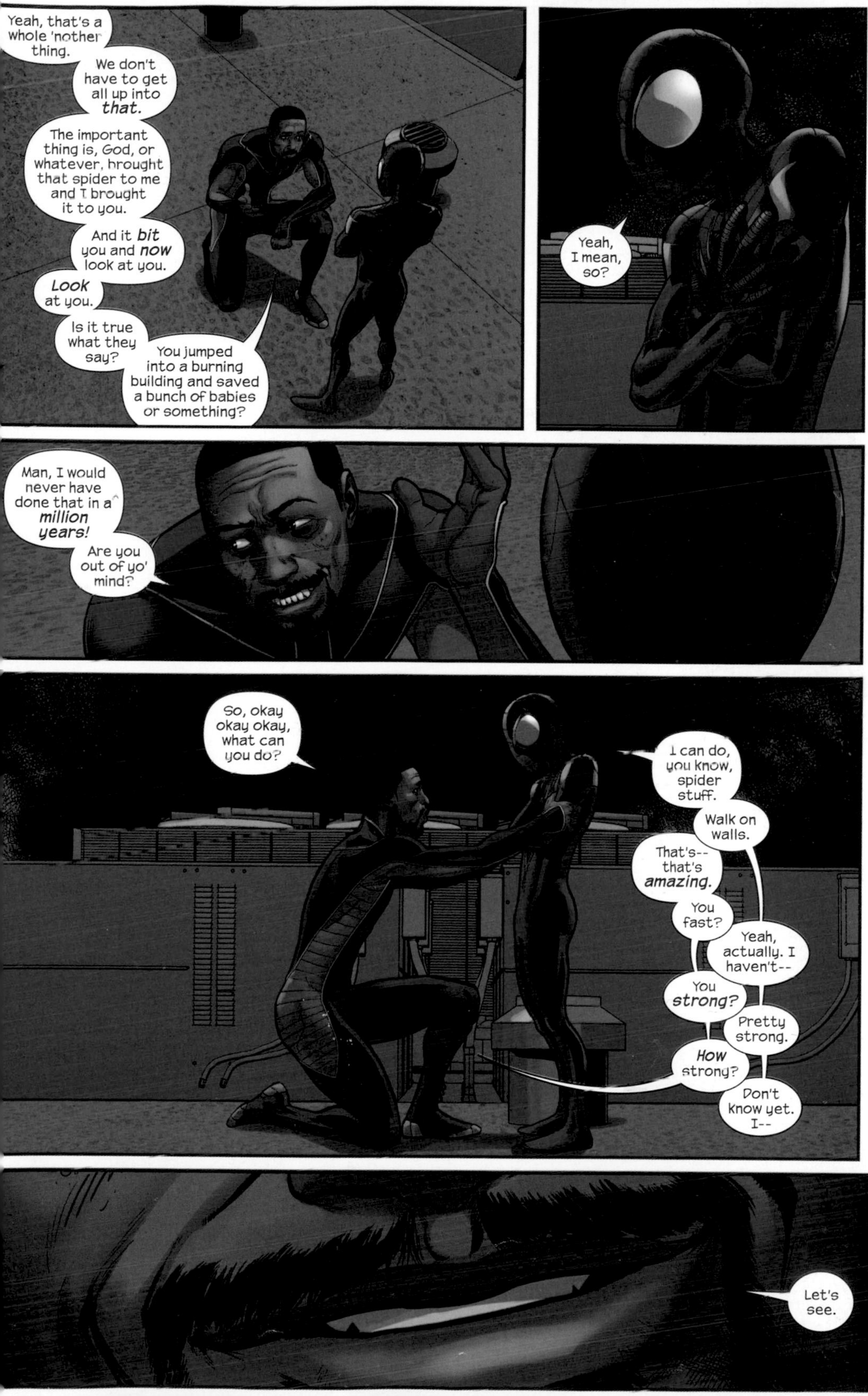
Yeah, that's a whole 'nother thing.
We don't have to get all up into *that.*
The important thing is, God, or whatever, brought that spider to me and I brought it to you.
And it *bit* you and *now* look at you.
Look at you.
Is it true what they say?
You jumped into a burning building and saved a bunch of babies or something?
Yeah, I mean, so?
Man, I would never have done that in a *million years!*
Are you out of yo' mind?
So, okay okay okay, what can you do?
I can do, you know, spider stuff.
Walk on walls.
That's-- that's *amazing.*
You fast?
Yeah, actually. I haven't--
You *strong?*
Pretty strong.
How strong?
Don't know yet. I--
Let's see.

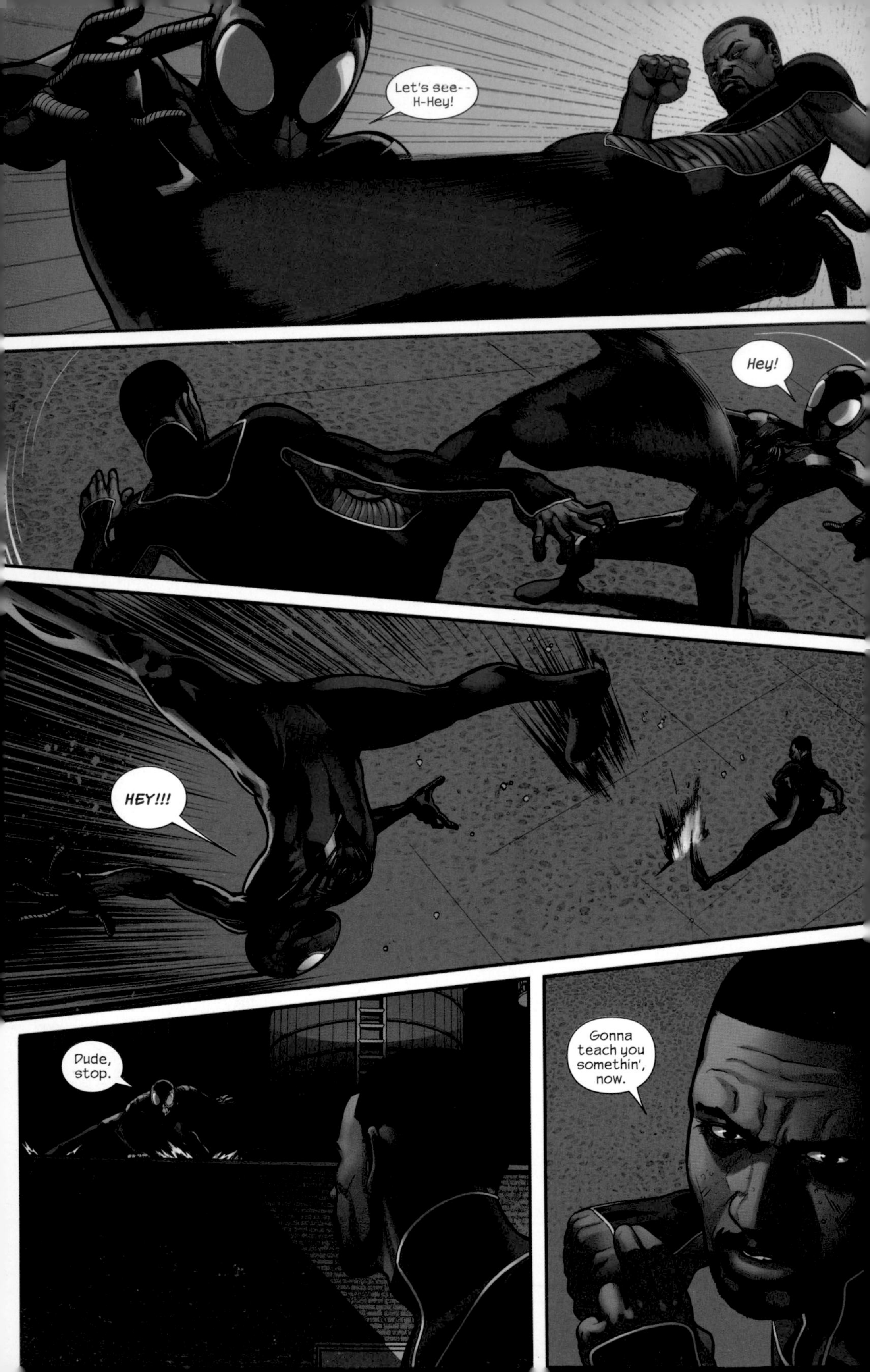
Let's see--
H-Hey!
Hey!
HEY!!!
Dude, stop.
Gonna teach you somethin', now.

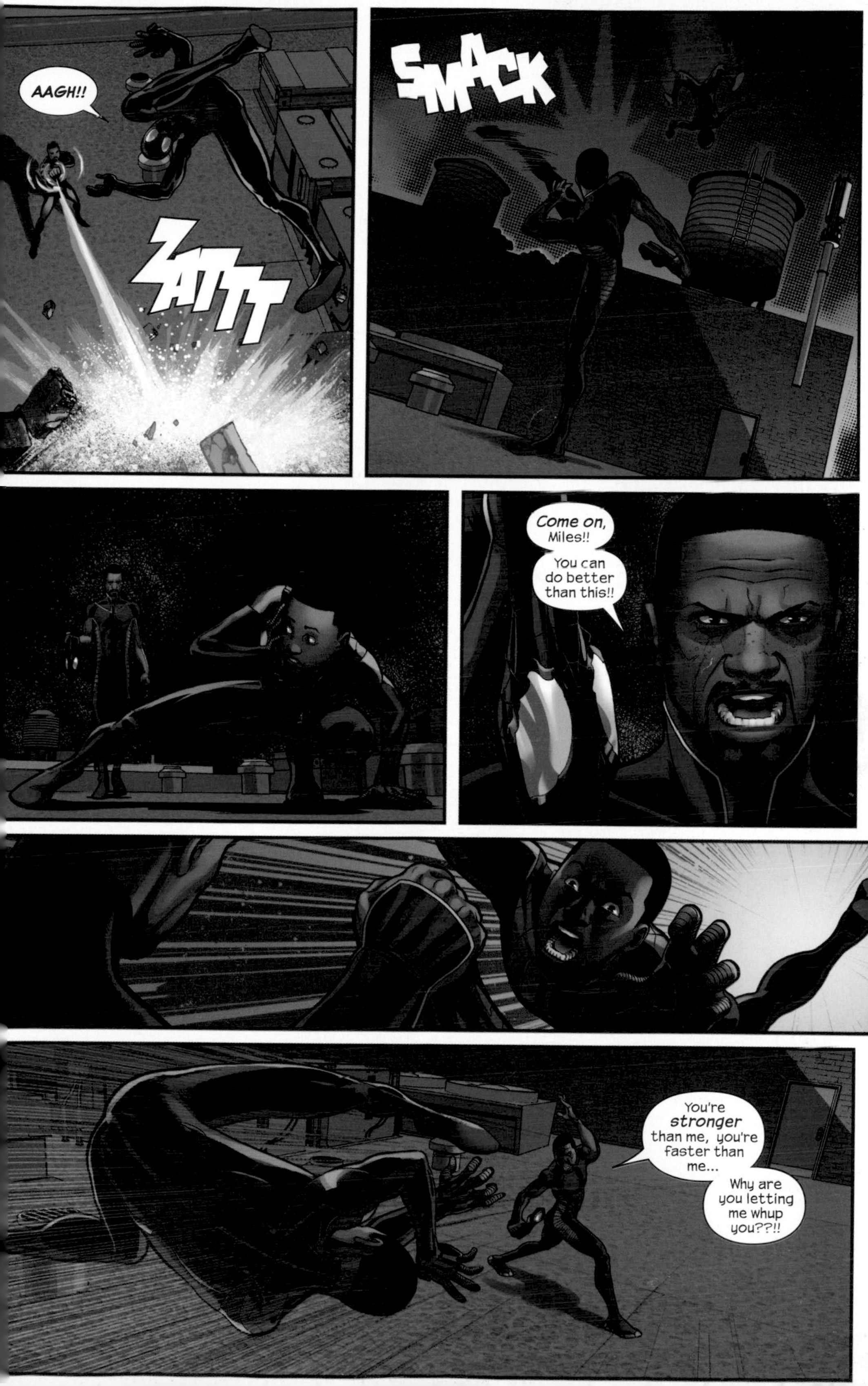
AAGH!!
ZATTT
SMACK
Come on, Miles!!
You can do better than this!!
You're stronger than me, you're faster than me...
Why are you letting me whup you??!!

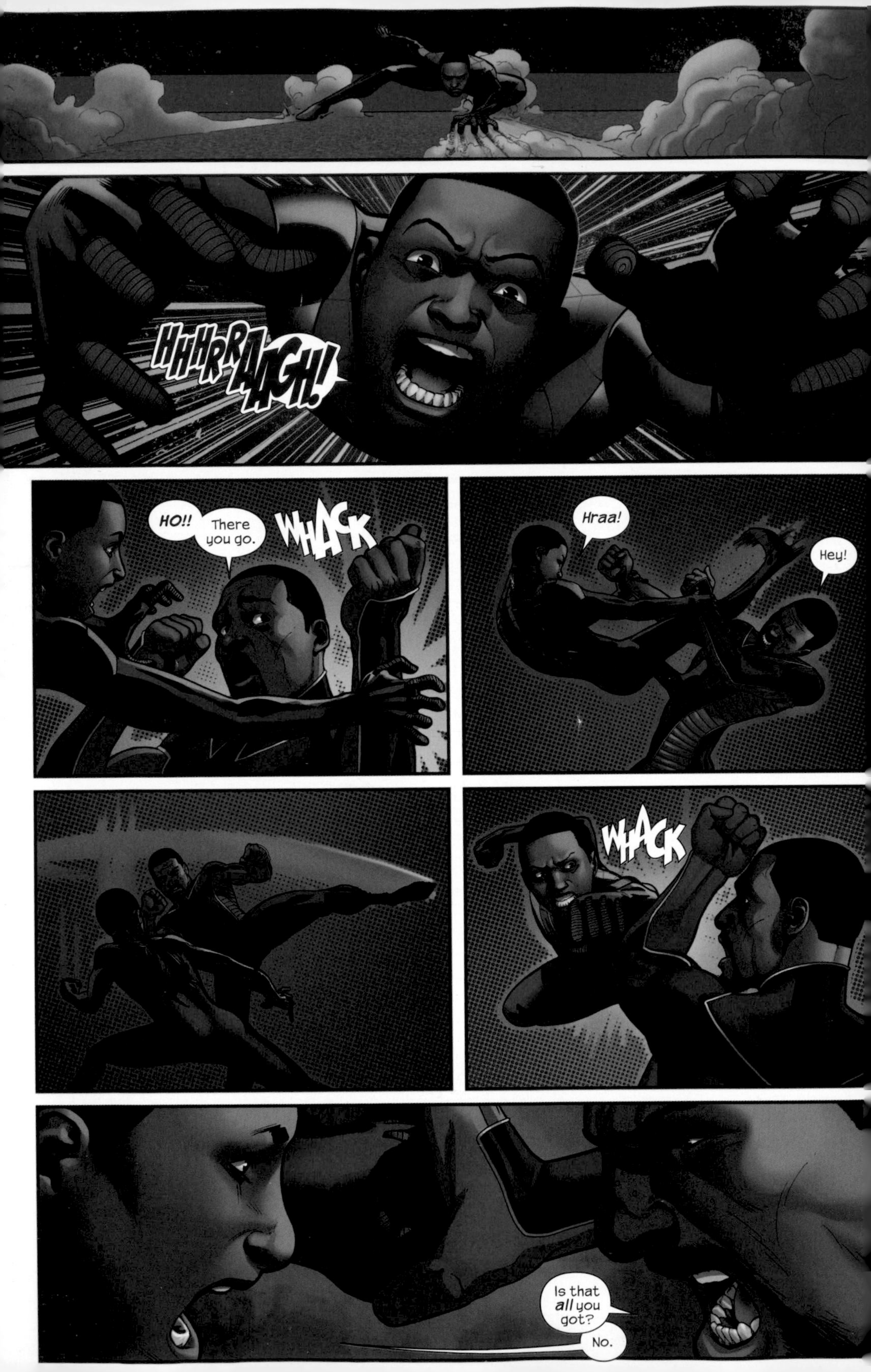
HHHRRAAGH!
HO!!
There you go.
WHACK
Hraa!
Hey!
WHACK
Is that *all* you got?
No.

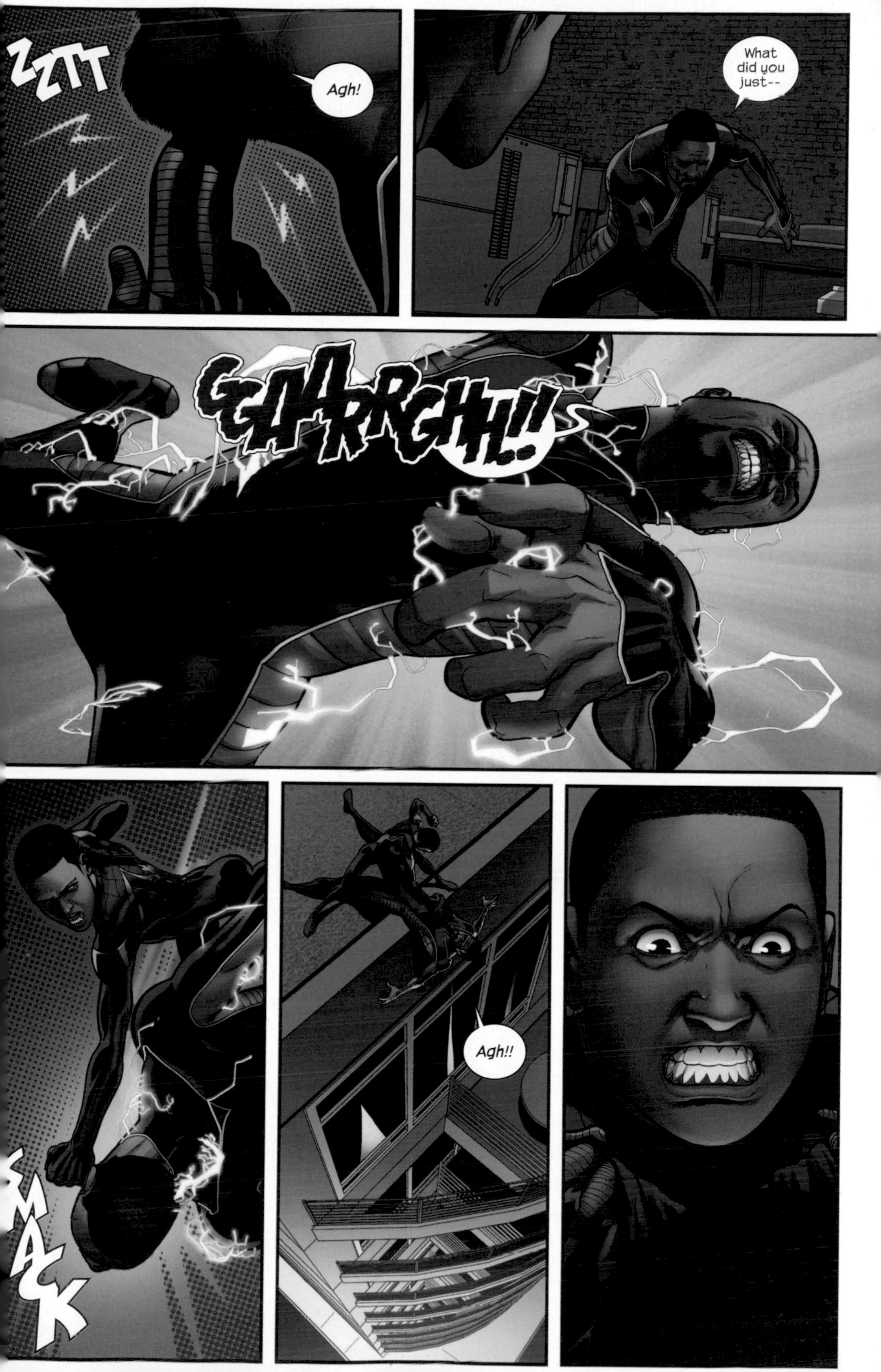
ZZTT
Agh!
What did you just--
GGAARRGHH!!
SMACK
Agh!!

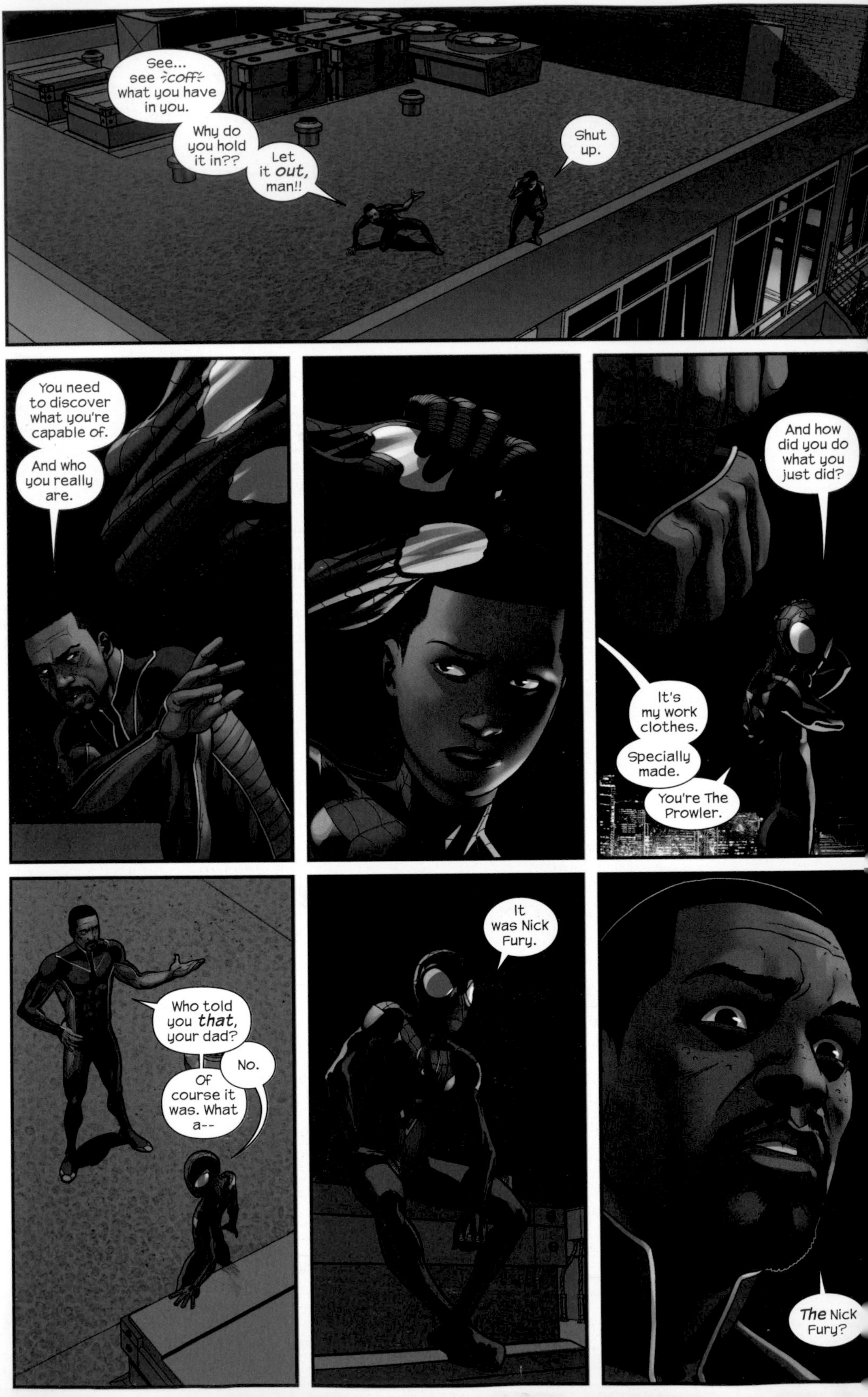
See... see ≈COFF≈ what you have in you.
Why do you hold it in??
Let it *out,* man!!
Shut up.
You need to discover what you're capable of.
And who you really are.
And how did you do what you just did?
It's my work clothes.
Specially made.
You're The Prowler.
Who told you *that*, your dad?
No.
Of course it was. What a--
It was Nick Fury.
The Nick Fury?

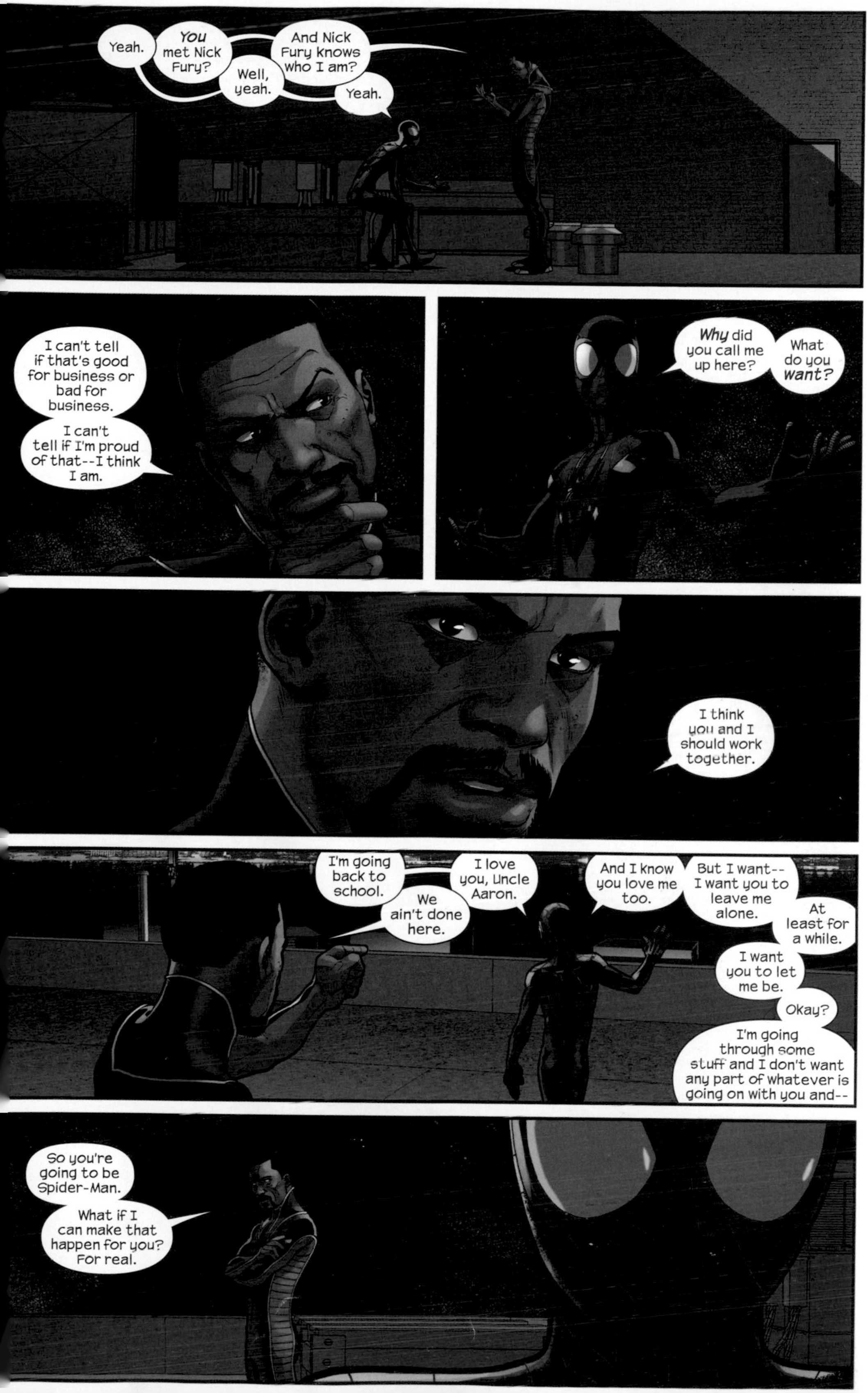
Yeah.
You met Nick Fury?
Well, yeah.
And Nick Fury knows who I am?
Yeah.
I can't tell if that's good for business or bad for business.
I can't tell if I'm proud of that--I think I am.
Why did you call me up here?
What do you *want?*
I think you and I should work together.
I'm going back to school.
We ain't done here.
I love you, Uncle Aaron.
And I know you love me too.
But I want-- I want you to leave me alone.
At least for a while.
I want you to let me be.
Okay?
I'm going through some stuff and I don't want any part of whatever is going on with you and--
So you're going to be Spider-Man.
What if I can make that happen for you? For real.

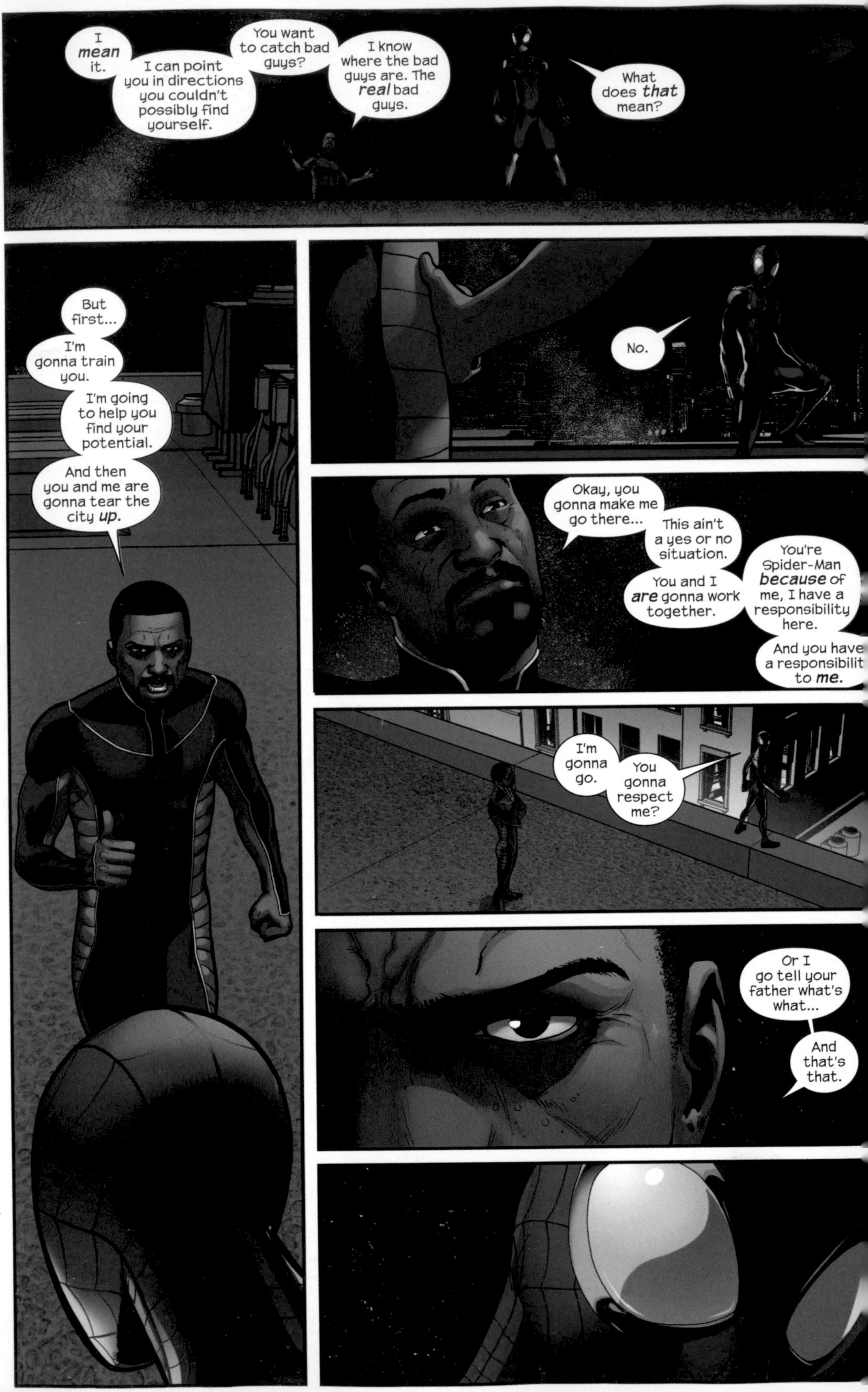
I *mean* it.
I can point you in directions you couldn't possibly find yourself.
You want to catch bad guys?
I know where the bad guys are. The *real* bad guys.
What does *that* mean?
But first...
I'm gonna train you.
I'm going to help you find your potential.
And then you and me are gonna tear the city *up.*
No.
Okay, you gonna make me go there...
This ain't a yes or no situation.
You and I *are* gonna work together.
You're Spider-Man *because* of me, I have a responsibility here.
And you have a responsibilit to *me.*
I'm gonna go.
You gonna respect me?
Or I go tell your father what's what...
And that's that.

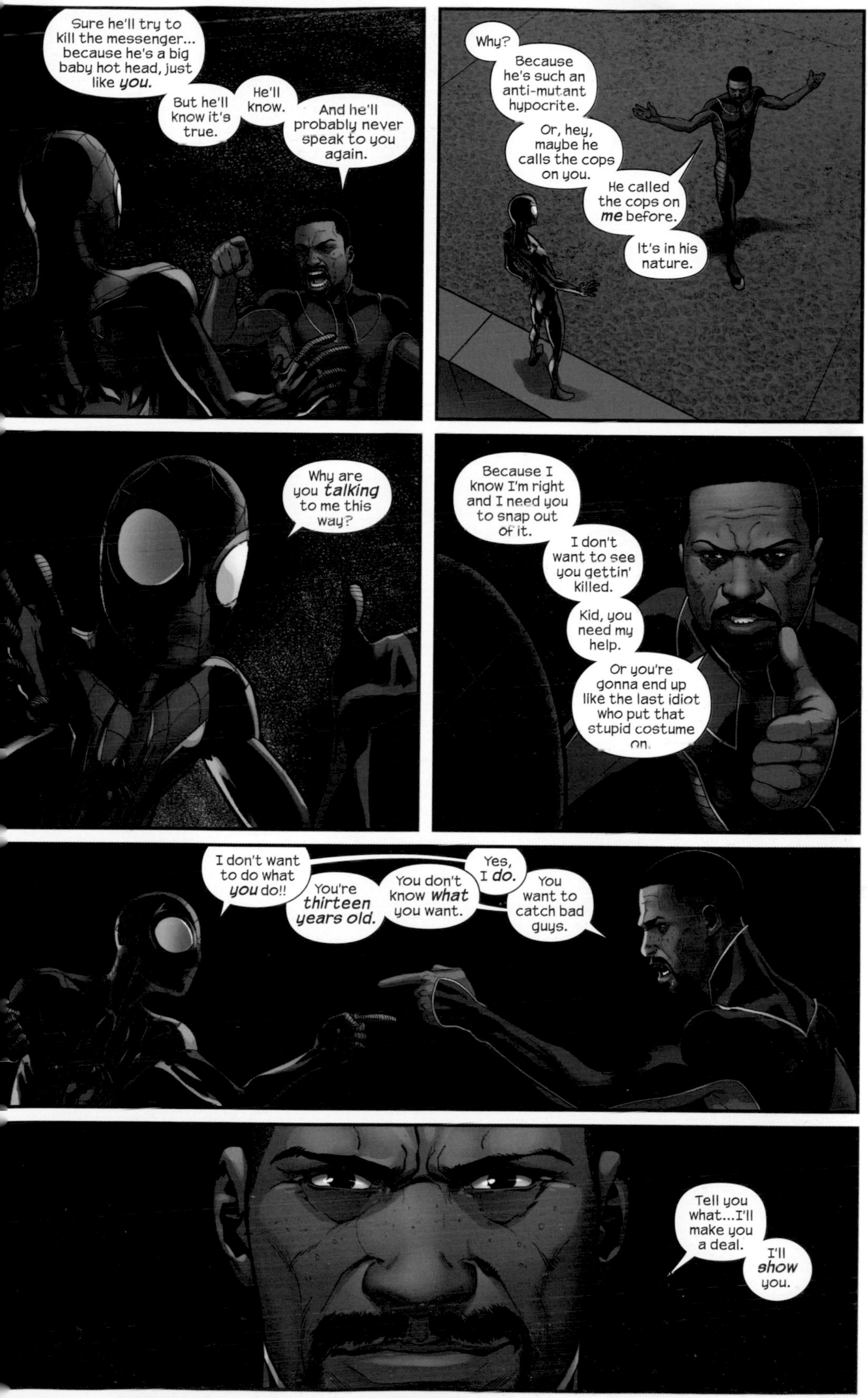

Sure he'll try to kill the messenger... because he's a big baby hot head, just like *you.*
But he'll know it's true.
He'll know.
And he'll probably never speak to you again.
Why?
Because he's such an anti-mutant hypocrite.
Or, hey, maybe he calls the cops on you.
He called the cops on *me* before.
It's in his nature.
Why are you *talking* to me this way?
Because I know I'm right and I need you to snap out of it.
I don't want to see you gettin' killed.
Kid, you need my help.
Or you're gonna end up like the last idiot who put that stupid costume on.
I don't want to do what *you* do!!
Yes, I *do.*
You're *thirteen years old.*
You don't know *what* you want.
You want to catch bad guys.
Tell you what...I'll make you a deal.
I'll *show* you.

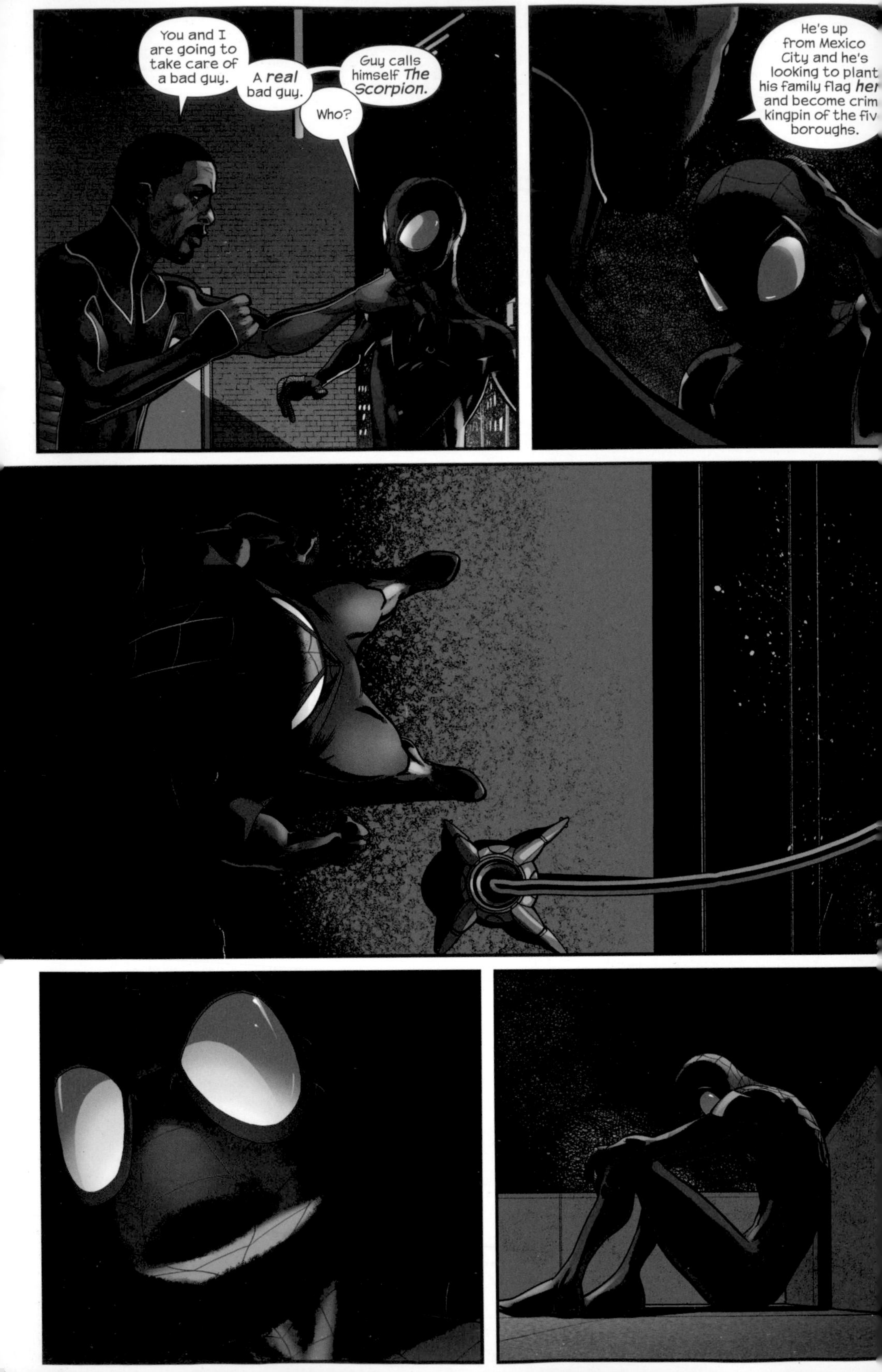
You and I are going to take care of a bad guy.
A *real* bad guy.
Who?
Guy calls himself *The Scorpion*.
He's up from Mexico City and he's looking to plant his family flag *her* and become crim kingpin of the fiv boroughs.

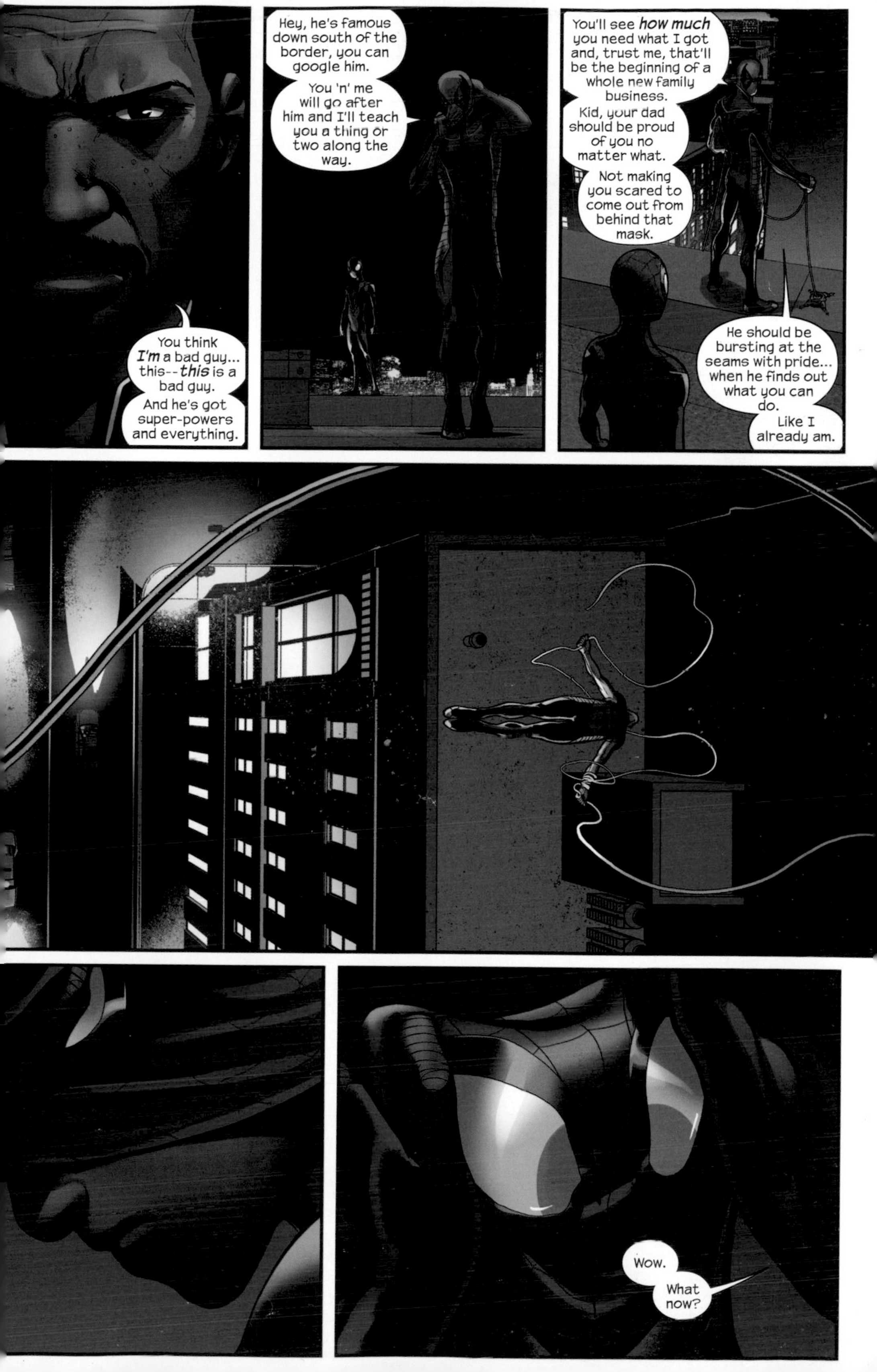
You think I'm a bad guy... this--this is a bad guy.
And he's got super-powers and everything.
Hey, he's famous down south of the border, you can google him.
You 'n' me will go after him and I'll teach you a thing or two along the way.
You'll see how much you need what I got and, trust me, that'll be the beginning of a whole new family business.
Kid, your dad should be proud of you no matter what.
Not making you scared to come out from behind that mask.
He should be bursting at the seams with pride... when he finds out what you can do.
Like I already am.
Wow.
What now?

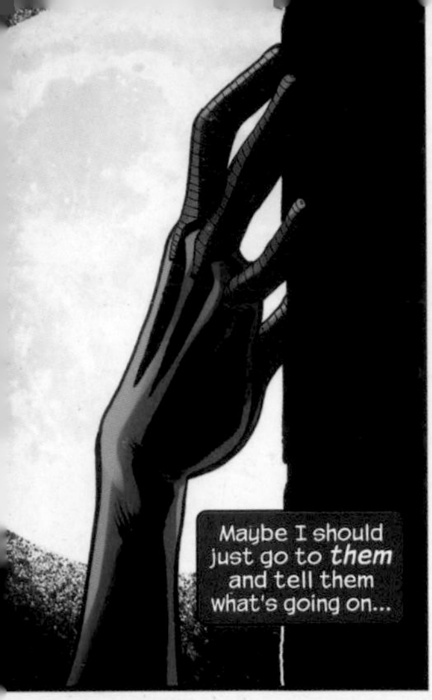
Maybe I should just go to *them* and tell them what's going on...

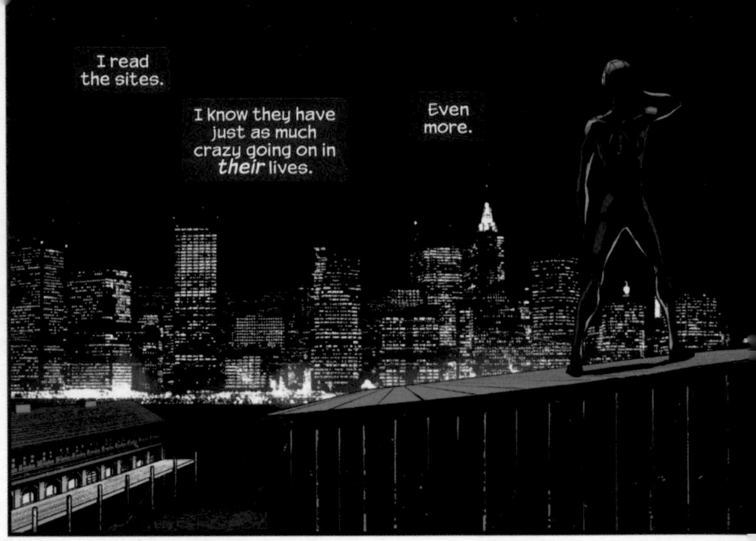
I read the sites.
I know they have just as much crazy going on in *their* lives.
Even more.

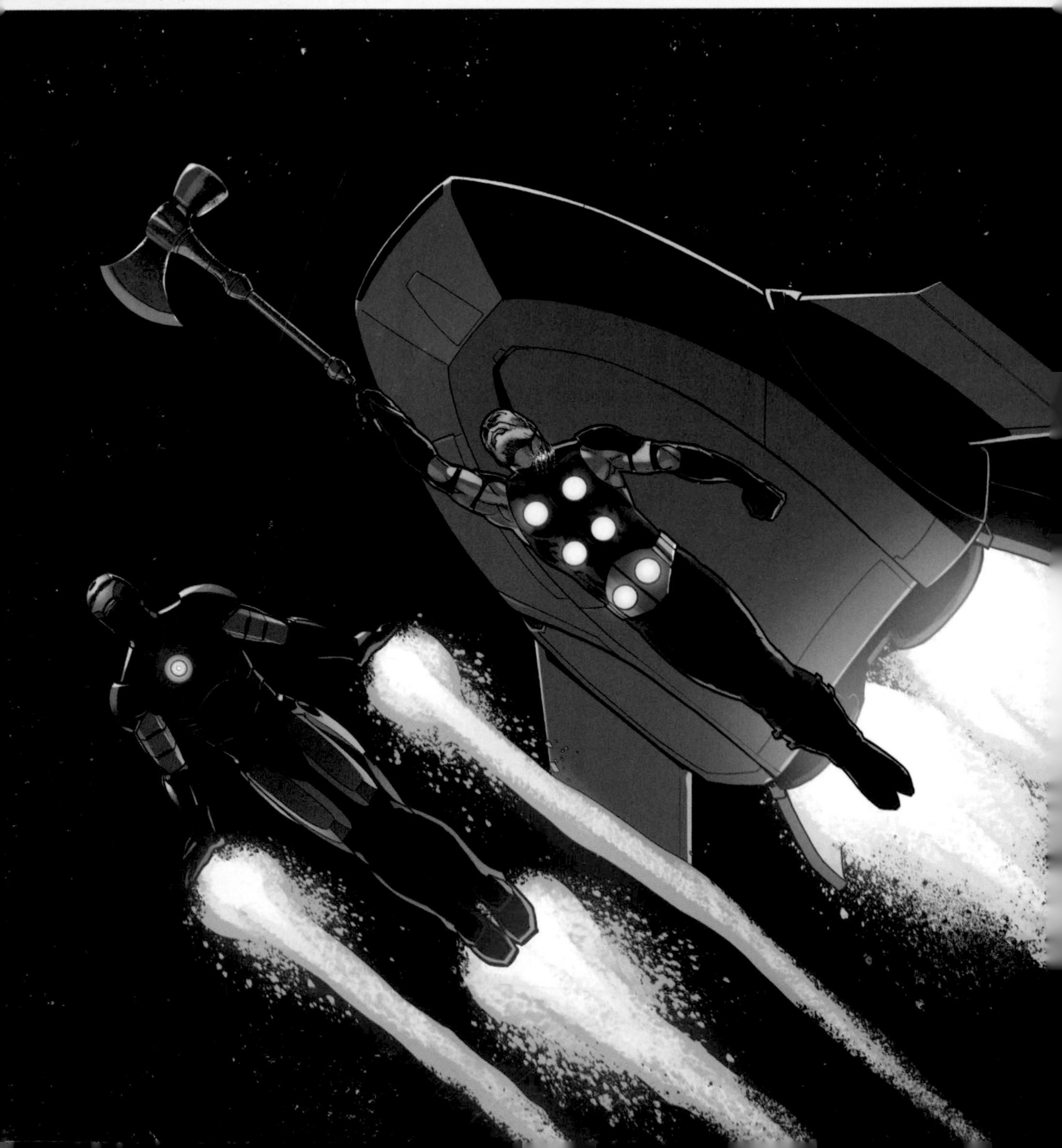

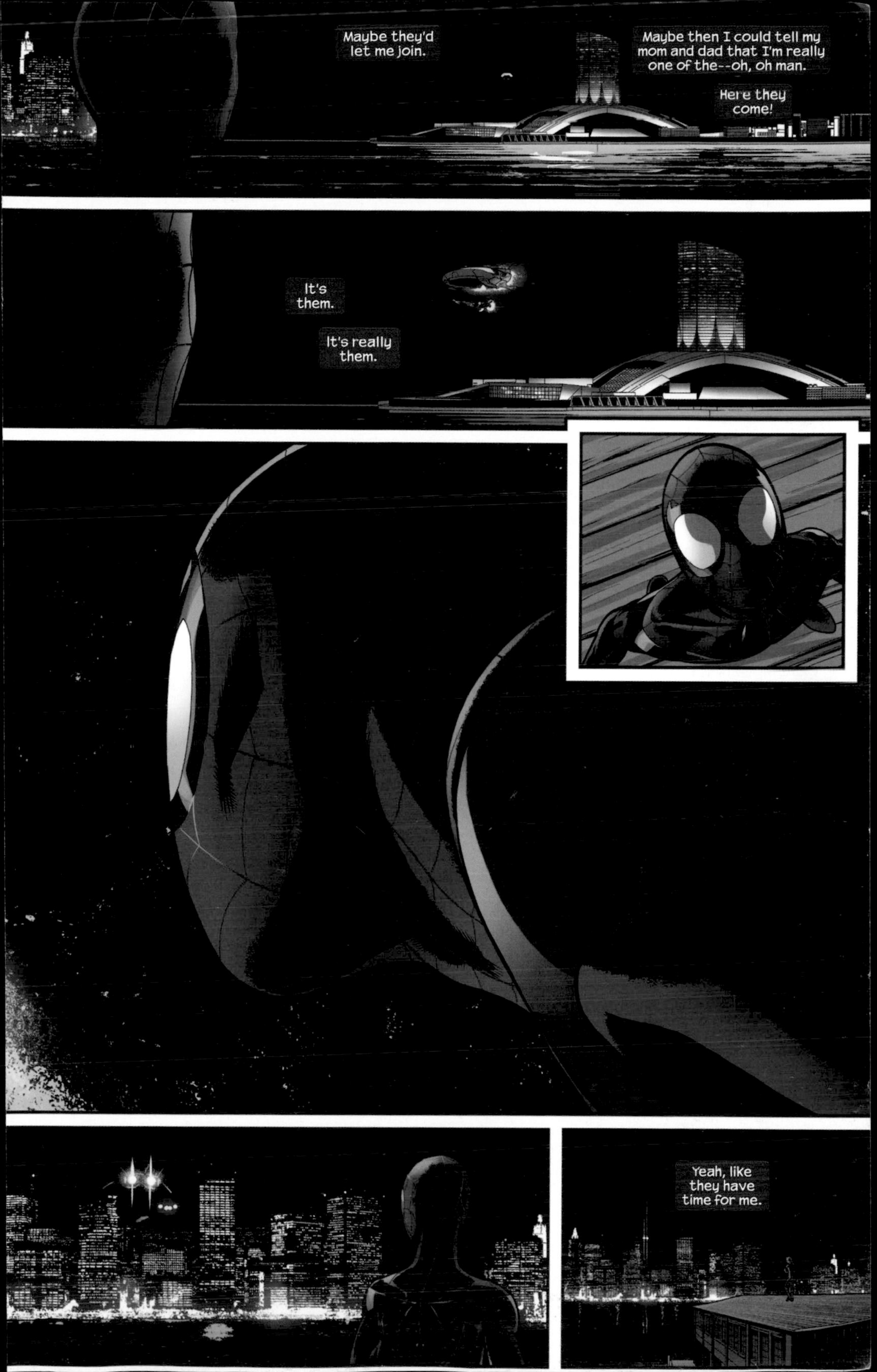
Maybe they'd let me join.
Maybe then I could tell my mom and dad that I'm really one of the--oh, oh man.
Here they come!
It's them.
It's really them.
Yeah, like they have time for me.

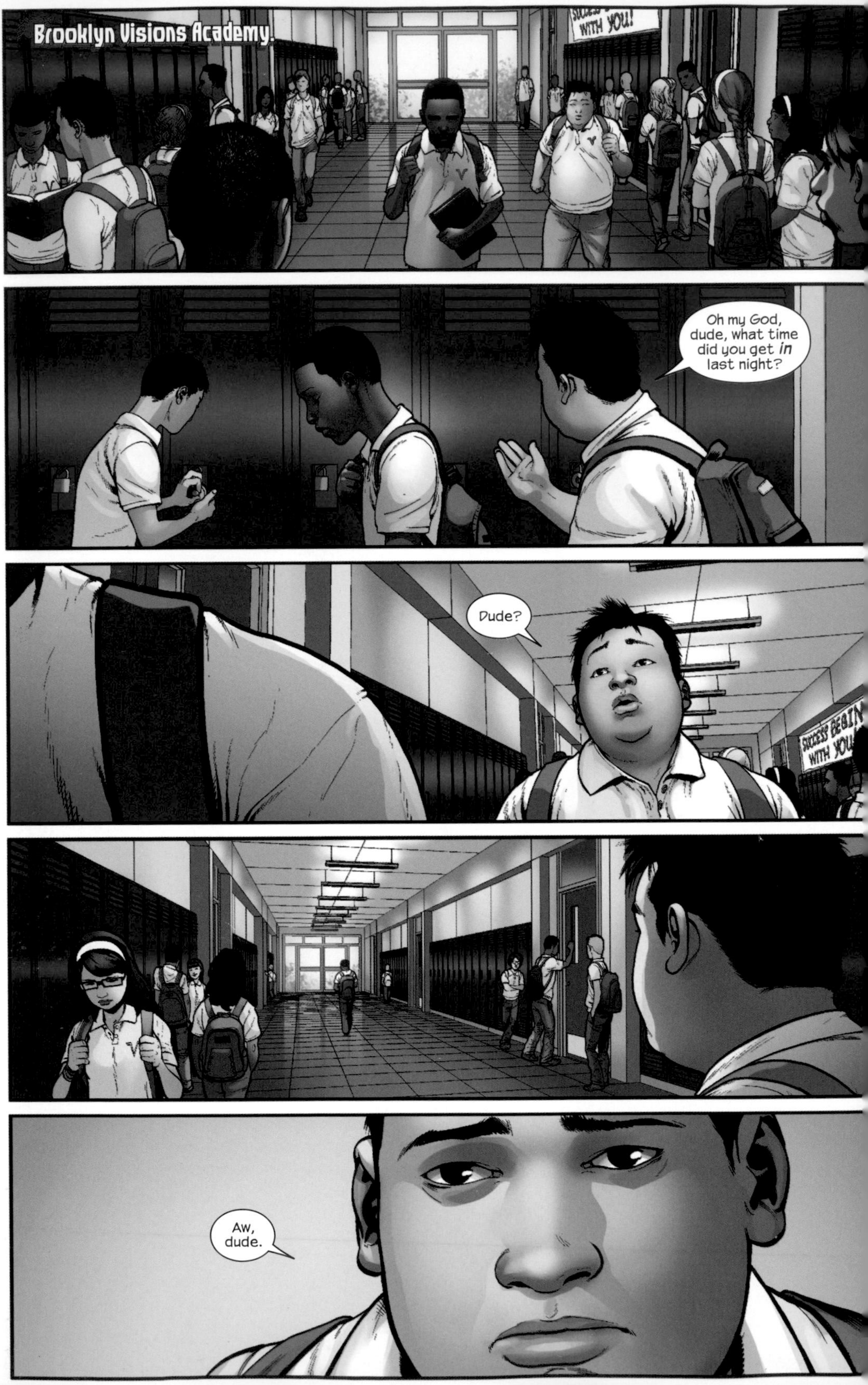
Brooklyn Visions Academy.
SUCCESS ... WITH YOU!
Oh my God, dude, what time did you get *in* last night?
Dude?
SUCCESS BEGIN... WITH YOU
Aw, dude.

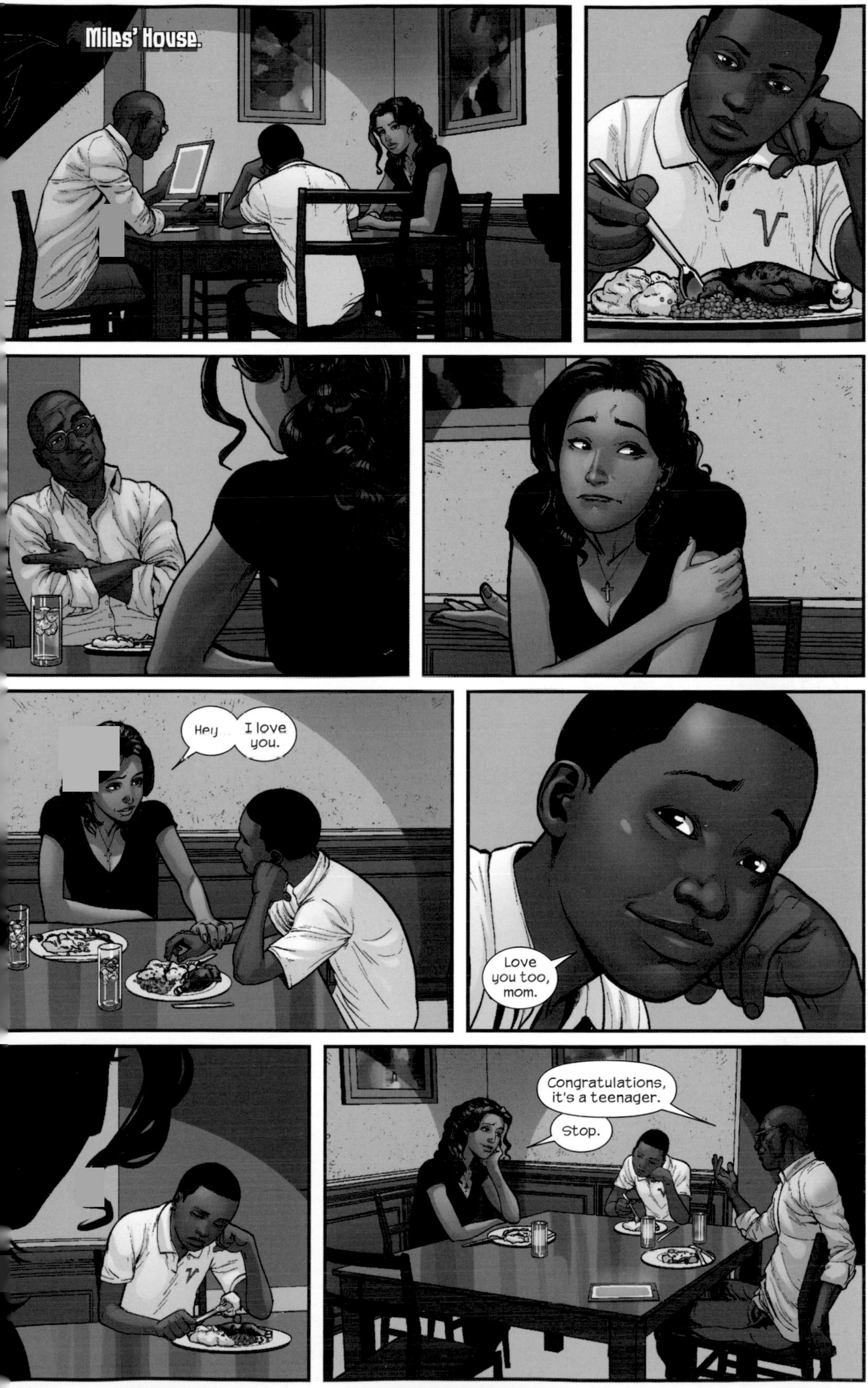
Miles' House.
Hey...
I love you.
Love you too, mom.
Congratulations, it's a teenager.
Stop.

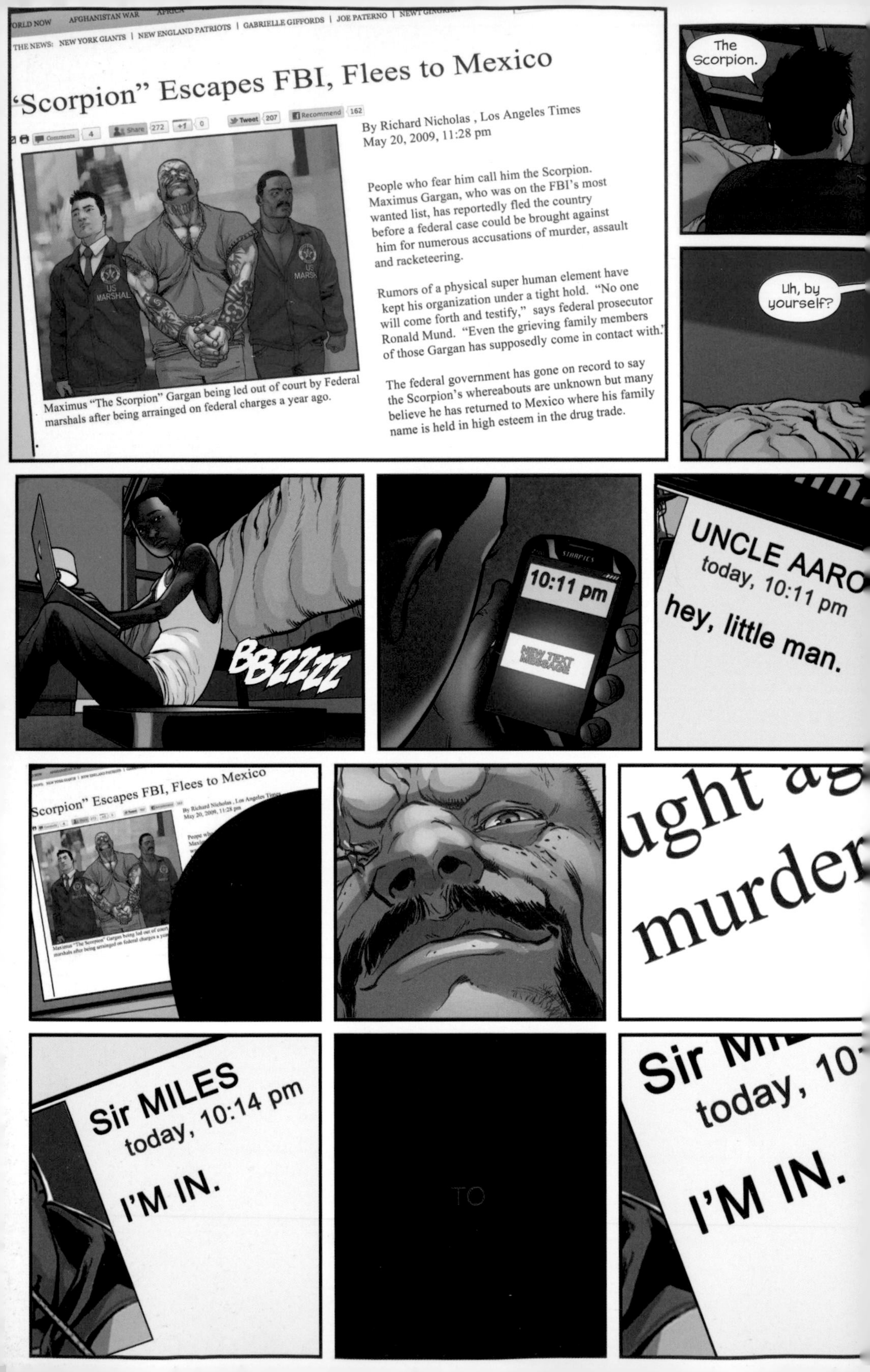
ORLD NOW | AFGHANISTAN WAR | AFRICA
THE NEWS: NEW YORK GIANTS | NEW ENGLAND PATRIOTS | GABRIELLE GIFFORDS | JOE PATERNO | NEWT GINGRICH
'Scorpion" Escapes FBI, Flees to Mexico
Comments 4 | Share 272 | +1 0 | Tweet 207 | Recommend 162
By Richard Nicholas , Los Angeles Times
May 20, 2009, 11:28 pm
People who fear him call him the Scorpion. Maximus Gargan, who was on the FBI's most wanted list, has reportedly fled the country before a federal case could be brought against him for numerous accusations of murder, assault and racketeering.
Rumors of a physical super human element have kept his organization under a tight hold. "No one will come forth and testify," says federal prosecutor Ronald Mund. "Even the grieving family members of those Gargan has supposedly come in contact with."
The federal government has gone on record to say the Scorpion's whereabouts are unknown but many believe he has returned to Mexico where his family name is held in high esteem in the drug trade.
US MARSHAL
Maximus "The Scorpion" Gargan being led out of court by Federal marshals after being arraigned on federal charges a year ago.
The Scorpion.
Uh, by yourself?
BBZZZZ
10:11 pm
NEW TEXT MESSAGE
UNCLE AARO
today, 10:11 pm
hey, little man.
Scorpion" Escapes FBI, Flees to Mexico
ught ag
murder
Sir MILES
today, 10:14 pm
I'M IN.
TO
Sir MI
today, 10
I'M IN.

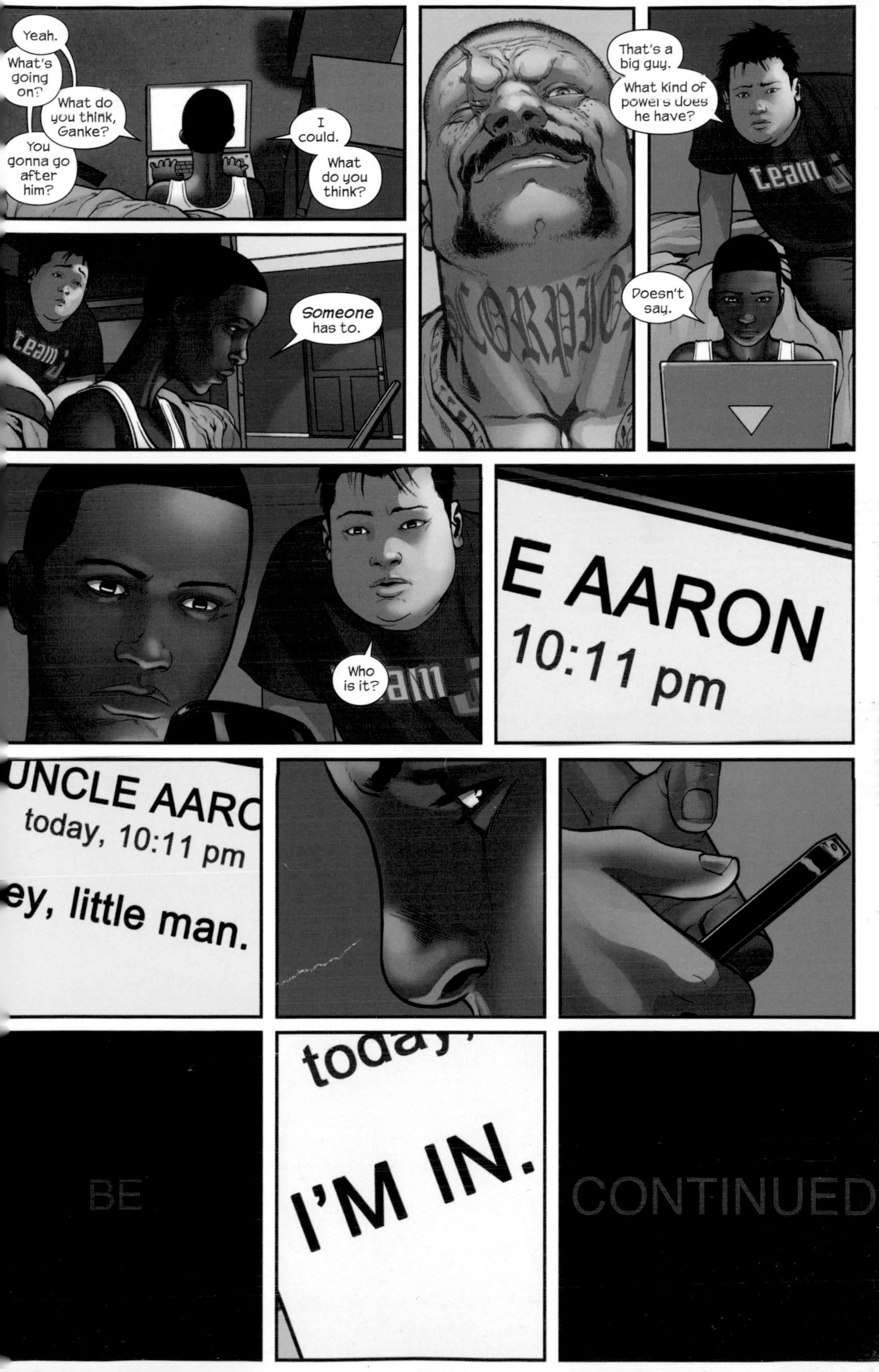

Yeah.
What's going on?
You gonna go after him?
What do you think, Ganke?
I could.
What do you think?
That's a big guy.
What kind of powers does he have?
Doesn't say.
Someone has to.
Who is it?
E AARON
10:11 pm
UNCLE AARO
today, 10:11 pm
ey, little man.
today,
I'M IN.
BE
CONTINUED

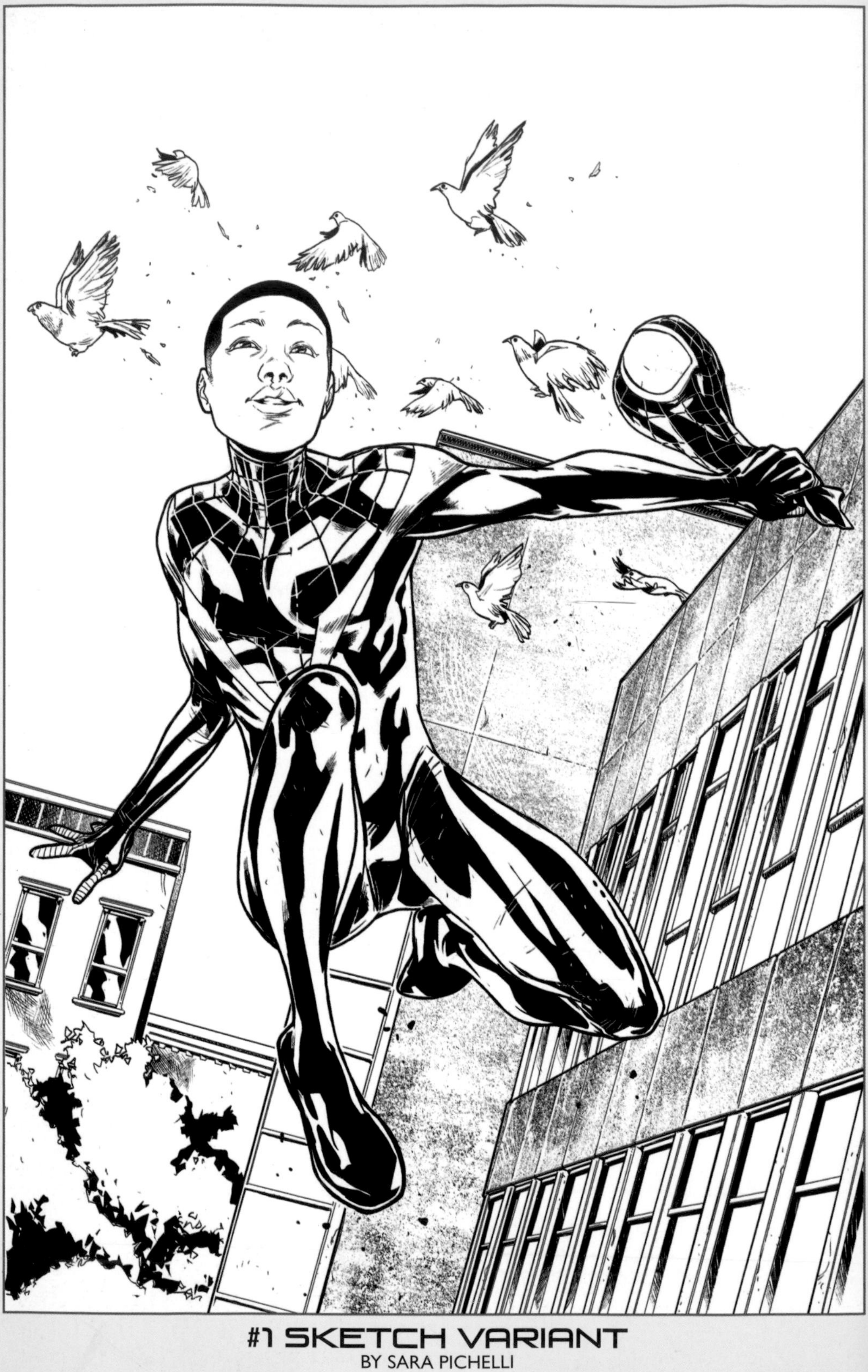

#1 SKETCH VARIANT
BY SARA PICHELLI

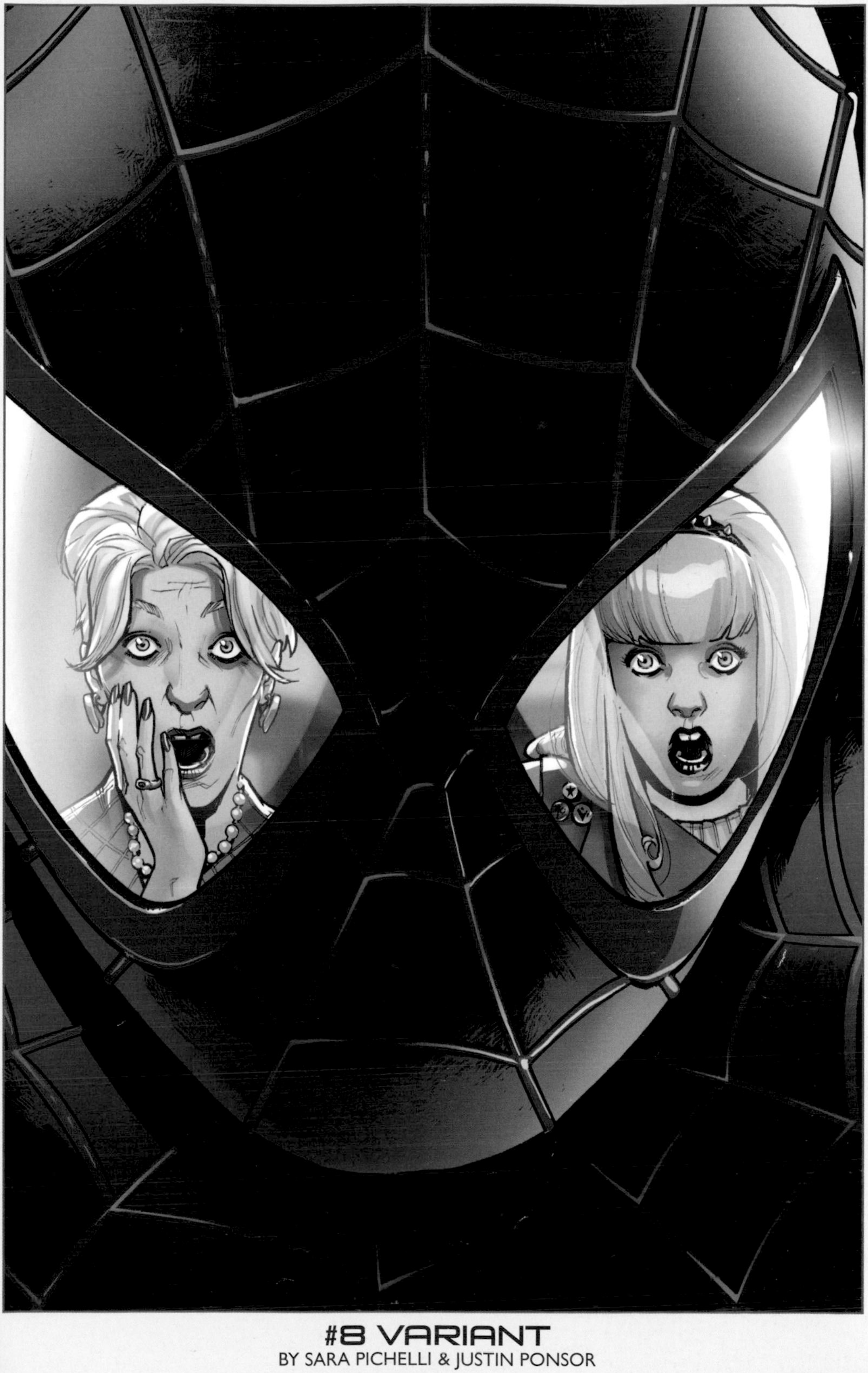

#8 VARIANT
BY SARA PICHELLI & JUSTIN PONSOR

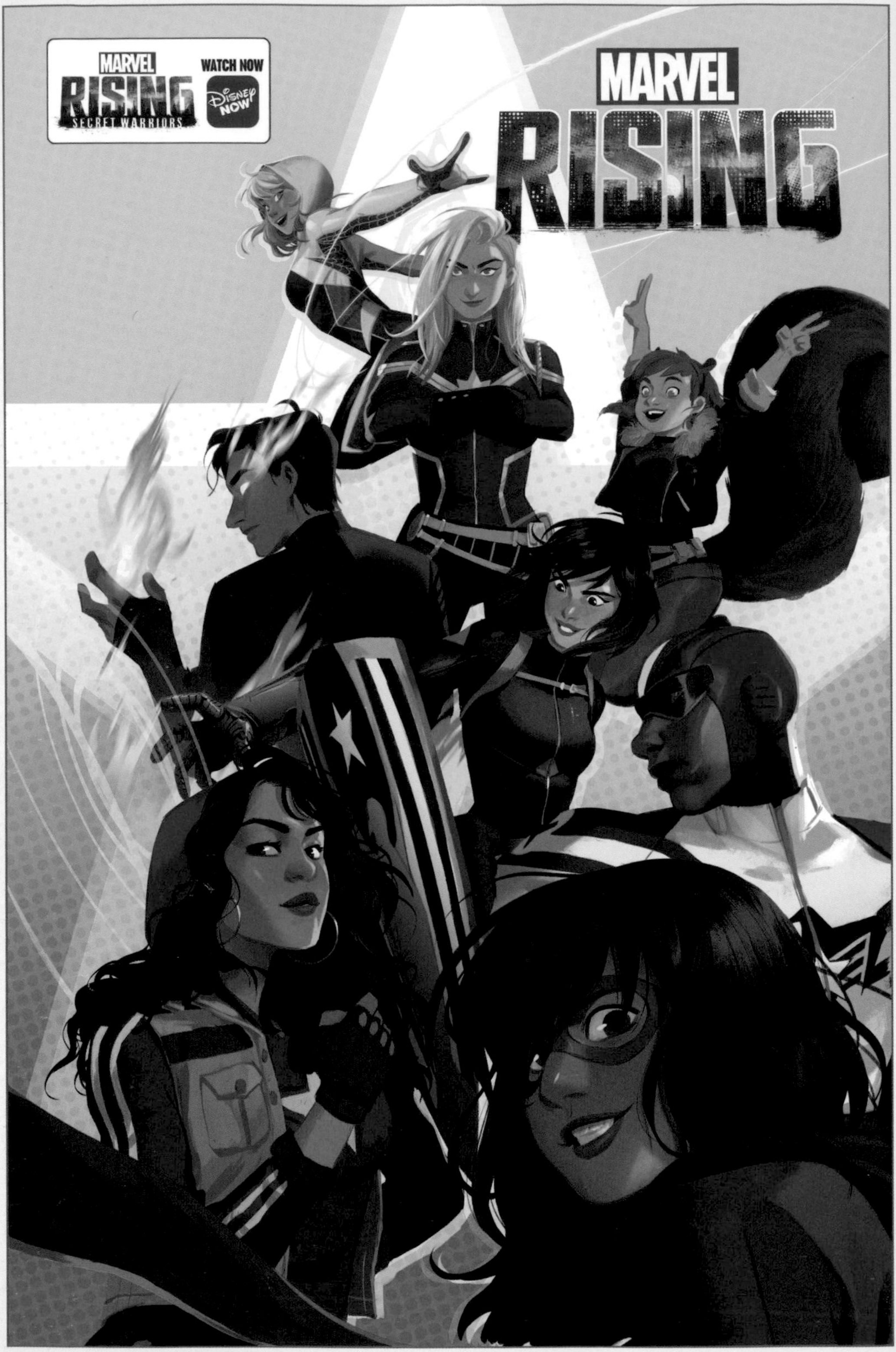
MARVEL
RISING
SECRET WARRIORS
WATCH NOW
DISNEY NOW
MARVEL
RISING

INTRODUCING *MARVEL RISING*!

MARVEL RISING

THE MARVEL UNIVERSE IS A RICH TREASURE CHEST OF CHARACTERS BORN ACROSS MARVEL'S INCREDIBLE 80-YEAR HISTORY. FROM CAPTAIN AMERICA TO CAPTAIN MARVEL, IRON MAN TO IRONHEART, THIS IS AN EVER-EXPANDING UNIVERSE FULL OF POWERFUL HEROES THAT ALSO REFLECTS THE WORLD WE LIVE IN.

YET DESPITE THAT EXPANSION, OUR STORIES REMAIN TIMELESS. THEY'VE BEEN SHARED ACROSS THE GLOBE AND ACROSS GENERATIONS, LINKING FANS WITH THE ENDURING IDEA THAT ORDINARY PEOPLE CAN DO EXTRAORDINARY THINGS. IT'S THAT SHARED EXPERIENCE OF THE MARVEL STORY THAT HAS ALLOWED US TO EXIST FOR THIS LONG. WHETHER YOUR FIRST MARVEL EXPERIENCE WAS THROUGH A COMIC BOOK, A BEDTIME STORY, A MOVIE OR A CARTOON, WE BELIEVE OUR STORIES STAY WITH AUDIENCES THROUGHOUT THEIR LIVES.

MARVEL RISING IS A CELEBRATION OF THIS TIMELESSNESS. AS OUR STORIES PASS FROM ONE GENERATION TO THE NEXT, SO DOES THE LOVE FOR OUR HEROES. FROM THE CLASSIC TO THE NEWLY IMAGINED, THE PASSION FOR ALL OF THEM IS THE SAME. IF YOU'VE BEEN READING COMICS OVER THE LAST FEW YEARS, YOU'LL KNOW CHARACTERS LIKE MS. MARVEL, SQUIRREL GIRL, AMERICA CHAVEZ, SPIDER-GWEN AND MORE HAVE ASSEMBLED A BEVY OF NEW FANS WHILE CAPTIVATING OUR PERENNIAL FANS. EACH OF THESE HEROES IS UNIQUE AND DISTINCT--JUST LIKE THE READERS THEY'VE BROUGHT IN--AND THEY REMIND US THAT NO MATTER WHAT YOU LOOK LIKE, YOU HAVE THE CAPABILITY TO BE POWERFUL, TOO. WE ARE TAKING THE HEROES FROM MARVEL RISING TO NEW HEIGHTS IN AN ANIMATED FEATURE LATER IN 2018, AS WELL AS A FULL PROGRAM OF CONTENT SWEEPING ACROSS THE COMPANY. BUT FIRST WE'RE GOING BACK TO OUR ROOTS AND TELLING A MARVEL RISING STORY IN COMICS: THE FIRST PLACE YOU MET THESE LOVABLE HEROES.

SO IN THE TRADITION OF EXPANDING THE MARVEL UNIVERSE, WE'RE EXCITED TO INTRODUCE MARVEL RISING--THE NEXT GENERATION OF MARVEL HEROES FOR THE NEXT GENERATION OF MARVEL FANS!

SANA AMANAT

VP, CONTENT & CHARACTER DEVELOPMENT

▶ **DOREEN GREEN** IS A SECOND-YEAR COMPUTER SCIENCE STUDENT – AND THE CRIMINAL-REDEEMING HERO THE UNBEATABLE SQUIRREL GIRL! THE NAME SAYS IT ALL: AN UNBEATABLE GIRL WITH THE POWERS OF AN UNBEATABLE SQUIRREL, TAIL INCLUDED. AND ON TOP OF HER STUDYING, NUT-EATING AND BUTT-KICKING ACTIVITIES, SHE'S JUST TAKEN ON THE JOB OF VOLUNTEER TEACHER FOR AN EXTRA-CURRICULAR HIGH-SCHOOL CODING CAMP! AND WHO SHOULD END UP IN HER CLASS BUT...

▶ **KAMALA KHAN**, A.K.A. JERSEY CITY HERO AND INHUMAN POLYMORPH MS. MARVEL! BUT BETWEEN SAVING THE WORLD WITH THE CHAMPIONS AND PROTECTING JERSEY CITY ON HER OWN, KAMALA'S GOT A LOT ON HER PLATE ALREADY. AND FIELD TRIP DAY MAY NOT BE THE BREAK SHE'S ANTICIPATING...

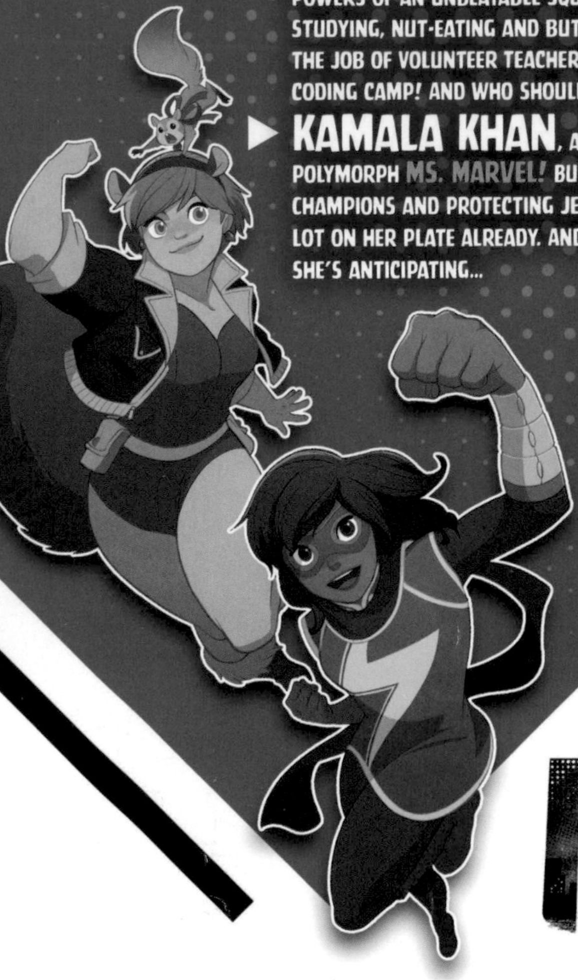

MARVEL RISING

PART 0

DEVIN GRAYSON WRITER

MARCO FAILLA ARTIST

RACHELLE ROSENBERG COLOR ARTIST

VC's CLAYTON COWLES LETTERER

HELEN CHEN COVER

JAY BOWEN DESIGN

HEATHER ANTOS AND **SARAH BRUNSTAD** EDITORS

SANA AMANAT CONSULTING EDITOR

C.B. CEBULSKI EDITOR IN CHIEF

JOE QUESADA CHIEF CREATIVE OFFICER

DAN BUCKLEY PRESIDENT

ALAN FINE EXECUTIVE PRODUCER

SPECIAL THANKS TO RYAN NORTH AND G. WILLOW WILSON

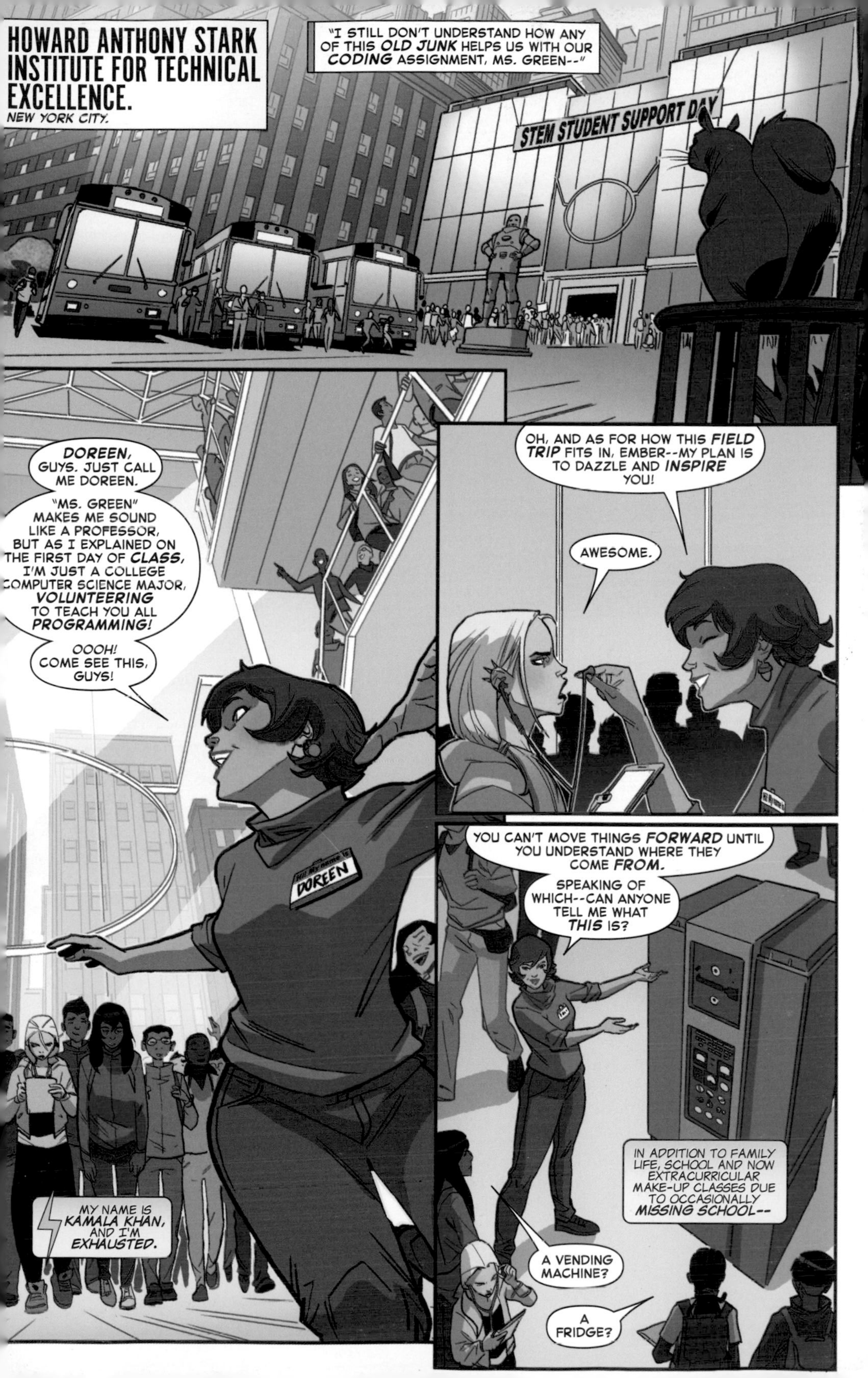
HOWARD ANTHONY STARK INSTITUTE FOR TECHNICAL EXCELLENCE.
NEW YORK CITY.
"I STILL DON'T UNDERSTAND HOW ANY OF THIS OLD JUNK HELPS US WITH OUR CODING ASSIGNMENT, MS. GREEN--"
STEM STUDENT SUPPORT DAY
DOREEN, GUYS. JUST CALL ME DOREEN.
"MS. GREEN" MAKES ME SOUND LIKE A PROFESSOR, BUT AS I EXPLAINED ON THE FIRST DAY OF CLASS, I'M JUST A COLLEGE COMPUTER SCIENCE MAJOR, VOLUNTEERING TO TEACH YOU ALL PROGRAMMING!
OOOH! COME SEE THIS, GUYS!
HI! My name is DOREEN
MY NAME IS KAMALA KHAN, AND I'M EXHAUSTED.
OH, AND AS FOR HOW THIS FIELD TRIP FITS IN, EMBER--MY PLAN IS TO DAZZLE AND INSPIRE YOU!
AWESOME.
YOU CAN'T MOVE THINGS FORWARD UNTIL YOU UNDERSTAND WHERE THEY COME FROM.
SPEAKING OF WHICH--CAN ANYONE TELL ME WHAT THIS IS?
IN ADDITION TO FAMILY LIFE, SCHOOL AND NOW EXTRACURRICULAR MAKE-UP CLASSES DUE TO OCCASIONALLY MISSING SCHOOL--
A VENDING MACHINE?
A FRIDGE?

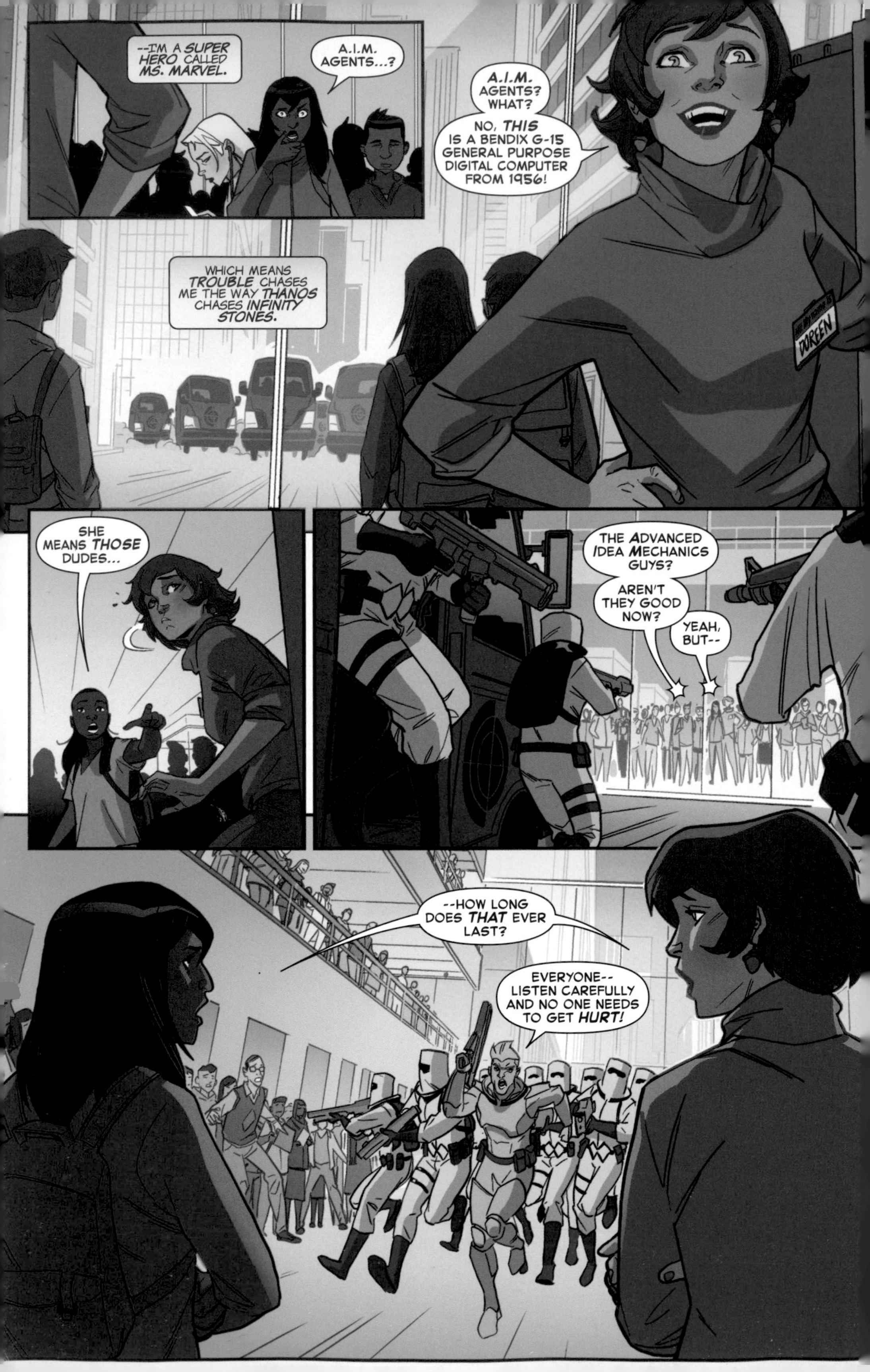

--I'M A SUPER HERO CALLED MS. MARVEL.
A.I.M. AGENTS...?
A.I.M. AGENTS? WHAT?
NO, THIS IS A BENDIX G-15 GENERAL PURPOSE DIGITAL COMPUTER FROM 1956!
WHICH MEANS TROUBLE CHASES ME THE WAY THANOS CHASES INFINITY STONES.
DOREEN
SHE MEANS THOSE DUDES...
THE ADVANCED IDEA MECHANICS GUYS?
AREN'T THEY GOOD NOW?
YEAH, BUT--
--HOW LONG DOES THAT EVER LAST?
EVERYONE-- LISTEN CAREFULLY AND NO ONE NEEDS TO GET HURT!

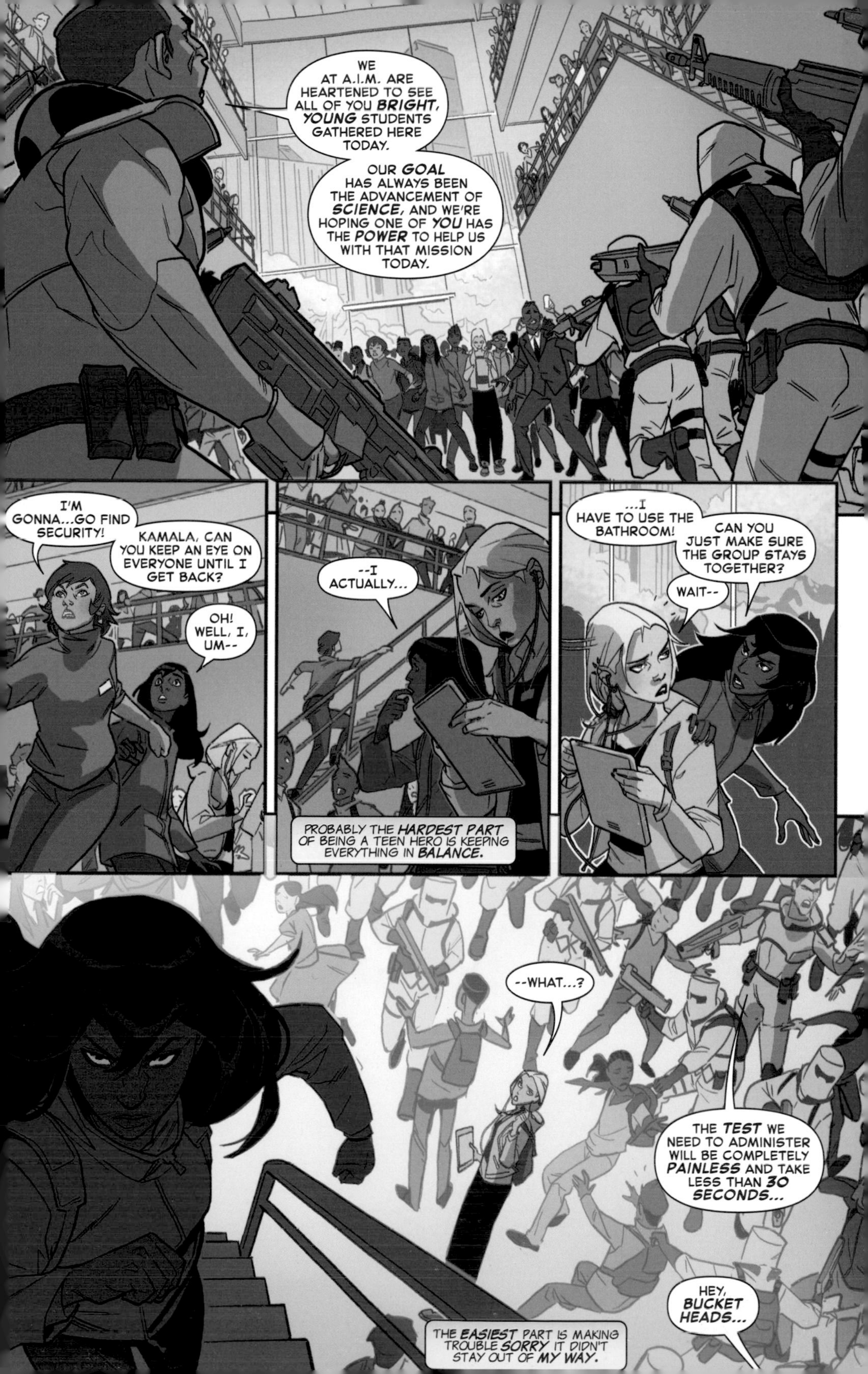
WE AT A.I.M. ARE HEARTENED TO SEE ALL OF YOU BRIGHT, YOUNG STUDENTS GATHERED HERE TODAY.
OUR GOAL HAS ALWAYS BEEN THE ADVANCEMENT OF SCIENCE, AND WE'RE HOPING ONE OF YOU HAS THE POWER TO HELP US WITH THAT MISSION TODAY.
I'M GONNA...GO FIND SECURITY!
KAMALA, CAN YOU KEEP AN EYE ON EVERYONE UNTIL I GET BACK?
OH! WELL, I, UM--
--I ACTUALLY...
PROBABLY THE HARDEST PART OF BEING A TEEN HERO IS KEEPING EVERYTHING IN BALANCE.
...I HAVE TO USE THE BATHROOM!
CAN YOU JUST MAKE SURE THE GROUP STAYS TOGETHER?
WAIT--
--WHAT...?
THE TEST WE NEED TO ADMINISTER WILL BE COMPLETELY PAINLESS AND TAKE LESS THAN 30 SECONDS...
HEY, BUCKET HEADS...
THE EASIEST PART IS MAKING TROUBLE SORRY IT DIDN'T STAY OUT OF MY WAY.

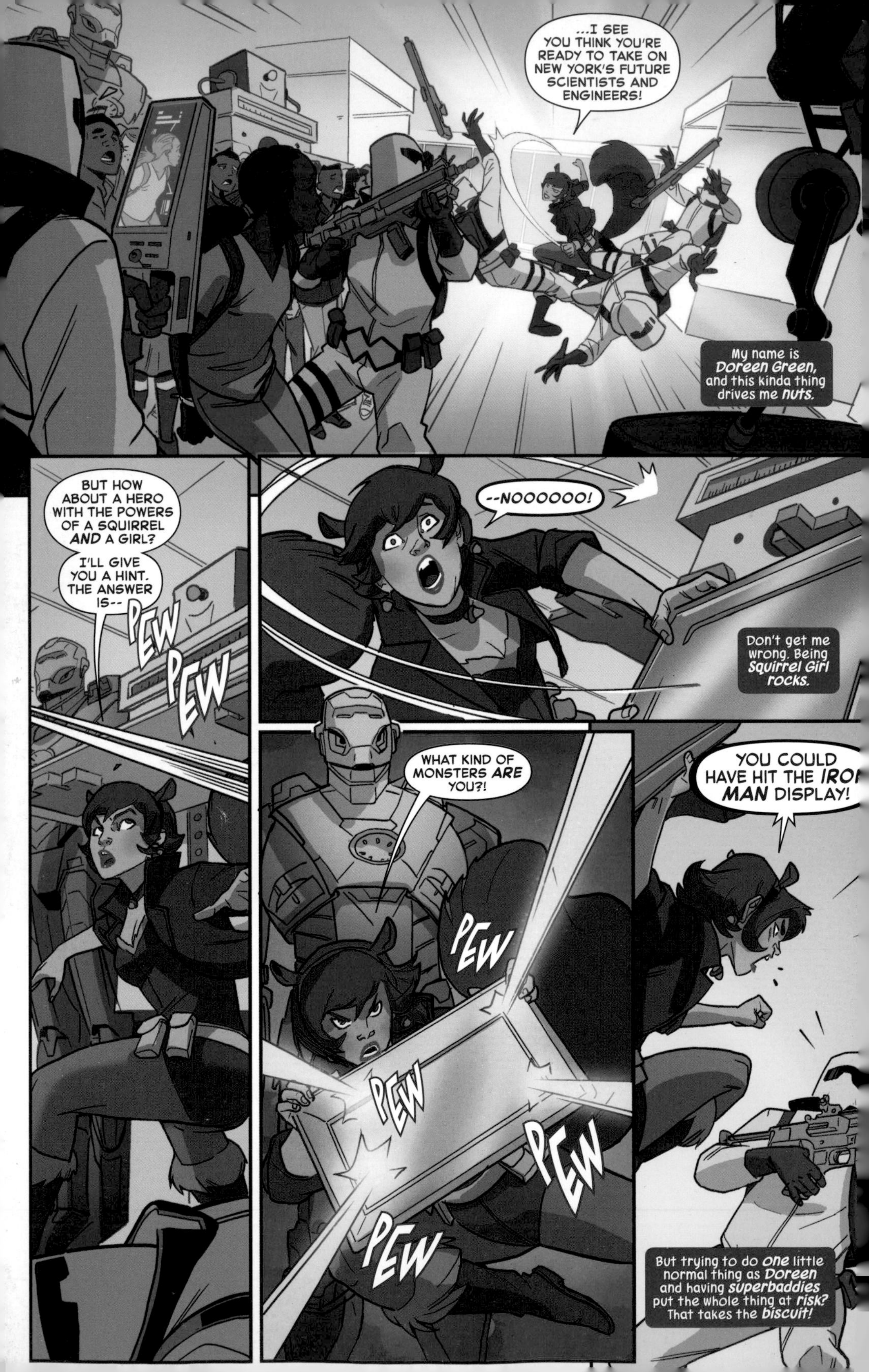
...I SEE YOU THINK YOU'RE READY TO TAKE ON NEW YORK'S FUTURE SCIENTISTS AND ENGINEERS!
My name is *Doreen Green,* and this kinda thing drives me *nuts.*
BUT HOW ABOUT A HERO WITH THE POWERS OF A SQUIRREL *AND* A GIRL?
I'LL GIVE YOU A HINT. THE ANSWER IS--
PEW
PEW
--NOOOOOO!
Don't get me wrong. Being *Squirrel Girl* rocks.
WHAT KIND OF MONSTERS *ARE* YOU?!
PEW
PEW
PEW
PEW
YOU COULD HAVE HIT THE *IRON MAN* DISPLAY!
But trying to do *one* little normal thing as *Doreen* and having *superbaddies* put the whole thing at *risk?* That takes the *biscuit!*

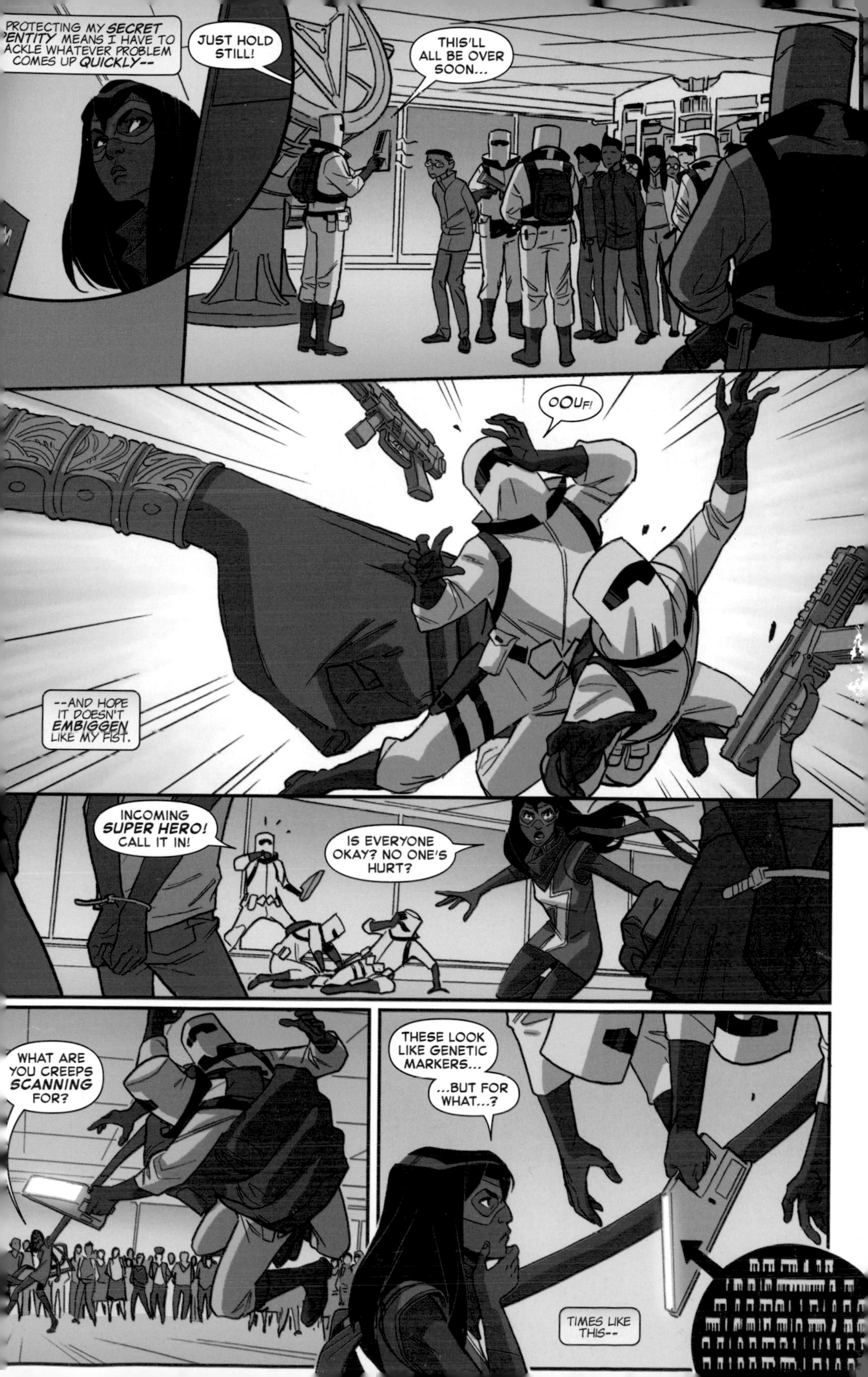
PROTECTING MY SECRET IDENTITY MEANS I HAVE TO TACKLE WHATEVER PROBLEM COMES UP QUICKLY--
JUST HOLD STILL!
THIS'LL ALL BE OVER SOON...
OOUF!
--AND HOPE IT DOESN'T EMBIGGEN LIKE MY FIST.
INCOMING SUPER HERO! CALL IT IN!
IS EVERYONE OKAY? NO ONE'S HURT?
WHAT ARE YOU CREEPS SCANNING FOR?
THESE LOOK LIKE GENETIC MARKERS...
...BUT FOR WHAT...?
TIMES LIKE THIS--

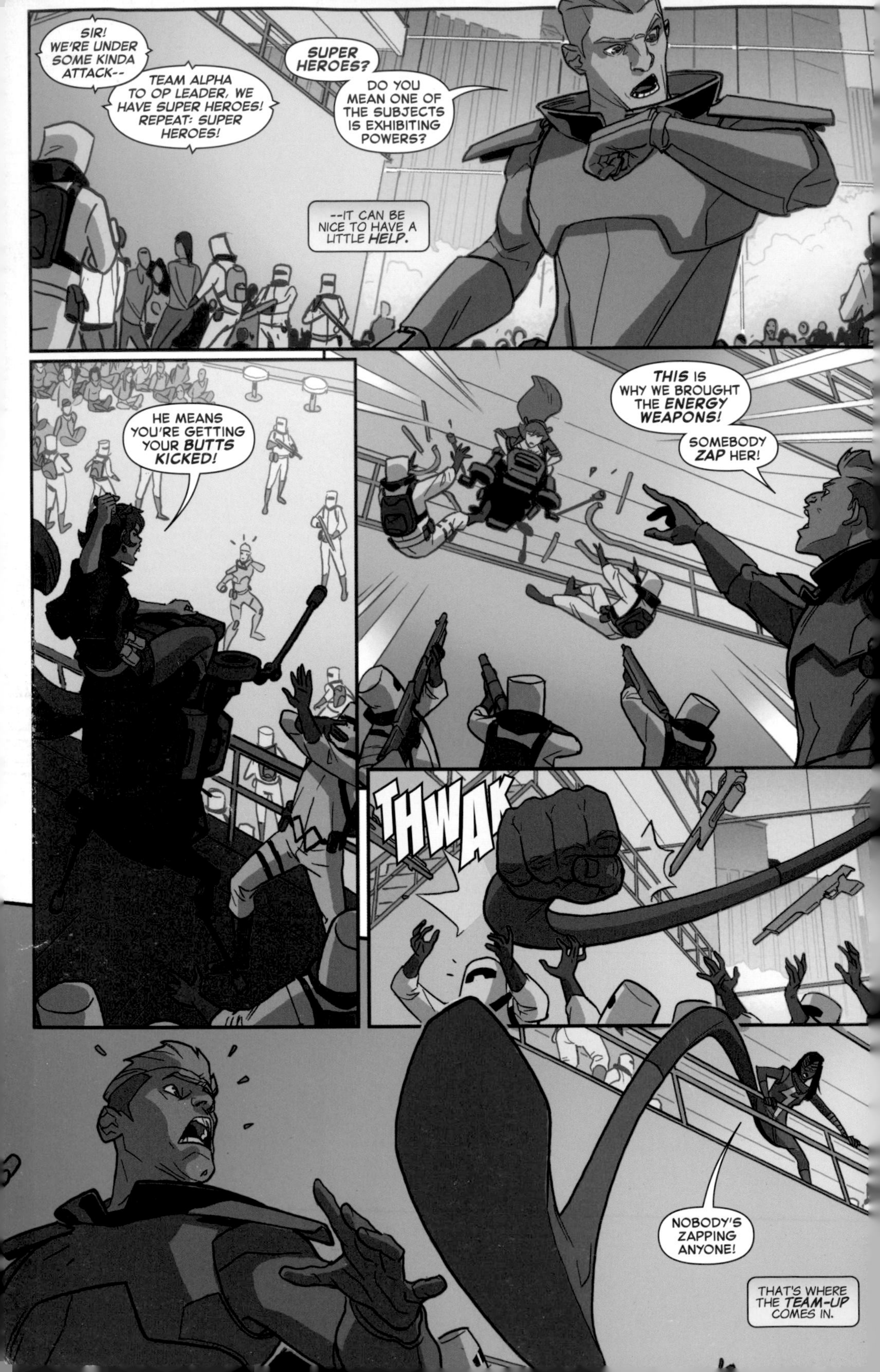
SIR! WE'RE UNDER SOME KINDA ATTACK--
TEAM ALPHA TO OP LEADER, WE HAVE SUPER HEROES! REPEAT: SUPER HEROES!
SUPER HEROES?
DO YOU MEAN ONE OF THE SUBJECTS IS EXHIBITING POWERS?
--IT CAN BE NICE TO HAVE A LITTLE HELP.
HE MEANS YOU'RE GETTING YOUR BUTTS KICKED!
THIS IS WHY WE BROUGHT THE ENERGY WEAPONS!
SOMEBODY ZAP HER!
THWAK
NOBODY'S ZAPPING ANYONE!
THAT'S WHERE THE TEAM-UP COMES IN.

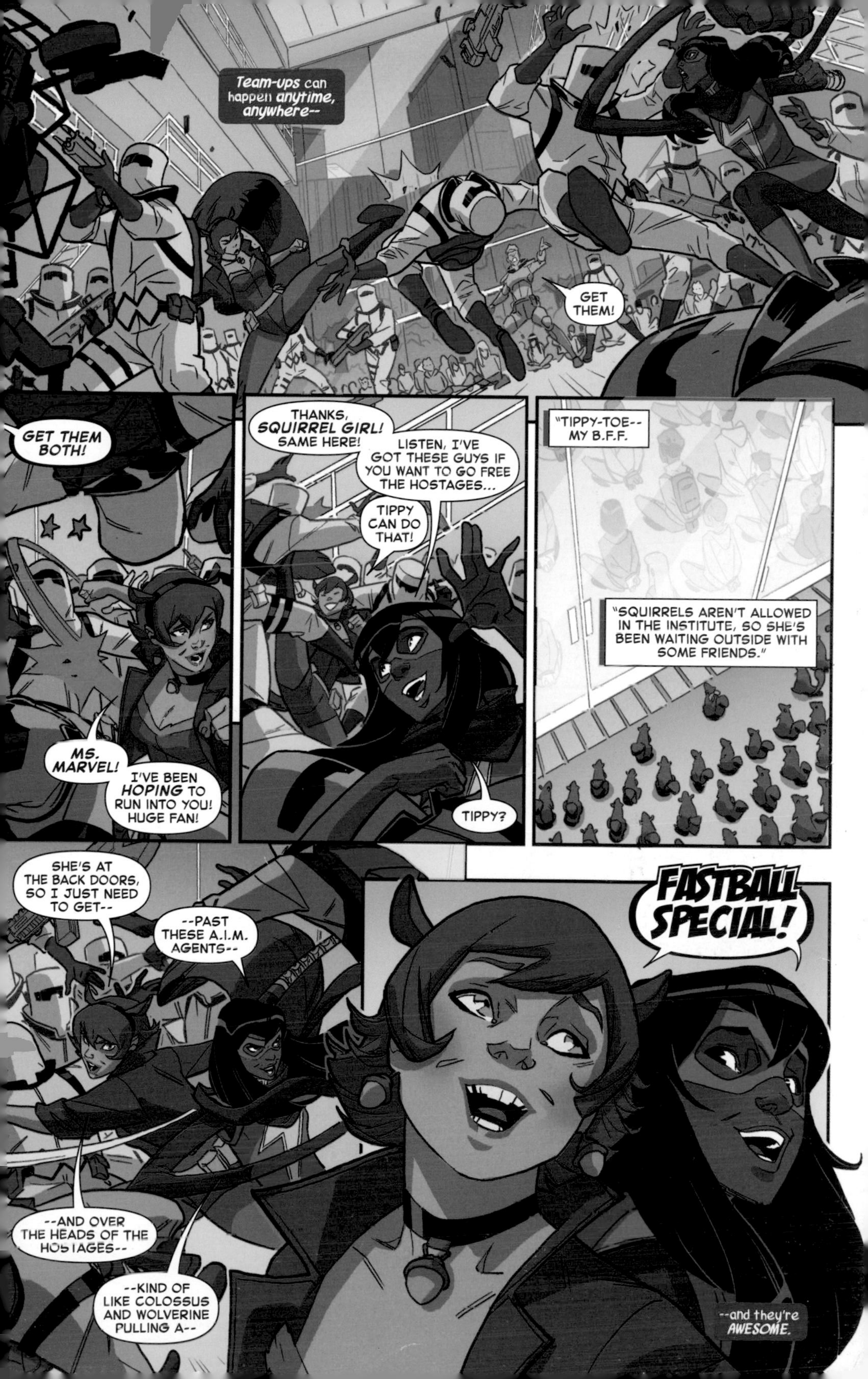

Team-ups can happen anytime, anywhere--
GET THEM!
GET THEM BOTH!
MS. MARVEL!
I'VE BEEN HOPING TO RUN INTO YOU! HUGE FAN!
THANKS, SQUIRREL GIRL! SAME HERE!
LISTEN, I'VE GOT THESE GUYS IF YOU WANT TO GO FREE THE HOSTAGES...
TIPPY CAN DO THAT!
TIPPY?
"TIPPY-TOE-- MY B.F.F.
"SQUIRRELS AREN'T ALLOWED IN THE INSTITUTE, SO SHE'S BEEN WAITING OUTSIDE WITH SOME FRIENDS."
SHE'S AT THE BACK DOORS, SO I JUST NEED TO GET--
--PAST THESE A.I.M. AGENTS--
--AND OVER THE HEADS OF THE HOSTAGES--
--KIND OF LIKE COLOSSUS AND WOLVERINE PULLING A--
FASTBALL SPECIAL!
--and they're AWESOME.

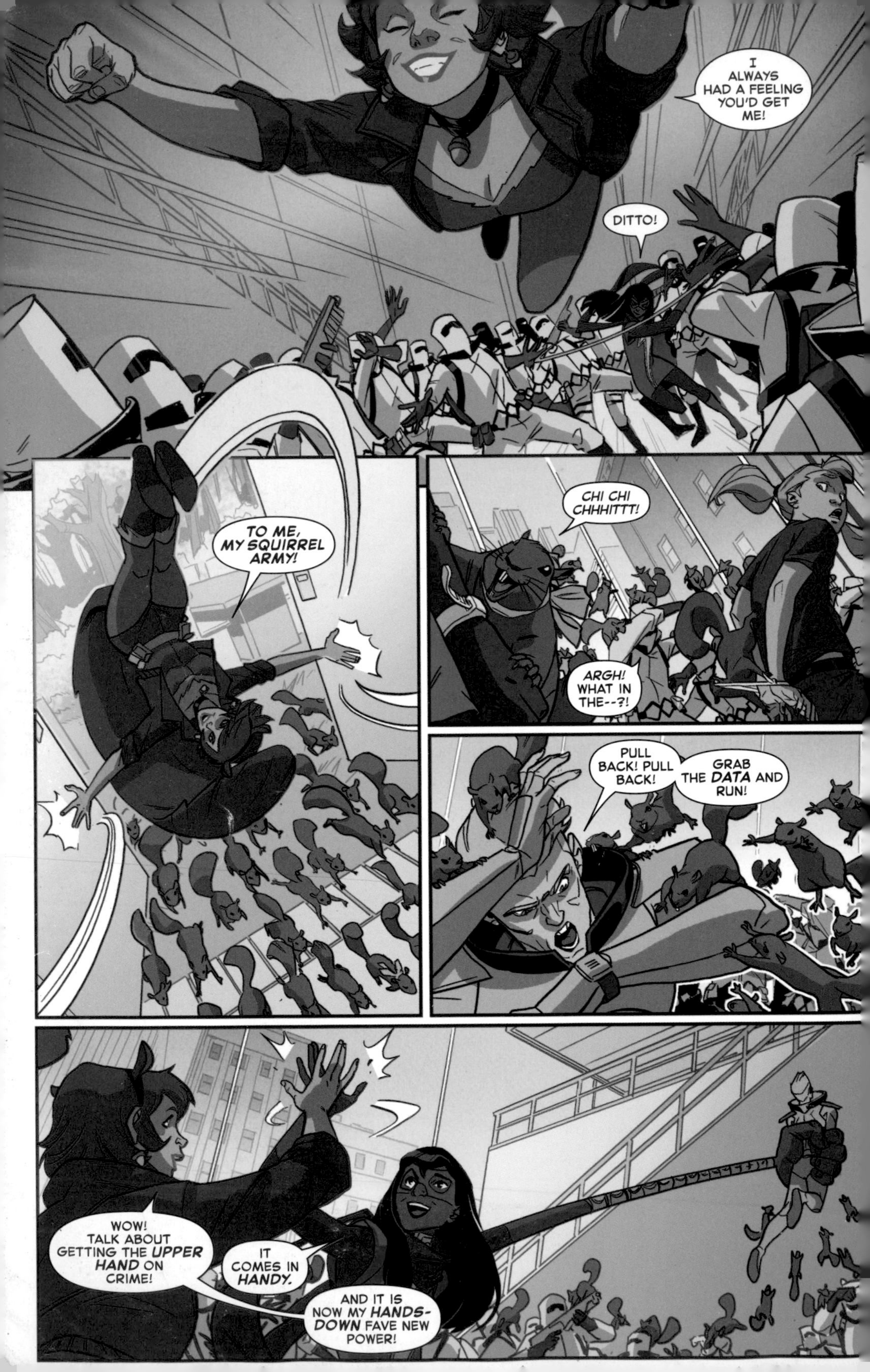
I ALWAYS HAD A FEELING YOU'D GET ME!
DITTO!
TO ME, MY SQUIRREL ARMY!
CHI CHI CHHHITTT!
ARGH! WHAT IN THE--?!
PULL BACK! PULL BACK!
GRAB THE DATA AND RUN!
WOW! TALK ABOUT GETTING THE UPPER HAND ON CRIME!
IT COMES IN HANDY.
AND IT IS NOW MY HANDS-DOWN FAVE NEW POWER!

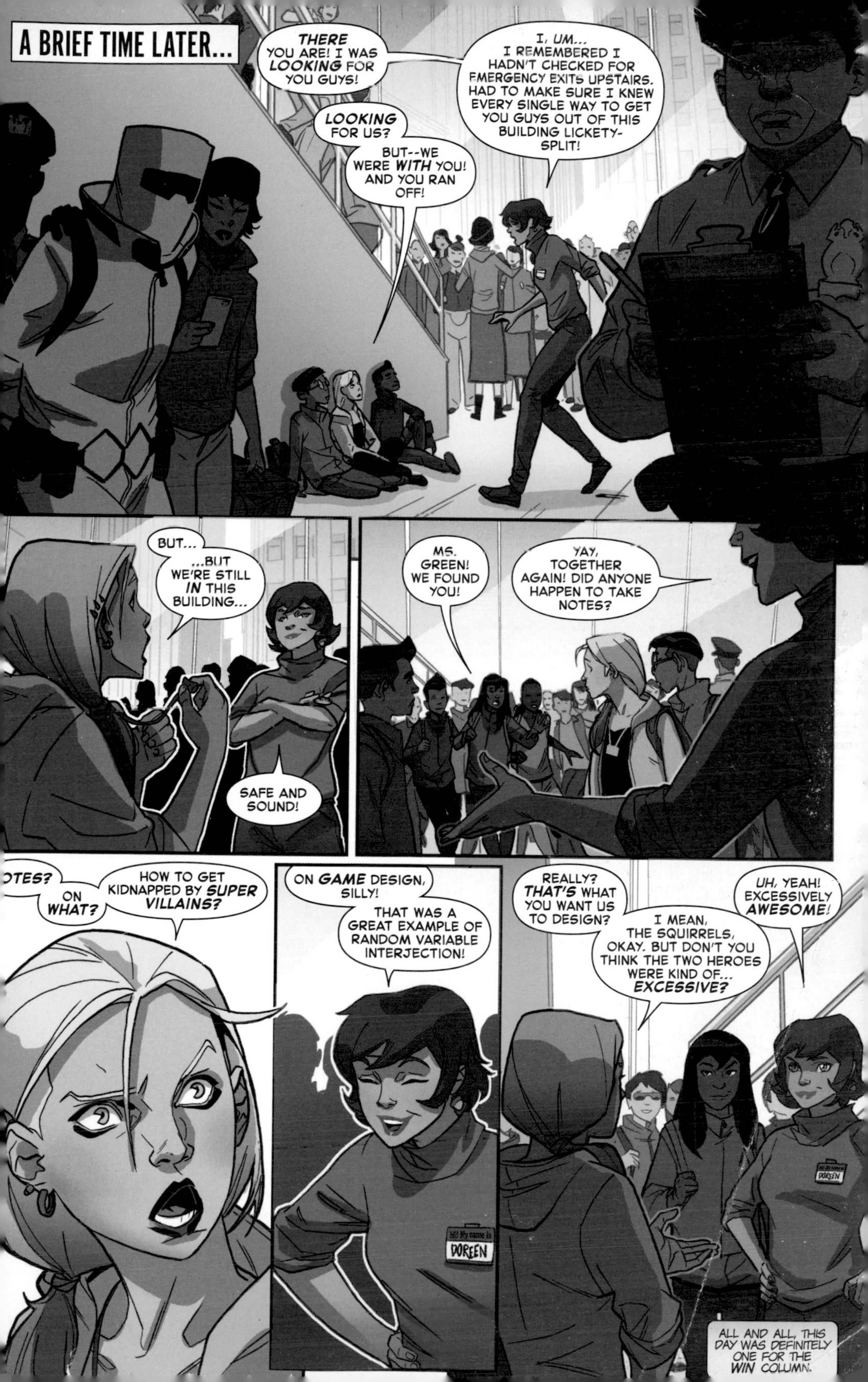
A BRIEF TIME LATER...
THERE YOU ARE! I WAS LOOKING FOR YOU GUYS!
I, UM... I REMEMBERED I HADN'T CHECKED FOR EMERGENCY EXITS UPSTAIRS. HAD TO MAKE SURE I KNEW EVERY SINGLE WAY TO GET YOU GUYS OUT OF THIS BUILDING LICKETY-SPLIT!
LOOKING FOR US?
BUT--WE WERE WITH YOU! AND YOU RAN OFF!
BUT... ...BUT WE'RE STILL IN THIS BUILDING...
SAFE AND SOUND!
MS. GREEN! WE FOUND YOU!
YAY, TOGETHER AGAIN! DID ANYONE HAPPEN TO TAKE NOTES?
OTES? ON WHAT?
HOW TO GET KIDNAPPED BY SUPER VILLAINS?
ON GAME DESIGN, SILLY!
THAT WAS A GREAT EXAMPLE OF RANDOM VARIABLE INTERJECTION!
REALLY? THAT'S WHAT YOU WANT US TO DESIGN?
I MEAN, THE SQUIRRELS, OKAY. BUT DON'T YOU THINK THE TWO HEROES WERE KIND OF... EXCESSIVE?
UH, YEAH! EXCESSIVELY AWESOME!
HI! My name is DOREEN
DOREEN
ALL AND ALL, THIS DAY WAS DEFINITELY ONE FOR THE WIN COLUMN.

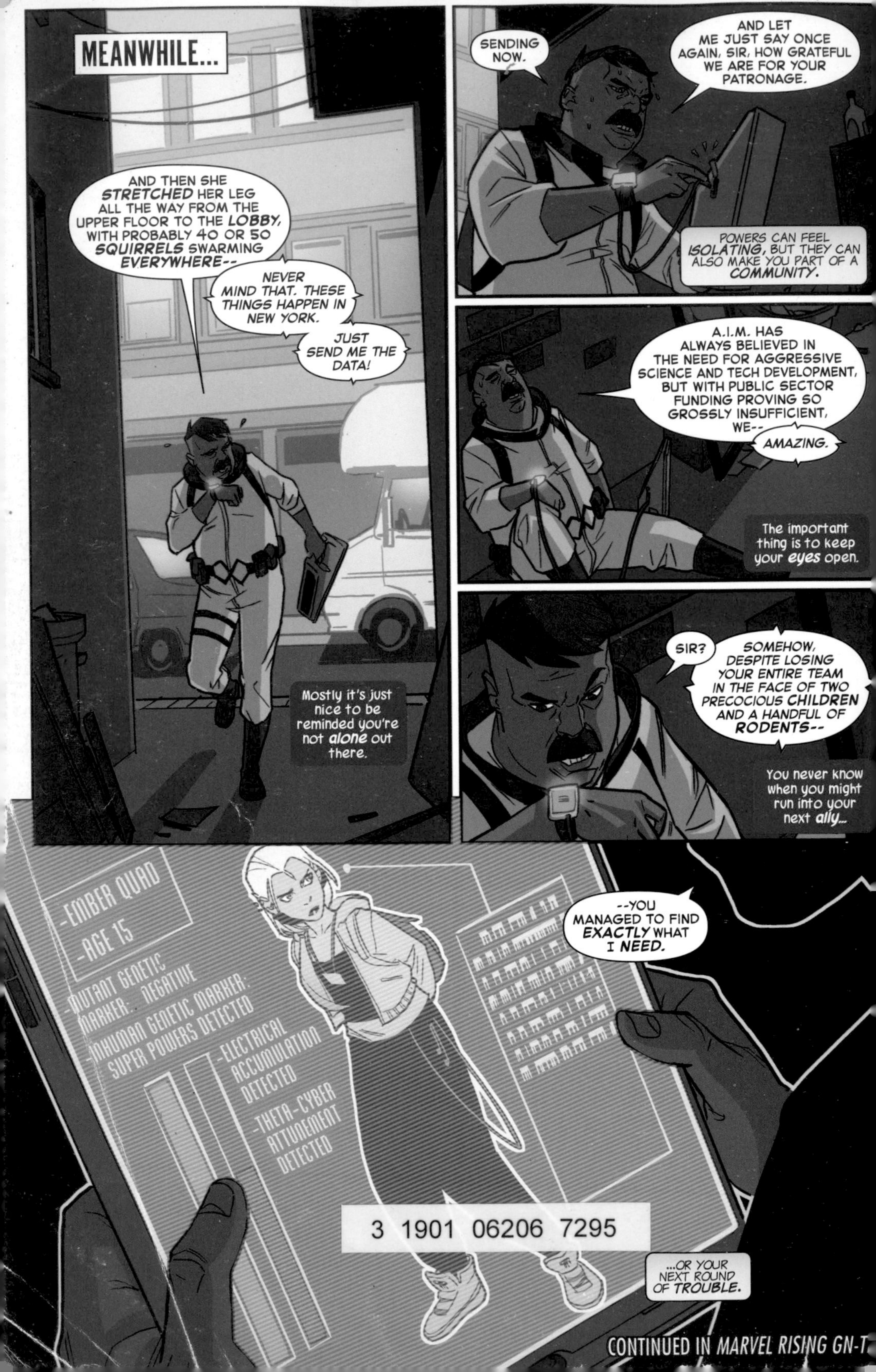
MEANWHILE...
AND THEN SHE STRETCHED HER LEG ALL THE WAY FROM THE UPPER FLOOR TO THE LOBBY, WITH PROBABLY 40 OR 50 SQUIRRELS SWARMING EVERYWHERE--
NEVER MIND THAT. THESE THINGS HAPPEN IN NEW YORK.
JUST SEND ME THE DATA!
Mostly it's just nice to be reminded you're not alone out there.
SENDING NOW.
AND LET ME JUST SAY ONCE AGAIN, SIR, HOW GRATEFUL WE ARE FOR YOUR PATRONAGE.
POWERS CAN FEEL ISOLATING, BUT THEY CAN ALSO MAKE YOU PART OF A COMMUNITY.
A.I.M. HAS ALWAYS BELIEVED IN THE NEED FOR AGGRESSIVE SCIENCE AND TECH DEVELOPMENT, BUT WITH PUBLIC SECTOR FUNDING PROVING SO GROSSLY INSUFFICIENT, WE--
AMAZING.
The important thing is to keep your eyes open.
SIR?
SOMEHOW, DESPITE LOSING YOUR ENTIRE TEAM IN THE FACE OF TWO PRECOCIOUS CHILDREN AND A HANDFUL OF RODENTS--
You never know when you might run into your next ally...
-EMBER QUAD
-AGE 15
-MUTANT GENETIC MARKER: NEGATIVE
-INHUMAN GENETIC MARKER: SUPER POWERS DETECTED
-ELECTRICAL ACCUMULATION DETECTED
-THETA-CYBER ATTUNEMENT DETECTED
--YOU MANAGED TO FIND EXACTLY WHAT I NEED.
...OR YOUR NEXT ROUND OF TROUBLE.
CONTINUED IN MARVEL RISING GN-T